W9-CYU-716

Confessions of a Thug

Philip Meadows Taylor

Edited by Matthew Kaiser

CONFESSIONS OF A THUG

PHILIP MEADOWS TAYLOR

EDITED WITH AN INTRODUCTION BY

MATTHEW KAISER
HARVARD UNIVERSITY

cognella™
San Diego, CA

First published in the United States of America in 2010 by University Readers, Inc.

Cover design by Monica Hui

14 13 12 11 10   1 2 3 4 5

Printed in the United States of America

ISBN: 978-1609279-95-0

www.cognella.com 800.200.3908

CONTENTS

Editor's Introduction

I N English, the word "thug" generally refers to a violent person or hardened criminal. The conceptual and lexical roots of "thug" can be traced to nineteenth-century colonial India, to a period of British military and political expansion on the subcontinent. Of the numerous criminal gangs and secret societies that the British suppressed in India in the 1820s and 1830s, one in particular—a religious death cult that claimed the lives, according to some estimates, of 20,000 people annually—loomed large in the Indian popular imagination, becoming synonymous with *thagi* (robbery). The very existence of the Thugs, who strangled and robbed their victims, was proof, to the British, of the incompetence and corruption of native law enforcement. To eradicate *Thuggee*, as the British called this mysterious sect, and validate the East India Company's guarantees of economic and political stability, the Company tightened its administrative grip on India, transforming the Thug into a powerful symbol of a dysfunctional and inscrutable land.

Captain Philip Meadows Taylor's *Confessions of a Thug*—which takes the form of a deposition given by a captured Thug to an unnamed British law enforcement officer—stands at the forefront of this reformist campaign to recast British imperialism as a political cure to India's ills. An instant bestseller when it appeared in 1839, Taylor's imperial "true-crime" novel was inspired by his work as Assistant Superintendent of Police in the southwestern districts in the Nizam's Dominions. The novel alerted the British public to the existence of Thuggee and urged the government to allocate more resources to anti-Thuggee operations, which were underfunded and undermanned. *Confessions of a Thug* also introduced "thug" into the English lexicon. That the novel was written by an imperial "insider," a man who had interrogated actual Thugs, gave it an aura of authenticity. With its alluring blend of Orientalism and documentary realism, *Confessions of a Thug* became the most widely read, ideologically influential representation of India in English of the nineteenth century. It sparked a craze in England for all things Thug-related. While the novel is an unabashedly propagandistic work of British empire writing, presenting India as teeming with con artists and predators, it is also a politically courageous protest, as Taylor's "Introduction" indicates, against those who have failed to keep the Indian population safe, against those in Britain who view Indians as exploitable resources rather than people to protect. Through the eyes of Ameer Ali, who confesses to strangling over seven hundred people, Taylor re-imagines India, making the case for a more humane, self-critical imperialism.

What made the Thugs especially dangerous, from a British perspective, was not the brutality with which they killed and robbed wayfarers; nor was it their disruption of trade routes. It was their seductiveness, cunning, and charm: their ability to hide in plain view. From the Sanskrit *sthag*, "to conceal" or "to veil," and from the Hindi *thagna*, "to deceive," "to trick," or "to swindle," the word *thag* (pronounced *tug*) not only refers to a deceptive person but a cutthroat or trickster who gains the confidence of his victims by extending the hand of friendship. Disguised as soldiers or merchants, Thug inveiglers convinced unsuspecting travelers to join their well-armed caravans for protection against robbers. Once the omens proved propitious, the Thugs strangled their victims, burying them in remote graves, occasionally dismembering or beheading the corpses. Because so much portable wealth—jewels, bullion, and silks—was transported on foot across India every day, Thugs managed to steal vast sums of money and property, leaving behind little trace of their crimes. Though devotees of the Hindu goddess Kali (who is sometimes called Bhowanee or Devi), to whom their victims were nominally sacrificed, many Thugs were devout Muslims, viewing Kali as an extension of Allah's will. Thugs attracted little attention from the British until 1829, when several mass graves were uncovered. Subsequent investigations by Taylor's colleague and rival, Captain William Henry Sleeman, who, like Taylor, interrogated Thugs and recorded their confessions, revealed the extent to which Thugs colluded with native officials, or bribed dubious rajahs in exchange for protection. By the mid 1830s, in the wake of Sleeman's discoveries, Thuggee appeared disturbingly ubiquitous, woven into the fabric of Indian society. As *Confessions of a Thug* makes clear, many Thugs were respectable men. Taylor's narrator describes Ameer Ali as "more than gentlemanlike." Some Thugs were even prominent figures in their communities.

If the Thugs threatened to undermine the economic and political stability that the British sought to establish in India, they also presented them with a golden opportunity to expand and consolidate their control of the country. The Thug became a complex and contradictory symbol. He reminded the British that seductive India was not what it seemed, that friendship was seasonal, allegiances uncertain. He was proof of India's backwardness and savagery. At the same time, however, the very existence of Thugs, the ease with which they plied their trade, was a sign of Indian vulnerability, of the deadly threats faced by a country destabilized, in large part, by British interference. The decentralized state of the government in India, the dilapidated condition of country roads and infrastructure, and the political chaos and demographic upheaval triggered by British military incursions had contributed, some reformers argued, to the spread of Thuggee in the first place. The Thug was a symptom of a landscape in flux, of a country in need of centralized control. If the Thug was proof of the inadequacy of native constabularies, he shamed the British, too, reminding them of their neglect of their Indian subjects. For decades, Thuggee had sprouted in jungly profusion behind the Company's back. British representations of Thuggee might be shaped by paranoid fantasies and xenophobic misinformation about Indian culture; these representations are simultaneously informed by imperial soul-searching, by guilty projections, by debates within British society about one's moral obligations to the people one subjugates. The Thug is the shadow cast by Empire.

The British government's anti-Thuggee campaign, which reached its apex in the 1830s, and which Sleeman, to Taylor's frustration, spearheaded, functioned in part as a public-relations campaign to convince the Indian and British populations of the benign and intrinsically *just* nature of the East India Company's heavy-handed and costly presence in India. In suppressing Thuggee, imperial reformers like Governor-General Lord William Bentinck sought to rescue India, recasting themselves as India's liberators and protectors, rather than its exploiters. If, as some historians suggest, British expansion had inadvertently accelerated the spread of Thuggee, then Britain would devote its energies, reformers insisted, to protecting its Indian subjects from the consequences of its antiquated model of imperialism. A rallying cry for further intervention, the figure of the Thug had become by the late 1830s an opportunity for imperial redemption.

———•———

Philip Meadows Taylor's fascination with Thuggee began in 1829. As a twenty-year-old Assistant Superintendent of Police in the employ of the Nizam, a native prince under the military protection of the British, Taylor was confronted one morning with a gruesome discovery. Near a village in the southwestern district of the Nizam's territories, hungry jackals or hyenas had succeeded in dragging two decomposing corpses from a newly-made grave. Though the bodies were partially eaten, their faces disfigured, it was clear they had been strangled. Several more bodies were discovered nearby. Taylor began to investigate. His suspicions fell on a band of Muslim merchants who regularly passed through his district. Though it seemed unlikely these respectable traders—sellers of copper pots and silver ornaments—had a hand in the murders, Taylor ordered his men to watch them closely.

To Taylor's frustration, however, his investigations ended abruptly when the elderly Nizam died and the new Nizam, in a show of independence, terminated the employment of all Europeans in his civil administration. Taylor returned to his regiment in Hyderabad. The key to unlocking the mystery of the murders, to exposing the Thuggee conspiracy, was just out of reach. It was a bitter moment: it would haunt him for the rest of his life.

Five years earlier, an ambitious fifteen-year-old Taylor had arrived in Bombay from Liverpool to work as a clerk in what he assumed was a prosperous trading firm. When the firm proved little more than a crude retail shop, Taylor took a position as a lieutenant in the Nizam's Army. Though commanded by former British military officers who were loyal to the British Crown, the Nizam's Army was not under the direct control, technically, of either the Crown or the East India Company. In all his years in India, in fact, Taylor never worked for the Crown or the Company, finding employment instead in the British-staffed bureaucracies of the Company's semi-autonomous client states. At sixteen, Taylor moved to the bustling city of Hyderabad in the Deccan. The city features prominently in *Confessions of a Thug*. Taylor's personal charm, his facility with Indian languages, and his easy friendships with native officials enabled him to rise through the ranks relatively quickly. At eighteen, he was named Assistant Superintendent of Police. He was responsible for the safety of over a million people across eleven thousand square miles. Two years later, on the verge of uncovering the Thuggee conspiracy, of making a name for himself in the annals of law enforcement, Taylor was relieved of his command, his destiny thwarted.

His frustration, however, would only increase. That same year, hundreds of miles to the north, near Sagar, another ambitious young officer, William Henry Sleeman, had also discovered the unearthed bodies of strangled travelers. Sleeman's subsequent investigations, his interrogations of Thug informers, including Amir Ali of Rampur, who claimed to have murdered over seven hundred people, blew the lid off the Thuggee system. Sleeman became famous. Over the next decade, Sleeman's investigative efforts and his growing network of "approvers" or informers led to the apprehension and execution of thousands of Thugs. Taylor respected and admired Sleeman. He offered to assist him however he could. Nevertheless, he envied his colleague's success. In his posthumously published autobiography, *The Story of My Life* (1877), Taylor confessed: "I felt sore that it had not fallen to my lot to win the fame of the affair."

Taylor yearned to be a leader in the anti-Thuggee campaign. Opportunity arrived in 1833. To alert the British public to the widespread problem of Thuggee in India, Taylor penned a short article, "On the Thugs," for Edward Bulwer-Lytton's

The New Monthly Magazine (The article is reproduced in its entirety at the end of this volume.). Intrigued by Taylor's bizarre tale of crime, and impressed with his familiarity with Indian culture, Bulwer-Lytton suggested he expand the article into a novel, adding a dash of romance to his ethnographic account of Thug culture, thereby reaching a wider audience. Spurred in part by his professional rivalry with Sleeman, who published his own account of Thuggee in 1836, Taylor took Bulwer-Lytton's advice, working on the manuscript throughout 1836 and 1837. The result was *Confessions of a Thug*.

The plot of the novel is loosely based on the lengthy deposition that Amir Ali gave Sleeman in 1832. Taylor's unnamed police officer is a stand-in, in fact, for Sleeman. While Taylor retains key details from Amir Ali's deposition, such as his childhood abduction, the plot of the novel diverges markedly from the original, which is a sixth its length. Taylor's fictional Ameer Ali is a composite of numerous people and sources. He even contains traces of Taylor himself. Punctuated by romantic, sentimental, touristic, and adventurous asides, Ameer Ali's tale is drawn from other Thug confessions, from journalistic and anecdotal accounts of Thuggee, from Taylor's extensive travels in India, and from his readings in Oriental literature. Taylor's fictional Ameer Ali outshines Sleeman's actual Amir Ali.

Confessions of a Thug was published in three volumes by Richard Bentley in 1839. It was wildly popular. Taylor's publisher had insisted he tone down its graphic violence. A young Queen Victoria read the finished product with relish. On furlough in England at the time of its publication, Taylor returned to India a famous man. He had become the new face of the anti-Thuggee campaign. The word "thug" was on the tip of the English tongue. Thanks to Taylor, in fact, the British public now saw India through the eyes of *his* Thug. Indeed, they saw themselves through Taylor's disconcerting interpretation of Indian eyes.

Invoking several literary genres, including the Oriental tale, the Newgate novel, the European travelogue, the eighteenth-century picaresque novel, and the ethnographic narrative, *Confessions of a Thug* is a formally, psychologically, and politically unsettling text. Its boundaries blur. Its villain is also its hero. The victimizer is a victim. The Thug is exotic yet familiar. Ameer Ali seems, at times, uncannily British. To underscore this parallel, Taylor heads various chapters with epigraphs from Shakespeare, Byron, Milton, and Scott. Ameer Ali repels and attracts the reader. His charm, his allure as a character and storyteller, is precisely what makes him so dangerous, for the Thugs, Taylor reminds us, are tricksters and seducers. Ameer Ali knows how to ingratiate himself. He wraps his narrative of personal suffering around the reader's heart like a discursive *roomal*, or strangling-cloth. In the dialogic and psychological showdown between Thug and police officer, between India and British Empire, one's sympathies as a reader gravitate inexorably toward the murderer. For all his efforts to view Ameer Ali with scientific detachment, even Taylor's narrator sympathizes, on occasion, with the unrepentant killer. *Confessions of a Thug* is a disorienting work of literature. It is a window onto Empire.

———— • ————

The text follows the 1873 edition, published by Henry S. King in one volume. In place of Taylor's "Glossary of Indian Words," which appears at the end of the 1873 edition, I have opted to footnote all Indian words and references. The number of translated words and phrases has been expanded substantially. To this end, Patrick Brantlinger's out-of-print 1998 edition has proven quite helpful, as have Sleeman's *Ramaseeana, or A Vocabulary of the Peculiar Language Used by the Thugs* (Calcutta: G. H. Huttmann, Military Orphan Press, 1836) and Edward Thornton's *Illustrations of the History and Practices of the Thugs* (London: William H. Allen, 1837). This Cognella edition would not have been possible without the assistance of Wes Ye, Monica Hui, Mieka Hemesath, Jessica Knott, and Bonnie Lee. Additional thanks go to Jan Alber, Frank Lauterbach, and Alan Richardson, as well as to Carol Dell'Amico and Ken Urban for their feedback.

Matthew Kaiser
Harvard University

MAP OF INDIA IN 1857

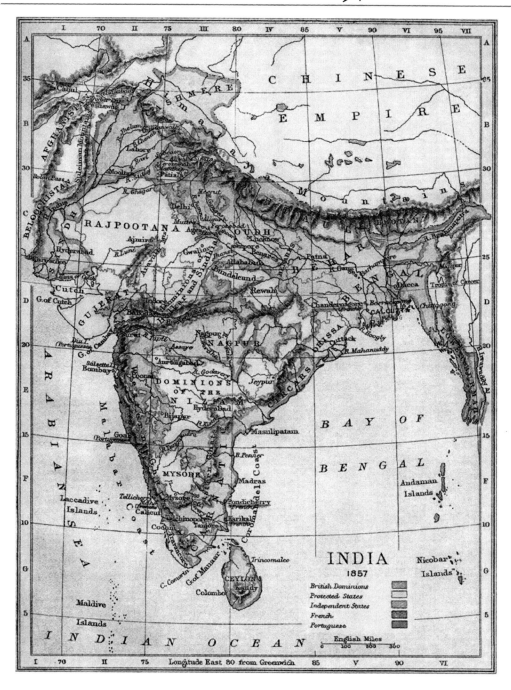

CONFESSIONS OF A THUG

"I have heard, have read bold fables of enormity,
Devised to make men wonder; but this hardness
Transcends all fiction."

—Law of Lombardy

To

THE RIGHT HONOURABLE

GEORGE, LORD AUCKLAND, G.C.B.,

GOVERNOR-GENERAL OF INDIA,

WHO IS VIGOROUSLY PROSECUTING THOSE

ADMIRABLE MEASURES

FOR THE SUPPRESSION OF THUGGEE, WHICH

WERE BEGUN BY THE LATE

LORD WILLIAM CAVENDISH BENTINCK,

G.C.B. AND G.C.H.,

HIS PREDECESSOR;

THESE VOLUMES

ARE, BY PERMISSION AND WITH GREAT RESPECT,

DEDICATED.

CHAPTERS

INTRODUCTION

THE tale of crime which forms the subject of the following pages is, alas! almost all true. What there is of fiction has been supplied only to connect the events, and make the adventures of Ameer Ali as interesting as the nature of his horrible profession would permit me.

I became acquainted with this person in 1832. He was one of the approvers or informers who were sent to the Nizam's territories[1] from Saugor,[2] and whose appalling disclosures caused an excitement in the country which can never be forgotten. I have listened to them with fearful interest, such as I can scarcely hope to excite in the minds of my readers; and I can only add, in corroboration of the ensuing story, that, by his own confessions, which were in every particular confirmed by those of his brother informers, and are upon official record, that he had been directly concerned in the murder of seven hundred and nineteen persons. He once said to me, "Ah! sir, if I had not been in prison twelve years, the number would have been a thousand!"

How the system of Thuggee[3] could have become so prevalent—unknown to, and unsuspected by, the people of India, among whom the professors of it were living in constant association—must, to the majority of the English public, not conversant with the peculiar construction of Oriental society, be a subject of extreme wonder. It will be difficult to make this understood within my present limits, and yet it is so necessary that I cannot pass it by.

In a vast continent like India, which from the earliest periods has been portioned out into territories, the possessions of many princes and chieftains—each with supreme and irresponsible power in his own dominions, having most lax and inefficient governments, and at enmity with, or jealous of, all his neighbours—it may be conceived that no security could exist for the traveller upon the principal roads throughout the continent—no general league was ever entered into for his security;

---

1 Hyderabad State in central India was ruled by a hereditary native administrator called a Nizam, who was under the protection of the British.

2 Sagar, city in central India.

3 The word *Thug* means *a deceiver*, from the Hindee verb *Thugna*, to deceive; it is pronounced *Túg*, slightly aspirated. [*Taylor*]

nor could any government, however vigorous, or system of police, however vigilant it might be in one State, possibly extend to all.

When it is also considered that no public conveyances have ever existed in India (the want of roads, and the habits and customs of the natives being alike opposed to their use); that journeys, however long, have to be undertaken on foot or on horseback; that parties, previously unknown to each other, associate together for mutual security and companionship; that even the principal roads (except those constructed for military purposes by the Company's[1] government) are only tracks made by the constant passage of people over them, often intersecting forests, jungles, and mountainous and uncultivated tracts, where there are but few villages and a scanty population; and that there are never any habitations between the different villages, which are often some miles apart;—it will readily be allowed, that every temptation and opportunity offers for plunderers of all descriptions to make travellers their prey. Accordingly freebooters have always existed, under many denominations, employing various modes of operation to attain their ends; some effecting them by open and violent attacks with weapons, others by petty thefts and by means of disguises. Beyond all, however, the Thugs have of late years been discovered to be the most numerous, the most united, the most secret in their horrible work, and consequently the most dangerous and destructive.

Travellers seldom hold any communication with the towns through which they pass, more than for the purchase of the day's provisions; they sometimes enter them, but pitch their tents or lie under the trees which surround them. To gain any intelligence of a person's progress from village to village, is therefore almost impossible. The greatest facilities for disguise among thieves and Thugs exist in the endless divisions of the people into tribes, castes, and professions; and remittances to an immense amount are known to be constantly made from one part of the country to another in gold and silver, to save the rate of exchange; jewels also and precious stones are often sent to distant parts, under the charge of persons who purposely assume a mean and wretched appearance; and every one is obliged to carry money upon his person for the daily expenses of travelling. It is also next to impossible to conceal anything carried, from the unlimited power of search possessed by the officers of customs in the territories of native princes, or to guard against the information their subordinates may supply to Thugs, or robbers of any description.

---

1   The East India Company, a British trading company that ruled India from 1757 to 1858, at which time the British Crown assumed direct administrative control of the subcontinent.

It has been ascertained by recent investigation, that in every part of India many of the hereditary landholders and the chief officers of villages have had private connection with Thugs for generations, affording them facilities for murder by allowing their atrocious acts to pass with impunity, and sheltering the offenders when in danger; whilst in return for these services they received portions of their gains, or laid a tax upon their houses, which the Thugs cheerfully paid. To almost every village (and in towns they are in a greater proportion) several hermits, fakeers,[1] and religious mendicants have attached themselves. The huts and houses of these people, which are outside the walls, and always surrounded by a grove or a garden, have afforded the Thugs places of rendezvous or concealment; while the fakeers, under their sanctimonious garb, have enticed travellers to their gardens by the apparently disinterested offers of shade and good water. The facilities I have enumerated, and hundreds of others which would be almost unintelligible by description, but which are intimately connected with, and grow out of, the habits of the people, have caused Thuggee to be everywhere spread and practised throughout India.

The origin of Thuggee is entirely lost in fable and obscurity. Colonel Sleeman[2] conjectures that it owed its existence to the vagrant tribes of Mahomedans[3] which continued to plunder the country long after the invasion of India by the Moghuls and Tartars.[4] The Hindoos claim for it a divine origin in their goddess Bhowanee;[5] and certainly the fact that both Mahomedans and Hindoos believe in her power, and observe Hindoo ceremonies, would go far to prove that the practice of Thuggee was of Hindoo origin. Though very remote traditions of it exist, there are no records in any of the histories of India of its having been discovered until the reign of Akbur,[6] when many of its votaries were seized and put to death. From that time till 1810, although native princes now and then discovered and executed the perpetrators,—I believe it was unknown to the British Government or authorities. In that year the disappearance of many men of the army, proceeding to and from their homes, in-

---

1   Muslim or Hindu ascetics.

2   William Henry Sleeman (1788-1856), British soldier and colonial administrator often credited with discovering and suppressing Thuggee in India.

3   English term for Muslims.

4   The Muslim Emperors of Turko-Mongol descent who ruled parts of India from the late fourteenth century to the early nineteenth century.

5   Also called Kali or Devi; the Hindu goddess of destruction.

6   Akbar Shah II (1760-1837), Mughal Emperor of India during a period of British imperial ascendency.

duced the commander-in-chief to issue an order warning the soldiers against Thugs. In 1812, after the murder by Thugs of Lieut. Monsell, Mr. Halhed, accompanied by a strong detachment, proceeded to the villages where the murderers were known to reside, and was resisted. The Thugs were discovered to be occupying many villages in the purgunnahs[1] of Sindousé,[2] and to have paid, for generations, large sums annually to Sindia's Government for protection. At this time it was computed that upwards of nine hundred were in those villages alone. The resistance offered by the Thugs to Mr. Halhed's detachment caused their ultimate dispersion, and no doubt they carried the practice of their profession into distant parts of the country, where perhaps it had been unknown before.

It appears strange, that as early as 1816 no measures for the suppression of Thuggee were adopted; for that the practices of the Thugs were well known, we have the strongest evidence in a paper written by Doctor Sherwood, which appeared in the Literary Journal of Madras, and which is admirably correct in the description of the ceremonies and practice of the Thugs of Southern India. One would suppose that they were then considered too monstrous for belief, and were discredited or unnoticed; but it is certain that from that time up to 1830, in almost every part of India, but particularly in Bundelkhund and Western Malwa,[3] large gangs of Thugs were apprehended by Major Borthwick and Captains Wardlow and Henley. Many were tried and executed for the murder of travellers, but without exciting more than a passing share of public attention. No blow was ever aimed at the system, if indeed its complete and extensive organization was ever suspected, or, if suspected, believed.

In that year, however, and for some years previously, Thuggee seemed to have reached a fearful height of audacity; and the British Government could no longer remain indifferent to an evil of such enormous and increasing magnitude. The attention of several distinguished civil officers—Messrs. Stockwell, Smith, Wilkinson, Borthwick, and others—had become attracted with great interest to the subject. Some of the Thugs who had been seized were allowed life on condition of denouncing their associates, and among others Feringhea, a leader of great notoriety.

The appalling disclosures of this man, so utterly unexpected by Captain (now Colonel) Sleeman, the political agent in the provinces bordering upon the Nerbudda

---

1 Districts.

2 In northern India.

3 Semi-autonomous states in central India.

river,[1] were almost discredited by that able officer;[2] but by the exhumation in the very grove where he happened to be encamped of no less than thirteen bodies in various states of decay, and the offer being made to him of opening other graves in and near the same spot, the approver's[3] tale was too surely confirmed. His information was acted upon, and large gangs, which had assembled in Rajpootana[4] for the purpose of going out on Thuggee, were apprehended and brought to trial.

From this period, the system for the suppression of Thuggee may be said to have commenced in earnest. From almost every gang one or more informers were admitted; and when they found that their only chance of life lay in giving correct information, they unequivocally denounced their associates, and their statements were confirmed by the disinterment of their victims in the spots pointed out.

In this manner Thuggee was found to be in active practice all over India. The knowledge of its existence was at first confined to the central provinces; but as men were apprehended from a distance, they gave information of others beyond them in the almost daily commission of murder. The circle gradually widened till it spread over the whole continent; and from the foot of the Himalayas to Cape Comorin, from Cutch[5] to Assam, there was hardly a province in the whole of India where Thuggee had not been practised, where the statements of the informers were not confirmed by the disinterment of the dead!

Few who were in India at that period (1831-32) will ever forget the excitement which the discovery occasioned in every part of the country; it was utterly discredited by the magistrates of many districts, who could not be brought to believe that this silently destructive system could have worked without their knowledge. I quote the following passage from Colonel Sleeman's introduction to his own most curious and able work.[6]

"While I was in civil charge of the district of Nursingpoor, in the valley of the Nerbudda, in the years 1822, 1823, and 1824, no ordinary robbery or theft could be committed without my becoming acquainted with it, nor was there a robber or

---

1   Narmada River, in central India.

2   I take this opportunity of acknowledging the obligations I am under to Colonel Sleeman for much valuable information, and also for a copy of his work. [*Taylor*]

3   Informer's.

4   Rajputana, large autonomous state in northwest India.

5   Kachchh, in western India.

6   The following passage is from Sleeman's *Ramaseeana, or A Vocabulary of the Peculiar Language Used by the Thugs*, 32-33.

thief of the ordinary kind in the district, with whose character I had not become acquainted in the discharge of my duty as a magistrate; and if any man had then told me that a gang of assassins by profession resided in the village of Kundélee, not four hundred yards from my court; and that the extensive groves of the village of Mundésur, only one stage from me on the road to Saugor and Bhopal, was one of the greatest bhils, or places of murder, in all India; that large gangs from Hindostan and the Dukhun used to rendezvous in these groves, remain in them for days together every year, and carry on their dreadful trade all along the lines of road that pass by and branch off from them, with the knowledge and connivance of the two landholders by whose ancestors these groves had been planted, I should have thought him a fool or a madman. And yet nothing could have been more true: the bodies of *a hundred travellers* lie buried in and among the groves of Mundésur, and a gang of assassins lived in and about the village of Kundélee, while I was magistrate of the district, and extended their depredations to the cities of Poona and Hyderabad."

Similar to the preceding, as showing the daring character of the Thuggee operations, was the fact, that at the cantonment of Hingolee, the leader of the Thugs of that district, Hurree Singh, was a respectable merchant of the place, one with whom I myself, in common with many others, have had dealings. On one occasion he applied to the officer in civil charge of the district, Captain Reynolds, for a pass to bring some *cloths* from Bombay, which he knew were on their way accompanied by their owner, a merchant of a town not far from Hingolee. He murdered this person, his attendants, and cattle-drivers, brought the merchandise up to Hingolee under the pass he had obtained, and sold it openly in the cantonment; nor would this have ever been discovered, had he not confessed it after his apprehension, and gloried in it as a good joke. By this man too, and his gang, many persons were murdered *in the very bazar of the cantonment*, within one hundred yards of the main guard, and were buried hardly five hundred yards from the line of sentries! I was myself present at the opening of several of these unblessed graves (each containing several bodies), which were pointed out by the approvers, one by one, in the coolest manner, to those who were assembled, till we were sickened and gave up further search in disgust. The place was the dry channel of a small water-course, communicating with the river, not broader or deeper than a ditch; it was close to the road to a neighbouring village, one of the main outlets from the cantonment to the country.

Once awakened to the necessity of suppressing, by the most vigorous measures, the dreadful system only just detected in its operation, the officers who were first appointed to investigate the reports and accusations of the informers, used their utmost efforts to arouse in the Supreme Government a corresponding interest, and happily succeeded. The matter was taken up most warmly by the Governor-General, Lord William Bentinck,[1] and the Supreme Council; and highly intelligent officers were appointed to superintend the execution of measures in those districts where Thuggee was discovered to be in practice. Most of the native princes gave up claims upon such of their subjects as should be apprehended upon charges of Thuggee, or who should be denounced by the informers; and although in many parts the landholders and patels[2] of villages protected the Thugs and resisted their apprehension, yet the plans for the suppression of the system were eminently successful. As suspicion was aroused, no body of men could traverse the country in any direction without being subject to the strictest scrutiny by the police, and by informers who were stationed with them upon all the great thoroughfares and in the principal towns.

The success of these measures will be more evident from the following table, which was kindly supplied to me by Captain Reynolds, the general superintendent of the department.

From 1831 to 1837, inclusive, there were

Transported to Penang, etc	1059
Hanged	412
Imprisoned for life with hard labour	87
Imprisoned in default of security	21
Imprisoned for various periods	69
Released after trial	32
Escaped from jail	11
Died in jail	36
	1727

Made approvers	483
Convicted but not sentenced	120
In jail in various parts not yet tried	936
	3266

---

1 As the last sheets of this work are passing through the press, the melancholy intelligence of the death of Lord W. Bentinck has reached England. I am thus prevented having the honour of placing his name, in conjunction with that of Lord Auckland, in the dedication of these volumes. [*Taylor*]

2 Head officers.

Added to the above, Captain Reynolds mentioned that, at the time he wrote, upwards of 1800 notorious Thugs were at large in various parts of India, whose names were known: how many besides existed, it is impossible to conjecture.

How enormous therefore must have been the destruction of human life and property in India before Thuggee was known to exist, or was only partially checked! How many thousands must annually have perished by the hands of these remorseless assassins! Awful indeed is the contemplation; for during the whole of the troublous times of the Mahratta and Pindharee Wars[1] their trade flourished; nor was it till 1831 that their wholesale system of murder received any serious check; and after its general discovery, the countless and affecting applications from families to the officers of the department to endeavour to procure them some knowledge of the places where their missing relatives had been destroyed, that they might have the miserable satisfaction of performing the ceremonies for the dead, showed how deeply the evil had affected society.

And not only as described in the following pages has Thuggee existed; since they were written, it has been discovered under several other forms, and been found to be extensively practised on the Ganges, by men who live in boats, and murder those passengers whom they are able to entice into their company in their voyages up and down the river. But the most refined in guilt are those who murder parents for the sake of their children, to sell them as household slaves, or to dancing women to be brought up to prostitution.

Throughout the whole of India, including all territories of native princes, only eighteen officers are employed as superintendents and agents for the suppression of Thuggee; many of whom, besides the labour of this office, which is excessive, have other civil and political duties to fulfil. By a reference to any map, it will at once be seen what enormous provinces or divisions of India fall to the superintendence of each person.[2] Whether it is possible for each to extend to every part of that under his charge the extreme attention and scrutiny which are so imperatively necessary to put an end to this destructive system (for there is no doubt that wherever one well-initiated Thug exists, he will among the idle and dissolute characters which everywhere abound in the Indian population find numbers to join him), must be best

---

1 Taylor is referring to the period from the 1790s to the early 1820s, a time of British imperial expansion and political instability in India.

2 I select at random from a list in my possession two of the superintendents. Captain Elwall, Bengal Infantry, at Bangalore, has Mysore and the *whole* of the southern peninsula of India; Captain Malcolm, the *whole* of the territories of H. H. the Nizam. [*Taylor*]

known to the Government of India. It is only sincerely to be hoped that *economical* considerations do not prevent the appointment of others, if necessary.

The Confessions I have recorded are not published to gratify a morbid taste in any one for tales of horror and of crime; they were written to expose, as fully as I was able, the practices of the Thugs, and to make the public of England more conversant with the subject than they can be at present, notwithstanding that some notice has been attracted to the subject by an able article in the Edinburgh Review upon Colonel Sleeman's valuable and interesting work.

I hope, however, that the form of the present work may be found more attractive and more generally interesting than an account of the superstitions and customs only of the Thugs; while for the accuracy of the pictures of the manners and habits of the natives, and the descriptions of places and scenes, I can only pledge the experience of fifteen years' residence in India, and a constant and intimate association with its inhabitants.

If these volumes in any way contribute to awaken public vigilance in the suppression of Thuggee, or if from the perusal of them any one in authority rises with a determination to lend his exertions in this good cause of humanity, my time will not have been occupied in vain.

LONDON, *July*, 1839.

M. T.

CHAPTER I

YOU ask me, sahib,[1] for an account of my life; my relation of it will be understood by you, as you are acquainted with the peculiar habits of my countrymen; and if, as you say, you intend it for the information of your own, I have no hesitation in relating the whole; for though I have accepted the service of Europeans, in my case one of bondage, I cannot help looking back with pride and exultation on the many daring feats I have performed. Often indeed does my spirit rise at the recollection of them, and often do I again wish myself the leader of a band of gallant spirits, such as once obeyed me, to roam with them wherever my inclination or the hope of booty prompted.

But the time is past. Life, sahib, is dear to every one; to preserve mine, which was forfeited to your laws, I have bound myself to your service, by the fearful tenure of denouncing all my old confederates, and you well know how that service is performed by me. Of all the members of my band, and of those with whom chance has even casually connected me, but few now remain at large; many have been sacrificed at the shrine of justice, and of those who now wander broken, and pursued from haunt to haunt, you have such intelligence as will lead to their speedy apprehension.

Yet Thuggee, capable of exciting the mind so strongly, will not, cannot be annihilated! Look at the hundreds, I might say thousands, who have suffered for its profession; does the number of your prisoners decrease? No! on the contrary, they increase; and from every Thug who accepts the alternative of perpetual imprisonment to dying on a gallows, you learn of others whom even I knew not of, and of Thuggee being carried on in parts of the country where it is least suspected, and has never been discovered till lately.

It is indeed too true, Ameer Ali, said I; your old vocation seems to be as flourishing as ever, but it cannot last. Men will get tired of exposing themselves to the chance of being hunted down like wild beasts and hung when they are caught, or,

---

1 Sir.

what is perhaps worse to many, of being sent over the kala-panee;[1] and so heartily does the Government pursue Thugs wherever they are known to exist, that there will no longer be a spot of ground in India where your profession can be practised.

You err, sahib; you know not the high and stirring excitement of a Thug's occupation. To my perception it appears, that so long as one exists, he will gather others around him; and from the relation of what I will tell you of my own life, you will estimate how true is my assertion.

How many of you English are passionately devoted to sporting! Your days and months are passed in its excitement. A tiger, a panther, a buffalo, or a hog, rouses your uttermost energies for its destruction,—you even risk your lives in its pursuit. How much higher game is a Thug's! His is man: against his fellow-creatures in every degree, from infancy to old age, he has sworn relentless, unerring destruction!

Ah! you are a horrible set of miscreants, said I. I have indeed the experience, from the records of murders which are daily being unfolded to me, of knowing this at least of you. But you must begin your story; I am prepared to listen to details worse than I can imagine human beings to have ever perpetrated.

It will even be as you think, said Ameer Ali, and I will conceal nothing. Of course you wish me to begin my tale from as early a period as I can recollect.

Certainly. I am writing your life for the information of those in England, who would no doubt like to have every particular of so renowned a person as yourself.

Well then, sahib, to begin. The earliest remembrance I have of anything, and until a few years ago it was very indistinct, is of a village in the territories of Holkar,[2] where I was born. Who my parents were I know not. I suppose them to have been respectable, from the circumstances of my always wearing gold and silver ornaments, and having servants about me. I have an indistinct recollection of a tall fair lady whom I used to call mother, and of an old woman who always attended me, and who I suppose was my nurse, also of a sister who was younger than myself, but of whom I was passionately fond. I can remember no other particulars, until the event occurred which made me what I am and which is vividly impressed on my mind.

From an unusual bustle in the house, and the packing up of articles of clothing and other necessaries, I supposed we were on the eve of departure from our home. I was right in my conjecture, for we left it the next morning. My mother and myself

---

1 Black water; the sea. Captured Thugs who were spared execution were transported to the British-held island of Penang in present-day Malaysia, or to the island of Mauritius in the Indian Ocean, where they were forced to work in labor camps or on plantations.

2 Maharaja Yashwantrao Holkar (1776-1811), military leader and ruler of Indore in central India.

travelled in a dooly,[1] old Chumpa was mounted on my pony, and my father rode his large horse. Several of the sons of our neighbours accompanied us; they were all armed, and I suppose were our escort.

On the third or fourth day after we left our village, after our march of the day, we as usual put up in an empty shop in the bazaar of the town we rested at. My father left us to go about on his own business, and my mother, who could not show herself outside, after repeated injunctions that I was not to stray away, lay down in an inner room and went to sleep. Finding myself at liberty, as Chumpa was busy cooking and the juwans[2] were all out of the way, I speedily forgot all my mother's orders, and betook myself to play with some other children in the street. We were all at high romps, when a good-looking man of middle age addressed me, and asked me who I was—I must have been remarkable from the rest of the ragged urchins about me, as I was well dressed, and had some silver and gold ornaments on my person. I told him that my father's name was Yoosuf Khan, and that he and my mother and myself were going to Indoor.[3]

"Ah, then," said he, "you are the party I met yesterday on the road; your mother rides on a bullock, does she not?"

"No, indeed!" retorted I angrily, "she rides in a palankeen, and I go with her, and father rides a large horse, and we have Chumpa and several juwans with us. Do you think a Pathan[4] like my father would let my mother ride on a bullock, like the wife of a ploughman?"

"Well, my fine little fellow, it shall be as you say, and you shall ride a large horse too, one of these days, and wear a sword and shield like me. But would you not like some sweetmeat? See how tempting those julabees[5] look at the hulawee's;[6] come with me, and we will buy some."

The temptation was too strong to be withstood by a child, and after a fearful look towards the shop where we stayed, I accompanied the man to the hulwaee's.

He bought me a load of sweetmeats, and told me to go home and eat them; I tied them up in a handkerchief I wore round my waist, and proceeded homewards. This transaction had attracted the notice of some of the ragged urchins I had been

1 Palankeen or covered litter.
2 Youths, soldiers.
3 Indore.
4 Pashtun; member of an Indo-Afghan ethno-linguistic group.
5 Kind of sweetmeat.
6 Confectioner's.

playing with, and who had longingly eyed the julabees I had been treated to; and as soon as the man who had given them to me had gone a short distance, they attacked me with stones and dirt, till one more bold than the rest seized me, and endeavoured to get my prize from me. I struggled and fought as well as I could; but the others having fairly surrounded me, I was mobbed, and obliged to deliver up my treasure. Not content with this, one big boy made a snatch at the necklace I wore, on which I began to bellow with all my might. The noise I made attracted the notice of my acquaintance, who running up, soon put the troop of boys to flight, and taking me under his charge, led me to our abode, where he delivered me up to Chumpa; at the same time telling her of the scuffle, and cautioning her not to let me out of her sight again.

I was crying bitterly, and my mother, hearing a strange voice, called me to her. Asking me what had happened, I told my story, and said that the person who had saved me was speaking to Chumpa. She addressed him from behind the cloth, which had been put up as a screen, and thanked him; and added, that my father was absent, but that if he would call again in an hour or two, he would find him at home, and she was sure he would also be glad to thank the person who had protected his child. The man said he would come in the evening, and went away. My father returned soon afterwards, and I received an admonition in the shape of a sound beating, for which I was consoled by my mother by a quantity of the sweetmeats from the hulwaee's, which had been the cause of my trouble, and I may add also of my present condition. You see, sahib, how fate works its ends out of trifling circumstances.

Towards evening my acquaintance, accompanied by another man, came. I was a good deal the subject of their conversation; but it passed on to other matters, among which I remember the word Thug to have been first used. I understood too from their discourse that there were many on the road between where we were and Indoor, and that they were cautioning my father against them. The men said that they were soldiers, who had been sent out on some business from Indoor; and as there were a good many of their men with them, they offered to make part of our escort. My friend was very kind to me, allowed me to play with his weapons, and promised me a ride before him on his horse the next day. I was delighted at the prospect, and with him for his kind and winning manner; but I did not like the appearance of the other, who was an ill-looking fellow—I shall have to tell you much more of him hereafter.

We started the next morning. Our two acquaintances and their men joined us at a mango-grove outside the village, where they had been encamped, and we proceeded on our journey. In this manner we travelled for two days, and my friend performed his promise of taking me up before him on his horse; he would even dismount and lead him, allowing me to remain on the saddle; and as the animal was a quiet one, I used to enjoy my ride till the sun became hot, when I was put into the dooly with my mother. On the third day I remember my friend saying to my father, as they rode side by side,—

"Yoosuf Khan, why should you take those poor lads of yours on to Indoor with you? why not send them back from the stage we are now approaching? I and my men are ample protection to you; and as you will belong to the same service as myself there can be no harm in your trusting yourself and family to my protection for the rest of the journey; besides, the dangerous part of the road, the jungle in which we have been for the last two days, is passed, and the country before us is open. The only fear of Thugs and thieves existed in them, and they are now far behind."

"It is well said," replied my father; "I dare say the lads will be thankful to me for sparing them a part of the long march back, and they have already accompanied us some fifty or sixty coss."[1]

On our arrival at the stage, my father told the lads they must return, at which they were highly pleased; and on their departure about noon, I gave many kind messages to my old companions and playfellows. I remember too giving an old battered rupee[2] to be delivered to my little sister, and of saying she was to hang it with the other charms and coins about her neck, to remind her of me. I found it again, sahib; but, ah! under what circumstances!

At this period of his narrative, Ameer Ali seemed to shudder; a strong spasm shot through his frame, and it was some time before he spoke; at last he resumed:

Tell a servant to bring me some water, sahib—I am thirsty with having spoken too much.

No, said I, you are not thirsty, but you shall have the water.

It was brought, but he scarcely tasted it—the shudder again passed through him. He got up and walked across the room, his irons clanking as he moved. It was horrible to see the workings of his face. At last he said, Sahib, this is weakness. I could not conceal it; I little thought I should have been thus moved at so early a period of my story; but recollections crowded on me so fast, that I felt confused and very sick. It is over now—I will proceed.

Do so, said I.

---

1   One coss is equivalent to two miles.

2   Basic unit of money in India.

The juwans had been gone some hours, and it was now evening. My friend came to our abode, and told my father that the next were two short stages, and if he liked they might be made in one, as it would shorten the distance to Indoor; but that we should be obliged to start very early, long before daylight, and that the bearers who carried the dooly could easily be persuaded to make the march by promise of a sheep, which the patail[1] of the village he proposed going to would supply free of cost, as he was a friend of his. My father seemed to be rather indignant at the idea of his taking a sheep for nothing, and said that he had plenty of money, not only to pay for a sheep, but to give them a present if they carried us quickly.

"Well," said my friend, "so much the better, for we sipahees[2] have rarely much about us but our arms."

"True," returned my father; "but you know that I have sold all my property at my village, and have brought the money to aid me in our service. Indeed, it is a good round sum."

And my father chuckled at the idea.

"What! have you a thousand rupees?" I asked, my ideas of wealth going no further.

"And what if it should be more?" said he, and the matter dropped; but even now I think I can remember that my friend exchanged significant glances with his companion.

It was then arranged that we should start with the rising of the moon, about the middle of the night.

We were roused from our sleep at the hour proposed; and after the men had had a pipe all round, we set off. I was in the dooly with my mother. The moon had risen; but, as well as I can remember, there was but little light, and a slight rain falling, which obliged us to travel very slowly. After we had proceeded a few coss, the bearers of the dooly put it down, saying that they could not get on in the dark and the mud, and proposed to wait till daylight. My father had a violent altercation with them; and as I was now wide awake, and it had ceased to rain, I begged to be taken out of the dooly, and allowed to ride with my friend. He did not assent as readily as usual; yet he took me up when the bearers had been scolded into going on. I remarked to him that some of the soldiers, as I thought them, were absent. My remark attracted my father's notice to the circumstance, and he asked our companion where they were. He replied carelessly, that they were gone on in advance, as we had travelled as yet so slowly, and that we should soon overtake them.

---

1 Head officer of a village.

2 Sepoys; Indian soldiers serving under British command.

We proceeded. We came at last to the deep bed of a river, on the side of which there was some thick jungle, when my friend dismounted, as he said to drink water, and told me the horse would carry me over safely. I guided him as well as I could; but before I had got well across the stream, I heard a cry, and the noise as if of a sudden scuffle. It alarmed me; and in looking back to see from whence it proceeded, I lost my balance on the horse, and fell heavily on the stones in the bed of the river, which cut my forehead severely. I bear the mark now.

I lay for a short time, and raising myself up, saw all the men, who I thought were far on before us, engaged in plundering the dooly. I now began to scream with all my might. One of them ran up to me, and I saw it was the ill-looking one I have before mentioned. "Ah! we have forgotten you, you little devil," cried he; and throwing a handkerchief round my neck, he nearly choked me. Another man came up hastily,—it was my friend. "He must not be touched," he cried angrily to the other, and seized his hands; they had a violent quarrel, and drew their swords. I can remember no more; for I was so much frightened that I lost all consciousness, and, as I suppose, fainted.

I was recovered by some water being forced into my mouth; and the first objects which met my eyes were the bodies of my father and mother, with those of Chumpa and the palankeen-bearers, all lying confusedly on the ground. I cannot remember what my feelings were, but they must have been horrible. I only recollect throwing myself on my dead mother, whose face appeared dreadfully distorted, and again relapsing into insensibility. Even after the lapse of thirty-five years, the hideous appearance of my mother's face, and particularly of her eyes, comes to my recollection; but I need not describe it, sahib; she had been strangled! She, my father, and the whole party had come to a miserable and untimely end! I heard a narrative of the particulars of the event, many years afterwards, from an old Thug; and I will relate them in their proper place.

When I recovered my consciousness, I found myself once more before my friend who had saved my life. He supported and almost carried me in his arms, and I perceived that we were no longer on the road. We were rapidly traversing the jungle, which extended as far as I could see in every direction; but the pain of my neck was so great, that I could scarcely hold up my head. My eyes seemed to be distended and bursting, and were also very painful. With my consciousness, the remembrance of the whole scene came to my recollection, and again I fell into insensibility. I recovered and relapsed in this manner several times during this journey; but it was only momentary, only sufficient to allow me to observe that we still held on at a rapid pace, as the men on foot were between running and walking. At last we stopped, as it was now broad daylight; indeed, the sun had risen. I was taken off the horse by one of the men, and laid under a tree on a cloth spread on the ground, and after some time my friend came to me. Desolate as I was, I could not help feeling that he must have had some concern in the death of my parents; and in my childish anger I bitterly reproached him, and bid him kill me. He tried to console me; but the more he endeavoured, the more I persisted that he should put me to death. I was in dreadful pain; my neck and eyes ached insufferably. I heaped all the abuse I could think of upon him, and the noise I made attracted the notice of the ill-looking man, whose name was Ganesha.

"What is that brat saying? Are you too turned woman," cried he fiercely, addressing the other, whose name was Ismail, "that you do not put the cloth about his neck, and quiet him at once? Let me do it, if you are afraid."

And he approached me. I was reckless, and poured forth a torrent of vile abuse, and spat at him. He untied his waistband, and was about to put an end to me, when Ismail again interfered, and saved me; they had again a violent quarrel, but he succeeded in carrying me off to some little distance to another tree, where some of the band were preparing to cook their victuals; and setting me down among them, bidding them take care of me, he went away. The men tried to make me speak, but I was sullen, and would not; the pain of my neck and eyes seemed to increase, and I began to cry bitterly. I lay in this manner for some hours I suppose; and at last, completely tired out, fell asleep. I woke towards evening; and when Ismail saw me sit up, he came to me, soothed and caressed me, saying that I should henceforth be his child; and that it was not he, but others, who had murdered my parents. I remember begging him to do something for my neck, which was swelled and still very painful. He examined it, and seemed to be struck with the narrow escape I had had of my life.

He rubbed my neck with oil, and afterwards put upon it a warm plaster of leaves, which relieved it greatly, and I felt easier for its application. He remained with me; and some of the other men, sitting down by us, began to sing and play to amuse me. I was given some milk and rice to eat in the evening; but before it was time to sleep, Ismail brought me some sherbet[1] of sugar and water, which he said would make me sleep. I suppose there was opium in it, for I remember nothing till the next morning, when I found myself in his arms on horseback, and knew that we were again travelling.

---

1   Cooling drink of sweet diluted fruit juices.

I pass over the journey, as I remember nothing of it except that Ganesha was no longer with us, which I was very glad of; for I hated him, and could not bear his presence. Even in after years, sahib, though we have been engaged together in Thuggee, I always bore a deep-rooted aversion to him, which never changed to the last.

Ismail and seven men were all that remained of the band; and we proceeded, by long and fatiguing marches, to a village in which he said he resided, and where I was to be given up to the care of his wife. We arrived at last, and I was introduced to a good-looking young woman as a child of a relation, whom he had long ago adopted as a son, and had now brought home to her; in fine, I was formally adopted by them as their own, and my sufferings were speedily forgotten.

———•———

Chapter II

I MUST have been at this time about five years old. It will strike you perhaps as strange, sahib, that I should remember so many particulars of the event I have described; but when I was imprisoned some years ago at Dehlie,[1] I used to endeavour, in my solitude, to recollect and arrange the past adventures of my life, one circumstance led me to the remembrance of another—for in solitude, if the mind seeks the occupation, it readily takes up the clue to past events, however distant, and thought brings them one by one before the imagination, as vividly fresh as the occurrence of yesterday—and from an old Thug's adventures, which I heard during that imprisonment, I found my memory to serve me well. I was in possession of the whole of the facts, as I have related them to you, and I have only perhaps supplied the minor parts from my own mind. I particularly recollect the scene with Ganesha, which he afterwards related to me, and told me that such was his rage at the abuse I poured on him, that had it not been for the dread of Ismail's vengeance, and of his power, he would have sacrificed me in his fury.

But to return to my story, if you are not tired of it.

No indeed, said I; I am becoming more and more interested.

Well, resumed Ameer Ali, I was kindly nursed and tended by Ismail and his wife. The curiosity of the villagers was a good deal excited by my appearance, and I have since suspected Ismail thought I might one day reveal what I knew of my origin; and for this reason I was never allowed out of his or his wife's sight. I must then however have speedily forgotten all about it, or at least have retained so confused and indistinct a recollection of the circumstances, that had I endeavoured to relate them to any one, I could not have made them intelligible, and should have been disregarded.

Ismail, in this village, carried on the trade of a cloth merchant, at least when he was at home. He daily sat in his shop, with different kinds of cloth before him for sale; but it was plain, even to me, to see that he was restless and uneasy. He would

---

1   Delhi, city in northern India.

very often be absent for days together, without his family knowing where he had gone; and he would suddenly return with large quantities of cloth and other goods, which were always exposed for sale. I continued to be the object of his greatest care, and I reciprocated his affection, for indeed I was more kindly treated by him than I ever had been by my father, who was a proud and ill-tempered man. My new mother, too, never gave me reason to be displeased with her; for having no child of her own, I was her pet, and she lavished on me all the means in her power. I was always well dressed, and had every indulgence that a child could wish for.

I was about nine years old, I think, when my kind protectress died of fever while Ismail was on one of his excursions, and I was taken by a neighbour to his house until he returned. I shall never forget his despair when he found his home desolate. Young as I was, I could do but little to console him; but he used to go and deck his wife's tomb with flowers every Friday, and bitter were his lamentations over her grave.

Poor Miriam! for that was her name—it was well for you that you died; had you lived, what would now have been your condition! As the wife of a noted Thug, your reputation would have been blasted, and you would have become an outcast!

Sahib! she never knew what Ismail was. He was to her a man in prosperous circumstances. She had everything she could desire, and not a want remained unsatisfied; and so deeply and well laid were his plans, that she would never have known, till the day of his capture, that she was the wife of a professed murderer!

I pass over the next four or five years of my life, as I can remember no incident in them worth relating. Ismail, soon after the death of his wife, removed from the village where he had hitherto resided, and took up his abode in the town of Murnae, which was then in Scindia's[1] possession, and I was put to school with an old man, who taught me to read and write Persian.

As I grew older, I observed that Ismail used very frequently to have a number of men at his house by night, and I was naturally curious to know who they were and why they assembled. One evening that I knew they were expected, I feigned to lie down and go to sleep as usual; but when they had all come, I got up cautiously, and hid myself behind a purdah or screen at the farther end of the room where they sat. After they had eaten what was prepared for them, they all drew together, and began conversing in a language[2] I only partially understood, and I thought this strange, as I knew Hindoostanee and the common dialect myself, having picked up the latter

---

1 The Sindhia dynasty ruled Gwalior State in north India in the eighteenth and nineteenth centuries.
2 Ramasee; a secret Thug language.

by associating with the boys of the town. By-and-by, Ismail went to a closet very near where I lay, and his movements alarmed me greatly, as I was fearful of being discovered; he took from it a box, which he placed in the circle, and opened it. Rich as I had always thought him, I had no idea of the wealth it contained; there were quantities of gold and silver ornaments of all kinds, with strings of pearls and other valuables; they seemed parceled out into lots, as equally as possible, and to each man he gave one, reserving a considerable share for himself. At last they began to speak in Hindoostanee, a language I understood. One of them, an elderly man with a venerable beard, said to Ismail,

"What do you intend doing with Ameer? He is almost a young man; and if he is to be one of us, it is high time he should be taught what to do. It is very dangerous to have him about the house; he might discover something, and be off before you knew anything of the matter."

"Oh, I have no fear of him," said Ismail; "he is too fond of me; besides, he has no other protector in the world but myself. He was the son of * * * * *"

And here the conversation was carried on by Ismail again in the language I did not understand.

"It does not matter," said another man, whose name was Hoosein, and whom I knew very well, as he was employed by Ismail, to all appearance, as an agent for selling his cloth; "the lad is a smart active fellow, and a great deal too knowing for you to let him go about everywhere with so little restraint; he will find out all one of these days, if he is not fairly brought among us. Besides, he is old enough to be of use in many ways, and he ought to be instructed in our profession, if he be ever to learn; depend upon it, the sooner he eats the goor,[1] the more relish he will have for it. I brought up a lad myself; and when once he got his hand in, he was a perfect tiger at the work, and became so expert, that our oldest hands could hardly compete with him."

"Well," said Ismail, "I believe you are right, and I foretell great doings from this boy. He is brave and stout beyond his years, and there are but few who can excel him in his qusrut,[2] which I have taught him ever since he was a child; but he is of so kind and gentle a disposition, that I do not know how to break the matter to him. I almost fear he will never consent."

"Pooh!" said a third man, whom I had never seen before; "these very kind-hearted boys are the best we could have; they are the more easily led and won over, and one

---

1   Raw sugar; molasses.
2   Gymnastic exercise.

has more dependence upon them. Put the matter in the proper light; talk to him of the glory of the business, and of our surety of heaven. Describe to him all about the houris[1] which our blessed prophet,—may his name be honoured! has promised us, and tell him too of the heaven of Indra,[2] all of which you know we are sure of; the one by our faith as Moslims, and the other by our profession. He will soon be won over, I am certain."

"I think," said Ismail, "you have hit on the right way; the lad goes to the old foolish moolla[3] of the mosque whenever he can get a moment's leisure, who has so filled his head with stories about paradise, which he reads to him out of the blessed Koran, that he is at times half beside himself, and this is the only point on which he is assailable. I will talk him over, and have no doubt he will soon belong to us."

"The sooner the better," said Hoosein, laughing; "I like to see the first attempt of a beginner: he always looks so simply innocent when the cloth is put into his hand, and he is told—"

"Silence!" cried the old man. "Suppose he were now to hear you (and you were going on with a relation of the whole matter), he might take a different view of the subject, and be off, as I said, before."

"No; there is no fear of that," said Ismail; "but are you not tired with your march? remember, we have far to travel tomorrow, and, by Alla! it is for some good too."

"Ay!" said all, getting up; "let us go to sleep; it is too hot to rest here; we shall be cooler in the open air," and they left the room.

You may believe, sahib, that my curiosity was at the highest pitch. Who was Ismail? who were the rest? what was it I was to know, or to be taught? My mind was in a whirl. I could not sleep that night; I never closed my eyes; I seemed to be in a fever, so intense was my curiosity, and, I may say, my desire to know everything, and to become a partner with Ismail in whatever he was. Hitherto I had been looked upon, and treated as a child; now that was to be cast aside. I was, like a snake, to throw off my old skin, and to appear in a new and brighter form. Who could my parents be? I had gathered enough from the conversation, that Ismail was not my father, and I taxed my memory to recollect such portions of my previous existence as might throw some light on the subject; but all was dark within me. I could remember nothing but poor Miriam, my mother as I had used to call her; beyond this, though hard did I endeavour, I could recollect nothing. It was only in after times, as

---

1 Beautiful virginal women who serve as companions to the Muslim faithful in Paradise.

2 Hindu god of war and storm.

3 Islamic priest.

I have told you, and during a long imprisonment of twelve years, that my memory aided me.

The old moolla of the mosque had hitherto appeared in my eyes the most learned of men; he had stored my mind with passages from the Koran, which had made me an enthusiast. When he spoke to me of the glories of heaven; of the thousands of houris who would be at the command of every true believer, described their beautiful forms, their eyes like sapphires, their teeth of pearls, their lips like rubies, and their breath like the perfume of musk; the palaces of jewels, and the fountain of immortality and never-ending youth;—I believed that I was destined to enjoy all. They had inflamed my imagination; and as I used to repeat them to Ismail, he too appeared as delighted as I was, and used to regret that he had never studied the blessed book, that he might enjoy its beautiful descriptions; yet the moolla was called a fool by Hoosein, and I understood from him that theirs was a higher calling, their rewards more splendid than even those of the Moslim! What could they be? I burned to know! and resolved, that if Ismail did not break the matter to me, I would, of my own accord, lead him to the subject.

I said, I think, that my eyes never closed that night; when I rose in the morning, I found that Ismail and the others were gone. He did not return for some days. This was nothing uncommon, certainly; but his proceedings had become mysterious to me for a long time before, and I could not help connecting his frequent and long absences with his true profession, whatever that might be. He could not be *only* a cloth merchant; there was nothing in that plodding business to hold out to him or to me the splendid hopes which Hoosein and the rest evidently entertained, and with which I had no doubt he was familiar. It must be something beyond this, which I could not compass; and to see whether I could get any clue to it, I betook myself to the old moolla.

Azeezoolla, for that was his name, received me with his usual kindness, but remarked that I must be ill, as my face, he said, was full of anxiety, and as though I was suffering from fever. I said I had had ague, but that I was better, and that it would soon pass from me. I took my usual lessons in the forms, positions, and words of a Mahometan's[1] daily prayers; and when these were ended, I begged him to open the Koran, and explain again to me my favourite passages. The old man put on his spectacles, and rocking himself to and fro, read to me passage by passage of the book in Arabic, explaining the meaning to me as he read. They were the same I had

---

1   English term for a Muslim.

heard often before; and when he had finished, I asked him whether there were not other portions of the book which he had concealed from me.

"No, my son," said he; "I have concealed from you nothing. My knowledge of this blessed book is indeed very limited; but oh, that you could have seen and heard the commentaries which my revered preceptor, peace be to his memory! had written upon it! In them, so deep was his knowledge, that every sentence of some chapters, in which the true meaning is purposely hidden from the uninspired, formed a separate treatise; nay, in some passages every word, and indeed every letter, was commented upon. But he is gone, and is now enjoying the delights of the paradise I have revealed to you. All I can do is to read to you, and I will do it again and again, till you have by heart the parts which most interest you, and which are the cream of the book."

"But," said I, "have you never heard of anything beyond what you have told me, in all your long experience? You are surely concealing something from me, which you fear to tell me on account of my youth."

"No, indeed," said the old man; "it is true that some professors of our religion, Sofees[1] and others, whose creeds are accursed, have from time to time promulgated heterodox doctrines, which are plausible enough, and entrap the unwary; but they lead to ultimate perdition, and I think you are now too well grounded in your belief to be led away by them, young as you are."

"Thanks to your kindness, I am," said I, "and it was only to try whether I had more to learn, that I have now questioned you as I have;" for I saw he either could not or would not reveal to me more. "But tell me, father, what profession ought I to adopt to carry your wise instructions into the best effect?"

"Become a moolla," said he; "you will have to undergo much painful study, but in the course of time this obstacle will be overcome; and depend upon it, there is no station or profession so acceptable to God as that of one of his ministers. I will instruct you in the rudiments of Arabic, and your father, when he sees your mind bent upon it, will not oppose you; nay, he will send you to Dehlie to complete the education I shall have begun."

"Well, I will think of it," said I. But it was very far from my intention to become a moolla. I could not disguise from myself that Azeezoolla was miserably poor, and was dependent upon contributions he with difficulty collected for his maintenance. Besides, Ismail was not a moolla, nor Hoosein, nor any of their set; and I must become one of them, be they what they might, before my mind could be at rest. I

---

1   Muslim mystics.

went no more to him. I had got from him his little store of knowledge, and if once I had broken the subject of my future life to him, I should only be subjected to continual arguments in support of his view of what would tend to my benefit; and as I did not like them, I thought it better to stay away.

Would to God I had become a moolla! Anything would be preferable to my state at present, which must now for ever remain as it is. It is my fate however, and I ought not to murmur at the decrees of Providence. If it had not been written, would my father have been murdered? If it had not been written, should I have ever become a Thug? Assuredly not! Who can oppose Fate? who can avert its decrees? Yet would you not, sahib, release me, and provide for me, if after many years you found me faithful?

Never! said I. You Thugs are too dangerous ever to be let loose again upon the world; your fingers would itch to strangle the first man you met, and before long we should hear of Ameer Ali Jemadar,[1] with a gang of forty or fifty fellows, who would give us infinite trouble to catch. Would it not be so?

I believe you are right, said Ameer Ali, laughing. In spite of my remorse at times, the opportunities would be too tempting for me to let them pass. And you know I have eaten the goor, and cannot change. I am better as I am, for if you caught me again you would hang me.

I have not the least doubt we should, Ameer Ali. But go on with your story; you will forget what your train of thought was, if you digress in this manner. He resumed.

Nearly a month elapsed, and after this weary time to me, Ismail returned, accompanied by Hoosein. My father, for so I shall call him, remarked a change in my appearance, which I accounted for as I had done to the moolla, and he seemed satisfied. But was I? Oh, no! I was consumed by my burning curiosity to know all that was hidden from me. I could not sleep at nights, and became sullen, and oppressed with thoughts which led me to no conclusions. At one time I had formed the determination to leave my father, and seek my fortune; and had actually packed up a few of my clothes, and a little money I had, and resolved to leave the town in the night, little caring where my fate should lead me; but when the time came, the sense of my desolation so pressed upon me, that I abandoned the idea, and remained. I trusted to time for clearing up the mystery that hung over me, but at the same time determined that I would be more watchful over my father and his companions than I had ever been before. And many were the resolutions I made to speak to him on

---

1 Officer; captain.

the subject nearest my heart; yet even when opportunities occurred, I could not bring myself to the task. It was not that I was timid—naturally I was brave—it was a mysterious consciousness that I should hear something (whenever I should hear it) that was strange, nay, fearful, that deterred me; but why this feeling should have so possessed me I cannot now tell, yet so it was.

One evening, Ismail sent for me to his sleeping-room. I had been rarely admitted to it, and my heart beat fearfully, with a presentiment that I was upon the crisis of my fate. Ismail seemed to me to be disturbed; he bade me sit down, and we sat silently for some time gazing on one another; there was only one small oil light burning in a recess of the wall, which made the apartment very gloomy, and this trifling circumstance contributed still more to increase the morbid feeling within me. I believe I almost gasped for breath; I could bear it no longer. I arose, threw myself at his feet, and burst into a passionate fit of weeping.

"Why, Ameer, my child, my son," said he kindly and caressingly, "what is this? what has troubled you? has some fair one bewitched you? have you got into any difficulty while I have been away? Tell me, my boy; you know you have no one in the world so fond of you as your father, and, alas! you have now no mother."

When my feelings gave me power of utterance, fearfully I repeated to him what I had heard from him and the rest, on the memorable night I have before related. When I had finished, I rose up, and with a throbbing heart said, "I have erred, my father; my curiosity, a boy's curiosity, overcame me, but since then my feelings have changed, why I know not; I am no longer a boy, for I feel that I can do anything, and only implore you to put me to the proof;" and I folded my hands on my breast, and stood silently. He was evidently much moved; dusk as it was, I could see his face working with emotions, and under expressions new to me.

At last he broke the silence, which had become to me insupportable. "My son," he said, "you know more than I had ever intended you should. I have now no alternative but to make you such as I am myself, and my knowledge of your character leads me to anticipate much from you."

"Trust me, only trust me!" I passionately exclaimed. "You shall never have cause to regret it!"

"I believe you," said he; "and now attend well to what I shall say, for upon it your future existence depends. There can be no hesitation, no falling back on the world, when once you know all. You will have to undergo a trial which will stretch your courage to its utmost. Will you go through with it? dare you to brave it?"

"I dare," cried I, for I was reckless.

He seemed to be absorbed in thought for a few moments, and then said,—

"Not to-night, but I swear to you that in three days at the farthest, I will conceal nothing from you."

I was disappointed, yet full of hope, and he dismissed me to my repose.

Ismail performed his promise; but I can hardly describe to you, sahib, the effect it then had on my mind. Shall I endeavour to relate what his tale was? I only hesitate, as it began by his giving me a sketch of his life, which I fear would lead me from my own story; yet it would interest you greatly.

I doubt not that it would, Ameer Ali, said I; and when you have finished your own adventures you can return to it.

You are right, sahib, I will omit it at present, all except his concluding words; which, with his tale of wrong, endured and revenged, made me hate the world, and cleave to Thuggee as the only profession and brotherhood in which I could hope to find good faith existing. They were these, and they have ever been indelibly impressed on my memory.

"Thus far, my son, have I related some events of my life for your instruction, and I have little more to add. I need hardly now mention that I am a Thug, a member of that glorious profession which has been transmitted from the remotest periods to the few selected by Alla for his unerring purposes. In it, the Hindoo and the Moslim both unite as brothers; among them bad faith is never known: a sure proof that our calling is blessed and sanctioned by the Divine authority. For where on this earth, my son, will you find true faith to exist, except amongst us? I see none in all my dealings with the world; in it, each man is incessantly striving to outwit and deceive his neighbour: and I turn from its heartlessness to our truth, which it is refreshing to my soul to contemplate. From the lowest to the highest among us, all are animated with the same zeal. Go where we will, we find the same brotherhood; and though differing perhaps, in many parts, in customs and points of practice, yet their hearts are the same, and all pursue the great aim and end of Thuggee with the same spirit. Go where we will, we find homes open to us, and a welcome greeting among tribes of whose language even we of Hindostan[1] are ignorant; yet their signs of recognition are the same as ours, and you need but to be thrown among them as I have been, to experience the truth of my assertions. Could this be without the aid of God? So clashing are human interests, and so depraved is the social state of our country, that I own no such feeling could exist without the Divine will. Some repugnance you will feel at the practice of the profession at first, but it is soon overcome, for the rewards held out are too glorious to allow us to dwell for a moment on the means we

---

1   Northern India.

use to attain them. Besides, it is Fate,—the decree of the blessed Alla! and who can withstand it? If he leads us into the undertaking, he gives us firm and brave hearts, a determination which no opposition can overcome, and a perseverance which never yet failed to accomplish its object. Such, my son, is what I would make you. You will enter on your calling at once in a high grade, under my auspices, a grade which others spend years of exertion to attain; you will never know want, for all my wealth shall be shared with you. Be firm, be courageous, be subtle, be faithful; more you need not. These are the highest qualifications of a Thug, and those which ensure honour and respect among our fraternity, and lead to certain success and high rank. As for me, I look but to see you at the head of a band of your own to retire, and in quiet pass the remainder of the years allotted to me, content with hearing the praise which will be bestowed upon Ameer Ali, the daring and enterprising son of Ismail! till then I shall be your guardian and instructor."

Chapter III

Falstaff.—He's no swaggerer, hostess; a tame cheater he; you may stroke
him as gently as a puppy greyhound. He will not swagger with a
Barbary hen if her feathers turn back in any show of resistance.
                    —*2nd Part of King Henry IV.*, Act ii., Scene 4.

"MY father," said I, "you need say no more; I am yours, do as you will
with me. Long ere I heard this history from you, I had overheard
a conversation between Hoosein, yourself, and some others, regarding me, which has caused me great unhappiness; for I feared I was not thought
worthy of your confidence, and it weighed heavily upon my mind. That was in
fact the cause of the sorrow and heaviness you have remarked; and I longed for an
opportunity to throw open my heart to you, and to implore of you to receive me
among you. I am no longer a child, and your history has opened to me new feelings
which are at present too vague for me to describe; but I long to win fame as you
have done, and long to become a member of the profession in which you describe
true faith and brotherhood alone to exist. As yet I have seen nothing of the false
world, and assuredly what you have said makes me still less inclined to follow any
calling which would lead me to connection with it. Heartless and depraved I have
heard it to be from others beside yourself, and I feel as though I was chosen by Alla
to win renown; it can only be gained by treading in your footsteps, and behold me
ready to follow you whithersoever you will lead me. I have no friend but yourself,
no acquaintance even have I ever formed among the youths of the village; for when
I saw them following what their fathers had done, and what appeared to me low
and pitiful pursuits, my spirit rose against them, and I have cast them off. My only
friend is the old moolla, who would fain persuade me to become one like himself,
and spend my days reading the Koran; but there is nothing stirring in his profession, though it is a holy one, and it consequently holds out no inducement to me,
or any hope of gratifying the thirst for active employment which is consuming me.
I have wished to become a soldier, and to enter one of the bands in the service of
Scindia to fight against the unbelieving Feringhees;[1] but this too has passed away,

---

1   Europeans.

and now I desire nothing but to become a Thug, and follow you, my father, through the world. I will not disappoint you; my thirst for fame is too ardent for anything but death to quench it."

"May God keep it far from you," said Ismail with feeling. "You are the only solace to a life which has now no enjoyment but what is produced by the development of your thoughts and actions. I know, my son, you will not disappoint me. You see the state of prosperity I am blessed with, but you little know the power I have; my authority is owned by every Thug in this part of Hindostan, and a week's notice would see a band of a thousand men ready to obey any order I should give them. This will be proved to you in a few days, at the festival of the Dusera.[1] We shall all assemble, at least as many as will be requisite for the opening operations of the year, which will be undertaken on a scale of unusual greatness, for we have determined to take advantage of the confusion at present produced by the wars of Holkar and Scindia with the Feringhees. We anticipate much work and a stirring season, and the men are impatient for employment, after a long period of inactivity. I will take you to Sheopoor,[2] which we have decided on as our place of meeting, as the zemindar[3] is friendly to us and assists us in many ways. I will introduce you to my associates, and you will be initiated as a Thug in the usual manner."

Thus, sahib, our conversation ended; the night had passed in its relation, and I went to rest a different being from what I had been for many days before. I rose, and found all my former energy and spirit had returned to me; and whereas a few days before I went about like a love-sick maiden, I now held up my head, threw out my chest, and felt a man. It was true I was still a boy, I was only eighteen years old, but I did not suffer my thoughts to dwell upon this; a few years, thought I, and, Inshalla![4] I shall be somebody. To prove to you, sahib, the excitement that possessed me, I shall relate to you the following circumstance. I might have joined in the action before, but never should have dreamed of doing the deed of daring I then did, in the presence too of men who were soldiers by profession, but who hung back at the moment of danger.

It happened, a day or two after the conversation with my father which I have related, that a tigress with a cub came into a small tract of jungle which lay near our village; the first day she was seen she killed a shepherd, the second day another

---

1   Hindu festival typically celebrated in October.
2   Sheopur, city in Sindia in northern India.
3   Powerful landowner who collects the land taxes of his district.
4   May it please Allah!

man who had gone to look for his body, and the third she grievously wounded the patail of the village, a man who was held in universal estimation, and he died during the night. A general meeting of the villagers was held at the place set apart for deliberations, and it was determined that all the active men should proceed in a body and attack the beast in her lair. The next morning we all assembled before daybreak. There was one man, a huge large-whiskered and bearded Pathan, who volunteered to be our leader; he was literally hardly able to move for the weapons he had about him. Two swords were in his belt, which also contained an assortment of daggers of various sizes and shapes; a long straight two-edged sword hung over his left shoulder, the point of which nearly touched the ground; he had also a shield across his back, and in his right hand a matchlock with the match lighted. He addressed my father as we came up.

"Salaam aleikoom![1] Ismail Sahib," said he, "is a quiet person like you coming out with us, and the Sahib Zadah too?

"Yes, khan,"[2] replied my father, "it is incumbent on all good men to do their utmost in a case of need like this; who knows, if the brute is not killed, but that some one else may become food for it?"

"Inshalla!" said the khan, twisting up his moustachios and surveying himself, "we have determined that the beast dies to-day. Many a tiger has fallen from a shot from my good gun; and what is this brute that it should escape? May its sister be defiled; the only fear is, that it will not stand to allow us to prove that we are men, and not dogs before it."

"As to that," said my father, "we must take our chance; but say, khan, how will you move with all those weapons about you? Why, you could not run away, were she to rush out."

"Run away!" cried the khan. "Are our beards to be defiled by a brute? What are you thinking on this morning, to suppose that Dildar Khan ever turned from anything in his life? Only let it come out, I say, and you will see what use the weapons will be! Trust to me single-handed to finish it. First I shall shoot it with my matchlock; it will be wounded; then I shall advance on it thus," said he, drawing the long sword and flourishing it, at the same time twirling round and round, and leaping in every possible direction.

---

1   Safety and good health to you!
2   Muslim chief or ruler.

"There!" said he quite out of breath, "there! would not that have finished it? Why I am a perfect Roostum[1] in matters of this kind; and killing a tiger is only child's play to Dildar Khan! why, I could eat one, tail and all. But come along, and when the play begins, let no one come in Dildar Khan's way," said he to the assembled group, "for, Inshalla! I mean to show you poor ignorant people how a tiger can be killed by a single man."

"I know the khan to be as arrant a coward as ever breathed," said my father to me; "but come, let us see what he will do, for I confess I am anxious to behold him capering before the tigress."

"By Alla!" said I, "if he does perform such antics, the brute will dine on him to a certainty."

"That is no concern of ours," said my father; "it is a matter of destiny; but I would venture a great deal, he never goes within an arrow's flight of her."

We all set out headed by Dildar Khan, who still flourished his long sword, holding his matchlock in his left hand, now and then smoothing up his moustachios, which grew, or had been trained to stick upwards from his lips, and reached nearly to his eyes. We soon reached the jungle, and on entering it, I thought the khan showed signs of fear.

"The beast can be but a panther after all," said he, "and it is hardly worth the while of Dildar Khan to put himself to trouble. See, boys," continued he to some of us, "I will wait here; if it should really turn out to be a tiger you can let me know, and I will come and kill it."

Against this, however, we all protested, and declared that all would go wrong without him; and after some demur he again proceeded.

"I told you," said my father, "how it would be; but let us see how he will end the affair."

We went on till some bones and torn clothes, and the head of one of the unfortunate men who had been killed, lying near a bush, proved very plainly that the animal was not far off; and at these the khan showed fresh signs of fear.

"They say it is a purrut bagh,"[2] said he, "a beast into whom the unsainted soul of that mad fakeer,[3] that son of the Shitan,[4] Shah Yacoob, has entered, and that it is proof against shot. Why should we risk our lives in contention with the devil?"

---

1   Valiant Persian hero.

2   A man transformed into a tailless tiger.

3   Muslim or Hindu mendicant.

4   Devil.

"Nay, khan," said a young dare-devil lad, the scamp of the village, "you are joking. Who ever heard of a purrut bagh that was a female? Besides, we will burn the beards of fifty Shah Yacoobs."

"Peace!" cried the khan, "be not irreverent. Do we not all know that purrut baghs can be created? Mashalla![1] did I not see one near Asseergurh, which a fakeer had made, and turned loose on the country, because they would not supply him with a virgin from every village?"

"What was it like?" cried a dozen of us; and for a moment the real tigress was forgotten.

"Like!" said the khan, rubbing up his moustachios with one hand, and pressing down his waistband with the other, "like! why it had a head twice the size of any other tiger, and teeth each a cubit long, and eyes red as coals, which looked like torches at night; and it had no tail, and—"

But here he was stopped short, and our laughter too, by a loud roar from a short distance; and a moment afterwards, the tigress and a half-grown cub, rushed past us with their tails in the air.

"Well, khan," said the lad before mentioned, "that is no purrut bagh at any rate. Did you not see the tail of the big one, how she shook it at you?"

"I represent," said he, "that, tail or no tail, it holds the accursed soul of that wretch Yacoob, may his grave be defiled! and I will have nothing to do with it; it is useless to try to kill the Shitan; if he choose, you know, he could blow us all into hell with a breath."

"Namurd! namurd! coward! coward!" cried some of us; "you were brave in the village; how are you now?"

"Who calls me namurd?" roared the khan; "follow me, and see if I am one or not," and he rushed forward, but not in the direction the tigress had gone.

"That is not the way," cried some, and at last he turned.

"This is child's play," said my father; "come, if we are to do anything, we had better set about it in good earnest."

And we went on in the direction the beast had taken.

It led to an open glade, at one side of which there was a large rook, with some very thick bushes upon it.

"She is there, depend upon it," said an old hunter; "I never saw a more likely place in my life."

---

1 Allah be praised!

We were all about thirty steps from the rock and bushes, and Dildar Khan did not at all relish his proximity to them.

"I beg to represent," said he in a low voice to us all, "that having killed so many of these brutes, I know best how to manage them, and as I am the best armed of the party, I shall take up my position near yonder bush, by which runs the pathway; she will take to it when she is driven out, and then you will see the reception she will meet with from Dildar Khan. Inshalla! I shall present the point of my sword to her, and she will run on it, then I shall finish her with one blow of my tegha."[1]

We all looked in the direction he pointed, and sure enough there was a bush, about two hundred paces off, on the pathway to the village.

"Not that one surely," said my father; "why, man, you will never see the beast from thence."

"Trust me," said the khan, and off he went.

"I told you how it would be," continued my father; "directly he sees the animal, he will be off down the road as fast as he can. But come," said he to the men, "since the khan thinks he will be of more use down yonder, I will lead you on, and we will see whether this eater of men cannot be got out."

We were immediately divided into three parties, one to go on either side of the bushes, the other by a circuit to get behind the rock and if possible upon it, in order to shoot her from above if she was to be seen; if not, at any rate to dislodge her by throwing stones. The arrangements were quickly completed, and though we were all within only a few yards of the bushes, there was no sign of the tigress. She expressed no displeasure at our near approach or preparations, as she had been disturbed before, and of course could not easily be driven out of her place of refuge. I was with one of the parties on the side, and had no arms but a sword and a light shield; indeed, I had gone more as a spectator than aught else. We waited a few minutes, and one of the party who had been sent round, appeared on the top of the rock; he was soon followed by three others.

"Are you all ready?" cried one of them; "I shall heave down this stone."

"Bismillah![2] Away with it!" cried my father.

Three of then applied their strength to it, and at last it rolled over the face of the rock, and thundering down, split into a thousand fragments. There was a moment of intense anxiety and suspense, but no tigress followed.

---

1 Short, crooked saber.

2 In the name of Allah!

"Try whether you cannot see her," cried my father; "if you do, fire; we are all prepared."

The men looked down in every direction, but said nothing. At last one of them was observed to be pointing to a particular spot, as though he showed the others something.

"By Alla!" said my father, "he sees her. Look out; she will rush forth before you are thinking of her."

Every man blew his match, and planted his feet firmly. At last one of the men on the rock raised his matchlock and fired; it was answered by a tremendous roar which rent the skies, and out rushed the cub, apparently badly wounded, for before he had come a few yards he lay down and roared horribly; he was fully half-grown, and made a dreadful noise. One of the men of our party fired at him, and he did not move after the shot struck him.

"Now we shall have tough work," said my father; "she will be savage and infuriated beyond description; it is hardly safe to be here; but mind your aim, my lads, she will never reach us; I never yet missed mine, but the shot may not be fatal; so look out for yourselves."

Again my father called to the men on the rock to heave over another fragment. There was one very large one just on the brink. After a good many pushes it gave way, and as the former had done, shivered into atoms with a great noise. It was successful, the tigress rushed out towards our side, and stood for a moment. I had never seen a tiger before, and could not help admiring her noble appearance. There she stood, her tail erect, the end of it only waving from side to side, glaring on us with her fearfully bright eyes, apparently irresolute as to what she would do, and not noticing the body of the cub, which was close to her. We were all as silent as death, each man with his matchlock to his shoulder. My father fired, and then the others; I could see the whole distinctly, for I had no gun. She staggered when my father fired, he had evidently hit her; but the rest had missed, and she charged with another tremendous roar, right at our party; but the shout we set up and the waving of our weapons turned her, and she set off at a low canter towards the bush where Dildar Khan had stationed himself.

"Ya Alla!" cried my father, "coward as he is, he will be killed! she will spare nothing now! what can be done?"

By this time the other party caught a glimpse of her, and every matchlock was discharged; she must have been hit again for she stopped, turned round, growled, and showed her teeth, but again sprang forward. I imagine Dildar Khan had no idea that she was approaching him, as he had hidden himself behind the bush and could have seen nothing of what had passed. "He may escape," said my father; it is possible, yet scarcely; what can be done?" No one made a reply, but an instant afterwards I had drawn my sword, and set off at full speed after the enraged brute.

"Ameer Ali, my son! come back, come back instantly! Ya Alla, he too will perish!" cried my father in an agony of apprehension.

But I heeded not, and who of that company had my fleet foot? yet some of them followed me. As I ran, I saw the tigress was weak, and was badly wounded, but still she ran fast. I saw her approach the bush, and the miserable man Dildar Khan rush from behind it, and stand in her very path, with his arms stretched out, apparently paralysed with fear. Another instant she had crouched as she ran, and sprang upon him; he was under her, and she fiercely tearing his body. It did not stop me; I heard the cries of those behind me to turn off, but I did not. I do not think I gave the danger a thought; if I did, the excitement overpowered it. Another bound had brought me close to the brute, whose head was down gnawing the body beneath her. I made but one stroke at her, which, praise be to God! was successful; the blade buried itself deep in the back of her neck, and she seemed to me to drop dead; I bounded off to one side, and watched for a moment. She was indeed dead, and lay, her limbs only quivering, upon the body of the man beneath her. Unfortunate coward! wounded as she was, she would not have turned after him, had he even had the presence of mind to avoid her; but he had thought to fly, and the sight of the animal had paralysed his faculties. Though all passed in a moment, methinks now, sahib, I see him, his eyes starting from his head, and his arms raised and expanded, as though wooing the animal's fatal embrace. Coward! had he remained behind the bush, he was safe, and might have shot her as she passed; but there he lay, a fearful spectacle, his face all bitten and lacerated, and the blood pouring from wounds in his stomach! He was quite dead. My father came up immediately; he embraced me, and burst into tears.

"How could you risk your life, my boy?" said he; "how could you be so rashly venturous of your life for so poor a wretch as he?" pointing to the body; "did I not tell you he was a coward? Yet I am proud of you now, my son, and you have shamed us all. See!" continued he to the whole assembly, "our faces are blackened this day by a boy; who among you could have planted so well-aimed and deep a cut? See: the blade has buried itself, and is half through the bone. Mashalla! it is a brave boy!" and again my father hugged me to his breast.

"I beg to represent," said old Benee Singh, my instructor in my athletic exercises, "that some of the praise is due to me for my good teaching. I always told you, Ismail

Sahib, that the Sahib Zadah[1] would be worthy of his father; may his riches increase, and may live a thousand years! Yes, sir," said he to me, "often have I taught you that cut. You see, you were running along, and cut over your left hand; it is few that can do that with any certainty, but you have caught the knack, and you want but a little practice to become as good a swordsman as myself. Perhaps too," continued he to me laughing, "the heart of your teacher may be made glad to-day; under such an auspicious commencement, the Sahib Zadah will remember the old Rajpoot."[2]

"That reminds me," said my father, "that I owe you a present; come to me this afternoon. Inshalla! we know how to be grateful for kindness, and it shall have its reward." And he received when he came a handsome gift.

I must say, however, that under his tuition I had become highly expert at all manly exercises; I could use a gun, throw a spear, wrestle, knew the exact use of every description of sword, straight or crooked, single or double-edged, long or short, and in all these exercises there was not a lad of the village, and I may say of the country round, who could in any way compete with me.

That night my father said to me, "Ameer, my son, to-morrow you accompany me to Sheopoor. I need not tell you how to-day's exploit will raise you in the eyes of your future companions. Already have I despatched intelligence of our proposed departure to-morrow, and some account of to-day's affair, enough only to make them curious to see the hero of it; and I have mentioned no particulars, which will make them the more anxious to hear them from me. You have hitherto been looked on with some suspicion by many members of my band; and were it not for my rank of jemadar, I should have been obliged to explain my intentions in regard to you long ago to them. I look therefore upon this event as particularly fortunate; as, knowing you are to be publicly brought amongst them, they will receive you with greater warmth and respect, as having given so undeniable a proof of your bravery, in the presence too of old soldiers, who have most of them seen many a tough fight."

"It was God's will," said I; "else what power had a boy like me to do such a thing?"

"You are now no child," replied my father; "you have this day, or I mistake you much, thrown off every lingering feeling of boyhood; the change has been sudden, but it has been complete, and it will last, or I mistake you much."

"You do not," I replied, "I am not what I was; to-day's is the first blood I have seen spilled; I feel that it will not be the last."

———◆———

1   Male child; son.
2   A member of a powerful landowning and military caste of northern and central India.

CHAPTER IV

1st Murderer.—How dost thou feel thyself now?
2nd Murderer.—Faith, some dregs of conscience are yet within me.
                                        —*Richard III.,* Act i., Scene 4.

2nd Murderer.—... I am one, my liege,
        Whom the vile blows and buffets of the world
        Have so incensed, that I am reckless what
        I do to spite the world.
                                        —*Macbeth,* Act iii, Scene 1.

THE day after my adventure with the tiger, I left our village with my father. We travelled on horseback, and on the fourth morning afterwards reached Sheopoor, the town from which the grand expedition was to set out. It was here too, that I was to be admitted into the band of Thugs, and I looked forward to my inauguration with much impatience, and perhaps some dread, for I knew not what ceremonies I had to go through. We put up in the house of Moedeen, where several other Thug leaders were also; and after refreshing ourselves, my father bid me accompany him to the council which was to determine on the future operations. I was presented to the members, ten in number, who were the jemadars of the different bands. I could see, from the respect and consideration with which my father was treated, that he was looked upon as the chief of the whole; I was gratified by the reception I met with; and my conduct in the affair with the tiger, the whole circumstances of which were related by my father, raised me at once to a high station in their respect.

As it still wanted two days of the festival of the Dusera, my inauguration was postponed to that day; for it is esteemed a particularly fortunate one by the Thugs, and indeed by all classes. On it, you are already aware, that all great undertakings are commenced by armies, and, in like manner, by us Thugs; for the breaking up of the rains gives a hope that the adventure will not be impeded by them; and the continuance of fine weather which follows it, allows the band to travel in comfort, and with better hope of booty from the chance of falling in with travellers, who also take advantage of the break in the weather to commence long journeys. Above all, it is a day peculiarly sacred to Bhowanee,[1] our patroness and goddess. Still, being a Moosulman,[2] I could not then see why such respect was paid to the festival of the Dusera, or indeed why it was kept at all; and I applied to my father for a solution of my doubts on the subject.

"It is necessary to your fully understanding this," said he, "that I should give you an outline of our belief in the Divine origin of our profession, which is intimately connected with the faith of the Hindoos, and by whom we Moosulmans have been instructed in the art of Thuggee."

"This is wonderful indeed," said I; "how do you reconcile any connection between the faith of unbelievers and that of the blessed prophet?"

"I cannot pretend to solve the difficulty," said my father; "but as their religion is far more ancient than ours, and no doubt had a Divine origin, there are many points in it which one of the true faith may follow without offence, so that he does not join them in all their forms and professions. Indeed, this is impossible, as no one can become a Hindoo; but, as I told you before, Thuggee is one of the means by which Alla works out his own ends; and as the profession of it has been handed down to us from ages, and becomes the fate of those who are called to follow it, there is no possibility of avoiding the profession though one desired to do so; and, as a direct consequence, no sin in associating with Hindoos in the practice of it, from whom it has had its origin. Do you understand me?"

"Perfectly," said I; "it was not to question its propriety that I asked the question, but only to know how it was that Hindoo festivals were acknowledged and kept by us Moosulmans."

"The Dusera is the only one," said my father, "which is observed; and the reason of this is, that it is the fittest time of the year to commence our enterprises, and has been invariably kept sacred by all Hindoo Thugs. But I must tell you of the origin of Thuggee, that you may judge for yourself how ancient it is, and how well the instructions then given by Divine command have been followed up. In the beginning of the world, according to the Hindoos, there existed a creating and a destroying power, both emanations from the Supreme Being. These were, as a matter of consequence, at constant enmity with each other, which still continues. The creative power, however, peopled the earth so fast, that the destroyer could not keep pace with him, nor was he allowed to do so; but was given permission to resort to every means he could devise to effect his objects. Among others, his consort Devee, Bhowanee, or Kalee,

---

1 Kali or Devi, Hindu goddess of destruction.
2 Muslim.

for she is known under these names and many others, constructed an image, into which, on this occasion, she was empowered to infuse the breath of life. No sooner was this effected, than she assembled a number of her votaries, whom she named Thugs. She instructed them in the art of Thuggee; and to prove its efficacy, with her own hands destroyed before them the image she had made, in the manner which we now practise. She endowed the Thugs with superior intelligence and cunning, in order that they might decoy human beings to destruction, and sent them abroad into the world, giving them, as the reward of their exertions, the plunder they might obtain from those they put to death; and bidding them be under no concern for the disposal of the bodies, as she would herself convey them from the earth. Ages passed on in this manner, and she protected her votaries from human laws, and they were everywhere found to be faithful: but corruptions crept in among them with the increased depravity of the world; and at last, a gang more bold and curious than the rest, after destroying a traveller, determined, instead of following the old custom of leaving the body unnoticed, to watch and see how it was disposed of. They hid themselves, as they thought, secure from observation in the bushes by the side of the road, and waited the arrival of the goddess. But what mortal can escape the eye of Divinity? She quickly espied them, and called them before her. Terror-stricken by her splendid and terrific appearance, and in the utmost dread of her vengeance, they attempted to fly; but she arrested their steps, and in an awful manner upbraided them for their want of faith.

"'You have seen me,' said she, 'and looked upon a power which no mortal has ever yet beheld without instant destruction; but this I spare you; henceforward, however, I shall no longer protect you as I have done. The bodies of those whom you destroy will no longer be removed by me, and you must take your own measures for their concealment. It will not always be effectual, and will often lead to your detection by earthly powers, and in this will consist your punishment. Your intelligence and cunning still remain to you. I will in future assist you by omens for your guidance; but this my decree will be your curse to the latest period of the world.'

"So saying, she disappeared, and left them to the consequences of their own folly and presumption: but her protection has never been withdrawn. It is true, the remains of those who fall by our hands are sometimes discovered, and instances have been known of that discovery having led to the apprehension of Thugs, at least so I have heard; but during my lifetime I have never known of one, and it is my firm belief that such instances have been permitted on purpose to punish those who have in some way offended our protectress, by neglecting her sacrifices and omens. You therefore see how necessary it is to follow the rules which have guided our fraternity for ages, and which cannot be changed without incurring the displeasure of the Divine power; nor is there anything in our creed to forbid it. We follow the blessed precepts of our prophet; we say our Namaz[1] five times a day; we observe all the rules of our faith; we worship no idols; and if what we have done for ages, ever since the invasion of India by our forefathers,[2] was displeasing to the apostle, surely we should have had, long ere this, some manifestation of his displeasure. Our plans would have been frustrated, our exertions, rendered of no avail; we should have dragged on a miserable existence; and, long ere this, should have abandoned Thuggee, and our connection with its Hindoo professors."

"I am convinced," said I; "for your relation is wonderful. Truly have you said that we are under the especial protection of Providence; and it would be sinful to question the propriety of any usages which have been transmitted from a period so remote, and followed without deviation. I will allow that I had thought this open connection with Kafirs[3] as offensive, because I was led, from the representations of the old Moolla who was my instructor, to believe them sunk into the lowest depths of depravity and bad faith; but he must have been ignorant, or a bigoted old fool."

"I will say nothing more than this," said my father, "that you will be thrown much into the society of Hindoos, all of good caste, and you will find them as faithful and as worthy of your friendship as any Moosulman; such, at least, has been my experience of them."

On the day of the Dusera the ceremony of my inauguration as a Thug commenced. I was bathed and dressed in new clothes which had never been bleached, and led by the hand by my father, who officiated as the gooroo, or spiritual director, and to whom seemed to be confided the entire direction of the ceremonies. I was brought into a room, where the leaders of the band I had before seen were assembled, sitting on a clean white cloth, which was spread in the centre of the apartment. My father then, advancing towards them, asked them whether they were content to receive me as a Thug and a brother, to which they all answered, "We are."

I was then conducted into the open air, accompanied by the whole number, when my father, raising his hands and eyes to the sky, cried in a loud voice, "O Bhowanee! mother of the world! whose votaries we are, receive this thy servant—vouchsafe to him thy protection—grant to us an omen which may assure us of thy consent!"

---

1   Daily prayer.

2   A reference to the Mughal Emperors, Islamic rulers of India from the early sixteenth century to the mid eighteenth century.

3   Infidels.

We waited for some time; and at last, from a tree over our heads, the loud twittering of the small tree-owl was heard.

"Jey[1] Bhowanee! Victory to Bhowanee!" cried the whole of the leaders; and my father embraced me, saying,—

"Be of good cheer, my son; the omen is most favourable. We could hardly have expected such an one; thy acceptation is complete."

I was then reconducted to the apartment, and a pickaxe, that holy symbol of our profession, was placed in my right hand, upon a white handkerchief. I was desired to raise it as high as my breast; and an oath, a fearful oath, was then dictated to me, which I repeated, raising my left into the air, and invoking the goddess to whose service I was devoting myself. The same oath was repeated by me on the blessed Koran, after which a small piece of consecrated goor, or coarse sugar, was given me to eat, and my inauguration was complete. My father received the congratulations of the assembly on the fortunate issue of the ceremony, and he then addressed me as follows:—

"My son, thou hast taken upon thee the profession which is of all the most ancient and acceptable to the Divinity. Thou hast sworn to be faithful, brave, and secret; to pursue to destruction every human being whom chance, or thy ingenuity, may throw into thy power, with the exception of those who are forbidden by the laws of our profession, which are now to thee sacred. These are particular sects, over whom our power does not extend, and whose sacrifice is not acceptable to our Divine patroness; they are Dhobees,[2] Bhats,[3] Sikhs,[4] Nanukshahees,[5] Mudaree Fukeers,[6] dancing-men, musicians, Bhungees,[7] Tailees,[8] Lohars,[9] Burraes,[10] and maimed or leprous persons. With these exceptions, the whole human race is open to thy destruction, and thou must omit no possible means (but at all times dependent upon the omens by which we are guided), to compass their destruction. I have now

---

1 Victory to.

2 Washermen.

3 Bards or scribes.

4 Practitioners of the monotheistic religion of Sikhism.

5 A class of mendicants.

6 A sect of Muslim mendicants.

7 Sweepers.

8 Oilmen.

9 Blacksmiths.

10 Carpenters.

finished; thou art become a Thug; and what remains of thy profession will be shown to thee by our gooroo, who will, under the necessary ceremonies, instruct thee in its details."

"It is enough," said I; "I am yours to death; and I only pray that an opportunity may soon be afforded me to prove to you my devotion."

Thus I became a Thug. Had I commenced my career under other and ordinary circumstances,—I mean, had I not been introduced to my profession by one so powerful and well esteemed as my father then was,—I must have entered the lowest grade of all; and had I proved myself to be active, intelligent, and brave, I might have risen in time to the highest. But this was spared me; and though too young myself to become a leader, I was in a rank above the rest, and was considered to be, and looked up to as, the person who was hereafter to fill my father's place, whenever it should suit him to retire from active employment.

The business which the Thug leaders had assembled to deliberate upon, was a plan of my father's, for a large body under himself and two other leaders (one of whom was Hoosein), to take the high road to the Dukhun;[1] to advance together as far as Nagpoor,[2] from whence my father was to proceed to Hyderabad;[3] and the others separating, one to go to Aurungabad,[4] thence through Khandesh,[5] by Boorhanpoor,[6] to Indore, and back to Sheopoor; the other also to Aurungabad, but from thence to Poona;[7] afterwards, if possible, as far as Surat,[8] and from thence homewards; but if the season should be too far advanced, they were to get to Boorhanpoor and home in the best way they could; finally, we were all to meet at Sheopoor by the commencement of the next rainy season.

No opposition was made to this; on the contrary, it was highly approved of, as, under the personal direction of Ismail, it could not fail of success, and as an expedition had not been made to the Dukhun for many years before. The other gangs were to proceed in various directions about Hindostan as far as Benares,[9] and round

---

1   The Deccan, the vast peninsular plateau that makes up most of southern India.

2   Nagpur, large city in central India.

3   Capital city of the Nizam's Dominions in central India, and ruled by a hereditary administrator.

4   Aurangabad, a city located in the northwestern region of the Nizam's Dominions.

5   Region in central India on the northwestern corner of the Deccan plateau.

6   Burhanpur, central Indian town north of the Nizam's Dominions.

7   Pune, western Indian city seized by the British in 1817.

8   City in western India ruled by the British.

9   Varanasi, holy city in northern India under British control.

through the Saugor and Nerbudda country,[1]—their proceedings to be guided by circumstances, which could not now be foreseen.

Thus planned, but a few days elapsed before we set off on our journey. With us there were sixty men, with Hoosein forty-five, and with the other jemadar, whose name was Ghous Khan, thirty; making in all one hundred and thirty-five.

Before we commenced our journey, however, it was necessary to consult the omens; and as the ceremonies are somewhat curious, I shall relate them to you,— observing, that no expedition, whether of a large or small body, can be undertaken without them.

The morning we were to separate on our different destinations, everything hav- ing been duly prepared, we repaired to a spot which had been chosen on the road, a short distance from the village, and the whole band was in attendance. Bhudrinath, a man of much intelligence and respectability, and who was learned in the con- ducting of ceremonies, bore the sacred pickaxe, which had been previously duly consecrated, and was immediately attended by my father and three other jemadars. My father, as the leader of the whole, carried a lota[2] filled with water, suspended by a string which he held in his mouth, down his right side. Had that lota fallen, what a dire omen would it have been to him! Nothing could have averted his death in that year, or at furthest in the year following.

We moved slowly, till we reached the spot fixed on, and there my father stood. Turning his face to the south, the direction we were to take, he placed his left hand on his breast, reverently lifted his eyes to heaven, and pronounced in a loud voice the following invocation to Bhowanee:

"Mother of the universe! protectress and patroness of our order! if this expedition be pleasing to thee, vouchsafe us thy help, and give us an omen of thine approbation!"

He was silent, and every mouth repeated the prayer aloud.

Now every one looked impatient for the omens; the band scarcely breathed, so intensely anxious was the suspense. Long we waited, perhaps half an hour; no one spoke; and the reverent silence of the assembled numbers had something exceed- ingly impressive in it. At last the pilhaoo, or omen on the left hand, was vouchsafed: a jackass brayed, and was almost instantly answered by one on the right, which was the thibaoo. What could have been more complete! such an omen had not been known for years, and promised the utmost success, and splendid booty. Loud and

---

1   The Saugor and Nerbudda Territories, a region of British India.
2   Small drinking vessel.

fervent were the cries of praise to Bhowanee; and each turning to his companion, congratulated him on the prospect.

Seven long hours my father sat on that spot, during which time all was prepared for the journey. At its expiration he arose, and we took the nearest road to Guneshpoor.[1]

At the stage where we stopped for the evening, the thibaoo and pilhaoo were heard by Bhudrinath, who carried the nishan, the pickaxe, or as it was now called, having been consecrated, *khussee;* and these renewed favourable omens produced an increased confidence in the expedition and its leaders. At the first streamlet we passed the next morning, the band all sat down, and some goor and dall,[2] which had been brought with us, was shared to all. Proceeding, favourable omens were again seen, and all declared that we should speedily gain a rich booty.

To me this was all strange and unaccountable; but the implicit faith which every one seemed to place in the omens, and the regularity with which the ceremonies were conducted, impressed me with a strong idea of their necessity; though, to my shame I say it, as I acquired confidence in myself, I scorned them as foolish; until misfortune, no doubt sent by Bhowanee, brought me to my senses, and made me penitent.

In a few days we arrived at Guneshpoor, and as yet we had no adventure. On reaching the town, the sothaees or inveiglers, whose duty it is to entice travellers into the power of the Thugs, were sent into the town, while we remained under a mango-grove on the outside. They were absent most part of the day; and when they returned they were eagerly questioned for intelligence. The men who had been sent on this duty were two Hindoos, one by name Bhudrinath, whom I have mentioned before, a Brahmin,[3] and the other a man of inferior caste, by name Gopal; but both were persons of the most bland and persuasive manners, and I was told that they rarely failed in their object. I was, among the rest, highly curious to hear their adventures in the town, and joined my father on his taking his place in the assembly.

Bhudrinath told us, that he had gone through the whole of the bazaar without success, when he was attracted to a bunnea's[4] shop by a respectable old man, who was in high dispute with the bunnea. He went up to him, and the old gentleman, who was in a violent passion at some attempted exaction on the part of the merchant,

---

1   Town in central India near Nagpur.

2   Boiled pulse.

3   A member of the highest Hindu caste, priesthood.

4   Huckster's.

immediately accosted him, and begged him to be witness to the transaction, expressing at the same time his intention of having the man brought before the kotwal[1] for his dishonesty.

"The bunnea was very insolent and abusive," Bhudrinath went on to say; "and after some altercation, I contrived to settle the matter by dint of threats and persuasions. The old man seemed highly pleased with me; and it naturally led, after we left the shop together, to a conversation about whither I was going, and who I was. I took advantage of this, to convince him that the town was no safe residence for a traveller, even for a night, and discovered that he was a Persian mootsuddee, or writer in the service of the Rajah of Nagpoor, whither he was travelling with his son.

"I of course alarmed him as much as I could with accounts of the thieves and Thugs on the road, and represented ourselves to be a company of travellers proceeding also to Nagpoor, on our way to the Dukhun, and associated together for mutual protection; and that we always rested outside the villages, as being the safest places when our number was so large. He seemed so struck with the proposal I made to him to come out and join us, that I lost no time in pressing him to leave the town, and I have succeeded. I have left Gopal, who joined us, to show him the way out, and assist him in packing up his things, and I have no doubt they will be here before sunset."

"Barik Alla!"[2] exclaimed my father; "your face is bright in our eyes, Bhudrinath; and I have no doubt, lads," said he to the knot of listeners, "that the old khayet[3] has abundance of money and jewels, and his plunder will help to see us on to Nagpoor; so if he does not come to us of his own freewill, we must even waylay him, and that too in the next march. A short time will decide this; and if he does not come, some of you lughaees[4] must be off to prepare the bhil or place of burial."

But we were saved the trouble; for the khayet came into our camp, as he had said, by sunset, and was met at the confines of it by my father and the two other jemadars. The respectability of his appearance struck me forcibly; he was evidently a man of polished manners, and had seen courts and good society. After arranging his travelling cart to sleep in, by placing some tent walls around it for protection to his women, he and his son, an intelligent handsome-looking youth, came to the spot

---

1   Town magistrate.

2   Blessings of Allah!

3   A caste of Hindus, usually clerks.

4   Those Thugs responsible for burying the dead.

where my father and the other leaders had spread their carpets; and many of the band being assembled, there ensued a general conversation.

Who could have told, sahib, the intentions of those by whom he was surrounded? To me it was wonderful. I knew he was to die that night, for that had been determined when he arrived in our camp, and while he was arranging his sleeping-place. I knew too that a spot had been fixed on for his grave, and that of those with him; for I had accompanied my father to it, and saw that it was begun; and yet there sat my father, and Hoosein, and Ghous Khan, and many others. The pipe and the story passed round, and the old man was delighted at the company he had fallen into.

"I thank you," said he to Bhudrinath, "that you brought me out of that unsainted village; truly here is some enjoyment in the society of gentlemen who have seen the world. There I should have been in perpetual dread of robbers, and should not have slept a wink all night, while here I need not even to be watchful, since I am assured by the Khan Sahib," pointing to my father, "that I shall be well taken care of."

"Ay!" growled out in a whisper an old Thug who sat behind me, "he will be well taken care of, sure enough, I will see to that."

"How?" said I.

He gave the sign, by which I knew him to be one of the bhuttotes or stranglers who had been selected.

"I have an old grudge against him," he continued, "and the time is come when I can repay it."

"Tell me how it happened," said I in a low tone, for the man's face wore a savage expression as he said it.

"Not now," said he, "how can I? I will tell you to-morrow night when we meet in the mujlis.[1] That man is Brij Lall, as great a rascal as ever lived, one who has committed more murders and more villanies in his life than any of us Thugs. But his cup is full, his breath is already in his mouth; one squeeze from me, and it will go forth never to return."

"And the boy," said I, "that fair, fine boy,—surely he will be spared."

"To tell all he saw, I suppose," said the man; "to deliver us up at the first place we come to! No, no, Mea,[2] we know better, and so will you one of these days."

And he went round and seated himself just behind the old man, who turned about as though he were intruded upon.

---

1 Assembly.

2 A term of endearment for a boy.

"Sit still, sit still," said my father; "it is only a companion. In an open camp like this every one is privileged to hear the conversation of the evening mujlis, and we usually find some one among us who can enliven the evening with a tale, until it is time to rest for the night."

So the old Thug sat still. I could see him playing with his fatal weapon, the hand-kerchief, now pulling it through one hand and now through the other; and I gazed on the group till my brain reeled again with excitement—with intense agony I might call it with more truth. There sat the old man, beside him his noble looking boy, behind them their destroyers, only awaiting the signal; and the old man looked so unconscious of danger, was so entirely put off his guard and led into conversation by the mild, bland manners of my father, that what could he have suspected? That he was in the hands of those from whom he was to meet his death? Ah, no! And as I gazed and gazed, how I longed to scream out to him to fly! had I not known that my own death would have followed instantaneously, I had done it. Yet it would have been of no use. I turned away my eyes from them; but they returned to the same place involuntarily. Every movement of the men behind seemed the prelude to the fatal ending. At last I could bear the intensity of my feelings no longer. I got up, and was hurrying away, when my father followed me.

"Where are you going?" said he. "I insist on your staying here; this is your initia-tion; you must see it, and go through with the whole."

"I shall return directly," said I, "I go but a pace or two; I am sick."

"Faint-hearted," said he in a low tone; "see you do not stay long, this farce must soon end."

A turn or two apart from the assembly restored me again, and I returned and took up my former place, exactly opposite the old man and his son. Ya Alla![1] Sahib, even now I think they are *there* (and the Thug pointed with his finger), father and son; and the son's large eyes are looking into mine, as my gaze is riveted on them.

Ameer Ali looked indeed as though he saw them, and stared wildly, but passing his hands across his eyes, he resumed.

Taajoob! said he, wonderful! I could have sworn they both looked at me; but I am growing old and foolish. Well, sahib, as I said, I gazed and gazed at them, so that I wonder even now they saw nothing extraordinary in it, and did not remark it. But no; the old man continued a relation of some treaties the Nagpoor Rajah was form-ing with the English, and was blaming him for entering into any league with them against his brethren, when my father called out "Tumbako lao (bring tobacco)!" It

---

1 Oh Allah!

was the signal. Quicker than thought the Thug had thrown his handkerchief round the neck of the old man, another one his round that of the son, and in an instant they were on their backs struggling in the agonies of death. Not a sound escaped them but an indistinct gurgling in their throats; and as the bhuttotes quitted their fatal hold after a few moments, others who had been waiting for the purpose, took up the bodies and bore them away to the already prepared grave.

"Now for the rest," cried my father in a low tone; "some of you rush on the servants; see that no noise is made; the bullock-driver and others can be dealt with easily."

Some of the men ran to the place the khayet had chosen, and surrounded the unsuspecting cart-driver and the other servants, who were cooking under a tree. I saw and heard a scuffle, but they also were all dead ere they could cry out.

"Come!" said my father and Hoosein taking me by the arms and hurrying me along, "come and see how they are disposed of."

I went, or was rather dragged along to one side of our encampment, where there was a ravine some feet deep, in the bottom of which a hole had been dug, and by the side of which eight bodies were lying. The father and son, his two wives, the bullock-driver, two male servants, and an old woman; also a servant, who was in the inclosure with the women. The bodies were nearly naked, and presented a ghastly spectacle, as they lay in a confused heap, but just visible from the brink of the ravine.

"Are they all here?" asked my father.

"Yes, Khodawund,"[1] said one of the lughaees, whom I knew.

"Then in with them!" cried my father; and they were quickly deposited in their last resting-place, the head of one over the feet of another, so that they might lie close.

"We had better open them," said the lugha, "for the ground is loose and they will swell."

So gashes were made in their abdomens, and the earth quickly filled in on them; it was stamped down, the top smoothed, and in a few moments no one could have discovered that eight human beings had been secreted beneath the spot. We turned away from it, and every one betook himself to repose.

Sahib, can I describe to you how I passed that night! Do what I would, the father and son appeared before me; the old man's voice rung in my ears, and the son's large eyes seemed to be fixed on mine. I felt as though a thousand devils sat on my breast, and sleep would not come to my eyes. It appeared so cold-blooded, so unprovoked

---

1   My lord.

a deed, that I could not reconcile myself in any way to have become even a silent spectator of it. Yet my father had joined in it, my father whom I loved intensely, and Hoosein too. But all would not do; I could not tranquillize myself. I crept from beneath our little tent, and sat down in the open air. The moon shone brightly as ever, as now and then she emerged from beneath a passing cloud, and there was a cool breeze which fanned my burning face and soothed me. I watched her as she appeared to travel along in the heavens till she became overcast; and a few heavy drops of rain, as if she wept over the deed she had witnessed, drove me again under the tent. I crept close to my father, who was sound asleep, and embracing him with my arms sleep came to my eyelids, and I woke not till the usual hour of prayer arrived, when I was roused by my father to join in the morning supplication.

We spread our carpets, and I repeated the form with him; but my thoughts were with the old man and his son, and the event of the preceding night.

Immediately after it was over, our horses were saddled, and we set out on what proved to be a long march; for it was necessary to get as far as possible from Guneshpoor, that no suspicion might attach to us.

In due time we arrived at the stage, and a man was sent into the town to purchase one rupee and a quarter's worth of goor, or coarse sugar; what this was intended for I could not imagine, but it was soon made known to me when I asked my father.

"This," said he, "is the sacrifice of the Tupounee,[1] in which we all join after any adventure similar to what you saw last night; it is a rite of the utmost solemnity, and must never be neglected."

The man returned with the sugar, and a place having been chosen, Bhudrinath, the bearer of the khussee,[2] was seated on a blanket spread for him, his face towards the west. All the best men and noted bhuttotes seated themselves on each side of him, looking in the same direction as he did. My father then made a small hole in the ground near the blanket, upon which was placed the sacred pickaxe and the pile of sugar, and a piece of silver as an offering. A little of the sugar was then put into the hole by my father. He raised his clasped hands to heaven, and in a supplicatory manner cried aloud,—

"Powerful and mighty goddess! who hast for ages vouchsafed thy protection unto thy votaries, and who particularly to Joora Naik and Khudeek Bunwaree gavest one

---

1   The sacrificial ceremony Thugs perform after a murder.
2   Consecrated pickaxe.

lac[1] and sixty thousand rupees in their need, we beseech thee in like manner to aid us, and fulfil our desires!"

This prayer was devoutly repeated by all around, and my father taking water in his hand sprinkled it upon the pickaxe and into the hole. He then took pieces of the sugar and presented them to each of the Thugs in succession, who ate it in silence; they then drank some water, and the pile of sugar was distributed among the rest of the assembled band, who likewise ate their portions in silent reverence; all except myself, for not having as yet strangled a man, I was not eligible to partake of it with the rest. However, my father had reserved a portion of his own for me, which he made me eat. After I had swallowed it he said,—

"You have eaten the goor, and are now a Thug in your heart. Were you to desire to forsake us you could not, such is the power it has when consecrated as you have seen it over the hearts of men. Were any one to find a portion and eat it, whatever might be his rank or condition in life, he would assuredly become a Thug; he could not avoid it, the power it would exercise over him would be irresistible."

"This is wonderful indeed," said I. "Have such things been known?"

"I could relate hundreds of instances had I time," he replied; "but ask Hoosein, or any one, they will all tell you the same."

In the evening, when all were assembled as usual, my father took me to task about my faint-heartedness, as he termed it.

"This will never do, my son," said he; "you, who ran in upon the tiger so nobly, ought not to shrink from such child's play as this; you must be a man, and behave better, and remember you have eaten the goor."

"For shame, brother!" said Hoosein. "Do not speak so to the Sahib Zada;[2] remember you were no better yourself at first. Do you not recollect the business at——, and what difficulty I had to persuade Ganesha that you were in reality good stuff? Let the Sahib Zada but see one or two more of these affairs, and he will be quite a different person, he will become a tiger at the work. I do not fear, my son," said he, turning to me and slapping me on the back; "worse men than you have begun better, and ended in being chicken-hearted fellows, only fit to dig graves and be scouts. Old Hoosein never yet was mistaken in any one, and you, Inshalla! will surpass your father. Only let him," continued he, again addressing my father, "let him see one or two more affairs, and then try his hand himself; you will then see whether I am wrong or not."

---

1   100,000 (also *lakh*).

2   Son.

"It is well," exclaimed my father. "Believe me, my son, I meant not to upbraid you, but I was fearful the feeling you displayed might grow upon you. Be kind as you will to those around you, affectionate to your connections, pity the poor, give alms to the needy; but remember that you are a Thug, and have sworn relentless destruction to all those whom Alla may throw in your way."

"I am rebuked," said I, "and your words have sunk into my heart. Never more shall you have to say of me that I flinched from my duty. Whenever you think fit, I am ready to take the handkerchief." And to turn the subject I said, "I beg to represent, that Mahomed the bhuttote promised to tell me some history of the man who died last night, and I call on him to fulfil his word."

"Well spoken!" cried a dozen of the men; "Mahomed is a sure hand at a story, let us have it."

Mahomed, after stuffing a large quantity of paun-leaf[1] and tobacco into his mouth, crunched it several times between his teeth, and after a copious discharge of red saliva, settled himself upon his heels, and addressing my father spoke as nearly as I can remember as follows:—

"I was born at Boree, which is a small village in the Nagpoor territory; my father was a Thug, as you all know, and my ancestors were the same for generations before. Tales of their feats have been handed down in our family from father to son, and they are worth relating, but they have nothing to do with my story. They had been prosperous however, and had saved money enough to give a large sum at the court of Nagpoor for the office and lands of the patelship (chief magistracy) of our village; nevertheless they pursued their profession of Thuggee. My grandfather Kasim, as many of you know, was as famous a leader of Thugs as any one has been since he died; and my father, who was then young, succeeded to his property and situation. Long he held it, and none arose to dispute his claim.

"But his prosperity was not fated to last. Well do I remember the day when some soldiers, sent by order of the peshkar[2] of the court arrived at the village with an order to bring him to 'the Presence.' My father vainly endeavoured to learn from them the reason of this sudden call for him, as he was regular in his payments to the Government; and finding reasoning would not avail, he strove to bribe the leader of the party into conniving at his absence. But all would not do; he was obliged to accompany them, and he took me with him at my earnest entreaty. I was then a young man, probably about the age of the Sahib Zada there. We reached Nagpoor

---

1   Betel leaf, used as a stimulant.
2   The rajah's secretary.

after some long marches, and on our arrival we were cast into a vile prison, our legs loaded with irons, and we were denied the commonest comforts. We had no paun or tobacco, no clean clothes, were not allowed to see any one, and were given the coarsest and most wretched food to eat. In this manner we passed three long months. My father in vain entreated to know what he was accused of, or who was his accuser; and equally in vain were his attempts to have his situation made known to his family and friends. We wearied ourselves in our lonely prison with conjectures as to what the cause of the misfortune could be, but without success. At last, one day that wretch Brij Lall, who died last night by my hand, came into our prison attended by soldiers. My father gave himself up for lost, and thought his hour of death had arrived; but recovering, he appeared to recognise Brij Lall, and instantly assailed him with imprecations and abuse.

"When he had finished, Brij Lall, eyeing him with a grim look, said,—

"'Pateljee![1] perhaps you will now condescend to give the Government some account of the effects of Jeysookhdas the merchant, who lived in your village, and about whose affairs you well know I was sent some years ago. You may also remember the reception and treatment you gave me, for which, by the blessing of God, I will now see whether I cannot effect a return.'

"'Thou art a liar, and a base-born rascal of a mootsuddee![2] cried my father, 'and not one word shalt thou ever know from my lips. Send some one more fit to confer with Kasim Patel, and he will tell what he knows; but not one word to thee, thou dog and son of a dog.'

"'We will see,' said the vile wretch; and making a sign to the soldiers with him, my poor father was seized, and a horse's nosebag filled with hot ashes being tied over his head, he was thumped violently on the back till he was forced to inhale the hot dust, which nearly killed him. This was repeated several times, on every refusal to tell to Brij Lall what he desired to know. At last nature could bear no more, and he fainted. The wretch then left the prison, particularly ordering that no water should be given. But in this his vile intentions were frustrated; for fortunately some had remained from our morning's supply, and after sprinkling my father's face, and forcing a draught into his mouth, he recovered sufficiently to sit up and drink some more, which revived him."

---

1   A formal name for the head of a village.

2   Scribe.

Chapter V

WHEREIN THE OLD THUG ENDS HIS TALE

"'I THOUGHT I should have died, my son,' said my father at length; 'and see what a black heart that villain must have to treat an old man after that fashion. My curses on him and his! he will prosper awhile, but judgment for this and all his villanies will at last overtake him.'

"'Tell me,' said I, 'what quarrel there is between you, and what cause he has to persecute you in this manner.'

"'Listen,' he replied, 'and you shall know. Some years ago, when you were but a boy, Jeysookhdas, who was the principal sahoukar[1] in the village, died. On his death-bed he sent for me, and delivering over his family to my care, entreated me as a Moosulman, and one of the faithful, to protect them against this Brij Lall, whom he had in the public durbar[2] at Nagpoor beaten with a shoe, for slandering him in the vilest manner with the intent of ruining his reputation. In fact Brij Lall had accused him of making away with some of the revenue—for Jeysookh was the channel of payment not only of the revenue of our village, but of those around us, amounting in the year to nearly a lakh of rupees. Fortunately for him, the character of Jeysookh stood too high for the aspersions of a low wretch like this to hurt it, and no notice was taken of what he had said. But the insult he had received never left the mind of Brij Lall. He brooded over it, and made every attempt to ruin my old friend; who, as he had powerful enemies at the court, was ever afterwards kept in continual dread of being plundered under some false accusation, or cast into prison. At length however he died; and in our last interview he implored me to lose no time in sending off his wife and family to their country, Marwar,[3] with their jewels and what money I could collect. I did so as soon as I possibly could, under an escort of our own people, in case they should fall in with other Thugs on the road.

---

1 Banker.
2 Court.
3 Desert region in western India.

"'They had scarcely been gone a week, when this Brij Lall and another moot-suddee came with an order from his master Narayun Pundit, the peshkar, to seize Jeysookh's family and effects. The order was a verbal one, and this being a very unusual circumstance, I directly refused to give any intelligence about the family, or account of the effects of the deceased. Brij Lall began to threaten, and at last became grossly abusive to me, on which I beat him with my shoe, had him turned out of the village, and he was pelted with mud and stones by all the idle lads as he was conducted beyond the boundaries.

"'I never heard anything more of Brij Lall, but I knew he was my enemy at court, as I could get no justice for many complaints I made against the ill conduct and aggressions of a neighbour, who had not only encroached on my boundaries, but had seized grain which had been cut on several occasions. This annoyance at last reached such a height, that I determined to send a deputation to the court to petition for redress. It was however fruitless. My people were openly opposed by Brij Lall, who it seemed had risen into great favour and power; I was openly accused as a usurper of the patelship of our village; a person was set up by Brij Lall as the descendant of the real patel; and so much countenance and support was given him that my people returned to me in great alarm and utterly discomfited.

"'Since that time, my son, now about five years ago, I have been constantly alarmed by reports which have reached me through my friends at Nagpoor. I have been warned to beware of assassination, to allow no strange men to come into the village, nor to go anywhere without a sufficient escort. This, however, has not, as you know, interfered with our profession, which I have not neglected to follow; but in other respects I have been careful. In spite of all, however, we are fairly in his hands, and may Alla deliver us out of them!'

"We remained some days without another visit from our tormentor; but at last he came again, and my poor father was again tortured in various ways, but without effect: he would tell nothing.

"'You dare not kill me, cowardly kafir as you are,' cried he to Brij Lall; 'and, Inshalla! were I once out of this vile prison, you should see what a true Moosulman could do for himself. And I bid you beware.'

"Brij Lall laughed at my father's impotent threats, and again left us.

"We had remained in confinement for nearly three months, when one day one of the soldiers of our guard, won over by my father's promises and really struck with the injustice of our case, agreed to convey a petition, which my father had drawn up, to a sahoukar, with whom he was acquainted, who then managed the money affairs of our village, and resided in the city of Nagpoor.

"He was extremely astonished to hear of our situation, and immediately set to work to procure our liberation. But this was no easy task: Brij Lall possessed the ear of the minister of the court, and every attempt our friend made was frustrated. At last he laid our case before the chief sahoukar of Nagpoor, a man of great influence, who went to the minister himself expressly on our behalf. We were told that the next day we were to appear in the durbar and answer the accusations which had been made against us; and at the hour appointed we were taken to the house where the peshkar resided, and where he heard the various suits and cases which were brought before him.

"Narayun Pundit was then a young man, but he was looked up to with much respect by all who had any dealings with him. He was considered just, and one who patiently listened to both sides of a question before he gave his decision. But our bitter enemy Brij Lall was his confidential mootsuddee, and conducted himself in so plausible a manner that his tyrannies were never discovered.

"Brij Lall made his accusation against my father. He said that, by the laws of the kingdom, accounts of the effects of sahoukars and other wealthy persons ought to be furnished to the Government when they died without male children; that it was well known that Jeysookhdas was wealthy; that he had two or three daughters, but no sons; and that they had no right to have touched a rupee of the property, until the accounts of the Government had been settled. Again, that my father was not the rightful patel of Boree, and that the person who was descended from the original possessors claimed the office and the lands which were then in my father's possession. Brij Lall concluded his representation by saying to the pundit, 'I will refrain from dwelling, O incarnation of Brahma![1] on the usage I have met with at this man's hands. Twice did I visit his village, and twice was I received with such indignity that my blood boils at the recollection. My intentions in going there were solely for the good of the Government; and had I but then complained, the wrath of my lord would have descended on this man's head, and annihilated him and his family. But I devoured my grief, and it was not until provoked by his repeated refusals to come to the Presence, and his contempt of the messages sent to him about the effects of Jeysookhdas, that I became aware that the dignity of the Government was set at nought, and I ordered his arrest and imprisonment.'

"'Ya Alla! Alla!' cried my father; 'my lord, it is all a lie. I call Alla to witness that I never disobeyed any order of the Government when sent to me in a proper form. Have I not eaten the salt of the Government before that pitiful wretch was born?

---

1   The Hindu creator god.

and who is he that my lord should suffer him to abuse so old a servant of the state in his presence? If I have permission, I will represent to my lord that I am not in fault, but that this devil ought to be severely punished for the treatment he has subjected your slave to."

"'We will hear you to-morrow,' said the pundit,[1] 'and in the meantime it will be proper for you to draw up a statement of what you have to say in your defence, in order that its relation may be more succinct and more readily comprehended.'

"My father then begged not to be confined like a thief, and offered the two sahoukars as his securities to appear whenever he might be called on. This was admitted, in spite of Brij Lall's protestations that no securities would bind us, and we walked away in company with our friends; my father, as he passed him, twirling his mustachios and looking askance at him, with many a muttered Inshalla and Mashalla, all of which Brij Lall answered with looks of the most deadly spite and hatred.

"In the course of the evening an account was drawn up in Persian of the whole of Brij Lall's conduct from first to last; and we took it to the durbar in every expectation of seeing him disgraced before our eyes, for his unwarrantable treatment of us. But we were doomed to 'eat disappointment.' The petition was read by Narayun Pundit, and he proceeded to pass judgment in the case; which was, that Brij Lall had much exceeded his authority in imprisoning my father, that he had acted wrongly in persecuting Jeysookh and his family, for that on an examination of the accounts there did not appear to be any claim against him.

"On the other hand, that my father had behaved ill to Brij Lall, in having had him turned out of the village; disrespectfully to the State, in not readily giving the accounts demanded to an agent who was known to have the power to ask for them, and in resisting for so long a time his repeated orders.

"My father was going to reply, when his friend the sahoukar stopped him. 'Better,' said he, 'is it to come out of a battle with half your life than with no life at all. Be quiet, consider that you have escaped, which is what very few do, from the net which was thrown round you by that low rascal, and be thankful.'

"My father had only to pay a small fine for what he had done to Brij Lall. He considered that he had obtained a victory, and so the matter ended.

"I never shall forget the advice which the old sahoukar gave my father, when after some days' sojourn with him, and being entertained at his expense, we were about to set out for our village.

---

1 Teacher; a learned Hindu.

"'Pateljee,' said he, 'I know that Brij Lall well; he will never give up his revenge; you have seen that he behaves like a cow before his patron, but absent from him he is a tiger in heart and in manners; and such is the influence he has obtained that no one dares to oppose him. You have indeed got well out of his clutches; but had not your affairs been taken up our séth,[1] you would have remained in your miserable prison until his hate had been satisfied by your death, from the constant torment and ill-usage he would have subjected you to.'

"'Shookr Alla!'[2] said my father, 'I am at least safe now.'

"'Not without great caution,' said the sahoukar; 'his emissaries will beset you wherever you go, and it will require your utmost vigilance and wariness to avoid them. By your soul, O Patel, I beseech you not to disregard what I say, or you will repent it.'

"'I will not,' said my father; 'your words are friendly, and I drink them in as grateful sherbet. But this Brij Lall must have long arms and powerful if he can reach Mahomedjee Patel.'

"In a very few days after, we took our leave and returned home; but, as had been predicted, in a few months strange men began to be seen about the village, and my father, strange to say, disregarded all our prayers to stay at home, especially after dusk. He would not listen to us, called the men we had seen travellers, and stayed from home late at nights out of bravado. However, my mother grew at last so anxious and so alarmed about these repeated visits of unknown people, that she begged of me never to leave my father's side by day, and always to bring him home with me from the fields in the evening. This I did for a long time; but one night, one cursed night—would that I had never seen the dawn of the day preceding it!—having been delayed in a field of sugar-cane to arrange about the cutting of it the following day, we were late in returning home.

We were accompanied part of the way by some men of a neighbouring village, but they separated from us about half a coss from ours; and the remainder of the way (if we followed the straight road) was one which was not thought safe, and by which no one went after nightfall if he could help it. I attempted to take another, but the old man observed it, and said sharply, 'That is not the way, that road will keep us out an hour longer.' I had no reason to give to dissuade him from the road I wished to avoid, though an ill-defined feeling that there was danger in the one before us had led me to endeavour to take the other. But, my friends, who can avoid his fate? If it

---

1   Merchant; rich man.
2   Thank Allah!

is the will of Alla that one is to die, of what use is human foresight? We went on, and soon reached the inclosed fields, between the high milk-bush hedges of which the path wound. It was scarcely light enough to see our way, but we knew every foot of the road. All at once, as we proceeded, I thought I saw in a hedge which crossed the road a glimmer as if of the match of a gun.

"'Look!' said I to my father, 'we are waylaid, there are people behind the hedge. Look, there are three lighted matches!'

"'You are a fool,' cried he, 'they are fireflies. Are you afraid? has my son become a coward?'

"The words were hardly out of his mouth when there were three sharp cracks close to us. My father fell on his face without uttering a sound, and I felt a coldness and numbness all down my back, with a sharp pain, and the same feeling in my leg. I became sick, staggered a few paces, and then fell; but I was not insensible. Three men rushed out from the hedge, and ran towards us with drawn swords. Seeing that neither of us moved, one of them turned me over on my back and looked into my face. I shut my eyes, for I knew if they were open I should not live an instant.

"'This is not the man,' said the fellow standing over me; 'we have missed them.'

"Another came up."

"'It is nearly as good,' said he, 'it is the young devil the son, the father, depend upon it, is the other; come and see.' And they left me.

"They went to where my poor father lay, but I could not see what they did. I suppose they examined him, for one cried, 'Alhumd-ul-illah![1] we have been successful; our faces will be bright in our employer's sight for this. And only think, to have succeeded so easily after this long watching! The old dog was as wary as a fox."

"'You may thank me,' said another, who had not as yet spoken; 'if I had not dogged him to the sugar-cane field, and found out his nearest way homewards, we might have had a long continuance of our fruitless watching, of which I was heartily tired. Come,' continued he, 'we must not stay, the country will be too hot to hold us. Madhoo will help us on to Nagpoor, and the sooner we get to him, the better; the horses I know are all ready."

"I heard no more. I was sick and faint, and lay almost insensible for a long time. The pain of the wounds was horrible, and I writhed in torment; the night too was dreadfully cold, and I became so stiff I could not move. I tried even to get as far as my poor father's body, which I could just see lying on its back; but motion was denied me. I lay and moaned bitterly. I heard the voices of persons not far of, and

---

1 Praise be to Allah!

shouted as loud as I could, but they did not hear me. There were shots fired, as I afterwards heard, as signals to us; but I could not answer them. What could I do, lying as I did like a crushed reptile? My senses went and returned, as though I were dead, and again alive. Oh, my friends, how can I describe to you the misery of that night? At last I was roused out of a faint by some persons with a torch standing over me. I quickly recognized them as some of the labourers of the village. They had searched every lane, and at length found me. I knew not what they said or did; but they broke out into lamentations on seeing my father's body, and taking me up in a blanket they carried me to the village, and set me down at the door of my father's house: alas! his no longer.

"My friends, all of you have seen the grief of women when death has come into the house and struck down a father, a brother, a son; all of you know how the shrieks and moans of women pierce into the heart, and turn men's livers into water. Till my father's body arrived there was no cry—no scream. My mother sat in a corner rocking herself to and fro, calling on my father's name in a low tone, and every now and then beating her breast; my sister attended to me, and moistened my mouth with water, as I still lay unable to speak, but fully aware of all that was going on around me. Some old women of the village sat near my mother, shivering in the cold wind which whistled through the house, and speaking among themselves in whispers. There was but a small lamp in a niche in the wall, which with its flickering light now revealed one group now another, causing the shadows of the whole to leap about, over, around, above me, until my disturbed brain fancied them a legion of devils sent to torment me before my time.

"'Sister,' said I, 'call our mother to me, I am dying, I think,' for at the moment I felt fainter than ever.

"'No, no! you must not die; you must not leave us now,' said the affectionate girl. 'It is but a wound; the barber is coming and will take out the ball; and a fomentation is being prepared by the hukeem.[1] You will soon be well.'

"As she spoke this a sudden gleam of torches lighted up the whole space outside; and immediately after, four men, bearing my poor father's body, walked slowly towards the house. I summoned energy enough to sit up, leaning against the wall, and the body was brought, all bloody as it was, and laid down. I should not say laid down, for as the men who carried it were preparing to let it down gently, one of the corners of the blanket slipped, and the corpse fell heavily to the ground, giving a horrid dull squelch, the sound of which thrilled through every nerve.

---

1 Physician.

"For an instant there was not a word spoken; bat when the bloody features were exposed to view, the uproar was dreadful. Headed by my mother, all the old women rushed to the side of the body, and began the most heartrending shrieks; those who had carried it were also affected, and the cry reached to the outside, where the crowd assembled took it up, till the heavens were cracked with the noise of the lamentations. It was in vain that I endeavoured to make myself heard. But on a sudden the noise ceased, and silence was ordered by the kazee[1] of the village, who entered. He cast a look on the dead body, and then asked for me. 'Who has done this?' said he; "whom do you suspect? Tell us, by your soul, tell us, ere it be too late to overtake them, whoever they may be.'

"'Mahdoo, Patel of Etare,' said I; 'but the villains have horses, they are gone ere this, there is no use sending.'

"'Who have horses? who have gone, did you say?' cried he with impatience. 'Rally for a time, and strive all you can to let us know how this was,—how it happened.'

"I had barely strength, but I gave a short relation of the whole.

"'By Alla, it is the work of Mahdoo himself,' said one, 'and we will burn his village before the morning breaks.'

"'It is the doing of Rheim Khan,' cried another.

"Rheim Khan was my father's brother-in-law, and they had been at bitter enmity.

"'Who takes the name of Rheim Khan?' cried my mother. 'May his tongue be blistered and rot in his mouth! May his end be like this!' pointing to the corpse; and again she resumed her howls and lamentations.

"'Did you hear the woman?' said one fellow close to me; 'she would not curse at that rate if Rheim Khan was free from suspicion.'

"'Silence!' said I, as loud as I could. 'I know who is the author of this, at least I have a right to have the strongest suspicions. Mahdoo Patel had no hand in it, he is a coward; Rheim Khan, though he hated the old man, could never have done or planned this; no, it is neither. It is one whom we poor people can never reach from his height of station, one whom the pleasure of Alla alone can bring down to the condition of him who is there; I mean Brij Lall, the accursed, the merciless.' I was exhausted with speaking, and sank down.

"'Who spoke?' said my mother raising her head; 'I surely heard the voice or my son!'

"'I am here, my mother,' said I; and she turned to me.

---

1 Muslim judge.

"'Thou here! thou alive! Coward! hast thou come to me to see thy father a bloody corpse in his own house? Where wert thou that thou diedst not with him? Did I not caution thee never to leave the headstrong old man, who would persist in disregarding all advice, and in exposing himself at night?'

"'I cannot answer thee now, my mother,' said I; 'but I was with him. See here, I fell also; though I did not die then, I feel that I shall do so soon.' I opened my vest and showed her the hole the ball had made, out of which a drop or two of black blood every now and then oozed; she looked at it, and threw herself at my feet.

"'Thou art no coward!' she sobbed out, 'thou art no coward! Thou hast bled in thy father's defence, and I can say nothing but that it is the will of Alla, and his fate. Who can avoid his destiny? But it is hard to lose both. Husband and son, husband and son, and I an old woman.'

"And she went from me, and resumed her place at the side of the body.

"One by one the neighbours left us. The name of Brij Lall had silenced every one; and in a very short time there remained only the watchers by the corpse, my sister, and myself. She was but a girl, my friends, but she watched by me and fomented my shoulder and leg with warm water, until the coagulated blood dissolved, and I was easier. How I wished for the light to be put out! but they would not hear of it. I have seen death in many, many forms since, but never have I seen anything that I could compare with my remembrance of my father's appearance. His features were pinched up, his lips drawn tightly across his mouth showing his upper and under teeth; his eyes were wide open, for they could not be closed; and the flaring light now rising now sinking, as it was agitated by the wind, caused an appearance as if of the features moving and gibbering, with that ghastly expression on them. I could not take my eyes off them, and lay gazing at them till the day broke.

"The barber, who had been absent at a neighbouring village, soon afterwards arrived, and examined my wounds. One ball had entered my shoulder and had passed into my neck. He groped in the wound for some time with a pair of pincers, and after putting me to horrible pain, succeeded in getting hold of it and drawing it out. I was then easier: the blood flowed copiously; the wound in the leg was only through the flesh, and having taken some opium I soon fell asleep, and awoke, though still in pain, yet easier than I had been.

"My father had by this time been buried, I was left with the consciousness of having one enemy, and one too who would not forego his revenge even to the son of his victim.

"The old kazee could recommend nothing, could suggest no measures to be pursued to bring the murderers to conviction. So, as he said, we sat down on the carpet of patience, to smoke the pipe of regret, and to drown our affliction in the best way we could. Matters continued to run smoothly for the period of a year. I was considered to have succeeded to my father's rights, when one day the man who had been set up by Brij Lall as the real patel, in opposition to my father, arrived at the village with a body of armed men, and with orders for his installation. The villagers were too weak to resist this tyranny, and I was forced to resign all my claims to the newcomer. By this time my sister had gone to the house of her father-in-law, and I sent my mother after her, for I had no longer a home. I left the village with an aching heart, to see if my father's friends, the sahoukars, could do anything for me at the court. But they too had changed, as I might perhaps have expected, and would do nothing.

"Brij Lall, they said, was too powerful to be interfered with; and they recommended me to give up all hopes of justice, as the attempt to fix the crime of murder upon him, with the insufficient evidence I possessed, would be attended with my certain destruction. Nor would they assist me to regain my lost rights; so that I was friendless, and, as it were, forsaken in the world. I had but one resource: I joined the first band of Thugs I could discover, though I had previously not practised the profession, and I have since lived a lonely and wretched life in the world. My mother is long since dead. My sister still lives, and has some children; she is happy, and has no remembrance of the past. I pay her a visit now and then, and am received with affection and kindness. She is the only one in this world except you, my friends, who cares for me. She believes me to be a soldier in the service of Holkar, and she will never know to the contrary. Praise be to Alla! however, my enemy has died by my own hand; and I am content, for I am revenged. Some of you, my friends, will lay me in my grave when my time comes, and it will not be long. I have lived hitherto for the deed I did last night. There is no excitement for me in the future, and it matters not how soon the old Thug is laid in the earth. This is my story, such as it is; if I have arrested your attention and gratified the Sahib Zada, my intentions have been fulfilled, and I am content."

The whole assembly was struck and affected by the old man's story, and all joined in consoling him for his misfortunes. But I was particularly interested in them, as they went more to convince me that the hand of Alla was upon all our doings than even my father's history. Both were striking instances, but the Thug's particularly so. It really seemed as though Brij Lall had been given into our hands, nay to the very hands of him he had so oppressed, to receive his punishment on earth previous to the eternal fires of Jehunum.[1] "Henceforward," said I to myself, "no one shall have it to say of Ameer Ali that he hung back when occasion required his personal exertions. I will emulate my father, and the country shall know and feel that I am a scourge on its wickedness. No one shall escape me; I will act up to the utmost of the oath I have taken, wage unrelenting war with the whole human race, and, Inshalla! they shall see whether Ameer Ali cannot lead his men on to actions which will by far surpass any of the present times, and equal those the traditions of which remain among us."

From that day I put myself under the tuition of the gooroo, or teacher of the band,—an old Thug who was worn out with age, but had been considered to be one of the most dexterous bhuttotes, or stranglers, who had lived within the memories of any of the men of our company. He was a Hindoo, a Rajpoot; and though his frame was dry and shrivelled, yet from his height, breadth of shoulders, and sinews, which were developed the more by the absence of flesh to cover them, it was easy to see that he had been a man of immense strength and power; and, added to this, if his great dexterity in using the handkerchief was considered, the stories of his superior prowess might easily be credited. I had hitherto not associated much with him, and beyond a courteous demeanour to each other, we had been but little acquainted; so I begged my father to take me to him, deliver me over to his care, and request of him to initiate me thoroughly in the practice of a bhuttote.

He was delighted at this spontaneous offer on my part, readily acceded to my wishes, and at once put me under the care of Hoosein and Roop Singh, the old Thug I have mentioned, who belonged to Hoosein's party.

"For a few days," said my father, "I will not see you; you shall remain with them; and when you return to me, let me welcome you as ready and willing to take a part in the next affair we may be engaged in."

The day after we began in earnest. Roop Singh repeated incantations over me. I ate no meat, indeed tasted nothing but milk for four days. Numerous sacrifices were made to the sacred pickaxe; every omen was observed, and as I sat under the trees after our daily march, scarcely a bird alighted on them but there was some conclusion drawn from it; and the appearances of different animals and birds as we commenced our march in the mornings were particularly observed and noted. I was naturally very inquisitive as to the meaning of all that was done to me and for me; but the old gooroo would not enlighten me.

---

1 Hell.

"My son," said he, "when I was your age, these ceremonies were performed over me to make me fearless and stony-hearted, active and cunning, so as to ensnare all who came within my reach, and to avoid my enemies, to make me fortunate, and to cause me to win fame. In all these I have never failed. Two others upon whom I have performed them are rising fast to be jemadars, such is their address and courage; and you too will be the same; therefore ask no questions. Content yourself with knowing that everything is going on properly and to my complete satisfaction, for I have not observed one unfavourable omen."

On the fifth morning, the handkerchief was put into my hand; and after having been bathed, anointed with sweet-smelling oils, and marked on the forehead with vermilion, as a votary of Bhowanee, I was declared a bhuttote.

"One thing I forgot," said the old man laughing, as he gave me the cloth, "and that was the principal perhaps. I have not shown you how to use it, and I have a peculiar knack of my own, which is easily communicated. You will soon learn it."

He took the cloth, tied a large knot at one end, with a piece of silver inserted in it; this he held in his left hand, the plain end being in his right, and about as much space between them as would nearly compass a man's neck; the closed hands had the palms uppermost.

"Now," said he, "mark this; and when you throw the cloth from behind, and have got it tight, suddenly turn your knuckles into the neck, giving a sharp wrench to either side that may be most convenient. If done in a masterly manner, instant death ensues."

I took the cloth, and held it as he directed, but it did not please him.

"Give it me back, that I may show you more exactly on your own neck," said he.

"Indeed, no," cried I laughing; "you might think I was a traveller, and have me down in an instant, without intending it; but I perfectly understand the method."

"Then try it on *me*, Ameer Ali; I shall see by the position of your hands whether you know anything about it."

I obeyed him; the old man shook his head and laughed.

"That will never do; you could not kill a child in that way," he said. "When you feel my hands round your neck you will understand."

So I submitted with as good a grace as I could, though I did not at all like the idea. My blood ran cold through me as I felt his chill, clammy hands about my neck. But he did not hurt me, and I saw where my error had been. I tried it on him as he had shown me several times, and was declared at last to be perfect.

"Now you only want practice, Ameer Ali," said he.

"Inshalla! Roop Singh," I replied, "we shall have plenty of it. One beginning, and I fear not for the rest. Like a tiger, which, once having tasted human blood, will if possible take no other, and runs every risk to get it, so I feel it will be with me." And it was so. Sahib, I knew myself—I had spoken truly.

CHAPTER VI

IN WHICH THE READER WILL BE INFORMED HOW AMEER ALI
KILLED HIS FIRST MAN

NOTHING of any moment occurred during the rest of our march to Nagpoor, if I except the deaths of a few solitary travellers, who had fallen by the hands of a small portion of the band who had been sent to another road, which ran parallel to the one on which we marched; and as I know no particulars of them worth mentioning, I shall at once lead you, sahib, to our encampment at Nagpoor.

Outside the city is a large tank,[1] on the margin of which the majority of the band encamped. My father and a few others put up in the town, for the purpose of converting the booty already obtained into money. It was not a difficult task, for as the property which had belonged to Brij Lall was easily saleable, we soon found purchasers among the numerous goldsmiths and sahoukars of the city.

In one of his dealings with a sahoukar, my father casually stated that he was proceeding to Hyderabad with some men he had brought from his village, and for whom he was in hope of procuring employment under, as he said, his brother, who was in the service of the then reigning prince Sikundur Jah. The sahoukar at once proposed to accompany us, and to give my father and his men a handsome remuneration if he would protect him on the road; as he had, he said, been for some time on the look-out for an opportunity to put himself under the escort of a respectable man who might be travelling there with a number of followers.

At that time, sahib, in consequence of the unsettled state of the country, and the many rumours there were of wars, any man of respectability, who was idle in his village, and could persuade a few companions to accompany him as their leader, was sure of employment as a soldier, if he presented himself at any of the courts of Hindostan or the Dukhun. Sindea, Holkar, the Peshwah,[2] every prince in fact had a large army which was tolerably paid; and it was better to serve with them, than to pursue any other occupation. We had met several bands of such men on our road

---

1   Reservoir; lake.
2   Hereditary rulers of the Maratha Empire in central India.

down to Nagpoor, so that our company presented no extraordinary or suspicious appearance, especially under my father, who looked like a soldier, was always well armed and dressed, rode a fine horse, and on occasions of residing in, or even passing through, a city, was always attended by a number of the Thugs as his escort; and his appearance was certainly what he represented himself to be to the sahoukar.

My father readily agreed to the sahoukar's terms, and bound himself down in a day or two afterwards to be at his disposal, and to afford him protection as far as Hyderabad. At a secret conference they had that day, the sahoukar, as my father told me, informed him that he was going to take down a good deal of treasure, some valuable jewels and some merchandise, by which he hoped to get a handsome profit at Hyderabad. Nay, he even went so far as to show him what he was going to take with him; and you cannot imagine, sahib, the joy that was diffused in our camp at the certainty of so rich a booty.

In order to give our band as much of the appearance of soldiers as possible, my father purchased for those who had none, matchlocks, swords, and shields, and distributed them; and, in truth, when all the men were drawn up to be examined, they were a fine-looking set of fellows; for as this expedition had been considered one of extreme adventure, none but the youngest and most able-bodied had been selected for it. They were all informed of the agreement which had been made with the sahoukar, cautioned to put on as military and swaggering an air as possible, and, in short, to behave as soldiers would, during the part of the journey they would have to appear as his escort.

This was in the evening, and during the night the camp was a scene of jollity; the booty in view, nay, almost within their grasp, was sufficient to cheer them. A set of dancing girls was invited from the city, and in listening to their songs the best part of the night was passed.

We expected the sahoukar anxiously all the day, and just at nightfall he came to our camp in a small travelling cart, with one or two servants and two or three small ponies, on which a tent and his baggage were laden, and ten bullocks with their two drivers. Altogether, there were eight men, including himself.

We saw but little of him during our march to Oomraotee;[1] my father and Hoosein used sometimes to sit with him in his tent during the evening, and I was also introduced to him. He was a large, unwieldy man, and I began to think whether he would not be a good subject for my first trial. I mentioned my thoughts to my father, and he was much pleased with me.

---

1   Hinganghat, a town in the north district of the Nizam's territories.

"I had intended to have appointed you to be his bhuttote," said he; "he is too fat to make any resistance, and he will be the easier work for you, who have not as yet tried what you can do."

So from that time I looked upon him as my first victim.

I daily went to my instructor to gain fresh insight into my profession, and practised the handling of the cloth in every way he pointed out to me. He one day proposed to inveigle a lonely traveller into our camp, in order that I might try my hand upon him first; but I objected to this, as I felt confident in my own powers, and was determined, as I had selected the sahoukar, that he should be the first man.

I pass over our journey, as nothing worth mentioning occurred on the road. We arrived at the town, and took up our quarters in the bazaar. I was much struck with its apparent opulence and prosperity; but it was not to be wondered at, as it was the place where all the merchandise and manufactures of Hindostan were brought to be distributed over the Dukhun, and where all the spices, drugs, and other articles of trade arrived from the south, to be sent to different parts of Hindostan.

The town seemed to be full of sahoukars' houses and large shops; and in the bazaars were displayed every article that I had ever heard of, besides many others from the Europeans at Bombay which I had never seen before; and I wandered about every day in company with my father, admiring and wondering at all I saw.

The sahoukar's business detained him some days at this place, at the end of which we again set forward, with an addition to his people of three men, who drove a few bullocks heavily laden with cloths, which we heard were of the most costly description, being those of Benares, which are justly celebrated for their richness and beauty. Nor did this addition at all disconcert our plans, for in consequence of the sahoukar having accompanied us, Hoosein's party still remained; and, indeed, if it had not, there were plenty of my father's to have secured the whole without trouble.

From Oomraotee to Mungloor is three stages, and "there," said my father, "I shall decide on the place for the ending of this matter. If I remember right, there are some low hills and ravines not far beyond it, which will give us excellent opportunities for concealing the bodies. And do you, Hoosein, inquire who among your men know the ground, for it will be necessary to send some one who does with the lughaees."

Inquiries were accordingly made when we reached our first stage, a village named Baum, and it was discovered that three men were intimately acquainted with the whole of the road, and had been on the point of coming forward to recommend that one spot in particular should not be neglected. They were closely questioned by my father and Hoosein; and they gave a very clear description of a place, which seemed to be so well fitted for the purpose that it was at once determined on, and the men promised extra reward if they would exert themselves.

I now felt that my time had come; that in a very few hours I might take my place with the rest, having established my right to be their equal.

Perhaps it was weakness, sahib, but from that time I avoided the sight of the sahoukar as much as possible. I saw him once or twice on the road; but an involuntary shudder crept through me, and, like a fool, I almost wished I were back again at our village. But it was too late to retract; I had a character to gain, and the esteem of him who best loved me, my father, to secure. To turn back was impossible, and to evince the smallest cowardice was to degrade myself irretrievably. I had therefore no resource but to do my best; and, in truth, when the sahoukar was not before me, I felt no reluctance to perform my part, but, on the contrary, the same desire I had before experienced to distinguish myself.

We reached Mungloor. It is a large town, full of Mahomedans, and celebrated for the shrine of Meer Hyāt Kalundur, a saint of great antiquity. His tomb is held in particular veneration, and it was judged highly expedient that we should offer up our prayers for the success of our enterprise. Accordingly, my father, myself, Hoosein, and some other Mahomedans went to the tomb, and having observed all the ceremonies required and directed by the attendant moollahs, we were sitting in conversation with two of them, when we discovered, by a casual sign made by my father to Hoosein, which was recognised by them, that they were Thugs! Most extraordinary, thought I; here are sacred ministers of our faith Thugs as well as ourselves. But after some conversation with them, I could see that my father esteemed them lightly.

"These fellows can hardly be Thugs," said my father to Hoosein, as we descended the steps of the shrine into the outer court, where many of the men had put up for the day, "and we had better caution the people against getting acquainted with them. I do not think they will notice us further as it is, but they might do so did they know whom we have with us."

"You are right," said Hoosein; "it might perhaps be better were the men told not to disclose whom we have with us."

They were accordingly cautioned; and it turned out that we had done right, as we heard afterwards that the moollahs were most inquisitive, and could not understand how it was that we had come so far and were going so much farther without an object; and I have no doubt had we not acted as we did, and disclosed our intentions to, or asked for assistance from them, that they would have either betrayed us to the village authorities, or insisted on such a share of the spoil, which we dare not have refused, as would have materially lessened ours.

After prayers we returned to the place where we had put up, and found a man belonging to the sahoukar waiting for us. He said his master would stay that evening where he was, with a friend, instead of coming outside the village to our encampment, but that my father was to leave some men with him as a guard; and that he would set out early in the night, as he was determined to go on to Bassim, a town some distance off, where he had another friend, whom he wished to visit; that as it was so long a march we must start early, so as to allow time for a halt for refreshment at a village half way.

My father did not like the idea of sending the men into the village, lest they should be recognised as Thugs by any of the Thug villagers; yet he could not but acquiesce, and some were sent as soon as night closed in, that there might be hardly a chance of their being known. In the meantime every preparation was made by the party of gravediggers who were to precede us, and at nightfall they also left the ground, fourteen in number, with the two who knew the spot in company with them. They were confident as to the precise place they should fix on, and described the hills as little more than low mounds, caused by some high land breaking into ravines; that, if they remembered right, the road was very stony, and crossed by several small streams, whose banks were lined by thick brushwood, and that in any one of these in which there might be no water, the bhil, or grave, should be prepared. They were also desired to place men in advance to give information, that we might all take our places, and fall on, when the signal was given.

It was now generally known to all that I was to have the sahoukar to myself, and many thronged about me to see how I looked forward to my first trial; every one cheered me, and I must own this gave me great confidence. As the time approached, my soul burned for the work like that of a young and brave soldier to see the first flash of his bright sword in anger. My father enjoyed my demeanour in silent satisfaction; he spoke not, but there was exultation in his eye as he looked fondly upon me, and I felt that I should not disappoint him.

The whole band seemed to be impressed particularly with the importance of the present matter, for they collected into groups, and though each man knew exactly what he had to do, and what was appointed for his comrade, yet they seemed to be discussing the whole, till one by one they separated, and each stretched himself out to gain the little rest he could, before the time arrived which would call him into active, nay, deadly strife,—my father and Hoosein too, all except myself. I was sitting outside our slight tent, when Roop Singh came to me.

"Baba!"[1] said he as he sat down, "how feel you? is your heart firm and your blood cool?"

"Both," said I; "nothing can change my heart; and feel my hand, is my blood hot?"

"No," said the old man, taking it in his; "it is not, nor does it tremble; this is as it should be. I have seen many prepare for their first trial, but never one so coolly and calmly as you do; but this is all in consequence of the blessed muntrus[2] which have been read over you, and the ceremonies you went through."

"Perhaps so," said I; "but I think I should have been much the same without them."

"Now, may Bhowanee forgive you, proud boy," he replied; "you know not their efficacy. Was there ever a prouder being than I was,—a Rajpoot by birth, and one of the purest tribes? Had I not slain wild beasts, or helped to slay them from my childhood? but when a man was shown me, and the handkerchief alone put into my hands to destroy him with, indeed I trembled; nor was it for a long time that I could be brought to attempt it. But," continued Roop Singh, "you have one more ceremony to go through, which on no account must be neglected; go, call your father, Hoosein, and Bhudrinath, that they may be present."

"We were all soon assembled, and the gooroo[3] led the way into an adjoining field. He stopped, and turning to the direction in which we were to proceed, raised his hands in a supplicatory manner, and cried, "O Kalee! Maha Kalee![4] if the travel-ler now with us should die by the hand of this thy new votary, vouchsafe us the thibaoo!"[5]

All of us stood silently; and wonderful to relate, even at that late hour an ass brayed on the right hand. The gooroo was overjoyed.

"There!" cried he to the others, "was there ever so complete an acceptation of a votary? The omen almost followed the prayer."

"Shookr Alla!" exclaimed my father, "it is now complete; he will go forth and conquer. There only remains for you to tie the knot."

"That I will do when we return," said the gooroo; and when we reached our encampment, he took my handkerchief, and untying the knot which had been

---

1   Father.

2   Prayers; mantras.

3   Spiritual leader.

4   Great Kali!

5   Omen on the right hand.

previously made, he retied it, placing a piece of silver in it. Presenting it to me, he said,—

"Receive this now sacred weapon; put your trust in it; in the holy name of Kalee I bid it do your will."

I received it in my right hand, and carefully tucked it into my waistband, that I might not lose it, and that it might be ready for action when required.

"We remained in conversation for some time, and then threw ourselves on our carpets to snatch a short rest, till one of our men from the village came and told us that the sahoukar was preparing to move, and had sent him on to warn us.

The band were quickly roused and our beasts laden, and we drew up by the side of the road to await his arrival. He was not long in coming, and we all moved on together.

The night was beautiful, the road excellent, and we pushed on in high spirits. The booty we were to possess, the tact with which the whole matter had been managed from the first, would mark it as an enterprise of a superior description, one that any one of us would be proud to mention, and which would cause a considerable sensation, not only in the country, but among the numerous bands of Thugs of Hindostan, more especially those we were to rejoin at the conclusion of our season.

We had proceeded about two coss, when there was a murmur among the men who led, and one of the scouts was an instant afterwards seen making his way to where we were. My father recognised him as one of those he had sent on.

"Bhilla manjeh?" [Have you cleared the hole?] he eagerly inquired.

"Manjeh!" said the man. "It is cleared, and it is all ready. See you yon low hills? A streamlet, as I told you, runs from them; and it is a rare bhil[1] that we have made, Jemadar Sahib. You will say we have done well."

"And how far may it be?" demanded my father.

"About half a coss," said the man. "A short distance from hence, the road becomes stony, and continues so till you are above the pass—take advantage of it;" and he fell in among the others.

The men were silently warned to be at their posts; and each man, or two men, as it was necessary, placed himself close to the one to whom he had been assigned. By designed obstruction in front, the bullocks belonging to the sahoukar, with their attendants, were brought immediately about the cart in which he rode, and the whole being gathered into one place, were the easier to be secured. The preparations again roused me, and I grasped the handkerchief firmly, thinking every moment that the

---

1 Grave.

signal was about to be made; but we still crept on at a slow pace, for the road was narrow and lined by thorny bushes; and the men in front proceeding as slowly as possible, we were kept exactly in our proper place, and expected every moment to reach the spot.

As we approached the small hills, the jungle became pretty thick, and appeared doubly so by the moonlight, and we passed many places where I thought the deed might have been done with advantage. But I was wrong, for the lughaees[1] had selected an admirable one.

A man came from the front, whispered a few words to my father, and again went on. This increased my anxiety. We crossed a small hollow, ascended a bank, and below us I saw what I was sure was the place. The banks of the rivulet were high and steep, covered with thick underwood matted by trailing creepers. A few higher trees nearly met over its bed, in which could be just discerned a small thread of water, looking like a silver snake as the moon's rays fell on it through the dark foliage. A hundred thieves might lie there, thought I; and who could ever know the fate of a traveller who might so easily be surprised in such a spot?

I was roused from my train of thought by my father, as he called out "Hooshiaree!" (caution). This was the preparatory signal. He went to the side of the cart, and represented to the sahoukar that we had reached the stream, and that the bank was so steep, and the bed so stony, that he must get out and walk over to the other side, if no farther. This was quite sufficient; the man got out, and after seeing the cart safely down the steep bank was preparing to follow himself.

The whole scene is now before me. The bullocks and their drivers, with the Thugs, were all in a confused group in the bed of the little stream, the men shouting and urging on their beasts; but it was easy to see that every man had a Thug close to him awaiting the signal. They were only a few feet below us, and the stream was so narrow that it was with some difficulty all could stand in its bed, especially when the cart reached the bottom. Above, stood my father, Hoosein, and myself, the sahoukar, one of his servants, and several Thugs.

I was eagerly waiting the signal; I tightly grasped the fatal handkerchief, and my first victim was within a foot of me! I went behind him as being preferable to one side, and observed one of the other Thugs do the same to a servant. The sahoukar moved a step or two towards the road—I instinctively followed him; I scarcely felt

---

1 Those of the Thugs responsible for burying the dead.

that I stirred, so intensely was I observing him. "Jey Kalee!"[1] shouted my father: it was the signal, and I obeyed it!

As quick as thought the cloth was round his neck; I seemed endued with superhuman strength. I wrenched his neck round—he struggled convulsively for an instant, and fell. I did not quit my hold, I knelt down on him, and strained the cloth till my hand ached; but he moved not—he was dead! I quitted my hold, and started to my feet. I was mad with excitement! My blood boiled, and I felt as though I could have strangled a hundred others, so easy, so simple had the reality been. One turn of my wrists had placed me on an equality with those who had followed the profession for years,—I had taken the first place in the enterprise, for I had killed the principal victim! I should receive the praise of the whole band, many of whom I was confident had looked on me as only a child.

I was roused from my reverie by my father.

"You have done well," he said in a low and kind voice; "you will receive the reward of this soon. Now follow me, we will go to the grave. Ere this the bodies have been collected, and I myself must see that they are properly disposed of. There will be a noise about this business, and it will need great exertion for us to get out of the road we are now travelling."

I followed him. We descended into the bed of the stream, and were led to the grave by one of the men; others bearing the body of the sahoukar followed. We passed up the bed of the stream for a short distance; and near the mouth of a small tributary, the bed of which was dry, a number of the men were standing;

"The grave?" asked my father.

"It is up there," said one. "You will have to creep, and the thorns are very bad."

"It matters not," he replied; and we entered the place.

The banks of the rivulet were perhaps two or three yards high, and the bed was so narrow that but two persons could advance abreast. The creepers and trees were matted overhead, and the sides so thick that it was impossible that any one could have got down from above. The tangled character of the spot increased as we proceeded, until it became necessary to free our clothes from the thorns which caught us at every step. In a few moments we heard the sound of voices, and after creeping almost on all fours through a hole which had apparently been forced through the underwood, we came upon the grave.

There was only one; it occupied almost the entire breadth of the stream; it was very deep, and the earth, or rather sand, had been thrown out on each end. The

---

1 Victory to Kali!

lughaees were sitting there, sharpening stakes cut from the jungle; but they could scarcely be seen from the darkness of the place, which the thick wood above only partially allowed the moonbeams to penetrate. They were conversing in a low tone in the slang of the band, which I had not yet learned; my father spoke to them, or rather to their leader.

"You have had your wits about you," he said, "and we will think well of you when we make the distribution; this is a grave that even a jackal could not discover. Again I say, Peer Khan, you have done this properly, and it is well I have seen it that I may speak of you as you deserve; but you must be quick,—the night advances."

"It is finished, khodawund," replied the man. "We do but wait for another body which they say is coming, and the filling up will be done immediately."

As he spoke, the body of the sahoukar was brought up by three men, who railed at it for its weight.

"It is their wont," he said. "Do not speak to them; only watch what they do; for you must see all, that you may be fully acquainted with your duties."

I was silent. The corpse was dragged to the brink and thrown in, as also that of the servant who had been killed close to the sahoukar. Incisions were made in their abdomens, and sharpened stakes driven through them.

"Were it not for the precaution you see," said my father, "the ground might swell, and the jackals would drag out the bodies; in this way, however, it is impossible."

When all was finished, quantities of stones which had been collected were thrown upon the bodies, afterwards thorns, and the whole was covered up with sand, which was carefully smoothed

"I think this will do, Jemadar Sahib," said Peer Khan; "we may now leave the place. It is not likely that any one will come here to look for the sethjee[1] or his people, and the Sahib Zada has seen how cleverly we have done our work."

"Enough," said I, "I shall know how to act as a lugha myself should I ever need it."

My father beckoned me to follow him. I stayed to see some dry sand thrown over the place, and proceeded with the others. The hole in the underwood made by us was closed up with great care; and a branch of a bush being broken off, and trailed after him by the hindermost man, obliterated every footmark in the dry sand of the nulla.[2]

---

1 Respectful term for a rich man.
2 Ravine.

Chapter VII

A NEW ADVENTURE, WHICH PROVES AN UNUSUAL PRELUDE TO AN EVENING'S ENTERTAINMENT

THE rest of the band, with the cart and laden bullocks, had proceeded some way before we overtook them. "We passed through a thin jungle for some distance, emerging from which, we found ourselves on a wild, bare plain, here and there studded with straggling brushwood. We all collected together, and lighting fires, the hooka[1] passed round, and each one related his achievement, and gloried in the prospect of a speedy division of the booty we had acquired.

To arrange our future proceedings was by no means an easy matter, as it was necessary to get past Bassim, where the sahoukar had friends, and his cart and bullocks might possibly be recognised in the town. My father's advice was to travel till daylight, and then to withdraw to one side of the road as far from observation as possible; to remain there as long as we could, and then to push on beyond Bassim. At this halt too there was to be a grand division of the spoil, at least as much of it as could be divided; and Hoosein's party was to separate from us and pursue their road in the best way they could, in the direction which had been pointed out to them. Accordingly we again started, and after passing some villages halted about sunrise, at some distance from the road, near a grove of trees, in which there was a well of water. Before the men betook themselves to cooking their meal after the march, they were all assembled: and the quantity of goor having been brought, the ceremony of the tupounee was performed as I have before described. I was now entitled to a seat on the blanket with the other bhuttotes: I was their equal! The ceremony ended, I untied the knot of my handkerchief, as directed by my father, and taking out the piece of silver, presented it with some rupees to my gooroo, touching his feet at the same time in reverence. This was the last of my ceremonies of initiation. I was a bhuttote, had fairly killed my man, and held myself to be the equal of any of my associates.

After this my father and Hoosein brought forth all the plunder of our late enterprise. It was magnificent. There was a good quantity of gold and silver in money; but

---

1   A tobacco pipe with a water filter.

the principal valuables were the jewels which the sahoukar was taking to Hyderabad for sale, and the cloths and brocades on the bullocks—they were of the richest description.

The distribution of these was a matter of great difficulty, and it was impossible to satisfy every one; besides, the pearls and diamonds would have lost a great deal of their value by being divided among the men. So it was agreed to share the ready money, cooking-utensils, and other effects of the sahoukar, also the least valuable cloths, into two equal portions as nearly as possible, in proportion to the number of men of each band; that my father was to have charge of the jewels, which he was to sell at Hyderabad to the best advantage, as also of the most valuable cloths; and that the proceeds of these were not to be divided until we again reached our place of rendezvous.

The division of the ready money, upwards of three thousand five hundred rupees, gave to each man a considerable sum, enough at any rate to support him for some time, the more especially as the share of the former booty was not nearly expended; for every man lived as frugally as possible, and all seemed intent upon vying with each other as to who should have the largest share at the general division. Nay, many even denied themselves the meanest luxuries, and it was not uncommon to see a man eating his cakes without ghee,[1] or anything but pure water.

Bhudrinath, however, one of the most skilful of the band, was a complete exception to what I have said. He was a short, stout, active fellow, a man who aspired to be a jemadar, and with some reason. I have mentioned him before as the bearer of the sacred pickaxe. He was one of the most enterprising among us, and had conducted small expeditions, in which he had acquitted himself much to the satisfaction of those who had entrusted him with them.

It was curious to see that man eat. He consumed every day that he could get it, two seers[2] of flour made into cakes, a quarter of a seer of ghee, and a large pot of milk containing upwards of a seer. It seemed impossible that one man could demolish the pile of cakes when he had baked them, and fairly sat down to eat them; but one by one they disappeared, accompanied by such draughts of water as would alone have filled any ordinary person. Towards the end of the pile, however, it was easy to see that his jaws could hardly perform their office, and it was almost painful to behold the distension of his stomach. He would stretch himself first on one side, then on the other; get up and stroke down the mass collected, apparently from his throat

---

1 　 Clarified butter.
2 　 One seer is equivalent to two pounds.

downwards, and again essay to finish what remained, and after many attempts he would sometimes succeed.

Often have I seen two or more village dogs sit opposite to him, during the consumption of the mountain of cakes, looking wistfully at it, in the hope that a portion of each as he ate it might be thrown to them, watching and envying every mouthful as it passed into the apparently insatiable maw; but in vain! Sometimes Bhudrinath would divide the last two or three cakes between them, when every means of eating more had been tried and had failed; but it was oftener that desire of eating predominated. He would appear on the point of gratifying the dogs' expectations,—nay, would even break a piece off and hold it in his hand as if offering it, the dog would move towards him, but the coveted morsel disappeared as the rest had done, and he would return to his expectant station, to resume a watch which too often ended in disappointment.

We often jeered him on his enormous consumption of food; but he used to declare that nothing under the daily allowance I have mentioned could satisfy him, or enable him to perform his duty.

Our encampment broke up towards evening. Friends were seen embracing each other, and wishing mutual success; at length they all departed. We watched them over the brow of an eminence not far off, and then started ourselves.

Leaving the beaten road to Bassim, we struck on into one to the left; and as it promised to lead to some large town we followed it, as well to avoid discovery as to court new adventures. By the light of a bright moon we travelled most of the night, passing through a dreary country, in many parts covered with jungle, and never entering a village save to ask the road, or to get fire to light our hookas. Indeed we were often repulsed in this. There appeared to be a general dread of robbers, and the walls and gates were usually manned by armed men, on the intimation of our approach being given by the dogs as we passed; but no questions were asked us, as to who we were or where we were going, although perhaps our numbers might have excited suspicion.

In this manner, and without knowing where the road we had taken would lead us, we travelled for some days; and as we had purposely avoided the principal roads, it was not to be expected that we should meet with anything in the way of adventure, or with any travellers whom we could entice into our society. At last we came upon a broader road than that on which we had been travelling; and as we had left every danger from our late deed far behind us, we determined to follow it, in the hope that it would lead us towards Hyderabad, or some large village in its direction, from whence we could get upon a well-travelled road and carry on our vocation. As it was, we had gained a respectable booty even for a whole season; but scarcely two months had passed, and we could not afford to go on so far as Hyderabad in inactivity.

The road led us on for some hours, till large mango groves, with here and there the white top of a Hindoo temple peeping over them, gave us intimation that we were approaching a place of consequence. It turned out to be the town of Oomerkhér, a wealthy place surrounded with most luxuriant cultivation of wheat and other descriptions of grain.

"It will be our own fault," said my father, "if we find not some game here. Having encamped on the other side of the town, the sothaees[1] must carefully pass through the bazars, and this evening may bring us booty enough to recompense us for staying here."

The duty of a sotha was one which I had also to learn. Men were even more proud of excelling in it, than in that of a bhuttote; for it required the greatest tact and powers of dissimulation, ability to support characters and disguises, a smooth tongue and polite demeanour. Bhudrinath was one who united all in an eminent degree; he was a short, stout, active man as I have mentioned, but extremely handsome, and with a most winning manner. It was his constant boast that he never marked out a victim whom he did not strangle with his own hands.

We passed through the town, describing ourselves as merchants from Hindostan; and as the bales of cloth when stopped by the collector of tolls were readily shown by my father and the duty demanded on them cheerfully paid, our assertion was credited, we were civilly treated by the authorities, and shown an excellent piece of ground for our encampment.

"Now dress yourself in your best clothes," said Bhudrinath, "and come with me into the town. Remember, your father is a merchant, you are a jemadar commanding his escort, I am a bhulaadmee (respectable person) belonging to you. We will take with us Peer Khan, who although a lugha is an excellent sotha, and a respectable fellow when he is dressed and armed; and it is hard if we do not pick up somebody."

Our meal was soon cooked and eaten; and after carefully attiring ourselves we set off into the town to seek for adventures. It astonished me to see the indifference with which the practised hands proceeded, considering the object they had in view; for to me there was as much excitement in this, as in what I had already learned and practised. I confess our appearance was remarkable. I was very noticeable from my dress and arms, which were of the richest description, consistent with the appearance I had assumed. My face, then much fairer than it is now, sahib, with a mustachio

---

1 Inveiglers.

already well formed, and a figure which, though perhaps somewhat slender, gave promise of future strength and power. Contrasted with my companions, I felt I was superior to them in appearance; and a little pardonable vanity gave me an air and swagger which were not unfitting the military profession I had set up.

We entered the town, and betook ourselves to the chowree[1] where the kotwal and some respectable persons were sitting, surrounded by a few armed men as is usual. As we passed by them we were invited to enter, and received with great politeness. I was placed in the seat of honour by Bhudrinath, who took his station at some distance. A desultory conversation began. My father's name was asked, where he was going, and what he had brought for trade, who we were, and in short the general object of our journey by, as they told us, an unfrequented road, at least from Hindostan. The tone in which this question was asked seemed to me so suspicious, that I thought for an instant we were suspected, and I was endeavouring to frame a reply, when Bhudrinath stopped me.

"I represent," said he, addressing the man who had asked the question, "that we were set astray at that abode of unsainted people, Nagpoor. Either with a view to deceive us, or (God knows it may be so, I have heard of such things) perhaps of robbing us, persons from whom we asked information, told us the best and most frequented road was by this place; and truly the town you have the fortune to dwell in is a place of great beauty and fertility, and is evidently in the hands of a most wise governor, and one who protects his people. How, Jemadar Sahib, have I not said truly?"

"Indeed," said I, "you have; and the kindness we have as yet met with shows that the servants of the governor are worthy of their master. Truly it is not to be wondered at if the town is prosperous and beautiful in such hands; and such is the mellifluous speech of the kotwal, that we are impressed with the greatest opinion of the discernment of the exalted person who has selected him."

"May your condescension never diminish," said the kotwal; "your slave is not worthy of these encomiums; he is less than the least. If my lord could but see the dispenser of benefits under whose beams he lives, he would indeed say that the court of Hyderabad is worthy of being compared with any in Hindostan, as having formed such a pattern of excellence."

"Well," said I, "we shall only be too glad to lay our nuzzurs[2] at the feet of this patron of yours; and no doubt we shall see in him a pattern of noblemen, a specimen

---

1 Public hall.
2 Offerings.

of what we may expect to see at the capital of the Dukhun. When may we hope to be admitted to the presence?"

"In the evening, after prayers," replied our acquaintance; "it is then that justice is dispensed to these poor unbelieving cultivators, and the durbar is enlivened by the presence and heavenly music of a set of dancing-women, whom my lord has brought with him from the city."

"We will come," said I; "and I pray you to give your lord notice that we have accepted your invitation to visit him; nay, that we are desirous of paying our respects to him."

As I finished speaking, an elderly man of decent appearance had entered the chowree; he was a Hindoo, and looked like a merchant. He demanded, in rather a peremptory tone, a place to rest in, declaring that if he did not get it immediately he would go and complain to the ruler of the town.

The spirit of the old kotwal seemed to be roused by the man's behaviour, and he declared in round terms that he would not give a foot of ground, or an empty shop, without he was civilly asked.

"Look you, gentlemen," said he to us; "I ask you to decide between us. I swear by the Prophet I care no more than a snap of my fingers for him, I have seen twenty thousand better; and if he goes to complain, why let him go—he will be driven from the presence with stripes. People like him come in hundreds every day, and who can trouble themselves in looking after them?"

"You and your master may be the portion of the devil," said the old merchant; "ever since I have entered the territories of the Nizam I have been treated in this manner. But it is only what I have heard before. Not a night have I passed without an alarm of thieves; and God knows, if I had any protection, I would rather lie outside your wretched walls than in the zenana[1] of your amil[2] himself. Your bunneas are rascals: I am offered grain at nearly double the price I paid yesterday; I am refused shelter at night. In God's name, what am I to do? Gentlemen," cried he to us, "what am I to do?"

Bhudrinath answered, as I was going to speak, and to my astonishment angrily,—

"What would you have, O discontented man! I suppose some place has been offered to you, and you have thought it not good enough; or are you drunk with opium? or has hunger after your journey spoilt your temper? Go, betake yourself to

---

1 Harem.

2 Subordinate official.

the bazaar; be thankful that you can get any place; and, if no one will shelter you, lie in the street; bethink yourself that many a better man has done so before you."

The man stood aghast; he looked first at us, then at the kotwal and his men, while expressions of delight at his discomfiture ran through the kotwal's party: "Well said!" "Proper fellows!" "He ought to be turned out of the village," &c. At last, without saying a word, he threw down his turban and ran out, bellowing as loud as he could.

"We all burst into a hearty fit of laughter. "That is a queer fellow," said I to the kotwal; "I doubt not you have often such to plague you. But send for him back, we will make him ashamed of himself, and I will beg you give him a place to stay in."

"As you will," replied he; "but for your intercession I should not have troubled myself about him. Many such have I to deal with. One day a fellow comes swearing he is cheated by every one; another, that he can get nothing to eat, when perhaps both are too stingy to buy; another that he has no shelter, when he will not pay the trifle demanded by the bunnea for the use of his shop. Again, a third must have every delicacy to be found in a city, and he is furious because he cannot get them; when, if they were all before him, he could not afford to buy one. In short, sirs, there is no end to the fancies, foolishnesses, and I may say tyranny of travellers, and who think me, I suppose, to possess superhuman power, and to have jins (genii) at my command, to bring them whatever their foolish ideas may desire."

"You have indeed no easy situation, and to please every one is impossible," said I. "But here comes the merchant;" and he entered.

"Take up your turban, good fellow," said the kotwal, "and do not be angry; you are no child to be quarrelling with decent people; have you never travelled before, that you should be angry and throw dust on our beards in this manner? In God's name take up your turban; and do some one of you go and see that the good man gets a place for himself."

The man looked irresolute for an instant, then took up the turban and walked sulkily out, accompanied by the person desired to attend him. Bhudrinath gave me a sign, and we took our leave. We had scarcely got out, when he said, "That man is ours; now see how I will manage him. I dare say he has but few persons with him, and he will be easily disposed of."

We kept our eye on him and his attendant, and watched him take possession of a shed of wretched appearance, with many symptoms of dissatisfaction. We loitered purposely, till we saw that he was alone, and then went up to him.

"Ram! Ram![1] Sethjee," said Bhudrinath, addressing him; "what a place is this they have put you into after all, not fit for hogs to lie in! That rascally kotwal, for all his smooth tongue, is an arrant knave I warrant; and I have heard," continued he, lowering his voice, "that he has in his employ a number of thieves, whose business it is to cut away travellers' saddle-bags from under their heads at night, and when the poor man goes to complain in the morning he is beaten out of the village. Did we not hear so, Jemadar Sahib?"

"Yes, indeed," said I; "don't you remember the man who met us at the village some coss from this, and warned us of the thieves of Oomerkhér, and said he had been robbed of everything he possessed, and then driven out with scarcely a rag to cover him? It was then that I determined to encamp outside, where we might have our own sentinels, and where, if we were robbed, it would be our own fault."

"God help me! I am a lost man!" cried the merchant; "I know not what to do;" and he beat his head with his clenched hand. In those bags is all I am worth in the world; I fled from Surat to save myself from oppression, and it appears that the farther I fly the worse usage I meet. It was only two nights ago,—after watching till my eyes nearly started from my head from want of sleep, and not being able to sit longer, I lay down and my eyes closed, —that an attempt was made to cut my bags from under me; and as I woke, the thieves snatched away two of my cooking utensils and the cloth I had about me. What could I do? Had I run after them, some fellow would have been off with my bags; so I sat still, and screamed for help. The villagers were soon assembled about me, and when I told them what had happened, a villain who called himself the patel, abused me for defaming his village; and I was actually thrust without the gates, and left to pursue my way in the dark, in momentary dread that I should be pursued, and perhaps robbed and murdered. Oh, my unhappy fate!" cried he; "what will it lead me to! Fool that I was to leave my own country, to become the sport of unblessed brutes, such as I have met in this wild country!"

"Well," said Bhudrinath in a compassionate tone, "you have been used very ill, and you ought to go and complain to the hakim[2] here; report says he is a just man, although those under him may be thieves and rascals."

"No, no, no!" cried the man; "go and complain! and be fleeced of my last rupee! The great man would require a nuzzur, and every dependent would ask for one; did I dare to refuse, my situation would be worse than it is now. No, no! I have not been

---

1 Rama, Hindu deity.
2 Governor.

robbed as yet, and please God, if I could only get out of this town, I would attach myself to some party of respectable persons going the same road."

Bhudrinath turned to me, and took me a few paces aside. "The bait has taken," said he; "our net is now round him; you must draw it tightly."

"How?"

"By inviting him to our encampment; I will propose it, and you shall pretend to disagree at first, and then, after some persuasion, consent. Do you understand?"

"I do;" and we turned back.

Bhudrinath again addressed him, while I turned away. "Sethjee," said he, "you are a man in misfortune, and if we don't help you out of this place you will assuredly be robbed of everything you possess. You must come and put up in our encampment; that is to say, if the Jemadar Sahib will permit it; but the truth is, we are very careful, and allow no one to approach it, as we are escorting a merchant from Benares to Hyderabad, who has a large amount of goods with him."

"For God's sake! for the sake of your father and mother!" cried the poor wretch, "for the sake of your children, intercede for me! do not suffer me to be robbed and murdered here! Ai! Jemadar Sahib," he said to me, catching me by my dress, "you are my father and my mother; a word from you, and I am safe, and my poor merchandise will reach its destination. God knows, if anything happens to me on the road, my house will be made desolate, my employers will seize my wife and children. Jemadar, you can protect me from this, you can save my life from these fears, which make me most wretched, and are consuming my soul!"

"Thooh![1] good man," cried I, spitting on the ground, "do not be so abject. Inshalla! I am able by God's favour to afford protection to one who is a prince among merchants, and you are too poor to think of. In His name follow us, and we will take care of you; we are going to Hyderabad ourselves, and you can remain among the servants; do you, Peer Khan, bring this man out to us."

Peer Khan remained, and we returned to our camp. On the way we determined that he should die before evening, or when it should become dusk, and we would then go into the town and visit the evening durbar of the hakim.

In a short time we beheld the merchant and Peer Khan, with another man, driving two ponies apparently heavily laden towards our camp.

"Come, this is more than I hoped for," said my father, "there are two of them; and two ponies well laden must afford something worth taking; we cannot expect this to be as profitable work as the last, but much may come out of it."

---

1 Fie!

The men approached, and the merchant was presented to my father.

"To your kindness," he said to me, "I owe all I possess, and if these poor bags might but be allowed to remain along with the rest of the merchandise you are protecting, it would increase the favour and they would be safe."

"Surely," I replied, "you can unload your beasts; and there is the pile of goods, you can put your bags on the top of it."

It was curious to see the behaviour of the men of the band; they appeared to have an instinctive knowledge of the purpose for which the men had been brought into the encampment. They did not evince the smallest savageness of demeanour, as perhaps might have been expected; on the contrary, every one was most civil and attentive to the strangers: one offered to rub down the ponies, another to make a place for cooking, a third to bring grass from the town, or anything they might require for their meal. In a short time we observed the appearance of care and anxiety on the face of the merchant to give place to a cheerful expression, and long before evening both the men were among a knot of the Thugs, listening to their stories, and themselves relating their adventures. Little did they think what preparations were making, and that in a few short hours they would cease to be counted with the living.

Chapter VIII

MEANWHILE a consultation was held as usual at my father's tent, and the different parts were assigned to us. The office of bhuttote[1] fell to me, and the merchant was delivered to my hands. I now experienced none of the hesitation which had formerly troubled my mind; I only longed for objects to exercise myself on, to perfect my hand in the peculiar knack it required. I had before me the example of those I most looked up to, and to equal or excel them was my sole ambition. I was determined to excel, and the excitement of the whole system proved a powerful stimulus. In this matter too I had acted a prominent part as a sotha; and I began to pride myself on my ingenuity in seconding, as I had done, one so completely an adept as Bhudrinath.

We agreed to put the men to death immediately after evening prayer.

We had in our camp a boy about twelve years old, the son of one of the Thugs, who sang very beautifully, and his father used to accompany him on the saringee.[2] It was our custom of an evening after prayers to send for the youth and be entertained by his songs; and he sang so well, that he often collected a considerable sum from among us. On this occasion he was called, and when he had begun, a message was sent to the merchant to come and partake of our entertainment. He came, and his servant also; the latter was a fine stout man, whiskered and mustachioed, and from the dialect he spoke I concluded him to be a Rajpoot of Meywar,[3] whose inhabitants are a noble race and brave to a degree. I eyed him, as he sat down in his place, with a half-formed determination to change the merchant for him. Bhudrinath had been allotted to him; and as I reflected on my own powers and his, I felt assured that if he was thought equal to it, I was superior to him, though I might not be considered so. Another thought, and my determination was made; I proposed the exchange to Bhudrinath.

---

1 Strangler.
2 Indian violin.
3 Mewar, a region in southeast Rajputana.

"As you please," said he in a whisper, "but yonder is a tough fellow; these Meywaree Rajpoots are active as panthers, and to tell you the truth I did not half like the idea of being allotted to him; but there is no help for it, and if I were to fail there are twenty others who would finish him. But do you think yourself equal to him?"

"Yes, I do not fear him; I have, besides, a reputation to win, and do not care running a little risk."

"As you will," he replied; "but you must mention it to your father."

I did so. The merchant was too much absorbed in the boy's song to attend to us, and the servant was in ecstasies, as it was one of his own country.

"Are you able to do it? do not try else," said my father; "the man is armed, and has a dagger at his girdle; a sword I do not fear, but daggers are awkward things, and you might be wounded.

"And suppose I was," I replied, "do you think the fear of that deters me? No, no; I have taken this on myself, and I will, with your permission, go through with it."

"As you like, my son, I will not oppose you; you have a name to gain, and you do well to run some risk. I will observe you narrowly, and be ready to succour you should you require it."

The usual phrase, "Pān lao" (bring pān),[1] was to be the signal; and as we changed places, myself and Bhudrinath, I fancied the servant eyed us with some suspicion; I thought I saw him loosen the dagger in his girdle; perhaps it was fancy, and yet he must have thought there was danger. He stood up and looked round at us; and as I contemplated his brawny form, naked from the waist, his chest covered with hair, and his muscular arms, I thought for an instant I had overrated my strength; but to recede would have been cowardly. The only plan was to attack him standing; I moved towards him, and cast a keen look on my father, by which I intended that he should give the signal as soon as I had taken my post; he understood me. I had gained my place, the man had just turned round to look at me and to get out of my way, and I was just telling him not to move, as I was passing on, when the signal was given.

Was it that I was a moment late, or that he had caught a glimpse of the fate of his master? or that in reality he suspected that all was not right, that he was in danger? I know not; but as I threw the cloth around his neck, he drew his dagger: to have loosed my hold would have been followed by instant death, he would have plunged it into me; and he struggled so much that, in spite of my great strength, he almost succeeded in getting his other hand between his neck and the cloth. All

---

1 Betel leaf.

this happened in less time than I take to say it. My danger was imminent, but as fortune would have it a Thug attempted to seize the hand which held the dagger; this diverted his attention from me for an instant: although half choked, he made an immense effort, which nearly shook me off, and as he reached the unfortunate man, he plunged the weapon into his heart!

The man uttered a loud groan and fell, and the blood spouted forth over us both; but the action had given me a fresh hold, I was able to use my knuckles, and who could live under the strength I put forth? The Rajpoot's dying struggles were tremendous, but I would not quit my hold; my father rushed to me.

"Where is the cord?" he cried; "he will not die in this manner; where is the cord? pass it about his neck, and let two of you pull."

"No, no!" I exclaimed, "he is nearly finished; let me alone, this work is my own, no one shall interfere." Fortunately, having thrown the man on his face, I was able to kneel on his back, and he was soon past the ability to use his dagger. At last there was one convulsion stronger than the previous ones, and he lay still—he was also dead—my second victim!

I arose, breathless and exhausted; and as I looked on the prostrate corpse before me, I felt indeed that there had been danger— that I had escaped from a deadly struggle, and that my art had triumphed over strength. Almost beside the body lay that of the man who had aided me, who had received a desperate wound. All had been so occupied with me, that they had overlooked the poor sufferer; he was lying with his face to the ground groaning.

"For God's sake," said I, "turn him round, the wound is in his stomach; can nothing be done for him?"

Some of the men accordingly turned him; but it was plain to see that there was no hope of life—the blood poured in a stream both from the wound and from his mouth. He made several attempts to speak, but in vain; he died almost instantly. While I was engaged in the struggle, I several times fancied that the Rajpoot's dagger had reached me, as I endeavoured to avoid it by screwing my body as far away from him as possible; but the excitement was too great for me to feel the wound, if there was any. Yet now on putting my hand to my side, I found, by the blood on my garment, that I was wounded! the blood too was observed by my father.

"Protection of God! he is wounded!" he cried. "My son, my son, did I not warn thee? did I not bid thee beware of that Rajpoot? thou wast no match for him, my son; and now thou art wounded, and what can be done?" and my father sat down, fairly overpowered with his emotions.

I felt that the wounds were but scratches, and hastened to open my vest. "There," said I, showing the wounds, "I said he would do me no harm; and what are these? a thorn from a hedge would have caused a deeper and more painful one."

"Shookur Khoda!"[1] exclaimed my father, "you are not hurt after all" (and the old man's eyes fairly ran over with tears as he looked at the wounds); "but I had feared the worst after that horrid sight. Ai,[2] Mahomed! thou wast a faithful servant."

The bodies of the merchant and the Rajpoot were instantly stripped, and removed to the grave which had long before been prepared for them; it was made inside a small tent, where my father, myself, and some others slept, and where it was secure from observation. I never was more struck with the despatch and ingenuity of the lughaes than on this occasion. I had but delayed to have my slight wounds dressed, and to bathe and cleanse myself from the blood I was covered with, when I went to see the grave, thinking to find it still open. I was perfectly astonished,—there was no sign of the earth having been disturbed; the place where the hole had been dug had been carefully beaten down, plastered over with mud; and, but that it was wet, no one could have told that it had been touched by the hand of man. My father's sleeping-carpet and mine were then laid over the place.

"Now," said I to Bhudrinath, "let us put on our best clothes and visit the hakim.[3] Will you come too, my father?"

"No, béta (no, my son), I have enough to do to keep all quiet here: some one must remain; and you and Bhudrinath have deserved your amusement, so go and take it. And here," cried he to some of the Thugs, "take your shields and swords, and accompany my son; and see that you look like soldiers, and not like Thugs, for the night."

Six or eight were soon ready, dressed in clean clothes and armed; and by this time, the moon having risen, and it being the hour appointed by the kotwal for the evening durbar,[4] we set off to the town.

Truly, dressed as we were in the handsomest clothes we could select, we looked not only soldiers but handsome fellows. Each of us had given a knowing cock to his turban; and mine, of the richest gold tissue, passing several times under my chin, set off my face by giving me a particularly martial appearance. My arms were of the richest description: a sword with a hilt inlaid with gold, its scabbard covered with

---

1   Thank the lord!

2   Ah.

3   Governor.

4   Assembly.

crimson velvet, with a ferrule to it of silver, of an open pattern, which covered nearly half of it. In my girdle, which was a cashmere shawl, were a pesh-kubs, or knife, with an agate handle, inlaid also with gold, and a small jumbea, or Arab dagger, also highly ornamented with gold and silver. I carried too a shield of rhinoceros' hide, the manufacture of Sylhet,[1] and painted and gilt in the beautiful manner of Hindostan, the bosses being of silver, richly chased and ornamented. My dress was of the finest muslin, which showed my shape through it to the greatest advantage; and rich cloth-of-gold trousers completed a dress at once elegant, and calculated not only to impress an observer with my correct taste, but to convince him that I was a person, if not of rank, of respectability.

Bhudrinath and Peer Khan's appearance was something less showy than mine; but they looked good and true men, and fair seconds to one of my pretensions.

So we set off to the town, and passing the gate went to the kotwal's chowree,[2] where we hoped to meet with him, or with some one who would direct us to the durbar. As it happened, the kotwal was there; and, relinquishing his employment of caring for travellers, he accompanied us to introduce us.

We walked through some of the streets, picking our way through tethered cattle and all the abominations of a Mahratta town, and at last reached a respectable-looking gateway, around which a number of soldiers were standing and lounging. Our friend the kotwal passed us through them; and after traversing two open courts, we reached the place where the entertainment and assembly was going on. A fine-looking old man questioned us as to who we were, to which the kotwal replied for us, that we were respectable persons desirous of paying our respects to the Nuwab Sahib;[3] to which I added, that, having heard much of his great name and hospitality, we considered that it would be unpolite to pass through his town without paying our compliments to him, and becoming acquainted with so estimable a person.

"You are welcome," said the old man; "there is nothing pleases the Nuwab Sahib so much as to see strangers, wherever they may come from; and, Inshalla! you will have no cause to regret having taken this trouble."

"On the contrary," I replied, "we cannot think it trouble, but an honour seldom allowed to such poor persons as we are. But pray lead us to the presence."

We ascended a few steps into the hall, where sat the Nuwab, surrounded by a number of persons. Before him were a group of dancing women, displaying their

---

1   City in Assam, in eastern British India, present-day Bangladesh.

2   Public hall.

3   His Excellency the Governor.

charms, and entrancing their hearers with songs of Persia and of Hindostan. Our conductor bade us wait for a moment; and going up to the Nuwab, said a few words to him, intimating our arrival.

"Khamoosh!" (silence!) cries the Nuwab, and it was repeated by a dozen voices; "let the strangers be admitted."

We were ushered on, leaving our shoes at the edge of the pure white cloth which was spread over the part of the room which led to the Nuwab's musnud.[1] On seeing us he made a polite salutation; and I stepped forward, and enveloping the hilt of my sword in an embroidered scarf I had thrown loosely about my shoulders, I presented it as a nuzzur.[2]

"Kubool hooa,"[3] said the old gentleman, placing his hands upon it, "it is accepted; sit down near us. Inshalla! we are much pleased with your appearance, and bid you heartily welcome to this our poor durbar."

To be polite I resisted this civility, protesting that I was by far too humble an individual to allow myself so much honour; but he was not to be denied, and accordingly I seated myself in the most respectful attitude, with my heels under me; and placing my sword and shield before me, in the best manner to display their beauty, I turned to the Nuwab, who seemed to be contemplating my appearance.

"Mashalla!"[4] said he to me, "thou art a brave-looking young fellow. Now tell me who thou art, and who these respectable persons are that accompany you?"

"I beg to represent in your service," I replied, joining my hands, "that I am nothing but a poor soldier, a syud[5] by birth. I have a few men with me, for whom and myself I am going to Hyderabad to seek service. I am come from Hindostan; my father, who is at our camp, is a merchant going to the city with merchandise. These persons," I continued, pointing to Bhudrinath and Peer Khan, "are two of my associates; and being superior to the rest, I have ventured to bring them to present their nuzzurs to the presence."

"By all means, Meer Sahib; we delight to see good and stout-looking fellows. Any one such is a pearl in the eye of an old soldier like myself. Let them be brought forward," said he to an attendant; and both advancing made the requisite salutations, and presented the hilts of their swords as I had done.

---

1 Throne.
2 Gift.
3 It is accepted.
4 Allah be praised!
5 A male Muslim who claims to be descended from the Prophet Muhammad.

The ceremonies of introduction being concluded, the musicians and dancing women were desired to recommence, and I had a moment's leisure to survey the apartment and the scene before me.

The apartment opened through three large wooden arches, into the courtyard which we had crossed; and between them were hung large purdahs or curtains of English scarlet cloth, which could be let down as occasion required. The room was lofty, and behind where we sat the walls were ornamented with stucco-work in rich designs. Above, on one side, was a small gallery thickly screened, from whence the inmates of the zenana[1] could observe all that was passing below without being seen; Before us the dancing-girls were moving with their peculiar floating motion, and singing while they expressed the amorous words of their song by their gestures. Another set were sitting down by their side, waiting for their turn to be called, and both were splendidly dressed and covered with jewels.

Nuwab Hoosein Yar Jung Buhadoor, a fine-looking wiry old soldier, polite and courtly in his manner, was a good specimen of the noblemen of the Dukhun; though perhaps not so effeminately polished as those of Dehli, yet he was one whose appearance commanded respect; and his bright keen eye, and the seam of a wound on his right cheek, showed that he had seen battle-fields and was familiar with war. His dress was of plain Dacca[2] muslin; but a string of large pearls round his neck, which he used as a rosary, and the beautiful sword lying before him on the carpet, would prove to the most casual observer that he was a man of rank and consequence.

He observed me looking round, and addressed me thus:—

"We are in a poor place here, my friend; but what can be done? The duty of the Government must be performed, and we cannot carry our house about with us. However, we have made the place as decent as it could be, considering we are in the jungle; and by the favour of the prophet, we have brought bright eyes and sweet voices with us, so that we do not lack amusement. Say, what thinkest thou of our selection? Yonder is Zora, sitting down, second to few in Hyderabad either for beauty of person or sweetness of voice: the other, now singing, is one we picked up on the way hither; but, Inshalla! in a short time she will be fit company for the other, and we shall take her to the city with us, to astonish our acquaintances."

The dancing-girl Zora, hearing her name mentioned, turned round and looked towards me. I was instantly dazzled by her beauty. She was not so fair as some of her profession I had before seen; But if she was not so fair, her features were small and

---

1   Harem.
2   Dhaka.

regular; and her large antelope-like eyes, when turned full on me, seemed to pierce me through. It was not a quick glance, but one that was fixed slowly upon me, and was not withdrawn. I was then young and modest, and I was fairly abashed. She observed it, and turned round and smiled to one of her companions.

"Come," said the Nuwab, smiling, you are not to steal the hearts of my tuwaifs.[1] You are a dangerous-looking fellow; and that handsome face of yours will do much mischief if I mistake not. Tell me the news from Hindostan; report speaks of war in that quarter, and that the Mahrattas[2] and Pindarees[3] are arming."

"Why," I replied, "there are such reports. "We heard that there was service to be got either with Sindea or Holkar, and that they and the Feringhees[4] would soon be at war; but we preferred trying our fortune in the Dukhun—for we heard the pay offered by both was very small to soldiers armed as we are, as they place their principal dependence on the troops under the Francese[5] generals, by whom alone the Ungrez[6] Feringhees are to be opposed."

"Ay," said the old Nuwab, "the times of fair fighting are passing away, and the inventions of Europeans are fast supplanting the bravery of the men of Hind.[7] God knows where it will end! Even at Hyderabad the Feringhees have got such a hold of the place, that God knows whether they will ever be driven out. And they train the miserable kafirs of Telingana[8] to fight in ranks and perform evolutions which are truly wonderful; but the power of Alla is great, and they are in favour with him."

"One comfort, however," said I, "is that the Francese and Ungrez are at bitter enmity; and if there is a fight, one or other, by the blessing of God, must be beaten. Then will be the time for true believers to rouse themselves, and free their country from the yoke of both."

"You talk like a young, hot-blooded boy: this cannot be. We of Hyderabad are too much beholden to the Ungrez Feringhees for freeing us from the demands of the

---

1 Dancing-girls.

2 The armies of the once-powerful Hindu Maratha Confederacy of central India, defeated by the British in 1819.

3 Pashtun mercenaries who accompanied the Maratha armies.

4 Europeans.

5 French.

6 English.

7 India.

8 Region within the Nizam's territories.

Mahrattas and the oppression of Hyder Ali[1] and Tippoo,[2] to quarrel with them; and after all I question whether we could do much against them. Tippoo fell, and he had the advice of the Francese in building his fort.[3] God protect me! it was only a mud wall before the Ungrez."

"You saw it then?" I inquired.

"Yes, indeed," said he kindling, "I saw the whole; and if you had also, you would have wondered to see the 'soger'[4] battalions scrambling up the breach like cats, headed by their officers, in the face of a fire of guns and matchlocks which would have scattered the people *we* call sipahees[5] like chaff. Truly they are something like men; and if we of India had fought like them, would they have possessed one foot of ground? Inshalla! they would not; but it is no use regretting. And now Sikundur Jah has made a treaty with the Ungrez, and sits in his zenana like a eunuch, leaving them to take care of him and his country."

"Then you think," said I, "that I have no chance of service at the city?"

"By no means," said he; "you are, I think, pretty sure of it. There are plenty of openings for a fine young fellow like you, and your appearance will take with some of those who command troops. Inshalla! you might have had it here, but my list is full; and you are not likely to separate from your men?"

"No," said I, "that I could not; the poor fellows would starve in a strange land; and having collected them, I must perform my promise of taking them to the city."

"Now you must see my pride, Zora, dance," said the Nuwab. "Inshalla! your heart must be hard if she does not make it ache, as she has done that of many a one."

The group who had hitherto been singing were desired to be seated, and Zora prepared to stand up. The bells for her ankles were brought, and she tied them on. The musicians to accompany her tuned their instruments, and after a short prelude she stood up. If I had been struck with her appearance sitting, how much more splendid was it now! She was not tall, but exquisitely formed, as far as could be judged from her peculiar dress, which was so loose from under her arms as completely to hide her form to her ankles; but it was of the richest description.

---

1   Haider Ali (1722-1782), ruler of Mysore in southern India.

2   Sultan Fateh Ali Tipu of Mysore (1750-1799), son of Haider Ali; fierce opponent of British rule in India and of the East India Company's puppet government in Hyderabad.

3   At Seringapatam.

4   Camp.

5   Sepoys.

It was made of a dark lilac-coloured gauze, in bands alternately with gold tissue; the bottom trimmed with gold tissue very broad, as far as her knees, upon which there was rich embroidery in gold thread and seed pearls. Around her she had thrown with extreme grace a scarf of the lightest muslin and silver, of the same colour as her dress; so thin was it, that as she moved, it seemed almost to float away from her in the air caused by her motion. The colour of the scarf round her head in contrast with her complexion, made it appear much fairer than it really was, and her large soft eyes still more brilliant and swimming.

The musicians began their usual prelude, and with it one of Zora's companions, a pretty girl, the slow movements of the dance. After a few turns she resumed her place, and Zora herself, like the full moon emerging from a cloud, sailed towards us with a slow and graceful motion. How shall I describe to you, sahib, her exquisite movements! Every turn displayed her form to greater advantage, and I gazed till my soul was fairly entranced. But how much more was I affected when she began to sing! Having performed the dance, both the slow and quick, she ceased; and after a prelude by one of the musicians behind her, she broke out into an impassioned ghuzul.[1]

It was one I was very fond of myself. I listened till I could have fallen at her feet, and worshipped her as a peri[2] from heaven. My soul was so intoxicated with the blessed sounds I heard, that I was insensible to all around me.

She at length ceased; and the Nuwab, who had been observing me attentively, asked me what I thought of the songstress and her dancing.

"Most wonderful is it," I replied; "my liver has become water before her fascinations. It is fortunate for me that I am not to live within their influence, or I were lost for ever. I could forego fame and my profession to lie at her feet and dream away my existence."

"You talk like a foolish boy," said the Nuwab, and must not give way to such fancies; many a man has been ruined for ever by them. Persons like her are greedy and insatiable of money, as we are told of the sea, which swallows up everything that is cast into it, without showing a sign on its surface beyond that of the transient ripple."

"Cannot they love?" I asked; "are they so utterly mercenary?"

"Utterly. Alas! young man, I have known and felt it; but let us change the entertainment; I have some rare bhyroopeas[3] with me, who arrived from Hindostan the

---

1   Love song.

2   Supernatural girl.

3   Comedians; comic actors.

other day. I have but heard them once, and my sides ached with laughter. You, no doubt, are well acquainted with their style; yet it is somewhat new to me: they shall be produced."

"May your condescension increase, Nuwab," said I; "truly your favour is great on your poor servant, and of which he is utterly unworthy. Nevertheless, he will not fail to make known the fair name and hospitality of Hoosein Yar Jung Buhadoor wherever his fate may lead him, which is the only return he can make for it."

"You will prosper, I hope," he replied; "young fellows of your appearance rarely fail to make friends. But here come the bhyroopeas; let us see what new amusement they have prepared for us; something to laugh at, I doubt not."

They were three in number; and twisting their faces into comical expressions, so as to cause the whole assembly to burst into a simultaneous fit of laughter, one of them stepped forward and said, that in the country whence he came there was once a Nuwab, a very wise man, who governed his country as no one had done before, and was a lord victorious in war; and that, if the hoozoor[1] pleased, his slaves were prepared to relate some of his adventures.

"Go on," said the Nuwab, "we are attending; see there is nothing indecent, for you are in the presence of the khanum."[2]

"Asteferalla!" (God forbid!) cried all, making their salutation towards the screen; "may the favour of the khanum be upon us, and may Alla give her a long life and posterity to bless her. Inshalla! we shall find favour in her sight, and take away our garments filled with gold."

They commenced: one of the men, dressed ridiculously as a child, personated the Nuwab. The story begins with his youth, how he is petted in the zenana; and the two others changing their dresses to those of females, one is his mother, the other his nurse. The young Nuwab is pampered, spoiled, becomes unruly, is declared to be possessed by the Shitan; a moollah is called in, and charms and wonderful potions, prepared by the aid of magic, are administered. The great child screams and roars, kicks his mother and nurse out of the assembly, upsets all about him; and the confusion and noise created by all this, especially among the tuwaifs, made a scene of fun, at which we all laughed heartily.

---

1   Highness.
2   A khan's wife.

In an incredibly short time the men again made their appearance, and the second act began. The child had grown up to be a youth, and to be fiery and uncontrollable. Women, wine, horses, and arms are his enjoyments; reckless of everything, he plunges into dissipation, sets his parents at defiance, runs into debt, is surrounded by sharpers and parasites, who despoil him of all he possesses, and he has given himself up to harlots and debauchery: and this ends the second part.

His father dies—he is now Nuwab; he is the head of a proud house, has men and soldiers at his command, and his territory to manage. He forthwith kicks out his former companions, discards every one he had formerly had near him, good and bad together, and gives himself up to a new set of rogues who had preyed upon his father—men with hoary beards, only the greater adepts in villany. He has a quarrel with a neighbouring noble, and the two prepare for war.

The troops are described: how they eat mountains and drink rivers, and the Nuwab himself as going forth like a bridegroom to meet his bride, like the lightning from the thundercloud, or a river overrunning its bounds, terrible, irresistible, before whose glance men quail as before a lion! His horse and arms,—the former large of carcass, small of limb, feet large and broad, fleet as the antelope, courageous as the panther. Of the arms, the sword which, wielded by his father, had cut through a buffalo's skin and divided the thickest quilting.

He goes forth, and the fight commences; the horse charge, and the Nuwab and his enemy meet (each is mounted on the back of a man). They fight; sword after sword (made of wood) is splintered. One of the horses is killed; it is the Nuwab's! He too is killed! he is at the mercy of his foe! No, he is up again; the fight is renewed; it is long doubtful; fresh weapons are given by attendants; at last he is victorious. Alla Akbar![1] the victory is won, the enemy is routed.

Then follows the torture of the prisoners, the rifling of the zenana. There is one slave beautiful, small, delicate in form, an eye like the gazelle's, fair as the beauties of Room[2] or the fabled ones of England. She falls at his feet: he is captivated. She conquers, and the nika[3] is performed. They live happily for some time; but the fame of the beauty of the daughter of a neighbour reaches him. His soul is on fire, his former love is neglected. He proposes marriage; it is accepted; the bride comes home, and a deadly jealousy ensues between the rival wives. The quarrels of the zenana

---

1   God is great!

2   Ottoman Empire.

3   Marriage.

are described; and by the shrieks of laughter from behind the screen, it was easy to believe how naturally all had been described and acted.

The Nuwab has reached middle age; he is now a father of a family, a respectable man, a religious man, surrounded by moollahs, who flatter him, and have usurped the places of his former companions. He is as debauched as ever; but it is not known. He passes for a just and good man, and his durbar is described, and his judgments. What was Solomon compared with him? or Hatim Tai,[1] or Lokman[2] the wise? And at each enumeration of his virtues the assembly loudly applauded, and directed their looks to the real Nuwab who sat as the spectator.

Again the Nuwab is shown, old and decrepit, worn out by disease, surrounded by quacks, from whom he demands nostrums to make him young and vigorous. His zenana is fuller than ever of women, who flatter his vanity, tell him he is as young as ever he was, and yet are false to him; but he has a son who promises to excel his father, who is a Mejnoon[3] in form, a Roostum in valour, before whom his father's enemies are scattered like chaff from the grain before the wind.

The old Nuwab is growing more and more decrepit and querulous. His fancies and longings are described in a most laughable manner; and as the final event approaches, he sinks into his eternal sleep, sure of the seventy houris of paradise and the eternal youth, which is the portion of true believers.

Having concluded, they stepped forward for the largesse promised.

"Well, Meer Sahib," said the Nuwab to me, "how like you this? have the men done ill or well?"

"Ul-humd-ul-illa!"[4] said I; "the works of Alla are wonderful, and assuredly these fellows are of his especial handiwork. I have seen many of their caste before, but never any like these."

"They shall be well rewarded," said the Nuwab; "and yet, despite of our having laughed at the whole story, there is much of a moral in it, and much satire. Would that many of the rising generation could receive a lesson from it; they might become wiser and better men."

"Ameen,"[5] I replied; "my lord's remarks are just. I did not notice the satire when I heard it; but now I feel it, and it is just."

---

1   Hatim al-Tai, sixth-century Arab poet and symbol of generosity.
2   Luqman, holy man and author of fables.
3   Majnun, legendary hero driven mad with love for the beautiful Layla.
4   Praise be to God!
5   Amen.

The night was far advanced; and requesting leave to depart, I rose to be gone. I was passing the tuwaifs, when an old woman pulled me by the sleeve, and said hurriedly, "If you seek an opportunity, there is another who desires one. Be secret, you shall hear more from me." My blood boiled; I slipped a piece of money into her hand, and departed.

CHAPTER IX

IN WHICH AMEER ALI PROVES HIMSELF AN EXCELLENT HAND AT MAKING A BARGAIN, AND THAT HIS AMOUR HAS A CHANCE OF SUCCESS

I SAID my blood boiled; could it be that one so lovely, one who had kept company with the nobles and men of wealth of Hyderabad, had seen aught to admire in me, who was unused to courtly scenes, and was even yet a boy, deficient in manner and address? Could it be that from my dress and appearance she thought me rich, one who would squander my substance upon her? These thoughts were passing through my mind, and we had nearly reached our encampment without my having interchanged a word with my companions. The silence was broken by Bhudrinath.

"How is this, Meer Sahib?" said he; "what has tied your tongue? have you nothing to talk about after our night's entertainment, no remarks to make on the beautiful kunchinee?[1] By Alla! though it is a Mahomedan oath, I would almost be content to give up the heaven of Indra, and turn Moosulman, were I sure of being attended in the paradise of Mahomed by a set of houris just such as she. And to think of her belonging to that old wretch the Nuwab, and to be buried in this hole of a Mahratta village, when she might have half the nobles of Hyderabad at her feet were she there! By Alla! I say again, it were worth the while to try and entice her away from the old sensualist, and it would be something to talk about, not to mention her company on the road, and the rare addition she would make to our evening amusements."

"Why," I replied carelessly, "the girl is, as you say, of surpassing beauty, and no doubt feels herself uncomfortable in this abode of swine; yet to get her away would be no easy task, and what should we do with her when we got her?"

"I shall try and see if her coming with us is any such marvellous difficulty," he rejoined; "and you know if afterwards there is any pursuit, she and the rest of her people are easily provided for."

"Now you speak like a cold-blooded Thug," I retorted angrily (for deny it as much as I would to myself, I could not but feel that the dancing-girl had more than

---

1 Dancing-girl.

interested me), "and I would sooner quit you all, and get back to Hindostan the best way I could, than that a hair of her head should be injured."

"I did but jest, Meer Sahib; you know I am not one who wars with women, except when they come before me in the fair and lawful exercise of my vocation. No, if we get the girl, it must be by fair means; and strait-laced as your father is on many points, he is too fond of a good song and good music to deny us having her in company; so do not mind what I said, and do not go to sleep upon your anger to your poor friend, if indeed you have any."

"I am not angry," said I, "though I certainly felt my blood rise when you alluded to her. We will consider about the rest in the morning, and if we can but persuade my father that the girl comes of her own accord, I do not anticipate any objection; but we must be sure that she will go first, and to this end I have a kind of clue which may guide me."

"How? did she say aught to you?" he eagerly inquired.

"No," said I; "how could she in that crowd? But you know I understand Persian, thanks to the old moollah my teacher, and you do not; and from the words of the last plaintive song she sang, and her mode of expressing them, I have a shrewd guess that she is tired of confinement and of her mate. You know the old proverb, 'Kubootur bu kubootur, bāz bu bāz'—Pigeons mate with pigeons, and hawks with hawks."

"Well," said Bhudrinath, "according to that, she is more likely to look to you than to me; and you know I am a Brahmin; therefore I leave her and the matter to your management; I am ready to assist when I can be of use. Inshalla! as you people say, we shall make a corner-stone of the old fellow's beard and laugh him to scorn."

"Ameen!" said I, "we will try at all events, and you shall hear from me in the course of to-morrow more upon this subject." We then separated for the night; and I was glad Peer Khan and the rest of the men had been so far behind us, as not to have been able to overhear any part of our conversation. I confess that, as I lay down to sleep, I earnestly desired the success of our scheme, though as yet it could hardly be called one; and though I had in some degree struggled with it, I had not been proof against the fascination of the dancing-girl; nor indeed was it to be wondered at after the words of the old woman.

Soon after the morning prayer, the leaders of the band were assembled to see the opening of the bags of him who had died the evening before. My father presided in the assembly, and one by one they were brought from the pile of merchandise. We had indeed got a prize; and it was not to be wondered at that the care of them had cost the man they belonged to so much anxiety. In each of them, among a quantity of old clothes, rags, and old copper vessels, were concealed small boxes filled with precious stones, pearls, small diamonds, rubies, and emeralds, and in two of the boxes were sets of ornaments made up, and set with jewels; and two in particular, a bazu bund, or ornament for the arm, and a sir-pésh, or ornament for the turban, were particularly splendid.

My father, who had a good deal of experience in these matters, pronounced the whole to be worth at least fifteen thousand rupees, and offered the band the alternative of distributing the whole in as equal portions as he could, or of waiting till our arrival at Hyderabad, where they could easily be sold for ready money. The latter, after some deliberation, was determined on, as had been the case with the former booty.

I proposed, as I knew that we might perhaps run short of money on the road, especially if we met with no more rich travellers, to offer one of the two ornaments for sale to the Nuwab, and as I had made his acquaintance to take it to him myself. The proposal was agreed to, and I was not without hope that by some lucky chance I might fall in with the old woman who had spoken to me the night before, and might be able to arrange a meeting with her, which should guide us in our future plans; so accordingly about noon I called Bhudrinath to accompany me, and we proceeded to the palace, as it was called by the villagers.

By the way we met with our friend the kotwal; but I cut him short with "Another time, Kotwaljee,"—for it seemed as though we were to have a long story,—"another time, my friend, we will pay you a visit; but at present the matter we have in hand is urgent, and it being past noon we are afraid of being denied admittance, and so you must excuse us."

"Of course," said he, "I will not detain you, and I shall not fail to present myself at your camp this evening to receive your further commands."

"That means," said Bhudrinath as we moved on, "that he expects a present. These worthies have been my study for many years."

"Ay," said I, "we must pay him well, and he will be the first to cry up our praises should anything happen; but do you anticipate anything?"

"Not I," said he. "I wish we could always do our work as securely, and get as well paid for it; but here we are at the Nuwab's gate."

An attendant at our request took in our names to the Nuwab, and after a short delay we were again ushered into his presence, and received with the same civility as we had been the night before. After some desultory conversation, I opened the object of our visit.

"Khodawund," said I, "my father pleads an attack of fever and cold for not attending to present his nuzzur at your feet, and he trusts you will pardon his seeming neglect. In his behalf I have brought a rare piece of jewellery for your inspection, which he hopes may please you; and by its purchase you will not only materially assist him, but it will become the property of one worthy to possess and wear it."

Thus saying, I produced the ornament for the turban, and laid it before him. He was evidently much struck with its beauty and the fine water of the precious stones, and after turning it in every position he could to catch the exact light for it, laid it down with a kind of sigh.

"It is indeed beautiful, and worthy of the turban of Bundugan Ali[1] himself; but," said he, "I am too poor to buy it; its value must be very great."

"No doubt," said I, "my grandfather must have paid handsomely for it; but times have altered with us, and we have been glad to sell our family property for whatever it would fetch. In this instance, far be it from your slave's intention to put a price upon an ornament without peer in its fashion; yet methinks it would so well become the forehead of my lord that he ought not to let slip such an opportunity of possessing it, to be enabled to show it one day at the court of his prince."

"Thou sayest truly; and if I may, I will but show it in the mahal,[2] and see how the persons of my household like it. Inshalla! they will approve of it, and then we will see if we can come to terms about it."

"Certainly," said I; "the time has been when it would have been nothing for our house to have presented a tray of such to one of my lord's power and rank; but we are reduced, as I said, and are no longer fit possessors of what we dare not wear."

The Nuwab took the jewel, and went into his zenana. He was absent a long time, but we could see by his face on his return that it had been approved of.

"They have looked at it in a thousand ways, and have discovered that there is good fortune to come with it; not that I need any, but you know what a parcel of old women are," said he. "And now I will ask what may be the price. You know we nobles of Hyderabad are not overburdened with money, and you must be moderate in your demand."

"Why," said I, "I am flattered by the opinion of those who have seen it, and can only say that my grandfather (may his memory live for ever!) paid so large a sum for the jewel that I am afraid to mention it. My lord must observe particularly its exquisite water. He, I say, collected the stones one by one during a long period of his life, and they cost him alone six thousand rupees; the gold around them is somewhat

---

1 His Highness.
2 Private apartments.

more; but my father will esteem himself fortunate if five thousand rupees be given for it."

"It is too much," said the Nuwab with a sigh; "where have I five thousand rupees to lay out in such a bauble as this? My friends, I have been gratified by the sight of it, but to purchase it is out of the question: the money I have not. Yet stay; allow me to have it valued by a jeweller, and we may perhaps come to terms."

"By all means," said I; "I have told my lord no lie in stating the price of it. But let the jeweller see it; he may fix a smaller sum; and such is our urgent necessity for a little ready money that perhaps we may be induced to take something less."

The jeweller was accordingly sent for, and arrived after a short time. He was shown the jewel; and from the expression of admiration on his countenance, I could see we had not overvalued it. He took it to the light, and putting on his spectacles, examined it in every possible way. At last he returned, and taking the spectacles from his nose, asked the price we had fixed on it. I told him.

"At the time this was made up," said he, "no doubt it was worth the sum you mention, for the stones are of rare water; nevertheless, we all know that men cannot afford to expend money as they used to do, and all things considered, perhaps at present four thousand rupees would not be too much, and indeed a fair price."

"It is too little; we must be content to sell other articles to supply our necessities. So Nuwab Sahib," said I, "with our profound thanks for your condescension, we ask leave for our departure;" and I took up the jewel and arose.

"Stay," said he; "I offer you three hundred rupees more: four thousand three hundred, surely that is sufficient."

"Make it five hundred," I replied, "and it is yours." And after much haggling on both sides, the price was fixed at four thousand four hundred and fifty. Of this, two thousand five hundred were paid by the Nuwab's treasurer in money, and for the rest, at my request, a bill was made out by a sahoukar[1] of the village on Hyderabad. And after again offering our thanks to the Nuwab, we took leave of him for ever.

"Not a bad morning's work," said I to my companion as we walked homewards, attended by some of the Nuwab's soldiers, escorting the men who carried the bags of money; "the sight of the coin will gladden my old father's heart; and it will be something to divide among the men, who are really in want of money, and will keep them comfortably till we reach the city, even though we should fall in with no more rich prizes."

---

1 Banker.

"Indeed, you may congratulate yourself on your address and good manners; for without them you could not have carried the matter off in the way you have done," said he. "Now if I, though I am a far older Thug, had tried it, I should have most likely failed for want of a plausible story. The old fellow swallowed the account of your grandfather, as if it had been as true as that we are now here. By Krishna,[1] thou art a rare boy!"

"These matters sharpen one's intellect; and though I could not deceive an unfortunate traveller as you can, you see I am of some use at a pinch, Bhudrinath."

"All will come in time," said he; "I do not despair of you after this; and if you accompany me in my work, you will soon excel me I think."

"We shall see," I returned; "but our errand is not complete: we have not met the old woman."

"Ha! so that plan is still in your head," cried he; "I warrant it you dreamed of the kunchinee last night, and your young heart is all on fire."

"No," said I laughing, "not quite that; but I have some hope, and I shall return to the kotwal's chowree after a little time, and perhaps the old creature may be in the bazar and may see me."

"Shall I accompany you?" asked he.

"No," said I; "I think it would mar the business. I will go alone; the presence of another besides myself might prevent her, if I meet her, from being communicative."

"As you will," said he; "as you are determined to carry the matter to the utmost, you have a better chance of success than I have; and besides you are a principal, while I could only be an agent."

Thus conversing, we arrived at the tents; and dismissing the soldiers and money-carriers with a handsome present, I had the bags moved into my father's tent, who was asleep; I ranged them before him, and awakening him, pointed to them.

He rubbed his eyes, grumbling at being aroused from his slumber; but they were quickly fascinated by the sight of the bags, and I could not help laughing heartily at his astonishment, as he took them up one by one, guessing at their contents.

"What, my son! Ameer Ali, where hast thou got all this? there must be five hundred rupees in each of them! One, two, three, four, five," said he, counting them; "two thousand five hundred! impossible! My son, what hast thou been doing? my brain is in astonishment. Where didst thou get it?"

"There is just what you say, father," said I; "each contains five hundred, or nearly. It is the price of the jewel you gave me to sell, which it seems was worth more than

---

1 Popular Hindu deity.

we thought for. I asked at a venture five thousand rupees, and I have brought you four thousand four hundred and fifty, which was as much as I could get; here are hoondees[1] for two thousand, and the rest is in the bags."

"As much as you could get, boy!" cried my father; "why thou hast done wonders. Mashalla! we are rich indeed; this is more than I ever expected;" and, his eyes fairly running over with tears, he embraced me warmly.

"Now," said I, "as I have done good service, I have in return a favour to beg, which I hope my father will grant; and it is a matter I dared not settle without his sanction."

"Say on," said my father; "I can deny thee nothing."

"Why," continued I, "there is a tuwaif of surpassing beauty, who sings like a bulbul,[2] and who is anxious to accompany us to Hyderabad. I dared not allow it without speaking to you."

The old man's visage clouded. "A tuwaif!" said he; "and dost thou not remember, my son, all the cautions I have given thee against persons of her condition, and hast thou so soon forgotten them as to get into their company on the first occasion which presented itself?"

"I represent," said I, "that neither have I forgotten them, nor have I gone into her company. I saw her at the Nuwab's durbar last night, but did not even speak to her."

"Then how knowest thou that she desires to go from hence?"

"I have heard it," said I, "from one who is attached to her, an old woman, who, I doubt not will be here before the evening."

My father shook his head. "I do not disbelieve thee, my son," said he; "but I mistrust thy young heart and hot temper. It is a danger too great to be encountered; for once with us, and she would get thee into her toils, and then father, duty, and profession will be alike forgotten, and I should lose thee, my son, which would kill me.

"Do not think so, I pray, my father," said I; "there is not the danger you anticipate; she would follow us, and we should see but little of her, except we desired her presence to sing to us on the dreary evenings of our journey. And grant me this request, I pray you; 'tis the only one I have ever asked, and perhaps I deserve something for what I have done hitherto."

"Thou dost indeed," he replied; "anything else would have been gladly granted without a demur on my part. However, I have confidence in thee, my son, and therefore have it as thou wilt, I will not gainsay thee in the matter."

---

1   Bills of exchange.
2   Nightingale.

So far therefore there was no objection; yet my heart smote me as I thought on the concealment I had made of her being in the pay and service of the Nuwab, and that her connection with him might bring us all into trouble. However, thought I, women have sharp wits; and if she truly desires to get away from him, she will take her own measures.

As soon as I could, therefore, I set off to the bazaar; and after loitering along the row of shops, and purchasing articles that were really required by us, I ascended the steps which led to the chowree, and was soon in conversation with the kotwal, who entertained me with the gossip of the town, and did not fail to endeavour to impress me with a high sense of his power and influence. More than once I was on the point of confiding to him my plan, and offering him a bribe to assist me; but I checked myself, on the consideration that he might take my money and afterwards play me false. As it happened, however, I was not long in suspense, for I saw the old woman in the bazar beneath me, making the best of her way in the direction of the gate of the town by which I had entered; so I took my leave of the worthy kotwal, begging him to come to the camp in the evening for a reward for his civility and exertions.

I had, however, lost sight of the old woman before I got fairly down into the street; and following the direction she had taken, overtook her just beyond the gate.

"Mother," said I, "am I he whom you seek?"

"Ai mere jān! (ah, my soul!) have I at last found thee, my prince? Surely I have not ceased in my endeavours since last night to meet thee; I saw thee enter the palace, but my old limbs would not carry me quick enough to overtake thee." And she threw her hands over my head, and cracked every joint of her fingers by pressing them against her temples.

"Are we secure against observation here?" she continued, "for I have much to say to thee, and that quickly."

"Not here," I replied; "I will go on to our tents yonder, and you can follow me; I will wait for you near them."

The old woman hobbled up to me as I stood under a mango-tree secure from observation. Quite out of breath, she sat down. When she had recovered herself, she untied a corner of the cloth about her person and presented me with a small ring.

"This," said she, " is from her you know of; and for the love of Alla, my soul! do you exert yourself for her: she is dying in this place, and is subject to all the torments the caprice of that unblest Nuwab can think of. She is one day in favour and loaded with kindnesses; another, in a fit of jealousy or rage, he deprives her of every comfort, shuts her up in a lonely room, and will not even allow me to go to her. You, my son, are young and brave; you will not suffer her to continue in this state, she who is the pearl of Hyderabad, who has found favour in the sight of princes and nobles. For the sake of Alla, exert yourself, and she is free, and will accompany you to the end of the world. She has seen you, and your beauty has entered into her soul and is consuming her liver; and between this and her former miseries, she is to-day in a state of madness, so that even I cannot pacify her."

"I am ready, mother," said I. "'Tis true I have never been blessed with hearing a word from her, save in her songs; but I can understand them; and there was one she sang which has been ringing in my ears ever since I heard it. Say, had it any reference to me and herself?"

"You have guessed well," she replied; "I told her to sing it, in the chance of its being understood, and, blessed be Alla, it was not in vain; but the time is passing fast, my son, and what can be done?"

"Nay," said I, "that I wish to hear from yourself, for I know not how to proceed; neither do I know this town, nor the house where she lives, so what can I advise? I am helpless in this matter, yet willing to the utmost."

"Listen then," said the old woman; "I will describe the place, and you must come after me and see it from the outside, that you may know it in the night. The place she is now in, and where she will most likely sleep to-night, is a small tiled house, at the corner of the wall of the zenana toward the street. There are two windows, some distance from the ground, yet not so high but that she might get out, if any one helped her on the outside. There is no other way of her escaping; for it would be impossible for her to get through the zenana, and afterwards through the open courts, which are full of soldiers. Say, will you dare the adventure; or be a coward, a namurd, who would not risk a drop of blood for a woman, and one so fair as she is?"

"I am no coward, I believe," said I, "though I have no deeds of arms to boast of. I accept the risk, and I pray Alla to defend us! Are there soldiers near the place?"

"No," said she, "not one; the only danger is at the village-gate, which is always guarded. How will you pass this?"

"If that is all," said I, "trust to me; and Inshalla! we will all laugh at the Nuwab's beard in the morning. But tell me, how do you intend to contrive to accompany us?"

"Ah, I have arranged that already. I am allowed free egress at any hour of the night, upon the various pretences or necessities of my mistress; and I can get out at midnight and meet you anywhere you may determine."

"This is good," said I; "now come and show me the place."

She guided me through the gate we had just passed, and turning down a narrow alley desired me to mark the various windings as we went along, which I did. We at last reached a street between two high walls, one of which was the Nuwab's zenana;

and passing on we arrived at length under a small tiled house, which answered the description she had given of it.

"This is the place," she said; "and that is the window from whence she must descend. It is not very high, as you see, and there will not be much difficulty in her getting out."

"I see none," I replied, "if she has only a stout heart. Tell her to tie her sheets together and drop them over; we will be below, and take care she reaches the ground easily."

"I will," said she; "and now away! we may be seen, and if so Alla be our help!"

"She sees us!" cried I; "for there is a hand stretched forth from the window."

"It is she!" said the old woman; "and oh! what joy it must be to her to know that there are persons anxious and willing to serve her! Now, my poor bird, thou shalt no longer have a cage, though it be a gilded one. But away, my soul, away! do not loiter here; a smile from her were dearly purchased now, and to-night you will have thousands, ay with her blessings too."

"I go," said I; "but fail not, nurse; for your life see that all is right; you must meet us at the corner we last passed."

The old woman nodded her assent, and I withdrew as quickly as possible from the spot, though I would have given worlds for one glance, for one approving smile, from the object of my love. As soon as I reached the tents, I summoned Bhudrinath, told him of my success, and unfolded to him the plan as it stood at present. He was rejoiced, and saw nothing objectionable in it.

"I have one thing, however," said he, "to represent, which you may do or not, as you please."

"What is it? Say on."

"Why," he replied, "although it will be, as you say, an easy enough matter to get out of the town, I by no means think it so easy to get in."

"By Alla! you say truly," said I. "What advice can you give to aid my plan?"

"You see," rejoined he, "that the gates are guarded. I tried myself to get in last night, before midnight, as I had an affair of my own to look after, and the fair one expected me; but the sons of dogs at the gates (may their sisters be defiled!) swore I was a thief, and after interchanging abuse for a long time they finally shut the wicket in my face, and I was forced to return in the worst of all possible humours. So my advice is, that we go in before nightfall, and take up our quarters in the shop of a bhutteara[1] with whom I have scraped an acquaintance; the fellow will not suspect

---

1 Eating-house keeper.

anything if we leave his place in the night, as I hinted my bad fortune of last night to him to-day, and he was the one to propose my coming to his place in the evening, to go wherever I pleased afterwards. So what say you? Shall we go to the fellow, or trust to our wits to get in the best way we can?"

"Your plan is a good one," said I, "and I thank you for your bad luck last night; but for it, we might have gone and knocked our heads against the gate to no purpose; to be sure we might climb over the wall, and I wonder you did not think of it."

"I did," he replied, "and was undecided about attempting it; but some fellow might have seen me, and, taking me for a thief, have thought no more of sending a ball through me than if I were a dog; so I came away."

"Thou hast a wonderful deal of discretion," said I; "now my hot blood would have led me into some scrape, whereas thou hast eaten thy ill-humour."

"And am now at thy service," rejoined he. "So we sleep inside to-night, which I am glad of, and we will get out through the farther gate; it will be some way round, but that is better than facing the fellows at this gate, who, I suspect, know me, or will recognise my voice, for I was too angry to disguise it."

"We will," said I; "and now I must in and eat, for I have fasted since the morning, and an enterprise is ill done on an empty stomach."

After evening prayer Bhudrinath and myself went into the town; and it was well we did so, for the men at the gate knew him perfectly, and good-naturedly joked him about his bad success the night before.

"Thou art beforehand with us to-night, my friend," said one fellow; "and thou art wise, for hadst thou come later we should have shut the door in thy face as before."

"You might have been more civil," said Bhudrinath, laughing. "I suppose, though you would not let me in, you will let me out in case I should bring any one with me?"

"Why, that is not against orders exactly, but you would have to pay toll; so, if you have not brought money with you, you had better stay where you are."

"I may find some probably," said Bhudrinath to the speaker, "enough at any rate to fill your hookahs for some days, if there is occasion."

"Agreed," said all the fellows; "a bargain, by Alla! a few rupees, and you may take any one you please, the Nuwab's harem too to boot, though there is not much in it by all accounts."

"Who is your wughyra, your officer?" said I; and one of the men stepped out. "I am he, may it please your nobility, and I can wink at an honest fellow's doings as well as another."

"Provided you are paid for it," said I.

"Of course," said he, laughing; "we are lucky when chance throws gentlemen like you in our way."

"Here then," said I, "are five rupees, to entertain yourselves with; and see that you don't get drunk, or the blame will fall on us."

"May your condescension increase!" cried the whole; "we are your worship's devoted servants."

"Now how do you mean to get out?" asked Bhudrinath as we passed on.

"Not this way," said I, "if I can help it, for there will be a disturbance about the matter; and if we go out here it will give a clue to our discovery. We will try the other gate first."

"I would lay a wager they are all drunk in an hour," said he, "and we may then open the gate for ourselves; but here is the bhutteara's shop, and those kabobs smell very savoury; I sometimes wish I was not a Brahmin, that I might eat them as you do."

"Ah," said I, "it is well for you to say that; but perhaps they may have proved too tempting at some time or other."

"By Krishna! I swear you wrong me," cried he; "Brahmin I am, and will be. You know my creed tells me that I have been successively transformed through every grade of suffering humanity; and now that I have reached the top, I am not such a fool as to descend to the bottom and undergo the whole pain again for the sake of a few kabobs."

"You are right," said I; "nevertheless I will try them; I could not eat when I wished at my tent, but their smell has raised my appetite wonderfully." And in a short time my fingers were pretty deep in a smoking dish of kicheree[1] and kabobs, as hot as pepper could make them.

"Friend Bhutteara," said I when I had done, "surely the Shitan himself must visit your shop now and then, for no other could eat those scraps of meat, except he had a mouth of brass."

"I beg pardon," said the fellow, "but I was away on business, and I suspect my daughter must, as you say, have put too much pepper in them; but I can make my lord a cup of sherbet, a poor imitation of what true believers will drink in Paradise, and it will cool his mouth."

"And a hookah, if you please," said I, "then I shall feel more comfortable."

---

1   Rice with legumes, ghee, and spices.

CHAPTER X

"Sleep you or wake you, lady bright,
  Sing Megan oh, sing Megan ee!
Now is the fittest time for flight,
  And thy lover waits to set thee free."
                              —Old Song.

I HEARD the bhutteara bustling about in the interior of his house for a while, and was gratified to see that he so evidently exerted himself to please me. In a short time more the sherbet was prepared, and its grateful coolness, with the rose-water which had been mingled with it, allayed the irritation of my mouth, and enabled me to enjoy a hookah, which, if served in a less costly apparatus than that the Nuwab had offered me, was as good in flavour; its pleasing fumes composed me, and quieted the feverish excitement I had hitherto been in.

"You appear comfortable," said Bhudrinath.

"I am so," I replied; "and I doubt not you envy me, in spite of your Brahminical belief."

"Perhaps I do," said he; "yet having never tasted the luxuries of meat and other things you set such value upon, I cannot estimate them sufficiently, and I care not about them; nay more, the very idea of meat, the sight of it in its raw state, the blood, the garbage accompanying it, are loathsome to me; and I very much question, were I to become a Mahomedan, whether I could ever bring myself to eat it. Pah! the idea is horrible."

I could not help laughing heartily at his disgust, and he was not angry. "But," said I, "how are we to wake at the proper time? an hour too soon or too late, and our enterprise is ruined."

"I was thinking of the same thing," he replied; and turning to the bhutteara, he asked him how late he remained up; "For," he continued, "my friend and I have a small matter on our hands about midnight. Can we trust you to awaken us if we sleep?"

"Certainly," said the man; "I never shut up my shop till after midnight, for sometimes travellers drop in, and poor hungry souls, the first place they seek is the bhutteara's shop; and were there not something hot for them woe be to me!"

"Here is a trifle over and above the price of the kabobs," said I, throwing him a few rupees, "to keep you awake."

He picked up the money with many salams[1] and good wishes, and my hookah being smoked out, and feeling drowsy, I laid myself down and slept, but not long. As is often the case, excitement overpowered sleep, and I woke in alarm lest I had overslept the time; I had not however done so. Looking round me, I saw the bhut-teara busily employed in cooking cakes, while his little daughter was turning some kabobs on the fire; he observed me, and said, "You are soon awake, sahib, it wants a good hour yet of your time; you had better go to sleep again; you see I have work in hand which will keep me up beyond that time, for some travellers have arrived, and it is as much as I can do to satisfy their hungry stomachs."

"I cannot sleep again," said I; "I am refreshed, and another hookah or two will keep me awake till it is time to go."

"I understand you," said he; "you young men are hot-blooded, and are always seeking adventures. But it is only as it ought to be; I would not give a couree[2] for a young fellow who had not the spirit you appear to possess."

"May you prosper," said I; "but let me have another hookah, for truly the first has left a grateful flavour in my mouth."

He disappeared into the interior of his house for a short time and returned with it.

"Now," said he, "if the first pleased you, you cannot but be gratified with this; it is prepared from a choice receipt, and it is only persons of rank and taste like yourself to whom I ever give it; it would be lost on the multitude."

It was, as he said, delicious; and my pipe had been refilled several times to my great satisfaction, when he told me the time I desired was come.

"Yonder star," said he, "rises over the houses a short time before midnight, so rouse your companion; you will be expected."

I did so; Bhudrinath was soon awake, and ready to accompany me. We took leave of our host, and directed our way through the now deserted streets to the place of assignation.

"We are wonderfully like two thieves," said he to me; "what if the village watch should catch us? we should look very foolish."

"I see no danger of it," said I; but hardly were the words out of my mouth, when we saw the patrol coming down the street before us. There was an open gate close

---

1   Bows.

2   Small shell coin.

to us, and stepping inside we hid ourselves behind the large doors. We had however been observed, and as the men passed, one said he was sure he had seen two men lurking there.

"Nonsense," said another fellow, "you are always seeing men in the dark. Come along! it is just midnight, and I am sleepy; we will go a little farther and then beat the duphra;[1] if there are any thieves about, they will run away."

A loud yawn was a pretty good proof of the truth of his assertion, and they passed on. Just as we emerged from our hiding-place, the duphra and horns were sounded, and answered from the other sides of the town; and then all was again still as death, save when a village dog howled his wild cry to the moon.

"There is now no danger," said I; "come on, we are near the place."

A few paces farther brought us to the corner where the old woman said she would await our coming, and there to our great joy we found her.

"My blessings on ye that ye are come," said she; "I thought the night would never wear away, and I have been waiting here for some hours.

"Is all prepared?" said I; "is she ready?"

"Ay, that she is; I warrant the hours have gone as slowly with her as with me; and listen," said the old woman, "she has hit upon a rare device, which will mislead suspicion;" and she laughed heartily.

"For the love of Alla be quiet!" said I; "were we heard or seen we are undone."

"For that matter there is not much to apprehend, for this house on one side is deserted, and inside the wall, on the other, is nothing but the Nuwab's garden, where no one stays at night."

"Tell me then what her plan is; can we assist it?"

"Oh no," said the woman; "it is her own invention, and a rare one it is. I had just come to her, when she sent me out to get a bladder full of blood. I could not make out what she wanted it for, but I went and bought it, though I had to get a kid killed on the pretence that the meat was suddenly required. Well, no sooner had I returned, than she poured some of it on her bed, rumpled and daubed the sheets, tore off pieces of her dress and scattered them about the room, also some of the beautiful hair from her head, which she also threw about, and in short made the place look as if she had been wounded, and there had been a scuffle to get her out. Ah, it was a rare device! and the best of it is, that a Nuwab who lives at a distance, and who has been trying to get this one to give her up (and there has been much

---

1 Tambourine.

quarrelling between them on the subject), will be suspected, and it will never be thought that she has run off of her own accord."

"'Tis wonderful," said I; "and, proverbial as is woman's wit, yet, by Alla! this is an instance which ought to be written in a book; but we are delaying here to no purpose."

"Come, then," said the old woman; "it is but a few steps farther."

We stationed ourselves under the window, in which there was a strong light burning; and the old woman giving a sharp but low cough, a figure was seen at the casement; it opened; it was she!

"Is he here?" said a low, sweet voice, which thrilled through me.

"Yes, lady, the humblest of your slaves is here, and prays you to be quick, for the sake of Alla; there is no time to lose."

"I will be with you instantly," replied she.

"Do so," said I; "but be quick, or we are lost."

She withdrew from the window, and a few instants after re-appeared and let down a box and bundle. I unfastened them, and she drew up the sheet.

"Now," said she, "I come; but what is to be done with the sheet? I must fasten it inside ere I descend."

"Leave that to me," said I, "only come down."

A few instants more were occupied in fastening the cloth, and she then stepped out on the ledge. My heart beat audibly lest she should fall and hurt herself, and we should be observed; but I and Bhudrinath placed ourselves underneath, to catch her if she fell. It was however unnecessary, for she was on the ground in an instant, and I had pressed her to my heart!

"The rest must not be left undone," said I; and ascending by the sheet, I entered the window. The room was a small one, and, by the hasty glance I threw around it, it appeared indeed as though there had been a scene of violence and bloodshed. Clothes were strewn about, the floor and bed were stained with blood, and pieces of torn apparel, lying here and there, gave to the whole the appearance of what was intended. I did not stay a moment, but unfastening the sheet, threw it down, and getting outside the window dropped to the ground. The shock hurt me considerably, but it was not the time for complaint. We held a hurried consultation as to which gate we should go out by, Bhudrinath again preferring the one by which we entered. This, however, was overruled by all of us; and, guided by the old woman, we took our way to the other. We met not a soul in the lonely streets, and, by the blessing of Alla, on reaching the gate we found the wicket open, and the man who should have guarded it fast asleep, with his shield under his head and his sword by his side.

Stealthily and slowly we passed by him, lest our footfall should awake him; and gaining the outside, we hurried along under the shadow of the walls until we gained the plain on which was our encampment.

When fairly within our guards, who were stationed round the spot, the fair being, who had hitherto clung to me, suddenly sank down. To fetch water for her was the work of a moment; and after forcing some into her mouth she recovered.

"I was overcome with joy," said she, throwing herself at my feet; "and indeed, if you knew the anxious suspense I have been in ever since last afternoon, you would believe me. At one time I was overjoyed at the prospect of deliverance from my hateful servitude, and again, as the night wore on, and I tried to count the hours, I sometimes thought that the time had passed, and that my preparations had been but a mockery. And now to find myself free and with you, ah! my lord, it is too much joy—my heart is like to burst."

I raised her up and caressed her, and seating her under a tree, put my arm around her, and we sat in the lovely moonlight in silence; she could not speak, and I would not break the current of her thoughts, whatever they might be.

How long we sat there I cannot tell; we were interrupted by the old woman. "This is no time for dalliance," said she; "my lady requires rest; and methinks, sir, were you to get us on before morning breaks, we should elude pursuit, and you could follow us."

"You say truly," said I, "and it shall be cared for."

Fortunately the cart of the sahoukar had not been sold, and though it was still laden with his effects, there was plenty of room in it for the two females.

I went to Bhudrinath, whom I found fast asleep after his night's work; when he was fully awakened, he seemed to comprehend that his services were again required.

"What, more work!" said he. "Well, Meer Sahib, I am ready; what is it?"

"It is too bad for me to rouse you so soon," said I, "and to require you to go on with this matter; for Alla, who sees my heart, alone knows how grateful it is to you for your assistance this night."

"Do not say so, my young friend," cried he laughing; "I would do anything for a little fun and excitement."

"Why," I rejoined, "you must know the old woman has advised instant flight from hence; so you and some of the men must be ready to be off before daylight; and as I have prepared the old sahoukar's cart for her, you will be easily able to get eight or ten coss from hence to-morrow, and the same the next day, when you must halt till we come up. Remember you are a Moosulman for the time, and she must be protected and screened as though she were the wife of one."

"I understand," said he, "and will do my trust faithfully."

"I believe you," I replied; "and now for the road,—which to take I am undecided. I have heard that two branch off from this to Hyderabad."

"Stay," said Bhudrinath; "I think Peer Khan knows both. I will go and bring him; you know he is one of my set."

He went and returned with the man. "I have explained all to him," said he," and now hear what he has to say."

"I beg to represent," said Peer Khan, "that I know both roads, but not perfectly; still I should think what the Meer Sahib counsels the best, for the other is a sad lonely one, and few travellers go by it; as to the chance of being pursued, we must trust to our good tukdeer (destiny), which has brought us thus far without an accident, and, Inshalla! will carry us on."

"Well, Peer Khan," said I, "you must be the guide; you are the only person who knows anything about the road, and I can only say that if you are steady and faithful I will make you a handsome present when I overtake you at Nirmul."

"May your condescension increase, Meer Sahib," said he; "but putting the gift out of the question, you know very well that there is not a man among us who would not give his blood to-morrow, or any time he might be called upon, for you. But come, Bhudrinath, I had better get the men together, and be ready."

I returned to the tent, where I found Zora and the old woman sitting covered up in their sheets, and warming themselves over a fire they had lighted. In a few words I told them of the necessity of flight, and added, "Alas! I do not accompany you now; we have had a consultation on the subject, and have determined that, for the sake of mutual safety, we must for the present separate. Alla, who sees my heart, knows that it will burn with anxiety and care while I am absent from you; for know, lady, that from the time I first beheld you in the durbar, my soul hath been consumed by your beauty, and as then I was plunged into despair at the thought that you never could be mine, so now is the excess of grief that I must part with you."

She was silent for some time; but at last throwing back her veil, and again displaying her beautiful face to me, she put her hand into mine. "I trust you," said she; "I have no fear now, except for you; I will go without a murmur, for I see how necessary it is for us to separate; yet assure me, my beloved, that you will not be long away, and I am content."

"I repeat," said I, "only two days at the furthest. We shall follow you to-morrow evening, or the next morning; and once that we are in motion, I will push on till I overtake you, where we will wait for my father and the rest."

"By what road do we travel?" asked the old woman.

"By Nirmul," said I; "it is out of the way, and we have therefore chosen it; it is not probable that the Nuwab's people, if he sends any out, will take that direction."

"You are right," she replied; "they will not. But I would give much to see him to-morrow, when the flight of this pretty bird is known."

"What shall we care," said I, "except to laugh at his old beard? I will go into the town as soon as the alarm has spread, and you shall have all the news when we meet again."

"Now bid me start," said Bhudrinath, who then entered the tent, "and I am off. For the present I am Jumal Khan, by which name inquire for me on the road."

"May God protect you all! You have a precious charge, my friend," said I, "and would that I could even now take your place."

The women were soon ready, and I saw them comfortably settled in their vehicle.

"Now I am off," cried Bhudrinath. "Drive on the cart; and do some of you fellows keep about it, as though it were a decent man's zenana."

"Alla Hafiz!"[1] said I, "and may the Prophet guide you safely!" They went on; I stood watching them, until a turn in the road hid them from my sight, and I betook myself to my tent, where, throwing myself down, sleep soon came over me.

I was awakened by my father, who came into the tent where I was lying; he seemed angry with me for having been out all night, as he said, on some unprofitable if not unworthy business; "but," said he, "it is time for the morning prayer, and after that I will hear what you have been about." I accompanied him to the skirts of our camp, where, spreading our carpets, we watched for the blush of dawn to go through the usual forms; when they were over, he seated himself and desired to hear what I had done; "I fear me no good," said he, "but tell me."

So I recounted the events of the night, and was prepared for a severe lecture, and a great deal of advice and reproof. I was for once agreeably disappointed; instead of being angry, he laughed heartily at the whole affair, and applauded our arrangements in having sent Zora out of the way.

The sun was barely risen, when there arose a noise from the town, and it was plain enough to us that the discovery had taken place. The whole place was in a ferment; people hurried out of the gates and collected into groups, and by the pointing to our camp, and their gesticulations, we were obviously the suspected persons; and, as we had anticipated, about twenty horse and some foot soldiers issued from the gate nearest to us, and came directly towards us. They surrounded our little camp; and

1 Allah protect you!

one or two who appeared the leaders of the party rode up, and in an authoritative manner demanded to see our leader.

I had previously arranged with my father that he was to continue to support his character as a merchant, and to put me forward as the jemadar of the party; and as he knew that I had appeared in the character at the Nuwab's durbar, and supported it well, he had readily acceded to my request.

"You see the leader," said I, "in my poor person; and what may be the demands of the Nuwab Sahib so early? Is there anything his poor servant can do to prove how much he is impressed with the kind treatment he has received?"

"You must be content to be our prisoner," said the man haughtily, "until your camp is searched; a strange event has happened, and you are suspected."

"Of what?" said I, appearing thunderstruck; "of what can I be suspected? But the camp is before you, sirs; by all means search it. Perhaps," said I bitterly, "your town has been robbed, and it is not wonderful that persons of respectability should be suspected in this unmannerly country."

"Peace!" cried the man, "we must do our duty; and I for one, for the sake of appearances, should be glad to find you had not requited the Nuwab's hospitality with treachery."

"I am dumb," said I, "notwithstanding that I am in utter astonishment at your words; but by all means search the place, and afterwards perhaps you will in kindness unravel this mystery to me."

He rode with me to my tent, and dismounting entered it with me, followed by two or three of his men. There was nothing in it but the carpet and mattress on which I had slept, a few cooking utensils, and some bales of plunder piled up at the farther end.

" She is not here," said Azim Khan, the leader of the Nuwab's party, "let us go to the other tent."

I accompanied them, and making a salam to my father, told him that the Nuwab's people wished to search his tent, as they had done mine, and added, "Do not oppose them, lest the Nuwab should in truth see reason to suspect us."

"Certainly not," said my father; "here is the tent, and I am the Nuwab's slave; it is not likely that an old man like me should have women concealed here."

So his tent was searched as mine had been, and afterwards the temporary screens of the men; but nothing was found, and the party were evidently disappointed.

"We are on the wrong track, and I told you so," said Azim Khan to the leader; "depend upon it, as I told the Nuwab, it is that rascal Sheffee Khan's work: we all know him to be in the employ of the hakim of Nursee, who wanted to get the girl, and we had better be after him than wasting our time here."

"A girl!" cried I; "truly this is most wonderful; for the sake of Alla satisfy my curiosity; what is all this about? By your head," said I to the leader, "but that it seems a serious matter, I feel much tempted to laugh at the idea of my poor camp being searched for a girl,—some slave, I presume, who has run away or been carried off by her lover; say, sahib, what has happened?"

"Why, it is no laughing matter to us, whatever it may be to you," said the leader; "send your men out of hearing, and you shall have the whole story."

"Away with you!" cried I to our men, who had crowded round; "this is no tale for your ears."

"The affair is this," said the man: "until last night, there was in the zenana of the Nuwab a dancing-girl of surpassing beauty and accomplishments; but early this morning her apartment was found empty, marks of violence everywhere about it, blood on the sheets of her bed, and some of her hair and portions of her clothes strewn about the room. There was no alarm in the night, the gates of the town were closed and guarded as usual, and it seems some work of the Shitan that this should have taken place, and that we should have had dirt thrown on our beards without knowing by whom. There is the Nuwab raving and swearing like a madman, his zenana is all in confusion; and, what is worst of all, he threatens to discharge every one of us, without we either bring back the girl or get him intelligence of her within three days."

"Protection of Alla!" cried both I and my father, "this is most extraordinary. And have you no suspicion who has insulted you in this manner?"

"Why," said the man, "you were first suspected, as being strangers and a large party, and we were desired to search your camp; but here we find nothing but bales of goods: and indeed you are not likely persons to have carried her off, for I question whether you ever saw her."

"I dare say," said I, "she was one of the women who were in the durbar the other night, when I paid a visit to the Nuwab."

"Very likely," he returned; "were those you saw good-looking?"

"They were both so," said I: "one was tall and fair, the other was shorter and not so fair, but very handsome."

"That was the girl," said the man; "I have seen her myself once or twice, when I could get inside of a night. But I am wasting my time here, and must return; you may depend upon my fully exonerating you from any suspicion in the matter."

"Your favourable opinion," said I, "will no doubt have its due weight; and I pray you to carry our condolence to the Nuwab, and say that if we have permission we will wait on him to express it."

"I will deliver your message," said he; "but I think you will not be admitted, as really he is in great grief, more on account of the insult, perhaps, than the loss of the girl. I take my leave."

He saluted us and rode off; and not long after a servant of the Nuwab came, with a civil message and some fruit, to say that his master regretted he could not see us, and was sorry that he had been under the necessity of searching our camp. We dismissed him with a present, and reiterated our condolences, which he promised to deliver. "And now," said I to my father, "this is no place for us longer; we must be off. What say you to a march in the afternoon?"

"It is good," said he; "we will go. Tell the men to be prepared."

Chapter XI

WE were on our way towards Nirmul in the afternoon, and as we had
heard no more of the Nuwab and his distress, we were relieved from
our anxiety; but I was in great dread the whole time we remained at
the town after the Nuwab's people had left us, lest some chance should open to
them a clue to detect us. The bhutteara might possibly reveal what he knew of our
proceedings; for although he knew not our object, still our remaining with him for
so short a time (as he must have formed a notion that we were after some woman),
coupled with the disappearance of Zora, might have led him to suppose, and very
naturally so, that we had carried her off. Fortunately, however, no ill effects did
ensue, and on the third day after leaving Oomerkhér we reached Nirmul.

As I entered the town I saw Bhudrinath in a shop, sitting with his back to the
street, in conversation with a decent-looking man, a Moosulman by his appearance.
He did not observe me, but on my calling out his assumed name he hastily rose, and
assisting me to dismount embraced me cordially.

"Is she safe?" I asked in a low tone, so as not to be overheard by his acquaintance.

"She is," he replied; "you have nothing to fear; and she is all impatience to behold
you again."

Sahib, I did not lose an instant in again beholding my beloved and pressing her
once more to my heart. She was more lovely than ever; and after some fond chidings
for my delay, and a relation of all the anxiety she had suffered in my absence, and
the fatigues of her journey, we gave ourselves up to that voluptuous feeling of joy
and security which those only know who have loved and been separated from each
other under circumstances of doubt or danger. After passing some time with her I
rejoined Bhudrinath.

"Why," said he, "from what I have picked up as yet, I suspect he has urgent reasons
for getting away from hence as fast as he can; in other words, he has been helping
himself to more than he ought in some revenue affair, and his safety depends upon

flight. I told him I expected you and your party, and that he would have a good opportunity of getting away if he chose to mix with us. You see," added Bhudrinath, "that when once I have fixed my eye upon any one, it is against my principles to let him escape me; now, as this is the case, we must have that man,—first, because of my principles, as I said, and, secondly, because of the money, which most assuredly he has in his possession; do you comprehend?"

"Perfectly," said I, laughing. "Your argument is an admirable one; therefore I will second your endeavours with all my heart. How shall we proceed?"

"Why," said Bhudrinath, "that is a somewhat difficult matter to determine, for I do not know where the fellow lives; but he promised to be with me soon, and I dare say he will not be long away."

"We must spread the carpet of patience," said I, "and sit on it, I suppose, till he makes his appearance; meanwhile I see no reason why I should not eat."

Well, sahib, I went inside the purda,[1] where my well-dressed meal awaited me, and Zora and I had our fingers very soon buried in a smoking dish of kicheree and a very good currie.[2] While I was thus employed, I heard the usual salutation pass between Bhudrinath and his acquaintance; and when I had satisfied the cravings within me, which had been grievous to bear, I joined them.

"This is my brother, of whom I have spoken to you," said Bhudrinath, presenting me to him; "he has now, as you see, overtaken me, and we shall journey on together. All his men are encamped outside the town, but as he is more comfortable with me, you see him here."

We exchanged salutations, and, by way of drawing him to the subject, I asked Bhudrinath when we should start.

"I cannot delay," said I; "that detention at Nursee was most inconvenient, and but for that we should have been far on the road by this time."

The man stared at me, and at last said to Bhudrinath, "Surely you must be joking when you say this gentleman is your brother; why, you are much older, and your features do not resemble in the least."

"We are not real brothers," he replied, "but cousins: you know that cousins usually call themselves brothers."

"But how comes it," said he, "that he is the jemadar of your men, and not you, who are the elder?"

---

1 Screened enclosure for Muslim women.
2 Curry.

"Why, it is a long story, and would not interest you," said Bhudrinath, "suffice it to say, that he is the son of the elder branch, who married long after my father, having lost his first wife; so, by the consent of the family and my own, he was declared leader, though he must confess I am his adviser."

I pretended to be ashamed of my dignity, and allowed, though I was nominally superior, yet that I could not get on at all without my *cousin*.

"Well," said the man, "you have curious customs in your country, but in every one they differ. Here your relative situations would be reversed; and so I suppose I must treat with you, Jemadar Sahib; I dare say your cousin has told you all about me?"

"He has," said I, "at least as much as you have told him; but we are both present, and what you say to one equally concerns the other; so I pray you speak on without reservation."

"I will not then recur to the past," said the man; "suffice it to say, that I have every reason to wish to get out of this place, as far as Hyderabad; there I shall be secure from mine enemies. I therefore propose to accompany you, if you will guarantee me protection and concealment on the road."

"We are ready to do that," said I; "but you will allow we shall run some risk; for besides protection and concealment on the road, we must defend you if necessary, and all this requires some recompense."

"True, and I am in no condition to drive a bargain, therefore you must name your own terms."

"You are liberal, I see," I rejoined, "and you shall find us to be so also. Perhaps one hundred and fifty rupees will not be thought by you exorbitant?"

"It is not; half I will pay you now, and the other half when we arrive."

"Agreed," said I, "it is satisfactory; and now say how you intend to travel. If I have permission, I would advise a mode which would be certain to escape detection."

"What is it?" cried he eagerly.

"That you should hire or buy a cart, and travel in it, at any rate for a few marches; my brother has his zenana with him, and you could not be discovered; no one would dare to search a cart which held females."

"By Alla, it is a rare plan!" said the man; "I wonder it never entered into my head. Yet cart I have none; and how to get one without giving a clue to my flight——"

"Do not distress yourself about it," said Bhudrinath; "furnish us with the money—about one hundred rupees will be enough—and I will go and purchase one, and account to you for whatever may be over."

"And my camels, and horses, and servants," said the man, "what can be done with them?"

"How many of them are there?" I asked.

"There are two camels and two horses; and I have three or four servants, whom I wish to accompany me."

"Then send them all to our camp at night," said I; "they will not be seen; and if necessary they can be sent on a march."

"You are ready witted people," cried he, "and what has cost me days and nights of anxiety, you have settled satisfactorily in a few moments. Now I clearly see there is no time to be lost; and I go to bring the money, and give directions to my people."

So he left us.

"Well done," cried Bhudrinath to me, "you fairly took the words out of my mouth, and I think the fish has taken the bait."

"I think so too," said I; "the fellow may be a very sharp revenue collector, but he is no match for you and me; and you see he is a greater man than we thought for, as he speaks of his horses, camels, and servants. No doubt we shall have a good round sum from him."

I hurried to my father, leaving Bhudrinath to manage everything his own way if I should not return in time to meet the man we expected.

He was surprised to see me, and exclaimed, "I did not think you would have left your adored so soon; to what am I indebted for this early visit?"

"Nay," said I, "father, do not mention her; it sounds like banter, and I have other work in hand just now than attending even to Zora."

"Ay, indeed! and now tell me, my son, what thou hast in view."

"Why," said I, "Bhudrinath and I have secured a man in the town, who promises to be almost as good a prize as either we have had before; and when you see two horses, some camels, and servants come into your camp this evening, do you allow them to remain, and start them off as early as may be to-morrow morning towards Hyderabad."

"I will do as you wish," said my father; "but tell me, Ameer Ali, what is this you are about? Are you sure there is no risk, no danger?"

"As far as I can see, there is not; but hear what has been done already, and then judge whether the matter ought to be persevered in or not. If you do not like it, we will drop it at once." So I told him all.

"You are both of you doing your work well, and I approve of it greatly," said the old man; "I will on my part receive the camels, etc., and will send on a party of gravediggers this very night. We will set off to-morrow night or early the next morning."

Bhudrinath was absent when I reached the house in the town, and I had to wait a long time for his return, which was not till near evening; however, I had the society I best loved, and the hours fled quickly. I was nevertheless overjoyed to see him return with a cart and two fine bullocks. He had purchased the whole from a set of dancing girls, and the cart was fitted with curtains, in the manner of those used to carry women.

When it was brought up to the house he dismissed the driver with a small present.

"There," said Bhudrinath, "is ninety-five rupees' worth, and the concern is cheap enough; our only care is now for the person who is to ride in it."

"Where is he?" said I; "are you sure of him?"

"As sure," said Bhudrinath, "as I ever was of any one; he is now gone to take leave of the hakim of the place, and will pretend he has done all his business. He has sent his camels and people to the camp, with strict orders to obey whoever there may be there in authority, and I myself directed them to go to your father and receive instructions from him. The man himself will be here at nightfall."

"Inshalla!" cried I; "truly may we say we are fortunate, nothing has gone wrong."

Just as we had completed all our preparations our friend came, and by this time it had become quite dark, so that he joined us unobserved; and as we had sent word to him that the cart had been purchased, he brought with him what we supposed to be his valuables; one of his servants carried the bundle, which appeared carefully tied up in waxed cloths, his hookah, and his bedding.

"Are you sure you have omitted nothing?" he asked.

"Certain," said I; "everything is ready. I have been to the gate, and have told the guard that we have a long march before us, and will pass out a little after midnight with two carts and our people."

"Well," said he; "then here is your money;" and he counted out seventy-five rupees to me.

"Now we have nothing to desire," said I; "but to be informed of your name, which hitherto you have not told us."

"Call me Kumal Khan for the present," he replied; "you shall know my real name at Hyderabad."

"As you will," said I; "doubtless you have good reasons for not discovering yourself to us. Meanwhile, as you say, Kumal Khan will do as well as any other name; therefore, Khan Sahib, I think the sooner we take some rest, the more we shall be refreshed for our journey to-morrow."

"I can lie down anywhere," said he; "I dare say I shall sleep moreover, which my care and anxiety have prevented my doing for some nights past."

He spread his carpet and covered himself up. Bhudrinath followed his example, and in a short time they were both asleep, as their deep breathing testified.

Strange destiny, I thought; there lies the man who has but a few hours to live, side by side in peaceful slumber with one who will be actively employed in his destruction. A few hours, and their situations will be changed, oh, how changed! one to lie senseless in the earth, and the other to live and breath, and to tax his wits to gain fresh victims. "Ya, Alla!" I exclaimed involuntarily, "thy purposes are inscrutable!"

We were roused at the time appointed by the men, and our preparations for departure quickly completed. I saw Zora safely deposited in her cart, as also her old attendant, next Kumal Khan in his; and putting myself at the head of the party, we were soon beyond the gates of the town and at the encampment. Here I sent on Zora's cart, and desired one of the men to come back and give us due notice should he meet the tillaees, or scouts, on the road. I then sought out my father, and inquired whether he had allotted bhuttotes and shumsheas (persons to hold the hands) to the servants and grooms.

"I have settled everything," he replied; "and given every man his instructions; there will be no difficulty if all is ready before us. But are you sure that Kumal Khan, as you call him, is not armed?"

"He has a sword," said I; "but what of that? Bhudrinath and I will easily manage him, and he will not be on his guard."

"Then keep well behind," said my father; "if there is any scuffle he will not hear it, and I will send a man back to you when we meet the first of the scouts. You can then do as you please; either bring him on, or deal with him there, as you like."

"Very good," said I; "we will be guided by circumstances."

I saw with secret exultation how beautifully everything had been arranged, as our men and our acquaintance's servants passed me. To every one of them was attached one of the most expert bhuttotes, with two others to assist if necessary; yet they disposed themselves so carelessly that suspicion was out of the question. Each one as he passed threw a look of intelligence towards me, as much as to say, "Here is work we delight in;" and I felt truly excited as the whole band was before me, their arms glancing brightly in the moonbeams.

This, thought I, is the joy my father told me of; and what could raise such feelings within me in the common plodding pursuits of life? When these fellows are but my own, then shall the name of Ameer Ali be dreaded and feared; men shall wonder at it; many a timid woman's heart shall beat as she listens to stories of me, and allows her fancy to picture to her him of whom she hears such deeds of daring bravery. "Yes," cried I aloud, for I could not control myself; "the time will come, ay, and soon; the present is poor work to what I have thought of and will put into execution!"

The voice of Bhudrinath recalled my ideas. "In the name of Narayun[1] and all the gods," said he; "what are you talking about? Come, we wait for you."

I urged my horse down the bank, and was with him in an instant. Kumal Khan put his head out of the curtains, and asked if we had assembled our men.

"Yes," said I; "they are all before us, except my cousin, myself, and a few of our attendants, who will stay round you."

"That is right," said he; "I shall sleep if this vile jolting will let me. Oh that I were on my horse, instead of being cooped up in this cart!"

"Patience," said Bhudrinath; "I dare say you will soon be out of it again."

"That I shall, my friend," said he; "when I dare show myself;" and so saying he shut the curtains.

Bhudrinath and I rode on some time in silence; at last we reached a rising ground, which apparently led down to the bed of a river, for I thought I saw the water glistening in the moon's rays. The jungle was thicker than before, and I involuntarily turned to Bhudrinath.

"Surely this is the spot," cried I; "we must wait for the cart," for we had preceded it a long way.

"We had better do so," he replied; "it will soon be up."

We had just heard the rumbling sound of the wheels, when the man I had sent on with it came up to us.

"What news?" I asked; "is all prepared?"

"By this time it is," said the man; "when I met the first scout I returned to tell you; they have fixed on a beautiful spot, and I doubt not that the band are waiting for you, having done their share of the night's adventure."

"Well," said I; "we don't want you here, so go on again." But he begged hard to remain, and I allowed him.

As Kumal Khan passed us, Bhudrinath gave the driver the signal; he nodded his head in compliance; and telling the men who were to hold our horses to be near and in readiness, we got behind the cart and followed it down the descent. About half-way down, the bank of the road sloped into it, and rose into a small eminence. I marked the place, and saw that the driver had done the same; the cart gradually

---

1 Vishnu, supreme Hindu god.

diverged from the track; one wheel went up the bank, it leaned fearfully over, and at last came down with a terrible crash.

We were off our horses in an instant, and ran up; Kumal Khan was groaning beneath it.

We lifted it up and got him out; but he was either so frightened or hurt he could not speak. At last he recovered; and the first words he uttered were a volley of abuse at the driver.

"Look!" cried he; "a smooth road, not a stone or a pebble, and yet that son of a base mother must needs drive up yonder bank, and has nearly killed me."

"He shall be well punished for his carelessness," said I; "but are you hurt, Khan?"

"My right arm is very painful," said he, holding it; "and I wish to Alla I had a horse to ride, instead of going farther in that concern."

"It cannot now be helped," said Bhudrinath; "and it is well none of your bones were broken. We will keep nearer you in future, and see that the fellow drives more carefully."

The cart had been by this time set fairly in the road again, and Kumal Khan's mattress and pillow arranged. As he turned away from us, and laid hold of one of the posts of the curtains, and had his foot on the wheel to get in, I threw the handkerchief round his neck.

"What—what is this?" was all that escaped him; the rest was an indistinct gurgling in his throat for an instant. The wrench I gave to his neck must have extinguished life, for he relaxed his hold of the post, and fell to the ground without sense or motion.

"Neatly and cleverly done," cried Bhudrinath; "I could not have managed it better myself; you see he does not stir—he is dead enough. Now, Meer Sahib, believe that a man can be killed before he touches the ground."

"I must see you do it," said I; "this fellow held on by the cart for some moments. But come," I added to the men, "lift the body into the cart, we have no time to lose." They bundled it in, and we set off as rapidly as the bullocks could trot.

"What if he should revive with this jolting?" said I to Bhudrinath.

"Never fear," he replied; "if he does, he will only have to be killed over again; but depend upon it he is dead enough; no man ever survived the wrench you gave him—his neck is broken. The old gooroo has taught you well, I see plainly."

"I own I feel more confidence every time I do it," said I; "and I should not care if even now I had one or two more fellows to try my hand upon."

"Nay," said Bhudrinath laughing, "rest you content with what we have done. See, we are at the bhil,[1] and yonder is the whole band collected."

We rode up to the spot, and the first inquiry was from my father: "Have you brought him?"

"Yes," said I; "the earth that held him is in the cart."

"Did *he* do it?" he eagerly asked of Bhudrinath, and pointed to me.

"Ay, did he," he replied, "and most properly too. He had him all to himself; I did not interfere."

"Al-humd-ul-illa!"[2] cried my father; "he is a worthy son. Come," continued he to all the men, "do not loiter here, but make the best of your way to the river-side; we will follow, and I dare say overtake you."

Seeing there was no more to be done, I pushed on to the river, the Godavery,[3] and finding that all had been ferried over, I urged on my horse to overtake Zora's cart; for I knew not what she would think of my absence, nor how I could well account to her for it satisfactorily; but I trusted to chance to frame some excuse. I passed the men, who were straggling along in parties of ten or twelve; but still I did not see the cart, though I had desired those who were in charge of it not to drive fast. I became anxious, and urged my horse into a gallop.

Well it was that I did so, for when I had proceeded some distance I heard a confused clamour before me. Could she have been attacked by thieves? was my instant thought. It was probable; for the road was narrow and the jungle thick on both sides, and seeing the few men with the cart, thieves might have surprised them. I drew my sword, to be prepared, as the noise and screams seemed to increase, and in a few moments more arrived at the spot. There indeed was a scene of violence! the moon was still shining brightly, and I could see all before me.

The cart was surrounded by the five or six men I had sent on with it, and who were defending their charge bravely; two of the robbers, as I supposed, were stretched on the ground; the rest were aiming cuts at my men, which they parried; but just as I got up, one of my men fell, and the rest looked exhausted. I suspect neither party observed my arrival, so intent were they on their own proceedings, and I could see that my cry of "Bismilla!"[4] accompanied by a cut which struck down one of the

---

1 Burial site.

2 Praise be to Allah!

3 Godavari River.

4 In the name of Allah!

robbers, was as startling to them as unexpected; while my faithful men, who now saw me plainly, set up a shout, and attacked their opposers with renewed spirit.

The scuffle lasted only a few moments longer: throwing myself from my horse, I drew my pistol from my girdle, and discharged it at a thief who was coming up to me with his sword uplifted; the ball passed through his body, and he fell. On this the rest of the band turned and fled. We pursued them for a short distance, and secured a youth who was one of them; the rest got clear off.

Chapter XII

SHOWING HOW JUSTICE IS OFTEN SUMMARILY DISPENSED

WHEN we returned to the cart, my first business was to soothe my poor Zora, whose screams, added to those of the old attendant, and the oaths, execrations, and shouts of the contending parties, had made a din which defies description. I found her terribly alarmed of course, but the rascals had not been suffered to approach her; and when she was assured by me that I should not again quit her side, she was calm, and gave me a history of the attack; which was, that as they were going along, the thieves began to pelt them with stones from the bushes on the sides of the road; and at last, perhaps not thinking them armed, rushed from their concealment, and the fight began.

The wounded thief was unable to walk, so he was put into the cart with the dead body; the boy's arms were tied behind his back, and a cord passed round his neck I tied to my own saddle. Leaving twenty men to guard the wounded, we then quickly proceeded.

We arrived at a large village before the sun rose; but the villagers were up, and the herds of cattle were pouring out of the gates on their way to the pastures. We desired the men to take up the encampment under some tamarind trees, and my father, myself, and Bhudrinath went to the gates, and desired to see the patel or whoever might be the chief authority.

After waiting a long time we were told that the amil[1] expected us, and were ushered into his house, where he sat in a verandah, apparently used by him generally to transact business in. He was a Hindoo, a khayet[2] by caste, and, as those persons usually are, was polite and courteous in his manners. My father was spokesman on this occasion, and after introducing himself as a merchant, and us as leaders of the men who escorted him,—the old Oomerkhér story,—he told him of the attack which had been made on us, of which however he seemed for a time to be perfectly incredulous.

---

1   Municipal official; governor.
2   Clerk.

"Impossible!" said he; "there has not been a highway robbery, or an attempt at one, for years, ever since some notorious thieves were caught and beheaded here: you must be under some mistake."

"You have not mentioned our wounded men, and that several of the thieves have been killed by us," said I to my father. "Perhaps this worthy gentleman will believe us when he sees them, or finds the bodies of the rascals; and again, you forget that two of them are in our custody."

"Indeed!" cried the amil, "that alters the case; but the truth of the matter is, that so many travellers beg for escorts from village to village, and set forth their having been threatened between here and Nirmul, that I am become difficult to satisfy, or to be persuaded that any danger has existed."

"We require no escort," said my father; "we are strong enough to take care of ourselves, having, as you have heard, beaten off these thieves; all we want is a few men to bring up our wounded, and justice done on the rascals we have caught."

"It would be well for us," said Mohun Lall, "if all travellers were to defend themselves like you; we should have but few thieves in the country, for they would find theirs a losing trade. But I think you said you had one of them unhurt. Where is he? We may perhaps get something out of him."

I sent for the lad, and he was questioned for some time about the gang, and where it was probable they had gone; but he would not answer a word, and the man who was interpreting for us gave up questioning him in despair.

"He will not say a word in this manner," said Bhudrinath; "give him the lash. I dare say that will make him speak."

"True," said Mohun Lall; "I was going to send for a korla;"[1] and he called to one of his men to bring one.

The thief shuddered as he saw it, and was again asked if he would confess; but he remained silent.

"Throw him down," cried Mohun Lall, "and cut the skin from his back."

In an instant he was thrown with his face to the ground, and the lash, wielded by a stout fellow, brought blood at almost every stroke; but in vain: he would not speak a word—not even a cry for mercy.

"This is of no use either," said one of the men who held him; "get a bag full of ashes. I'll warrant he speaks fast enough when that is put over his face."

A leather bag, such as is used to give grain to horses, was filled with burning-hot ashes, and brought. It was tied over his mouth, and at the same time he received

---

1 Whip.

some hard thumps on his back to force him to breathe. This apparently had the desired effect; for after a short time, during which the torture must have been great, he muttered something and the bag was withdrawn.

"You think to make me confess," said the rascal as soon as he could speak, "but it is in vain. I know well where my people are gone, and I curse the authors of their discomfiture;" and he poured a torrent of abuse on me. "Yes," continued he, pointing to me, "it was you who struck down my father, and as he is dead I want no more than to die also; you may hang me as soon as you please."

"Ha," said Mohun Lall, "I had forgotten him; let him be brought."

I had left the fellow badly wounded, but did not think there was any danger of his life. When he arrived, however, carried on a bed, it was evident he was dying; he scarcely breathed, and the rattle was in his throat. We did not, therefore, trouble ourselves further about him, but endeavoured to make the son confess; the whip and hot ashes were both resorted to again without effect, and all our endeavours only produced fresh execrations and abuse.

"There is no bearing this any longer," cried Mohun Lall; "the fellow must be hung. I know those rascals, and were we to keep him for a year we should never get a word of intelligence out of him, so there is no use in delay."

"As you will," said my father; "perhaps he will confess when the rope is round his neck."

"We shall see," replied Mohun Lall; "but I do not think it. Send for the mangs."[1]

These wretches, everywhere the vilest of mankind, were soon present, and the thief was made over to them.

"You see," said Mohun Lall to him, "you have no chance to escape; will you now confess and take service with me? I will protect you."

The fellow hesitated, looked at his father, and appeared irresolute; but a second glance at his expiring parent again rallied him.

"Not for all the wealth you could give me," cried he, drawing himself up, and looking at us proudly. "Had *he* been alive, and in your power, I might have taken your service; but you could not protect me now, and I would rather die by the hands of your people than by those of my associates, from whom I could not escape."

"Away with him!" cried Mohun Lall to the mangs; "see that you do your work properly."

"And our mamool (customary present), Maharaj,[2] you must not forget that."

---

1 Leather-workers; the lowest Hindu caste.
2 Great leader.

"No, no," cried he; "but away with ye; I am polluted by your presence. Go to the kotwal after you have done, and he will have received orders to give you a sheep and as much liquor as will make you all drunk."

The fellows made many most profound salams, and went off with their wretched companion.

"Where will they hang him?" said I; "I should like to see him again, and try if I can't persuade him to live to become a decent fellow."

"Somewhere beyond the gate," said Mohun Lall. "I do not know the place myself, but my people will show you. You will do little good, however, I am afraid; and after all, why should you trouble yourself about him?"

"It is no trouble," I replied, "I have simply a curiosity upon the subject, and will see the last of him."

"I will accompany you," said Bhudrinath; and we took our leave and followed the executioners.

About an arrow's flight from the gate were two scraggy, gnarled and almost leafless neem-trees, beneath which stood the group we sought, and round them all the urchins and idle men of the village. We hastened up to them and found that everything was prepared: a rope with a noose in it hung over a branch, and one of the mangs was coolly sharpening a knife upon an old stone idol which lay beneath the tree,—for what purpose I could not make out; however, my business was not with them, but with the wretch who was so near his death. He had seen us approach, and I thought was urging the mangs to despatch him before we came up; but they did not do so, as they imagined we brought some other orders to them. I addressed myself to the robber: "Will you not live?" said I; "so young as you are, have you no love of life? I now again promise you protection if you will confess, as you have been asked to do before."

"Let the cords be somewhat loosened which bind my arms," said the robber, "and I will speak to you; at present I am in too much pain to talk."

"Loosen them," said I to the mangs; "and one of you hold the rope in case he attempts to escape."

The robber smiled faintly at what I said, and continued:

"You have taken an interest in me, and although I owe my present condition to you, yet sooner or later I should have come to the same end, or fallen by some shot or cut of a sword; therefore I forgive you my death. But again I repeat I have no wish to live; nor, miserable as I am, can you suppose I would purchase my life by an act of treachery to my companions. Had my father lived and remained in Mohun Lall's power, I would have promised anything; but he is dead. My uncle too fell by the hands of one of your men in the attack on your cart; and whom have I left in this world to care for that I should live? One day has seen the end of my family; and it was our fate. Yet bear to Mohun Lall my hate, and the curses of a dying man. It is he who has killed me, and for this he will have to pay a fearful retribution. And now," said he turning to the mangs, "do your horrible office; I have no more to say."

I was going to speak again, but Bhudrinath stopped me.

"What is the use?" said he; "the fellow is obstinate, and, depend upon it, if he were spared, it would only be to lead good men into danger, if not into destruction: let him die, he deserves it."

The mangs looked to me for orders, and I told them to proceed: it was clearly of no use to delay. The robber was again tightly pinioned and thrown on the ground, and the mang who held the knife he had been sharpening, dexterously cut both sinews of his legs close above the heel; he was then raised up, the noose put round his neck, and in another instant he was pulled up to the branch and struggling in his death agony.

"Pah!" said Bhudrinath, turning away, "it makes me sick. What a contrast this is to our work, where he who is to die scarcely knows that the handkerchief is about his neck before he is a dead man!"

"You say truly," said I; "we have the advantage; but these mangs are miserable outcast wretches. What else could you expect from them? Now let us go to the camp; my father will be there, and we will see what this Kumal Khan had with him."

When we arrived, we found that all his baggage had been examined. There were two boxes, the contents of which we looked to see with some impatience. One was nearly filled with papers relating to his business as a revenue-collector, and these were burned as fast as they could be looked over by me. In the bottom, however, was a bag filled with gold, which Bhudrinath held up in triumph.

"This is something better than musty paper," said he, putting it on one side; "now for the other box."

It was broken open, and proved a rich prize indeed. After the clothes with which the top was covered had been removed, a number of bars of silver met our expecting eyes.

The box was not, however, emptied, and under another layer of clothes were ten bars of gold of the same size as the silver ones.

"Here is the cream of the matter," cried Bhudrinath, as he took up the first; "Alla knows how much there is; but it is clear the man was worth killing; and finely indeed must he have plundered the unfortunate cultivators."

The bars of gold and silver were made over to my father, to be placed among the other plunder we had got; and all that now remained to be seen were the clothes he had worn and his waist-bag. There was not, however, much in it.

"Stay," said Bhudrinath, "here is another bundle, which was in the humeanah."[1]

I took it from him, and unrolled fold after fold of clean paper. "Why, there is nothing here," said I; "I suppose he kept this to write on."

"Go on to the end, nevertheless," said my father; "let us see all."

After removing three more folds I came to another small packet, which was tied up with thread. "Here is something at last," said I, breaking it open. "Bills of exchange, in the name of the blessed Prophet! and, I doubt not, of value too. Have we any one who can make them out?"

"I cannot read the writing," said Bhudrinath, "but I can make out the figures if they are not written in Persian."

"Ah, no," said I, "they are Nagree or Guzerattee; so try your skill."

"This," said Bhudrinath, after examining one, "is for two thousand rupees: see, these are the figures."

"I dare say you are right," said I, handing the rest to him; "what are these for?"

"Here is a second for four hundred."

"Not much," said my father; "but go on."

"The third is for—let me see again," said Bhudrinath; "ah, I am right, it is for two thousand two hundred; and the last is for two hundred and forty."

"That is, let me see," said I, "four thousand eight hundred and forty. Well, we have got a good prize."

"Yes!" cried my father, "we should be well off if they were worth anything to us; but they are no better than the waste paper we have burned."

"How?" said I; "we should get the money if we presented them, surely?"

"You do not reflect," said my father, "that if we did so, it would lead to our detection in this matter: so destroy them."

"Indeed," said I, "I will not, but will keep them for stolen money; and I dare say were we to affect to be this Kumal Khan's agents, we might get the amount."

"As you will," said my father; "but remember you take no steps about them without consulting me."

So I kept them, and had afterwards reason to be glad that I had done so.

---

1 Purse; bag.

CHAPTER XIII

*HOW KUMAL KHAN'S HEAD WAS CUT OFF, AND STUCK UP NEAR
THE GATE OF THE TOWN*

AS we were to leave the village the next morning, I thought I might as well go and take leave of Mohun Lall, and accordingly went to his house in the evening.

"So you could make nothing of that rascal who was hung up," said he when we were seated; "these thieves are hardened vagabonds, and though I have hung several in this way, I have never been able to get anything out of them."

"I could not," said I; "the fellow was, as he called it, faithful, and died worthy of a better cause."

"It is no use speaking of him," said Mohun Lall; "the fellow is dead, and I would that all his brethren were hanging as high as he is; but I have heard a strange piece of news since you left me, Meer Sahib, which I do not care telling you, and you may perhaps be able to give me some assistance."

"Command me," said I; "anything that I can do will be but a poor return for your attention."

"The matter is this," said he: "a person by name Syud Mahomed Ali, who is very respectably connected at Hyderabad, came from the city with letters to the governor of Nirmul, two or three years ago, directing him to be employed as a collector of any small district which might become vacant. He lived some time with him, and when an opportunity offered, was appointed by him his naib, or deputy, in a district not far from Nirmul. Latterly, the governor has made a good deal of difficulty in getting him to remit the revenue collections, and one or two complaints which reached him privately made him suspicious. This feeling was increased by hearing that he had sent off his baggage in a clandestine manner,—whither, no one knew, and this morning both he and his people have suddenly disappeared."

"It is most extraordinary," said I; "but as I never heard of this person before, I do not see exactly how I am to be of any use to you or your friend."

"It is only a chance that you may be so," said Mohun Lall; "and my request is, that you keep a look-out for him during your journey, and, should you meet him, that you will arrest him instantly, and send him to me under an escort of your people, to whom I promise a handsome reward for their delay and trouble. One thing I must tell you, that on many occasions he has assumed the name of Kumal Khan,—the name I believe of a relative of his who adopted him, and perhaps he may have taken this name in travelling."

"I will not forget it," said I, "and you may depend upon my doing my utmost to secure him, should I fall in with him; and could you give me a paper relating his delinquencies, under your own seal, to serve me as a kind of authority for arresting him?"

"Certainly," said Mohun Lall; "your thought is a good one; I will forthwith write one myself." So saying, he drew up the document, and handed it to me.

"I am an indifferent scholar," said I, "but I dare say I can make it out;" and taking the paper I read what he had written, which was in substance what he had told me.

"And now I pray you to give me my dismissal, for I have business among my people, and the day is nigh closed."

"I will not detain you," said Mohun Lall; "and if there is anything you or your people want which my poor village can afford, you have only to send for it. I shall write too to my friend to tell him of the arrangement I have made, and the confidence I have in you."

"I thank you for your kindness," said I, "and should I want anything more I will not scruple to send for it. Salam, Sahib!"

"Salam!" he returned; "I wish you a safe journey and a successful one."

"Thanks again to you, good Amil, for your last words," said I to myself as I went away; "Inshalla! it will be as successful as it has hitherto been. Well, indeed, Mahomed Ali has met his deserts; and it is better perhaps for him that he lies cold and dead as he is, than that he should have lived to be haunted by an evil conscience, and to fall into the hands of those he has cheated and deceived, who would have tortured him to death if they had not immured him in a miserable prison to pine out the remainder of his days.

"Verily a good deal has been done, and my old father will laugh heartily when he hears how I have behaved, and how I have baffled suspicion by the commission I have brought with me, of which these papers are good proof. I have got his true name too, and it is hard if with this clue I do not get hold of the money for the bills of exchange which my sagacious parent would have destroyed. Shabash![1] Ameer Ali, do thou go on in this way, and whose dog is he who shall compete with thee, either in cunning or in daring!"

---

1 Bravo!

As I thought he would, my father laughed heartily at the business I had undertaken.

"It would be a good joke," he said, "to send for Kumal Khan's head, and put it at the gate of the village; they would then be at rest about him, and Mohun Lall's friend would be obliged to disgorge a little of the coin I have no doubt he has helped himself to out of the revenue."

"By Alla," said I, "it is an excellent thought, and I will send a couple of lughaees to bring it."

"No, no," said my father; "I did but jest; it is now nearly evening, and it would not do to risk them on that lonely road at nightfall; besides, they could not well be back before we start."

"As you will," said I; but at the same time I made an inward determination to mention it to one or two of them.

When I reached my tent, I sent for three lughaees, enterprising fellows. "Now," said I, "my lads, I have got an adventure for you, and here are five rupees apiece if you will do it."

"Your commands are on our heads and eyes," said they; "you have only to order us, and we will perform your wishes."

"Well then," said I, "what I want is the head of Kumal Khan: do you know the place you put him in? and is the grave deep?"

"We know the spot exactly," said one of them, a Hindoo, by name Motee-ram; "what lugha ever forgot a spot where he had buried any one! the grave is not deep, and he is at the top of all. But what are we to do with the head? and why is it wanted?"

I detailed to them what Mohun Lall had said, and repeated what a good joke it would be to get the head, and place it in some conspicuous place.

"Then," said Motee-ram, "if I may offer advice, I recommend its being put under the tree whereon the thief was hung this morning; the worthy amil will think Kumal Khan has fallen by the hands of some of his gang."

"A capital idea," said I; "and therefore, if you find no one about when you return, place it there, for I have no wish to look at it."

"It shall be done to your satisfaction," said all three; "and we will start immediately."

So they left me. Yet I was in dread all the time they were absent lest anything should befall them, and I often wished I had not sent them on such an errand; but it was too late, and I could not recall them. Anxiously and sleeplessly did the hours pass till near midnight; and poor Zora could not imagine what was the matter with me. I excused myself to her, however, on the plea of having a headache and feeling unwell, and suffered her and the old woman to put quicklime on my temples, and use other remedies which she said were infallible in such cases; and at last pretending I was going to sleep, she lay down and was soon really so.

It was about midnight that I was relieved from my suspense, and gladly did I hear the voice of Motee-ram at my tent door calling to me. I arose and went out. "Is all safe?" I eagerly asked.

"All is safe," said he; "and we have brought the head and put it where you told us. It was well we went, for we found a troop of jackals busily scratching at the grave; and they would have got to the bodies before morning, for they had made a large hole when we arrived. However we scared them away, and put a quantity of dry thorns just under the earth on the top; they will not try it again, and if they do it does not matter, as no one will ever find that spot—it was too well chosen."

"You have done your work well and bravely," said I, "and you shall have your money to-morrow morning." They left me, and, the excitement past, I lay down and slept soundly.

The next morning we rose before day; the omens were consulted, and proved favourable, and all prepared for prosecuting our march. We were soon ready, and finding that Zora was comfortable in her cart, and that she needed nothing, I could not resist the temptation of going as far as the tree where the thief had been hung, to see whether in reality the head of Kumal Khan had been brought. Accordingly I separated from the party, and ran as fast as I could to the spot, which was not far distant. I know not why, but an involuntary shudder crept over me as I reached the tree and looked about for the object of my search.

The wind which had been still all night, suddenly rose with the breaking day, and its first sigh through the withered branches of the neem almost seemed to have a voice in it—a deprecation of the deed we had done the night before, and of which so foul an evidence as that before was present; for at that instant my eyes fell on the head, which had been placed on a projecting knot of the trunk to protect it from the jackals. I recoiled from it with loathing, for the eyes were protruding from the sockets and the mouth open, and the expression of the features was hideous in the extreme. I gazed at it for a moment. "This must not be," said I; "those eyes will betray us:" so taking the cold head down, I forced them into their sockets, and shut the eyelids, which I was able to do, as the stiffness of death was past. I then placed the head on a large stone close to the tree, on which some rude idol was sculptured, and quitting the place, ran as fast as I could to a small puddle I had passed as I came, in which I cleansed my hands from the blood which had adhered to them.

"Alla be praised, they are pure again!" said I inwardly, as I washed them eagerly with some earth and water. "Brave as I know myself to be, and caring for nothing alive, I would not have gone with Motee-ram and his people, have dug up that body and decollated it—no, not for the wealth of Delhi. Pah! the idea is horrible!" and I arose and ran again at my uttermost speed till I reached the party.

My absence had not been remarked, which was well; and having mounted my horse, I stationed myself near Zora's cart, which was in front.

After we had reached the stage, and were resting ourselves for the day, a horseman came from the amil with a letter, at which we were all greatly amused. It related how the head had been found and recognised, but at the same time implored me to keep the event secret, in order that the amil's friend, the ruler of Nirmul, might gain time to meet the demand caused by the defalcation of the man we had killed. This exactly suited my purpose, as I had now no doubt that I should be able to get the amount of the bills.

On the fifth morning after this we were to reach Hyderabad. It was estimated as seven coss distant, so we did not start so soon as usual; we wished to reach it when the day was well advanced, in order to attract as little attention as possible, for our numbers were considerable. We therefore divided into three parties, one under my father, one under myself, and the other under Surfuraz Khan, a friend of my father's whom we had met on the road, and who with his men had been admitted into our company; and we agreed to meet again in the karwan,[1] which was the usual resort of all travellers, and where we were told we should find accommodation in the serais which were used by them. Mine was the first division to move, and my father said he should remain with the baggage, and bring it leisurely along, as he should have to pay the usual duties upon the property we had secured, at the various toll-houses.

Accordingly at full daylight we set out. It was a lovely morning, cold, yet not so cold as in our own country, where the frost is often seen on the ground, and the grass feels crisp under the foot of the traveller until the sun rises; still, a good shawl was a welcome addition to my usual clothing.

Wreaths of mist spread themselves over some hills to the left of the road, and concealed from our view an immense tank which lay at their foot; while, as a gentle breeze arose, the mists were set in motion, revealing one by one piles of the most stupendous rocks I had ever seen, and which appeared as though they had been heaped on each other by human agency. I had been struck by these extraordinary rocks on our first entering Telingana, and remarked them now to Bhudrinath; he gave a ready solution to my conjectures as to their origin.

1　Inn; caravanserai.

"You perhaps have heard of one of our sacred books called the Ramagan,"[1] said he; "in it are related the wars of the gods. The origin of one of them was the forcible carrying off of Seeta, the wife of Ram. She was taken to the island of Lanka (Ceylon), and there detained by the rakshas or evil spirits of the place, assisted by the king with powerful armies; they defied Ram, and he was in utter despair at the loss of his beautiful wife, nor could he find any trace of whither she had been carried. You know that Hunooman, our monkey-god, was a wise and astonishing being; in the monkeys of the present day his form only is perpetuated; the intelligence is gone, and cunning alone is left to them. But it is also a sad fact that, like them, mankind has also degenerated, and we are no more like the beings of those days than the present monkeys are like Hunooman. Well, as I was saying, Ram in his perplexity was visited by Hunooman, who pitying his state proposed to go in search of the lost fair one, and accordingly departed. Long did he wander, and at last discovered her in Lanka, in a state of as great distress as he had left her lord in. Quickly he returned with the intelligence, and an army was assembled for the conquest of the island. But a difficulty arose when it reached the end of the land; before them certainly lay Lanka, but a wide and rough sea ran between them, the roaring waves of which appalled the stoutest hearts—nor did even the glorious Ram himself escape the general fear. Boats were not to be procured, and if they had, what would have been their use to transport an army which consisted of millions of god-like beings, each of whom was ten cubits in height! Bam gave himself up to despair; but Hunooman at one bound clearing the channel, quickly returned with assurances that a bridge could soon be constructed, and that he and his companions would labour night and day till it was completed.

"Quick as thought, legions of monkeys departed to the Himalayas. Huge mountains and rocks were torn from their foundations and transported by relays of these indefatigable beings to the shores of the ocean. One by one they were dropped into it from above, and the splashing of these huge masses is described as terrific, the water ascending to the heavens and extinguishing the stars! At last the bridge was completed, the vast armies marched over it, the country was conquered, and the beauteous Seeta restored to the arms of her devoted lord.

"Now these rocks are part of those brought from the Himalayas and have remained piled upon each other just as they were set down by the monkeys; for this country being half way, it was here that the relay was established, and, when the bridge was completed, these remained, not being required. To prove the truth of what I have

---

1 Ramayana; ancient Sanskrit epic.

said (and may Bhugwan[1] grant that no one doubt it!), I must tell you that remains of the bridge are visible to this day. Many pilgrims with whom I have conversed, who had been to Ramisseram,[2] declared that they had gone in boats along the side of the bridge, and traced it by the points of rocks appearing above the water, almost in a direct line from one land to the other, with here and there a small island where the waves have not been able to make an impression; that farther, heaps of rocks similar to these are met with in various parts between here and Ramisseram, which no doubt were not required; and you will remark that in no other part of the country north of this do any similar ones appear. There cannot, therefore, be a stronger proof of the truth of our ancient religion than these hardened witnesses, which will last to the end of the world, to the confusion of all unbelievers and sceptics."

"Mashalla!" said I; "it is a wonderful story, and true enough, for I have heard of the bridge myself. We Moslims have it, that Baba[3] Adam, who was placed by Alla in the paradise of Serendeeb,[4] which is Lanka, got tired one day of his confinement to so small an island; and seeing the mainland at a distance, made the bridge by throwing mountains into the sea, each at seven coss distance, to get there. When it was completed, he easily stepped from one to the other, and so gained the land; but this action displeased Alla, who soon afterwards ejected him from the paradise, and man has been a wanderer ever since."

"Yes," said Bhudrinath; "but is not my story the most probable, especially when you see all these rocks piled up in so extraordinary a manner, as if in loads? Why, if a man wanted to carry a heap of stones, he would pile them up in the same way; and see, these are in separate heaps, just as they were laid down, some large, some small, according, no doubt, to the strength of the parties who bore them."

"Alla ke Qoodrut,"[5] exclaimed I,—"it is the power of God. Mashalla! they were great monkeys! It is well we have none of them nowadays, or they would pelt us out of the land."

---

1   His Highness.
2   Town near Madras (Chennai).
3   Father.
4   Anglicized version of *Swarnadip*, Sanskrit word for Sri Lanka, from which the English word "serendipity" derives.
5   It is the power of God.

Chapter XIV

HOW AMEER ALI ARRIVED AT HYDERABAD

WE passed the village of Ulwal, its white pagoda peeping from among groves of tamarind and mango trees, and its large tank now glistening in the rays of the sun; and pursuing our way, we saw on passing a ridge of rocks, the camp of the army at the far-famed Hoosain Sagor,[1] or, as it is more often called, Secunderabad.[2] The tents of the English force glittered in the bright sun, and behind them lay a vast sheet of blue water.

We had heard much of this lake from many persons on our journey, and as we passed it a strong breeze had arisen, and the surface was curled into thousands of waves, whose white crests, as they broke, sparkled like diamonds, and threw their spray into our faces as they dashed against the stonework of the embankment. We stood a long time gazing upon the beautiful prospect, so new to us all, and wondering whether the sea, of which we had heard so much, could be anything like what was before us. I have since then, sahib, twice seen the sea. I need not attempt to describe it, for you have sailed over it; but when I saw it first, methought I could have fallen down and worshipped it, it appeared so illimitable, its edge touching as it were the heavens, and spread out into an expanse which the utmost stretch of my imagination could not compass,—a fit type, I thought, of the God of all people, whom every one thinks on; while the hoarse roar of the waves as they rolled on, mountain after mountain, and broke in angry fury against the shore, seemed to be a voice of Omnipotence which could not fail to awaken emotions of awe and dread in the most callous and unobservant!

We passed the embankment of the tank. As yet we had seen nothing of the city; but there was a ridge not far off, and as we ascended it I could no longer control my impatience. I spurred my horse, and before I reached the top shut my eyes, that whatever was before me might burst upon my view at once.

---

1   Hassain's lake.
2   British military settlement near Hyderabad.

My horse slackened his pace when he reached the top, and allowing him to go on a few steps I opened my eyes, and glorious indeed was the prospect before me.

Beneath lay Hyderabad, the object of many a conjecture, of many an ardent desire to reach it—the first city of the Dukhun, justly celebrated throughout the countries I had passed. I had imagined it, like every other I had seen, to be in the midst of a plain, and that all that would be visible of it would be here and there a minaret rising out of large groves of trees; but Hyderabad presented a different aspect.

I stood on the crest of a gentle slope, which to my right hand was broken at some distance by rocky hills, and to the left appeared gradually to descend into a plain, which stretched away almost uninterruptedly to the horizon. Before me, on the gentle rise of the valley, and beyond where I supposed a river to be, lay the city, its white terraced houses gleaming brightly in the sunlight from amidst what seemed to me at the distance, almost a forest of trees. The Char Minar[1] and Mecca Musjid[2] rose proudly from the masses of buildings by which they were surrounded; and here and there a white dome, with its bright gilt spire, marked the tomb of some favourite or holy saint, while smaller mosques, I might say in hundreds, were known by their slender white minarets.

Beyond the city rose another connected chain of rocky hills which ran along until they met those on the right hand, and shut in the valley on that side. The city seemed to be of immense extent; but I thought from the number of trees, that it was composed principally of gardens and enclosures, and was much surprised afterwards, when I entered it, to find its streets so filled with houses, and the whole so thickly peopled.

It was altogether a most lovely scene: the freshness of the morning, the pureness of the air, and the glittering effect of the city and its buildings caused an impression which can never be effaced from my memory. I have seen it since, and though it is ever truly beautiful, it never struck me as it did that day. But I was then young, full of spirits, and flushed with the consciousness of my own powers, just developing, and assuring me that they would lead me to eminence.

One by one, as the Thugs came up, each ejaculated his praise of the beautiful scene, and all declared that the capital was worthy of the encomiums they had heard lavished on it. Inquiring the nearest road to the karwan, we descended the slope, and threading our way through numberless suburbs we reached the place, and were at the end of our journey. We were grateful for it, and for the protection and success

---

1 Mosque of the Four Minarets in Hyderabad.
2 Mecca Masjid; huge seventeenth-century mosque in Hyderabad.

we had met with. We took up our abode for the present in a serai[1] which surrounded a large and richly ornamented mosque; and for our greater convenience I went in search of an untenanted house, and after some difficulty succeeded in hiring a small place, the property of a merchant who resided next door. It contained only three rooms and the verandah, which was the shop; but it was enough for my father and myself and there was a small room with a strong door, in which we stowed away all our plunder.

Zora was overjoyed at reaching the place of her birth, and what was in reality her home. She could talk of nothing but the delight of meeting with her relatives and friends, and the surprise her arrival would excite in them all, as she said they had considered her lost to them ever since the Nuwab had carried her off. The almost certainty of her being separated from me as soon as she was again in their power never occurred to her, and I determined that before she visited them I would lay all my fears before her, convinced that her affection for me would be the best guide for her conduct.

Our landlord the merchant was very civil and attentive to our wants, though his civility evidently proceeded in a great measure from curiosity as to who we were and what was our object. I stated to him in a few words our old story—of my father being a merchant, and myself a soldier of fortune who had accompanied him in search of employment. He was now curious to know of what my father's stock in trade consisted; but we were resolutely silent upon the subject, although he offered his agency to dispose of our goods.

"For," said my father to me afterwards, "our goods I know are valuable, and I know not their worth; nor have we as yet opened the bales; we will do so to-morrow morning, and assort them; we will then go into the city to the shops of the sahoukars, and inquire for articles similar to them, find out their prices, and by this means be enabled to value our own. Were we to offer them in ignorance of their market prices, we might be suspected; and though we may not get what they are intrinsically worth, we shall no doubt be able to sell the whole for a handsome sum."

I agreed with him perfectly, and the next morning we set to work to open the bales.

Their contents were indeed costly,—brocades, cloth of gold, fine muslin scarves, also woven with gold and silver patterns, plain muslins, and a few shawls, besides fine cloths of different kinds for wearing apparel, and sarees[2] with silk and tissue

---

1   Inn.
2   Saris; women's garments.

borders, the latter from the looms of Nagpoor. These, and the jewels in our possession, when laid out and assorted, made a display on which we feasted our eyes for some time, wondering at their magnificence: after I had made an inventory of the whole, my father and myself, attired in handsome clothes and mounted on the best of our horses, attended by a few of the men, took our way into the city.

Crossing over an old but massive bridge, below which ran the river, now a shallow stream, we entered by the gate at the head of it, and inquiring our way went direct to the chowke, or marketplace, where we trusted we should find goods exposed for sale similar to our own. The streets were narrow and dirty, and the interior of the city certainly did not answer the expectations we had formed from its outside and distant appearance; still there were evident tokens of its wealth in the numbers of elephants, on the backs of which, in canopied umbaras,[1] sat noblemen or gentlemen, attended by their armed retainers. Crowds of well-dressed persons paraded the streets, and as the festival of the Mohorum[2] had just commenced, cries of "Hassan! Hoosein![3] Doola![4] Deen! Deen!"[5] and a thousand others familiar to us resounded on every side.

We made our way as well as we could through the throng, and our attendants were often obliged to clear us a passage, which exposed them to the jeers and abuse of the multitude, as they were recognised as strangers from their dress and language. Once or twice I observed a hand laid on a sword by some respectable person who had been jostled or pushed by our men, and heard a deep threat muttered; but we managed to get along, and at length came to a broader street, where the crowd was less dense; and here that noble building the Char Minar, burst at once upon our view.

"How grand!" I exclaimed, stopping my horse and looking up to the huge minarets, which seemed to pierce the clouds; "to see this alone is worth a journey from Dehli."

The minarets formed the four corners of the building, and from them sprang immense arches which supported a roof, upon the top of which a small mosque was built. It did not look capable of supporting the immense weight of the whole, and yet it had stood for centuries, and the fabric was unimpaired.

---

1 Canopied seats.
2 Festival in honor of Islamic martyrs.
3 Hasan ibn Ali and Husayn ibn Ali, grandsons of the Prophet Muhammad, revered as martyrs.
4 Bridegroom!
5 Faith! Faith!

"It is the hour of prayer," said my father, interrupting my gaze; "and hark! the muezzin[1] calls from the Mecca mosque; thither we will now proceed, and afterwards transact our business."

I followed him, and passing by the Char Minar, we turned up a street to our right, and stopped our horses at the gate of the mosque.

A feeling of awe mingled with admiration came over me as we entered the court-yard and advanced along a raised causeway to the foot of a flight of steps which led up to the interior. On either side of us were the graves of princes and nobles, many of them of elegant forms and richly carved; but the building itself engrossed my entire admiration. Five lofty and wide arches opened to view the interior of the edifice, where an equal number appeared in depth; and where the arches met, the eye was perplexed by the innumerable points and ornaments, which, running into each other, completed a roof of exquisite design and workmanship. To add to its beauty, the whole was of stone, carefully smoothed, whereas the Char Minar and the other buildings I had as yet seen were of stucco.

But I had little time to observe more; the sonorous and melancholy call of the muezzin had ended, and the few attendants for the afternoon prayer had spread their carpets and commenced their devotions. We joined them, and kneeling on our outspread waistbands, went through the usual forms, while the low murmur of the prayers of all ascended to the fretted roof and added to the solemnity of the scene.

To the majority of those present there was, perhaps, nothing new or uncommon; but I, who had escaped the dangers of our journey and those attendant on our profession, felt that it went to my heart; and, murderer as I was, though not as yet callous, I was softened, and my tears flowed fast as I repeated the words of prayer, and the impressive language of the blessed Koran in which they were couched.

The ceremony concluded, we rose, and though I was well disposed to linger in the sacred edifice and observe more of its beauties, my father hurried me away, and we returned to the Char Minar.

"Here," said my father; "those useful rogues the dullals[2] are to be met with. They will try to cheat us, no doubt, as it is their trade; but as we are not purchasers, we may avail ourselves of their aid to find out the houses of the merchants who deal in our articles, and it may be that the fellow we fix on will be intelligent and assist us to dispose of our property."

---

1   The man who calls Muslims to prayer from the minaret of a mosque.
2   Brokers.

We stopped on reaching the building, the lower part of which was sadly dis-figured by numbers of wretched huts and stalls, where vendors of vegetables and sweetmeats sat, and served out their goods to the passers-by. My father, calling to a decent-looking young Hindoo, of intelligent countenance, asked him where he could meet with a dullal, as he was a stranger in the city, and wished to see some clothes and other goods, which he did not know where to find.

"I am one at your service, noble sir," he replied; " and I know well the richest warehouses, and can lead you to any you wish; and," added he, "there is not a sahou-kar or dealer in the city who will not readily give your poor servant, Mohun Das, a character for sobriety and trustworthiness."

"You had better not say much of your good qualities till they have been proved," said my father; "your tribe has not the best reputation on these points."

"Ah," said the man, "my lord is well aware of what (alas that I should say it!) the majority of our tribe are, a sad set; nevertheless, his slave will not be found to be like them, for having begun by being honest, he has not found it worth his while to be otherwise."

"That is as much as to say you would be dishonest if it suited your interests," said I; "but come, the day wears fast, and we are anxious to be out of this crowd before dark."

The fellow gave me a knowing look, accompanied by a shrug of his shoulders, which could not be mistaken; what I had said had proved to him that we were on our guard.

"What description of goods may you be in search of?" said he; "any may be pro-cured, from the shawls of Cashmere and brocades of Benares to the meanest article."

"Benares fabrics are what we require," said I; "a few handsome roomals[1] and doputtas,[2] and a turban or two, to adorn ourselves for the minister's durbar."

"You shall see them," said the dullal, girding his shawl about his waist. "Now follow me, and keep a good eye on me, lest you lose me in the crowd." And so say-ing, he descended the steps of the building, and led us along some of the principal streets, till he dived into an obscure alley, and stopped at the door of a house which certainly promised nothing from its exterior.

"A very unsatisfactory search we should have had," said my father; "had we en-deavoured to find out a merchant ourselves. It is well we took this fellow with us."

---

1 Handkerchiefs.
2 Scarves.

"These merchants, I have heard, usually choose these secluded places on account of their security," replied my father. "It would not do in a lawless place like this to expose goods for sale as they do in other cities. But they are well known, and easily found out by strangers if they apply to the dullals as we have done."

We were ushered into the interior of the house, and were received by a large fat man, the very counterpart of the sahoukar I had killed. I started involuntarily at the resemblance; but soon recovering myself, and assured by his civility, I seated myself, as did also my father, and we quickly entered on the object of our visit.

One by one bales were opened and their contents spread before us. The sahoukar's stock seemed to be interminable and of great value. We selected several articles, and inquiring the prices of those which we inspected, of which I made memoranda, we desired them to be kept for us, saying that we would call the next day with money to pay for them. The sahoukar pressed us to take them with us, and the dullal offered his security for us; but for obvious reasons we declined, and took our leave of the merchant.

The dullal accompanied us as far as the Char Minar, where my father, slipping a piece of money into his hands for his trouble, told him we now knew our way home, and bid him come early in the morning to the karwan and inquire for the house of Rugonath das Sahoukar, where he would get tidings of us.

"So far I am satisfied," said my father; "our goods, as you will have observed, are equal in quality to those we saw, and by the prices affixed to them we have a good earnest of a large sum of money, if we can only dispose of them, a matter I apprehend of no difficulty if properly managed."

The next morning came the dullal.

"Canst thou be secret?" asked my father at once, and throwing him a couple of rupees. The fellow started and trembled.

"If such is my lord's will," said he, his teeth almost chattering with fear, "I can; but I am a poor man, a very inoffensive man. I am my lord's slave, and rub my nose on his feet," cried he at last, fairly throwing himself on the ground, and rubbing his forehead against the ground, as he saw my father's brow contracting, and his face assuming an expression of anger at the evident suspicion which the man had of us.

"Why," cried my father, as the fellow lay on the floor whimpering, "what is this? what chicken-hearted son of a vile woman art thou? In the name of Alla get up! Because a man who, Inshalla! is somebody, asks thee whether thou canst be secret, must thou of necessity think thou art going to have thy throat cut?"

"Do not talk of it," cried the wretch, shutting his eyes and shuddering. "I am a poor man and a miserable Hindoo; what would my lord get by cutting my throat?"

"Nay," said my father, "this is beyond bearing; the fellow has not the soul of a flea. Kick him out into the street, and beat him on the mouth with a slipper: there are plenty of dullals to be found beside him."

"Pardon, noble sir!" cried the fellow,—the mention of his trade leading him to suppose that he was required in the way of his calling,—"pardon my foolishness. My lord's threatening aspect turned my liver into water; but now that he smiles again, I am assured that no harm is meant."

"Harm! surely not to such a wretch as thou," said my father; "but since thou art inclined to listen to reason, sit down, and hear what we have to say to thee."

"I can be secret," cried the dullal; "let my lord speak."

"It will fare badly with thee if thou art not," said my father, again looking grimly at him; "but listen. I am a merchant; I have never been at this city before; but hearing at Dehli that an investment of valuable goods, such as we saw yesterday, was likely to sell well here, I have brought one down with me. I knew not the selling prices here, and therefore engaged thee to show me some goods, that I might be able to regulate the sale of my own. Now, canst thou manage it for me?"

"Surely, surely," said the fellow in delight," nothing is more easy. My lord will not of course forget my perquisites on the sale?"

"Thou shalt have five rupees in every hundred's worth disposed of," said my father; "will this content thee?"

"It is a princely offer, and worthy of my lord's generosity," said the dullal. "Might I be permitted to see the goods?"

"It is necessary that you should see them, and here they are," rejoined my father; and he opened the door of the room where they were, and one by one displayed the contents of the bales.

"This is indeed a rich stock," said the dullal; "you may be able to sell most of the cloths, but I question whether the whole, without you intend to remain here some time."

"That depends upon circumstances over which I have no control," said my father; "if I cannot sell them all here, I shall take what remains to Poonah."[1]

"Well," said the man, "if I am permitted, I will make memoranda of all that there is here, and in the course of to-morrow will let you know what can be done. I cannot do so earlier, for I shall have to visit all the dealers."

---

1 Pune.

"Do what you think best," said my father, "and here are ten rupees for your expenses. Now begone, and let me see you again at this time to-morrow."

The fellow made many salams and took his leave.

"Did you ever see so pitiful a wretch?" said my father. "For two couries I would have strangled him on the spot, to put an end to so disgraceful a coward."

"Let him pass," said I; "he is but a Hindoo, and not worth thinking of. But you are not going to let him off with all the money you have promised him?"

"Of course not," replied my father; "you understand I suppose what is to be done?"

"Perfectly," said I; "leave him to me."

I went to Zora, my own gentle Zora. She had been speaking much of visiting her kindred, and though I had put her off as well as I could since we arrived, I saw with concern that I had no longer any pretext for detaining her. I could have fled with her—I think I could. Such was the intensity of my love for her, that, had I had the courage to speak of flight and she had agreed to accompany me, I verily believe I should have forsaken father, associates, and profession, and committed myself to the world.

And if I had, said the Thug, musing, should I have been worse off than I am now? should I ever have worn these disgraceful fetters? have ever doomed myself to perpetual imprisonment and a state of existence which I would to heaven were ended, and should be ended, but that I have (and I curse myself for it!) a mean, base, ay, cowardly lingering for life! Sahib, I tell you it would have been well for me had I then fled,—fled from guilt and crime, into which I daily plunged deeper. With my soldierlike figure, my address, my skill in the use of arms, I might have gained honourable service, I might have led armies, or have met a soldier's death on some battlefield! But it was not so written; it was not my fate, and I am what I am,—a curse to myself, and to all with whom I have ever been connected.

Zora! she thought not of my anxiety; all she hoped for, cared for now, was to see her mother and her sister. She assailed me with importunities that I would send her, and assured me that she would not be long absent, but go to them she must,—they would so rejoice to see her again, and would welcome me as her deliverer. After seeing them she would return to me, and we should never again be parted.

"Alas!" I said, "my Zora, you know not what you ask. Do you think that those charms are of no value to your mother and sister? You have owned to me that you are far more beautiful and attractive than any of those you are connected with. In your absence they will have sunk into obscurity, and they will hail your return as the earnest of more wealth and more distinction."

"Nay, these are cruel words, my beloved," she replied; "you well know that I have never deceived you, and that, as true as that I breathe, my soul is yours for ever. So let me go, I pray you, and in a few hours I shall be again with you, and pressed to your honoured breast."

"Be it so," said I sadly; for though I hardly dared think it, I felt as if this was our parting for ever. "Go then; and if you return not, I will come to you by the evening."

A covered zenana cart was easily hired; and the driver seeming perfectly to understand where she wished to go, she stepped joyfully into it, attended by her old servant, and, with two of my men to attend her, she left me.

They soon returned, but they knew nothing, save that there was great joy in the house when her relatives saw her. Towards evening I could no longer control my impatience; and taking one of them with me, I mounted my horse and rode to her house.

It was situated nearly opposite a fountain, which is in the centre of the street below the Char Minar, and I had passed it the day before. I was easily admitted; and oh! what joy was evinced when I entered the room where Zora, her sister, and mother were seated! "He is come!" cried my poor girl, and she rushed into my arms. She strained me to her breast for an instant, and then holding me from her, "Look, mother!" she cried; "look on him; is he not as I said? is he not as beautiful and brave?"

The old lady approached me, and passing her hands over my face cracked her knuckles and every joint of her fingers by pressing the backs of her hands against her temples, while the tears ran down her cheeks: this she did as often as there was a joint to crack; and then she caught me in her arms and hugged me, crying at the same time like a child.

The sister received me, I thought, rather coldly. Had I been less handsome, perhaps, she would have been more cordial; she did not seem to like Zora's having so handsome a lover.

"May the blessing of the Prophet and the twelve Imams[1] be on you and your posterity!" cried the old lady when she had recovered breath to speak. "May the gracious Alla keep you in His protection, and may the lady Muriam[2] and the holy Moula-ali bless you! You have made a desolate house full again, and have changed our weeping to joy. What can I say more? Who could have thought it was our Zora when a cart stopped at the door? Zenatbee was just saying that it was that vile

---

1   The spiritual successors to the Prophet Muhammad.
2   Maryam; the Arabic name for the Virgin Mary.

wretch Sukeena come to pretend condolence, while in reality she rejoiced at our misfortune, which left her without a rival; and I was saying—no matter what I was saying—when we heard, a faint cry, as if of astonishment, and a bustle, and we did not know what to think; when in rushed our lost Zora, our pearl, our diamond; and then I thought my old heart would break with joy, for my liver seemed to be melted; and I have done nothing since, Meer Sahib, but sit opposite to her, and stroke her face with my hands, and gaze into her eyes, to assure myself that I am not mistaken. Inshalla! to-morrow I will send five rupees to every shrine in the city, and distribute sweetmeats to fifty beggars in the name of the Imam Zamin; besides, I will have a tazea[1] made, and will no longer wear these mourning garments. Ah! Meer Sahib, if you knew how I have sat day after day, and wept till I am reduced to a mere shadow of what I was! and all my friends tried to console me, but in vain, I would not be comforted." And her tears flowed afresh at the recollection.

What the old lady was before her grief commenced, I cannot pretend to say; but in her present plight she appeared the fattest woman I had ever looked upon. She could now talk; she rolled from side to side when she stirred, and lifted her feet as an elephant would do among a dense crowd of people. It was painful to see her in her tight trowsers; at every movement she made, especially when she sat down, they appeared about to split, and let out a mass of flesh which was in rebellion against its confinement. She ought to have worn a petticoat; but no, the old lady had her vanity, and still prided herself on the beauty of her limbs, which I heard afterwards had really been strikingly symmetrical in her youth.

We sat conversing and relating our adventures, until the evening fell, and I spread my carpet for prayer.

"Ah, he is a good syud," said the old woman; "I like to see the young fond of their devotions; but it is ever thus with the noble race from Hindostan."

I was preparing to take my departure, when they one and all cried out against it. "What! leave our house before you have broken bread and drunk water with us?" It was not to be thought of,—I must stay: dinner was prepared; they were just on the point of sending for me when I came, and above all it was the ninth day of the Mohorum, and I must stay, were it but to see the procession of the Nal Sahib. That sacred relic, one of the shoes of the horse the blessed Prophet rode when he fled to Medina, would be carried in grand procession, and I should never have a chance of seeing the like again. These reasons, and many imploring looks from Zora, made me speedily determine; so sending away my horse and the man, with a message to my

---

1   Miniature tomb in honor of Islamic martyrs.

father to say I should not return, I gave myself up to a night of enjoyment, such as I little expected when I parted with Zora in the morning.

The dinner was excellent, and the old lady's cooking unexceptionable. There were all sorts of curries, with but a mouthful in each little cup, but still sufficient of each to leave an exquisite flavour in the mouth, only to be replaced by another surpassing it—pilaus[1] of various kinds, and sweetmeats—and, to crown all, some delicious wine of the infidels called the Francees,[2] which the old lady pronounced not to be wine, but sherbet, and allowed to the Huzoor[3] himself, the great Sikundur Jah.[4] It certainly was very delicious, and elevated the spirits. At the end, after taking a whiff or two, she carefully wiped the mouth-piece, and presented me with her own hookah, the fragrance of which was beyond that of ambergris or musk. I was in paradise! I was intensely happy!

"You have heard me sing," said Zora to me, "when I was in captivity, and after the fatigues of travel in our little tent, where there was no scope for my voice; now my heart is glad and bounding, and you shall hear me again—may the Prophet pardon me for singing during the Mohorum!—and you shall say which you like best; my sister shall accompany me till I am tired, and I will then accompany her."

A saringhee was brought; Zenat tuned it, and taking the bow played a short prelude. It was one to the most entrancing sounds I had ever heard. Zora surpassed all her former attempts, it was ravishing to listen to her; and her sister, who was a perfect mistress of the instrument (a strange thing for a woman), gave it its full force of melody and expression. You know, Sahib, how nearly it accords to the human voice; and now, as accompaniment and song rose and fell together, it appeared as though two of the richest, fullest voices were pouring forth strains such as angels might have come down from the skies to hear.

But at last the noise of drums and shouting outside became so great, that both gave up in despair.

"A plague on them all," said she; "and I in such voice that I could have sung to you all night! And have I sung well?"

---

1   Rice dishes; pilaf.
2   French.
3   His Highness.
4   Mir Akbar Ali Khan Siddiqi Sikander Jah (1768-1829), Nizam of Hyderabad.

"Ay, have you," said I; "but methinks the first song you ever sung to me, at the palace in Oomerkhér, will dwell longer on my memory than any I have heard since."

"Ya Alla!" exclaimed Zenat, who had moved to the window; "was there ever a sight so magnificent! Come and see; 'tis passing fast, and will be soon out of sight."[1]

---

1   Here ends the First Volume of the 1839 edition.

Chapter XV

SETTING FORTH HOW AMEER ALI SPENDS THE NINTH NIGHT
OF THE MOHORUM, AND HOW HE LOSES HIS MISTRESS

ENAT'S exclamation drew us to the window. "Quick!" she said; "look out, or you will lose the sight; they are even now passing the Char Minar."

We did look out, and the sight was indeed magnificent. A crowd of some hundreds of people were escorting a punjah,[1] that holy symbol of our faith; most of them were armed, and their naked weapons gleamed brightly in the light of numberless torches which were elevated on lofty bamboos; others bore aftab-geers,[2] made of silver and gold tinsel, with deep fringes of the same, which glittered and sparkled as they were waved to and fro by the movements of those who carried them. But the object the most striking of all was the Char Minar itself, as the procession passed under it; the light of the torches illuminated it from top to bottom, and my gaze was riveted, as though it had suddenly and startlingly sprung into existence.

The procession passed on, and all once more relapsed into gloom: the Char Minar was no longer visible to the eye, dazzled as it had been by the lights; but as it became more accustomed to the darkness, the building gradually revealed itself, dim and shadowy, its huge white surface looking like a spectre, or I could fancy like one of the mysterious inhabitants of the air whom, we are told, Suleeman-ibn-Daood[3] and other sages had under their command, and were thus enabled to describe. Again, as we gazed, another procession would pass rapidly, and a sudden flash as of lightning would cause the same effect; interior and exterior of the edifice were as bright, far brighter they seemed, than at noonday.

I was enraptured. Zenat had left us to ourselves, and we sat, my arm around my beloved, while she nestled close to me, and we murmured to each other those vows of love which hearts like ours could alone frame and give utterance to.

Long did we sit thus. Sahib, I know not how long—the hours fled like moments.

---

1   Large sculpture of a metal hand, emblematic of the Creator.
2   Large umbrellas; sun screens.
3   Abu Dawood, ninth-century Islamic scholar.

"Look!" cried Zora, "look at that mighty gathering in the street below us; they are now lighting the torches, and the procession of the Nal Sahib will presently come forth."

I had not observed it, though I had heard the hum of voices; the gloom of the street had hitherto prevented my distinguishing anything; but as torch after torch was lighted and raised aloft on immense poles, the sea of human heads revealed itself. There were thousands. The street was so packed from side to side, that to move was impossible; the mass was closely wedged together, and we waited impatiently for the time when it should be put in motion, to make the tour of the city.

One by one the processions we had seen pass before us ranged themselves in front, and as they joined together, who can describe the splendour of the effect of the thousands of torches, the thousands of aftab-geers, of flags and pennons[1] of all descriptions, the hundreds of elephants, gaily caparisoned, bearing on their backs their noble owners, clad in the richest apparel, attended by their armed retainers and spearmen, some stationary, others moving to and fro, amidst the vast mass of human beings!

One elephant in particular I remarked,—a noble animal, bearing a large silver umbara, in which sat four boys, doubtless the sons of some nobleman from the number of attendants which surrounded them. The animal was evidently much excited, whether by the noise, the lights, and the crowd, or whether he was "*must*,"[2] I cannot say; but the mahout[3] seemed to have great difficulty in keeping him quiet, and often dug his ankoos[4] into the brute's head with great force, which made him lift his trunk into the air and bellow with pain. I saw the mahout was enraged, and, from the gestures of some of the persons near, could guess that they were advising him to be gentle; but the animal became more restive, and I feared there would be some accident, as the mahout only punished him the more severely. At last, by some unlucky chance, the blazing part of a torch fell from the pole upon which it was raised on the elephant's back; he screamed out with the sudden pain, and raising his trunk, rushed into the crowd.

Ya Alla, what a sight it was! Hundreds as they vainly endeavoured to get out of the way, only wedged themselves closer together, shrieks and screams rent the air; but the most fearful sight was when the maddened beast, unable to make his way

---

1 Pennant; triangular flag.

2 Wild.

3 Elephant driver.

4 Spiked stick used to drive elephants.

through the press, seized on an unfortunate wretch by the waist with his trunk, and whirling him high in the air dashed him against the ground, and then kneeling down crushed him to a mummy with his tusks. Involuntarily I turned away my head; the sight was sickening, and it was just under me.

When I looked again, the brute, apparently satisfied, was standing quietly, and immediately afterwards was driven away; the body of the unfortunate man was carried off and deposited in a neighbouring shop; and all again became quiet.

All at once the multitude broke out into deafening shouts of "Hassan! Hoosein! Deen! Deen!" the hoarse roar of which was mingled with the beating of immense nagaras. The sound was deafening, yet most impressive; the multitude became agitated; every face was at once turned towards the portal from which the sacred relic was about to issue, and it came forth in another instant amidst the sudden blaze of a thousand blue lights. I turned my eye to the Char Minar. If it had looked brilliant by the torch-light, how much more so did it now! The pale sulphurous glare caused its white surface to glitter like silver; high in the air the white minarets gleamed with intense brightness; and, as it stood out against the deep blue of the sky, it seemed to be a sudden creation of the genii—so grand, so unearthly—while the numberless torches, overpowered by the superior brightness of the fireworks, gave a dim and lurid light through their smoke, which, as there was not a breath of wind, hung over them.

All at once a numberless flight of rockets from the top of the Char Minar sprang hissing into the sky, and at an immense height, far above the tops of the minarets, burst almost simultaneously, and descended in a shower of brilliant blue balls. There was a breathless silence for a moment, as every eye was upturned to watch their descent, for the effect was overpowering. But again the shouts arose; the multitude swayed to and fro like the waves of a troubled sea; every one turned towards the Char Minar, and in a few instants the living mass was in motion.

It moved slowly at first, but the pressure from behind was so great that those in front were obliged to run; gradually, however, the mighty tide flowed along at a more measured pace, and it seemed endless. Host after host poured through the narrow street; men of all countries, most of them bearing naked weapons which flashed in the torch-light, were ranged in ranks, shouting the cries of the faith; others in the garbs of fakeers chanted wild hymns of the death of the blessed martyrs; others again in fantastic dresses formed themselves into groups, and, as they ran rather than walked along, performed strange and uncouth antics; some were painted from head to foot with different colours; others had hung bells to their ankles, shoulders, and elbows, which jangled as they walked or danced; here and there would be seen a man painted like a tiger, a rope passed round his waist, which was held by three or four others, while the tiger made desperate leaps and charges into the crowd, which were received with shouts of merriment.

Some again were dressed in sheepskins, to imitate bears; others were monkeys, with enormous tails; and they grinned and mowed at the crowd which surrounded them. Now, some nobleman would scatter from his elephant showers of pice[1] or couries among the crowd below him; and it was fearful, though amusing, to watch the eager scramble and the desperate exertions of those undermost to extricate themselves,—not unattended by severe bruises and hurts. Bodies of Arabs, singing their wild war-songs, firing their matchlocks in the air, and flourishing their naked swords and jumbeas,[2] joined the throng, and immediately preceded the holy relic, which at last came up.

It was carried on a cushion of cloth of gold, covered by a small canopy of silver tissue; the canopy and its deep silver fringes glittering in the blaze of innumerable torches. Moollas dressed in long robes walked slowly before, singing the Moonakib and the Murceas.[3] Men waved enormous chourees[4] of the feathers of peacocks' tails, incense burned on the platform of the canopy and sent up its fragrant cloud of smoke, and handfuls of the sweet ubeer[5] were showered upon the cushion by all who could by any means or exertions get near enough to reach it.

Gradually and slowly the whole passed by. Who can describe its magnificence? Such a scene must be seen to be felt! I say *felt,* sahib, for who could see a mighty multitude like that, collected for a holy purpose with one heart, one soul, without emotion? Hours we sat there gazing on the spectacle; we scarcely spoke, so absorbed were we by the interest of the scene below us. At length, however, the whole had passed, and the street was left to loneliness and darkness; the few forms which flitted along here and there, looked more like the restless spirits of a burial-ground than human beings,—and the silence was only now and then broken by a solitary fakeer, his bells tinkling as he hurried along to join the great procession, the roar of which was heard far and faintly in the distance.

Just as we were about to retire, a number of men formed themselves into a circle around a pit in which were a few lighted embers; but some bundles of grass were

---

1   Coin worth one hundredth of a rupee.

2   Swords.

3   Mohorum hymns.

4   Fans.

5   Scented and colored powder.

thrown on them—the light blazed up—and drawing their swords they danced round and round the fire, waving their weapons, while all shouted aloud in hoarse voices the names of the blessed martyrs. The blazing fire in the centre lighted up their wild forms and gestures as they danced, tossing their arms wildly into the air. Now they stood still, and swayed to and fro, while the fire died away and they were scarcely perceptible. Again more fuel was thrown on, the red blaze sprang up far above their heads, and their wild round was renewed with fresh spirit.

The night was now far spent, and the chill breeze which arose warned us to retire. Indeed Zenat and her mother had done so long before, and we were left to ourselves.

Sahib! that was the last night I passed with my beloved, and the whole of our intercourse remains on my memory like the impression of a pleasing dream, on which I delight often to dwell, to conjure up the scenes and conversations of years past and gone—years of wild adventure, of trial, of sorrow, and of crime.

I can picture to myself my Zora as I parted from her on the following morning; I can again hear her protestations of unalterable love, her entreaties that I would soon return to her; and above all I remember her surpassing loveliness, and the look of anguish I might call it with which she followed me as I left her, after one long passionate embrace. These impressions, I say, still linger on a mind which has been rendered callous by crime, by an habitual system of deception, and by my rude intercourse with the world—my deadliest enemy; and they are refreshing and soothing, because I have no wrong toward her to charge myself with. I rescued her; she loved me, and I loved her too; we wanted nought but a longer intercourse to have strengthened that affection, which would have lasted till death. But why should I talk thus? Why should I, a convicted felon and murderer, linger on the description of such scenes and thoughts? Sahib, I have done with them; I will tell you of sterner things—of the further adventures of my life.

I returned to my father; he was not angry at my absence, and I found Mohun Das, the dullal, closeted with him, and also another sahoukar-looking[1] person. Mohun Das had been eminently successful. The sahoukar I saw was the assistant in a wealthy house, which had need of all our goods, and he was come to see them before the bargain was finally closed. They were displayed to him, both goods and jewels; he approved of all, said he would return shortly with an offer for them, and having made a list of the whole he departed.

"Now," said Mohun Das, "about the price; what do you ask?"

---

1 Tradesman-like.

"You know better than I do," said my father, "therefore do you speak, and remember, the more they sell for the more you get."

"I have not forgotten your munificence," said the dullal, "and I say at once the cloths are worth sixteen, and the jewels ten thousand rupees; but you must ask thirty thousand,—you will get twenty-five I dare say."

"It is too little," said my father; "they cost me nearly that sum; and how am I to pay my guards if I get no profit? I shall ask thirty-five for the whole."

"Well," said the dullal, "if you do, so much the better for me; but mark what I say, you will get no more than my valuation; however, if you will trust me and leave it to my judgment, I will get a fair price."

"I will, but recollect, twenty-five thousand is the least." "Certainly," said the dullal; "I go to do your bidding."

"Go," said my father; " Alla Hafiz![1] be sure you return quickly."

It was noon before he returned, but it was with a joyful face when he did come.

After many profound salams, he exclaimed to my father: "You have indeed been fortunate; your good destiny has gained you a good bargain. I have got thirty thousand six hundred rupees for the whole. We had a long fight about it and wasted much breath; but, blessed be Narayun! your slave has been successful. See, here is the sahoukar's acknowledgment."

My father took it and pretended to read; I was near laughing outright at his gravity as he took the paper and pored over the crabbed Hindee characters, of which he did not understand one,—nor indeed any other; for he could neither read nor write.

"Yes," said he gravely, "it is satisfactory; how am I to be paid?"

"The sahoukar will arrange that with you in any way you please," said the dullal; "ready money or bills are equally at your service; but as all transactions are generally at six months credit, the interest for that time at the usual rate will be deducted."

"And if I take bills, I suppose the interest will be allowed till I reach Benares, or whatever place I may take them upon?"

"Certainly."

"Good," continued my father; "do you attend here with the sahoukar, and we will settle all about it, and he can take away the merchandise whenever he pleases."

So the dullal departed.

---

1 Allah protect you!

It was now about the time when the tazeas[1] were to be brought to the edge of the river to be thrown into the water, and as the karwan was not far from the spot, I proposed to my father to send for our horses and ride thither to see the sight.

He agreed, the horses were quickly brought, and we rode to the bridge over which the road passes into the city. Taking our stand upon it, we beheld beneath us the various and motley groups in the bed of the river; there were thousands assembled; the banks of the river and the bed were full,—so full, it seemed as if you might have walked upon the heads of the multitude. The aftab-geers, and the tinsel of the various tazeas glittered in the afternoon sun,—the endless variety of colours of the dresses had a cheerful and gay effect,—and, though it was nothing to the grand appearance of the procession at night, still it was worth looking at. The tazeas were brought one by one, by the various tribes or neighbourhoods to which they belonged, and thrown into the pools in the bed of the river, for deep water there was none; but there was sufficient for the purpose, and as each glittering fabric was cast in, it was assailed by hundreds of little ragged urchins, who quickly tore the whole to pieces for the sake of the ornaments; and there was many a warm contest and scramble over these remains, which excited the laughter of the bystanders.

One by one the various groups returned towards their homes, looking wearied and exhausted; for the excitement which had kept them up for so many days and nights was gone. In many a shady corner might be seen lying fast asleep, an exhausted wretch—his finery still hanging about him, his last couree perhaps expended in a copious dose of bhung,[2] which, having done part of its work in exciting him almost to madness during the preceding night, had left him with a racking brain, and had finally sent him into oblivion of his fatigue and hunger.

The Mohorum was ended. We stayed on the bridge till the time for evening prayer, when, repairing to an adjacent mosque, we offered up our devotions with the others of the faithful who were there assembled. This done, I told my father I should again visit Zora, and most likely remain at her house all night; he bid me be sure to return early in the morning on account of our business; and having promised this, I departed.

I rode slowly through the now silent and almost deserted streets. The few persons whom I met were hurrying along to their homes, and had no common feeling or interest with each other as before; I passed along the now well-known track, and was soon at the house which held all that was most dear to me on earth. I sent up

---

1   Miniature tombs in honor of Islamic martyrs.
2   Bhang; cannabis.

my name and dismounted; I expected the usual summons, and that I should see that countenance I longed to behold welcoming me from the window. I waited longer than I could assign a cause for in my own mind; at last my attendant returned, and as he quitted the threshold the door was rudely shut after him, while at the same time the casements of the windows were both shut. What was I to think of this? Alas! my forebodings were but too just. My attendant broke in upon my thoughts by addressing me.

"Her mother, whom I have seen," said he, "bid me give you her salam, and tell you that her daughter is particularly engaged and cannot receive you. I ventured to remonstrate, but the old woman became angry, and told me that she had behaved civilly to you, and that you could not expect more; and further, she said, 'Tell him from me, that he had better act the part of a wise man, and forget Zora, for never again shall he see her; it will be in vain that he searches for her, for she will be beyond his reach; and I would rather that she died than become the associate and partner of an adventurer like him, who, for all I know, might inveigle her from home, and, when he was tired of her, leave her in some jungle to starve. Go and tell him this, and say that if he is a wise man he will forget her."

"And was this all?" exclaimed I in a fury; "was this all the hag said? I will see whether I cannot effect an entrance;" and I rushed at the door with all my might. In vain I pushed and battered it with the hilt of my sword, it was too securely fastened within to give way. I called out Zora's name—I raved—I threatened as loud as I could to destroy myself at the door, and that my blood would be upon the head of that cruel old woman. It was all in vain, not a bolt stirred, not a shutter moved, and I sat down in very despair. A few persons had collected, observing my wild demeanour; and as I looked up from my knees, where my face had been hidden, one of them said, "Poor youth! it is a pity his love has been unkind, and will not admit him."

"Pooh!" said another, "he is drunk with bhung; Alla knows whether we are safe so near him! He has arms in his hands; we ought to get out of his way: your drunken persons are ticklish people to deal with, let alone their being a scandal to the faith."

I was ashamed; shame for once conquered anger. I walked towards my horse, and mounting him rode slowly from the place. How desolate everything appeared! The night before, I had reached the summit of happiness. I cast one look to the window where I had sat in sweet converse with her whom I was destined no more to behold; I thought on her words, and the glittering scene was again before me. Now all was dark and silent, and accorded well with my feelings. I rode home in this mood, and throwing myself down on my carpet, gave myself up to the bitterness of my feelings and unavailing regret. A thousand schemes I revolved in my mind for the recovery of Zora during that night, for I slept not. One by one I dismissed them as cheating me with vain hopes, only to be succeeded by others equally vague and unsatisfactory. I rose in the morning feverish and unrefreshed, having determined on nothing. There was only one hope, that of the old woman, the nurse; if I could but speak with her, I thought I should be able to effect something, and as soon as I could summon one of the men who had attended Zora, I sent him for information.

Chapter XVI

BHUDRINATH RECOUNTS HIS ADVENTURES. THE DULLAL FINDS TO HIS COST
THAT A BARGAIN IS OFTEN EASY TO MAKE AND EASY TO BREAK

I HAD not seen Bhudrinath now for some days, and fearing he might think me neglectful, I went to the serai in which he and the men had put up.

"Ah!" cried he when he saw me approach, "so we are at last permitted to see the light of your countenance! What, in the name of Bhowanee, have you been about? I have sought you in vain for the last three days.

"Tell me," said I, "what you have being doing, and you shall know my adventures afterwards."

"Well then," said he, "in the first place, I have made a series of poojahs[1] and sacrifices at the different temples around this most Mahomedan of cities; secondly, I have seen and mixed in the Mohorum; and lastly, I have assisted to kill seven persons."

"Killed seven persons!" I exclaimed in wonder. "How, in the name of the Prophet, did you manage that?"

"Nothing more easy, my gay young jemadar," he replied; "do you not know that this is the karwan, where travellers daily arrive in numbers, and from which others are as frequently departing? Nothing is easier than to beguile them to accompany us a short distance, pretending that we are going the same road; why a Thug might live here for ever, and get a decent living. The people (my blessings on them!) are most unsuspicious; and thanks to Hunooman and his legions, there is no want of rocks and wild roads about the city, which give capital opportunities for destroying them."

"Ajaib!"[2] I exclaimed, "this is very wonderful; and who were they?"

"Not in the least extraordinary," said Bhudrinath coolly, "if you think on it;—but to answer your question. The first was a bunnea[3] who was going to Beeder;[4] we took him to Golconda,[5] and buried him among the tombs, and we got seventy rupees and

---

1 Acts of worship.

2 Wonderful!

3 Grocer.

4 Town to the northwest of Hyderabad.

5 Golkonda; a ruined Islamic city outside Hyderabad.

some pieces of gold from him. The second were two men and their wives, who said they were going to Koorungul: where that is Bhugwan[1] knows! but it is somewhere in a southerly direction. We killed them about three coss from the city, among some rocks, and left them there."

"That was wrong," said I, "you should have buried them."

"Not at all wrong, my friend; who will take the trouble of inquiring after them? Besides, we had not time, for the day had fully dawned, and we feared interruption from travellers; we got above two hundred rupees, and two ponies, which I have sold for thirty rupees."

"Well," said I, "these make five; and the other two—"

"They lie there," said Bhudrinath, pointing to where a horse was picketed; "they were poor devils, and not worth the trouble of taking out; we only got forty-two rupees from both."

"Dangerous work," said I; "you might have been seen."

"Oh! no fear of an old hand like me; every one was off to the city to gape at the show, and we were left alone. I was deliberating whether we should not accompany them on the road we came in by, and by which they were going; but Surfuraz Khan cut short my doubts and uncertainties by strangling one fellow on the spot, and I followed his example with the other; the bodies were concealed till night, and then buried."

"But is there no fear of the grave bursting?" I asked.

He laughed. "Fear! oh no, they lie deep enough; and you know our old tricks."

"Well," said I, "it is most satisfactory; and I have missed all this, have been a fool, and have lost my mistress into the bargain."

Bhudrinath laughed immoderately; but seeing the gravity of my face, he said,—

"Never mind, Meer Sahib, care not for my merriment; but truly thy face wore so lack-a-daisical an expression, that for my life I could not have refrained. Cheer up, man, there is plenty of work in store for you; women will be faithless, and young and hot-brained fellows will grieve for them; but take a friend's advice, make your profession your mistress, and she at least will never disappoint you."

"Your advice is good," said I; "nevertheless the mistress I have lost is, as you know, worthy of regret, and I shall miss her for many a day. But tell me, what have you now in hand,—anything in which I may have a share?"

"Why no," he replied, "nothing; but if you are so inclined, we will take a ramble this evening through the bazars, we may perhaps pick up somebody."

---

1   God.

"Of course I will be with you, for in truth my hand will get out of practice if I neglect work. But have you seen my father?"

"I have not," said Bhudrinath; "I hear he is very much engaged about the property, and do not like to disturb him."

"You are right, he is," said I; "but he will finish all to-day, and get the money. I suppose after that we shall not stay long here, and for my part I care not how soon we set off; I am anxious for new scenes and adventures, and we are not likely to do much here. Is not Surfuraz Khan here?"

"No; he is gone with a party of seven travellers towards Puttuncherroo,[1] and has taken ten or fifteen of the best of the men with him; he will not be back probably before night, if then."

"Who were the travellers?"

"Bunneas, I heard," said Bhudrinath carelessly; "I did not see them myself, and Surfuraz Khan was in too great a hurry to give me any information."

"Out upon me!" I exclaimed, vexed at my idleness; "here have I been amusing myself while all this has been going on. For the sake of the Prophet, let us do something soon, that I may settle scores with my conscience, for I have hardly assurance enough to look you in the face after my behaviour."

"Well," said he, "come this evening; if we can't decoy any one, we will kill somebody for amusement and practice."

"I agree," said I; "for by Alla! I must do something. I am as melancholy as a camel, and my blood, which boiled enough yesterday, seems now scarcely to run through me;—it is not to be borne."

I found when I reached home that the dullal had arrived, and with him the sahoukar's clerk, and some porters to carry the goods, as well as fellows with matchlocks and lighted matches and others with swords and shields to escort them. I stared at them.

"One would think you were going to battle, Séthjee," said I, "with all those fierce fellows; I am half afraid of them."

The fellows laughed; and the clerk replied, "They are necessary, and we always have them. If our goods were stolen, nay, carried off before our eyes, should we get any redress? no, indeed. We therefore protect our property the best way we can."

"Now," said my father, "take your goods and be off with them; they are no longer mine, and I fear to allow them to remain under my roof."

---

1 Small town north of Hyderabad.

"Surely," said the clerk, "they will be out of your way directly; and now let us speak about your money, or will you take some merchandise as part of it?"

"Not a bit, not a bit," replied my father; "I want all my money in rupees—no, stay, not all in rupees; give me five thousand in silver and the rest in gold, it will be easier carried."

"I suppose you mean five thousand rupees, and the rest in gold bars; well, you must purchase gold according to weight, and the best is twenty rupees a tola;[1] but you had better take bills, and the exchange is favourable."

"No, no; no bills," said my father, "but the gold; if I remember rightly, the price of gold was high when I left Dehli, and was likely to remain so; and I have plenty of persons for my guard if robbers should attack me."

"You forget me," cried the dullal, "and my percentage."

"Make yourself easy," said I; "it will be paid out of the five thousand rupees; it will be about fifteen hundred I think."

"What did you say? fifteen hundred. To whom?" asked the clerk.

"To this dullal," said I; "I suspect the rascal is cheating us."

"Cheating! surely he is. Why, Mohun Das, good man, what have you been about? Are you mad, to ask so much?"

"Ah, it was my lord's offer and promise," said he, "and surely I shall now get it. Pray what business is it of yours?"

"What ought he to have?" asked my father.

"One per cent is ample," replied the other; "and you might have saved this too if you had only applied yourself to the different sahoukars."

"We were strangers," said I, "and knew not their places of residence; so we were obliged to have recourse to this rascal, who offered his services."

"What! did you not take me from the Char Minar? Did you not promise me five per cent, and bind me to secresy about the sale of your goods?" cried the dullal.

"Listen to him," said my father; "he raves. Now, Meer Sahib, did not this rascal come begging and beseeching for employment, and when I said I would try him, and asked his terms, he said he was miserably poor, and would take whatever was given him; was it not so? And now, Punah-i-Khoda,[2] we are to be bearded in this manner, defrauded of fifteen hundred rupees, where we have not as many couries to give, and made to eat dirt into the bargain. Beat him on the mouth with a shoe!

---

1   One tola is equivalent to 11.663 grams.
2   The Lord protect.

spit on him! may he be defiled so that Ganges' water would not purify him! may his mother, sisters, and all his female relatives be—"

"Nay, my good friend," said the sahoukar's clerk, "be not thus rash and hot-headed, nor waste your breath upon so mean a wretch since you have employed him, something must be given, it is the custom, and next time you will know better; say, may I pay him the one per cent, which will be three hundred and six rupees?"

"Three hundred and six rupees! Alla, Alla! where am I to get the half?," cried my father. "For the love of the Prophet, get me off what you can; I swear by your head and eyes that I am a poor man, and only an agent; is it not so, Meer Sahib? Am I not miserably poor?"

"You certainly cannot afford to pay so much money as one per cent, on this large sum," I replied; "nevertheless, as such appears to be the custom, you had better give something, say one hundred and fifty rupees."

"Certainly," said my father; "I am ready; I will not refuse any thing in reason; but so large a sum—I was quite astounded at the impertinence of the demand, and lost my temper like a fool."

Mohun Das stood all this time with his eyes and mouth wide open; looking from one to the other, every word that was uttered increasing his astonishment and disappointment.

"Do you pretend to fifty," screamed he at last, "do you pretend to say that I am not to get my money, my fifteen hundred rupees, for which I have toiled night and day? And do you pretend to say I came to you first? Did you not take me with you from the Char Minar?"

"Nay, here is the Char Minar again; for the sake of Alla," said I to the clerk, "if you really know this fellow, advise him to be quiet. What have I, who am a soldier, to do with his filthy traffic? He may provoke a patient man once too often, and people with weapons in their hands are not safe persons to play jokes with;" and I twisted up my mustachios.

I have told you, sahib, what a coward the fellow was; he fell instantly on the ground and rubbed his forehead against the floor.

"Pardon! pardon!" he cried, "most brave sirs! anything, whatever you choose to give me, even ten rupees, will be thankfully received, but do not kill me, do not put me to death; see, I fall at your feet, I rub my nose in the dust."

"You fool," cried the clerk; holding his sides with laughter, for he was a fat man; "you fool; ah, Mohun Das, that I should have seen this! In the name of Narayun, who will do you any harm? Are you a child—you with those mustachios? Shame on you, man; dullal as you are, be something less of a coward; get up, ask for your money boldly, ask for whatever these gentlemen please to give you, though indeed you deserve nothing for your impertinent attempt at deception."

He got up and stood on his left leg, with the sole of the right foot against the calf, his hands joined, his turban all awry, and the expression of his face most ludicrously miserable.

"Ten rupees, my lord," he faltered out; "your slave will take ten rupees."

We all once more burst into a peal of laughter; the gomashta's[1] sides appeared to ache, and the tears ran down his cheeks.

"Ai Bhugwan! Ai Narayun!" cried he, catching his breath; "that I should have seen this! Ai Seetaram! but it is most amusing. Ten rupees! why, man," said he to the miserable dullal, "you just now wanted fifteen hundred!"

"Nay," said my father, "let him have his due. You said one hundred and fifty,—that he shall have. Do you, Meer Sahib, go with this worthy sahoukar to his kothee,[2] and bring the money; I dare say he will give you a guard back, and you can hire a porter for the gold and silver."

"Certainly, you shall have the men," said the gomashta; "and now come along; I shall have to collect the gold, and it may be late before it can be weighed and delivered to you, and the rupees passed by a suraff."[3]

As we went on, the dullal said to me, "You will pay me at the kothee, will you not?"

"We will see," said I; "the money is none of mine, and I will ask advice on the subject."

"Not your money! Whose then?"

"Why his who has employed you, and from whom you are to get one hundred and fifty rupees," I said. "Are you a fool? why do you ask?"

"Ah nothing, only I was thinking—"

"Thinking of what?" I asked; "some rascality, I doubt not."

"Ah," said he, "now you speak as you did at the Char Minar."

"By Alla!" said I, stopping and looking at him, "if ever you mention that word again—"

"Never, never!" cried the wretch, trembling; "do not beat me; remember it is the open street, and there will be a disturbance; the words escaped me unawares, just as I was thinking—"

---

1 Agent's.

2 House.

3 Money-lender.

"That is twice you have said that, and by Alla! I think you have some meaning in it. What *would* you be at?"

"Nothing, nothing," said he; "only I was thinking—"

"Well!"

"I was only thinking that you are an adventurer, who has accompanied that rich merchant from Hindostan."

"Well, and what of that? you knew that before."

"You are not rich?"

"No indeed," said I, "I am not."

"Then," said the wretch, "why not both of us enrich ourselves?"

"How?" I asked.

"Refuse the guard, or take some men I will guide you to: they will do whatever you like for five rupees apiece; we will fly with the money, and there is a place in the rocks close to this where I have plunder hidden—we will go thither and share it."

"Where is the place you allude to—is it far?" I asked.

"No," said he; "will you come. I can show it you from a distance; we need not get up the rocks—there is danger of being seen in the daytime."

I followed him for a little distance, and he pointed to a huge pile of rocks at the back of the karwan and Begum Bazar.

"There, do you see a white spot about halfway up on a rock?"

"I do," said I.

"That is the spot," he replied; "it is known but to myself and a few others; whatever I can pick up I put there."

"What do you get?"

"Ah, little enough; sometimes a shawl, a brocade handkerchief, or some gold, anything in fact. But why do you ask? will you do what I said, and join us? There are sixteen of us; one is yonder, disguised as a fakeer, the rest are hard by and will accompany us."

"Dog!" cried I dashing him to the earth, "dog! dost thou know to whom thou speakest? Here there is no one" (for we had got to the back of the houses), "and it were an easy task to send thee to Jehanum;[1] one blow of my sword, and that false tongue would cease to speak for ever;" and I half drew it. I knew the effect this would have; there was the same grovelling cowardice he had displayed before. He clung to my knees; I spurned him and spat on him. "Reptile!" cried I at length, wearied by his

---

1 Hell.

abjectness, I would scorn to touch thee; a syud of Hindostan is too proud to stoop to such game as thou art. Lead me to the sahoukar, for, by Alla, I distrust thee!"

"Nay, in this matter I have been honest," said the wretch; "the money is sure."

"It will be well for thee that it is," said I, "or I swear to be revenged. Lead on and beware how you go; if I see one attempt at escape I will cut you in two, were it in the middle of the bazar."

"Then follow me closely," said he; and he gathered up his garments, which had become disordered, and we again entered the crowded bazar.

We were soon at the sahoukar's, who awaited us; the money and gold were told out, and a receipt I had brought with me given; and, accompanied by the guard of soldiers, I took the treasure to my father.

"Meer Sahib, kind Meer Sahib," said the dullal, as we approached our dwelling, "you will forget all that has passed; Bhugwan knows I was only jesting with you; I love to play such tricks,—nay, I have always been of a jesting disposition;" and he laughed in his terror. "You will not forget my little perquisite, my hundred and fifty rupees, I know you will not."

"Peace!" cried I, "if you wish to get a courie. Has it not been promised to thee on the word of two of the faithful? Thou shalt get the uttermost farthing."

I dismissed the sepoys[1] with a small present, when the money had been lodged in our strong-room; and as they went, the miserable dullal looked after them as though he thought with them had departed his last chance for existence. It certainly drew to a close.

"Give me my money and let me depart," said he in a hollow voice.

"Wait," said I, "till it is counted out for you."

"Ah, I had forgotten the dullaljee," cried my father; "I will get out his due."

———— • ————

---

1 Soldiers.

CHAPTER XVII

Cheel ké ghur men, mas ka dhér.
—*Hindee Proverb.*
There's always meat in a kite's nest
—*Free Translation.*

M Y father counted out the money and handed it over to the dullal; his countenance brightened as he viewed it, and he made numberless salams and protestations of thanks. "Now you must write a receipt for the money," said my father.

"Surely," replied the fellow, taking a pen out of his turban, "if my lord will give me paper and ink."

"Here they are," said I; "write."

He did so, gave me the paper, and tied the money up in a corner of his dhotee,[1] which he tucked into his waistband. "Have I permission to depart?" he asked; "my lord knows the poor dullal, and that he has behaved honestly in this transaction. Whenever my lord returns to Hyderabad, he can always hear of Mohun Das, if he inquires at the Char Minar; and he will always be ready to exert himself in his patron's service."

"Stay," said I, "I have somewhat to say to thee;" and I related to my father the whole of the conversation I have just described.

"Is it so?" said he to the miserable being before him; "is it so? Speak, wretch! let me hear the truth from thine own lips. Wouldest thou have robbed me?"

But the creature he addressed was mute; he stood paralysed by fear and conscious guilt, his eyes starting from his head, his mouth open, and his blanched lips drawn tightly across his teeth.

"Thou hast deserved it," continued my father; "I read in that vile face of thine deeds of robbery, of murder, of knavery, and villany of every kind; thou must die!"

"Ah, no, no! Die? My lord is pleased to be facetious; what has his poor slave done?" And he grinned a ghastly smile.

---

1   Waist-garment.

"Thou wouldest have robbed me," said my father, "when I trusted thee with my whole substance; thou wouldest have left me to starve in a strange land without compunction; thou hast robbed others, and cheated thousands; say, art thou fit to live, to prey longer upon the world thou hast already despoiled?"

He threw himself at my father's feet; he grasped his knees; he could scarcely speak, and was fearfully convulsed and agitated by extreme terror. "I am all that you say," he cried, "thief, murderer, and villain! but oh! do not kill me. My lord's face is kind—I cannot die—and my lord has no sword, and how will he kill me?" He had only just perceived that we were both unarmed, and he made a sudden rush at the door. "The kotwal shall know of this," he cried; "people are not to be terrified with impunity." The door was fastened; he gave several desperate pulls and pushes at it; but I was at his back, and the fatal handkerchief was over his head: he turned round and glared on me—the next instant he was dead at my feet.

"There," said my father exultingly, "judgment has overtaken him, and the memory of his crimes will sleep with him for ever; we have done a good deed."

"Yes," said I, "a good one indeed; he confessed himself to be a murderer, robber; and knave—what more need you? and so young too for this accumulation of crime!"

"Drag him in here," said my father, "I like not to look on him; and go for the lughaees; he must be buried at night in the small yard of the house; I dare not have the body carried out in this crowded city."

"It shall be done," I replied; "but think what an escape we have had. Had you not told me to go with the wretch, we should have lost our money."

"Yes, my son, and even had we got it, had you not suspected that five per cent, was too much, I should certainly have paid the sum; but I saw your drift, and I think took up the clue admirably. We have cheated the knave both out of his money and his life."

"True," said I, "it has been a good adventure, and amusing withal; besides, it promises further advantage."

"From the rock and the fakeer?"

"Yes; there will be good booty."

"Take care," said my father; "the band may be there, and they will give you a warm reception."

"I will go and consult with Bhudrinath," said I; "the adventure will just suit him and Surfuraz Khan; we will do nothing rashly."

Bhudrinath was at the serai waiting for me.

"So, Meer Sahib," said he, "you are still in the humour for a frolic; how many lives will satisfy your worship to-night? There is no lack of men in this abode of villany."

"I am in the humour," said I, "but not for what I intended; I have better game in view."

"Ha!" said he, "so *you* have been acting sotha; and pray what may this game be?"

"One that will require stout hearts, and, may be naked weapons," I replied; are you willing to accompany me?"

"To death," said Bhudrinath; "but I cannot for my life see what you are driving at."

"Listen," I replied; and I related to him the whole history of the dullal.

"Cleverly done, very cleverly indeed, my young jemadar," said he, when my relation was ended. "No one could have managed it better from first to last; the rascal deserved his rate; and now I suppose we must search out these hidden treasures in the rock."

"Exactly," said I; "I would do so this very night if I knew how to go about it properly."

"Let me see," said Bhudrinath musing; "we shall not want many men, six or eight resolute fellows will be sufficient. You and I, Peer Khan, Motee-ram, and four others, are ample; there is no use waiting for Surfuraz Khan, he will not now be back before the morning. But how to get intelligence of the place, and whether any of the rascals are there at night?"

"Can no one personate a fakeer?" said I; "a kulundur,[1] anything will do. He might go up now, as the spot is close by, and bring us news in an hour or so."

"I have it," cried Bhudrinath, "Here, some one, call Shekhjee to me."

Shekhjee came. He was an old man, with a long beard; but he was an able fellow and a rare good hand with the handkerchief.

"Shekhjee," said Bhudrinath, "sit down, I have something to say to you. You can personate a fakeer, if necessary, can you not?"

"Certainly," replied the old fellow, "Moosulman or Hindoo, all kinds are familiar to me. I know all their forms of speech and have many of their dresses."

"It is well," said Bhudrinath; "now listen. You must go and disguise yourself this instant; we have an enterprise in view;" and he related our purposed scheme and what had preceded it. "And now," continued Bhudrinath, "you must be wary, and by dark you must return and tell us of the place and if there are men there."

"Is the fakeer who lives there a Hindoo or Moosulman?"

"I saw the impression of spread hands in whitewash on the rock, so he must be a Moosulman," said I.

---

1 Muslim mendicant.

"Then I know how to act," cried the Thug. "Sahibs, I take my leave, and will not fail you. I shall be with you by the time I am required."

"Will he manage it?" I asked of Bhudrinath. "Methinks it is a delicate business."

"Never fear him," said Bhudrinath; "he is a most accomplished rogue, and is a capital hand at disguise, especially as a fakeer, and once got us considerable booty by enticing five Nanukshaee fakeers[1] among us who had picked up a good deal of money and were going to build a well with it. Besides, he is as brave as a lion, and you have seen his other work."

As we were talking Surfuraz Khan came in.

"Ours has been a good business," he cried exultingly, "and there is good spoil. We have killed all the men, and the plunder is coming in charge of our fellows."

"That is so far good," said I; "but is there any ready money, or is it all goods?"

"Both, Meer Sahib, both; but methinks you need not be so ready to ask, when we have not seen your face ever since we have been in the city. We might all have been taken and safely lodged in Puntoo Lall's huwélee[2] for all you knew of the matter. I do not like such conduct."

I was enraged at his speech, and was about making an angry reply when Bhudrinath interfered.

"Peace!" said he, "no brawls: it is disgraceful, and only fit for drunkards and smokers of ganja;[3] listen to me. Surfuraz Khan, you are no boy, and ought not to let your anger have sway; listen, and hear what our young jemadar has been about, and I swear by Bhowanee I think he will yet put us all to shame."

He then related all I had told him, on hearing which Surfuraz Khan's angry feelings gave way in a moment; he rose and embraced me.

"I was wrong," said he, "and you must forgive me; and to prove that I am more than ever your friend, I beg you to allow me a place in this adventure, for, by Alla! it promises to be a strange one."

"Willingly," said I; "we thought you would not arrive in time, but now you are come I would not on any account that you did not accompany us."

"So you have strangled the fellows you took out," said Bhudrinath. "Had you any trouble?"

"None whatever," replied the khan. "We took them out on the Masulipatam road, and found a spot on the other side of Surroonuggur; we threw the bodies into a

---

1   A class of mendicants.

2   Large house.

3   Marijuana.

well and returned by another road. Soobhan Alla![1] this is a rare place, and we might remain here for years and have some amusement every day. I think I shall stay here."

"You may do as you please about that," said I, "when we have shared the spoil we have got. You will then be free; but I should be sorry to lose you."

In such conversation we continued till it was dusk, and then assembling the men we intended to take, eight in all, and seeing that our arms were in good order, we waited in great anxiety for the return of our emissary.

At last he came.

"There is no time to be lost," said he. "I went up to the place and found the fakeer. He is a fine sturdy young fellow, and at first warned me to descend; but when I told him I was hungry and weary, that I had just arrived from Hindostan, and did not know where to lay my head, and begged for a crust of bread and water in the name of the Twelve Imaums, he was pacified, and admitted me into his cave, gave me some food and a hookah, and we sat carousing for some time. I pulled out my opium-box and took a very little; seeing it, he begged for some, and has taken such a dose that he will not wake till morning. I left him fast asleep."

"He shall never wake again," said I; "but did you observe the place? Where can the plunder be hidden?"

"He lives in a cave, between two enormous rocks," said Shekhjee. "It was nearly all in darkness, but I saw a corner at the back of it built up with mud and stones, which he said was his sleeping-place, and I suspect it is there that the plunder is concealed."

"Come then," said I; "there is not a moment to be lost; if we delay we may chance to find the rest of the gang. This is just the hour at which they are all out in the bazars, stealing what they can."

We all sallied out, and conducted by our guide, crept stealthily along the foot of the rocks till we gained the narrow pathway by which we were to ascend.

We held a moment's conference in whispers, and bidding five of the men stay below until we should tell them to ascend, Bhudrinath, myself, and Surfuraz Khan crept up the narrow track to the mouth of the cave, whither the old Thug had preceded us.

"He still sleeps," said he in a whisper; "but tread softly, lest you wake him. He lies yonder, close by the lamp."

"Mind, he is mine," said I to Bhudrinath; "do you and Surfuraz Khan hold him;" for as I looked on the powerful form before me, I felt this precaution to be necessary.

---

1 Praise be to Allah!

But he slept; how was I to throw the roomal about his neck? Bhudrinath solved the difficulty; he gave the fakeer a smart blow with the flat of his sheathed sword upon the stomach, and the fellow started up to a sitting posture.

"What is this? Thieves!" was all he could say; my handkerchief was ready, and now it never failed me—he was dead in an instant.

"Now trim the lamp," said I to Bhudrinath. "Call up three of the men, and let the others remain below to look out."

Bhudrinath tore a piece of rag off the clothes of the dead fakeer, which he twisted up into a thick wick and put into the oil vessel; its strong glare lighted up the interior of the cave, and we saw everything distinctly.

"Here is the wall which I spoke of," said Shekhjee, "and we had better search behind it."

"We did so. There were piles of earthen jars in one corner, which we at first supposed to contain grain or flour, and indeed the first two we uncovered had rice and dal in them; the third felt heavy.

"This has something in it beyond rice," said I; "examine it closely." The mouth was stuffed with rags, but when they were removed we beheld it filled with money—rupees and pice mixed together.

"This was not wise," said Bhudrinath; "the Shah Sahib ought not to have mixed his copper and silver, the silver will be tarnished; but we can clean it."

The next pot was the same; the last was the best: it was full of gold and silver ornaments, rings, anklets, and armlets. "We shuddered to see that many of them were stained with blood.

"The villains!" I exclaimed; "that wretch then told the truth when he confessed himself to be a murderer; the city is well rid of him. But we must not stand talking. Do one of ye tie these things up and be ready for a start, while we look but for further spoil."

But there was nothing else in this corner, no bales of cloth or other articles as we had expected. We were looking about to find any other place of concealment, and had nearly given up our search, when Surfuraz Khan, who had gone outside, called to us.

"Come here," he cried; "there is a place here which looks suspicious."

We ran to the spot, and found the hole he had discovered to be between two rocks; it was dark within, and a man could but just enter by crawling upon his hands and knees.

"Give me the light," said I; "I will enter it if the devil were inside."

"Better the devil than any of this infernal gang," said Bhudrinath to me as I entered.

I found no one, and the space within, which was so low that I could scarcely stand upright, was filled with bundles.

"Neither the devil or any of the gang are here," cried I to those outside, "so do some of you come in quickly and see what I have found."

I set myself to work, as did also the others, to untie the different bundles, and we were all busily employed. I had just opened one which contained, as I thought, brass cooking-pots and water-vessels, and was overjoyed to find some gold and other silver, when the alarm was given from outside. We all got out as quickly as we could and inquired the cause.

"There are two men," said the scouts, "whom we have watched come round the corner of the houses yonder and approach the bottom of the rocks; they do not walk fast, and appear to be carrying loads of something."

"Only two," said I, "then they are easily managed. Put out the light, and conceal yourselves at the entrance of the cave; we must fall upon them as they enter."

We had just taken our posts behind a rock which was close to the mouth, our roomals ready, and two with their swords drawn, when one of the fellows called out, "Ho! Sein! Sein! come down and help us up. Here we are, laden like pulla-wallas,[1] and thou hast not even a light to show us the way."

"Not a word," said I, "as you value your lives. Let them come."

"May his mother be defiled!" said the other fellow. "The beast is drunk in his den and does not hear us. I will settle with him for this."

I suppose he stumbled and fell, for there was another series of execrations at the fakeer, the load, and the stones; but in a few moments more they both reached the platform and threw down their bundles, which clanked as they fell.

"Where is this drunken rascal?" said one, a tall fellow as big as the one we had killed. "No light for us, and I warrant the brute has either smoked himself dead drunk or is away at the bhung-khana[2] just when he is wanted."

The other sat down, apparently fairly tired and out of breath.

"Go inside," said he; "you will find the lamp and cruse of oil behind the wall. I will not stir an inch."

The first speaker entered, cursing and abusing the fakeer. Surfuraz Khan and I rushed on him and despatched him; but the other hearing the scuffle cried out and

---

1 Porters; coolies.
2 Bhang shop.

attempted to escape. He was not fated to do so, however: his foot slipped, or he stumbled over one of the bundles he had brought, and fell, and before he could rise had received his death-wound by a cut in the neck from one of the men behind the rock, who darted out upon him.

"Enough of this work," said I; "we had better be off; first, however, let us pay one more visit to the hole and get what we can, and do one of you see what is in the bundles."

We again entered the hole, and each taking a bundle we got out. Those the fellows had brought only contained cooking-pots and a few cloths, so we left them behind, and made the best of our way to the serai laden with our booty.

I have forgotten to tell you, sahib, how many more proofs we discovered in that cave of the bloody trade of these villains. Many of the bundles were of wearing apparel, and most of them covered with blood. One that I opened was quite saturated; and as the still wet gore stuck to my fingers, I dropped it with mingled disgust and horror.

———◆·◆———

Chapter XVIII

WHEN we returned we had a good laugh over our success. The adventure was novel to us all; and we pictured to ourselves the mortification and chagrin of the robbers, when they should arrive, at finding their stronghold plundered of all its valuables, and their friends lying dead at the threshold, instead of being ready to receive them and recount their adventures of the evening.

As a better place of security, I took the jewels and silver vessels I had found to our house and locked them up in the strong-room, to be disposed of afterwards as best they might be.

My father, I need not say, was overpowered with joy; and every new feat that I performed seemed to render me more dear to him. He caressed me as though I had still been a child.

"Wait till these actions are known in Hindostan, my son," said he with enthusiasm; "I am much mistaken indeed if they do not raise you to a rank which has been attained by few,—that of subadar."[1]

I did not reply to him, but I made an inward determination to venture everything to attain it. I was aware that nothing but a very successful expedition, coupled with large booty and a deed of some notoriety and daring, could raise me to the rank my father had mentioned; but that it could be attained I had no doubt, since others had reached it before me: and why should not I, whose whole soul was bent upon winning fame through deeds which men should tremble to hear?

Two days after our adventure at the robbers' cave, the whole of the karwan and adjacent neighbourhood were thrown into great excitement from the discovery of the dead bodies by their smell and the number of vultures they attracted. Various were the conjectures as to the perpetrators of the violent deed, and many attributed it to the treachery of some of the band of robbers; however, all agreed that a great benefit had been done by unknown agents. Much of the stolen property was

---

1   High-ranking officer.

recovered; among it was some of great value which had been stolen from a sahoukar a short time before, and which in our hurry and confusion had escaped us; but, as it was, we had got a considerable booty. All the gold and silver was secretly melted into lumps by one of our men who understood how to do it, and it was valued by weight at upwards of seven thousand rupees.

On a general division of the proceeds of the booty being proposed, which amounted in a gross sum, by the sale of the camels, horses, bullocks, carts, and various valuables, to about fifty thousand rupees, all the Thugs agreed that it had better be reserved until the return of the expedition to our village; and meanwhile twenty rupees were disbursed to each inferior, and fifty to each jemadar, for their present wants. My father now talked of leaving the city; but I entreated a further stay of ten days, as, in concert with Bhudrinath and Surfuraz Khan, I had laid out a plan for dividing our gang into four portions, one to take post on each side of the city, and to exercise our vocation separately, the proceeds to be deposited as collected in one place, and to be divided when we could no longer carry on our work.

The plan was favourably received by him, and that day it was put into execution. We paid the trifling rent of our house, and on the pretence that we were about to leave the city and return to Hindostan, quitted the karwan and took up our quarters on the other side, in a suburb which bordered upon the Meer Joomla tank. Bhudrinath and his party went into the Chuddar Ghat bazar, near the magnificent mansion of the Resident; as, being a grand thoroughfare, it was frequented by numerous travellers, and from thence branched off many roads, both to the north and east. Surfuraz Khan with eight men continued at the karwan, as he was less known than we were. Another large party took post on the western road from the city towards Shumshabad, under Peer Khan and Motee-ram, who were resolved by their exertions to merit the trust which had been confided to them.

Our plan succeeded wonderfully; not a day passed in which the destruction of several parties was not reported; and though the booty gained was inconsiderable, yet it was probably as much as we could expect, and it was all collected and deposited in our new abode, from whence my father disposed of such as met a ready sale.

I pass over my own share in these little affairs. I had thought, when I selected the quarter I did, that there would have been more work than turned out to be the case; I was disappointed in the small share which fell to my lot, in despite of my utmost exertions to the contrary, and entreated Bhudrinath or Surfuraz Khan to exchange places with me. They, however, would not: they had laid their own plans; and as I had myself selected my station I had no right to any other, nor ought I to have been dissatisfied.

It was very early in the morning of the eighth day after we had commenced operations, that Bhudrinath came to me in great alarm.

"We must fly," said he; "the city is no longer safe for us."

"How?" I asked in astonishment; "what has happened? Has aught been discovered, or have any of the band proved faithless and denounced us?"

"I will tell you," replied Bhudrinath; "it is a sad affair—some of our best men are taken and in confinement. You know Surfuraz Khan to be daring, far beyond the bounds of discretion, and that for this reason few hitherto have liked to trust themselves to his guidance; and but for this fault he would ere now have been one of our leading jemadars, for he is a Thug by descent of many generations, and his family has always been powerful."

"But the matter," cried I impatiently; "what in the name of Shitan have we to do with his ancestors? By Alla! you are as bad as a—"

"Nay, I was not going to make a story about it," said Bhudrinath mildly, for nothing could provoke him, "so do not lose your temper; but listen. Surfuraz Khan, then, yesterday evening had got hold of two sahoukars, who were on the eve of departure for Aurungabad; he persuaded them to put up in the serai with him, and they were to start the next morning. They were supposed to be rich, as their effects in two panniers[1] were brought into the serai, and carefully watched by them. By some unlucky chance, just as the evening set in, they were visited by two or three other merchants whom they seemed to know, and who persuaded them to wait for another week, and to join them in their journey up the country. To the extreme mortification of Surfuraz Khan they agreed to the proposal; but as they said there would be danger in removing their bags from the serai at night, they told their friends they would sleep there, and join them in the morning. Surfuraz Khan, I hear, made every exertion by persuasion to induce them to alter their determination, but in vain. So you know there remained but one alternative, which was to put them to death in the serai, and to dispose of the bodies as well as they could; besides, the circumstance of the men being afraid to risk their bags by removal at night, looked as though they were of value. I must own, Meer Sahib, it was tempting; it would even have been so for you or me,—how much more for the Khan! Had he even waited till towards morning, done the business, and started, leaving the bodies where they were, he could have got clean off with the booty, which was large, and he could have come round the back of the city and joined you or me; any one of us could have taken his post in the karwan, and no one would have been at all suspicious. But no, he did

---

1   Pairs of baskets carried by beasts of burden.

not reflect; the men were killed almost immediately after their friends left, and their bags plundered. As it is, we have got some of the spoil in the shape of two strings of pearls, but the best are gone."

"And how was the matter discovered? you have not said."

"Why," continued Bhudrinath, "one of the sahoukars' friends shortly after returned with a message. Surfuraz Khan made some excuse that they had gone out, but would soon return. The fellow waited for a long time; but at last growing suspicious he went away, and returned with the others, who insisted upon a search for their friends. Surfuraz Khan had contrived to bury the bodies in the yard, but some articles were found on his person which the others positively swore to, as also the bags in which they had been; and the upshot of the whole was, that they were all marched off to the city by a guard which was summoned from somewhere or other for the purpose, except one of them, by name Himmat Khan, one of Surfuraz's own people, who happened to be absent."

"It is a sad business truly," said I, "and I do not exactly see what is to be done to extricate them."

"Nor I," replied Bhudrinath; "but this evil comes of not taking the omens, nor attending properly to them when they are taken."

"Nonsense!" said I; "you are always prating about these foolish omens, as if success lay in them more than in stout hearts and cunning plans. I believe them not."

"You will rue it then one day or other," said Bhudrinath; "depend upon it you will rue it. I tell you I could mention a hundred instances of the disastrous effects of disregard of omens, and what I say will be readily confirmed by your father."

"Pooh," said I, "he is as superstitious and absurd as yourself; why do you not make your lamentations on my want of faith to him, instead of troubling me with them?"

"I would," he replied, "but that he seems to have given over the charge of the whole expedition to you, and to have forgotten his station as the leader and conductor. Did any one ever hear of a whole band being separated, and each pursuing a separate course, without the omens being taken, or a solemn sacrifice offered to Bhowanee?"

"I thought you had performed all the rites you seem to think so necessary," said I sneeringly; "and if you have not, to whom else have we to look but to you, who are the nishan-burdar?[1] By Alla and his prophet! Bhudrinath, methinks you have deceived us all; and," said I, my anger rising, "I bid you beware how you speak of my father as you have done; remember that I am able and willing to avenge any word which may be spoken against him, and I will do it."

---

1 Bearer of the sacred pickaxe.

"Young man," said Bhudrinath gravely, "you well know me to be one who never enters into idle brawls or quarrels, and these angry words of yours are wasted; keep them, I pray you, for those who will gratify you by taking offence at them—to me they are trifles. Your placing no dependence upon the omens which have been considered by Thugs both of your faith and mine to be essential to our success, is only attributable to your inexperience; the necessary offerings have been neglected by us, and behold the punishment. Though at present it has fallen lightly upon us, there is no saying how soon the whole of us may be in danger; suppose any of those taken are put to the torture and denounce us, how could we escape?"

"Then what do you counsel?" said I.

"I would first propose an offering to Bhowanee, and then such measures for the deliverance of those who have been seized as may be hereafter determined on by us all."

"Perform the ceremonies by all means," said I; "you and my father know how to do so. My ignorance might mar your object, so I will keep away from you till they are over."

"You are right, it might, and I am glad to hear you at length speak reasonably; where is your father?"

"You will find him asleep within," said I, "and you had better go to him."

Sahib, the sacrifices were made, the omens watched, and declared to be favourable. What they were I know not; I cared so little about these ceremonies then that I did not go near them, or even ask what had been done. It was only in after days that their value and importance were impressed upon me by a series of misfortunes which were no doubt sent to check my presumption; since then my faith in them has been steadfast, as you shall hereafter learn.

My father and Bhudrinath returned to me with joyful countenances. "Bhowanee is propitious," said they, "in spite of this little display of her anger. The truth is, we have in some manner neglected her; but she is now satisfied."

"Since that is the case," said I, "we had better be stirring and doing something for the poor fellows; but what to do I know not. When did you say they were seized, Bhudrinath?"

"About the middle of the night."

"Then they are now in confinement somewhere or other, and it will be impossible to effect their release by day. A bribe I dare not offer, for they say Hussein Ali Khan, the kotwal, is an upright man. When is it likely they will be brought before him?"

"I know not," said Bhudrinath, "but it can easily be ascertained;" and he went into the street, and soon returned: "I asked an old bunnea the question, or rather at what time the kotwal held his durbar,[1] and he told me in the first and second watches of the night."

"Then," said I, "they must be rescued by force, and I will do it."

"Impossible!" cried both at once.

"But I tell you I will do it," said I; "where is Himmat Khan? With him and six of our best men I will do it, if they will stand by me. Do any of them know the kotwal's house?"

They were summoned, but none knew it.

"Then," said I, "I will go even now and find it out, and will return when my plan is perfected."

"And I will go and bring some of my men," said Bhudrinath; "I will be back by noon."

"See that they bring their swords and shields, Bhudrinath; some of them may volunteer to accompany me."

"I will do so for one, Meer Sahib; I have confidence in you in spite of your want of faith;" and he laughed.

"I understand you," said I; "you forgive me?"

"Certainly; did I ever quarrel with you?"

"No, indeed, though you had cause; I was foolish."

"Why, what is all this?" said my father. "You have not surely been offended with each other?"

"It is nothing," I replied, "for you see the end of it; but I am losing time, I must depart."

I went into the city, and easily got a person to show me the kotwal's habitation. It was in a long, narrow street, which did not appear much of a thoroughfare. This exactly suited my purpose, for we could have done little in a crowded place. It seemed very practicable to surprise the men who should escort our friends, and I had no doubt if suddenly attacked, they would scamper off, and leave their prisoners to their fate.

I returned and laid the result of my inquiries before my father. He was not averse to the undertaking, but was in much alarm at the prominent part I should have to play, and the chance of our being defeated.

"But," said he, "my son, these thoughts are the cowardly ones which affection often suggests, and Alla forbid they should have any effect with you; go, in the name of the Prophet, to whose protection I commend you."

---

1 Court.

Towards evening, therefore, myself, Bhudrinath, and six others, two of whom were Rajpoots, who swore to die rather than come back unsuccessful, went into the city. We separated but kept in view of each other, and they all followed me to the street in which the kotwal resided. There we lounged about for some hours, and I grew very impatient. Would they ever come? had they even before this been tried, condemned, and cast into prison? were questions I asked myself a thousand times. That the durbar was being held I knew by the number of persons who went in and came out of the house, but still there were no signs of our brethren.

I was sitting listlessly in the shop of a tumbolee,[1] almost the only one in the street, when Himmat Khan came up to me. I saw by his face that he had news, and descended from the chubootra[2] upon which the man exposed his goods, and turned round a dark corner.

"They come," said he, panting for breath from anxiety. "I have been watching one end of the street and Khoseal Sing the other; they are coming by my end, and will be now about half way up."

"And by whom are they guarded?" I asked.

"Oh," said he, "a parcel of line-wallas,[3] about twenty soldiers with old muskets; we could cut through a hundred of them."

"Have they their bayonets fixed?" I inquired.

"They have; but what of that? they are cowardly rascals, and, you will see, will run away."

"Then," said I, "run and tell Bhudrinath, who is yonder; tell him to walk down that side, I will go down this; when we are near them I will give the jhirnee."[4]

My four men had now joined me, as I told them to do if they saw me speak to any one; Bhudrinath was joined by his, and by Khoseal Sing who had given up his watch at the other end and arrived at the critical moment. Our parties proceeded down the street exactly opposite to each other. I thought not of danger, though it was the first time I had ever drawn a sword in anger against a fellow creature, and I was about to precipitate myself into what might be a sudden and desperate combat. Our shields apparently hung loosely and easily on our arms, but they were tightly grasped, and our swords were free in their scabbards. I saw the party approach; they marched carelessly, and had not the arms of my companions been tightly bound,

---

1 Seller of tobacco and betel-leaf.
2 Raised platform.
3 Infantrymen.
4 Signal for murder.

and the whole tied together by a rope, which the leader of the party held in his hand, they might have easily escaped.

Our men joined together in the middle of the street, and when we were close to the coming party, I cried in a loud tone, "Bhaee Pān lāo!"[1] It was the signal: our swords flashed from their scabbards, and we threw ourselves on the sepoys. I cut right and left, and two men fell; the others were as successful. I rushed to the prisoners, and a few strokes of my sword and of those who were nearest cut their bonds and they were free. As Himmat Khan had said, the whole of the sepoys fled on the instant of the attack.

"Fly to the gates, my brothers, or they will be shut!" I cried; "fly through these narrow dark streets; no one will know who you are nor trouble themselves about you."

We all dispersed in an instant. I cast a hurried look around me as I returned my bloody sword into its scabbard, and saw five poor wretches lying on the ground and groaning. It was enough; I too fled down the nearest street which offered, reached the gate I had entered by, and when I got on the embankment of the Meer Joomla Tank, I plunged among the gardens and enclosures which are below it, and by the various lanes which led through them soon reached my father's house.

The attack on the escort of the prisoners, sahib, was so sudden, and over so quickly, that I can give you but a faint idea how soon it was made and finished. It occupied less time than I have taken to tell it, and I have often wondered since that the noise and confusion not only caused by us, but by a few passengers who witnessed the fray, did not alarm the whole street, and cause the inhabitants to rise on us.

By morning all our companions were present at the different places of rendezvous; but thinking we were no longer safe about the city, my father sent them all out of the way to the camp at Hassain Sagor, where he bade them wait, for we knew that it would never be searched for us.

Nothing now remained to detain us but to dispose of the plunder we had gained during the last ten days, and there was none of much value: a few strings of pearls, several shawls, and some unset precious stones were the best, and they were soon sold; the gold and silver as before had been melted down.

---

1 Brother, bring betel-leaf!

CHAPTER XIX

IN WHICH THE READER WILL PERCEIVE THAT AMEER ALI PASSED A BUSY AFTERNOON

I HAD now only two matters on my hands: one to discover Zora if I could, the other to endeavour to get the bills of exchange I had brought with me cashed. Of the first I had but little hope: for since the day I went to her house, although I had constantly men on the watch about it, I could discover nothing of her or the old nurse; the latter I had bribed handsomely, and I knew if it was possible to convey to me any information of her I loved, she would do so. I had several times passed the house myself in the hope of seeing Zora by some accident or other, but it was in vain; and at the time I now speak of, I had almost given her up in despair. Had it not been, sahib, for the wild interest of my trade, I should have sunk into apathy and wretchedness, so fondly, so deeply did I love her. It was this which rescued me from myself, for I could not be behind the rest in seeking adventures; and once that I had a band entirely under my own direction, I was incessantly occupied in finding employment for it, and taking my own part in the catastrophes which ensued.

The day after the rescue of our brethren we held a consultation, at which the principal members of the band were present. I need not relate particulars; suffice it to say, that all agreed in thinking we had remained long enough consistently with our safety, and it was resolved to depart in the course of the next day, or at most the day after. One by one the parties, as they were then divided, were to take the nearest road towards Beeder, which led through Puttuncherroo; and the last mentioned place was to be the rendezvous whence we should proceed in company.

Little time therefore remained to me; and as soon as I possibly could I took Bhudrinath and Motee-ram with me, and we went into the city. We sat down on the steps of the Char Minar. Wonderful indeed were the stories we heard of our skirmish with the kotwal's soldiers; the accounts of the killed and wounded on each side were ludicrously inconsistent, and you may imagine how we enjoyed the various relations we heard, all either from persons who declared they had been eye-witnesses of the matter, or who had heard it from undoubted authority. But it was not our errand to waste time by listening to idle tales, not one of which contained a word of truth, but to get the money for the bills we had found among the effects of Syud Mahomed Ali, *alias* Kumal Khan, and we had repaired to the Char Minar as the most likely place to meet with a person who could read them, and without suspicion tell us upon whom they were drawn.

Observing as we sat a miserable half-starved looking wretch, with a pen stuck between his turban and his ear, an ink-bottle hanging by his side, and a roll of paper under his arm, I fixed upon him as a likely person to suit our purpose. I beckoned to him, and he ran eagerly towards us. "Canst thou read Goozerattee?"[1] I asked.

"Noble sir, I can not only read but write it, for it is my native tongue; what are my lord's commands?"

"Simply," said I, "to read a hoondee[2]—no great matter;" and I handed him one of the bills.

"It is an order, sahib, drawn in favour of Kumal Khan (my lord's name I presume), by Bearee Mul of Nandair, upon Gopal Chund Bisn Chund of the Begum Bazar, for four hundred rupees, at nine days' sight."

"Is it correctly drawn?" I asked.

The fellow looked at the bill, and turned it round and round, examining every part of it.

"Does your worship suspect it?"

"Alla forbid!" said I; "for if it is wrong, I and these worthy associates of mine are ruined, for we have more like it, and for larger sums."

"I see nothing wrong in the bill," said the man; "but let me see the others." I showed them.

"They are all correct," said he; "you have only to take them for acceptance, and you are sure of your money."

"Is the firm upon whom they are drawn well known?"

"They have a great deal of country business in hoondees," said the man, "and are on that account perhaps less known than many of our leading bankers; but nevertheless the firm is most respectable.

"Where did you say they live?"

"In the Begum Bazar. If your worships wish it, I will accompany you thither."

"Good," said I, "do so; we are strangers, and might not readily find the house. You shall be rewarded for your trouble."

"We went out of the city by a small gate at the end of a street which led down from the Char Minar,—I think it is called the Dehli gate,—and turning to the left,

---

1   Gujarati.

2   Bill of exchange.

after crossing the river, we were soon in the midst of the populous and wealthy suburb in which the bankers we sought resided. The road through the principal street was almost blocked up by bags of grain, bales of merchandise, tethered bullocks belonging to the grain-carriers, and empty carts; and it was as much as we could do to keep together, both from these causes and the crowd of people. The noise, too, of the crowd, of the buying and selling in the bazar, the curses and execrations of bullock-drivers and unloaders, the cries of men measuring grain, and a thousand others, made a din and confusion which I had never heard equalled. However, by dint of pushing and elbowing our way, we reached a respectable-looking house, and were introduced to one of the partners by the man we had taken with us.

I put a bold face on the matter, and presented one of the hoondees. The sahoukar was an old man, and taking a pair of spectacles from a fold in his turban, he placed them on the end of his nose and carefully read the hoondee; he afterwards turned it round and round, and examined it most carefully, looking from time to time most suspiciously at me over his glasses.

I own this would have been unpleasant had I been alone, but with the two companions I had brought with me I cared not; had it come to the worst, our weapons were ready, and we would have used them for our liberty.

"I wish to speak a few words with you, if you will follow me into the next room," said the sahoukar, pointing to one which led from that in which we sat. He rose, and I followed him.

"How came you to be possessed of this?" said he anxiously; "and who are you?"

"It matters not who I am," I replied; "and it must suffice for you to know that I am to receive the money for that hoondee, and for these also; and I showed him the others.

"Most extraordinary!" he exclaimed after he had examined them. "I cannot understand it. It is most strange that they should be presented by another. Young man, by what authority are you here to receive this money?"

"By his for whom they were drawn," I replied.

"His name, and the sahoukar's who drew them?"

"Kumal Khan,—and the sahoukar's, Bearee Mul."

"That will not do," said the sahoukar; "you have blundered in your errand, young man; the drawer's name any one could have told you."

"Perhaps this may enlighten you further upon the subject," said I, and I took from my waistband the seal of the syud.[1]

---

1   Male Muslim who claims to be descended from the Prophet Mohammad.

He examined it, and going to a box in the room he took from it a bundle of papers. He turned them over rapidly.

"Ay, here they are," said he reading, "'Accounts of Syud Mahomed Ali'; and now, young man, if there is deceit in that seal it can be easily proved, for behold the seal of the worthy syud himself;" and he showed me an impression on one of the papers.

I confess I had been in much suspense, for had I by any unlucky chance got hold of the wrong seal my detection would have certainly followed; but still I had taken the ring from the man's own finger, and it was not likely that he had any other. The instant I saw the impression, however, I was satisfied that it was the right one.

"Now for the proof," said the sahoukar, rubbing the seal over with ink and wetting a piece of paper with his tongue. "If you have attempted deceit, young man, your detection is certain. Shall I stamp it?"

"Certainly," said I, "I am innocent of any attempt to deceive you. The worthy syud gave me the seal in order that you might be satisfied."

He pressed the seal to the paper and withdrew it; the impression was perfect, and exactly corresponded with that on the paper of accounts.

"This is correct," he said at length; "though I cannot read Persian, the letters appear the same, and the size is exact. I cannot therefore doubt longer; but still it is most strange."

"I can only say," said I, "that I am the syud's confidential agent, whom he has sent to you for the money; if you will not pay it, say so, that I may write to him."

"By no means," said the sahoukar; "the money is here. But why did not the syud come himself? the bills are made payable to him alone."

"True," said I, "they are; but if you are in his confidence, as you seem to be, you will know that there are good reasons for his absence from the city at present, and as he wanted the money he has sent me for it."

"And where is he?"

"That I cannot tell you," said I; "it can be divulged to no one. Suffice it for you to know that when the proper time comes he will emerge from his place of concealment." And I told the truth, sahib, for will he not rise at the day of judgment?

And Ameer Ali laughed heartily at his own conceit.

"Well," said the sahoukar, "no doubt remains as to your right to the money. When do you want it? the bills are at nine days' sight."

"Now; I have no time to lose, I must depart in the morning. You can deduct the interest for nine days. But stay," I continued, "the syud told me that if he owed you anything you were to deduct it, and if any balance of his remained in your hands you were to pay it to me."

"Good," replied the sahoukar; "I will see;" and he turned to his books. "Ah, here is the account. Last balance struck the fifteenth of Suffer,[1] nearly a year ago,—in his favour three hundred and twelve rupees, four annas."[2]

"So much the better," said I; "now pay me the moneys and write a receipt; I will sign it with the seal, which I must take back with me."

The sahoukar called to a man inside.

"Here," said he, "register these hoondees, and get the money for them, and make out a receipt. Your name?" said he to me.

"Ameer Ali, an unworthy syud."

The money was duly counted out, a trifling deduction made for interest, and the whole paid to me. I put my own seal as well as that of the syud to the receipt, and after seeing the balance in the sahoukar's books duly cancelled, there was no longer cause to delay.

"How will you carry all that money?" said the sahoukar; "this is not a safe place for people to be seen out at so late an hour" (for the evening was now closing fast) "with such a sum in their possession."

"Content yourself," said I; "we are three stout fellows, and well able to defend our charge."

"You had better take two of my men, at any rate, to carry the money."

"I will carry some, if I am permitted," said the man we had brought with us. "Bhugwan knows I have eaten nothing to-day, and knew not where to get a meal till these kind gentlemen met me; and I may perhaps earn a trifling sum above what they have promised me."

"Good," said I; "how much can you carry?"

"Two thousand rupees," he replied, "if my lord will try me."

"Very well, then, take up that bag." The rest we divided between ourselves, and departed. We did not return as we had gone, but avoiding the city, passed by the house of the English Resident,[3] crossed the river below it, and on the other side struck into some close lanes, which led to the suburb we lived in. As we went along, I said to Bhudrinath in Ramasee, which I had now learned, "That fellow must not live; our secret is safe with the sahoukar, but not with another. What do you say?"

---

1   Safar; the second month in the Islamic calendar.

2   An anna is a currency unit equal to one-sixteenth rupee.

3   The chief representative of the East India Company in Hyderabad and de facto British Ambassador at the court of the Nizam.

"I agree with you," said he. "We can throw the body into a well; and there is one not far off, I think; I bathed there this morning.

"Very well," said I; "when you see the place give the signal. I will settle all our accounts with him for his trouble and carriage of our money."

We came to the well, and the signal was given; I was ready and my victim also, but he struggled hard, as the bag of rupees was on his shoulders, and my roomal had not fair play. He died, however, and we threw him into the well with a large stone tied in his clothes to sink him.

Strange, sahib, that after protesting his poverty as he had done, we should have found forty-three rupees in his girdle!

You may judge of my father's joy at my success; and to prove his sense of the value of my address and ready wit, he presented me with five hundred rupees out of the sum I had brought.

With this at my disposal, I determined to make a last attempt for Zora, for I thought that with it I might bribe the old woman who called herself her mother; and, late as it was, I pleaded some excuse and set off for the city. I soon reached the now well-known street, and finding the door open I entered, and was ushered into the presence of the old woman and Zora's sister Zenat.

They rose on seeing me, and welcomed me kindly.

"You have not been with us, Meer Sahib, since the Mohorum," said the old woman as she cracked all her fingers against her temples. "You knew that you would always be our most favoured guest, and yet we have not seen you. Why has there been this estrangement from us?"

I did not like to accuse the old woman of turning me from the door, as I have related before, so I said I had been absent from the city, and having only just returned had come to pay my respects to her.

"And now, mother," said I, "where is Zora? "Why is the rose separated from the nightingale?"

"Zora!" said the old woman; "why, have you not yet forgotten that foolish girl? Is there not Zenatbee, who is dying for you, and has raved about you ever since she saw you?"

"Touba! touba!"[1] cried Zenat, covering her face affectedly. "For shame, mother; how can you speak so? how can you tell such lies?"

"I say the truth, Meer Sahib; I swear the foolish girl's head has been turned by your beauty;" and she stroked my chin caressingly.

---

1 For shame! For shame!

What could I do? I saw at once that if I did not affect love for Zenat I should never hear aught of Zora; but I could not forget her so easily, and I hated Zenat for her love. I thought it better to come to terms at once if I could.

"Mother," said I, "I am proud of your daughter's love, and to one so young as I am such marks of preference as you say she is inclined to show me are most flattering; nevertheless I cannot forget Zora; and tell me, by your soul, am I to see her or not? Now hear me; I am not a rich man, not one who could lavish thousands upon her, but what I have is hers for ever, and yours too, if you will give her to me. Will you part with her?"

"What do you offer?" said the old woman. "Methinks you must be one of our nobles in disguise to come here with such a proposition."

"I am no noble," said I, "but a poor syud. I have five hundred rupees, and they are yours if you make Zora mine for ever; say the word, and to-morrow I will be present; we will send for a moolla, and the nika[1] shall be performed."

"Five hundred rupees!" cried the old woman, and she and her daughter burst into an uncontrollable fit of laughter. "Five hundred rupees!" continued she at length, when she could speak; "O man, thou art either mad or drunk!"

"I am neither the one nor the other," I replied very angrily; "I am as sober as either of you, nay far more so."

"Then if you are so," said the old wretch, "what, in the name of Alla, has come to you, that you think we would part with Zora for five hundred rupees? Five thousand, and twice as much, would not be sufficient."

"Then," said I, "you are a pair of the devil's children, and I spit at you. Not content with spurning me from your house like a dog, you now deny me the only happiness I looked to on earth. Women, have you no hearts?"

"Yes," cried the old hag in a fury; "yes, we did spurn you, as I do now. Begone! and never dare to intrude as you have done this night, or I will see if I cannot bring a few stout fellows together to beat you out with sticks like a dog and a son of a dog as you are."

"Peace! woman," cried I; "beware how you revile my father."

"May his mouth be filled with earth and his grave defiled! May your mother—"

I could bear this no longer. I ran to the door for my shoes, and held one in my hand threateningly.

"Now," said I, "another word of abuse, and I will beat you on the mouth."

---

1 Marriage ceremony.

It did not check her. A fresh torrent poured from her lips, and I was really provoked. I could bear it no longer. I rushed at her, beat her on the face with my shoe, and spit on her. The daughter hurried to the stair-head and raised cries of alarm.

"Thief, thief! He is murdering us! Kasim, Mahomed Ali, where are ye? We are murdered—we are defamed! Bring your swords, and kill him!"

I had pretty well belaboured the old woman, and thought it high time to be off; so I rushed to the door, and seizing Zenat threw her to the other side of the room with all my force. I saw that she had a heavy fall, and I ran down the stairs. About halfway I met a man with a drawn sword; he stood, and was about to make a cut at me, but I seized his arm and hurled him down the steps, and as he rolled to the bottom I leaped over him and was outside the house in a moment.

Well, thought I, as I went along, I have not got Zora, but I have slippered the old devil her mother, which is some satisfaction, and Bhudrinath will laugh rarely when he hears of my exploit.

Chapter XX

Cil.—Madam, your song is passing passionate.
Alv.—And wilt thou not then pity my estate?
—*Old Play.*

"FOR the love of Alla, young man!" cried a low and sweet voice as I passed under the gateway of a respectable-looking house; "for the love of Alla, enter, and save my mistress!"

Fresh adventures, thought I, as I looked at the speaker, a young girl, dressed like a slave. "Who are you?"

"It matters not," said the speaker; "did you not pass this way yesterday afternoon, in company with two others?"

"I did, and what of that?"

"Everything; my mistress, who is more beautiful than the moon at its full, saw you and has gone mad about you."

"I am sorry," said I, "but I do not see how I can help her."

"But you must," said the girl; "you must, or she will die. Follow me, and I will lead you to her."

I hesitated, for I had heard strange stories of lures spread for unwary persons— how they were enticed into houses for the gratification of wicked women, and then murdered. But the thought was only momentary. "Courage! Ameer Ali," said I to myself; "trust to your good fate and follow it up. Inshalla! there will be some fun."

"Look you," said I to the girl, "you see I am well armed. I will follow you; but if violence is shown, those who oppose me will feel the edge of a sharp sword."

"I swear by your head," said the girl, "there is no danger. My lord is gone into the country, and has taken all the men with him; there is no one in the house beside myself but two slaves and three old women."

"Then lead on," said I; "I follow you."

She entered the gateway and conducted me through a court into an open room, where sat a girl, richly dressed and of great beauty; but she covered herself immediately with her dooputta,[1] and cried when she saw me, "Ya Alla! it is he; am I so fortunate?"

"Yes, lady," said I, "your slave is at your feet, and prays you to remove that veil which hides a houri of paradise from the gaze of a true believer."

"Go," said she faintly; "now that you are here I dare not look on you. Go, in the name of Alla! what will you not have thought of me?"

"That your slave is the most favoured of his race," said I; "I beseech you to look on me, and then bid me depart if you will."

"I cannot," said the fair girl, "I cannot, I dare not; ah, nurse, what have you made me do?"

The old woman made me a sign to take the veil from her face, and I did so gently. She faintly opposed me, but it was in vain. In an instant I had removed it, and a pair of the loveliest eyes I had ever seen fixed their trembling gaze upon me—another, and I had clasped her to my heart.

"That is right," said the old woman; "I like to see some spirit in a lover. Mashalla! he is a noble youth;" and she came and cracked her fingers over my head.

"Now I will leave you," said she; "you have a great deal to say to each other, and the night is wearing fast."

"No, no, no!" cried the girl; "do not leave us; stay, good nurse, I dare not trust myself with him alone."

"Nonsense," cried the old woman, "this is foolishness. Do not mind her, noble sir;" and she left the room.

"Lady," said I, "fear not, your slave may be trusted;" and I removed from her, and sat down at the edge of the carpet.

"I know not what you will think of me, sahib," she said, "and I am at a loss how to confess that I was enamoured of you as I saw you pass my house yesterday; but so it was. My liver turned to water as I looked on your beauty, and I pined for you till my attendants thought I should have died. They said they would watch for you, and Alla has heard my prayer and sent you."

"He has sent a devoted slave," said I; "one whose soul burns with love, such as that of the bulbul[2] to the rose. Speak, and I will do your bidding."

"Hear my history, and you will know then how I am to be pitied," said the fair girl; "and it is told in a few words. I was the daughter of humble parents, but I was as you see me—they say I am beautiful; they married me to my husband,—so they

---

1 Veil.
2 Nightingale.

said,—but they sold me. Sahib, he is old, he is a tyrant, he has beaten me with his shoe, and I have sworn on his Koran that I will no longer remain under his roof. Yes, I have sworn it. I would have fled yesterday, but I saw you, and I prayed Alla to send you, and he has done so. Now think of me what you please, but save me!" And she arose, and throwing herself at my feet clasped my knees. "You will not refuse me protection? if you do, and your heart is hard towards me, one thing alone remains—I have prepared a bitter draught, and to-morrow's sun will look upon my dead body."

"Alla forbid! lady," said I. "He who has sent me to you has sent you a willing and a fearless slave; fly with me this instant, and I will lead you to a father who will welcome you, and a land far away where our flight will never be discovered."

"Now—so soon?" she exclaimed.

"Ay, lady, now; leave your house this moment; I will protect you with my life."

"I dare not, sahib, I dare not; ah, what would become of us if we were discovered? You would escape, but I—you know a woman's fate if she is detected in intrigue."

"Then what can be done?" said I. "Alas! I am a stranger in the city, and know not what to advise."

"I will call my nurse; let us leave all to her,—Kulloo!"

The old woman entered. "What are your commands?" said she.

"Listen," said I; "I love your fair charge with an intensity of passion; this is no place for us to give ourselves up to love, for there is danger, and we must fly; I am a stranger in the city, and am on the eve of departure for my home, which is in Hindostan, and whither I will convey her safely; she is willing to accompany me, and your aid and advice are all that is required."

"To fly! to leave home and every one for Hindostan, and with one unknown! Azeemabee, this is madness; how know you who he is, and where he will take you? I will not assist you. I was willing that you should have a lover, and helped you to get one; but this is mere madness—we shall be ruined."

"Mother," said I, "I am no deceiver; I swear by your head and eyes I can be faithful. Do but help two poor creatures whose affections are fixed upon each other, and we will invoke the blessings of the Prophet on your head to the latest day of our lives. I leave here to-morrow; my father is a merchant and accompanies me; he has ample wealth for us both, and I am his only child; we shall soon be beyond any chance of pursuit, and in our happiness will for ever bless you as the author of it. Ah, nurse, cannot you contrive something? is there no spot on the road past Golconda which you could fix on for our meeting? I can reward you richly, and now promise you one hundred rupees, if you will do my bidding."

Azeema gathered courage at my words, and fell at the feet of the old woman.

"Kulloo!" she cried, "have you not known me as a child? have I not loved you from infancy? Alas! I have neither mother nor father now; and has *he* not beaten me with a shoe? have I not sworn to quit this house? and did you not swear on my head you would aid me?"

"What can I do? what can I do?" cried the nurse; "alas, I am helpless; what can an old woman like me do?"

"Anything, everything," I exclaimed; "woman's wit never yet foiled at a pinch."

"Did you not say you had made a vow to visit the durgah[1] of Hoosain Shah Wullee?" cried Azeema; "and did not you say you would take me to present a nuzzur at the shrine of the holy saint, if I recovered from my last illness?"

"Thou hast hit it, my rose," said the nurse; "I had forgotten my vow. Sahib, can you meet us at the durgah to-morrow at noon?"

"Assuredly," said I, "I will be present. Good nurse, do not fail us, and another fifty shall be added to the hundred I have already promised."

"May your condescension and generosity increase!" cried she. "Sahib, I have loved this fair girl from her infancy, and though it will go sorely against my heart, I will give her into your hands rather than she should be further exposed to the indignities she has already undergone."

"Thanks, thanks, good nurse, I believe you; but swear on her head that you will not break your faith."

"I swear," said the old woman, placing her hands on Azeema's head, "I swear she shall be thine."

"Enough," I cried, "I am content; now, one embrace and I leave you. I shall be missed by my father, and he will fear I am murdered in this wild city."

We took a long, passionate embrace, and I tore myself from her.

"To-morrow," I cried, "and at the durgah we will meet, never again to part. So cheer thee, my beloved, and rouse all your energies for what is before you. To-morrow will be an eventful day to us both, and I pray the good Alla a prosperous one."

"It will, it will," cried the nurse; "fear not for anything. Nurgiz is faithful, and shall accompany us; the rest are long ago asleep, and know not you are here. But now begone; further delay is dangerous, and Nurgiz will lead you to the street."

She called, and the same slave who had ushered me in led the way to the door.

---

1 Shrine.

"By your soul, noble sir, by your father and mother, do not be unfaithful, or it will kill her."

"I need not swear, pretty maiden," said I; "your mistress's beauty has melted my heart, and I am hers for ever."

"Then may Alla protect you, stranger! That is your road, if you go by the one you came yesterday."

I turned down the street and was soon at home. My father was asleep, and I lay down; but, Alla! Alla! how my heart beat and my head throbbed! A thousand times I wished I had carried off the beautiful Azeema; a thousand times I cursed my own folly for having left her, when by a word from me she would have forsaken home and every tie and followed me; but it was too late. In the midst of conflicting thoughts and vain regrets I fell asleep; but I had disturbed dreams. I thought her dishonoured lord had surprised us as we tasted draughts of love, and a sword glittered over his head, with which he was about to revenge his disgrace. Again, I fancied one of the moollas of the durgah to be him, and just as she was about to depart with us, and was stepping into a cart, he rushed to her and seized her, and I vainly endeavoured to drag her from him. I woke in the excitement of the dream, and my father stood over me.

"What, in the name of the Prophet, is the matter with you, Ameer Ali, my son?" cried the old man. "It is the hour of prayer, I came to awake you, and I find you tossing wildly in your sleep and calling on some one, though I could not distinguish the name; it sounded like a woman's—Azeema, I think. What have you been about? Had you any bunij last night?"

Bunij was the cant phrase for our victims, and I shuddered at the ideas it called up.

"No, no," I said, "nothing. Let me go and perform my ablutions; I will join you in the namaz.[1] It will compose my thoughts, and I will tell you."

Our prayers finished, I related my adventures of the past night. He laughed heartily at my relation of the scene with Zora's mother, and declared I had served her rightly; but when I came to that with Azeema, his countenance was changed and troubled. However, he heard me to the end without interruption, and I augured favourably from it. I concluded all by throwing myself at his feet and imploring his sanction to our union.

"You have gone too far to retract, Ameer Ali," said he. "If you do not fulfil your promise to Azeema she will drink the poison she has prepared; you will be one cause

---

1 Prayers.

of her death, and it will lie heavy on your conscience; therefore on this account I give you my sanction. I am now old, a few years must see my end, and all I have long wished for is to marry you respectably and to see your children. I endeavoured to effect a marriage-contract in Hindostan before we left, but I was unable to do so. There is now no occasion for one; you have made your choice and must abide by it; Alla has sent you your bride and you must take her—take her with my blessing; and you say she is beautiful, in which you are fortunate. Money you will want, as you have promised some to her nurse; if she is faithful, give her from me an additional fifty rupees; and you had better take gold with you,—it will be easier carried."

"Spoken like my beloved and honoured father!" I exclaimed, "and I am now happy. I ask your blessing, and leave you to carry our plans into execution. We shall meet again at Puttuncherroo in the evening."

"Inshalla! we shall," he replied. "Be wary and careful. I apprehend no danger, but you had better take some men with you."

"I will," said I, as I rose to depart; "I will take some of my own, whom I can trust;" and I left him.

My horse was soon ready and my men prepared; but some conveyance was necessary for Azeema, and I ran to a house a short distance off where dwelt a man who had a cart for hire. I had been in previous treaty with him, to be ready in case I should get intelligence of Zora, and had engaged him to go as far as Beeder.

"Come," said I, "Fazil, I am ready and the time is come."

"And the lady?" said the fellow, grinning.

"Ah, she is ready too; only make haste, we have not a moment to lose."

"Give me twenty rupees for my mother, and I will harness the bullocks and put in the cushions and pillows."

"Here they are," said I; "now be quick—by your soul, be quick!"

"I will be back instantly," said he; and he disappeared inside his house, but returned almost immediately with the cushions and curtains of his cart.

"There," said he, as he completed his preparations and jumped on the pole, where was his driving-seat, "you see I have not been long. Now whither shall I drive? to the city?"

"No," said I; "to Hussain Shah Wullee's durgah. Do you precede, and we will follow you, for I know not the road."

"I know it well," said he; "follow me closely."

"Does it lead through the Begum Bazar or the karwan?" I asked.

"Through both, or either, just as you please."

"And is there no other way?"

"There is, but it is somewhat longer. We must go by the English Residence[1] and turn up towards the Gosha Mahal; the road will lead us far behind both the karwan and Begum Bazar."

"That will do," said I; "I wish to avoid both."

"Bismilla![2] then," cried the driver, "let us proceed;" and twisting the tails of his bullocks, a few gentle hints from his toes about their hind-quarters set them off into a trot, which however they exchanged for a more sober pace before we had got far. I allowed him to proceed to some distance, and then put my small party in motion.

---

1 Constructed in 1803 and surrounded by elaborate fortified gardens, the British Residency was a massive Palladian villa where the British Ambassador at the court of Hyderabad resided.

2 In the name of Allah!

Chapter XXI

WE soon passed the suburbs of the city, and held on our way towards the durgah. I was not without hope that we might fall in with Azeema on the road; but in this I was disappointed. As we passed over the brow of an eminence, the tombs of the kings of Golconda broke on our sight, occupying the whole of a rising ground in front. I had never before seen them, indeed I knew not of their existence, and they were the more striking on this account. I was astonished at their size and magnificence, even from that distance; but how much more so when we approached them nearer! We had plenty of time before us, and I proposed, if the durgah should not be much farther, to diverge from the road and examine them. I rode up to the driver of the cart, and asked him how far we were from the place of our destination.

"You cannot see the durgah yet," said the man, "but it is just behind the tombs, on the border of a large tank. You cannot miss it: you will see its white dome and gilt spire above the tamarind trees which surround it."

"Very good," said I; "do you go on thither, and if you are asked any questions, say that you belong to a party which is coming out from the city. We shall go to the tombs, and will join you shortly."

The driver kept to the road, and we, diverging from it, directed our way to the mausoleums of the departed kings. As we approached them, their immense size, and the beautiful groups which they assumed as our point of view shifted, struck forcibly on the mind, while the desolation around them added to their solemn appearance.

"What a pity," said Peer Khan, who accompanied me, "that the good people of the city do not make gardens about these proud buildings! The spot seems to be utterly neglected, even as a burying-ground."

"They are better as they are," said I; "the dust of the present miserable generation would hardly mix with that of so noble a one as that which has left such a monument of its glory. Ay," continued I, as we entered the first immense tomb, "these were kings and princes, who lie here; men who won their kingdoms at the sword's point, and kept them,—how different to the present degenerate race, who are indebted for the bread they eat to the generosity of the Feringhees!"

We ascended by a narrow stair to the top of the tomb, and from the terrace out of which the huge dome proudly reared itself the view of the city was superb; but it was not equal to the one I have before described to you, for we saw none of the white buildings; the Mecca Mosque and the Char Minar were alone distinguishable over the mass of trees, if I except the innumerable white minarets which rose out from the foliage in every direction. From the other side of the terrace the whole of the large tombs were seen at a glance—each by itself a noble and striking object, but rendered still more so when grouped with others of smaller size, whose contrast increased their massiveness. Not a creature was to be seen; the old fort itself, its grey mouldering walls covering the face of a huge pile of rocks, seemed tenantless, and was in unison with the abodes of the illustrious dead who had built it.

The silence and desolation were oppressive, and we scarcely made a remark to each other, as we traversed one by one the interiors of the noble edifices,—some of them dark and gloomy, and filled with bats and wild pigeons, whose cooing re-echoed within the lofty domes; and others whose wide arches admitted the light of day, and were more cheerful in appearance.

"Enough," said I, after we had examined some of the largest; "we do but loiter here while we may even now be expected. Yonder is the durgah, and we had better go to it and be prepared, she cannot now be long absent."

I saw as we approached the sacred edifice that our cart was ready; but there was no other, and my mind somewhat misgave me that Azeema had been unable to keep her appointment, and I resolved within myself that, should she not arrive before noon, I would return to the city and seek my bride, for such I now considered her. I could not leave so lovely a creature to the rude treatment she would experience from him to whom she was united—one who was undeserving to possess a jewel such as she was; but it was still early, and perhaps some hours must elapse before she could reach the durgah, which was farther from the city than I had anticipated.

I entered the holy precincts, and after offering up a gift upon the shrine of the saint, I put up a fervent prayer that the object we had come for should end successfully. This done, I sat down under the shade of the trees, and entered into conversation with one of the many moollas who attended on the tomb, and who were constantly employed in reading the Koran over the grave of the saint. He asked me who I was. I told him I belonged to the city, and had brought my wife to perform a vow to the saint, on her recovering from a dangerous illness. "But she is not yet come," said I; "I rode on with some of my attendants, and she will follow, and will soon be here."

Hour after hour passed, and yet Azeema did not come. Sahib, I was in a torment of suspense and anxiety. Could she have met with any misfortune? could her lord have returned home unexpectedly? could she have played me false? Ah, not the last! her grief, her misery, were too strong to be feigned, and what object could she have had in dissembling? Noon came, and the music of the nobut[1] began to play,—still no signs of her. My patience was fairly exhausted, and I went to the place where my horse stood, mounted him, and bidding the men remain where they were, I rode on towards the city. I had scarcely got beyond the small village by which the durgah was surrounded, when I saw three carts with curtains to them carefully closed approaching. My heart beat quickly with hope, and I determined to return; one of them surely is hers, thought I, and I will await her coming in the durgah.

"She comes!" cried I to Peer Khan, as he eagerly asked the cause of my quick return, "She comes! Bid Fazil have his cart in readiness, and take it round to the gate which leads towards Puttuncherroo."

I dismounted and stood at the gate.

The first cart arrived; it was filled with dancing girls, who had a vow to sing at the shrine, one of them having lost her voice some time before, but had recovered it, as they supposed, at the intercession of the holy Wullee. They passed me, and I soon heard their voices singing one of their melodies inside the tomb.

The second arrived; three old women got out, who were the bearers of some trays of sweetmeats for the moollas, the offering of some lady of rank, who was ill and begged their prayers and intercession with the saints for her recovery.

"Mother," said I to one of them, "saw you aught of a cart with three females in it, my zenana in fact, on the road from the city?"

"Yes," said the woman, "they are close behind us; their vehicle broke down in a rivulet we had to pass, and is coming very slowly, but it will be here directly; and the ladies are safe, for I spoke to them and offered to bring them on, but the damage had been repaired somehow or other, and they declined my offer."

"Alhumd-ul-illa!"[2] I cried, "they are safe then; I have been waiting here since morning, and in anxiety enough about them."

"No wonder," said the old lady, "for the khanum[3] seemed to be pale and weakly-looking; but, Mashalla! she is beautiful, and my lord too is in every way worthy of her."

---

1 Drum beaten at dawn, noon, and sunset.
2 Praise be to Allah!
3 Noblewoman.

"She has been ill," said I carelessly, "and her coming is in consequence of a vow she made."

"May Alla give her a long life and many children! I feel an involuntary interest in a pair whom he hath joined together, in every way so fitted for each other; but I go, noble sir, my companions await my coming."

She also passed on, and in a few moments more the cart I so longed to see turned the corner of some projecting houses, and advanced slowly towards the gate. How my heart throbbed! Was it her, my life, my soul, or was I doomed to a third disappointment? It stopped, and I could have fallen down and worshipped the old nurse, who first emerged from the closely-curtained vehicle; I ran towards her, but was stopped by the driver.

"It is a zenana, noble sir," he said, "and courtesy requires you to go out of sight, lest their faces should be seen in descending."

"Peace, fool! the women are my own."

"That alters the case," said the man; "and my lord's displeasure must not fall on his slave for this delay. The axletree cracked in passing a rivulet, which is a circumstance no foresight could have prevented, seeing that it was newly fitted after the Mohorum."

"It matters not," said I; "but you may now leave us. I will return and pay you your hire: there is an empty cart yonder which I will engage for them to return in."

The fellow retired to a short distance, and my breath went and came as I put my head into the curtains and saw my beloved sitting unveiled, beautiful beyond description, and her fine features glowing with the excitement of her success.

"Shookur khoda!"[1] she exclaimed, "you are here, my own best and dearest; you have not been unfaithful to your poor slave." I caught her in my arms, and imprinted numberless kisses on her lips.

"Touba! touba! for shame!" cried the old nurse; "cannot you refrain for a while? Assist her to dismount, and we will go into the durgah."

I did so, and closely enveloped in a boorka,[2] and leaning on the old woman and Nurgiz, Azeema followed me into the inclosure.

Our first care was to offer up at the shrine some money and a few sweetmeats which Azeema had brought with her; the old moolla to whom I had before spoken received them and laid them on the tomb.

---

1   Thank the Lord!

2   Burka; long loose garment covering head and body, worn by Muslim women.

"They are accepted," said he, "and whatever prayers you may offer up, our kind saint will intercede with the holy Prophet for you, that they be granted."

"Thanks, good moolla," said I; "all I desire is, that the pearl of my eyes may be protected in health, and long spared to me. Truly an anxious time have we had of it with her; but she is now restored to health, and may Alla grant it be continued!"

"It will be," he replied; "Alhumd-ul-illa! our blessed saint's prayers are wonderfully efficacious, and I could relate to my lord many miracles which have been performed here."

"No doubt," said I; "the fame of Hoosain Shah Wullee is spread far and wide, and we of the city have reason to be thankful that such blessed saints were led in days of old to take up their residence near it; for our present generation is so degraded, that without the aid of his prayers the displeasure of the Supreme One would fall heavily on us."

"My lord's words have a sweet and holy savour," said the moolla, "and show that, though his bearing is that of a soldier, his heart is filled with religion; and blessed is he in whom both are seen united. But I could tell my lord of many of the saint's miracles, if he has leisure to hear them; and as he will not return till the afternoon, we can sit down under the trees, and I will relate them."

"Excuse me, good moolla," said I; "time presses, and I have promised the syuda-nee's[1] mother that I will return before the cold of evening sets in, and it is now past noon."

"As you will," said he; "yet perhaps these few pages, which I have compiled during my leisure hours, may entertain as well as instruct, if my lord will accept them: of course he can read Persian?"

"Indifferently well," said I; "we soldiers are rarely good scholars; nevertheless I will keep the book, and here is a trifle which may prove acceptable;" and I put an ashruffee[2] into his hand.

The old man's eyes glistened as he saw it; and after a profusion of compliments he left us to ourselves.

"Now there is no time to be lost," said old Kulloo; "we must travel far and fast this day. You have brought a cart with you?"

"I have, it is ready; if there be aught in the one you came in, tell me, and I will have it put into the other."

---

1 Female Muslim who claims to be descended from the Prophet Mohammad.
2 Gold coin.

"Send a man or two with us," said the nurse; "I and Nurgiz will arrange the new vehicle, and return instantly."

They too left us, and we were alone. No one remained in the large inclosure, the women were still singing in the tomb, and all the moollas were sitting round them listening.

"Can you support the fatigue of further travel, Azeema?" said I.

"I am strong and can bear anything, so I am with thee and thou with me," she replied. "Dearest, I am now secure; but oh the suspense I have endured since I last saw you, and until I was fairly out of that vile city!"

"Tell me," said I, "how did you contrive to elude suspicion?"

"When you left us," replied Azeema, "I thought my happiness had fled for ever; I would have given worlds to have called you back, and to have fled with you then. I had seen your noble face, I had heard your vows of love; Alla had sent me a lover such as my warmest fancy had painted to me, while I was daily suffering torments which the fond and loving only can feel, when their affection is returned by severe and bitter insult; and I thought I had lost him, that I had only gained a few moments of bliss, which would appear like one of those dreams that had often cheated my sleeping fancy, to leave me when I awoke to the bitter realities of my sad lot—and I was inconsolable; but my kind old nurse and Nurgiz soothed me. They told me they would die for me, and assured me you would be faithful; so I gathered courage, and Kulloo proposed that we should make immediate preparations for flight. We packed up some clothes and my jewels, and all the money which had been left with us,—a few hundred rupees,—and before morning we lay down to take a little sleep. At daylight Kulloo told the other slaves and the two old servants that I was going to this durgah, and sent one of them for a cart; it came about sunrise, and concealing the articles we had packed up in two large bundles of carpets and sheets, which we said we should require to sit on at the durgah, we put them into the cart, got in ourselves, and the driver made the best of his way hither."

She had just spoken, when Kulloo came to us.

"All is prepared," said she. "I have dismissed the other cart, and your new one is now ready;—do not delay."

There was no occasion for her to hurry us, we were as well inclined to set off as she was, and we rose and followed her.

The cart was ready—my men with it, and Nurgiz already inside. Azeema got in, and her old nurse followed.

"You too?" cried I.

"Yes, Meer Sahib; my home is at Beeder,[1] whither I will accompany you; the city is no longer safe for me: my life would be forfeited were I ever to enter it again, and fall in with that prince of devils, Nusrut Ali Khan, whose house is now dishonoured, and whose beard we have spat upon."

"Drive on," I exclaimed to Fazil; "go as fast as you can; we must reach Puttuncherroo before night-fall."

The road from the durgah, after passing the tank upon which it was situated, led through a wild pass; piles of rocks frowned over us, and the road was at times so narrow that the cart could scarcely proceed.

"A rare place for a little work," said I to Peer Khan, as we reached a low barrier-wall thrown across the road, and pierced with holes for musketry; "many a wild deed has been done here in times past, I'll warrant."

"They tell queer stories of the place," he replied; "and we have used it ourselves in some of our late expeditions from the city. There lie the seven bunneas you heard of," and he pointed out a remarkable rock not far from the road. "A sad business we had with the grave: it was all rock underneath, and the bodies were hardly covered; but who asks about them in this country? Why, as we accompanied the travellers, we saw lying in this very pass the bodies of two men who had been murdered and dreadfully mangled."

"Well," said I, "we have left our marks behind us at any rate, and all things considered we have been lucky. It matters not if we get no more bunij[2] all the way to Hindostan."

"We have enough to make us comfortable for some years," said he; "nevertheless one's hand gets out of practice, and you are but young at the work; the more you have for a few years to come, the better."

We reached Puttuncherroo late in the evening, and to my inexpressible joy found my father and the whole band safely arrived, and comfortably encamped under a large banian tree, by which was a fakeer's tomb. One of our small tents had been pitched for Azeema, and after seeing her settled for the night I joined my father.

"You are a lucky fellow," said he, when I had told him of all my success; "I have been in anxious suspense about you, especially when the evening set in and you came not; but now there is no danger, we are once again in the country and the roads are our own. And now tell me, what is your new bride like? Is she as handsome as Zora?'

---

1   Bidar (Mohammadabad).

2   Victims.

"She is quite as handsome," said I; "the full moon is not more beautiful; she is tender in her love, and of an affectionate and kind disposition. You must see her to-morrow; she is now fatigued with travel."

"And you must be fatigued also, my son, and hungry too. I have a rare pilau ready for you."

It was brought; and after sending a portion to Azeema, my fingers were very soon busied with the rest of the contents of the dish; and I enjoyed it, for I had tasted nothing but a few of the sweetmeats Azeema had brought with her during the whole day.

CHAPTER XXII

Rosalind.—Now tell me how long you would have her, after you have
   possessed her.
Orlando.—For ever and a day.

—*As You Like It,* Act IV., Scene 1.

ON the fourth morning we reached Beeder. If not so striking in its outward appearance as we approached it as Hyderabad, this city was nevertheless interesting. The summit of a long table-land broke into a gentle descent, and from it Beeder suddenly opened on our view. The walls of the town occupied the crest of a high ridge; and over them one tall minaret, and what appeared another rude unfinished one, of great height, towered proudly. On the right hand the large white domes of some tombs peeped out of a grove of mango trees, with which the hill was clothed from top to bottom; and there was a quiet solemnity about the approach to the now nearly deserted capital of the Dukhun, the favourite residence of the once proud and powerful Bahmunee kings,[1] which accorded well with our feelings, and formed a powerful contrast to the busy city we had just left. Some of our men, who had gone on in advance, had chosen a spot for our encampment near the gate of the city upon the road we were to take in the morning; but separating from my party, I rode through the town, which, though now mean in comparison to what it must have been, was more striking than I had expected to find it.

I joined the encampment on the other side, which now presented its usual bustling appearance: some were already cooking their morning meal by the edge of the well, others were bathing, and all talking and conversing in that joyous manner which showed their minds were free from care and full of happiness, at the prospect of a speedier return to their home than they had anticipated, and well laden with a rich booty.

"My father, this is a city full of true believers," said I, as I joined him; "Moollas there must be in plenty, and I pray you to send for one, that the nika may be performed, and that I may receive Azeema at your hands as my wife."

---

1   The Bahmani Sultanate ruled the Deccan from the mid fourteenth century to the early sixteenth century.

"I will not oppose it, my son; but the old moolla, whoever he may be, will think it strange."

"He may think what he pleases," said I; "but I can no longer live without her; therefore pray consider the point settled, and send for him at once."

Accordingly Peer Khan was despatched for the holy person, who duly arrived. He was received with the greatest courtesy by my father, and the object for which he was required was explained to him. He expressed the utmost astonishment; it was a proceeding he had never heard of, for persons to celebrate a marriage on a journey, and was in every respect improper and indelicate.

When he had exhausted his protestations, my father replied to him.

"Look you, good moolla," said he, "there is no one who pays more respect to the forms and usages of our holy faith than I do. Am I not a syud of Hindostan? Do I not say the namaz five times a day, fast in the Ramzan,[1] and keep every festival enjoined by the law? And unwilling as I am to do anything which may be thought a breach of the rules of our faith, yet circumstances which I cannot explain render it imperative that this ceremony should be performed; and if you refuse, all I can say is, that there is no want of moollas in Beeder, and if you do not perform it some less scrupulous person must, and earn the reward which I now offer to you;" and my father laid two ashrufees before him.

"That alters the case materially," said the moolla, pocketing the money. "Since the ceremony must be performed, in Alla's name let it take place. It was no doubt fated that it should be so, and you will therefore find no person in Beeder more willing to read the form of the nika than myself. Let me I pray you return for my book,—I will be back instantly;" and he departed.

"There," cried my father, "I thought it would be so. No one can withstand the sight of gold. From the prince on the throne to the meanest peasant, it is the same; its influence is all-powerful. With it a man may purchase his neighbour's conscience, his neighbour's wife, or his daughter; with it a man may bribe the venerable Kazee of Kazees,[2] in any city he pleases, to declare him innocent, had he committed a hundred murders, forged documents, stolen his neighbour's goods, or been guilty of every villainy under the sun; with it a good man *may* be better—but that is rare—a bad man increases his own damnation; for it any one will lie, cheat, rob, murder, and degrade himself to the level of a beast; young women will dishonour their lords; old women will be bribed to assist them. A man who has hoards will practise every

---

1   Holy month of Ramadan.
2   Judge of judges.

knavery to increase them, yet is never happy; those who have no money, hunger and thirst after it, and are also never happy. Give it to a child to play with, and by some mysterious instinct he clutches it to his bosom, and roars if it be taken from him. In short, its influence cannot be opposed; old and young, rich and poor—all are its slaves. Men's wisdom is nothing, men's eloquence is nothing, their character nothing; their rank nothing, but this vile metal, which has no voice, no intellect, no character, no rank—this rules our destinies on earth as surely and as potently as Alla himself does in heaven."

"Alla ke Qoodrut!"[1] said I with a sigh, "your words are true, my father, now that one thinks on them; and we have had a precious specimen in the sudden change of opinion in the worthy moolla, who asked no further questions when he saw your gold."

"No!" cried my father, "and if one only had enough, one might rule the world. Who was Sikundur?[2] By all accounts, a petty prince, not half so powerful as he who rules this country; and yet, when he gained favour in the sight of the jins,[3] and afterwards by his magic got dominion over them, did they not place the treasures heaped up in the bowels of the earth at his disposal? and who could then stop his career? Is not this all written in a book, and is it not as true as the Koran?"

"It were heresy to doubt it," said I; "but here comes the subject of our conversation, with his book under his arm; I will prepare Azeema."

I went to her. "Dearest," cried I, seating myself and passing my arm round her waist, "dearest, the time is come, when, with the blessing of Alla and my father's sanction, you will be mine for ever, and when the law shall bind us together, for death alone to separate us. A moolla has come; and with your permission, now, even now, the nika shall be performed; further delay is idle, and I am consumed with the burnings of my love."

"So soon, Ameer Ali? Oh, not till we reach your home. What will your father think of my consenting to this wild union?"

"He sanctions it, beloved; 'twas he who sent for the moolla; 'twas he who persuaded him to perform the ceremony; and they but await my return to the tent to read the words which make you mine for ever."

"Alas! I know not," said the fair girl; "I am another's wife—how can this be done?"

---

1 It is the power of Allah!

2 Sikandar Lodi, Afghan Sultan who ruled north India in the late fifteenth century.

3 Genii.

"Forget the hateful marriage," I cried; "Azeema, these objections will kill me. Am I not your slave? Are we not now on our way to a distant land, where he from whom you have fled will never again hear of you? Ah, do not continue to talk thus, for it seems like a bitter mockery that you should have fled with me, now to deny yourself to me."

"No, no, no! do not say so, my lord; you saved me from insult, and from a miserable death to which I had doomed myself. I am your slave, not you mine; do as you choose with me; let it be even as you will. I will follow you till death." And she hid her face in my bosom.

"Then," cried I, "beloved, the preparations are soon made. Call Kulloo, and let her know all."

The old woman came, and was overjoyed to hear of my proposal.

"I had feared you would not have bound yourself by this tie, Meer Sahib," said she, "and my mind sorely troubled me on the subject; but now I am easy, and I will give my precious child to you with joy and confidence: may you be blessed in her, and see your children's children! Would that I could proceed with you! but I am old, and my bones and spirit would not rest easily in a strange land: your generosity and what I have scraped together is enough to make me comfortable for life, and when my hour comes I shall die content."

"Then be quick," said I; "put up a screen, and I will call the moolla; you can all three of you sit behind it while the ceremony is read."

A cloth was stretched from one side of the tent to the other, and fastened to the ground: my father, myself, and the moolla sat on one side, the females on the other.

"All is ready, moollajee," said I; "begin."

He opened his book and read the usual service in Arabic. I did not understand a word of it, neither indeed did he; but it was sufficient that it had been read—the ceremony was complete, and Azeema was mine for ever.

It would have been a pity to have left Beeder without seeing more of the town and fort, of which I had heard many praises; and in the evening, therefore, my father, myself, and a few others strolled into the town for the purpose of seeing what we could. First we passed the old Madressa,[1] a noble mass of ruins; the front was covered with beautiful enamel from top to bottom, and the immense minaret which we had seen from a distance in the morning was also covered with the same. The huge round fragments of another lay scattered about in every direction; and I could well picture to myself the noble building it must have been, ere by an unfortunate explosion of

---

1 Islamic college.

gunpowder, when used as a magazine by Aurungzebe,[1] its front was blown out, one minaret destroyed, and the whole rent and torn as if by an earthquake.

Passing onwards we arrived at an open space before the ancient and majestic ruins of the fort. Piles upon piles of old ruined palaces, in many places built upon the walls themselves, and all nodding to their fall, while they impressed us with a stronger idea of the magnificence of their builders than anything we had as yet seen, were a lesson to humble proud man, to teach him that he too must moulder in the dust as their founders had done. They had stood for centuries; yet now the owl, the bat, and the wild pigeon were the only tenants of these splendid halls, where once beauty had dwelt and had been the adoration of the brave and glorious.

Where were now the princely state, the pomp of royalty, the gallant warriors who had of old manned these lofty walls and towers, and so oft bidden defiance to hosts of invaders? All were gone; all was now lonely and desolate; and the stillness accorded well with the ruinous appearance of the scene before us. Not however that the walls were dilapidated or overthrown: *they* remained as firm and solid as ever; and here and there the muzzle of a cannon pointing from a loophole or rude embrasure showed that they were still capable of defence, though, alas! defenders there were none. We thought the place absolutely deserted, and went on to the gateway. It was massive, and highly ornamented with enamel work, such as we had seen before in the old Madressa and the tombs at Golconda.

While we thus stood admiring the outside, a soldier approached us and asked our business.

"We are strangers, who have put up in the town for the day," answered my father, "and we could not leave the spot without looking at the venerable fort of which we have heard so much. May we be permitted to enter?"

"Certainly," he replied; "persons of your respectable appearance are always gladly admitted. If you will follow me, I will show you over the interior, which is worthy your inspection."

We followed him, and passing through two gateways, which were defended by traverses so as to be impenetrable to invaders, we stopped under the third, and our conductor said,—

"The rooms above this are well worth seeing, if you will ascend."

"Surely," said I, "we would willingly see everything."

We ascended a narrow stair, which at the top opened into a small but beautiful suite of rooms, profusely adorned with enamel, far surpassing in its brilliancy

---

1 Aurangzeb (1618-1707), Mughal emperor.

of colours and minuteness of design any that we had before seen on the outside. Sentences of the Koran in white letters on a brilliant azure ground were all round the cornices, and the ceilings and walls were covered with flowers of every hue and design, their colours and the enamel in which they were worked being as fresh and bright as the day they were first painted.

"These are imperishable," said I to my father; "would that the buildings which held them could be so too, to remain to generations yet unborn a proof of the magnificence and wealth to which they owed their erection!"

"Ay," said he, "there requires no better proof than these of the present degeneracy. The monarchs of those times were just and liberal as well as powerful; the wealth their dominions brought them was freely expended in beautifying their cities, and raising edifices by which they might be remembered. Now, with the same dominions, the wealth they bring is either uselessly hoarded or wastefully expended; now, no buildings arise as monuments of a dynasty, no armies rejoice in the presence of a brave and noble sovereign, and, stimulated by his example, win for him renown at the points of their bright swords. All now is mean and sordid, from the poor pensioned descendant of Shah Jehan and Alumgeer to the representative of the once proud Soobahs[1] of the Dukhun."

"Yes," said our conductor; "what is the use of now calling oneself a soldier, with scarcely bread to eat? The few of us who are in the fort wander about the ruins of the noble palaces and the deserted walls, and our only enemies are the panthers and hyænas who have taken advantage of the yearly increasing jungle and desolation, and bid fair to expel us altogether. But look from the window, sirs; the open ground over which you came is called the Futteh Mydan, the plain of victory. Here the proud monarchs of Beeder, first the Bahmunee and afterwards the Beereed dynasties, used to sit, while their gallant troops poured forth from the gates, and amused while they gratified their sovereign with feats of arms. And yonder," added he, taking us to another window, "yonder are their tombs, where their mortal remains rest, though their spirits are in the blessed paradise of our Prophet."

We looked, and the view was lovely as it was unexpected. We were on the top of what appeared to be a lofty mountain, so far and so deep did the noble expanse of valley before us descend. The blue distance melted into the blue of the heavens, while nearer and nearer to us the villages and fields became more and more distinct, till, close under us, they seemed as it were drawn out on a map; and among them

---

1 Viceroys.

stood the tombs, a cluster of noble-looking edifices, their white domes glaring in the red light of the declining sun.

"Ay," cried I, "they must have felt that they were kings, while they gazed admiringly on their gallant soldiers, and looked forth over the lovely country which they ruled."

"Come," said my father, breaking in upon my reflections, which were rapidly peopling the open space of the Futteh Mydan with the troops and warriors of past ages, and picturing to me their manly games, their mock fights, the shouts of the contending parties, while from the spot whereon I stood the praises of the king and acclamations of his courtiers were ringing through the arched roofs and re-echoed by the multitudes without—"Come, it is growing late, and we must soon return."

We again followed our guide, and as we passed over a causeway which was built across the moat, we had a noble view of its great width and depth. The bottom was partially covered by stagnant pools, the remains of the water the monsoon had deposited; for the rainy season was now past. The fosse[1] was very curiously dug, with a view to defence, having been excavated out of the solid rock to a considerable depth; three walls had been left standing, with large intervals between each; and they would certainly oppose a most formidable interruption to an invader.

We entered the fort by a large gloomy archway, within which some soldiers were lounging; and from thence, traversing a large court-yard covered with fragments of ruins and rank brushwood, we emerged into an open space beyond. Here a scene of still greater desolation than even the outside presented opened on our view; ruins of all descriptions—of palaces, stables, offices, baths, magazines for arms and ammunition strewed the ground; it was a melancholy sight, but the whole was evidently far beyond repair, and fast hastening to destruction.

We left the spot, to see the only remaining real curiosity of the place, an immense cannon, the *sister,* as our guide told us, of one at Beejapoor.[2] It was on a high bastion, from which there was a magnificent view of the plain below us, over which the huge fort now flung its broad deep shadow, while the distant country was fast fading into obscurity under the growing darkness of the evening. The herds of the town, winding up the steep ascent from the plain, alone broke the impressive silence, as their lowings, the tinkling of their numberless bells, and the melancholy yet sweet notes of the shepherd's rude pipe ascended to our lofty station.

---

1 Fortified trench.

2 A reference to the famous *Malik-e-Maidan* (Master of the Plains), a fifty-five-ton cannon guarding the Lion's Gate in Bijapur, a city in southwest India.

But we could stay no longer; we returned by the way we had come; and though I longed to have roamed over the ruined and deserted palaces, and explored their recesses, it was too late; dismissing our guide therefore with a small present for his civility, we retraced our steps to our encampment.

From Beeder, sahib, we had no adventures worth relating till we reached Ellichpoor,[1] by which town we directed our route homewards. However we did not travel by the same road as we had done in coming down, which would have led us by Mungrool and Oomraotee, and we had good reason for avoiding both places: the re-membrance of the fate of the sahoukar would necessarily be fresh in the memory of the inhabitants of the latter place, and our appearance was too remarkable to be eas-ily forgotten. So we struck off from Nandair on the Godavery towards Boorhanpoor, and when we reached Akola in the Berar valley, we turned again towards Ellichpoor, and reached it in safety. You must not think, however, that during this long journey we were idle; on the contrary, we pursued our avocation with the same spirit and success with which we had commenced and continued our fortunate expedition; and no traveller, however humble, who joined our party, or was decoyed among us, escaped; and by this means, though our booty was not materially increased, yet we collected sufficient to support us, without taking aught from the general stock, which was to be divided when we reached our home.

At Ellichpoor we encamped under some large tamarind trees, close to the durgah of Rhyman Shah Doolah. It was a quiet lovely spot. Below the durgah ran a small river, which had its rise in the neighbouring mountains; and over its stream the hallowed buildings of the saint, embowered in thick trees, seemed to be the abode of peace and repose. Thither Azeema and myself, attended by some of our men, went, as soon as we had rested ourselves a little and changed our road-soiled gar-ments, to present our offerings at the shrine, and to offer up our thanksgivings for the continued care and protection of Alla.

This done, I sent her back to our camp, and entered into general conversation with the moollas, as was my wont, in order to gather information to guide us in our enterprises; and from so large a city as Ellichpoor I had some hope that we should gain a valuable booty.

We conversed upon many topics of everyday occurrence; at last, one of the moollas asked me where I had come from, and whither I was going. I said I was a horse-dealer, who had been down to Hyderabad with horses from Hindostan, and

---

1 Achalpur, in central India.

was now returning, having disposed of them. "And the men who accompany you, who are they?" asked the moolla.

"My father who is a merchant, is one," said I; "besides him there are the grooms and attendants who accompanied us, and several travellers who have joined us from time to time as we journeyed hither."

"Then you are a kafila?"[1] said the moolla.

"Exactly so," said I; "and feeling ourselves to be strong, we are determined to try the road to Jubbulpoor by Baitool, which, though unsafe for small bodies, presents no obstacle to our numerous party."

"Certainly not," he replied; "and the road will save you a long distance which you would have had to travel had you gone round by Nagpoor; and since you are bent on trying the jungle road, perhaps you would not have any objection to an increase to your party? and I think I could get you one."

"Certainly not," said I, "if the travellers are respectable."

"Highly so," said the moolla; "the person of whom I speak is a man of rank, no less than a Nuwab, who is returning to his nephew, who rules over Bhopal."

"Ah, I have heard of him, I think," said I; "you do not mean the Nuwab, Subzee Khan,[2] as he is called?"

"The very person, and a fine old soldier he is. It is a pity he is so addicted to the subzee or bhang, from which, however, he has gained a name which it is well known has struck terror into his enemies on the battle-field, and has fairly superseded any other he may have had."

"It is a pity," I said; "for report speaks well of the noble khan, and his deeds of arms are known to all who have sojourned in Hindostan. I shall be right glad to accompany him, for 'tis said also that he is a rare companion."

"You have heard rightly," said the moolla. "The Nuwab will be here before sunset, as he always comes to converse with us and drink his bhang; if you will step over from your encampment when I send to you, I will introduce you to him."

"Thanks, worthy moolla," said I; "you only need to summon me, and I will attend your call with pleasure."

I left him soon after. Here was the commencement of an adventure which promised fairly to eclipse all our former ones; the rank of the Nuwab, the number of followers he would necessarily have with him, and the noise there would be

---

1 Caravan.

2 Cannabis Khan (or Ruler).

made about him when he was missed,—all contributed to render this as pretty an adventure as a Thug seeking plunder and fame could desire.

I did not mention a word of my hopes to any one; I was determined to have this matter all to myself, both in plan and execution. If I succeeded, my fame and character were established for ever, and I could not fail with so many to back me. A momentary thought flashed across me—that the Nuwab was a man of war, that he would be armed to the teeth; and who was I that I could oppose him? but I dismissed it in an instant as unworthy. My confidence in my own prowess, both as a Thug and with every weapon whether on foot or on horseback, was unbounded; it had never as yet been checked, and I feared nothing living, I believe, in the form of man.

Yes, Ameer Ali, said I, you and all your tribe have ever feared us Englishmen. You have never yet attacked one of us, nor dared you.

The Thug laughed. No, sahib, you are wrong; we never feared you, but to attack any of you would have been impossible. When you travel on horseback you are not worth attacking, for you never carry anything about your persons. In your tents you are surrounded by a host of servants, and at night you are always guarded. When you travel post, we might possibly get a few rupees from your palankeens;[1] but you are generally armed, you usually carry pistols, and some of us must undoubtedly fall before we could effect our object. But, above all, there would be such a hue and cry if any of you were missing, that it would be impossible to escape, especially as any property we might take from you would assuredly lead to our detection.

Your reasons are weighty, said I laughing; but I suspect, Ameer Ali, you do not like the pistols, and that is the reason we have escaped you. But go on with your story; I have interrupted you.

Well then, sahib, to continue. I waited very impatiently till towards evening, when, as I was sitting at the door of my tent, I saw a man on horseback, attended by a small retinue, among whom to my great astonishment was a young good-looking girl mounted on a spirited pony, coming down the road from the city. He passed near our camp, and crossing the river, ascended the opposite bank and entered the durgah. Was this my new victim? I was not long in suspense; a message soon came from the moolla, requesting my company; and taking my sword and shield with me, I followed the man who had come to call me.

———•———

1 Covered litters for passengers.

Chapter XXIII

He was a stalwart knight and keen,
And had in many a battle been;
His eyebrow dark and eye of fire,
Showed spirit proud and prompt to ire.
—*Marmion.*[1]

SEATED with the old moolla I have before mentioned, the Nuwab, Subzee Khan Buhadoor (for by that name alone I knew him) was quaffing his bitter and intoxicating draught. Around him stood some of his retainers, fierce-looking fellows, one or two of them with deep scars on their rough visages, which showed they had bravely followed their noble master through many a hard-fought field. Behind him sat the slave I have mentioned, a slender fair girl, who was busily engaged in making a fresh bowl of the infusion the Nuwab was so fond of.

The moolla introduced me. "This," said he, "my lord, is the young man I spoke of. I need repeat no praises of him, for no doubt your discerning eyes will at once observe that he is a person of respectability and good breeding, and a fit companion for one my lord's exalted rank."

I presented the hilt of my sword as a nuzzur,[2] and after touching it with his hand, he bid me be seated near him on the carpet.

This I was too polite to do; so excusing myself on the ground of unworthiness of such honour, I seated myself on my heels on the edge of the carpet, and placed my sword and shield before me.

The sword immediately attracted his attention. "This is a noble weapon, Meer Sahib," said he; "may I be allowed to look at it?"

"Certainly," said I, presenting the hilt, "the sword is at my lord's service."

"Nay, Meer Sahib, I want it not; but I am curious in these matters, and have a choice collection, which I will one day show you."

---

1 *Marmion: A Tale of Flodden Field* (1808) by Sir Walter Scott (1771-1832), Scottish poet and novelist.
2 Symbolic offering.

He drew it carefully from the scabbard, and as the brightly polished blade gleamed in the sunlight, he looked on it with a smile of delight, such as one would greet an intimate friend with after a long absence.

I must, however, describe him. In person he was tall and strongly made; his arms in particular, which were distinctly seen through his thin muslin dress, were remarkably muscular, and very long; his figure was slightly inclined to corpulency, perhaps the effect of age, which had also sprinkled his curling beard and mustachios with grey hairs; or it might be that these had been increased in number by the dangerous use of the drug he drank in such quantities. His face was strikingly handsome, and at once bespoke his high birth. A noble forehead, which was but little concealed by his turban, was covered with veins which rose above its surface, as though the proud blood which flowed in them almost scorned confinement. His eyes were large and piercing like an eagle's, and, but that they were swollen and reddened by habitual intemperance, would have been pronounced beautiful. He had a prominent thin nose, large nostrils, almost transparent, and a mouth small and curved like a bow, which, when the features were at rest, wore an habitual expression of scorn. His flowing and graceful beard and mustachios, which I have already mentioned, completed a countenance such as I had never seen the like of before, and have not met with since. The whole was inexpressibly striking, and in the meanest apparel the Nuwab would at once have been pronounced by any one to be a man of high family and a gallant soldier.

A rosary of large pearls was about his neck, and with this exception he wore no ornaments. His dress was studiously plain, while it was neat in the extreme. I remarked two deep scars, one on the back of his head where it joined the neck, the other on his broad chest, and its deep seam was not concealed by the thin dress he wore. Such was Subzee Khan, who had won his renown in many a hard fight, and whom I was determined to destroy on the very first opportunity.

He continued looking at the blade so earnestly and so long, that I began to think that it had possibly belonged to some victim of my father's, who might have been known to the Nuwab, and I was mentally framing a reply in case he should ask me where I got it, when he suddenly said, as he passed his finger along the edge, "So you too have seen battles, my friend; there are some slight dents in this good sword which have not escaped the touch of an old soldier. How did it come by them?"

"Oh, a trifling skirmish with robbers as I came down from Hindostan," said I; and I related to him our affair with the thieves in the Nirmul road.

"It was well done," said he, when I ended my account; "but, methinks, you might have followed up your success and sliced some more of the rogues a little. This weapon would not have failed you if your heart had not."

"My heart never failed me yet, Nuwab," I replied; "those who know me well, also know that I burn for an opportunity to prove that I am a man and no coward; but what could I do in that instance? there were but few of us, and the jungle was terribly thick—we could not have followed them in the dark."

"You are right," he replied; "and what say you, my young friend, to following the fortunes of Subzee Khan? He has at present naught to give thee; but, Inshalla! the time is fast approaching when men of tried valour may win something. My friend Dost Mahomed writes to me to come quickly, for he has need of leaders in his new enterprises; and, methinks, your figure and address would find favour with him. What say you? You are not fit to sell horses all the days of your life; and if you have turned any money in your present expedition, you cannot expend it in a manner more befitting your appearance than in getting a few men together, and offering your service. Dost Mahomed has need of such youths as you, and, Inshalla! we will yet do something to win us fame."

"May your favour increase, Bundé Nuwaz!"[1] cried I; "it is the very thing my soul longs for; with your introduction I cannot fail of obtaining service: and if once we have anything to do, you will find I shall not be backward."

"Then you will accompany me?" said he; "I am glad of it. You have some men with you I perceive, and some travellers; what say you to taking the direct road to Jubbulpoor? it is a rough one, but I am pressed for time; and that by Nagpoor, though free from interruption or danger of robbers, is much longer."

"I had determined on taking it, Nuwab Sahib," I replied, "even before I saw you for we are a strong party and well armed; but now I can have no hesitation. As for thieves or robbers, I have no dread of them, and my lord assuredly can have none?"

"None, since you have joined me," he said; "but with the few fellows I have, I confess I hardly liked to brave the jungle; for the bands who roam through it are strong and merciless, and it would be a sorry fate for Subzee Khan to fall in an unknown spot, after a life spent in battle-fields,"

And yet you will do so, Nuwab Sahib, said I internally; your death-blow will reach you in that jungle you dread, and no monument will mark the spot where the remains of Subzee Khan will lie.

---

1 Benefactor of the slave!

"And when shall you be ready to move, Meer Sahib?" continued he; "have you aught to delay you here?"

"Nothing," I replied. "I had purposed marching to-morrow morning, but if my lord wishes I can wait a few days."

"Ah no,—to-morrow morning I cannot move conveniently; but the day after I will join you here by daylight, and we will travel together."

"Jo Hookum!"[1] I replied, "I shall be ready; and now have I permission to depart?"

"Certainly," he said; "I will no longer detain you, for I must be off myself. My friend Sulabut Khan has an entertainment of some kind to-night, and I have promised to attend it."

I returned to my tent, and though I longed to break the matter to my father, yet I refrained from doing so until the Nuwab had fairly joined us, when I would introduce him properly.

As we were preparing to start the third morning before daylight, the Nuwab rode into our camp and inquired for me.

I was speedily with him, and my father coming up to us I introduced them to each other. After the usual compliments had passed, my father, unobserved by the Nuwab, threw me a significant glance,—I returned it, and he understood me; a look of triumph passed across his features, which gratified me, because to me alone was the band indebted for the adventure which was to follow.

Our party was soon in motion, and as the light increased with the dawning day, it revealed to me the person and dress of the Nuwab, who now rode by my side. He was mounted on a splendid bay horse, which moved proudly and spiritedly beneath his noble master; the trappings of the animal were of crimson velvet, somewhat soiled, but still exceedingly handsome, for the saddlecloth and headstall were embroidered with gold thread in a rich pattern.

But the rider chiefly attracted my observation. He wore a shirt of mail, composed of the finest steel links, exquisitely polished, over his ordinary clothes; at his waist it was confined by a handsome green shawl, which he had tied round him, and in which were stuck two or three daggers, mounted in gold and silver. His arms were cased in steel gauntlets, as far as the elbows, and greaves of steel protected his thighs. On his head was a bright steel cap, from the top of which a crimson silk tassel depended, and a shawl handkerchief was folded round it to protect his head from the heat of the sun. At his back hung a shield of rhinoceros hide, richly painted and gilt; a long sword hung at his side from an embroidered velvet belt which passed

---

1 As ordered!

over his shoulder; and at his saddle-bow was fastened a small battle-axe, with a long and brightly polished steel handle.

Well did his appearance accord with his fame as a warrior. I had seen hundreds of soldiers at Hyderabad, but I had never yet looked on one so perfectly equipped as he who now rode beside me, nor one, could I but have attached myself to him, in whom I should have placed such confidence and followed readily into the deadliest strife. But what was the use of his weapons or his armour? they would not avail him,—his hours were numbered, and his breath already in his nostrils.

"You observe me intently," said he.

"I do," I replied; "for I have never yet seen so perfect a cavalier: horse, arms, and accoutrements all agree in setting off their noble owner. Do you always travel thus?"

"Always, Meer Sahib; a soldier should never be out of his harness. The short time I have spent in idleness with that luxurious dog Sulabut Khan has softened my body, and even now I feel my armour chafe me. But the time comes when I shall need it and I had as well accustom myself to it."

We continued the whole of the march together, and he beguiled the way with relations of his adventures, battles, and escapes. I was as much fascinated by them as by his powers of conversation, which were remarkable; and I often wished that I had met him as a friend, or enrolled myself under him, when I might have followed his banner and endeavoured to equal his deeds of valour. But he was marked: in our emphatic language he was become a "bunij," and he was doomed to die by every rule and sacred obligation of our profession.

We reached our first stage without any adventure. Beyond it the villagers told us that the jungle grew thicker and thicker, that the road was very bad and stony, and above all, that the Gónds[1] were in arms, and plundered all whom they met with.

"Let them try us," said the Nuwab as he listened to the relations, "let them try us! Inshalla! they will do us no harm, and it may be some of them will get broken crowns for their pains."

But the next morning we moved with more caution; our men were desired to keep well together, and I picked out a trusty few to surround the cart, which moved on with difficulty over the rough and stony roads; the Nuwab and myself rode at the head of the party.

As we advanced, the road grew wilder and wilder; in many places it was narrowed almost to a footpath, and the men were obliged to cut away the branches, which often nearly met across the road, so as to allow the cart to proceed. At other times it

---

1   The Gondi; an aboriginal people in central India.

ran between high banks, which almost overhung us, and from which missiles might have been showered on our heads, without a possibility of our being able to strike a blow in self-defence.

"That was an ugly place, Nuwab Sahib," said I, as we emerged from one of these narrow passes into a more open country, though still covered with jungle; "had we been attacked there we should assuredly have fallen victims."

"It was indeed," said he; "and I am thankful we have got out of it; if I remember aright, it has a bad name. From hence, however, I think there are no more; the jungle becomes a forest, and there is not so much underwood. But look," cried he, "what is that? By Alla! the Gónds are upon us. Shumshere Alum!"[1] cried he, in a voice which rang like the sound of a trumpet, "Shumshere bu dust!"[2] and his glittering blade flashed from the scabbard. Checking his horse, and at the same time touching its flanks with his heels, the animal made two or three bounds, after which the Nuwab fixed himself firmly in his seat, pressed down his cap upon his head, and cried to me to be ready.

I was not behindhand; my sword was drawn and my shield disengaged, which I placed before me to guard me from the arrows. A few bounds of my horse, which was scarcely second to the Nuwab's, brought me to his side, and we were followed by Bhudrinath and a few others mounted on ponies, and some men on foot with their matchlocks.

"Come on, ye sons of defiled mothers," cried the Nuwab; "come on and prove yourselves true men; come on and try your cowardly arrows against stout hearts and ready weapons! Base-born kafirs are ye, and cowards; Inshalla! your sisters are vile, and asses have loved your mothers."

I could not help laughing at the Nuwab's gesticulations and abuse, as he poured it upon the Gónds and shook his sword at them. They would not move, and perched up as they were on the side of a hill, they prepared their bows to give us a volley—and down it came certainly; the arrows whistled past us, and one wounded the nuwab's horse slightly in the neck, at which the Gónds set up a shout of triumph.

"Ah, my poor Motee, thou art wounded," cried he, drawing the arrow from the wound. "Meer Sahib, those rogues will never come down; you had better give them a volley and disperse them."

"Now, my sons," cried I to my followers, "whenever a fellow raises his body to fire, do you mark him."

---

1 Swords out!

2 Swords in hand!

They did so. One Gónd in particular, who was sitting on a rock drawing a large bow, which he placed against his feet, was a conspicuous object, and apparently careless of his safety. Surfaraz Khan aimed at him—fired—and in an instant he rolled over and over almost to our feet: the ball had hit him in the throat, and he was quite dead. The rest seeing his fate set up loud yells, and for a moment we thought they would have charged us; however, another of their number fell badly wounded, and carrying him off they rapidly retreated to their mountain fastnesses. Pursuit would have been vain as it was impracticable.

We met with no further adventure during our march, and duly arrived at our stage by the usual hour.

"Ameer Ali," said my father, coming to me shortly afterwards, "is the Nuwab to be ours or not? If you have invited him as a guest, say so; if not, you had better arrange something."

"A guest!" cried I; "oh, no, he must be disposed of: there can be no difficulty where there are so many good places to destroy him."

"Impossible!" said my father; "on horseback it would be madness. He is a beautiful rider, and his horse is too spirited: the least confusion would make him bound, and who could hold him? We must devise some other plan."

"Leave all to me," said I; "if there is no absolute necessity for selecting a place, I will watch my opportunity."

Chapter XXIV

Lear.—No, no, no life:

    Why should a dog, a horse, a rat have life,

    And thou no breath at all? O, thou wilt come no more,

    Never, never, never, never!

                —*King Lear,* Act v., Scene 3.

"I SUPPOSE you have long ere this guessed, my friends," said I to Bhudrinath and Surfuraz Khan, next day, "why the Nuwab in is our company?"

"We can have little doubt," replied the former, "since you have brought him so far; but, tell us, what are your wishes,—how is it to be managed? It will be impossible to attack him on the road; he would cut down some of us to a certainty, and I for one have no ambition to be made an end of just at present."

"You are right," said I; "we must not risk anything. Still, I think an opportunity will not long be wanting."

"How?" cried both at the same moment.

"Listen," said I, "and tell me whether my plan meets with your approval. During the march yesterday the Nuwab was regretting that we did not fall in with a good stream of clear water, that he might take his usual sherbet: you know that the slave girl he has with him always prepares it. Now I am in hopes that we may meet one in to-morrow's march, and I will try all I can to persuade him to alight and refresh himself; while he is engaged in conversation with me, if we find him off his guard, we can fall on him."

"Nothing is easier," replied Surfuraz Khan; "we cannot fail if he once sits down: his weapons will not then serve him."

"I do not half like the job," said Bhudrinath. "Suppose he were to be on his guard, he would assuredly escape; and though both myself and the khan here fear neither man nor devil, yet it is something out of the way to kill a Nuwab; he is not a regular bunij, and I think ought to be allowed to pass free of harm."

"Nonsense!" cried I. "This from you, Bhudrinath? I am astonished! What, if he be a Nuwab, is he not a man? and have I not fairly enticed him according to every rule of our vocation? It may be something new to kill a Nuwab; but think, man, think on the glory of being able to say we had killed Subzee Khan, that valiant among the valiant: why, our fathers and grandfathers never did such an act before."

"That is the very reason why I raise my voice against it," said he; "anything unusual is improper, and is often offensive to Bhowanee."

"Then take the omens upon it," said I, "and see what she says. Inshalla! we shall have the Nuwab yet."

"Ay," replied he, "now you speak like a Thug, and a proper one. I will take the omens this evening and report the result; should they be favourable, you will find Bhudrinath the last man to desert you."

In the evening the omens were duly taken, and proved to be favourable. Bhudrinath came to tell me the news with great delight.

"I said how it would be," I cried; "you were owls to doubt our patroness after the luck she has given us hitherto; and now listen, I have not been idle. I have found out from the villagers that about four coss hence there is a small stream with plenty of water; the banks are covered with jungle, as thick as we could desire, and I have fixed on that as the place. Shall we send on the lughaees?"

"Certainly," said Bhudrinath; "we may as well be prepared; but no," continued he, "what would be the use of it? If the jungle is as thick as you say it is, we can easily conceal the bodies; and at any rate, as there is a river, a grave can soon be made in the sand or gravel. But the Nuwab is a powerful man, Meer Sahib; you had better not risk yourself alone with him; as for the rest, the men have secured them,—that is, they have arranged already who are to do their business."

"So much the better," said I, "for there is little time now to think about it."

"I have selected one," continued Bhudrinath, "the fellow who calls himself the Nuwab's jemadar—I have scraped an intimacy with him, and am sure of him; the others have done the same; but we left the Nuwab to you."

"He is mine," cried I; "I did not wish to be interfered with. If Surfuraz Khan has not selected any one, I will get him to help me."

"He has not, Meer Sahib, that I know of, and he is as strong a man as any we have with us; with him and another of his men you cannot fail. But let Surfuraz Khan be the shumshea,[1] he is a good one."

"I scarcely need one if the Nuwab is sitting," said I; "though perhaps it is better to have one in case of any difficulty."

We made all our arrangements that night, and next morning started on our journey in high spirits. The Nuwab and I, as usual, rode together at the head of the party.

---

1   The Thug responsible for holding the victim's hands.

"This is an unblest country, Meer Sahib," said he, as we rode along. "Didst thou ever see so dreary a jungle, and not a drop of water to moisten the lips of a true believer from one end of the stage to the other? It is well the weather is cool, or we should be sorely tired in our long stages; and here have I, Subzee Khan, gone without my usual sherbet for three days on this very account. By Alla! I am now as thirsty as a crow in the hot weather, and my mouth opens in spite of me. Oh that we could light on a river or a well in this parched desert! I would have a glorious draught."

"Patience, Khodawund!"[1] cried I, "who knows but we may be near a stream? and then we will make a halt, and refresh ourselves. I am hungry myself, and should not care for an hour's delay to break my fast with some dates I have with me."

"Ha, dates! I will have some too; my fellows may find something to eat in my wallets, and thou sayest truly, the cold wind of these mountains makes one hungry indeed."

But coss after coss was left behind, and as yet no river appeared. I was beginning to think I had received false information, and was in no very good humour at my disappointment, when, to my joy, on passing over the brow of a hill, I saw the small river the villagers had spoken of below me.

"There," said I, "Khodawund! There at last is a river, and the sparkling of the water promises it to be good. Will you now halt for an hour? We can have a pipe all round, and your slave can prepare your sherbet."

"Surely," cried he. "We may not meet with another, and this is just the time when I like my sherbet best; send some one to the rear for my slave, and bid her come on quickly."

I despatched a man for her, and reaching the stream, we chose a smooth grassy spot, and spreading the covers of our saddles, sat down.

One by one, as the men arrived, they also rested, or wading into the water refreshed themselves by washing their hands and faces in the pure stream, which glided sparkling over its pebbly bed; the beasts too were allowed to drink, and all the men sitting down in groups, the rude hooka passed round among them, while they cheerfully discussed the merits of the road they had passed, and what was likely to be before them. Casting a hasty glance around, I saw that all the men were at their posts, three Thugs to each of the Nuwab's servants and retainers. They were therefore sure. Azeema's cart was standing in the road, and in order to get her away, I went to her.

---

1   My lord.

"Beloved," said I, "we have halted here for a short time, to allow of the people taking some refreshment, but you had better proceed; the road appears smooth, and we shall travel the faster to overtake you."

"Certainly," she replied; "bid them drive on, for I long to be at the end of the journey. Poor Nurgiz and myself are well-nigh jolted to death."

"Ah, well," I said, "bear up against it for another stage or two. I promise you to get a dooly, if I can, at the first large village or town we come to, and then you will be comfortable."

"Now proceed," said I to the Thug who acted as driver (for I had purchased a cart on the road, soon after we left Beeder, and he had driven it ever since), "proceed, but do not go too fast."

She left me, and I returned to the Nuwab. He was sitting in conversation with my father, and even now was partially intoxicated with his detestable beverage.

"Ho! Meer Sahib," cried he; "what dost *thou* think? Here have I been endeavouring to persuade this worthy father of thine to take some of my sherbet. By Alla! 'tis a drink worthy of paradise; and yet he swears it is bitter, and does not agree with his stomach. Wilt thou take a drink?" and he tendered me the cup. "Drink, man! 'twill do thee good, and keep the cold wind out of thee; and as to the preparation, I'll warrant it good; for there breathes not in the ten kingdoms of Hind a slave so skilled in the art of preparing subzee as Kureema yonder. Is it not so, girl?"

"My lord's favour is great toward his slave," said the maiden; "and if he is pleased, 'tis all she cares for."

"Then bring another cup," cried the Nuwab; "for what saith the song?" and he roared out the burden of one I had heard before—

Peyala pea, to myn né pea; phir kisse ko kya?[1]

"And what is it to any one? All the world knows that Subzee Khan drinks bhang, and is not the worse soldier for it. Now with a few fair girls to sing a ghuzul[2] or two to us, methinks a heaven might be made out of this wild spot."

"It is a good thought, Nuwab," cried I, chiming in with his humour; "we will get a set of tuwaifs from the next village we come to; I dare say they will accompany us for a march or two."

"You say well, Meer Sahib; yours are good words, very good words; and Inshalla! we will have the women," said the Nuwab slowly and indistinctly, for he had now swallowed a large quantity of the infusion, which had affected his head. "By Alla!

---

1 A cup (of wine) is drunk,—then I have drunk it; What is that to any one? [*Taylor*]
2 Love song.

they should dance too—like this—" continued he with energy, and he got up, and twirled himself round once or twice with his arms extended, throwing leering glances around upon us all.

It was irresistibly ludicrous to behold him. His splendid armour and dress but ill assorted with the mincing gait and absurd motions he was going through, and we all laughed heartily.

But the farce was proceeding too long, and we had sterner matter in hand than to waste our time and opportunity in such fooleries. So I begged him again to be seated, and motioned to Surfuraz Khan to be ready the instant he should see me go round to his back.

"Ho! Kureema," cried he, when he had again seated himself, "bring more subzee, my girl; by Alla! this thirst is unquenchable, and thou art excelling thyself to-day in preparing it. I must have more, or I shall never get to the end of this vile stage. I feel now as if I could sleep, and some more will revive me."

"Fazil Khan, bring my hooka," cried I, as loud as I could. It was the signal we had agreed on.

"Ay," cried the Nuwab, "I will beg a whiff or two, 'twill be agreeable with my sherbet."

I had now moved round behind him; my roomal was in my hand, and I signalled to Surfuraz Khan to seize him.

"Look, Nuwab!" cried he; and he laid hold on his right arm with a firm grasp.

"How dare you touch me, slave?" ejaculated Subzee Khan. "How dare you touch a Nuwab—?"

He did not finish the sentence. I had thrown the cloth about his neck, Surfuraz Khan still held his hand, and my father pulled at his legs with all his force. The Nuwab snored several times like a man in a deep sleep, but my grip was firm, and did not relax—a horse would have died under it. Suddenly, as he writhed under me, every muscle in his body quivered; he snored again still louder, and the now yielding form offered no resistance. I gazed upon his features and saw that the breath of life had passed from the body it had but now animated. Subzee Khan was dead—I had destroyed the slayer of hundreds!

But no one had thought of his poor slave girl, who at some distance, and with her back turned to us, had been busily engaged in preparing another rich draught for her now unconscious master. She had not heard the noise of our scuffle, nor the deep groans which had escaped from some of the Nuwab's people, and she approached the spot where Surfuraz Khan was now employed in stripping the armour and dress from the dead body.

Ya Alla! Sahib, what a piercing shriek escaped her, when she saw what had been done! I shall never forget it, nor her look of horror and misery as she rushed forward and threw herself on the body. Although master and slave, sahib, they had loved.

Her lips were glued to those of the unconscious corpse, which had so often returned her warm caresses, and she murmured in her agony all the endearing terms by which she had used in their private hours to call him, and implored him to awake.

"He cannot be dead! he cannot be dead!" cried the fair girl—for she was beautiful to look on, sahib, as she partly rose and brushed back her dishevelled hair from her eyes; "and yet he moves not—he speaks not"—and she gazed on his features for a moment. "Ah!" she screamed, "look at his eyes—look at them— they will fall out of his head! and his countenance, 'tis not my own lord's—those are not the lips which have often spoken kind words to his poor Kureema! Oh, my heart, what a pain is there!"

"This will never do," cried I; "some of you put her out of her misery; for my part, I war not with women."

"The girl is fair," said Surfuraz Khan; "I will give her a last chance for life."

"Hark you!" cried he to her, "this is no time for fooling;" and as he rudely shook her by the arm, she looked up in his face with a piteous expression, and pointed to the body by which she was kneeling and mourning as she rocked herself to and fro. "Hear me," cried the khan, "those who have done that work will end thy miserable life unless thou hearkenest to reason. I have no wife, no child: thou shalt be both to me, if thou wilt rise and follow me. Why waste further thought on the dead? And thou wast his slave too! Rise, I say again, and thy life is spared—thou shalt be free."

"Who spoke to me?" said she, in tones scarcely audible. "Ah, do not take me from him; my heart is broken! I am dying, and you would not part us?"

"Listen, fool!" exclaimed the khan; "before this assembly I promise thee life and a happy home, yet thou hearkenest not: tempt not thy fate; a word from me, and thou diest. Wilt thou then follow me? My horse is ready, we will leave the dead, and think no more on the fate of him who lies there."

"Think no more on him! forget him—my own, my noble lover! Oh, no, no, no! Is he not dead? and I too am dying."

"Again I warn thee, miserable girl," cried Surfuraz Khan; "urge me not to use force: I would that you followed me willingly—as yet I have not laid hands on thee."

A low moan was her only reply, as she turned again to the dead, and caressed the distorted and now stiffening features.

"Away with the body!" cried I to some of the lughaees, who were waiting to do their office; "one would think ye were all a parcel of love-sick girls, like that mourning wretch there. Are we to stay loitering here because of her fooling? Away with it!"

My order was obeyed; four of them seized the body, and bore it off in spite of the now frantic exertions of the slave; they were of no avail; she was held by two men, and her struggles to free herself gradually exhausted her.

"Now is your time," cried I to Surfuraz Khan; "lay hold of her in the name of the thousand shitans,[1] since you must have her, and put her on your horse: you can hold her on, and it will be your own fault if you cannot keep her quiet."

Surfuraz Khan raised her in his arms as if she had been a child; and though now restored to consciousness, as she by turns reviled us, denounced us as murderers, and implored us to kill her, he bore her off and placed her on his horse. But it was of no use; her screams were terrific, and her struggles to be free almost defied the efforts of Surfuraz Khan on one side and one of his men on the other to hold her on.

We proceeded about half a coss in this manner, when my father, who had hitherto been a silent spectator, rode up, as I was again vainly endeavouring to persuade the slave to be quiet and to bear with her fate.

"This is worse than folly," cried he, "it is madness; and you, above all, Surfuraz Khan, to be enamoured of a smooth-faced girl in such a hurry! What could we do were we to meet travellers? She would denounce us to them, and then a fine piece of business we should have made of it. Shame on you! Do you not know your duty better?"

"I'll have no more to say to the devil," said the man on the left of the horse doggedly; "you may even get her on the best way you can; what with her and the horse, a pretty time I am likely to have of it to the end of the journey;" and he quitted his hold.

"Ay," said I, "and think you that tongue of hers will be silent when we reach our stage? What will you do with her then?"

"Devil!" cried the khan, striking her violently on the face with his sheathed sword, "will you not sit quiet, and let me lead the horse?"

The violence with which he had struck caused the sword to cut through its wooden scabbard, and it had inflicted a severe wound on her face.

"There," cried my father, "you have spoilt her beauty at any rate by your violence; what do you now want with her?"

"She is quiet at all events," said the khan, and he led the horse a short distance.

---

1 Devils.

But the blow had only partly stunned her, and she recovered to a fresh consciousness of her situation; the blood trickled down her face, and she wiped it away with her hand; she looked piteously at it for an instant, and the next dashed herself violently to the earth.

"One of you hold the animal," cried the khan, "till I put her up again." But she struggled more than ever, and rent the air with her screams; he drew his sword and raised it over her.

"Strike!" she cried, "murderer and villain as you are, strike! and end the wretched life of the poor slave; you have already wounded me, and another blow will free me from my misery; I thought I could have died then, but death will not come to me. Will you not kill me?" and she spat on him.

"This is not to be borne; fool that I was to take so much trouble to preserve a worthless life," cried the khan, sheathing his sword; "thou shalt die, and that quickly." He threw his roomal about her neck, and she writhed in her death agonies under his fatal grasp.

"There!" cried he, quitting his hold, "I would it had been otherwise; but it was her fate, and I have accomplished it!" and he left the body and strode on in moody silence.

Some of the lughaees coming up, the body was hastily interred among the bushes which skirted the road, and nothing now preventing us, we pursued our journey with all the speed we could. Thankful was I that I had sent on Azeema in her cart; she was far beyond the scene of violence which had happened, and of which she must have guessed the cause had she been within hearing; but the driver of her cart had hurried on, and we had travelled some coss ere we overtook her. Strange, sahib, that after that day Surfuraz Khan was no longer the light-hearted, merry being he had used to be. He was no novice at his work; hundreds of human beings, both male and female, had died under his hand; but from the hour he killed the slave he was an altered being: he used to sit in silent, moody abstraction, his eyes gazing on vacancy, and when we rallied him upon it, his only reply was a melancholy smile, as he shook his head, and declared that his spirit was gone; his eyes too would on these occasions sometimes fill with tears, and sighs enough to break his heart would escape from him.

He accompanied us to our home, got his share of the booty, which he immediately distributed among the poorer members of the band, and after bidding us a melancholy farewell, stripped himself of all his clothes, covered his body with ashes, and went forth into the rude world, to bear its buffets and scorn in the guise of a fakeer.

I heard, years afterwards, that he returned to the spot where he had killed the girl, constructed a hut by the road-side, and ministered to the wants of travellers in that wild region, where his only companions must have been the bear, the tiger, and the wolf. I never saw him again after he parted from us, and many among us regretted his absence and his daring skill and bravery in the expeditions in which we afterwards engaged: his place was never filled among us.

I have no more adventures of this expedition to relate to you: we reached our home in due course without any accident or interruption; and who will not say that we enjoyed its quiet sweets, and appreciated them the more after our long absence and the excitement and perils of our journey? I was completely happy, secure in the increasing love and affection of Azeema, whose sweet disposition developed itself more and more every day. I was raised to a high rank among my associates, for what I had achieved was duly related to those who had stayed in our village, and to others who had been out on small expeditions about the country; and the immense booty we had acquired, and my father's well-known determination to retire from active life, pointed me out as a leader of great fortune, and one to whom many would be glad to entrust themselves in any subsequent expedition, as I appeared to be an especial favourite of our patroness.

The return of Hoosein's party, about two months after we had arrived, was an event of great rejoicing to us all when they reached our village. As we had agreed beforehand, at our separation, the whole of the proceeds of the expeditions of both parties were put into one, for general distribution, and on a day appointed it took place. Sahib, you will hardly believe it when I tell you that the whole amounted to very nearly a lakh of rupees.

It was carried by general acclamation that I should share as a jemadar, and according to the rules of our band I received one-eighth of the whole. Bhudrinath and Surfuraz Khan received what I did, but the latter only of such portion as we had won since he joined us. I forget how much it was, but, as I have told you, he divided it among the poorer members of the band; and having apparently stayed with us only for this purpose, he left us immediately, as I have before mentioned.

Upon the sum I had thus acquired I lived peacefully two years. I longed often to go out on small expeditions about the country, but my father would not hear of it.

"What is the use?" he would say. "You have ample means of subsistence for two years to come; my wealth you know is also large, and until we find the supply running short, why should you risk life in an attempt to gain more riches, which you do not need?"

But my spirit sorely rebelled against leading such an inactive and inglorious life; and every deed I heard of only made me more impatient to cast off the sloth which I feared would gain hold on me, and to mingle once more in the exciting and daring exploits of my profession.

Still I was fond of my home. Azeema had presented me with a lovely boy, who was the pride of my existence, and about the time I am speaking of I expected another addition to my family. I had already seen two seasons for departure pass, and a third was close at hand, but I suffered this also to elapse in inactivity, although I was repeatedly and strongly urged by Bhudrinath and others to try my fortune and head another band to penetrate into Bengal,[1] where we were assured of ample employment and success.

But much as I wished to accompany them, my father still objected: something had impressed him with an idea that the expedition would be unfortunate; and so in truth it turned out. A large gang under several leaders set out from our village at the usual time; but the omens, although not absolutely bad, were not very encouraging, and this had a dire effect on the whole. They had not proceeded far when jealousies and quarrels sprung up among the several leaders; they separated from each other and pursued different ways. One by one they returned disappointed with their expedition, having gained very little booty, scarcely sufficient to support them for the remainder of the year. But one party was never heard of more; it consisted of my poor friend Bhudrinath and six noble fellows he had taken with him. Years afterwards we heard his fate: he had gone down into Bengal, had visited Calcutta, and up to that period had been most successful; but there his men dissipated their gains in debauchery, and they set out on their return with barely sufficient to carry them a few marches.

They had nearly reached Benares, when, absolute starvation staring them in the face, they attacked some travellers, and, as they thought, killed them. They neglected, however, to bury their victims, and one, who was not dead, revived: he gave information to the inhabitants of the nearest village. My poor friends were overtaken, seized, the property they had about them immediately recognised, and the evidence given by the survivor of the party they had attacked was convincing. What could oppose this? The law had its course, and they were tried and hung.

Ameer Ali here stopped in his narrative, and promising to resume it in a few days, he requested permission to withdraw, and making his usual salam departed.

---

1 Northeast India.

A strange page in the book of human life is this! thought I, as he left the room. That man, the perpetrator of so many hundred murders, thinks on the past with satisfaction and pleasure; nay, he takes a pride in recalling the events of his life, almost every one of which is a murder, and glories in describing the minutest particulars of his victims, and the share he had in their destruction, with scarcely a symptom of remorse! Once or twice only has he winced while telling his fearful story; and what agitated him most at the commencement of his tale I have yet to hear.

With almost only that exception, his spirit has seemed to rise with the relation of the past; and his own native eloquence at times, when warmed with his tale and under the influence of his vivid imagination and faithful memory, has been worthy of a better pen and a more able translator than I am. But let this pass; I repeat, it is a strange and horrible page in the varied record of humanity. Murderers there have been in every country under heaven, from the time of Cain to the present,—murderers from hate, from revenge, from jealousy, from fear, from the instigation of any and every evil passion of our nature; but a murderer's life has ever been depicted as one of constant misery,—the worm that dieth not, the agony and reproach of a guilty conscience, gnawing at the heart, corroding and blasting every enjoyment of life, and either causing its wretched victim to end his existence by suicide, to deliver himself up to justice, or to be worn down by mental suffering—a more dreadful fate perhaps than the others. Such are the descriptions we have heard and read of murderers; but these Thugs are unlike any others. No remorse seems to possess their souls. In the weariness of perpetual imprisonment one would think their imaginations and recollections of the past would be insupportable to them; but, no: they eat, drink, and sleep like others, are solicitous about their dress, ever ready to talk over the past, and would, if released to-morrow, again follow their dreadful profession with a fresh zest after their temporary preclusion from it. Strange, too, that Hindoo and Moslem, of every sect and denomination, should join with one accord in the superstition from which this horrible trade has arisen. In the Hindoo perhaps it is not to be wondered at, as the goddess who protects him is one whom all castes regard with reverence and hold in the utmost dread; but as for the Moslem, unless his conduct springs from that terrible doctrine of fatalism, with which every true believer is thoroughly imbued from the first dawn of his reason, it is difficult to assign a reason for the horrible pursuit he has engaged in. His Koran denounces murderers. Blood for blood, an eye for an eye, and a tooth for a tooth, is the doctrine of his Prophet, which he trembles at while he believes. And Ameer Ali is a Bhula

Admee,[1] even in the eyes of his jailers; a respectable man, a religious man, one who from his youth up has said his namaz five times a day, is most devout in his life and conduct, is most particular in his ablutions, keeps the fast of the Ramzan and every saint's day in his calendar, dresses in green clothes in the Mohorum, and beats his breast and tears his hair as a good syud of Hindostan ought to do; in short, he performs the thousand and one ceremonies of his religion, and believes himself as sure of heaven and all the houris promised there as he now is of a good dinner.

And yet Ameer Ali is a murderer, one before whom every murderer of the known world, in times past or present (except perhaps some of his own profession), the Free Bands of Germany, the Lanzknechts,[2] the Banditti, Condottieri of Italy,[3] the Buccaneers and Pirates, and in our own time the fraternity of Burkes and Hares[4] (a degenerate system of Thuggee, by the bye, at which Ameer Ali, when I told him of them, laughed heartily, and said they were sad bunglers), must be counted men of small account.

Reader, these thoughts were passing in my mind, when at last I cried aloud, "Pshaw! 'tis vain to attempt to account for it, but Thuggee seems to be the offspring of fatalism and superstition, cherished and perfected by the wildest excitement that ever urged human beings to deeds at which humanity shudders."

"Did Khodawund call?" said a bearer, who had gradually nodded to sleep as he was pulling the punkah[5] above my head, and who was roused by my exclamation. "Did the sahib call?"

"No, Boodun, I did not; but since you are awake, bid some one bring me a chilum.[6] My nerves require to be composed."

———◆———

---

1 Respectable person.

2 Sixteenth-century mercenary bands in Germany.

3 Medieval Italian mercenaries.

4 In 1827 and 1828, Irish immigrants William Burke and William Hare suffocated seventeen people in Edinburgh, Scotland, selling the corpses to a doctor for the purpose of dissection.

5 Ceiling fan.

6 Hookah.

CHAPTER XXV

He is a man, take him for all in all, I shall not look upon his like again.
—*Hamlet*, Act i., Scene 2.

AT the expiration of a week, Ameer Ali sent word to me that he was ready to resume his narrative, and I lost no time in requesting him to repair to my residence. He arrived, and making his usual graceful obeisance, I desired him to be seated.

The reader will perhaps like to know something of the appearance of the man with whom he and I have had these long conversations; and no longer to keep him in the dark on so important a subject, I will describe Ameer Ali to him. He is what would be called a short man, about five feet seven inches in height; his figure is now slender, which may be the effect of his long imprisonment,—imprisonment it can hardly he called, except that to one of his formerly free and unrestrained habits and pursuits the smallest restraint must of course be irksome in the highest degree and painful to bear. His age may be about forty or forty-five years; but it sits lightly on him for a native of India, and it has not in the least whitened a beard and mustachios on which he evidently expends great care and pains, and which are always trimmed and curled with the greatest neatness. His figure, as I have said, is slight, but it is in the highest degree compact, agile, and muscular, and his arms are remarkable for the latter quality combined with unusual length and sinewyness. His dress is always scrupulously neat and clean, and put on with more attention to effect than is usual with his brother approvers, his turban being always tied with a smart cock, and his waist tightly girded with an English shawl or a gaily dyed handkerchief, where once a shawl of Cashmere or a handkerchief of brocade was better suited to his pretensions. In complexion he is fair for a native; his face is even now strikingly handsome, and leads me to believe that the accounts of his youthful appearance have not been exaggerated. His forehead is high and broad; his eyes large, sparkling, and very expressive, especially when his eloquence kindles and bursts forth in a torrent of figurative language, which it would be impossible to render into English, or, if it were rendered, would appear to the English reader, unused to such forms of speech, highly exaggerated and absurd; his cheeks are somewhat sunken, but his nose is aquiline and elegantly formed, and his mouth small and beautifully chiselled, and his teeth are exquisitely white and even; his upper lip is graced with a pair of small mustachios, which would be the envy of many a gay lieutenant of hussars;[1] while a beard close and wavy, from which a straggling hair is never suffered to escape, descends nearly to his breast, and hides a throat and neck which would be a study for a painter or a sculptor: to complete all, his chest is very broad and prominent, and well contrasts with the effect of his small waist.

His manner is graceful, bland, and polite,—it is indeed more than gentleman-like—it is courtly, and I have not seen it equalled even by the Mahomedan noble-men, with many of whom I have associated. Any of my readers who may have been in India, and become acquainted with its nobles and men of rank, will estimate at once how high is the meed of praise on this score which I give to Ameer Ali. His language is pure and fluent, perhaps a little affected from his knowledge of Persian, which, though slight, is sufficient to enable him to introduce words and expressions in that language, often when they are not needed, but still it is pure Oordoo;[2] he prides himself upon it, and holds in supreme contempt those who speak the corrupt patois of the Dukhun, or the still worse one of Hindostan. Altogether Ameer Ali is a character, and a man of immense importance in his own opinion and that of every one else; and the swagger which he has now adopted in his gait, but which is evidently foreign to him, does not sit amiss on his now reduced condition.

Reader, if you can embody these descriptions, you have Ameer Ali before you; and while you gaze on the picture in your imagination and look on the mild and expressive face you may have fancied, you, as I was, would be the last person to think that he was a professed murderer, and one who in the course of his life has committed upwards of seven hundred murders. I mean by this that he has been actively and personally engaged in the destruction of that number of human beings.

Now, Ameer Ali, said I, since I have finished describing your appearance, I hope you are ready to contribute more to the stock of adventures you have already related.

Your slave is ready, sahib, he replied, and Inshalla Ta-alla![3] he will not disappoint you. But why has my lord described my poor appearance, which is now miserable enough? Might your slave ask what you have written? and the tone of his voice implied that he had concluded it could not be favourable.

---

1 A cavalry officer.

2 Urdu.

3 If the sublime Allah wills!

Listen, said I, and I will read it to you. At every sentence the expression of his face brightened. When I had concluded, he said,

It is a faithful picture, such as I behold myself when I look in a glass. You have omitted nothing, even to the most, trifling particulars; nay, I may even say my lord has flattered me; and he arose and made a profound salam.

No, said I, I have not flattered your external appearance, which is prepossessing; but of your heart I fear those who read will judge for themselves, and their opinions will not be such as you could wish, but such as you deserve.

You think my heart bad then, sahib?

Certainly I do.

But it is not so, he continued. Have I not ever been a kind husband and a faithful friend? Did I not love my children and wife while He who is above spared them to me? and do I not even now bitterly mourn their deaths? Where is the man existing who can say a word against Ameer Ali's honour, which ever has been and ever will remain pure and unsullied? Have I ever broken a social tie? ever been unfaithful or unkind to a comrade? ever failed in my duty or in my trust? ever neglected a rite or ceremony of my religion? I tell you, sahib, the man breathes not who could point his finger at me on any one of these points. And if you think on them, they are those which, if rigidly kept, gain for a man esteem and honour in the world.

But the seven hundred murders, Ameer Ali, what can you say to them? They make a fearful balance against you in the other scale.

Ah! those are a different matter, said the Thug laughing, quite a different matter. I can never persuade you that I was fully authorized to commit them, and only a humble instrument in the hands of Alla. Did I kill one of those persons? No; it was He! Had my roomal been a thousand times thrown about their necks and the strength of an elephant in my arms, could I have done aught, would they have died, without it was His will? I tell you, sahib, they would not, they could not? but as I shall never be able to persuade you to think otherwise, and, as it is not respectful in me to bandy words with my lord, I think it is time for me to recommence my tale, if he is ready to listen, for I have still much to relate. I have been so minute in the particulars of my first expedition, that perhaps I need not make the narrative of the other events of my life so prolix; indeed were I to do so, you, sahib, would be tired of writing and your countrymen of reading, for it would be an almost endless task to follow me in every expedition I undertook. I shall, therefore, with your permission, confine myself to the narration of those which I think will most interest you, and which I remember to possess remarkable incidents.

Go on, said I; I listen.

Well then, said the Thug, Khodawund must remember that I told him I passed over three expeditions, and that I had partly determined to go on the third. It is of that expedition I would now speak, as it was marked by an extraordinary circumstance, which will show you at once that it is impossible for any one to avoid his fate if it be the will of Alla that he should die.

At the time I speak of I had been obliged to form another set of intimates in consequence of the loss of Bhudrinath and Surfuraz Khan, for both of whom I had the sincerest regard. Hoosein, though I loved and revered him as my father's dearest friend, was now too old and grave to participate in all my thoughts and perhaps wild aspirations for distinction. So, as Peer Khan and Motee-ram, with whose names you are familiar, had now risen to my own rank, and proved themselves to be "good men and true" in various expeditions, I took them into my confidence, and we planned an enterprise, of which I was to be the leader and they my subordinates. Fifty of the youngest, stoutest, and most active and enterprising of our acquaintance were fixed on as the band; and all having been previously warned, we met a few days before the Dusera of the year 18— in a grove near our village, which was shady and well adapted for large assemblies, and was always used as a place of meeting and deliberation; it was considered a lucky spot, no unfortunate expedition ever having set out from it.

We were all assembled. It was a lovely morning, and the grass, as yet not even browned by the sun and drought, was as if a soft and beautiful carpet had been spread on purpose for us. The surrounding fields, many of them tilled by our own hands, waved in green luxuriance, and the wind as it passed over them in gentle gusts caused each stalk of tall jowaree[1] to be agitated, while the sun shining brightly made the whole glitter so that it was almost painful to look on for a continuance. Birds sang in the lofty banian trees which overshadowed us; hundreds of green parroquets[2] sported and screamed in their branches, as they flew from bough to bough, some in apparent sport, others to feed on the now ripening berries of the trees; and the whole grove resounded with the cooing of innumerable turtle-doves, whose gentle and loving murmurs soothed the turbulence of the heart, and bade it be at peace and rest and as happy as they were.

My father and Hoosein were present to guide us by their counsels and experience, and the matter in hand was commenced by a sacrifice and invocation to Bhowanee; but as I have before described these ceremonies, it is needless to repeat them; suffice

---

1   Millet.
2   Parakeets.

it to say that the omens were taken and were favourable in the highest degree; they assured us, and though I had little faith in them notwithstanding all I had heard to convince me of their necessity, they inspirited the whole band, and I partook of the general hilarity consequent upon them.

My father opened the object of the meeting in a short address. He said he was old and no longer fitted for the fatigues and privations of a journey; he recapitulated all I had done on the former expedition, pointed out the various instances in which I had displayed activity, daring, and prudence beyond my years, and concluded by imploring the men to place implicit confidence in me, to obey me in all things as though he himself were present, and above all not to give way to any disposition to quarrel among themselves, which would infallibly lead to the same disastrous results as had overtaken the expedition which had gone out the previous year.

They one and all rose after this address, and by mutual consent swore on the sacred pickaxe to obey me, the most impressive oath they could take, and any deviation from which they all firmly believed would draw down the vengeance of our protectress upon them and lead to their destruction.

I will not occupy your time, sahib, by a narration of what I myself said; suffice it to say, I proposed that the band should take the high road to the Dukhun, and penetrate as far as Jubbulpoor or Nagpoor; from thence we would take a direction eastward or westward, as hope of booty offered, and so return to our home. Khandesh[1] I mentioned, as being but little known to us Thugs, and where I thought it likely we might meet with good booty, as I had heard that the traders of Bombay were in the habit of sending large quantities of treasure to their correspondents in Malwa for the purchase of opium and other products of that district. I concluded by assuring them that I had a strong presentiment of great success, that I felt confidence in myself, and that if they would only follow me faithfully and truly, we might return in a few months as well laden with spoil as we had on the former occasion.

Again they rose and pledged their faith; and truly it was a solemn sight to see those determined men nerve themselves for an enterprise which might end happily, but which exposed them to fearful risk of detection, dishonour, and death.

---

1   Western district in the Maratha Confederacy in central India.

Chapter XXVI

AMEER ALI STARTS ON A NEW EXPEDITION: THE ADVENTURES HE MEETS WITH

OUR meeting broke up, and I returned to prepare Azeema for my departure. I had invented a tale to excuse my absence. I told her that the money which I had gained on my mercantile expedition to the Dukhun was now nearly expended; and although, in her society, and in the enjoyment of happiness such as I had never hoped for, I had been hitherto unwilling to leave my home, yet I could delay to do so no longer without absolute ruin staring us in the face. I added, that my father had placed a sum of money at my disposal for the purposes of trade; with which, if I met with the success I had reasonable ground to hope for, from the letters of my correspondents at Nagpoor and other places, I could not fail of realizing a handsome profit—enough to allow us another continued enjoyment of peace and affluence.

Long and vainly she strove to overrule my determination, pointed out the dangers of the road, the risks to which I should be necessarily exposed, the pain my absence would cause to her; but finding these were of no avail, as I told her my plans had been long laid, and that I was even now expected at Saugor, where my agents had collected the horses I was to take for sale, she implored me to take her and our children with me, adding that travelling was a matter of no difficulty to her, and that the children would enjoy the change of scene and the bustle and novelty of the camp.

But this also I overruled. It would have been impossible to take her, not to mention the expense of her travelling-carriage; and at last, after much pleading and objections of the description I have mentioned, she consented to remain; and placing her under my father's care on the morning we were to depart, I took an affectionate farewell of her. Many were the charms and amulets she bound about my arms and hung round my neck, which she had purchased from various wandering fakeers and holy moollas; and with streaming eyes she placed my hands upon the heads of my children and bade me bless them. I did so fervently and truly, for I loved them, sahib, with a love as intense as were the other passions of my nature.

At last I left her. Leaving one's home is never agreeable, often painful; for the mind is oppressed with indistinct visions of distress to those one leaves behind, and is too prone to imagine sources from which it might spring, though in reality they exist not. It was thus with me; but the appearance of my gallant band, as they greeted my arrival among them with a hearty shout, soon dispelled my vague apprehensions, and my spirit rose when I found myself in the condition which had been the object of many a fervent aspiration. I was my own master, with men willing to obey me, and, Inshalla! I exclaimed to myself, now Ameer Ali's star is in the ascendant, and long will it gleam in brightness!

I have told you of the ceremonies which immediately preceded our departure on a former occasion, of course they were repeated on this; the omens were again declared to be favourable by Motee-ram, who was our standard-bearer and director of all our ceremonies, as Bhudrinath had been; and we proceeded, accompanied for some coss by my father and Hoosein, who stored my mind with the results of their long experience. Among other things both particularly urged me to avoid the destruction of women.

"In olden times," said my father, "they were always spared; even parties in which there might by chance be any, although in other respects good bunij, were abandoned on their account, as, our patroness being a female, the destruction of her sex was considered obnoxious to her, and avoided on every occasion. Moreover, men are the only fit prey for men; no soldier wars with women, no man of honour would lift a finger against them; and you of all, my son, who have a beauteous wife of your own, will be the last to offer violence to any of her sex."

"Rely upon me that I will not," said I; "I was, as you know, strongly against the fate of the unhappy women who died on my first expedition, and, you will remember, I had no hand in their deaths; but I was overruled in my objections, first by Bhudrinath and afterwards by Surfuraz Khan, and what could I do? And it would be terrible indeed to think that the distresses of their party and the unknown fate of poor Bhudrinath were owing to the tardy but too sure vengeance of our patroness."

"It may be so," said my father; "but let not that prey on your mind; both myself and Hoosein have killed many a woman in our time, and, as you know, no ill effects have resulted from it. But bear in mind what I have said, act with wisdom and discretion, and above all pay implicit attention to the omens, and your success and protection are sure."

We rode on, conversing thus, and when we arrived at the boundary stone of our village, we dismounted and embraced each other, and I left them and rode on with my men.

According to our rules, no one was to shave or eat *pān*[1] until our first victim fell; and as this was a matter of inconvenience to many of the men, you may be sure we had our eyes in all directions and our scouts well occupied in every village we passed through or halted at. But it was not till the fifth day that we met with any one who offered a secure and in every way eligible sacrifice. We had fallen in with bands of travellers, some going to and others departing from their homes, but they had invariably women in their company, and them I was determined to spare, as well for my wife's sake as from the injunctions of my father.

However, as I have said, on the fifth day, early in the morning, we came to a cross-road, and were glad to see a party of nine travellers, three upon ponies, having the appearance of respectable men, and the rest on foot, coming up the road a short distance from us. To our great joy they struck into the road we were about to take. We had halted in pretended indecision as to the road, and when they came up we asked it of them. They readily pointed to the one before us, and although expressing themselves astonished at our numbers, they agreed to accompany us to the village where we proposed to halt, and the road to which we had inquired of them. I soon entered into conversation with the most respectable of their party; and I replied, in answer to his inquiries, that we were soldiers, proceeding, after our leave to Hindostan, to Nagpoor, where we were in service. He told me in return, that he and his brother, one of the two others mounted, with a friend and some attendants, were on a traveling expedition; that they had come from Indoor and were going to Benares, as well for the purchase of cloths and brocades, as to visit that sacred place of Hindoo pilgrimage.

Ho, ho ! thought I, these are assuredly men of consequence going in disguise and I have no doubt are well furnished with ready cash. No time must be lost, as they have come by a crossroad, and have not been seen in our company; there can consequently be no trace by which we could possibly be suspected on their disappearance; so the sooner they are dealt with the better. To this end I lagged behind a little, and imparted my determination to Peer Khan, who rode in the rear of all; by him it was told to another, and thus it circulated throughout the band before we had gone far. I was gratified and delighted to see how, as they became aware of what was to be done, each took his station, three Thugs to each traveller, and the rest disposed themselves round the whole, so as to prevent any possibility of escape.

I remembered the road well, for it was that upon which we had travelled before; and what Thug ever forgets a road? I knew also that, although the country around

---

1 Betel-leaf.

us was open and bare, there was a river not far off, the sandy bed of which was full of the wild cypress, and the bodies could be easily disposed of in the brushwood.

When we arrived at the brink of the river, the man I had continued to converse with begged for a short halt.

"We have been travelling since midnight," said he, "and I for one am well tired, and should be glad of rest."

I made no objection, of course, for it was the very thing I wished; and dismounting, and leading my horse to the water, I allowed him to drink, and then joined the party, which had all collected, and were now seated: the travellers discussing a hasty meal they had brought with them, and the Thugs sitting or standing around them, but all in their proper places.

I was on the point of giving the *jhirnee,* and I saw the bhuttotes handling their roomals in a significant manner, when, thanks to my quick sense of hearing, I distinguished voices at a distance. It was well for us that I had not given the signal; we should have been busily engaged in stripping the bodies when the party I had heard would have come upon us. Of course they would have seen at a glance what we were about, and have taken the alarm. But our good destiny saved us. I hesitated, as I have said, and in a few minutes fourteen travellers made their appearance, and came directly up to where we were sitting. They were persons of all descriptions, who had associated for mutual protection, and I had half determined to destroy them also, which I think we could have done, when they relieved me greatly by taking their departure, wishing us success and a pleasant and safe journey.

On one pretence or another I delayed our associates until the other party had proceeded far beyond the risk of hearing any noise, should there be any; and now, seeing everything ripe for the purpose, I called out for some tobacco, the word we had agreed to use, as being least likely to attract attention or inspire suspicion. I had planted myself behind the man I had been speaking to, and as I spoke my handkerchief was thrown. Three years' rest had not affected the sureness of my hold, and he lay a corpse at my feet in an instant. My work was done, and I looked around to see the fate of the rest; one poor wretch alone struggled, but his sufferings were quickly ended, and the party was no more.

"Quick, my lads!" cried I to the lughaees, "quick about your work!" One of them grinned.

"Why," said he, "did you not observe Doolum and four others go away to you brushwood when we reached this spot? Depend upon it they have the grave ready, or they have been idle dogs."

And it was even so: the grave had been dug while the unsuspecting travellers sat and conversed with us.

We were so busily engaged in stripping the dead, that no one observed the approach of two travellers, who had come upon us unawares. Never shall I forget their horror when they saw our occupation; they were rooted to the spot from extreme terror; they spoke not, but their eyes glared wildly as they gazed now at us and now at the dead.

"Miserable men," said I, approaching them, "prepare for death! You have been witnesses of our work, and we have no resource but your destruction for our own preservation."

"Sahib," said one of them, collecting his energies, "we are men, and fear not to die, since our hour is come;" and he drew himself up proudly and gazed at me. He was a tall, powerful man, well armed, and I hesitated to attack him.

"I give you one alternative," said I; "become a Thug, and join our band—you shall be well cared for, and you will prosper."

"Never!" he exclaimed; "never shall it be said that Tiluk Singh, the descendant of a noble race of Rajpoots, herded with murderers, and lived on their unblessed gains! No; if I am to die, let it be now! Ye are many; but if one among you is a man, let him step forward, and here on this even sand I will strike one blow for my deliverance;" and he drew his sword, and stood on the defensive.

"I am that man," cried I, though the band with one voice earnestly dissuaded me from the encounter, and declared that he was more than a match for me; "I am that man. Now take your last look on the heavens and the earth, for, by Alla! you never quit this spot!"

"Come on, boasting boy!" he exclaimed; "give me but fair play, and bid none of your people interfere, and it may not be as you say."

"Hear, all of you;" cried I to them, "meddle not in this matter —'tis mine and mine only. As for the other, deal with him as ye list;" and in an instant more he was numbered with the dead.

"These are your cowardly tricks," cried the Rajpoot, now advancing on me, for he had stood contemplating the fate of his companion; "my end may follow his; but I shall die the death of a soldier, and not that of a mangy dog as he has done."

I have before told you, sahib, that my skill in the use of every weapon was perfect, thanks to my good instructor; and I had never relaxed in those manly exercises which fit a man for active combat whenever he shall be called into it. My sword was the one Nuwab Subzee Khan had so much admired, and I felt the confidence of a man when he has a trusty weapon in his hand and knows how to wield it.

I have said that the Rajpoot advanced on me. He had no shield, which gave me an immense advantage, but the odds were in his favour from his height and strength; yet these are a poor defence against skill and temper.

He assailed me with all his force and fury; blow after blow I caught on my sword and shield, without striking one myself; he danced round me after the fashion of his people, and now on one leg, now on the other, he made wild gyrations, and at intervals rushed upon me, and literally rained his blows at my person; but I stood fixed to the spot, for I knew how soon this mode of attack must exhaust him, and the loose sand of the river added to his fatigue.

At length he stood still and glared on me, panting for breath. "Dog of a kafir!" cried he, "son of an unchaste mother, will nothing provoke thee to quit that spot?"

"Kafir!" I exclaimed, "and son of a kafir, thy base words have sealed thy fate;" and I rushed on him. He was unprepared for my attack, made a feeble and uncertain blow at me, which I caught on my shield, and the next instant my sword had buried itself deep in his neck. He fell, and the blood gushed from the wound and from his mouth.

"Shookur Khoda!"[1] exclaimed Peer Khan, "you have settled his business nobly; let me embrace thee;" and he folded me in his arms.

The Rajpoot was not dead: he had sufficient strength remaining to raise himself up on his arm, and he looked at me like a devil. He made many attempts to speak: his lips moved, but no sound followed, as the blood prevented utterance.

"Some of you put him out of his pain," said I; "the man behaved well, and ought not to suffer."

Peer Khan took my sword and passed it through his heart; he writhed for an instant, and the breath left his body.

"Away with him!" cried I, "we have loitered too long already."

The lughaees took him by his legs and arms, to avoid his blood, and carried him away; others strewed a quantity of dry sand over the spot where he had fallen, and in a few minutes more we were pursuing our way as if nothing had happened.

After this proof of my personal courage and skill, I may safely say I was almost adored by the whole band. They all assured me that a Thug having killed a traveller and a soldier in fair open combat was an unprecedented circumstance, and only required to be known to make me the envy of old and young, and I gloried in what I had done; their praise was sweet incense to my vanity.

---

1 Thank the Lord!

The booty we got from the merchant and his brother was rich, and was of itself a fair amount of booty for any expedition. Some were even for turning back, but they were only two or three voices, and were easily overruled.

"It would be a shame," I said, "if while fortune favoured us we did not take advantage of our good luck."

Sahib, we continued our march, and when we had reached Saugor we had killed nineteen other travellers, without, however, having obtained much plunder: ten, fifteen, and on one occasion only nearly a hundred rupees, were as much as any of them afforded us.

The town of Saugor was, and is now, a large and busy place, built on the edge of an immense lake, nearly as large as that of the Hoosein Sagor. The cooling breezes which travel over it make it a delightful spot. We encamped on the border of the lake near the town.

For the four days we remained there, we daily perambulated the bazars, and frequented the shops of bhuttearas,[1] one of whom was well known to Peer Khan, and whom we paid handsomely for information. He promised to be on the look-out for us, and on the third day after our arrival, Peer Khan came to me in the evening, as I sat before the entrance of my little tent, smoking and enjoying the delightful breeze which came over the vast sheet of water spread before me.

"Meer Sahib," said he, "the bhutteara is faithful; he has got news of a sahoukar going our road, who is to leave this place in about a week; he says we are certain of him, but that we must quit this spot, and march about within a few coss of the town, leaving two or three men with him to carry information."

"Ul-humd-ul-illa!"[2] cried I, "he is a worthy man. We will listen to his advice, and be off to-morrow early. Three of the best runners shall stay here as he counsels to bring us the news."

"But he stipulates for a large reward in case we are successful."

"I see nothing against it," said I; "he will be worthy of it if he is true to his word."

"Oh, for that you need not fear; he is faithful so long as you pay him."

"Then he shall have it. How much does he want?"

"Two hundred rupees if we get five thousand," he replied; "double, if we get ten: and in proportion if between one and the other."

"If the sahoukar is rich, Khan," said I, "we can well spare what he asks; so go and tell him he shall have it."

---

1 Eating-house keepers.
2 Praise be to Allah!

"I go," he said; "should I not return, conclude that I have stayed with him."

He sought out the men he required to accompany him, and taking them and a small bundle of clothes with him, I watched him far beyond the precincts of our camp on his way to the town.

Chapter XXVII

HOW AMEER ALI PLAYED AT THE OLD GAME OF FOX-AND-GOOSE, AND WON IT

WE travelled from village to village for four days, meeting with no adventure; and in truth I was beginning to be weary of the delay and inactivity when, on the fifth morning, one of the men we had left behind to bring information arrived.

"Peer Khan, sahib, sends his salam," said he, "and requests you will return immediately, as the bunij has been secured, and is about to leave the city."

"Know you aught of who he is?"

"No, I do not," Meer Sahib. "I lived at the bhutteara's, and he and the jemadar were often in earnest conversation about him, but I was not let into the secret."

"'Tis well," I replied; "refresh yourself, and be ready to accompany us. How far are we from Saugor?"

"By the way I came about fourteen coss," said he, "but by a path which I know, the city is not more than half the distance."

"Then we may be there by evening?"

"Certainly; by noon if you please, and I will conduct you now."

Accordingly, guided by him through a wild track which I should never have found alone, we reached Saugor towards evening, and after occupying our former ground, I hurried to the bhutteara's, where I was pretty sure of meeting my friends.

Peer Khan was there, and welcomed me. "I was fearful the messenger would miss you," said he; "but, praise to Alla, you are come."

"And this is our worthy ally, I suppose?" said I, making a salutation to the bhutteara.

"The same," he answered; "your poor slave Peroo is always happy when he can serve his good friends."

"I have not forgotten what you are to get, my friend," said I, "and you may depend on the word of a true Thug for it. Are we sure of the man?"

"As sure," said Peer Khan, "as of those who have hitherto fallen; to-morrow he will take his last look on Saugor."

"Ul-humd-ul-illa!" I exclaimed; "so much the better. And he will be a good bunij you think?"

"He will be worth seven or eight thousand good rupees to you," said the bhut-teara; "and all *nugd* (ready money) too."

"Good again, friend; but why do you not take to the road? You are a likely fellow enough."

"Oh, I have tried it already," said he laughing; "I was out on two expeditions with Ganesha Jemadar. Do you know him?"

"I have heard of him," I replied; "he is a leader of note."

"He is," said the bhutteara; "but he is a cruel dog; and to tell the truth,—I fear you will think me a coward for it,—I did not like the way he treated the poor people he fell in with, so I quitted active work, and only do a little business as you see now, by which I pick up a trifle now and then."

"Well," said I, "you do good it appears; but beware how you act, and see that you do not bully poor Thugs out of their money by threatening to denounce them."

The fellow winced a little at my observation, but recovering himself he stoutly protested he had never been guilty of so base an act.

Peer Khan threw me a sly look, as much as to say, you have hit the right nail on the head; but I did not press the matter further, for we were completely in his power.

"Then," said I, "we start in the morning I suppose?"

"Do so," replied the man; "the sahoukar goes to Jubbulpoor. It would be as well not to show yourselves for some days, as he might take the alarm, and some people of note have disappeared of late on the road."

"Now," said I to Peer Khan, "we have no further business here, and I am tired; let us go to the camp. We can send two scouts to remain here, to give us intelligence of the sahoukar's departure if necessary."

The men were instructed in what they had to do, and we left them and the bhutteara.

"You probed that rascal deeply by what you said," said Peer Khan as we walked along; "it is the very practice by which he gets his money; the fellow is as rich as a sahoukar by this means, and never omits to levy a contribution on every gang which passes Saugor."

"Then," said I, "my mind is made up as to his fate. Such a wretch is not fit to live—a cowardly rascal, who sits at his ease, runs no risk, undergoes no fatigue, and yet gets the largest share of any one. He ought to die. What say you to putting him to death?"

"It is a rare plan," replied he; "but how to get him out of the town I know not—he is as wary as a fox."

"Oh," said I, "that is more easily managed than you think. The kafir is fond of money?"

"As fond as he is of his own miserable existence."

"Then, Peer Khan, we have him. Directly we get to the camp I will send a man with a message, which you shall hear me deliver, and if it does not bring him, call Ameer Ali a father and grandfather of jackasses."

"Good," said he laughing; "we will see this rare plan of yours; but I tell you the villain is most wary. I never knew him come but except in broad daylight, when there was no danger, and then only to small parties."

"Here, Junglee," said I to a smart young fellow who always attended my person; "you know Peroo, the bhutteara?"

"Certainty; my lord was with him this afternoon. I know his house, for I was in the bazar purchasing some flour, and saw my lord at the shop."

"Good," said I; "then you will have no need to inquire for it. Now go to the bhutteara, and take my seal-ring with you: mind you don't let it go out of your hand; tell him, with many compliments from me, that as we are so sure by his kindness of the bunij in prospect, and have some money with us, I will pay him what he asks, if he will come here to receive it. Say that I do so as our return by this road is uncertain and may be at a distant period, and that I shall have no means of sending him the coin; and add, that I do this favour to him, as I am convinced of his good faith, and have placed implicit reliance in his assertions. Now, can you remember all this? Mind you speak to him in Ramasee,—he understands it."

"Certainly," said the lad; "I know all." And he repeated what I had told him word for word.

"That will do," said I, "and here is the ring. Now be off; run, fly, and let us see how soon you will earn two rupees."

"I am gone, Jemadar Sahib," cried he joyfully. "I will be back instantly."

"That is a sharp lad," said Peer Khan; "he takes one's meaning so readily. But on, Meer Sahib, Peroo will never come for that message; he is too old a bird to be caught with chaff!"

"Depend on it he will; he will hear the tinkling of the silver, and will run to it as ever lover did to his mistress's signal. Besides he has no chaff in prospect, but rupees, man, rupees. The fellow would run to Dehli for as much."

"We shall see," said Peer Khan. "If it be written in his fate that he is to come, why, Alla help him! come he must, there is no avoiding destiny. What! Peroo the bhutteara come out of his house at night to visit Thugs! I say the thing is impossible; it has often been tried, and failed utterly; the fellow laughed at them, as well he might."

"For all your doubts, Khan," said I, "Inshalla! we will throw earth on his beard to-night; and as we may as well be ready, call Motee and two or three lughaees; the grave must be dug, and that immediately."

Motee came, but was as desponding of success as Peer Khan.

"You will never take him," he said; "did not Ganesha offer to divide a large booty here last year, and that Peroo should have a share if he would come to take it? and he sent word that he laughed at our beards, and we had better leave his share in the hollow of an old tree known to us, or he would send the whole police of Saugor after us in the morning."

"And so you left the share?"

"We did, and it was a good one too."

"Then Ganesha was an owl, and I will tell him so if I ever meet him. Peroo should not have had a courie from me; nor will he now unless he comes to take it."

We were silent for some time, and I could hear the dull blows of the pickaxe, as the sound was borne by the chill night-wind from the place where the grave was preparing. He will come, thought I, and his iniquity will be ended; shame on the cold-blooded coward who can sell men's lives as he does, without striking a blow against them! As I was thus musing, our messenger was seen, in the dusky light, returning at the top of his speed, and alone. "We told you so!" cried both my associates triumphantly; "we told you how it would be!"

I was vexed, and bit my lips to conceal my chagrin. "Let us hear what he says at any rate," said I.

"Well, what news, Junglee?" cried I, as he ran up quite out of breath.

"Wait a moment, Jemadar," said he, "till I can speak: I have run hard."

"Here, drink some water: it will compose you. What has happened? Is there any alarm?"

"Ah, no alarm," replied the lad, "but listen. I went as fast as I could without running, for I thought if I appeared out of breath when I reached him he might suspect something; so when I got to the town gate, I walked slowly till I reached his shop. He was busy frying kabobs for some travellers, and told me to go into his private room and wait for him. In a short time he came to me.

"'Well,' said he, 'what news? Why have you come? The bunij is safe. It was but just now that one of your scouts came and said he had heard orders given for his departure to-morrow. What do you want?'

"So I repeated your message, word for word as you delivered it to me, and he seemed much agitated. He walked up and down the room for some time, talking to himself, and I could hear the words, 'Ganesha,' 'treachery,' once or twice repeated. So at last I grew tired of this, and said to him, 'I cannot wait, I have orders to return immediately: will you come or not?' and this stopped him; he turned round and looked at me severely.

"'Tell me,' said he, 'young man, was Motee-ram present when this message was delivered?'

"'No, he was not,' I replied.

"'Did he know of it?'

"'No; he had not returned from the town when I received it; at any rate, neither I nor the Jemadar Sahib saw him.'

"'Was Peer Khan present?'

"'No,' said I stoutly, 'he was not.'

"'But he left this place in company with your master.'

"'He may have done so,' said I, 'but I did not see him. I was preparing the jemadar's bedding when he returned, and the message was delivered to me privately; for after he lay down to rest he called to me and delivered it: and I may as well tell you that he counted out the money from a bag which was under his pillow.'

"'How much was there set apart for me?'

"'Two hundred and fifty rupees; he was counting more, but he stopped short, put the rest into the bag, and said it would be enough.'

"'And how much is in the bag?'

"'Alla knows!' said I; 'how should I know anything about it?'

"'Who sleep in the tent with the jemadar?' he asked, after another silence and a few more turns about the room.

"'No one,' said I. 'I sleep across the doorway; but no one is ever allowed to enter.'

"'You are a good lad,' he rejoined, 'and a smart fellow. How should you like to be a bhutteara?'

"'Well enough,' said I; for I wanted to see what he was diving at, and I suspected no good."

"Did you ever hear of such a rascal?" said Peer Khan. "Oh, if we only had him, I would wring the base neck off his shoulders."

"Let him go on," said I; "don't interrupt him."

"Well," continued Junglee, "he paced to and fro again several times, and at last came and sat by me, and took my hand in his. I did not like it, so I laid my other on the hilt of my dagger, which was concealed in my waistband.

"'Junglee,' said he to me, 'thou art a good lad, and may be to me a son if thou wilt aid me in this matter. Young as thou art, this bloody trade can have no charms for thee; besides, I'll warrant your jemadar does not make a pet of you as I would, and obliges you to work hard?'

"I nodded.

"'Ay! it is even so,' said he, 'and thou wouldst be free? Speak, boy, and fear not; thou shalt be a son to me. Alla help me! I have neither wife nor child.'

"I nodded again.

"'That is right,' continued he; 'although you are ill-used, you do not like to abuse the salt you have eaten, and I like you the better for it. Now listen to me. I will come, but not now. You say you lie at the entrance of the tent? Good! You must sleep as sound as if you had taken opium—do you hear? I shall step quietly over you, and I know an old trick of tickling with a straw—do you understand?'

"'I do,' said I; 'you would have the large bag.'

"'Exactly so, my son,' said he, 'you have guessed rightly; trust me, I will have it. As I go away I will touch you; you need not follow me then, but you can watch your opportunity.'

"'But the scouts,' added I; 'you have not thought of them.'

"'Oh, I can easily avoid them; the night is dark and cloudy, and no one will see me, I shall strip myself naked, and throw a black blanket over me.'

"'Then I agree,' said I; 'and I will quit those horrid people and become an honest man. Now what am I to say to the jemadar?'

"'Say,' replied he, 'that the herdsman's flock had often been robbed by the wolf of its fattest sheep; and the herdsman said to himself, I will catch the wolf and put him to death. And he dug a hole, and suspended a fat lamb over it in a basket, and sat and watched. And the wolf came, and saw from afar off that there was something unusual in the generosity of the herdsman. And he said to himself, Wolf, thou art hungry; but why should one lamb tempt thee? The time will come when thou mayest find the herdsman asleep; so wait, although thy stomach is empty. Say this to the jemadar and he will understand thee.'"

"By Alla! thou hast done well, Junglee," said I, "and thy faithfulness shall surely be well rewarded. What think you, my friends, of this villain?"

"Ah, we are not astonished," cried both, "it is just like him; but Inshalla! he will fall into his own snare."

"Now," said I, "call two of the scouts;" and they came,

After I had told them of the plot Peeroo had formed, "My friends," I continued, "you must allow this rascal to come into the camp. One of you lie down close to my tent, and pretend to be asleep; but have your eyes open, and directly you see him enter, rouse Peer Khan and Motee, and bring them to the entrance; and do you two then place yourselves one on each side of the door, so that he cannot see you. I shall feign to be asleep, and shall let him take the bag, though he should even fall over me in doing so. As he comes out you can seize him and hold him fast; do him no harm till I come. And as for you, Junglee, if you do not sleep as sound as though a seer of opium was in your stomach, I swear by Alla you shall lie in the same grave with him!"

"Do not fear me," said the lad; "I have eaten your salt; you are my father and my mother, you have treated me kindly, and how could I deceive you? Had I intended it, I had not mentioned a word of what he told me."

"Then we are all prepared," said I. "Did he say when he would come?"

"He did," said Junglee; "in the second watch of the night, when he had no more business."

"Good; then mind you are all ready, and we will spit on his beard."

Anxiously to me did the hours pass, till the time came when I might expect him. I went out of my little tent repeatedly to see that all were at their proper posts, and returned as often satisfied that they were. Peer Khan was lying near my tent apparently in a sound sleep, but I knew he was awake; the scouts were wandering lazily about; above all, the night was so dark that I could not see my hand before me, and the splashing and murmuring of the tiny waves of the lake upon the shore would prevent any noise of his footsteps being heard. "Yes," I said, half aloud, as I retired to my carpet for the last time, "he will come; thief as he is, he will not miss such a night as this: but the darkness favours us as much as it does him."

"Now, Junglee," said I, "this is the last time I stir out; mind your watch, my good lad, and I will not forget you. Peer Khan is close at the back of the tent: I care not much about the rest, they will soon be collected when he is caught."

"Do not fear me," said the boy; "my eyes are not heavy with sleep, and when I move from this spot to call Peer Khan, a rat will not hear me."

I went in and lay down; I drew my trusty blade and laid it close to my right hand, so that I could grasp it in a moment; and covering myself up with my quilt, as well to hide it as to assure me when he came (for I knew he would endeavour to pull it off me), I continued to stare steadfastly on the entrance of the tent; and my eyes becoming sensible of the greater darkness of the inside than that of the outside, I was certain that if any one entered, or even passed the door, I should see him. Long, long did I lie in this position. I hardly stirred, lest Peeroo should be outside listening whether I was awake. It was now, I guessed, considerably past midnight. Still no one came, and I should have been inclined to despair, did I not feel certain that his fate would lead him to destruction. Why is it, sahib, that one has these presentiments? I have often felt them during my lifetime, but I never could account for them.

At last he came. I saw an object darken the doorway, hesitate for a moment, and then pass in over the body of Junglee, who snored so loudly and naturally that I could have declared he was asleep, had I not known the contrary by having spoken to him a short time before. Alla! Alla! sahib, how my heart beat! I could hear its throbbings, and they seemed to be so loud in my breast that I thought he would hear them too. Another thought flashed across me—Could he be armed? and would he attempt to destroy me? It might be; and I almost trembled as I thought how I was to lie inactive and in his power while he abstracted the bag; I was on the point of leaping up and passing my weapon through his body, but I dismissed the idea. He is a thief, a miserable thief, and has not the courage to bring a weapon, much less to use it; and he will want both his hands too—he cannot have one. So I lay quiet, with my hands on the hilt of my sword. The tent was very low, and he was obliged to advance stooping. He reached my side and knelt down, and as I feigned the hard breathing of sleep, I felt his warm breath when he looked over me and into my eyes to see whether I really slept or not. He appeared satisfied that I did, for he instantly thrust his hand under the pillow, but so quietly that I could not have felt it had I been asleep. But the bag was not on that side, it was under my other ear. He felt it, but found, I suppose, that he could not abstract it without his awakening me; so he felt about on the ground for a piece of straw or a blade of grass, and began tickling my ear on the side next to him. I obeyed the intention of the action, and turned towards him with a grunt. It startled him, and he was still for a moment; but again his hand was groping. I felt the bag recede—recede till it was withdrawn from the pillow. I heard the clink of the money as he placed it on his shoulder, and I was content. I saw, too, that Junglee was not at the door (though when he had gone I know not—having been too much occupied by my own situation), and that the bhutteara was aware of it. He stopped, and murmured in a low tone, "Strange that he should be gone; but he knows the way and will not disappoint me." Another step, and he was beyond the threshold, and in the rough grasp of Peer Khan, Motee, and a dozen others.

"Capitally managed!" cried I, as I ran to the door and joined the group." Strike a light, one of you; let us see the face of this Roostum among thieves—a fellow who dares to rob a Thug's camp and defy him to his beard."

A light was brought, and there stood the trembling wretch with the bag of rupees still on his shoulder, and clutching it as though it were his own.

"Ha!" said I, "so it is you, Peeroo, and the wolf who was so wary has fallen into the hands of the shepherds at last: he would not take the little bait, but the large flock was well watched, and he has fallen into the trap. And now, rascal," I continued, "thou wouldst have robbed us, and dost deserve to die; yet upon thy answers to the questions I will put to thee depends thy life or death."

"Name them, oh name them!" said the wretch. "Let me live,—I will set off without delay, I will even accompany you; you may turn me out from among you in the jungle, and if ever my face is seen in Saugor again or on this road, deal with me as ye list."

"Very good," said I; "now answer the following questions. Is the bunij you have promised false?"

"As true as that I breathe. Ah, Meer Sahib, have not your men seen the preparations, and will not you hear the same to-morrow from them? How could you doubt it?"

"How much money will you give us to let you go? I want two thousand rupees."

"Ai Méré Sahib! Méré Sahib!"[1] cried the wretch; "two thousand rupees! Where am I to get them? I have not a courie in the world."

"It is a lie," said Motee and several others; "you have thousands of rupees which you have bullied poor Thugs out of; we could name a hundred instances in which you have taken money from us: how dare you deny it?"

"Look here," said I, "here is the roomal, and you know the use of it; say whether you will give the money or not."

"I will give it," said he; "I will swear on the pickaxe to do so, and do you come with me and take it."

"Ay, said I, "and be taken too ourselves! No, no, friend Bhutteara, do not try to throw dust on our beards after that fashion. Inshalla! the people who could catch you have sharper wits than you seemed to give them credit for. No, man, I was but joking with thee—where is all thy wealth concealed?"

"You may kill me if you will," said he, "but I give no answer to that question."

"Ah, well," cried I, "you may think better of it when you are choking. Now you two hold him fast, and take the bag off his shoulders."

They did so. I threw the roomal about his neck, and tightened it till he was almost choked. He made several attempts to speak, and at last I relaxed my hold a little; but he could not utter a word—fear of death had paralysed his powers of utterance.

"Give him some water," said I, "it will wash down his fright."

---

1   My sir! My sir!

He took it, and fell at my feet, and implored me to spare him. I spurned and kicked him.

"Where is the treasure?" I said. "You have felt the tightening of the roomal once, beware how you risk it again. Where is the treasure?"

"Promise to let me live, and I will tell," cried the bhutteara, trembling in every limb.

"I will promise," said I, "you shall remain here, and I will send people to bring it. You well know we have no time for delay, and if you trifle with us you know the result—you have already half felt it."

"Where is Motee-ram? He knows the spot."

"Liar! I know it not," cried Motee, stepping forward: "Do you wish to make me out to be a participator in your base gains?"

"You know the spot," continued the bhutteara, "but you do not know that there is aught there. You remember the old hollow mango-tree on the other side of the town, where you left the last share I got from Ganesha?"

"I do."

"Well, then, you must dig in the hollow of the trunk; about a cubit deep you will find all I have—gold, silver, and ornaments."

"Now, said I, "villain, I have kept my word, you *shall* remain here; the grave is dug which shall hold thee, and has been ready for hours. I swore that I would spit on thy beard before morning; and Bhowanee, whose votaries thou hast bullied and threatened, has delivered thee into my hands." And I spat on him; all the men who were near me did the same.

"Again," cried I, "hold him fast, and bring the tobacco." He knew the fatal "jhirnee,"[1] and struggled to be free; but he was a child in the power of those who held him—in an instant more he was dead!

"Off with you, Motee!" cried I; "take ten men and go to the spot he mentioned: he may have told the truth, and we shall be the richer for it; then will many a man cry Wah! Wah![2] when he hears of this deed."

The body was taken away and buried, the grave was smoothed over and beaten down, the place plastered over, some fireplaces made and fires lighted to blacken them, and our work was concealed.

---

1 Signal for murder.
2 Bravo! Bravo!

Now did not that villain deserve his fate, sahib? To my perception, his cold-blooded work was far worse than our legitimate proceedings; and as for his treachery, he paid the forfeit of it.

It was a fearful revenge, said I; but you spoilt the justice of it by your vile love of plunder. Why should you have promised him his life, and then have murdered him? that was base.

I did not promise it to him: I said he should remain where he was, and he did remain—ay, he is there now.

It was a nice distinction certainly, Ameer Ali, and only shows the more how little you are to be trusted. But how did you get on afterwards? had he told the truth about his money?

He had, replied the Thug. Long before morning Motee returned, and rousing me, poured at my feet a heap of gold and silver coins, necklaces, armlets, bracelets, and anklets. They were worth nearly three thousand rupees, and not one article of them was there but had been given him by Thugs. Motee, Peer Khan, and others recognised most of the property. We melted all the ornaments, and divided the whole at our next stage, and it was a good booty, and enriched us for a long time; indeed I may say it lasted till our return home.

And the sahoukar, I asked, was the news true about him?

Oh, quite true, said Ameer Ali; I will tell you of him. We left Saugor early, and at a short distance on the road sat down to eat the goor, as is usual with us after any adventure. While we were thus employed, one of the scouts came up, and told us the joyful news that the sahoukar had left the town, and was close behind us, and that the other, whose name was Bhikaree, had taken service with him as far as Jubbulpoor as attendant, to watch at night while the sahoukar slept.

"And how does he travel?" I asked.

"He is on a tattoo,[1] a good strong beast," said the scout, "and has two others laden with him, and there are four men besides himself and Bhikaree."

"Good," said I. "Now, my lads, we must push on; the sahoukar must see nothing of us for some days, and till then I shall avoid all others."

We hastened on, and got to the end of our stage. Three days we travelled quietly, and from time to time observed the omens; they were all favourable, and cheered us on. On the fourth, as if by accident, we contrived to fall in with the sahoukar and his people; our faithful Bhikaree we rejoiced to see in his train. It was in the road that we met with him, or rather allowed him to overtake us, and the usual

---

1 Pony.

salutations passed. I was well dressed and well mounted, and looked a soldier. He inquired our destination and business, to which the old story was answered, and we proceeded merrily along. The sahoukar was a fat, jolly fellow, and witty in his way, and stories were interchanged, and we all laughed heartily at his jokes. It is astonishing, sahib, how soon these trifles engender good will and friendship among travellers: the loneliness of the road and the weariness of the stage are forgotten in such pleasant conversation; and before we had reached the end of the stage we were as great friends as though we had travelled together for months, or known each other for years. A kind farewell was interchanged as we parted at the village; he to put up inside it in the bazar, and we to our old plan of encampment.

"To-morrow," said I to the assembled men, "is a good day, it is Friday: we must finish this business." All were agreed upon it; and at midnight the bélhas and lughaees went on, the former to choose a spot for the affair, and the latter to dig the grave.

At daylight, a man (our Bhikaree it was), came to say the sahoukar would wait for us at the other side of the village, and begged we would be quick, as he liked our company, and wished for the safety of our escort.

"I have been frightening him a little," continued he, "and in truth he has been in alarm ever since he left Saugor, for he had heard of the disappearance of some parties on the road last year; so when we met you yesterday he was highly delighted, and afterwards spoke warmly of you, Jemadar Sahib, and said he could feel no fear in your society."

"Well done," cried I; "thou hast played thy part well, and it shall not be forgotten. But, my friends, the sahoukar waits, and we had better be moving; do you all surround his party as you did yesterday; ply them with tales and stories, and keep their minds quiet."

"Jey Bhowanee! Jey Ameer Ali!"[1] was the shout of the party as we quitted the ground and took our way to the spot where the sahoukar awaited us.

---

1   Victory to Bhowanee! Victory to Ameer Ali!

Chapter XXVIII

Catesby.—'Tis a vile thing to die, my gracious lord, When men are unprepared and look not for it.

—Richard III. Act iii., Sc. 2.

"RAM![1] Ram! Meer Sahib," was the salutation of the sahoukar as we met at the spot whither Bhikaree had guided us. "Ram! Ram! I am glad you have condescended to keep company with your poor servant, for truly the sweet savour of your fluent discourse has left a longing in my heart to hear more of it, and happily I am so far favoured."

I returned the usual compliments, and we set forward on our journey. Gradually my band arranged themselves around their new victims. All were at their places, and I eagerly looked out for the first scout who should give us intelligence that the bhil was ready. A strange feeling it is, sahib, that comes over us Thugs at such moments: not a feeling of interest or pity for our victim, or compunction for the deed we are about to do, as perhaps you might expect to hear, but an all-absorbing anxiety for the issue of the adventure, an intense longing for its consummation, and a dread of interruption from passing travellers; and though I had become now callous in a great measure, still my heart was throbbing with anxiety and apprehension, and my replies to the sahoukar's witty and jolly remarks were vague and abstracted; my whole thoughts were concentrated upon the affair in hand, and it was not be wondered at. He remarked my altered behaviour, and I rallied myself, and was soon able to amuse him as I had done before.

"Ah! that is like yourself, Meer Sahib," said he, as I had just given utterance to a joke which caused his fat sides to shake,—"that is like yourself. Why, man, whose face did your first glance on awaking from sleep rest on? Surely on some melancholy being, and you have partaken of his thoughts ever since."

"I know not, Séthjee," I replied; "but you know that a man cannot always command the same evenness of temper, and I confess that my thoughts were far away, at my home."

---

1   Hindu deity.

"Well," said he, "all I wish for you and myself is, a safe return to our homes; for this travelling is poor work, and I have been unlucky enough to start on a very indifferent day after all my waiting. I had determined on leaving Saugor nearly a month ago, but on consulting the astrologer, he delayed me from time to time, declaring this day was bad and that day was worse, until I could stay no longer; and it was all to little purpose, and I pray Narayun to protect me from all Thugs, thieves, and dacoos."[1]

"Ameen," said I; "I respond to your prayer most fervently, for I am on my way to my service, where we chance often to get harder knocks than we can bear. But do they say there are Thugs on the road? and who or what are they? the term is new to me."

"Why truly I can hardly tell you, Meer Sahib. The Thugs, they say, are people who feign one thing or other, till they get unwary travellers into their power, and then destroy them. I have heard, too, that they have handsome women with them, who pretend distress on the roads, and decoy travellers who may have soft hearts to help them; then they fasten on them, and they have some charm from the Shitan which enables them to keep their hold till their associates come up, despite of all efforts of the person so ensnared to gain his liberty. And that either thieves, or Thugs, or rascals of some kind or other do infest the highways is most true, for many travellers disappear in an unaccountable manner. But I do not fear; I am in the company of honest men, and we are a large party, and they must be stout men or devils who would assail us."

I laughed inwardly at the sahoukar's idea of Thugs, and had no doubt that Ganesha Jemadar was, if the truth were known, at the bottom of the disappearance of the travellers. But I answered gaily, "Ah! no fear, my friend. These Thugs, as you say, may now and then light upon an unsuspecting single traveller and kill him, but no one would dare to touch a party like ours; and, Inshalla! if any appear, we will let daylight into some of their skins: there is nothing I love better than making keema (mincemeat) of these rascals. I have done so once or twice already, and I never found them stand when a sword was drawn. But yonder, I see, is one of my men sitting; I wonder how he got on before us. I will ask him. He must have started early to get a rest on the road;" and as we reached him he slowly raised himself from the ground, and made his salutation to me and the sahoukar; he appeared tired, and acted his part well.

---

1   Gang robbers.

"How is this, Ameer Singh?" said I, "how is it that you are so much in advance of us?"

"Oh," replied he readily, "a thorn ran into my foot yesterday, and as I knew you would not wait for me, I started at midnight with a few others, who said they would be my companions, and we travelled on leisurely; but I could not proceed farther, as my foot was painful, and I determined to wait for the party here to get a lift on a pony."

"You shall have it," said I. "Mount the one which carries my baggage, and I will see that a barber examines your foot when we reach the end of the stage. But where are your companions?"

"They said there was a small river in advance, about half a coss off, and they would proceed thither and wash their hands and faces; they bade me tell you that, if I could not follow them, you would find them there."

"Good," said I, "and I am glad to hear there is water near; we can dismount and refresh ourselves, for the stage is a long one. How say you, Séth Sahib? you Hindoos are as particular about your morning ablutions as we Moslems are."

"True, true," he replied; "the news is welcome, for my mouth is dry, and I have not as yet washed it; we will stop for a short time. Besides, my stomach is empty, and I have sweetmeats with me which I will share with you, Meer Sahib; it is ill travelling without something in the inside."

"A good thought," I replied, "and I shall be glad of them; I usually bring some myself, but have neglected to do so in this instance."

The scout was right, the rivulet he mentioned was scarcely as far as he had said, and we reached it after a few minutes' riding; and, sure enough, there were my men sitting unconcernedly by the edge of the water, busily discussing a hasty meal of some cakes they had brought with them.

"Bhill manjeh, have you cleared the hole?" I eagerly inquired of the bélha.

"Manjeh,"[1] he replied.

"What did you ask?" said the sahoukar; "if they have not a clean vessel for you to drink out of, you can have one of mine."

"Thanks for your kindness," I replied, "but my good fellow here tells me that he has brought one, and cleaned it ready for me."

We all dismounted; the men rushed into the water, and were each and all busily employed in washing their mouths and teeth, and drinking of the pure element

---

1   It is cleared.

which murmured over its pebbly bed beneath their feet; but none of them quitted their stations, and only awaited the signal to do their work.

"Is the bhil far distant?" I asked of the bélha who presented me with a lota[1] of water for the purposes of ablution.

"About an arrow's flight," said he, "down yonder in that thicket. It is a good place, and a well-known one; it was on this spot that Ganesha Jemadar had a rare bunij last year. But do not delay, for the sun is high, and travellers may be coming from the stage before us; this is the only running water on the road, and all hasten to it to refresh themselves."

"Then I am ready," said I; "and when you see me close to the sahoukar, I will give the signal; I see the men are all prepared." And I walked towards him.

"Why don't you give the *jhirnee*," said Motee-ram to me as I passed him, "we are all waiting for it."

"Now," said I, "be ready; I go to my station."

The fellow, near whom he was standing, turned round, hearing us converse in a strange language; but he immediately afterwards sat down and resumed the operation of cleaning his teeth with great assiduity: there were two men behind him who would shortly save him the trouble.

"Why, Séthjee," said I, "I wonder you do not go up higher; here you have the water muddied by all the fellows above you. Come with me, and I will show you a deep place where I have just washed, and where the water is clear."

"Ah, I did not think of it," said he; "I will follow you." He had been washing low down, and as I got him into the middle of the party I gave the *jhirnee*.

Sahib, though I had not killed a man with the roomal for nearly four years, I had not forgotten my old trick; he was dead, I think, ere he reached my feet.

Stupid it was in us to delay, and I prevented the like in future. Every man resumed his employment of washing himself as though nothing had happened, and there lay the bodies on the sand. We were once again fated to be interrupted. Two travellers were seen approaching, and the bodies were hastily covered with sheets, as if those who lay beneath them were asleep; and I cried to the men for some of them to sit and others lie down, and all to feign great weariness. They did so, and the men came up; they were poor creatures hardly worth killing, and I proposed to Peer Khan to let them go, but he would not hear of it.

"Let them go!" he cried; "are you mad? Do you not think that these fellows already suspect who we are? Does a man ever come into the presence of the dead, be

---

1 Vessel.

they ever so well covered or disguised, without a feeling that they are dead? And, see, some of our men are speaking to them; they are true bunij, and Dévee has sent them."

"As you will," said I, "but there may be more of them."

"Hardly so soon," replied he; "these fellows must have left in the night to be here so early; but come, let us ask them." And we walked up to them.

"Salam!" said I, "where are you from so early? You have travelled fast if you have come from the stage we hope to reach in the course of the day; how far is it?"

"It is seven long coss," said the man, "and the sun will be high and hot before you reach it; but we are in haste and must proceed."

"Stay," said I," dare not to move till you are allowed; and tell me, how many travellers put up last night in the village from whence you have come?"

"Two besides ourselves," replied the other of the two, evidently in alarm at my question. "Why do you ask?"

"Are you sure there were no more?"

"Certain," he replied; "we travelled together from Jubbulpoor, and put up in the same house."

"And how far are they behind you?"

"They will be here immediately, I should think, for we started at the same time but have outstripped them."

"Good," said I; "now sit down there and wait till they come."

"Why is this?" cried both; "by what right do you detain travellers? We will go on."

"Dare to stir at your peril," said I; "you have intruded on us, and must pay the penalty."

"What penalty? Are you thieves? if so, take what you will from us and let us go."

"We are not thieves," said Peer Khan; "but stay quiet, we are worse."

"Worse! then, brother, we are lost," cried one to the other; "these villains are Thugs; it is even as I whispered to you when you must needs stop among them: they have been at their horrid work, and yonder lie those whom they have destroyed."

"Yes," said I, "unhappy men, you have guessed right; yonder lie the dead, and you will soon be numbered with them; it is useless to strive against your destiny."

I turned away, for I felt, sahib—I felt sick at the thought of destroying these inoffensive people. They might have passed on; but Peer Khan was right, they had detected the dead, though the bodies had been laid out and covered as if the senseless forms were sleeping—but they lay like lumps of clay. No measured breathing disturbed the folds of the sheets which covered them, and a glance had been sufficient to tell the tale to the unfortunate people who had seen them. But I shook off the feeling as best I could; had I given way to it, or betrayed its existence to my associates, the power I possessed over them would have been lost—and it was the spirit of my existence.

"They must die," said I to Peer Khan; "you were right, and they had guessed the truth; but I wish it had been otherwise, and the lazy lughaees had done their work quickly; they might have passed on, and we have had a good morning's work without them; they are not worth having."

"I would not exchange places with them for anything you could name, Meer Sahib, and perhaps it were well to put them out of their suspense."

"Do so, Peer Khan, and get the rest with them removed; I will deal with one of the other two coming up. These fellows are half dead already with fear, and the others I will fall on in my own way; I hate such passive victims as these will be."

Peer Khan and another went to the miserable wretches, who remained sitting on the ground where we had left them. I watched them; they stood up mechanically when they were ordered to do so, and stretched out their necks for the fatal roomal, and were slain as unresistingly as sheep beneath the knife of the butcher. The rest of the travellers were not long coming, and were only two, as the others had said.

"Now," said I to Motee, "these fellows must be dealt with at once: you take one, I will the other; they must not utter a word."

"I am ready," said he; and we arose and lounged about the road.

The travellers came up. One was a young and the other an old man. I marked the young one, and as he passed me a Thug laid hold of his arm; he turned round to resent it, and I was ready. These two were carried away, and after collecting our dispersed party, we once more pursued our route without interruption.

It had been a good morning's work, the sahoukar was as rich as the bhutteara had said, and four thousand three hundred rupees greeted our expectant eyes as the contents of the laden ponies were examined; besides these there were six handsome shawls, worth better than a thousand more, and a few pieces of cotton cloth, which were torn up and immediately distributed. The other four travellers had upwards of a hundred rupees, a sum not to be despised, and which I divided equally among the band, reserving the large booty, and adding it to the sum we had already gained.

Chapter XXIX

IN WHICH IT IS CLEARLY SHOWN HOW HARD IT IS TO STOP
WHEN THE DEVIL DRIVES

WE reached Jubbulpoor without another adventure of any kind, and rested there for two days. Peer Khan, Motee, and myself perambulated the bazars during the whole time, but not a traveller could we meet with, nor could we learn that any were expected. It was therefore of no use to remain, and as we had still plenty of time before us, we could travel as leisurely as we pleased; so on the third morning we again proceeded.

The country between Jubbulpoor and Nagpoor is a wild waste. Villages are not met with for miles and miles, the road is stony and uneven, and the jungle thick and dangerous for nearly the whole way. On this account the tract has always been a favourite resort of Thugs; and more affairs have come off in those few marches than perhaps in any other part of the country frequented by us. We were all regretting that we had not met with some bunij at Jubbulpoor, wherewith to beguile the weariness of the road, when, at our second stage, soon after we had arrived, Motee, who had gone to look out for work for us, returned with the glad news that there was a palankeen at the door of a merchant's shop, surrounded by bearers and a few soldiers, which looked very much as if it belonged to a traveller.

"But he must be of rank," said Motee, "therefore I humbly suggest that you, Meer Sahib, should undertake to see who he is, and to secure him if possible."

I followed his advice, and changing my travelling attire for a dress which would ensure my civil reception, I armed myself and attended by a Thug who carried my hooka, I sauntered into the village. I soon saw the palankeen and men about it, and in order to gain some intelligence to guide me, I went to a small tumbólee's shop directly opposite to it, and sitting down entered into conversation with the vendor of tobacco and pan.

"This is a wild country you live in, my friend," said I.

"Yes, it is indeed as you say," he replied; "and were it not for you travellers, a poor man would have little chance of filling his belly by selling pān and tobacco; but, as it is, my trade thrives well."

"There do not seem to be many on the road," said I; "I have come from Jubbulpoor without meeting a soul."

"Why, the roads are hardly much frequented yet," he rejoined, "but in a month more there will be hundreds; and there," he continued, pointing to the house over the way, "there is almost the only one I have seen for some time."

"Who is it?" I asked, "and where has he come from? he was not with us."

"I know not," replied the tumbólee, "nor do I care; whoever he is, he has bought a quantity of my stuff, and it was the first silver which crossed my hand this morning."

I saw there was nothing to be got out of this man, so I went to a bunnea¹ a little farther off, and after a few preparatory and indifferent questions asked him whether he knew aught of the traveller; but he knew nothing either, except that a slave girl had bought some flour of him. "They say," said he, "that it is a gentleman of rank who is travelling privately, and does not wish to be known; at any rate, sahib, I know nothing about him; I suppose, however, he will come out in a short time."

This is very strange, thought I. Here is a gay palankeen, eight bearers and some soldiers with it, come into this wretched place, and yet no one's curiosity is aroused; who can it be? I will return to the tumbólee and sit awhile; I may see, though I cannot hear anything of this mysterious person.

I sat down in the shop, and calling to my attendant for my hooka remained there smoking in the hope that some one might appear from behind the cloths which were stretched across the verandah. Nor did I stay long in vain; I saw them gently move once or twice, and thought I could perceive the sparkle of a brilliant eye directed to me. I riveted my gaze on the envious purdah,² and after a long interval it was quickly opened, and afforded me a transient view of a face radiant with beauty; but it was as instantly closed again, and I was left in vain to conjecture as to the beautiful but mysterious person who had thus partially discovered herself to me. It would not have suited my purpose to have personally interrogated any of the bearers who were lying and sitting about the palankeen, as it would have rendered them suspicious, and would have been impertinent: after all, it was only a woman,—what had I to do with women now? And had I not made an inward resolution never to seek them as bunij; nay, even to avoid parties in which there might be any?

So I arose, and took my way to our camp, firmly resolving that I would pursue my march the next morning; for, thought I, she must be some lady of rank travelling to her lord, and Alla forbid that I should raise a hand against one so defenceless and

----

1 Huckster.
2 Screen.

unprotected! and I thought of my own lovely Azeema, and shuddered at the idea of her ever being placed within reach of other members of my profession, who might not be so scrupulous as I was.

But, sahib, the resolves of men,—what are they? Passing thoughts, which fain would excite the mind to good, only to be driven away by the wild and overpowering influences of passion. Despite of my resolve, my mind was unquiet, and a thousand times fancy brought to my view the look she had cast on me, and whispered that it was one of love. I could not shake it off, and sought in the conversation of my associates wherewith to drive her from my thoughts; but it was in vain: that passionate glance was before me, and the beauteous eyes which threw it seemed to ask for another, a nearer and more loving.

In this state I passed the day, now determining that I would resist the temptation which was gnawing at my heart, and now almost on the point of once more proceeding to the village and seeking out the unknown object of my disquietude; and I was irresolute, when towards evening I saw a slave girl making towards the camp, and I went to meet her, but not with the intention of speaking to her should she prove to be only a village girl. We met and I passed her, but I saw instantly that she was in search of some one, for she turned round hesitatingly and spoke to me.

"Forgive my boldness, sahib," said she, "but I am in search of some one, and your appearance tells me that it must be you."

"Speak," said I; "if I can aid you in anything, command me."

"I know not," she replied, "whether you are he or not; but tell me, did you sit at the tumbólee's shop this morning for some time, smoking a hooka?"

"I did, my pretty maiden," said I; "and what of that? there is nothing so unusual in it as to attract attention."

"Ah, no!" said the girl archly; "but one saw you who wishes to see you again, and if you will now follow me I will guide you."

"And who may this person be?" I asked, "and what can be his or her business with a traveller?"

"Your first question I may not answer," said the girl; "and as to the second I am ignorant; but, by your soul, follow me, for the matter is urgent, and I have most express commands to bring you if I possibly can."

"I follow you," said I; "lead on."

"Then keep behind me at some distance," she said, "and when you see me enter into the house step boldly in after me, as if you were the master."

I followed her. But ah! sahib, observe the power of destiny. I might have sat in my tent and denied myself to the girl, who, something told me, had come to seek me when I first saw her approach. I might, when I did advance to meet her, have passed on indifferently, and even when she spoke to me I might have denied that I was the person she was sent after, or I might have refused to accompany her; but destiny impelled me on, nay, it led me by the nose after a slave-girl, to plunge into an adventure I fain would have avoided, and which my heart told me must end miserably. Sahib, there is no opposing fate; by the meanest ends it works out the greatest deeds, and we are its slaves, body and soul, blindly to do as its will works! I say not Thugs only, but the whole human race. Is it not so?

It appears to me, Ameer Ali, said I, that poor Destiny has the blame whenever your own wicked hearts fixed themselves on any object and you followed their suggestions.

Nay, but I would have avoided this, cried the Thug, and have I not told you so? Alla knows I would not have entered into this matter; but what could I do? what were my weak resolves compared with His will? and yet you will not believe me. Sahib, I do not tell a lie.

I dare say not, said I; but the beautiful eyes were too much for you; so go on with your story.

The Thug laughed. They were indeed, said he, and accursed be the hour in which I saw them. But I will proceed.

The slave preceded me; at some distance I followed her through the village and its bazars, and saw her enter the house before which I had sat in the morning. I too entered it, leaving my slippers at the door, and with the confident air of a man who goes into his own house. I had just passed the threshold when the slave stopped me.

"Wait a moment," said she. "I go to announce you;" and she pulled aside the temporary screen and went in.

In a few moments she returned and bade me follow her. I obeyed her, and in the next instant was in the presence of the unknown, who was hidden from my sight by an envious sheet, which covered the whole of her person, and her face was turned away from me towards the wall.

"Lady," said I, "your slave is come, and aught that he can do for one so lovely he will perform to the utmost of his power. Speak! your commands are on my head and eyes."

"Be seated," she said in a low timid voice, "I have somewhat to ask thee."

I obeyed, and seated myself at a respectful distance from her on the carpet.

"You will think me bold and shameless, I fear, stranger," said she, "for thus admitting you to my presence, nay, even to my chamber; but, alas! I am a widow, and need the protection you are able perhaps to afford me. Which way do you travel?"

"Towards Nagpoor," I replied; "I purpose leaving this miserable place early tomorrow, and I have come from Jubbulpoor."

"From whence I have also come," she said, "and I am going too to Nagpoor. Ah, my destiny is good which has sent me one who will protect the lonely and friendless widow!"

"It is strange, lady," said I, "that we did not meet before, having come the same road."

"No," she replied, "it is not, since I was behind you. I heard you were before me, and I travelled fast to overtake you. We have now met, and as I must proceed the remainder of my journey alone, I implore you to allow me for the stage to join your party, with which, as I hear it is a large one, I shall be safe, and free from anxiety."

"Your wish is granted, lady," I said; "and any protection against the dangers of the way which your poor slave can afford shall be cheerfully given. I will send a man early to awaken you, and promise that I will not leave the village without you."

She salamed to me gracefully, and in doing so the sheet, as if by accident, partly fell from her face, and disclosed again to my enraptured view the features I had beheld from a distance. Sahib, the shock was overpowering, and every nerve of my body tingled. Only that a sense of decency restrained me, I had risen and thrown myself at her feet; but while a blush, as though of shame, mantled over her countenance, and she hastily withdrew the glance she had for an instant fixed on me, she replaced the sheet and again turned to the wall, bending her head towards the ground.

I thought it had been purely accidental, and the action at the time convinced me that she was really what she represented herself to be; and fearing that my longer presence would not be agreeable nor decent, I asked her if she had any further commands and for permission to depart.

"No," said she, "I have no further favour to beg, save to know the name of him to whom I am indebted for this act of kindness."

"My name is Ameer Ali," said I; "a poor syud of Hindostan."

"Your fluent speech assured me you were of that noble race; I could not be mistaken,—'tis seldom one hears it. Fazil! bring the pān and utr."[1]

She did so; and after taking the complimentary gift of dismissal, and anointing my breast and beard with the fragrant utr, I rose and made my obeisance. She

---

1 Attar; fragrant oil made from rose petals.

saluted me in return, and again bade me not forget my promise. I assured her that she might depend upon me, and departed.

She must be what she says, thought I; the very act of presenting pān and utr to me proves her rank; no common person, no courtesan would have thought of it. I shall only have to bear a little jeering from Motee and Peer Khan, which I will resist and laugh away; and this poor widow will reach Nagpoor in safety, without knowing that she has been in the hands of murderers. But I said nothing that night to any of them. In reply to their numerous questions as to the fortune I had met with in the village, and whether I had discovered the unknown, I only laughed, and said I believed it was some dancing-girl, for I knew the mention of one would turn their minds from the thoughts of bunij, as it is forbidden to kill those persons by the laws of our profession; and with my supposition they appeared satisfied.

Great, however, was their surprise when, in the morning, after having delayed our departure longer than usual, I joined the party of the lady outside the village, and they understood that we were to travel in company.

I was overpowered by jokes and witticisms from Peer Khan and Motee, who declared I was a sly dog thus to secure the lady all to myself; and after protesting vehemently that I cared not about her, which only made them laugh the more, I became half angry.

"Look you, my friends," said I, "this is a matter which has been in a manner forced upon me. Who the lady is I know not. She has begged of me to allow her to accompany us, as she supposes us to be travellers, and I have permitted it; and whether she be old or young, ugly or beautiful, I am alike ignorant. We may hereafter find out her history, but, whoever she be, she has my promise of safe escort, and she is not bunij. You remember my resolution, and you will see I can keep it."

"Nay," said Motee, "be not angry; if a friend is not privileged to crack a joke now and then, who, in Bhugwan's[1] name, is? And as for us, we are your servants, and bound to obey you by our oath; so you may have as many women in your train as you please, and not one shall be bunij."

So we pursued our road. Several times I could not resist riding up to the palankeen and making my noble horse curvet and prance beside it. The doors were at first closely shut, but one was gradually opened, and the same sparkling eyes threw me many a smiling and approving look, though the face was still hidden.

Alas! sahib, those eyes did me great mischief,—I could not withstand them.

---

1 God's.

About noon, when we had rested from our fatigue, and my men were dispersed in various directions, scarcely any of them remaining in the camp, the slave-girl again came for me, and I followed her to her mistress.

We sat a long time in silence, and the lady was muffled up as I had before seen her. Despite of all my conflicting feelings, I own, sahib, that in her presence my home was forgotten, and my burning desire was fixed upon the veiled being before me, of whose countenance I was even still ignorant.

She spake at last, but it was to the slave.

"Go," said she, "and wait without, far out of hearing; I have that to say to this gentleman which must not enter even your ears, my Fazil."

She departed, and I was alone with the other, and again there was a long, and to me a painful, silence.

"Meer Sahib," she said at length, "what will you think of me? what will you think of one who thus exposes herself to the gaze of a man and a stranger? But it matters not now; it has been done, and it is idle to think on the past. I am the widow of a Nuwab, whose estate is near Agra;[1] he died a short time ago at Nagpoor, on his way from Hyderabad, whither he had gone to see his brother, and I was left friendless, but not destitute. He had abundance of wealth with him, and I was thus enabled to live at Nagpoor, after sending news of his death to my estate, in comfort and affluence. The messengers I sent at length returned, and brought me the welcome news that there was no one to dispute my right to my husband's property; and that my own family, which is as noble and as powerful as his was, had taken possession of the estate and held it on my account; and they wrote to me to return as quickly as I could, and among the respectable men of the land choose a new husband, by whom I might have children to inherit the estate. I immediately set off on my return—ah! Ameer Ali, how can I tell the rest! my tongue from shame cleaves to the roof of my mouth, and my lips refuse utterance to the words which are at my heart."

"Speak, lady," said I, "by your soul, speak! I burn with impatience, and you have excited my curiosity now too powerfully for it to rest unsatisfied."

"Then I must speak," she said, "though I die of shame in the effort. I heard at the last village that you had arrived; I say you, because my faithful slave, who finds out everything, came shortly after your arrival and told me that she had seen the most beautiful cavalier her thoughts had ever pictured to her. She recounted your noble air, the beauty of your person, the grace with which you managed your fiery steed, and, above all, the sweet and amiable expression of your countenance. The account

---

1   City in north India and location of the Taj Mahal.

inflamed me. I had married an old man, who was jealous of my person, and who never allowed me to see any one but my poor slave; but I had heard of manly beauty, and I longed for the time when his death should free me from this hated thraldom. Long I deliberated between the uncontrollable desire which possessed me and a sense of shame and womanly dignity; and perhaps the latter might have conquered, but you came and sat opposite to the hovel in which I was resting; my slave told me you were there, and I looked. Alla! Alla ! once my eyes had fixed themselves on you, I could not withdraw them; and as the hole through which I gazed did not afford me a full view of your person, I partially opened the curtain and feasted my soul with your appearance. You went away, and I fell back on my carpet in despair. My slave at last restored me to consciousness, but I raved about you; and fearful that my senses would leave me, she went and brought you. When you entered, how I longed to throw myself at your feet! but shame prevailed, and, after a commonplace conversation, though my soul was on fire and my liver had turned into water, I suffered you to depart. I told my people that I must return to Nagpoor, as I had forgotten to redeem some jewels I had left in pledge, which were valuable; and they believed me. Ameer Ali!" cried she, suddenly throwing off her veil and casting herself at my feet, while she buried her head in my lap, "Ameer Ali! this is my tale of shame—I love you! Alla only knows how my soul burns for you! I will be your slave for ever; whither you go, thither will I follow; whoever you are, and whatever you are, I am yours, and yours only; but I shall die without you. Alas! why did you come to me?"

CHAPTER XXX

Yet she must die, or she'll betray more men.
—*Othello.*[1]

AND where now were all my resolutions? By Alla! sahib, I had forgotten all—home, wife, children; I thought not of them, but I drank deeply of love, wild, passionate, burning love, from her eyes, and I caressed her as though she were mine own. There we sat, and though guilt was in my soul, and it accused me of infidelity to my oft-repeated vows, I could not tear myself away from her, and I suffered her caresses in return, though they often struck to my heart like the blows of a sharp knife. Hours passed thus—I thought not of them; she seated at my feet, and I with my hands entwined in her long silken hair, and gazing at her face, of such loveliness, that never had my wildest dreams pictured anything like it. Zora was beautiful, Azeema was even more so, but Shurfun surpassed them both in as great a degree as they excelled any of their sex I had ever seen. Fain would she have had me stay with her; fain would she, the temptress, have then and there separated me from my band, and led me with herself, whither she cared not, so I was with her and she with me. Wealth, she said, she had in abundance, and we could fly to some undiscoverable spot, where we should pass years of bliss together, and where she would, by communication with her family, procure such money from time to time as would enable us to live in affluence.

"Ameer Ali," said she, "you are young, you are unknown, you have to fight your way to fame upon a bare pittance, and for this will you risk your precious life, when I offer you everything I possess, and swear that I am your slave? Ah, you will not, you cannot now leave me to perish in despair, and die of unrequited love! Speak, my soul, you will not leave me?"

Wretch, and perjured that I was, I swore to obey her wishes. Sahib, it was a sore temptation, and it overcame me.

At last I tore myself away from her, but not till I had sworn by her head and eyes to return the following day, when being more calm we might arrange our plans for the future.

---

1 Othello's exact words are: "Yet she must die, else she'll betray more men" (V.ii.6).

I returned to my little tent, and there, in the agony of my soul, I rolled on the ground. I raved, I refused to eat, and was as one bereft of sense; I spoke rudely to Peer Khan, who having been called by my attendant came to comfort me; and I was almost on the point of driving my dagger to my heart to end a life which, though a splendid prospect was open to it, could never afterwards be aught than one of guilty misery. But the passion reached its height; and as a thunder-cloud, which after a burst of internal commotion, after its deep peal has gone forth and it has ejected the lightning from its bosom, gradually pours its pent-up flood of waters to soothe and refresh the earth, so did mine eyes now rain tears, and they calmed me. I can now ask and take advice, thought I, and Peer Khan, who is fondly attached to me, will give it as he would to a brother.

I sent for him, and after apologising for my rudeness, said he would find the cause of it in the relation I would give of the last few hours. I told him all, and awaited his answer. My heart was relieved of a load of oppressive thought, and I was the better for it.

He pondered long ere he spoke; at last he said,—

"Meer Sahib, this is a difficult business indeed, and I hardly know what to advise; go to her to-morrow; be a man, and give not way to this boyish passion, which ill suits you; try to persuade her that you cannot do as she wishes; speak to her kindly yet firmly of her home, of her relatives, and of the guilt which must cleave to you both from the connection she proposes. Tell her you have a wife and two children, and if she is a true woman she will be fired with jealousy, and will quarrel with you; do you then become irritated in your turn, and leave her to go her own way, and find some one who may not be so scrupulous, and may take advantage of her blind passions. And if all this fail, if no words of yours can drive these foolish ideas from her brain, we have only to make a long march in some unknown direction and at once be quit of her. I know the paths through the jungles, and by them, difficult as they are, we can easily reach Berar, where she will never again hear of us."

I thanked him cordially for his advice; and that part of it which related to Azeema and my children struck forcibly on my heart. I was as yet, thanks to the protection of the Prophet, pure, and by his aid I would remain so. I determined I would urge my previous ties to her so forcibly, and I would depict my love for my wife in such colours, that she should at once reject me.

Full of these resolutions I once more obeyed her summons, sent me by her slave, and followed the girl, and as we had made a long march, of twelve coss, it was now late in the day. I need not again tell you, sahib, of all her love for me, which she now poured forth without check or reserve. She had fairly cast away all shame, and would hear of nothing I could represent as to the consequences of our connection with her family. I had only now one resource, and as a man in alarm for his life fires the train of a mine, so did I, hurriedly and perhaps incoherently, mention my wife and children. The effect was, as Peer Khan had expected, instantaneous. She had been sitting at my feet, listening to my objections, and playfully reasoning with me against them; but, at these words, she suddenly started to her feet, and drew her noble figure up to its full height, while her eyes flashed, as she smoothed back her flowing hair from her brow; the veins of her forehead and neck swelled, and she was terrible to look on. I confess I quailed beneath the glances of scorn she cast on me.

"Man!" she cried at length, "ah, vile and faithless wretch, say, did I hear thee aright? Dare to say again that thou hast a wife and children! What dirt hast thou eaten?"

It was my time, and my good resolutions came to my aid; I rose, and confronted her with a look as proud and unflinching as her own.

"Yes, Shurfun," I said, "I have spoken the truth; one as beautiful as thou art believes me faithful, and faithful I will remain to her; long I reasoned with thee, and hadst thou not been carried away, and thy good feelings deadened, by an idle and sudden passion, thou hadst heard my words, and submitted to them, for the sake of thy family and hitherto untarnished honour. For my unfortunate share in this matter, may Alla forgive me! Lady, it was thy maddening beauty which caused me to err; but He has strengthened my heart, and again I implore thee to hear the words of friendship, and be thyself again."

How can I tell you, sahib, of her despair, and the bitterness of her expressions, as she upbraided me with my deceit? I deserved them all, and not a word did I answer in return. I could not, and I dared not approach her, lest my heart should again yield to her blandishments, for I felt that a kind word or action would renew them, and cause her to forget the past; and it was pitiable to see her as she now sat on the ground, moaning and rocking herself to and fro, while at intervals she tore her hair and beat her breasts in her agony of spirit.

"Leave me!" she said at last. "Ah, Ameer Ali, thou hast broken a heart which could have loved thee for ever. I do not complain; it is the will of Alla that the only man I could ever have loved and honoured should deceive me, and I submit. Shurfun is not yet reduced so low that she could put up with the second place in any man's heart, were he the monarch of Dehli itself. Go! the sight of you is painful to my soul; and may Alla forgive us both!"

I left her. I hastened to Peer Khan, and related the whole to him, and he was delighted.

"Now," said he, "to make the matter sure, let us retrace our steps; it is not attended with any risk, for we can put up anywhere, and we need not visit the village we before halted at; we have no hope of booty at Nagpoor, and if you like we can penetrate, as I said before, into Berar, and return by Khândésh which was our original idea."

"I agree," said I; "this woman must be avoided at every risk. To save appearances she must go on to Nagpoor with her people, and we shall, by following your advice, avoid her altogether."

Accordingly, the next morning, instead of pursuing the road we had taken, we turned back, and after a few hours' travel halted at a small village, a few coss distant from the one we had left. But little had I calculated on that woman's love and wild passions. Before the day was half spent, we saw her palankeen attended by her men, advancing towards the village by the way we had come. What was to be done? I was for instant flight into the wild jungles by which we were surrounded, and where she would soon have lost all traces of us. But Peer Khan and Motee would not hear of it.

"It would be cowardly," said they; "there is no occasion thus to run before a woman; and why should we expose ourselves to dangers from wild beasts and the unhealthiness of the forest on her account? And," added Motee, "if she follow us now, depend upon it it is not on your account, but because she is now determined to go to her home as quickly as possible."

"It may be so," said I; "whatever her plans may be they will not influence my determinations." Yet my mind misgave me that she would again follow us, and a short time proved that my suspicions were right. The slave came by stealth to my tent, disguised as a seller of milk, and I followed her, for I knew not why her mistress had sent for me, and why she now sought me after our last meeting.

I reached her presence, and again we were alone. I armed myself against her blandishments, and determined to oppose them with scorn, that she might again quarrel with me, and leave me for ever. I cannot relate to you, sahib, all that passed between us: at one time she was all love, seeking to throw herself into my arms, and beseeching me to have pity on her, for she felt that her reputation was gone, in words that would have moved a heart of stone; at another, violently upbraiding me for my perfidy, and bidding me begone from her sight; yet, each time as I turned to depart, she would prevent me, and again implore me to listen and agree to her proposals.

At last I could bear with her no longer. I was provoked with her importunities, and vexed at my own irresolute conduct. I bade her farewell, and was quitting the shed where she had put up for the day, when she screamed to me to come back. I returned.

"Shurfun," said I, "this is foolishness, and the conduct of children; why should we thus torment each other? You have heard my determination; and could you offer me the throne of Dehli, I might share it with you, but my heart would be hers who now possesses it, and you would live a torment to yourself and me. Jealousy even now possesses your heart and what would not that passion become when you were in intercourse with the object you even now hate, and whom you could not separate from me?"

"I care not for your words," said she; "I care not for the consequences: I have set my life and my fame on the issue of this,—and refuse me at your peril! As for your wife, I hate her not. Does not our law allow you four wives? Is it not so written in the blessed Koran? You cannot deny it. Even I, who am a woman, know it. I would love Azeema as a sister, and your children for your sake; and can you refuse wealth and a future life of distinction for them? O man, are you bereft of sense? See, I speak to you calmly, and reason with you as I would were I your sister."

"I would to Alla thou wert my sister," I said; "I could love thee fondly as a sister, but never, never can I consent to this unhallowed and disgraceful union. Yes, Shurfun, disgraceful! disguise it with all thy flattering and sweet words, yet it is disgraceful. Do you dream for a moment that your proud family would receive as your husband, as the sharer of your property and wealth, a man unknown to them, one who has no family honours, no worldly distinction to boast of, and with whom you have picked up a casual acquaintance on the road? I tell you they would not. Go, therefore, I beseech you, to your home, and in after years I will send my Azeema to see you, and she shall pray for blessings on the noble woman who preserved her husband to her."

She sat silent for some time; but the fire was not quenched within her; it burst forth with increased violence, when I vainly thought that my temperate words had quenched it for ever. Again she bade me go, but it was sullenly, and I left her.

I had not been an hour in my tent when the slave again came to me. But perhaps, sahib, you are tired of my minuteness in describing all my interviews with the Moghulnee?

No, said I, Ameer Ali; I suppose you have some object in it, therefore go on.

Well then, resumed the Thug, the slave came to me and I was alone.

"For the love of Alla," said she, "Meer Sahib, do something for my poor mistress! Ever since you left her she has been in a kind of stupor, and has hardly spoken. She just now told me to go and purchase a quantity of opium for her; and when I refused, and fell at her feet, imploring her to recall her words, she spoke angrily to me, and said if I did not go, she would go herself. So I have purchased it; but alas! I know its fatal use; and you alone can save her. Come quickly then, and speak a kind word to her. I have heard all that has passed, and you have behaved like a man of honour; but since you cannot persuade her to forget you and relinquish her intentions, at least for the time fall in with her humour, and agree to accompany her, on the promise that she will not seek to see you on the road; and say that when you reach her jagheer[1] you will have your marriage duly solemnized. Oh, do this for her sake! You said you could love her as a sister, and this would be the conduct of a brother."

"Well," said I, "since the matter has come to this issue, that her life or death is in my hands, I consent;" and I arose, and went with her.

Oh, with what joy the unhappy girl received me! Long she hung upon my bosom, and blessed me as her preserver, and kissed her slave when she related what she had said to me, and that I had agreed to her wishes. "It is to save your precious life," I cried, "that I thus expose myself to the sneers and taunts of my friends and your own. Think on the sacrifice I make in losing their love, and you will behave cautiously and decently on the road; we need not meet—nay, we must not, the temptation would be too strong for us both; but I swear by your head and eyes I will not leave you, and you shall travel in our company."

The slave had gone out, and she drew towards me. "Beware," said she, "how you deceive me, for I know your secret, and if you are unfaithful I will expose it; your life is in my hands, and you know it."

"What secret?" cried I in alarm. "What can you mean?"

"I know that you are a Thug," she said in a low and determined voice; "my slave has discovered you, and a thousand circumstances impress the belief that you are one upon my mind—your men, the way you encamp, the ceremonies my slave has seen your men performing, and the freedom with which you go forward or return at your pleasure. All these are conclusive, and I bid you beware! for nothing that you can say will persuade me to the contrary; you have even now the property of those you have killed in your camp—you cannot deny it, your looks confirm my words."

I inwardly cursed the prying curiosity of the slave, and feared she had discovered us through one of our men with whom I had seen her conversing, and I determined to destroy him. But I had now fairly met my match, and though abashed for a moment, I replied to her:

"Then, Shurfun, since you have discovered us, I have no alternative; we must be united—I, to save my life and the lives of my men, you, to save your own. It is a fearful tie which binds us, but it cannot be broken."

---

1 Estate.

"I thought so," she said; "fool that I was not to have urged this before! I might have saved myself the agony which I have endured. Now go; I will hear of you from day to day, and it may be that we shall have an opportunity of conversing unobserved. Now I am sure of you, and my mind is at ease."

I left her, but my thoughts were in a whirl; she had discovered us, and by the rules of our profession I could not conceal it from my associates. Alla! Alla! to what would the communication I must make to them lead! Alas, I dreaded to think; yet it must be done.

A long time I deliberated with myself whether I should expose the truth to my associates, and fain would I not have done so; but the peril we were in was so imminent, and the lives of my fifty brave fellows were so completely at the mercy of a woman, that I could not overlook the strict rules of my profession. I knew that it could only lead to one alternative; but it was her fate, and it could not be avoided either by her or me.

As I expected, the fatal mandate went forth among us. My men were astonished and terrified at the information Shurfun possessed, and after very brief consultation her fate was determined on. Sahib, you will think the worse of me for this, but what could be done? We could not leave her, she would have alarmed the villagers, and they would have pursued us. True, they could have done but little against us there; but they would have dogged us through the jungles, and at last have watched their opportunity and seized us. Our next care was to endeavour to find out the person from whom she had gained the information, and I mentioned the name of him with whom I had seen the slave conversing. Sahib, as I did it, his face bore the evidence of conscious guilt. He was a young man but little known to any of us, and was one of the lughaees. He had accompanied Peer Khan in his last expedition, and had behaved well, so well as to induce him to allow his accompanying us; but by this act he had forfeited everything, and it was but too plain that he had been seduced by the wiles of that intriguing and artful slave.

Observing his altered looks, I at once accused him of treachery; and my accusation was re-echoed by the voices of the band.

"He must die!" cried one and all; "we could never carry on our work with the knowledge that there was one treacherous person with us; and it is the rule of our order too. Who ever spared a traitor?"

"Miserable wretch," said I to him, "why hast thou done this? Why hast thou been unfaithful to thine oath and the salt thou hast eaten? Didst thou not know the penalty? Hast thou not heard of hundreds of instances of treachery, and was ever one pardoned? Unhappy man! thou sayest nothing for thyself, and the sentence must be passed upon thee. Shame, that the wiles of a wretched slave should so far have led thee from thy duty, and exposed us all to peril!"

"Jemadar," said he rising, "I have sinned, and my hour is come. I ask not for mercy, for I know too well that it cannot be shown me; let me die by the hands of my own people, and I am content; and if my fate be a warning to them, I am satisfied. I was pure in my honour till I met that slave; she told me that you were to marry her mistress, and that you had told her who you were. I thought it true, and I conversed with her on the secrets of our band; I boasted to her of the deeds we had done, and she consented to be mine whenever we could meet with a fitting opportunity. Fool that I was, I was deceived; yet I offer this as no palliation for my offence. Let therefore Goordut kill me: his is a sure hand, and he will not fail in his duty."

Goordut, the chief of our lughaees, stepped forward. "Forgive me your death," said he to the fated wretch; "I have no enmity against you, but this is my duty, and I must do it."

"I forgive you," he replied. "Let your hand be firm; I shall offer no resistance, nor struggle; let my death-pain be short."

Goordut looked to me for the signal,—I gave it, and in another instant his victim had expiated his crime by death; he suffered passively, and Goordut's hand never trembled. The body was taken from among us and interred; and henceforward we had no treachery among us, nor did I ever meet with another instance save one, and that was successful; you shall hear of it hereafter.

There but remained to allot to the different members of the band their separate places in the ensuing catastrophe; and this done, I felt that I had acted as a good Thug, and that a misplaced pity had not influenced me during the transactions of the day.

Strange was it, sahib, that Shurfun, knowing who we were, should not, when she had discovered it, at once have fled from us! How she, a woman unused to and unacquainted with deeds of blood, could have borne to look on, nay, more, to have caressed and loved one a murderer by profession, whose hand was raised against the whole human race, is more than I have ever been able to understand. I can only say it was her fate. She might, she ought to have avoided me; in every principle of human conduct her love for me was wicked and without shame, and a virtuous woman would have died before she had ever allowed it to possess her bosom. She might have cast me off when she said she would, and when her resolution was made to see me no more; but her blind passion led her on into the net fate had spread for her, and she was as unable to avoid it, as you or I shall be to die, sahib, when our hour comes.

We started in company with her the next morning. I was determined I would take no active part in her death, for I could not bear the thought of lifting my hand against one whose caresses I had allowed, and whose kisses were, I may say, still warm upon my lips. Motee and Peer Khan were allotted to her, and one of her attendants was my share. But hers was a large party; she had eight bearers, four sepoys as her guards, and her slave rode on a pony, which was led by another servant. In all therefore they were fifteen individuals, and to make sure, thirty-five of my best men were to fall on them whenever we should meet a fitting place. I knew one, a wild spot it was, where the jungle was almost a forest, and where for miles on either side there was no human habitation; and I intended, for greater security, to lead the party by a path which I had discovered on our way down, and which led into the thickest part of the jungle, where I knew our deadly work would be sure of no interruption.

We reached the spot where the road diverged, which I intended to take, and after much opposition on the part of her bearers, I succeeded in persuading them to follow me, by telling them, both that the road was a short one, and that there was a stream of water which crossed it, whereas on the main track there was none.

We gained the small rivulet, and I dismounted; my band surrounded their unsuspecting victims, and eagerly awaited the signal; but I wished to spare Shurfun the sight of the dead which she would-be exposed to were she not the first to fall. I went to her palankeen, and asked her to get out and partake of some refreshment I had brought with me; she objected at first, as she would have to expose herself to the rash gaze of my men; but I told her I had put up a cloth against a tree, that it was but a few steps off, and that veiled as she was, no one would see her. "Your slave is there already," said I; "so come, she is preparing our meal, the first we have ever eaten together."

She stepped out cautiously, closely muffled in a sheet, so that she saw not those who were with me, the palankeen too concealed her person, and as she arose from her sitting posture, the roomal of Motee was around her, and she died instantly. Peer Khan held her hands, and the moment her breath was gone, he put the body into the palankeen and shut the door.

"Now thus much is done," said he, "we must finish the rest, and that quickly; they are all off their guard, and washing and drinking in the stream; the men are at their posts. Bismilla! give the *jhirnee!*"

I sought my place and gave it. My own share was quickly done, and the rest too; but one or two were unskilful, and the shrieks of the unfortunate but too guilty slave, among the rest, smote on my ear, and caused a pang to shoot to my heart at the thought that they had all died for the wretched caprice of a wicked woman. I could not bear to look at Shurfun,—the sight of her beautiful features would have overpowered me. I saw the lughaees bear her away, but I followed not. Her palankeen was broken into pieces and buried with her.

Wretch! cried I. Ah, Ameer Ali, hadst thou no pity, no remorse, for one so young and so lovely?

I might have felt it, sahib, but the fate of him who had died the day before was too fresh in my mind to allow me to show it: that might have been mine had I done so. Besides, can you deny that it was her fate? and, above all, had I not eaten the goor of the Tupounee?[1]

---

1 The sacrificial ceremony performed after a murder.

Chapter XXXI

SHOWING HOW AMEER ALI PLAYED A DEEP GAME FOR A LARGE STAKE,
AND WON IT

AFTER all had been completed, we travelled on until we reached a small and wretched village some coss from the scene of our late adventure, where, after the customary sacrifice of goor, the considerable booty we had gained was produced and distributed. There soon arose a discussion as to our future proceedings. Some advised that we should return and go on to Nagpoor; many indeed were for this, and I also inclined to it. But Peer Khan gave better counsel, saying that by our thus going backwards and forwards on the same road, we should certainly be suspected and perhaps attacked; and that to expose ourselves to this, was not to be put in comparison with any chance of booty. He advised that we should make the best of our way towards Ellichpoor, avoiding that town, and keeping near the hills, until we got out of the jurisdiction of Sulabat Khan, who, if he heard of us, would assuredly suspect us of the death of the Nuwab, Subzee Khan, who had been his guest, and whose fate was generally known over the country, and attributed with justice to Thugs. After some further deliberation, we all agreed to his plan; and the next day, leaving the high road, we struck into a jungle track and pursued it; and I was heartily glad, after some days of weary travel, when, arriving at the pass near the deserted temples of Mookhtagherry,[1] we saw the wide valley of Berar stretched out before us, covered with the still green and luxurious crops of jowaree[2] and cotton.

For some days previous I had had shiverings and pains all over my body, and my mind was restless and ill at ease. In spite of my efforts to throw them off, horrible dreams haunted me at night, and the figure of Shurfun constantly presented itself to my fancy—now in the fulness of her beauty, and now changed and distorted as she must have been in death; while at one time she was pouring out her tale of love to me, and at another upbraiding me with her fate. I had mentioned this to my companions, and many were the ceremonies which they performed over me to

---

1   Town to the north of Achalpur (Ellichpoor) in central India.
2   Millet.

drive away the evil spirit which Motee declared had possessed me. But they were of no avail, and on the morning we reached the top of the pass I was so ill that I was obliged to be supported on my horse.

What was to be done? To go into Ellichpoor was to run into the tiger's mouth, and all seemed to be at a loss whither to proceed.

However, on clearing the mouth of the glen through which the road ran, some of the men discerned a large village a very short way off, and came back with the welcome intelligence. I was sitting, or rather lying, at a miserable Goand hamlet on the road; and when I heard their news I remembered the village they spoke of, which I had passed the morning we left Ellichpoor with Subzee Khan, though I had forgotten its name. Thither, therefore, I begged they would carry me; and placing me upon my good horse, I was soon there, and made as comfortable as circumstances would admit of in the empty shop of a bunnea. But the fever raged within me; my whole frame was first convulsed with violent shiverings, which were succeeded by intense burnings. I remember no more of that day, nor indeed of many days after, for I lay insensible, and my spirit hovered between life and death.

The first words I recollect after that terrible time were from my faithful attendant.

"Shookr khoda!"[1] he exclaimed; "at last he has opened his eyes!" and he ran and called Peer Khan and others to me.

"Where am I?" I faintly asked, for in the violence of the fever I had forgotten everything.

"Shookr khoda!" again exclaimed all; "he speaks at last!"

I again repeated my question, and it was answered by Peer Khan.

"Why, do you not remember?" said he; "here you are in the good village of Surrusgaum, within three coss of Ellichpoor; and now that you have spoken all will be right, you will soon recover; but we have been sadly anxious about you, for a worthy Moosulman, who is a hukeem,[2] said only yesterday that you would die, and bade us prepare for your burial. He was wrong, however, and, Inshalla! you will soon see yourself at the head of your brave fellows again."

"Alas, Khan, I fear not," said I, "for I am weak and helpless, and your staying with me here only delays you to little purpose. Leave me to my fate, and if it is the will of Alla that I should recover, I will rejoin you at our home. I feel that I should be only a useless clog on your movements; for if I even get over this fever, I shall scarcely be able to sit on my horse for many a day to come."

---

1   Thank the Lord!

2   Physician.

"Forsake you, Meer Sahib! never!" exclaimed all who were sitting round me. "Who will bury you if you die? or who will tend you if you recover? What words are these? Are you not our brother, and more, our leader? and what would become of us if we left you?"

"Well, my friends," said I, deeply affected by their kindness, "since you prefer the bedside of a sick man to roaming in the wide and open country, even be it so; a few days will end your suspense, and either you will have to bury me here, or, if it be the pleasure of Alla, I shall once more lead you to new enterprises."

"But you must be silent," said Peer Khan, "for the hukeem said so, and told us if you roused at all to send him word, as he had prepared some medicine for you which he would administer, and hoped it would hasten your recovery. I will go and tell him the good news."

In a short time the khan returned, accompanied by an old and venerable person who, after feeling my head and body, turned to the khan and declared that my state was satisfactory. "But," said he, "as the fever proceeded from cold, which is still in his stomach, we must give him the medicine I spoke of. I have prepared it, and, being compounded of heating drugs, it will soon expel the cold, induce perspiration, and, Inshalla! to-morrow he will be a different being, though he will be weak for some time to come."

The draught was prepared, and though nauseous in the extreme, swallowed it, and by his directions covered myself with quilts and horse-cloths. I was quickly in a profuse perspiration; and when the hukeem, who sat by my side all the time, thought I had been long enough under this treatment, he withdrew the coverings one by one, and taking my wet clothes from me I soon fell into a sound and refreshing sleep, from which I did not awake till the next morning's sun was shining on my eyelids.

I felt so much refreshed when I awoke that I arose, but my head swam round and I fell. I did not essay to repeat the exertion; but I was well: I felt that I had thrown off the disease, and I was thankful. Soon I had an inclination to eat, and after a slight meal of kicheree[1] I was indeed a different being.

Two days more restored me to convalescence, and I heartily wished to be again on the road towards home; but travelling on horseback was out of the question, as I could only walk a few steps with assistance; so, as Peer Khan volunteered his services, I despatched him to Ellichpoor to endeavour to hire a palankeen or dooly with bearers to carry me a few stages, or as long as I should find them necessary.

---

1   Dish with rice, legumes, ghee, and spices.

He returned with them, and the next day, having remunerated the good hukeem, I gladly set out once again in company with my gallant fellows.

"We took the best road to Boorbanpoor, that through the valley of Berar, and close to the hills; and when we reached the old town of Julgaum, I felt myself so strong that I dismissed the palankeen and once more mounted my good horse.

A joyful and inspiriting thing it is, sahib, to mount one's horse after a long and painful illness, and to feel once more the bounds of the generous animal under you, as though he, too, rejoiced at his master's recovery. He was, like myself, in high spirits, and I never enjoyed a ride so much as I did on that morning; the cool breeze fanned my thin cheeks as I rode along, now humouring my horse by allowing him to bound and caracole as he pleased, now exercising him on the plain, and again rejoining my band as they walked merrily along, apparently under the influence of the same joy as myself, and rejoicing to see me once more at their head.

We met with no adventure till we reached Boorhanpoor, where we arrived on the tenth day after leaving the village at which I had been so near dying: indeed we sought none. We found good quarters in one of the old serais in the town, and I was determined to stay there until we met with something to lead us on. Accordingly, men were daily sent into the different bazars; but seven days passed in idleness, and I began seriously to think that the death of Shurfun, which, though an inevitable deed, was against my faithful promises, had caused me to forfeit the protection of our patroness; in other words, I feared my good fortune had deserted me, and for once I proposed a grand sacrifice to Dévee, and that omens should be consulted, in order to afford us some clue to our future proceedings.

It was done, and the omens were good—"Propitious to a degree!" said Motee, who was our conductor in these matters; "we shall have good bunij soon, or these would never have been vouchsafed to us.

But another day passed, and still the sothaees[1] reported nothing.

The day after, however, about noon, Motee came to me.

"You may know," said he, "that this place, from its wealth, is frequented by rokur-reas, or treasure-carriers, who bring money from Bombay, and take it into Malwa to purchase opium."

"I do," said I; "what of that? I heard as much from my father, who bade me return this way in the hope of picking up some of them."

"Then," said he, "I wish you to come with me, you and Peer Khan; you have both sharp eyes, and I am much mistaken if I have not discovered eight of them. I have

---

1 Inveiglers.

killed others of their tribe before now, and I think I am not wrong when I say that these are some also."

"Good," I replied, "I will come;" and accompanied by Peer Khan and Motee we set forth to examine the men whom the latter had spoken of.

In an empty shop we found them. Wary as these people are, it was highly necessary that we should not excite their suspicion; so we hurriedly passed them, concealing our faces in our handkerchiefs; yet from the casual glance I threw at them I was certain, from their sturdy forms and the one camel they had with them, as well as from a kind of restless and suspicious bearing, that they were the men we were in search of. This was just the season too; they would be bearing treasure to make advances to the poppy cultivators in Malwa, as the seed of the plant would not be sown for another month at least.

I was satisfied; yet how to insure their company I knew not, and many schemes passed through my mind before I could determine on anything. At length I formed one, as I sat with my companions on a flight of steps leading down to the river, and whither we often resorted to enjoy the fresh breezes and pure air from the noble river which flowed beneath us.

"I have been thinking," said I, "what we are to do to secure these fellows; you know they are proverbially wary."

Both nodded assent.

"Well," I continued, "what think you of the following scheme? You and I, Peer Khan, will pretend to be travellers; we will go now to our serai,[1] throw dust and mud over our horses and dirty our clothes, and, taking two men and a pony heavily laden with us, we will go round the city, enter by the gate under the old palace, and pretending to be weary, halt close to them; we shall easily be able to worm ourselves into their confidence, and will then accompany them. You, Motee, I will leave in charge of the band, and send you word what road we are to take. You must be guided by circumstances, and contrive to let the men overtake me by twos and threes; some must go on before, so that we may come up to them; and in this manner, though the band will be scattered, yet, Inshalla! in a few marches we shall muster strong enough to do the work. We can keep up a communication with each other, so that, when the business is done we can assemble, and then hurry forward to our home. But on no account must you be more than a stage behind us; and you must contrive to reach our halting-place a short time after we have left it. Now say, my friends, will this plan do? or can you advise any other more practicable? if so, speak?"

---

1 Inn.

"It is excellent," cried both, "and had wisdom for its father. No time ought to be lost."

We returned to our serai, and towards the afternoon two as travel-stained and weary travellers in appearance as ever came off a long and fatiguing march were seen to enter the south gate of Boorhanpoor and traverse the bazars in search of shelter. These were myself and Peer Khan, attended by my good lad Junglee and two other Thugs. We passed and re-passed the shed, which was a large one, in which the rokurreas were; and feigning to have been denied room everywhere that we had applied, I at last rode up to them, and addressed myself to the most respectable among them, a fine tall fellow, with huge whiskers and moustachios.

"Yaro!"[1] said I," you seem to be travellers as well as ourselves, and, for the love of Alla, allow us a little room to spread our carpets. Here you have seen us pass backwards and forwards for many times, and yet there is not a soul who will say to us, Dismount and refresh yourselves. Nay, we have been refused admittance into many empty places. May their owners' sisters be defiled!"

"Go to the serai," said the man; "there is room there, and you will be comfortable."

"Indeed," said I, "we have tried it already, and it is full; some forty or fifty fellows were in it, who bade us begone in no measured terms; and in truth we liked not their appearance, having some valuables about us. They looked very like thieves or dacoos—did they not, brother?" said I turning to Peer Khan.

"Ah, indeed," said he; "who knows, if we had put up among them, whether we should not have had our throats cut? It was the mercy of Alla," continued he, looking up devoutly, "that the place was full, or, weary as we are, we should have been right glad to have rested ourselves anywhere, for indeed I can hardly sit on my horse."

"You see," said I, "how we are situated. Hindoos though you be, you will not refuse us. The evening is drawing in, and we have ridden all day; a slight meal is all that we can hope to get, and then sleep will be welcome."

"Well," said the fellow, "it will be uncivil to turn you away, so alight; and," cried he to one of his companions, "do you, Doorjun, and some others move the camel's saddles and those bags nearer this way, and there will be room for these Bhula Admees."[2]

As they were being moved I heard the money chink.

We dismounted, and in a short time our horses were rubbed down, and a meal prepared, for we had fasted that day on purpose. When we had eaten it, behold us

---

1 Friends!
2 Respectable people.

seated in conversation with the rokurreas; and having already possessed ourselves of their intended route, we agreed to accompany them for mutual security, and in short were on as good terms with them as if we had travelled hitherto together. Our appearance, our good horses and arms assured them that we were soldiers, for I had told them we were in the service of Holkar, returning from Poonah, where we had been on a mission to the Peshwa,[1] and bearing with us not only despatches, but some hoondees[2] of large amount. In proof of this I pulled forth a bundle of papers from my inner vest, and touching my head and eyes with them, praised the munificence of Bajee Rao,[3] and extolled the friendly terms he was on with Holkar.

This was my master-stroke; the idea had occurred to me when I was at the serai, and I had hastily collected a bundle of waste-papers and accounts, made them up into a packet, directed it to Holkar, and sealed it with my own seal, which was as large as that of any prince in the country. By Alla! sahib, they believed me to be what I represented, as surely as that they had heads on their shoulders, and forthwith began questioning me on the possibility of the Peshwa and Holkar uniting to over-throw the Feringhees; but I was mysteriously close in my replies, just hinting that it was possible, and turning off the conversation to the marks of favour which had been shown me by Bajee Rao, about which I told enough lies to have choked myself; and I pointed to my own noble horse as one of the Peshwa's gifts. They all declared that he was worthy of the giver and of the possessor; and, after agreeing on our stage for the morrow, which was distant eight coss, they went to sleep with the exception of two, who sat guarding the treasure with drawn swords, and all believing that they were in company with an unknown great personage.

Before I lay down to rest I despatched Junglee with the information to Motee. I spoke to him openly in Ramasee, and he set off on his errand.

"That is a queer language," said the jemadar of the rokurreas; "what is it?"

"'Tis Teloogoo,"[4] said I carelessly. "I picked the lad up at Hyderabad two years ago for a small sum, and he is my slave; he understands our Hindee, but does not speak it."

Perhaps it was unwise to have done it, but I spoke in so careless a manner that they concluded I had sent him out on some casual errand. Indeed, I told him to

---

1 The political leader of the Maratha Confederacy in central India.

2 Bills of exchange.

3 Baji Rao II (1775-1851), Peshwa of the Maratha Confederacy in the late eighteenth and early nineteenth centuries.

4 Telugu; language spoken in the southern region of the Nizam's Dominions.

buy some tobacco and pān on his way back, and as the serai was not far from where we were, the time occupied in his going to it would not exceed that of an ordinary errand.

He returned with the pān and tobacco, and told me they were ready, but that the majority would remain the next day, and that seven of the best, under Goordut, were then about to depart; the rest, leaving one of their number as a scout in the village we were to halt at, would push on as far as they could beyond.

I was satisfied, and so sure did I feel of the success of this adventure that I would have wagered all I possessed that I killed the rokurreas in three days. We started the next morning, and for two days saw none of our men; however Peer Khan augured well from it, saying the fellows were up to their work, and would appear in good time, and that if they came too soon our companions would take the alarm and be off.

On the fourth day one of our companions appeared; we overtook him on the road, and as I lagged purposely in the rear, I learned from him that Goordut and his remaining men were in advance of us one march, and that some would join us that day and the rest the next.

This was as it should be. Four men joined us at the village we encamped at; and as we were now nine to eight, I began to think on the probability of putting them to death by violence—I mean, attacking them with our swords on any opportunity which might offer. But it was dangerous, as they were individually stouter men than we were, good hands at their weapons, and as watchful as cats.

The second day Goordut and his party joined us, but it was as much as I could do to persuade the rokurreas to allow them to travel in our company. They declared it was directly against their rules, that we must be aware of this, and that, if it was known by their employers that they even admitted one traveller into their society on the road, they would lose their reputation and means of subsistence.

"But you," continued the jemadar, whose name was Bheem Singh, "you are respectable persons, who, for the honour of the government you serve, would assist us against thieves or robbers, and we travel in your company through these territories of Sindia as safely as though we had a rissala[1] of cavalry to guard us. However, for our sakes, let not the tales of wayfarers make any impression on your mind; depend on a rokurrea's experience, they are not to be trusted: and even when by yourself always avoid associating with any one; no good can come of it, and much harm may ensue."

---

1 Regiment.

I promised to take his advice, and as I saw clearly that they would not admit any more of our band into their company, and that a quarrel and separation from them would inevitably be the consequence if I persisted in forcing any more upon them, I determined to finish the matter as I best could with the twelve men I had. Junglee was worth but little, at least I counted not upon him, as he was a mere stripling; but the rest were the very best of my band, all noted bhuttotes, and fellows who had good swords, and knew right well how to use them.

In the day, therefore, we had a consultation; we met in a field of jowaree, which concealed us, and there we discussed the affair. Peer Khan proposed to send one of the men back for Motee and the rest, to tell them to pass us in the night without stopping, and to allow us to overtake them early in the morning; and as soon as the two parties were mingled together, in passing each other, that I should give the *jhirnee*.

The plan was very feasible, and the advice was good, as it placed the issue beyond a doubt; I inclined to it myself. Still there was no honour to be gained by it; it would be large odds against a few, and this I did not like, as I had a choice in the matter. At last I said, after musing some time, and listening to Peer Khan as he discussed the measure, "No, no, Peer Khan; we are all of us young, and fame is dear to us. If we kill these people in the old way, and the booty is large, we shall no doubt get praise; but think, man, on the honour to be gained, the good name! If we risk ourselves against these fellows, and are victorious, will not every Thug in the land cry Shabash![1] and Wah, Wah![2] and is not this worth an effort? I tell you a good name is better than riches; and if it is our time to die, we cannot avoid it by calling up Motee and his people. They are, after all, only the refuse; and are we not the picked men of the band, and those on whom the matter would fall, even were the whole now present? Say, therefore, will ye risk your lives against these fellows, and fall on them to-morrow morning?"

Sahib, they did not hesitate; one and all pledged themselves to follow me, and die with me should it be their fate.

"Then see your swords are loose in their scabbards," said I, "and let each of you plant himself within striking distance of his enemy, on his left hand. Peer Khan and myself are mounted, and we cannot fail. I feel assured that there will be no danger, and that we shall succeed."

---

1 Well done!
2 Bravo, bravo!

We dispersed, and rejoined our associates. The evening was spent in singing and playing on the sitar,[1] on which two of the rokurreas and some of my men were adepts; and we retired to rest at a late hour, fully prepared to do our work well and bravely on the morrow.

And the morrow came, and the sun rose in splendour; we set out soon afterwards, for the rokurreas would not travel before it had risen, for fear of surprise from thieves or dacoos, who generally fall on travellers in the dark.

Somewhat to my mortification, two of the rokurreas mounted the camel they had with them, saying their feet were cracked and sore and they could not walk. This disconcerted me for a moment, for I thought they had suspected us, and I knew that most, if not all, the treasure was laden upon it. But I affected no surprise, and was determined, if they showed the least symptoms of flight, to wound the camel, and thereby prevent its getting away from us by the great speed I knew it possessed, for they had put it to its utmost the day before, to show me that it could outstrip a horse.

We travelled along until mid-day, and the fatigue and heat made us glad to dismount at a stream which crossed the road. I thought it would be a good opportunity to fall on them, but I was disappointed: they all kept together, and I was then satisfied that they half suspected our intentions; but I could not delay the attack long, and was determined to make it under any circumstances, for the rapid rate at which the rokurreas travelled was exhausting my men, who had much ado to keep up with them.

By the merest good luck, about a coss after we left the nulla,[2] we entered on a rough and stony track, which diminished the speed of the camel, whose feet were hurt by the stones, and he picked his way cautiously, though I saw the men on his back used every exertion to urge him on. This slowness enabled my men to take their places, and we continued to proceed a short distance, but ready at any moment for the onset. I wished to get as near the camel as I could, in order to prevent its escape; but the road became worse, our pace still slower, and I was satisfied it could not be urged quicker. We were at this time all in a group, and I saw that the time had come. How my heart beat! not with fear, sahib, but with excitement—excitement like that of a gambler who has risked his all on a stake, and who, with clenched hands, set teeth, and half- drawn breath, watches the turn of the couries, which is either to ruin him or better his fortunes.

---

1 Long-necked Indian lute.
2 Watercourse.

Peer Khan threw a glance towards me: one of the rokurreas was trudging along at his horse's shoulders, another was at the same place near mine; and the fellows on the camel, with their backs turned towards us, were singing merrily one of the wild lays of the Rajpoots, in which from time to time they were joined in chorus by those on foot, and by some of my men who knew the words. Junglee was close behind the camel leading my pony, and the others in the rear, but all in their places. I cast but one look behind to see that they were so, and being satisfied, I gave the *jhirnee*—"Junglee, pān lao!"[1] I cried with a loud voice.

The swords of my party flashed brightly from their scabbards, and in an instant were buried deeply in the bodies of their victims and crimsoned with gore. As for myself, I had cloven the scull of the fellow beneath me, and my sword sticking in the wound escaped from my hand as he fell; I threw myself from my horse to recover it, and only then saw the camel prostrate on the ground, moaning terribly; the men upon it had fallen with it, but both had gained their legs: one had thrown himself upon Junglee, and the poor lad waged an unequal combat with him; the other rushed on me with his sword uplifted. Sahib, I thought my end was come; but I had time to disengage my shield from my back, and held it before me in defence, while I tugged in very desperation at my weapon.

Praise be to Alla! it yielded to my great exertion, and we were on equal terms. I have before told you of my skill as a swordsman, but I had met my match in the rokurrea: he, though all his men were lying around him save one,—who having sorely wounded my poor attendant, was now closely pressed by Peer Khan and another, was as cool and wary as myself. We fought well, and for a long time the contest was equal; we were both out of breath, and our shields hacked with the repeated blows we had each caught on them. At last, as my foot slipped on a stone, he made a stroke at my head; the blow was weak from his exhausted state, or it would have ended me: it cut through my turban, and slightly wounded my head.

I did not fall, though I was somewhat stunned by the stroke; he might have taken advantage of the moment, yet he neglected it. Maddened by the thought of defeat, I rushed on him, and by the violence of my attack forced him backward. At last, he too slipped as he retreated, and lost his balance; he raised his sword wildly in the air to recover himself, but I did not lose my opportunity as he had done; my blow descended with its full force, increased by a sudden leap I made towards him, and he fell to the earth cloven through the neck and shoulder,—he was dead almost ere he fell. A moment I gazed on the features of the brave Rajpoot, and then sought my

---

1 Junglee, bring betel-leaf!

poor lad, from whom the life-blood was fast ebbing away; his wound was also in the neck, and the blood rushing into his throat was choking him.

I tried to staunch it with my waistband, but ineffectually; it relieved him for a moment, and he asked for water. A leathern bag containing some had been tied to the camel by one of the men, and I put the mouth of it to his lips; he drank a little, and sat up, supported by Goordut.

"I am killed," said he, "Jemadar, I die—my own blood chokes me—I cannot recover. Do not leave my body to be eaten by the beasts, but bury it. That fellow," continued he after a short interval, and pointing to one of the dead, "that fellow's sword killed me. I cut the hind sinews of the camel's leg, and it fell; I thought they would both be stunned, but he got up and attacked me, and I was no match for him. All the rest of you were engaged, or you would have helped me. But it was my fate to die, and I felt it yesterday, the bitterness of death then passed over me, but now I am content—the pain will soon be over."

Here he sunk insensible, and we stood around him weeping, for he was an affectionate lad, and we all loved him as a brother. But he recovered again slightly, though the rattle was in his throat, and the blood hardly allowed him to speak.

"My mother!" he said faintly, "jemadar, my mother! You know her, and my little sister. They will starve now;—but you will protect them for poor Junglee's sake?" And he strove to bend his head on my hand, as though to supplicate my assistance for them.

"Fear not," said I, "they shall be well cared for, and while Ameer Ali lives they shall know no want." But I could hardly speak for weeping, for I knew the old woman, and many were the prayers she made for his safe return as she confided him to my care. Alas! how should we be able to tell her his fate?

The poor boy was satisfied with my words; he would fain have replied to them, and his lips moved; but a torrent of blood checked his utterance, and raising his dull and glazed eyes to mine, he bowed his head on my hand, and died in the effort. "Now," said I to the assembled Thugs, "I here swear to one thing, and ye are none of mine unless ye agree to it. I swear that whatever share would have come to this poor lad, it shall be doubled for his mother; as yet we know not what it is; but whatever it be, it shall be doubled."

"We agree," cried all; "nay, every man of us will add to it what he can. Had Junglee not hamstrung the camel, which none of us thought of doing, it might, nay, would, have escaped: for we saw its speed yesterday, and the two good Rajpoots who were on it would have carried it off."

"Ye are my own brothers for this good promise," I said; "and now some of you dig a grave for the poor lad. We must unload that beast, and strip the bodies. For myself, I am in some pain, and will wash my head and tie up the cut: so set about your work quickly."

The camel still lay groaning; they tried to raise it up, but in vain: the stroke had divided the sinew above the hock, and it could not raise itself; so one of the men cut its throat, and ended its pain. The bags of treasure were transferred to my pony and Peer Khan's horse and mine, and every man also filled his waistband, so that we were enabled to carry it all off. We took the swords of the Rajpoots; but everything else, and their bodies, were dragged into the jungle to some distance, and hastily covered with earth and stones. The bloody earth on the scene of the conflict was collected and thrown away, and in a very short time nothing remained to mark the spot but the carcass of the camel, which we could not dispose of; and leaving the usual marks for the guidance of Motee and his party, we continued our march on the main road.

Ah, how great was our joy when, before we reached the stage we were to encamp at, and as we sat at the edge of a stream washing ourselves, we saw, on the brow of a rising ground we had just passed, our party coming up! They ran towards us in breathless anxiety and hope.

Motee was first, and he threw himself into my arms. "We hastened on," he said, "from the last stage, hoping to overtake you in time; and when we saw the dead camel, how great was our suspense till we could find you! We saw the traces of the conflict, and some blood which had escaped your notice,—which I have removed,—and that added to our anxiety; but, Dévee be praised! we have found you at last, and you are all safe. Is it not so?"

"Not quite," I said; "we have lost poor Junglee, who was killed in the fight, and I am wounded; but 'tis only a slight cut, and a few days will heal it."

Some of the treasure was instantly distributed to the other ponies; and encamping outside the village, when we reached it, after the accustomed sacrifice I had my small tent pitched, and all the treasure was conveyed to it. One by one the bags were opened, and glorious indeed was the booty—well worth the risk we had encountered! It consisted of dollars, gold mohurs,[1] and rupees, to the value of sixty thousand rupees in all; and there were also six strings of large pearls in a small box, sewn up in wax-cloth, which could not be worth less than ten thousand more. I need not describe our joy: we had comfort, nay affluence, before us for years, and

---

1 Gold coins.

every one sat and gazed at the heap of treasure in silent thankfulness. Finally, it was all collected and put into bags, which I sealed with my own seal.

We now hurried to our home, for we sought no adventure, not needed any: only two unfortunate wretches, who insisted on joining us, were killed, and in less than a month we were within three marches of our village. I despatched a man in advance to give notice of our approach; and Alla! how my heart beat with love and fond anxiety to see Azeema, and to press once more my children to my heart, after all the perils I had encountered! How intense was my anxiety to reach my own threshold, when I saw the well-known grove appear in view, the spot from whence I had departed so full of hope, and the walls and white musjid[1] of the village peeping from amidst the trees by which they were surrounded! I urged my horse into a gallop, and I saw my father and Moedeen approaching to meet me, to give me the *istukbal*, the welcome of return; but, as I neared them, they hung their heads, and advanced with slow and mournful steps. A sudden pang shot through my heart. I threw myself from my horse and ran towards them. My father was weeping.

"Speak, for the sake of Alla!" I cried. "What can this be? Oh, say the worst at once, and tell me—is Azeema dead? this suspense will kill me."

A few words only the old man spake, as he told me that my child, my beautiful boy, was dead!

And Ameer Ali wept.

---

1 Mosque.

Chapter XXXII

Lear.—Dost thou know me, fellow?

Kent.—No, sir; but you have that in your countenance which I would fain
call master.

—*Lear*, Act i., Scene 4.

ALTHOUGH the mind would ordinarily reject sympathy with the joys or
sorrows of a murderer like Ameer Ali, one so deeply stained with crime
of the most revolting nature, yet for the moment I was moved to see,
that after the lapse of nearly twenty years by his account, the simple mention of
the death of his favourite child could so much affect him, even to tears, and they
were genuine. I leave others to speculate on the peculiar frame of the Thug's mind,
how this one feeling of tenderness escaped being choked by the rank guilt that had
sprung up around it, and will pursue my relation of his adventures.

Sahib, he said, why should I now trouble you with an account of my miserable
meeting with my loved Azeema? You can picture it to yourself. Our souls had been
bound up in that boy, and it was long ere we could bring ourselves to submit to the
blow which the hand of Alla had inflicted. But the poignancy of the grief passed
away, and our girl, growing up in beauty, occupied our thoughts and engaged our
care and attention.

Some time after we returned, my father one day came to me, and, with concern
on his countenance, declared there was a rumour that we were suspected, and that
he thought our village was no longer a safe abode for us. We could risk nothing;
there might or might not be truth in the report, but it was our duty to secure a safe
asylum; and accordingly he and I set out to make a tour of the different states as yet
independent of the English, and to find out whether any of their rulers would allow
us a residence on payment of a fixed tribute, such as our fraternity had used to pay
to Sindia's government when our village belonged to that prince. We accordingly
departed, and after visiting many rulers in Bundelkund[1] (for we were averse to going farther from our home), we were received by the Rajah of Jhalone,[2] and were

---

1   Bundelkhand; region in north-central India.

2   Jalaun.

introduced to him by Ganesha Jemadar, who was under his protection, and who made him handsome returns from the booty he collected for his friendly conduct.

Our negotiation was a long one: the Rajah was fearful for some time of the consequences of harbouring us, or pretended to be so in order to enhance the favour he was conferring; but we distributed bribes plentifully to his attendants and confidential servants, and at last succeeded in our object. We were to pay a tax of three hundred rupees a year to his government, present him with anything rare or valuable we might pick up, and, to preserve appearances, my father agreed to farm three villages situated a short distance from his capital. The whole concluded by our presenting to him one of the strings of pearls we had taken on the last expedition, my own beautiful sword, and other articles valued at nearly five thousand rupees. When we were thus mutually satisfied, my father and some of the men remained behind, while I and the rest returned to our village, to bring away our families.

I confess I left our home with regret; many, many happy days had been passed there, and we were beloved by the villagers, to whom we had endeared ourselves by our inoffensive conduct. We were now to seek a new country, and form new ties and connections—a disagreeable matter under any circumstances. But my father's wisdom had saved us. The information the English officers had obtained—Alla only knows how—was correct. In a very few months after we were settled in our new abode, we heard that the whole Purgunna[1] of Murnae had been attacked, village by village. Many of the best and bravest of the Thugs had died defending their homes; the survivors had fled, routed and utterly disorganized, and had taken refuge with those who had made previous settlements as we had done.

For my own part, so long as my money lasted I was in no humour to expose myself to fresh risks. I had, too, attained the highest rank possible among Thugs, for I had been declared a soobehdar[2] immediately upon my return from the last expedition; and I was content to enjoy my ease, and assist my father in the management of the villages which had been confided to us, and by which we realized a comfortable income. For the time, therefore, Thuggee was abandoned; and though often urged by Ganesha, who had a wild and restless spirit, to join him in an expedition, we refrained from doing so, and lived peacefully and respectably.

There was something about Ganesha which to me was mysterious, and the instant I saw him at the court of the Rajah, a thought flashed into my mind that I had met him before under painful circumstances. In spite of all my endeavours I could

---

1 District.

2 High-ranking officer.

hardly ever shake it off sufficiently to be on any terms of cordiality with him; and I viewed with suspicion and distrust his intimacy with my father, and the evident effect his counsels had upon him. In person, Ganesha was tall and strong, but his face was more forbidding than any one I had ever before seen, and there was a savage ferocity about his manner which disgusted me. But let him pass at present; he has now little to do with my story, hereafter I shall be obliged to bring him prominently and disagreeably before you.

Nearly three years passed quietly, and unmarked by anything which I can recall to my memory. I had no more children, and my daughter was growing up a model of beauty and grace. I was happy, and never should have dreamed of leaving home, had it not been for the bad faith of the Rajah, and one unfortunate season of drought; by the former we were obliged to pay five thousand rupees, which he demanded under threats of discovering us; and by the latter we lost considerably in the villages we farmed, which were now seven in number, and for which he obliged us to pay the full amount of revenue. These sums seriously diminished our resources; and I began to look about me for men, to compose a band to go in search of more plunder. But they were not easily collected, for my own men had dispersed to distant parts of the country, and could not be brought together save at great expense and sacrifice of time.

Just at this period it was rumoured through the country that Cheetoo[1] and other Pindharee chiefs of note would assemble their forces after the rains, at the festival of the Dusera, and had planned an expedition of greater magnitude than any ever before undertaken; an expedition which was sure to enrich all its members, and strike terror into the English Government. The idea suited me exactly: I was a soldier by inclination, if not by profession; and I thought, if I could join any of the durras[2] with a few choice men, well mounted, we might make as good a thing of it as if we went out on an expedition of our own. The latter scheme, moreover, promised no success, for the roads would be infested by straggling parties of Pindharees, who were well known to spare neither travellers nor Thugs; they looked on the last indeed with great enmity.

Accordingly I set to work to make my preparations. Peer Khan and Motee still remained near us, and when I disclosed my plans to them, they entered into them with great readiness and alacrity. They had enough money to mount themselves well, and after a short absence returned fully equipped for the journey. I had told

---

1 Chitu, the famous Pindari chief.
2 Regiments.

them to look out for a few really fine fellows to accompany us, whom they brought; but our united means would not allow of our purchasing horses for them, and on foot they would be of no use. In debating on our dilemma, an idea occurred to me that the Rajah would perhaps lend or sell the horses on the promise of after and double payment. I had heard of such things, and I determined to try what could be done.

To my great joy the Rajah consented, and with less difficulty than I had anticipated, for I had become a great favourite with him. I was allowed to take five horses from his stables, which were valued at three hundred rupees each, with their saddles and accoutrements, and this sum was to be doubled in case we returned successful. The Rajah indeed thanked me for the hint I had given him, and many others obtained horses on the same terms, on giving security for the performance of the conditions under which they took them.

My final arrangements were soon completed. We were all armed and accoutred in the handsomest manner we could afford; and a better-mounted or more gallant-looking little party never set out in quest of adventure than I and my seven associates. Before we started we consulted the omens, which were favourable, and we performed all the ceremonies of departure exactly as if we had been going on an expedition of Thuggee.

In due time we arrived at Nemawur,[1] the residence of Cheetoo. Here were collected men from every part of Hindostan, as various in their tribes as they were in their dresses, arms, and accoutrements. The country round Nemawur was full of them, and the town itself appeared a moving mass of human beings, attracted by the hope of active service, and above all of plunder. We lost no time in presenting ourselves at the durbar[2] of the chief, and were graciously received by him. I opened our conference in the usual manner, by presenting the hilt of my sword as a nuzzur; and having dressed myself in my richest clothes, I was instantly welcomed as if I had been a sirdar[3] of rank, and had the command, not of seven men but of as many hundreds.

Cheetoo was a fine-looking man, and a gallant leader. He ought to have died on the field of battle, instead of in the miserable manner he did.[4] No man that ever led

---

1   Nemawar; a town on the Narmada River in central India.
2   A ruler's public assembly.
3   Leader.
4   Having fled the British, Chitu was killed by a tiger in 1819.

a lubhur[1] was juster in the division of plunder; no one was ever more attentive to the wants and complaints of those under him than was Cheetoo Pindharee. It was this which gained him so many followers, while his personal activity and hardihood stimulated his soldiers to exertion and emulation. Nothing could tire him; often have I seen him after a long and weary march, when it was as much as most of us could do to sit on our horses, dash out to the front and exercise his noble steed, which bore him gallantly, as though he were only returning from a morning's ride of a few miles.

Cheetoo was, as I said, struck with my appearance, as I introduced myself as a poor syud of Jhalone, desirous of serving under him in his ensuing campaign.

"Oh," said he, "from Jhalone! you have travelled far, my friend; but nevertheless you are welcome, as every brave cavalier is who brings a good horse and a willing heart to the service of Cheetoo. You know my conditions of service: I give no pay, but as much plunder as your own activity can procure; the people will tell you what my share of it is; and I look to your honesty, for your face belies you if you are a rogue."

"I know the conditions," said I, "and will accept them; but I have brought a few friends with me who are desirous of sharing my fortunes, and, if it be the pleasure of the huzoor,[2] I will bring them."

"Surely," he replied; "but now I am engaged; meet me with your men at the place of assembly in the evening, and I will see them and your horses, for the station I shall allot you in the durra depends on their fitness."

I made my obeisance and retired. I had made the acquaintance of one of Cheetoo's sirdars, a man by name Ghuffoor Khan, a perfect savage in appearance and deportment, a fellow who had Pindharee written on his face, and had served with much distinction in the durras of Dost Mahomed and Kureem Khan. He had introduced me to Cheetoo, and now, as he accompanied me from the durbar, he gave me instructions how I was to proceed.

"You will meet us," he said, "on the plain beyond the town, and see that all your horses look well, that your men are well dressed and armed, and I will venture to declare that you are all placed in my division, which has the honour of leading, and is the first for fighting and for plunder. I shall be glad to have you, and I will try whether I cannot get you the command of a hundred or two of my own risala.[3]

---

1   Private army.
2   Highness.
3   Regiment.

We want leaders, and from your appearance I judge that you will do justice to my patronage."

"It is the very thing I have ever wished for," I said; "and if you will but favour me, I will do my utmost to please you. It is true I have as yet seen no service; but that is easily learned when the heart is willing."

We separated, and I hastened to my men to get them in readiness for the inspection of our new chief. Our horses had now rested from the fatigue of the journey, and were in high condition; our arms were cleaned and sharpened. We provided ourselves with the long spear which is peculiar to the Pindharees, and of which thousands were on sale; and at the appointed hour I led my little band to the place, where some hundred horsemen were already assembled. I had dressed myself in the armour of Subzee Khan, which was a magnificent suit; and my noble horse as he bounded and caracoled with me, seemed proud of his rider, and glad that he had at last got into a scene suited to his fiery spirit. Peer Khan and Motee were also striking figures, and nearly as well mounted as I was; and the rest were as good, if not better, than the majority of those who were now assembled.

"Keep all together," said I to them; "do not straggle, or our party will appear more insignificant than it really is. When you see the chief coming, watch my movements and follow me."

Long before sunset Cheetoo issued from the town, accompanied by as gallant a company as could well be imagined. The leaders of the different durras were all around him, each surpassing the other in the richness and martial air of his dress, his arms, and the trappings of his horse. Before him, making his horse leap and bound in a wonderful manner, rode Ghuffoor Khan, clad in chain-armour, which glittered in the red rays of the setting sun. No one equalled him in appearance, though many were noble-looking cavaliers; and no one appeared to manage his steed with the ease and grace that he did.

"That is the man!" I cried with enthusiasm to Peer Khan; "that is the man we are to serve under; is he not a gallant fellow? Now follow me." And I gave my impatient horse the rein, and dashing onwards was in an instant at the side of Cheetoo, accompanied by my men. I dropped my spear to the ground, as I threw my horse back on his haunches close to him, and making an obeisance down to my saddle-bow, said that I had brought my men as he had directed, and awaited his orders.

Cheetoo checked his horse, and for a moment surveyed me with delight.

"You are a fine young fellow," he said at length, "and your men are excellently mounted. I would there were as many hundreds of you as you have companions.

However, something may be done. What say you, Ghuffoor Khan, will the Meer Sahib serve with you? and have you a few hundred men to put under him?"

"May I be your sacrifice!" cried the khan, "'tis the very thing your servant would have proposed. I liked the Meer Sahib from the moment I saw him; and now that he is properly dressed, by Alla! he is a very Roostum,[1] and the only fit companion for himself (forgive my insolence) that Ghuffoor Khan sees."

"Then be it so," said Cheetoo; "take him with you, and see that you treat him kindly."

"Come," cried the khan to me, "come then, Meer Sahib, take a tilting-spear from one of those fellows; here is a rare piece of ground, and I must see whether you are master of your weapon."

"I fear not," said I; "I know little about the spear. On foot and with the sword I should not fear the best man of the army; nevertheless, to please you, I will try."

I took the spear, a long light bamboo, with a large stuffed ball of cotton at the end of it, from which depended a number of small streamers of red cloth, and following Ghuffoor Khan, dashed forwards into the plain.

"We pursued each other alternately, now advancing to the attack, now retreating, amidst the plaudits of the assembled horsemen, who looked on with curiosity to see how an utter stranger would behave against the most accomplished cavalier of the army. For a long time neither of us had any advantage over the other; our horses were admirably trained, and neither allowed the other to approach within reach of the spear-thrust. This was the great nicety of the tilt, and cries of "Shabash! Shabash!"[2] resounded at every baffling turn or successful escape from a meditated blow. At last the khan touched me; it was but a graze, which I received on my arm, having delayed for an instant to turn my horse, and he cried out that he had won.

"I own it," said I, as our horses stood panting for breath, "for I am, as you know, a novice at the use of the weapon; yet if you will give me another trial, I will again cross spears with you, and see if I have not better luck."

"Good," cried he, laughing; "but look out, for I warn you I shall not be merciful; a sharp blow on the ribs of a young hand teaches him his vulnerable point, and causes him to be careful ever after."

"Come on," cried I; "if I can I will return the compliment."

We again took a large circle, and at a good canter approached each other till we were nearly within spear's length. The Khan was as good as his word, and made

---

1 Mythological Persian hero.

2 Bravo! Bravo!

several desperate lunges at me. I avoided them, however, by the quickness of my horse, and I plainly saw that he could by no endeavour approach near enough to me to strike a decisive blow. His horse, too, being fatter, was more blown than my own; and after allowing him to weary it still more for some time in a vain pursuit of me, I suddenly changed my position and became his assailant. I believe I was more cool and wary than he was, for he appeared vexed that a stranger should be on such equal terms with him at his favourite exercise; he did not parry my lunges with the same precision as in the first encounter, when, notwithstanding all my efforts to touch him, he avoided and laughed at me. Still I had not touched him; and growing weary of my close pursuit, he endeavoured to turn again and become the assailant; but whether his horse was slow in wheeling round, or whether I was too near to allow of his avoiding the blow, I know not; but as he endeavoured to cross behind me, I wheeled my horse suddenly, struck my heels into his sides, and as he gave his accustomed bound of some yards, struck my spear full on the broad chest of the khan, who was somewhat stunned by the blow. A loud shout from those around us proclaimed my victory; and the khan himself, though abashed at his defeat, was one of the loudest in my praises to the chief himself.

"By Alla!" said he, "thou art no stranger at this work, Meer Sahib; thou hast played me a trick."

"I swear by your beard and the Koran, that I have not, Khan," I cried; "it was the result of chance. Alla knows that two days ago I had never had a spear in my hand. I only observed what you did when you hit me, and to my good horse I owe my fortune. But it was all chance, and though I prize the victory, yet I regret that such a chance should have hurt you."

"Nay, I am not hurt, Syud," he replied, "and I bear these things with good humour; but if you are as good a hand with the sword as you promise to be with the spear, there will not be a man in the camp to stand before you."

"It would be boastful in me to challenge any one," said I, "seeing that I am a stranger among you; yet if the noble Cheetoo wishes to try me, I will essay what I can do to-morrow."

"Good, good!" cried all; and Cheetoo himself, vastly pleased with the result of my encounter with Ghuffoor Khan, bade me present myself early at his residence, where he would invite a few good swordsmen to attend and see us exercise.[1]

---

1 Here ends the Second Volume of the 1839 edition.

Chapter XXXIII

THE next afternoon we were all assembled on a small plain outside the town; Cheetoo had spread his carpet after the manner of a Pindharee, and sat with his chiefs around him, promising by his demeanour to be an eager spectator of the encounter. He was remarkably civil to me, and asked me to sit by him until a few men, who were ready, had displayed their dexterity and prowess. On the signal being given by him, two stout Rajpoots leaped into the circle and clattered their sticks on each other's shields for some time without either touching the other.

"Does this please you?" said Cheetoo to me. "Those fellows are good hands, you see, at their weapons: neither would have drawn blood had they had swords in their hands."

"They are expert enough," said I, "but methinks they have played together before and know each other's ways; they make a great show, but if I may be pardoned, I think neither has much real skill. If my lord wishes, I will try either of them."

"Take care you are not over-matched," said he; "I would not have your fair fame sullied. You have already interested me much in your behalf."

"Do not fear for me," said I; "I will do my best."

I stripped myself to my trousers, and girding a handkerchief tightly about my waist, I stepped into the circle, where one of the men, who had now rested from his first encounter, awaited me. I took a stick and a small shield made of basket-work from Peer Khan, who had brought them, and advanced to the centre. There were murmurs among the assembly that I was over-matched, for they contrasted my slight form with the tall and brawny one of my antagonist; but I was not to be deterred by this. I knew my skill, and that mere personal strength would avail but little against it.

"How is it to be?" said I to the Rajpoot. "Does the first fair blow decide between us?"

"Certainly," he replied. "I shall strike hard, so be on your guard."

"Good," said I: "now take your post."

He did. He retired to one edge of the circle and advanced on me leisurely, now stooping and leaning his shield-arm on his knee as he rested a moment to survey me, and now circling round me, first rising on one leg and then on the other, and waving his stick in the air.

I stood perfectly still and in a careless attitude, but well on my guard, for I knew that I should hazard something in moving after him. It was evident to me that he did not expect this, for he seemed for a moment irresolute, but at last he rushed on me with two or three bounds, and aimed a blow at my head. I was perfectly prepared, for I knew his mode of attack; I received the blow on my shield, caught the stick under it, and rained such a shower of blows on his undefended person as completely astonished him.

The assembly rang with plaudits, and the other Rajpoot stepped forward and saluted me.

"You have had but short work with my friend Bheem Singh," said he; "but now you must try me."

"I am ready," I replied; "so get to your post."

I had now an antagonist worthy of me. He knew my system of play, and verily I thought myself for the moment engaged with my old instructor; but I had used to vanquish him, and I did not fear the man before me. "We were soon hotly engaged: he was as cool and wary as myself, and after a long conflict, in which neither had the advantage, we rested awhile, both out of breath.

"Enough, enough!" cried Cheetoo; "you have both done bravely; neither has won, and you had better let the matter stand as it is."

"Not so, Khodawund," said I; "let us finish it. One of us must win, and my friend here desires as much as myself to see which of us is the better man. Is it not so?"

"Ay," said the fellow laughingly, "the Nuwab Sahib knows that no one as yet has overcome me; but I have fairly met my match, and whoever taught you was a good master, and has had a disciple worthy of him."

"As you will," said Cheetoo, "only play in good humour; let no feud grow out of it."

We both saluted him, and assured him we could not quarrel, and that whoever was victor must entertain a high respect for his opponent.

And to it we set again, as we had now recovered our breath. Victory for a long time hovered between us, now inclining to the one and now to the other; we had both lost our footing once or twice, and the spectators would have had us leave off, but excited as we were it was impossible—we stopped not for their exclamations. I was put to my last shifts to avoid the well-directed blows of the Rajpoot;

he had better wind than I, and this obliged me to alter my mode of play: hitherto I had attacked him; I now only warded off his cuts, but watched my opportunity. In his eagerness, thinking by a succession of blows he could beat down my guard, he exposed his side, and my stick descended on his ribs with a sound which was heard by all, and with a force which fairly took away his breath; had my weapon been a sword, I think I should have cut him in two.

"Fairly won!" cried Cheetoo; "fairly and bravely won! Ramdeen Singh, thou hast lost, but it is no disgrace to thee. Come to me by-and-by, and I will reward thee."

The Rajpoot laughed, and I was glad he bore the defeat so good-humouredly, for I had expected the contrary; he allowed that he had been vanquished, and cried out to all that it had been a fair encounter, and that he had used the utmost of his skill: "So beware," he continued, "how any of you engage the Meer Sahib; you all know what I am, and I have been fairly beaten."

I was delighted with the noble fellow, and addressed Cheetoo himself.

"I crave a boon, Khodawund, and if I may hope to have it granted, I will speak."

"Say on," he replied; "I will grant it readily."

"Then," said I, "let this brave fellow be placed under me. By your favour, a stranger has been entrusted with the command of part of the harawul (advance-guard), and I would have both these Rajpoots with me, and be allowed to entrust fifty men to the one and twenty-five to the other."

"Good," said Cheetoo, "let it be so; and do you, Ghuffoor Khan, look to it that it is done; these are the men who will serve us best in the time of need."

A few days more I was fairly installed into my new charge. Fortune had favoured me far above my expectations, and I saw naught before me but a career of distinction under my new master. True, I was no longer a leader on my own responsibility, but the rank I held was honourable, and perhaps far above my deserts. I seized an opportunity which presented itself, and wrote a full account of the whole to my father and Azeema, for I knew that they would rejoice at tidings so new and unexpected.

Our time passed in the camp in the manner I have related. In the mornings I was a constant attendant upon Cheetoo, who rarely allowed me to leave his person during his inspections of the constantly arriving new adventurers; and the evenings closed with feats of strength and trials of skill, in which I sustained the reputation I had begun with. I never spent a happier time than the month I was at Nemawur, in every way so gratifying to me, and so consonant to my previously formed wishes.

At last the festival of the Dusera arrived, and it was held with great pomp and show. A grand review of all the assembled adventurers was held, a muster taken, and it was reported that five thousand good horsemen were present; and this number, with their followers, and with those indifferently mounted, was augmented to nearly eight thousand—a gallant band, ready to do the bidding of their chief, and to carry war and devastation into the countries before them.

It was planned that we should separate into two bodies soon after passing the Nurbudda, penetrate as far as the Kistna[1] river to the south, and, should we find that fordable, then press on as far south as we could, without exposing ourselves to encounters with the regular armies of the Feringhees, which we were assured, although at present inactive, could speedily be sent in pursuit of us. Accordingly, as the morning broke, the whole camp was in motion; and a noble sight it was to see durra after durra defile before their chief, and hurry onwards at a rapid pace. Boats had been provided at the Nurbudda, which we crossed the same day, and took up our ground near the town of Hindia on its southern bank.

At this point the army separated. I remained with my division and Cheetoo, and we pushed on the day after, taking a direction to the westward, so as to come upon the river Taptee,[2] up the valley of which we were to proceed till we should reach the territories of the Rajah of Nagpoor, with whom a treaty had been previously made to allow us a free and unmolested passage through his dominions, on the condition that they were not to be plundered. The other division, under Syud Bheekoo, a leader of note and only second to Cheetoo, took a direction to the eastward, along the bank of the Nurbudda, until they reached the grand road to Nagpoor, by which it was their intention to travel.

Meanwhile we proceeded by rapid marches; for we were eager to reach the scene of our operations, as our money was running short, and without plunder we should starve. We heard that there was a small detachment of regular troops under Major Fraser watching our movements; but our spies told us they were few in number, and we were under no apprehension of an attack from them: it was reported that they did not exceed three hundred men, and we vainly thought they would not dare to face as many thousands. But we had not sufficiently estimated their bravery. We knew they were upwards of fifteen coss distant from us, and what infantry could make that march and attack a body of horse like ours?

They did, however, attack us. We had arrived at our ground near a village on the Taptee, and some were cooking their morning meal, others lounging idly about the camp or lying at full length on their saddle-cloths, when the alarm was given that the Feringhees were upon us. The scene of confusion which ensued is indescribable.

---

1 Krishna River in central-southern India.
2 Tapti River.

Men hurried hither and thither; anything like organization was past all hope; each, as he could gain his horse, threw himself upon it and fled for his life: not a man stood. In vain I entreated those with me to rally, and make a charge on the small body of red-coats which was now drawn up in line close to our camp, and was pouring volley after volley amongst us with destructive precision. Not a man would hear me; and though my own Thugs and a few of my division swore they would die if I were to lead them on, I saw no chance of success; and as one or two of my men had fallen near me, we too at length turned our horses' heads and fled. We were not pursued, though there were some horsemen with the infantry, who, had they not been the most arrant cowards, would have charged after and engaged us.

I must say I longed that they should, and I kept my men, nearly a hundred, in a close body, while from time to time we faced about and shook our spears in defiance at the body of horse, about our own number, who, however, did not stir. We saw the infantry once more put in motion, take possession of our camp, which, with the thousands of temporary screens from the sun standing here and there, and the fires burning under half-cooked victuals, must have been a welcome resting-place to them after their long march. They must have gained a considerable booty, for many a man threw himself on the bare back of his horse, leaving a well-lined saddle behind him to the victors.

Our surprise and rout was complete; and if the enemy had had a larger body of infantry, or any good cavalry with them to have followed us, we might have bidden adieu to all hopes of future plunder, and most likely should have taken our way to our respective homes and abandoned the expedition. As it was, however, we found we had not lost more than a hundred men, and three days afterwards we were again reunited, and in as good spirits as ever.

At length we debouched by almost untrodden paths from the hills to the eastward of Ellichpoor, and from among the dense jungles I had before traversed, after the affair with the Moghulanee.[1] We entered the territories of the Nizam near the river Wurda,[2] which we crossed, and in one march of nearly twenty-five coss reached Oomraotee, which it appeared had been the object of our leader from the first. I have once before described its riches and prosperity, and it was then far richer than it is now.

As we rushed along, more like the flood of a mighty river than aught else, every village on our route was instantly deserted by its inhabitants and left to our mercy.

---

1 Persian woman.
2 Wardha River.

They were one by one ransacked for treasure, and in some of the largest much booty was obtained. I was fortunate in leading the advance-guard on this day, and well do I remember the excitement of the moment, as we passed the last defile in the hills, and rushed in a body into the plain. Well do I remember waving my sword to my companions,—whose numbers were now swelled to nearly five hundred splendid fellows, often increased by parties from the rear,—as I showed them the broad plains of Berar, and told them that we had unlimited power to plunder as we listed!

Ghuffoor Khan envied me that day; he had been detained with Cheetoo, who remained with the main body, while my own harawul[1] was increased, in order that I might advance and surround Oomraotee. On we dashed! The few villages we surprised were quickly laid under contribution; and rupees and gold and silver ornaments were tendered, almost without our asking, by their terrified inhabitants. As we proceeded, the news that we were coming had spread through every village, and thousands of the people were seen flying from their homes; while a few only remained in each, with an offering to me, accompanied by entreaties not to burn their villages. Nor did I; though from the pillars of smoke which not long afterwards arose in every direction behind us, I too justly thought the main body had been less merciful than we had. We reached Oomraotee towards evening. There were but few soldiers to guard this important post, and they had fled on the news of our approach; we therefore entered the town unchecked and unopposed. How different was my present from my former visit!

I directed my course to the main street, where I knew I should find the principal sahoukars; and, after stationing parties of my men at each end and at the different outlets, I rode into the middle of the chouke, or market-place, and dismounted among the leading men of the town, who had a carpet spread, and were prepared, as they said, to do us honour.

But few words of greeting passed, for ours was no cordial visit, and each party was bent on driving the hardest bargain.

"Come, gentlemen," said I, after I had listened for some time to their vain protestations of poverty and inability to raise a sum adequate to my desires, "this is mere fooling. You have offered a lakh[2] of rupees; do you think the noble Cheetoo will be satisfied with this? I swear by the Koran he will not, and you had better at once be reasonable and listen to my words. The whole lubhur will be here before it is dark, and if any of you will take the trouble to ascend one of your tall houses, or one of

---

1   Advance guard of an army.

2   100,000.

the bastions, you will see how Pindharees mark their progress. Many a fine village behind me has not now a roof or tree standing, and your good town will assuredly share the same fate if you trifle with us; and not only will it be burned, but your property will be handed over to the tender mercies of my men—ay, and your wives and daughters also; so I give you fair warning. You have no force to oppose us; and if you refuse, I am desired to tell you that we shall stay here for some days and amuse ourselves by inspecting the interior of your houses. Go, therefore, be wise, consult among yourselves, and before the shadow of this tree has lengthened the measure of my sword (and I laid it on the ground), bring me an answer worthy of your name for wisdom, and liberal withal; beyond that time I give you not a moment; your houses are close at hand, and Inshalla! we will help ourselves."

"Well spoken!" cried all the men who were around me; "but, Meer Sahib, why not help ourselves at once? These stingy merchants can have no idea of the wants of men of honour like us, who have a long journey before us."

"You shall hear what they say," replied I; "meanwhile, let us be quiet and orderly, and let none of you interrupt their consultations, or offer violence to any of the townspeople."

The time had nearly elapsed, and the hilt of my sword was all that remained in the sunlight. The council of the merchants was, from all appearances, as far from a decision as ever, if I might judge from their angry debate and the unsettled and anxious expressions of their countenances.

Eagerly I watched the increasing shadow, as from time to time I called to them that the period allowed had nearly elapsed; at last the bright hilt of my sword glittered no longer, and I took it up amidst a shout from my men. The merchants saw my action, and again advanced in a body towards me.

"Sit down, Meer Sahib," said the fattest of them, who appeared to be the chief, "sit down; let us talk over this matter calmly and deliberately. That business is always unsatisfactory which is done in a hurry and with heated minds."

"No!" I exclaimed, "I will not: standing as I am, I will hear what you have to say. Remember, when I draw my sword the plunder begins, and though I have some influence over these brave fellows while they expect a reasonable offer from you, yet the instant they are disappointed my power ends, and I will not answer for any of your lives."

"Come aside with me for a moment," said the chief merchant; "I would speak with you apart: you need fear no treachery from a sahoukar!"

We all laughed heartily. "No, no," said I, "I fear naught, and will come. And do you, my good fellows," I added, turning to my men, "see that none of these worthy persons escape."

"Well," said I, when we had gone a few paces from the group, "what would you say? Be quick: my men are impatient, and your houses and shops are provokingly and temptingly near."

"Listen then," replied he: "you are a leader, and by your conduct doubtless have the influence you appear to have. You have not more than five hundred men with you; we offer you, therefore, ten thousand rupees as your own share, one thousand to each of your sirdars,[1] and one hundred apiece to your men; this will be nearly a lakh of rupees, and we will take our chance with the main body. What do you say? be quick and tell me, for the money is at hand, and can be easily distributed before the main body comes up."

I pondered awhile; I knew Cheetoo would make his own terms, and I did not see any harm in getting as much as I could of the spoil before he came. I knew also that he expected ten lakhs, and would get it, or nearly the sum, by fair means or foul. "Listen again," said the sahoukar; you are in advance, you have naught to do but take your money and push on, and any village before you will shelter you for the night; what will Cheetoo know of it?"

"Nay," said I, "here we remain; after a march of twenty-five coss, we are in no humour to proceed. But I will take my men outside the town on the instant payment of one lakh of rupees; remember, one third of what we get goes to the chief, and our share after all is not much."

"Agreed," said he; "now come to your men, and persuade them to be quiet: they will not get so much by violence as by treating us well."

We returned to the group we had left, and I unfolded to them the proposition which had been made to me; it was welcomed with a loud shout which made the air ring, and was then succeeded by loud cries for the money.

The sum had evidently been collected previously, for in a few moments a line of men, heavily laden with bags of rupees, issued from a lane close to where we were sitting. Duffa[2] by duffa of the Pindharees, each headed by its own duffadar,[3] was brought up to the spot; each man received his hundred rupees, each leader his thousand, which were stowed away in the capacious bags of their saddles.

---

1   Chiefs.

2   Squadron.

3   Squad leader.

"You have not cared for yourself, Meer Sahib," said Peer Khan; "you have taken nothing."

"Oh, do not fear for me," I replied; "I shall get my share; the bag does not look large, but it will hold gold."

His eyes brightened. "That is right," he said; "the others must not know of it."

"Not a syllable; it is known only to you and myself. Now we must take care these rascals commit no excesses; they seem half in the humour to run riot in the town,"

"They seem content," he replied; "at least, I for one am. By Alla! Meer Sahib, this is rare work; a thousand rupees in a morning's ride is better than our own profession, though we have been lucky in our time."

"Choop!"[1] said I, "silence! This is no time for our secrets. Away with you! See that the men take up ground before the town. I will remain here with some others, and see what becomes of the place when Cheetoo arrives."

One by one the Pindharees left me, except a few who stayed by my desire; and our business at an end, I sat down and awaited Cheetoo's arrival.

"What do you think he will ask?" said my fat friend to me.

"I know not," I answered; "but you had better be liberal at once, or he will sack your town, and you know what Pindharees are; they have few scruples, and some of you may be tortured."

A general shudder ran through the assembly at the thought of the torture, and I saw I had made a hit. "Yes," I continued. "there are such things as korlas,[2] and your fat backs would soon be laid open; besides, there are fellows who are rare hands at tying up fingers and hitting them on the ends, which is not agreeable, I should think, also at mixing compositions for those bags to be tied over your mouths. I have heard of even still worse contrivances to persuade obstinate sahoukars; but ye are wise men—ye will be warned."

"Say at once, Meer Sahib," said another of the merchants who had not yet spoken, "say what we should offer, and how many Pindharees are there? We have heard there are five thousand."

"Somewhat below the mark, Sethjee," said I; "we are little under ten thousand, I think. However, you will see the lubhur, and judge for yourselves. As for the sum, I should say, in the first place, a lakh of rupees for Cheetoo himself—I know he expects as much; then there are three sirdars, Heeroo, Ghuffoor Khan, and Rajun—

---

1 Be silent!
2 Whips.

fifty thousand apiece; then each minor leader and duffadar a thousand, and every good Pindharee a hundred. Say, have I spoken well?"

"Bhugwan[1] protect us!" cried one and all, "we are ruined and dead men. Why this would be at least eight lakhs of rupees; where are we to get such a sum? We are ruined and better kill us at once."

"No, no, my good friends, not so," said I. "All the world knows that Oomraotee is the richest town in the country, ay, richer than Hyderabad itself, and that the money may be counted, not by lakhs, but by crores;[2] so talk not to Cheetoo of your poverty, for he will presently prove whether you lie or not. Trust me, your safest plan is to offer him a large sum at once, for he has a long journey before him; the men have got nothing since we left Nemawur, and they are hungry and thirsty."

"I tell you all," said the fat sahoukar, "the worthy Meer Sahib speaks the truth. Bhugwan has sent this gurdee (calamity), and we must be resigned to our fate. Better far is it to give the uttermost farthing, than to see our wives and daughters dishonoured before our eyes. I have spoken."

"Good!" cried I; "now you speak like wise men, and I will give you further advice. Cheetoo is a great man, and loves to be paid honour, as indeed is due to him; so also do the other leaders. Now get you pan, uttur, and spices, make up a proper tray of them, bring a few handsome shawls, and as he takes his seat, one of you throw a pair of the best over his shoulders and those of the other chiefs, and lay your nuzzurs before him as you would before Sikundur Jah[3] himself; Inshalla! you will find favour in his sight, and where you would have to pay ten lakhs you will get off with, half the sum, and save your town besides."

"By Gunga![4] 'tis well said!" cried several. "Meer Sahib, you are a kind friend and give good advice; without you we should not have known what to do."

"Again," said I, "let none of you have long faces, but all look as if you were rejoiced at his coming. Be none of you alarmed before you have cause. Pay you must, and therefore do it with as good a grace as you can."

The assembly drank in my words, as I by turns advised and alarmed them, in order to keep up the spirit I had infused; and in this manner the time passed until the dusk of evening, when, by the noise of the tread or many horses' feet and the firing of matchlocks, we were assured of the approach of the main body.

---

1   Divine one.

2   Tens of millions.

3   The Nizam of Hyderabad from 1803 to 1829.

4   Ganga, Hindu goddess.

"Now stick by us," cried the sahoukars as they crowded round me; "you are our friend and must present us; we will not be afraid." But their words belied them, for the teeth of one and all were chattering with fear, and their cheeks blanched at the thought of confronting the renowned Pindharee chief.

Cheetoo came, and riding into the chouke, surrounded by a crowd of wild-looking figures, the effect of whose appearance was materially increased by the dusk of the evening, his titles were screamed out by a dozen mouths, each vying with the other in exaggeration of his powers.

The group of sahoukars, headed by me, advanced towards him; and the head merchant, rubbing his forehead on the chief's stirrup, implored him to alight and refresh himself, adding that a zeafut[1] had been prepared, and all were desirous of presenting their nuzzurs.

I seconded the request, and he exclaimed, "Surely I know that voice; whose, in the name of Shitan, is it?"

"That of your slave, Ameer Ali," said I.

"Oh, then all is right," he cried; "and thou too hast turned sahoukar. How is this, Meer Sahib?"

"May I be your sacrifice, Nuwab!" said I; "I have but mingled with these worthy persons, because they declared they should be annihilated at the sight of the splendour of your appearance. I did but console them and keep up their spirits till my lord arrived."

"Thou hast done well," said Cheetoo. "Is everything prepared?"

"All," cried the sahoukars; "if the noble Cheetoo will but alight, we are prepared to do him honour."

He alighted, and led by the hand by the chief merchant, he was conducted into an adjoining house, which belonged to one of the merchants, and where a clean white floor-cloth had been spread, and a musnud[2] placed. The room too was well lighted. Cheetoo took his seat, and looked around him with evident gratification; savage as his countenance was, it now wore a smile of triumph, yet mixed with an expression of extreme pleasure.

"These are civilised people," said he to Rajun, his favourite, who was close to him. "I little expected this: did you?"

"Indeed, no," said he; "I thought we should have had to cut our way into the town. Depend on it, this is some of Ameer Ali's doing."

---

1 Feast.
2 Throne.

"Likely enough," said Cheetoo; "he is a gentleman, and knows how a gentleman ought to be received. But for him it is most probable these swine would have shut themselves up in their houses, and given us the trouble of pulling them out. But see,—what are they about?"

I was nudged by the sahoukar, who, whispering, implored me to ask Cheetoo to accept their nuzzur. "Five hundred rupees for you if he takes it," again he whispered as I pretended to hesitate. "Agreed," said I; "I will revenge myself if it is not paid."

"By Gunga! by my Junwa!"[1] again said he most earnestly, "nay, I will double it. Speak for us, good Meer Sahib, are you not our friend and our brother?"

"What are those sons of asses talking to you about?" cried Cheetoo. "Why don't they speak out?"

"Khodawund!" I said, "the terror of your name has preceded you"—and he smiled grimly,—"and your appearance is in every way so imposing and surpassing the accounts these men have heard, that, by Alla! they are dumb; and though they would fain lay a nuzzur at your feet, in every way befitting your high rank, they have not words to express their desires, and have begged your slave to inform my lord of them."

"Kubool, Kubool! I agree," cried Cheetoo; "let the trays be brought. Verily a nuzzur from the sahoukars of Oomraotee ought to be worth seeing."

Fifteen trays were brought in, covered with rich velvet coverings, and set down before the musnud; one by one their covers were removed, and indeed it was a goodly sight! Dates, pistachio nuts, sweetmeats, and sugar-candy filled four; the rest contained cloths of various kinds, European and Indian, muslins, chintzes, rich turbans, and Benares brocades. It was a nuzzur fit for a prince, and Cheetoo was delighted.

"Now," said I to the sahoukar, "this is a happy moment; where are the shawls and the ashruffees?[2] Have a stout heart, and throw the shawls over him, as you would over one of your own tribe at a marriage."

The sahoukar took the shawls from an attendant, and putting five ashruffees upon them, advanced to the feet of Cheetoo; and having made the tusleemat, or three obeisances, he presented the gold, and unfolding the shawls, which were very splendid, dexterously enveloped the chiefs person in them, and then retreating, stood with his hands folded on his breast in an attitude of respectful humility.

---

1 Sacred thread worn by Hindu men over the left shoulder.

2 Gold coins.

Chapter XXXIV

The sons of Fortune, she has sent us forth
To thrive by the keen action of our wits,
Which, backed by fearful dread of our bright swords,
Doth fill our purses speedily.

CHEETOO was evidently flattered by the distinction with which he had been received, and as he examined the beautiful shawls which now enveloped his person, a grim smile of delight lighted up his coarse features. "These men have sense," said he to Ghuffoor Khan, "and are evidently accustomed to the visits of persons of quality. "We little expected this civility, and in truth it is most acceptable after our long ride; but they have forgotten you."

"Not so, noble Cheetoo," cried the sahoukar, advancing with several pairs of shawls over his arm; "we are not forgetful of our distinguished guests;" and he threw a pair over each of the chiefs, which they received with complacency.

"Let the room be cleared," cried Cheetoo; "we have business with these worthy gentlemen, which I have sworn to do before we touch any refreshment."

It was quickly done, and there only remained our leaders. And the sahoukars, who huddled together like wild fowl on the approach of a hawk.

"Come forward," said Cheetoo to them; "come and sit near us; we would speak to you."

They all arose, and, as they were directed, seated themselves in respectful attitudes on the edge of the musnud.

"Now," continued Cheetoo, "you are doubtless aware of our object. "We want money; and money we will have, by fair means or foul. If ye are wise, ye will pay me handsomely to be rid of me and my people, who are savage fellows. I desire not to harm you, and on your own heads be it, if any disaster befalls you. Say, therefore, how much are ye prepared to give?"

"Truly," said the sahoukar, my friend, who was the spokesman, "we have been duly advised of your Highness's coming; and as a proof that we did not dread you, you see us here, and we have done our poor ability to welcome so distinguished a person. We have also received good counsel from your servant the Meer Sahib; and agreeably to his instructions we have drawn up a list of a few trifles and some ready money which we are desirous of laying at the feet of your Highness." And the sahoukar handed to him a paper written in Persian.

"This is unintelligible to me, for I am no moonshee;[1] but can any of you read, brothers?" asked Cheetoo of the other leaders.

"Not a word, not a letter," cried one and all: "none of us know one letter from another."

"I can send for a moonshee," said the sahoukar; "one is in attendance."

"If I am permitted," said I, "I will read the list: I may be able to make it out."

"Ha! thou art a clerk as well as a good soldier," cried Cheetoo, laughing. "Well, take the paper, and let us hear our good fortune."

"First then," said I, after I had glanced over the document, "this paper sets forth, that the sahoukars and others of the market-town of Oomraotee, in council assembled, having heard of the near approach of the mighty Cheetoo and his army, and being desirous of approaching his feet with a small tribute of respect, have put down the following articles and sums of ready money, which are prepared and ready for his acceptance,—on no condition save that they may find favour in his sight, and be the humble means of insuring his clemency to others."

"Good!" said Cheetoo. "Now get thee to the marrow of the matter as speedily as may be, for my stomach craves food, and I doubt not these worthy gentlemen's families have prepared a repast for me."

"It is ready, noble Cheetoo," cried the sahoukar; "and if the order is given, it will be set out; but the food of us poor Hindoos would be tasteless to my lord, and therefore we have had the repast cooked by the best bawurchees[2] of the town."

"Silence!" cried the chief; "speak when you are allowed to do so: we are in no humour to be interrupted."

The sahoukar shrank back intimidated, and raising my voice I proceeded.

"The first item, Protector of the Poor!" cried I, "is a sum of fifty thousand rupees for yourself."

"Is that all?" cried he, his brow contracting.

"Stay," said I; "more follows. 'A tray of choice jewels, gold, and silver, valued at fifteen thousand rupees, and three trays of shawls and brocades for my lord's muhal,[3] valued at ten thousand rupees: in all, seventy-five thousand rupees. Secondly, a sum of ten thousand rupees to each leader of rank, of whom we learn from the worthy

---

1 Scribe.
2 Cooks.
3 Palace.

syud, Ameer Ali, there are three; a tray of jewels to each, of five thousand rupees, and three trays, each valued at five thousand more: in all, twenty thousand rupees each.'"

"Go on!" cried Cheetoo; "you have not done yet, I suppose?"

"No," said I, glancing down the paper; "there is more following. 'Thirdly, a sum of one thousand rupees to each duffadar; We are uninformed of their number, but we have supposed thirty.'"

"Good!" cried Cheetoo; "what more?"

"'Fourthly, the sum of fifty rupees to each deserving person, to be given at the discretion of the mighty Cheetoo; by report we hear there are four thousand. Also food, grain, and forage for as many days as the army may remain with us.' This is all," said I; "what are my lord's orders?"

"The list is well enough," said Cheetoo; "but they are wrong in some particulars: first, there are fifty duffadars, are there not, Ghuffoor Khan?"

"There are," he replied; "I told them off myself."

"Put that down, Meer Sahib," said Cheetoo. "Again, there are five thousand good Pindharees; am I not right?"

"True again," cried all the leaders; "were they not counted at Nemawur?"

This was a lie; there were hardly four thousand, for nearly half the lubhur had gone off in a different direction from the Nurbudda; but it signified little, for Cheetoo, I knew, was determined to make the best terms he could with the sahoukars.

"Put down five thousand," said Cheetoo; "and now see how much you have got."

I hastily arranged the amount, and read the paper to him. "First," said I, "there is your Highness's share, seventy-five thousand rupees; secondly, on account of the leaders, sixty thousand rupees; then the fifty duffadars, each man a thousand, fifty thousand rupees; lastly, five thousand men, each forty, two hundred thousand. And the sum of the whole is three lakhs and eighty-five thousand rupees."

"And," said Cheetoo to Ghuffoor Khan, "the horses' shoes must be worn out, I think? we require new ones."

"Certainly," cried the Khan, with a merry grin.

"Put down fifteen thousand rupees for the horse-shoes: this, Meer Sahib, will make the sum an even four lakhs; and, gentlemen," continued he to the sahoukars, "I must trouble you to pay with as little delay as possible, or we must help ourselves."

There was a hurried conference for a few moments among the sahoukars, and a few angry words passed among them; but they were wise: my fat friend rose, and making a lowly obeisance, declared the money was at hand, and should be brought immediately.

"Good!" cried Cheetoo; "now let me have my dinner, and do you all see that the duffadars are present at this house by to-morrow's dawn, to receive their shares and those of their men. The lubhur must move on, for after this kind reception, I would not have my friends the sahoukars exposed to the chance of being plundered by my lawless bands."

The chiefs separated, and I was preparing to leave the room with them, when Cheetoo called me back: "Come and take your dinner with me," said he; "I doubt not your friends the sahoukars have prepared enongh for us two."

I obeyed the order, and seated myself at the edge of the musnud. The dinner was soon brought, and a choice repast it was. We did justice to it, for in truth our travel had sharpened our appetites. These satisfied, and inhaling the fragrant smoke of our pipes, Cheetoo asked me how I had managed to bring about so advantageous a reception as he had met with.

I related the whole to him, suppressing, however, the fact that I had secured for myself so large a sum as ten thousand rupees; for had I disclosed that, he would presently have helped himself to half of it at least. Peer Khan was the only person who knew of it, and to him alone was I determined to entrust it.

He was delighted; he had, I knew, determined to raise a large sum, and I had purposely exaggerated his probable demand to the sahoukars; this, and my threats and hints of the place being given up to plunder on the least demur on their parts of paying handsomely, had been successful.

"You see, Meer Sahib," said he, "by your excellent conduct I have secured, first, seventy-five thousand rupees; and what is over, after every proper Pindharee has got his forty rupees, will make the sum pretty near a lakh: which is, you will say, a good beginning."

"May your prosperity increase, noble Cheetoo," said I; "if your slave can help you to a few more sums like the present, he will only feel himself too happy, and too honoured by distinction like the present. For the men I had with me, I made the same terms as you have accepted for the whole, and they were well satisfied."

"And for yourself, Meer Sahib?"

"I have not got much," said I; "perhaps I might have arrogated to myself the distinction of one of the leaders, but I refrained; they gave me five thousand rupees however, and I am satisfied."

"Nay," said Cheetoo; "it was too little, my friend, and I advise you to get as much as you can—next time. And as you have behaved so well in this instance at the head of the advance party, I will give it into your command in future, and must satisfy Ghuffoor Khan as well as I can; he is a good soldier, but a thick-headed fellow, who is always for helping himself, and setting fire to towns and villages, by which we seldom get half as much, especially from these rich places, as we could do by a little management and a few soft words."

"May your condescension increase, Nuwab!" cried I; "your servant, Inshalla! will never disappoint you."

I took leave of him soon afterwards, and joined the sahoukars, who were sitting below counting the money, which lay in large heaps on the floor.

They received me joyfully, and expressed in forcible language how much they were indebted to me for my active interference in their behalf. They would have pressed on me the five hundred rupees they had promised when I presented them to Cheetoo, but I refused it.

"No," said I; "if I have done you service, and I think I have, I will not sell my good offices. You have dealt as well by me as I have by you, so the balance is even; all I pray of you is to let me have my money in gold bars, which I can easily conceal, except a few hundred rupees for present expenses."

"It is granted," said the sahoukar; and I had shortly afterwards the gold in my possession; and taking a few of the sahoukar's men to guard me, I bent my way to the camp, the bright fires of which sparkled through the darkness on the plain beyond the town, revealing many a wild group which huddled round them to warm themselves from the effects of the almost chilling night breeze. I was soon at my little tent, which consisted of a cloth stretched over three spears, two of which were stuck into the ground, and another tied across them as a ridge pole; and assisted by Peer Khan, I put the gold into the bags I had had made in the flaps of my saddle, and sewed them over. I was ten thousand rupees richer in one night!

"This is grand work," said Peer Khan; "here we have had no trouble; and if we go on at this rate, we shall return far richer than after the toil and risk of a hundred Thuggee expeditions.

"I am to have the advance-guard always," said I; "and it shall be my own fault if we do not always secure a good share; for my own part, I have foresworn Thuggee, as long as there is a Pindharee chief to erect his standard."

"And we will all follow you," he replied; "Motee and the others are delighted with their success, and are in high spirits: there is not one of them but has got a good share of to-day's work, for we stuck near you, and were bribed well to use our influence with you; they thought us all duffadars, and you know Motee and myself shared as such."

"It shall not be my fault," said I, "if you are not all duffadars in reality before long. Let the men make themselves active, and dress handsomely: you are all well mounted, and will catch the eye of the chief."

By dawn the next morning I was with Cheetoo. The sahoukars had collected the whole of the money, by subscriptions among themselves and collections from the town; and the whole was distributed fairly, I must say, among the Pindharees. Each duffadar bore away the share of his duffa, and they knew too well the risk they would run if they defrauded any man of his just due.

A few hours elapsed, and after a hurried meal, every man was on his horse, and the lubhur departed to seek fresh plunder in the country before them. Yet before he set out, Cheetoo promised, in consequence of the ready payment of the sum he received, that in every future expedition he might undertake, the town of Oomraotee should be exempted from contributions; and he kept his word. Oomraotee was never again plundered, and a large body of troops, which were stationed there afterwards, effectually deterred small and straggling parties from surprising it as we had done.

Onwards we dashed. I, at the head of my band, who had now implicit confidence in me, caracoled along on my gallant horse, with a heart as light and happy as the unlimited freedom of action I possessed could make it. No thought of care intruded, and I was spared the pain of seeing the villages we passed through (from each of which we levied as much as we could, which was instantly laden on the Shootur camels[1] that accompanied us) burned or plundered, and the inoffensive inhabitants subjected to the cruel tortures of the men in the rear, who were often disappointed of booty.

We halted at Karinjah; a few soldiers who were in the town made a feeble defence, and wounded a few of my men as we rushed into the place; but they were soon killed or dispersed, and, as a warning to other villages, it was given up to sack and ruin. I could never bear the sight of wanton cruelty, and I repaired to my place in the camp; shortly afterwards I could see, from the bright blaze which rose from different parts of the village almost simultaneously against the clear grey evening sky, that it was doomed to destruction. Rapidly the fire spread, while the shouts of the Pindharees engaged in their horrid work, and the screams of inhabitants—those of the women were fearfully shrill and distinct—made a fit accompaniment. But it was work in which the Pindharees delighted; order, which never existed save when there was no excitement, was completely at an end, and any attempt to have checked the mad riot which was going on would have been attended most likely with death to the

---

1   Riding camels.

interferer. My own Thugs, too, sat around me, for a Thug is not savage, and they had no inclination to join in the excesses.

We sat in silence, but our attention was soon arrested by the figure of a man dragging along a girl, who resisted to the utmost of her power, but who was evidently nearly exhausted. I rushed forward to her rescue, and my eyes fell on the person of Ghuffoor Khan, his savage features exaggerated in their ferocious expression by lust and the scene he had been engaged in.

"Ha!" cried he, "Meer Sahib, is that you? Here have I been working like a true Pindharee, and have brought off something worth having; look at her, man! is she not a peri, a houri? The fool, her mother, must needs oppose me when I got into their house, but I silenced her with a thrust of my sword, and lo! here is her fair daughter, a worthy mate for a prince. Speak, my pretty one, art not thou honoured at the prospect of the embraces of Ghuffoor Khan?"

By Alla! Sahib, I could have killed him, and it would have been an easy matter to have done so, as he stood unprepared. I had half drawn my sword from its scabbard, but I returned it; I made an inward determination as to his fate, and I kept it. I vainly endeavoured to induce him to give up the girl and let her go, but he laughed in my face, and dragged her off. She would fain have fled from him, and attempted to do so, but he pursued and caught her, for her tender feet were cut by the rough ground, and I lost sight of them both in the quickly closing darkness. Miserable girl! she was a Brahmin's daughter, and was spared the degradation of seeing the light of another day, and the misery of returning to her desolate home polluted and an outcast: Ghuffoor Khan told me in the morning, with a hellish laugh, that he had murdered her, as she tried to possess herself of his dagger, to plunge into her own heart. "I spared her the trouble," he said.

Gradually the fire lessened in its fury, as there remained but few houses unconsumed, but the Pindharees were still at their wild and horrible work, as the shrieks borne to us on the night wind too well testified. I had heard that these excesses were sometimes committed, but I had formed no idea of their terrible reality. A thousand times I formed the resolution to quit the lubhur and return to my home; but again the thought, that a few straggling horsemen, who could give no proper account of themselves, would be immediately taken for Pindharees, and sacrificed by the now infuriated people of the country—this and, I must add, a restless desire for further adventures, caused me to dismiss it from my mind. It began to rain, too, and we all huddled together in my little tent, and passed a weary night till the morning broke. Then we were again in motion, and the ill-fated town of Karinjah, now a heap of smouldering ruins, was soon far behind us.

We passed Mungrool; and beyond the town, now in the broad daylight, I had an opportunity of seeing the spot where my first victim had fallen. I had thought that the place where he fell was in a large and dense jungle, so at least it appeared that night in the moonlight,—but it was not so; the rivulet was the same as when we had passed it, and I stood once more on the very spot where the sahoukar had fallen! A thin belt of bushes fringed the stream, and Peer Khan pointed with a significant gesture a little higher up than the place at which we crossed. It was the *bhil* where they were buried, and it now seemed a fearfully insecure spot for the concealment of our victims,—so close to the road, and apparently so thinly screened from observation. Yet many years had now passed since they were deposited in their last resting-place, and a succession of rainy seasons had either washed away their remains or covered them still deeper with sand.

We passed the spot, too, where our bands had encamped and separated; and before me was now a new country, though it little differed in character from that we had already traversed.

We halted at Basim,[1] and I greatly feared a repetition of the scenes of the past night; but the men were, to my astonishment, quiet and orderly; and a handsome contribution levied in the town in all probability saved it. From hence, in five marches, we reached Nandair on the Godavery,[2] a rich town, and one which promised as large a supply to our army as we had got at Oomraotee. We had feared the news of our approach would have reached it, and that the sahoukars and wealthy inhabitants would have fled; but it was not so: they were completely surprised and at our mercy, for not a single soldier worth mentioning was there to guard the place. A few there certainly were, who shut themselves up in an old fort which overhangs the river and commands the ford; but they kept within the walls, only firing a matchlock-shot or two whenever any of our marauders approached too near; we did not molest them, but set ourselves to work to levy as large a sum as possible.

As before, the advance-guard had been entrusted to me, and I pursued the same system I had done at Oomraotee.

I will not weary you with a repetition of almost the same tale; suffice it to say, that one lakh and a half of rupees were collected and paid to the army, and I got for my own share nearly three thousand rupees, some jewels, and a pair of shawls. The town was not destroyed; indeed, that would have been impossible, as the houses were substantial ones, with terraced roofs; but the suburbs suffered, and the huts of the

---

1 Washim.
2 Godavari River.

unfortunate weavers were sacked for the fine cloths for which the place is famous,—nor in vain, for half the army next day appeared in new turbans and waist-bands.

The river was not fordable, and there was but one boat; we therefore pushed along the northern bank till we reached Gunga Khair, where we were told there were boats and a more convenient ferry; nor were we disappointed. We crossed with ease during the day on which we arrived opposite the place, the men swimming their horses across, and the plunder and baggage being brought over by the boats. A few hundred men attempted to defend the town, but it was carried by forcing open the gate, and plundered. We lost some of our men, and I was grazed on the leg by a bullet, and disabled from taking active part in the sack of the place. Peer Khan and Motee were however not idle, and brought a goodly heap of jewels and coin to swell the general stock.

From hence we penetrated southward. Beeder, Bhalkee, the fine and flourishing town of Hoomnabad (a second Oomraotee), were severally plundered or laid under heavy contributions; while every village which lay in our route was sacked, and too often burned and destroyed. From Hoomnabad I led three hundred men to Kullianee, a few coss distant; but we found the alarm had been given, and that all the rich inhabitants had taken refuge in the fort, which is a very strong one, and to us was impregnable. Such was the dread we inspired, however, that the defenders of it remained quietly within it, and allowed us to keep quiet possession of the town till the next morning, when we again rejoined the main body.

We descended by a pass in the hills to the village of Chincholee, which was of course plundered, and we followed a direct southwardly route, burning and plundering every place in our way, till the broad and deep stream of the Krishna effectually opposed our farther progress. Here the lubhur halted for some days; forage was plentiful, every one was loaded with money, and we enjoyed ourselves in our encampment as true Pindharees. Dancing-girls were seized from all parts of the surrounding country, though no violence was ever offered to them, and they amused us with their songs and performances, and left us when we were again put in motion, well satisfied and well rewarded, and regretting that they could not accompany us.

Cheetoo was wrong to have halted, for the alarm that Pindharees were out had flown through the country, and in our march towards Koolburgah we got no plunder worth mentioning. Koolburgah we found garrisoned and prepared for our reception; so relinquishing our designs upon Sholapoor and the rich towns of Barsee and Wyrag, we struck off in the direction of Bheer, Pyetun and Aurungabad, hoping to surprise the latter, though we feared it would be well garrisoned.

But I was determined to surprise Barsee and Wyrag if I could, and I laid my proposals for the expedition before Cheetoo. He readily acceeded to my request, at which Ghuffoor Khan was extremely savage; and taking with me three hundred men, the best I could select, and dividing them into duffas under my own Thugs, I left the main body at the town of Allund, and dashed on towards Toljapoor, from whence there is a pass into the low country.

Toljapoor has little to recommend it but the temple of Bhowanee, which is a place of pilgrimage; and thongh I knew there were hoards of jewels in the possession of the Brahmins, yet, as many of my men were Hindoos, they would not hear of the temples being sacked, and I was forced to content myself with levying a few thousand rupees from the inhabitants.

Wyrag was our next aim, and we were successful. Our force was supposed to be a risala[1] of Mahratta horse who were known to be in the district, and we were allowed to enter the town unopposed. We sacked it, and got a large booty, for there was no time for a proposal of contribution; indeed I thought not of that alternative, nor could I restrain my men after their long march. Yet they were not cruel, nor did I hear of any of them having tortured any one, and the inhabitants gave up enough of their valuables to satisfy them easily. Here we heard that the risala we had been mistaken for was at Barsee, and as that place lay in our direct road to Bheer, where we were to join the main body, I was obliged to give up my intention of proceeding through it; there was also a large body of the Nizam's horse at Puréndah, and I feared that we might be cut off. An instant return by the road we had come was our only alternative; and after a few hours' rest we were again in our saddles, and travelling as fast as we could urge our horses towards Toljapoor. Nobly did my gallant horse carry me that day; most of the men dosed theirs with opium to insure their bottom, but my good charger needed it not, and he was almost as fresh when we again reached Toljapoor, as when he had left it.

Here we rested a day to refresh ourselves, and after that, pushing on, we overtook the main body at Bheer, where they were encamped. I had been baffled in part of my design, yet Cheetoo received with great complacency ten thousand rupees in money, and nearly the same amount in jewels, which I presented to him in full durbar as the results of my enterprise; for this he invested me with a dress of honour, and presented me with a good horse from among his own.

———————•———————

1 Regiment.

Chapter XXXV

RELATES HOW, ENCOURAGED BY HIS SUCCESS, CHEETOO PLANS ANOTHER EXPEDITION ON A LARGER SCALE, AND HOW AMEER ALI JOINED IT

BHEER was sacked and given up to rapine and excess for two whole days; and when we left it scarcely a rag remained to the miserable inhabitants. It was piteous to see them raking together a few posts of wood, many of them half burned, and erecting wretched hovels, which they covered with green boughs, to screen themselves from the cold winds of the night. They suffered the ravage of their town passively, for there were no soldiers to protect it; and what could they have done against a well-armed and savage horde like ours?

Pyetun, on the Godavery, shared the same fate; and though many of the rich inhabitants had fled for refuge to Aurungabad, yet enough remained for our purpose. You know, perhaps, that this place is celebrated for a manufacture of brocaded muslins, only inferior to those of Benares; and at that time there was an active demand for them, to supply the courts of Poona and Hyderabad: you may judge, therefore, of the value of the plunder we got. Cheetoo's camels and elephants were laden to the utmost; none of us fared badly; and our own stock was now so large of one valuable or another, that I hardly thought we should have been enabled to carry it with us. I need not follow our track much farther with minuteness; suffice it therefore to say, that we passed the Adjuntah Ghat, not however without being closely pressed by some troops of the Feringhees; but we eluded them by a rapid march or two, and after a vain attempt on Boorhanpoor, we struck off to the right by the valley of the Taptee, and in a few days were safely returned to the camp at Nemawur.

In little more than three months we had traversed the richest part of the broad territory of the Nizam; we had eluded his troops and those of the Feringhees, and laughed at their beards; we had plundered his richest towns with impunity; and we had returned, with scarcely the loss of a man, laden with plunder of enormous value. So rich was it, that the sahoukars of Nemawur, after purchasing all they could from us, were unable to find further funds to buy up the whole; and merchants from Oojein, and Indoor, and all the neighbouring large cities, were sent for to our rich market.

In due time all had been purchased, and every man prepared to return as quickly as he could to his home, with the proceeds of his booty. I need not say how my heart bounded at the prospect of again seeing mine, and laying at my Azeema's feet the wealth I had acquired, nor the pleasure she would experience in hearing me recount the wild adventures I had gone through. I accordingly purchased all the gold I could, as also did my men, and hiring two swift camels, I loaded them with it and the valuable cloths we had received for our own use, and was ready for a rapid march to Jhalone when I could receive my dismissal from Cheetoo's durbar. This it was not an easy matter to attain, for I had served the chief faithfully, he had confidence in my address and activity, and was loath to part with me, fearing I would not return to his standard.

The day I went to take leave he would not receive my parting gift, nor give me the usual ceremonial return of utr and pān on my departure; and I sat in the durbar in gloomy thought, that perhaps treachery was intended towards me—a poor return for my exertions. But I was wrong: he called me towards him when but few remained, and appointing a late hour in the night for an interview and private conversation, desired me to be punctual, for that he had matters of importance to reveal to me.

I returned to my abode in better hope, yet still suspecting, and almost inclined to follow the advice of Peer Khan and the rest, who would fain have had me fly, as the only means of preserving our money. I did not however entirely mistrust Cheetoo; but I determined, if he put me off with further words, and caused me more delay, that I would at once leave him in the best way I could.

I accordingly attended at the hour appointed, which was past midnight. I found the chief alone. I had never before been so honoured as to be admitted to an entirely private conference, though I had been allowed a seat in his councils, and my suggestions had been followed on more than one occasion. I could not divine what was to ensue.

"Be seated, Syud," said Cheetoo; "I have much to say to thee."

"Speak on, Nuwab," I replied; "your words are sweet to your servant, and they will fall on ears which will convey their meaning to a heart devoted to your service."

"Listen then," said he. "But first I will ask you what you thought the object of the last expedition to be?"

"Its object!" cried I. "Why, I suppose, only to get as much money as you could for yourself and your men, so as to be ready to take advantage of the war which sooner or later must ensue between the Mahrattas and the Feringhees—may their race be accursed! I never could divine a deeper object, though I have thought upon the subject myself, and heard many opinions expressed by others."

"You are partly right," said he, "but not entirely; now you shall hear the whole, and what my further projects are."

I settled myself into an attitude of profound attention, and drank in his words as he proceeded.

"You have had a watchful eye upon the times, Meer Sahib, and I expected it from you. You may have heard that Tippoo Sultan[1]—on whose memory be peace!—would fain have enlisted the Nizam and the whole of the Mahrattas in one confederacy to overthrow and extirpate the Feringhees. Had his plans been successful he would have done it; but, a curse on his avarice! he had an underplot to divide the Nizam's territories with the Mahrattas, which was discovered, Alla only knows how; and a curse on the luck of the Feringhees, who overthrew the only power which, while it lasted, upheld the dignity of the Moslem's faith! Tippoo is gone, and his power. Perhaps you are not aware that at this moment, though Holkar is sorely disabled from what he was, and Sindia has made a base league of passiveness with the Feringhees, a deep confederacy exists among the Mahratta states, and particularly between those of Poona and Nagpoor, to rise simultaneously and declare war against the usurping and never-satisfied Europeans. Sikundur Jah[2] will join with the Feringhees—not that he can do much, for his army is miserable, and his leaders have neither skill nor bravery; but still he will befriend them to the utmost, and his dominions are open to the passage and subsistence of their troops, and in them positions can be taken up which will sorely harass the future operations of the Mahratta leaders. My last expedition was therefore intended (and by the favour of Alla it has succeeded) to impoverish Sikundur Jah's country, to keep the people in a constant state of alarm, and, need I add, to fill our own purses.

"Now listen again. To effect my purpose thoroughly, and to distract the attention of the Europeans from the preparations of the Mahrattas, these expeditions must be rapid in succession to have their due effect. One half of the Huzoor's[3] dominions have been sacked, and the other half remains; Inshalla! it shall share the same fate. The Feringhees will be kept in a perpetual state of alarm; they will follow us vainly from place to place, but I fear them not. I have laughed at their beards once, and will do so again. They shall know who Cheetoo Pindharee is, and to their cost. Not only shall the cowardly Nizam suffer, but the rich provinces of the Feringhees shall be wasted. I will cross the Krishna; the river will be fordable, or nearly so; and the

---

1   Sultan Fateh Ali Tipu (1750-1799), ruler of Mysore and fierce opponent of British rule in India.

2   The Nizam.

3   His Highness's.

whole of the provinces which are not overrun by their troops shall be prostrated before my power. This will exhaust their resources and paralyze their efforts. The Mahrattas will then rise to a man. I will join them; for I have been promised a high command in their armies, and territories after their conquest; and we will rise, Meer Sahib—yes, *we*, I say, for these stirring times are the fit ones for such as myself and you—Inshalla! we will take advantage of them, and win fame for ourselves which posterity shall wonder at."

"It is a rare plan," said I, "and a deep one, while the game seems easy to play. I can find no fault with it; but will not the Feringhees be prepared for us, and meet us wherever we show our faces?"

"No!" cried he vehemently, "they will not! cunning as they are, I will be before them in the field. They now think that, glutted with plunder, we shall remain quietly here, and be fools enough to wait for another Dusera before we are again on the move; but they are wrong to a man: and here has lain the cause of my apparent secrecy with you. I could not proclaim it in my durbar that I had planned another expedition; some prating fool would have blabbed of it at his home, and the news would have flown over the country in a week. No; I have kept it secret, except from a few, and they are my chief leaders, every one of whom has a thousand men at his back. Hear me: I am determined, by the favour of Alla, to move hence at the head of a larger army than the last has been, in a space of time under two months. Say, will you come? I will give you the command of a thousand horse, for I love you and depend upon you. Can you return from Jhalone in that time? I have no wish to detain you here: a man's home is dear to him wherever it is, and you are right to return to it. Yet tell me that you will join me within two months, and what I have promised I will perform."

"I will," cried I; "may your condescension increase, your slave will take advantage of your bounty. In less than two months, though I travel night and day, I will come, and bring more men with me."

"The more the better," said Cheetoo. "Take the best horse from my stable if you wish it, he cannot be in better hands than your own; and as you will want camels, take, too, as many as you require from my own fleet ones. Load them lightly and they will keep up with you. And now go: I am weary in mind and body, and need repose; you, I doubt not, will start with the morning's dawn. Go, and may peace be with you!"

I left him, and joyfully rejoined my associates. I knew the secret was safe with them; and as I unfolded the deep plan to them, they were lost in wonder and admiration at Cheetoo's sagacity and forethought. To a man they swore to join me, and to follow my fortunes through good or ill. Merrily we set off the next morning, and quickly miles and miles of road disappeared under the hoofs of our fleet and hardy steeds. In far less time than it had taken us to come, we had reached Jhalone, unlooked-for and unexpected, and with a joyful bound I crossed my own threshold, and was again clasped in the embrace of my Azeema. What words can paint our joy? I cannot describe it; my heart was too full for utterance, as I was again seated in my own zenana, and beheld the frolics and gambols of my beauteous child. My father, too, rejoiced with me; but there was an eye of evil upon us: our cup of joy was fated to be no sooner filled to the brim than to be dashed from our lips. That eye was the Rajah's. But more of that hereafter.

Not that I neglected him: the prices of his horses were duly paid, and I presented to him a valuable string of pearls, with some beautiful cloths, the plunder of Pyetun, and a tray of fifty-one gold pieces. One would have thought he would have been satisfied, but it was not so; yet he was all smiles and congratulations. I was invested with a dress of honour, and encouraged privately (for he secretly knew of the new enterprise), to further exertions, and cheered on by him to win distinction and renown. Base liar and murderer! he deceived me; but who could have guessed his thoughts?

As soon as I could, I despatched Peer Khan and Motee with two of the others in various directions, to offer terms of employment and the prospect of booty to as many Thugs as they knew to be good men and good horsemen—the latter was a qualification in which but few Thugs excelled; nevertheless, in the space of ten days they returned with twelve others, some of whom I knew, and all were stated to be resolute men, well acquainted with the use of their weapons. They were easily provided with horses from the Rajah's stables, as the first had been, for he had received more than double their value, and would now have risked his whole stud on the same terms. I examined their arms, and rejected such as were defective, supplying them with others. Our saddles were newly stuffed, and every preparation which our experience could suggest was made for even a longer and more arduous enterprise than that from which we had just returned.

But little time now remained to me to enjoy the quiet peacefulness of my home; and now that I was there, I would fain have never again left it. Wealth I had in abundance, enough for many years; and I was in a situation from which I could have risen to a high civil employment, in the management of revenue in the Rajah's country. Still, the desire for adventure was not blunted, and above all, the promise I had given to Cheetoo could not be evaded or neglected; and had he not promised me the command of a thousand men? This had many charms in my sight; and should his plans succeed, to what rank might I not rise by my exertions, when the Mahrattas overthrew the Europeans and the Nizam, and their broad dominions were portioned out to the government of their faithful leaders! These thoughts urged me to a speedy departure; and tearing myself from my wife I left the town, with the blessings of my father and the apparent goodwill of the Rajah, who wished me every success, and presented me with a valuable sword as a mark of his especial favour.

I was soon again with Cheetoo, who received me with great joy. I found him busied with the large preparations he was making for his intended expedition. By this time the news of the immense booty he had collected in his first expedition had spread through all lands far and near; thousands had flocked to Nemawur, to offer themselves to his service, in the hope that they might partake in the next; and hundreds were arriving daily, to swell the numbers of the already assembled multitude. A difficult task it was to allot the various tribes and individuals to the command of the different leaders; and my aid was asked by Cheetoo, and as readily given, to organise as far as we could the heterogeneous mass.

It was no easy task, for the men would have preferred acting independently, and on their own account; but this did not suit Cheetoo's intentions, as his irruption, though for the sole purpose of ravage and plunder, was to be of a more regular kind than the preceding. Ghuffoor Khan was there in all his savageness, looking forward to the burning of towns and the torture of inoffensive persons, with a desire which had received additional zest from his previous experience. We were on civil terms, but I had never forgotten that night at Karinjah, and the memory of the wretched Hindoo girl, and her sufferings and murder. In this expedition I felt assured that he would give no check to his passions; and I only waited a favourable opportunity to arrest his career of crime by a stroke of retributive justice; until this arrived, I was determined to cultivate his acquaintance as closely as possible, in order that he might be the more surely my own.

Our preparations were now made; upwards of ten thousand good horse were already enrolled, and the number of their followers was beyond computation. How they existed on their own resources I know not, but they did so, and right merrily too, for our camp was one scene of revelry and enjoyment. As a final ceremony, Cheetoo held a general durbar, at which all the chiefs and leaders were present: he disclosed his plan of operations, which was, to penetrate through the territories of the Rajah of Nagpoor to the south-eastward, and passing through the forests and jungles of Gondwana,[1] to pour his forces on the almost unprotected provinces north

---

1   Central India.

of Masulipatam; from thence to cross the Krishna, to ravage the country as far as Kurnool, and to return from thence in the best way we could to Nemawur. This plan of operations was received with glad shouts by the assembly, the army outside the tent took them up, and the air was rent with cries of exultation. It was a spirit-stirring moment, all partook of the joy, and the chiefs eagerly besought Cheetoo to lose no time in his departure. Nor did he. Prepared as the whole were to move at a moment's warning, the order was given that the army should cross the Nurbudda the next day.

CHAPTER XXXVI

Duke.—I am sorry for thee; thou art come to answer
    A stormy adversary, an inhuman wretch
    Incapable of pity, void and empty
    From any show of mercy.
            —*Merchant of Venice.* Act iv., Sc. 1.[1]

AT the head of the advance, which consisted of my thousand splendid horsemen, I was the first to cross the river, now fordable; and we encamped on its farther bank, in the same spot we had occupied scarcely five months before, almost doubled in numbers, and with the prospect of a brilliant foray before us. I shall not speak of how we traversed the Rajah of Nagpoor's territories, or penetrated through jungles and forests which till now had hardly ever been traversed by armies. We suffered often sad straits for the want of water, but all bore up nobly; and at last our horde rushed upon the fertile plains of the northern Circars,[2] and everything fell before it. Mercy was shown to none, our army spread itself over a tract of country many miles in breadth, and every village in its route was sacked and reduced to ashes.

On we rushed, at the rate of ten and fifteen coss daily; neither mountains nor rivers impeded us; in the language of hyperbole, we devoured the former and drank up the latter. Troops there were none to oppose us; and if there had been any, they would have been trampled under the feet of our victorious squadrons. Yet we had no disposition to fight; it was no part of our plan. If we heard of resistance likely to be offered, we diverged from the spot, for what would have been the use of exposing

---

1   The Duke's exact words are:

    I am sorry for thee. Thou art come to answer
    A stony adversary, an inhuman wretch,
    Uncapable of pity, void and empty
    From any dram of mercy (IV.i.3-6).

2   British territory in eastern India along the Bay of Bengal.

ourselves to encounters, in which, though sure of victory, we should have lost many of our men and crippled our future operations?

After some days we reached Guntoor,[1] where we knew there was a large treasure collected, the revenue of the province we had desolated. To gain this was an object on which Cheetoo had set his heart, as he had heard it amounted to many lakhs of rupees, and it belonged to the detested Europeans. My men rushed with yells more like those of demons than men upon the devoted town. To restrain them would have been vain, and I did not attempt it. It was thoroughly sacked in the presence of the British officers, who confined themselves to a building in which was the treasure; and I must say they defended their charge nobly. No Pindharee could show himself near the spot without being a target for a volley of musketry; and though I importuned Cheetoo to allow me to storm the building at the head of my risala, he would not hear of it. He had been deceived, he said, about there being troops to defend it; and though I always thought there were but few, yet he exaggerated their numbers, and relinquished his determination.

In revenge, however, for our disappointment, we plundered the houses of the officers, broke all their furniture, and set fire to many of them afterwards, in the hope that this would draw them from their post, and expose them to the charge of the horse. They were too wise however to venture forth, and reluctantly we left the place from which we had promised ourselves so large a booty; not, however, that what we did get was inconsiderable, though many were disappointed.

I was not so. I had, with my own Thugs, seized upon a respectable looking house, which we defended against the Pindharees who attempted to enter, and we despoiled its inmates, a large family of rich Hindoos, of all their wealth and ornaments, to the amount of nearly thirty thousand rupees. We did it too without torture, for I never permitted that, though we were obliged to use threats in abundance.

Laden with our spoil we left the town in the afternoon, and by eight the straggling army was again encamped at a distance of nearly ten coss from it, secure against any pursuit.

We crossed the Krishna, and penetrated nearly as far as Kurpah, where we heard there was more treasure belonging to the English Government. But we were disappointed in this also. The officers who guarded it were on the alert, and the station was guarded by troops; we therefore avoided any collision with them, and directed our course towards Kurnool. Here, also, we were beaten off; but we crossed the river, and again entered the Nizam's territory, closely pursued by a body of English

---

1 Guntur; city in eastern India under British rule.

cavalry, who, however, did not cross after us. A consultation was now held, and it was determined that our lubhur should separate into three bodies, both for the sake of destroying and ravaging a larger tract of country than we could do united, and of more easily evading the troops which now watched our movements in every direction. One body therefore took a western course along the banks of the river, another an eastern one, and a third a middle course.

That which took the eastern road was the one with which Cheetoo remained, and with it were Ghuffoor Khan and myself. We were to pass through the country to the eastward of Hyderabad, and regain the Nagpoor territories by the great north road through Nirmul. I was now the sole companion of Ghuffoor Khan; so long as the other leaders remained, he was mostly in their company, but now their absence drew us together, and I may almost say that we lived in the same tent, if tent it could be called, which served to shelter us from the excessive heat of the weather. Need I mention that I was a constant witness to his cruelties? They were of every-day's occurrence, and to show you the man's nature, I shall relate one as a specimen of thousands of a similar kind that he committed.

We reached a town, the name of which I forget, nor does it signify now; as usual, it was entered pell-mell by the horde, and the work of destruction commenced. Why should I conceal it? I was as busy as the rest, and not a house or hut of any description escaped my followers and myself. Ghuffoor Khan was busy too. I had completed my work; I had torn ornaments from the females, terrified their husbands and fathers into giving up their small hoards of money; and having got all I could I was preparing to leave the town in company with my Thugs, who never separated from me. We were passing through the main street on our return, when our attention was attracted to a good-looking house, from which issued the most piercing screams of terror and agony.

I instantly dismounted, and bidding my men follow me, we rushed into the house. Never shall I forget the scene which met my eyes, when we reached the place from whence the screams proceeded. There was Ghuffoor Khan, with seven or eight of his men, engaged in a horrid work. Three dead bodies lay on the floor weltering in their blood, which poured from the still warm corpses. Two were fine young men, the other an elderly woman.

Before Ghuffoor Khan stood a venerable man, suffering under the torture of having a horse's nose-bag full of hot ashes tied over his mouth, while one of the khan's followers struck him incessantly on the back with the hilt of his sword. The miserable wretch was half choked, and it was beyond his power to have uttered a word in reply to the interrogations which were thundered in his ear by the khan himself as to where his treasure was concealed. Three young women of great beauty were engaged in a fruitless scuffle with the others of Ghuffoor Khan's party; and their disordered appearance and heart-rending shrieks too well told what had been their fate previous to my entrance.

What could I do? I dared not openly have attacked the khan, though I half drew my sword from the scabbard, and would have rushed on him; but he was my superior, and had I then put him and his men to death, it could not have been concealed from Cheetoo,—and what would have been my fate? So checking the momentary impulse, which I had so nearly followed, I approached him, and endeavoured to withdraw his attention from the horrible work in which he was engaged.

"Come, Khan Sahib," I cried, "near us is a house which has resisted my utmost efforts to enter; I want you to aid me, and, Inshalla! it will repay the trouble, for I have heard that it is full of money and jewels, as the family is rich." I did not tell a lie, for I had endeavoured to break open the gate of a large house, but desisted when I was informed that it was uninhabited.

"Wait awhile," said he; "I have had rare sport here. These fools must needs oppose our entrance with drawn weapons, and I got a scratch on the arm from one of them myself. But what could they do—the kafirs! against a true believer? They fell in this room, and their old mother too, by my own sword. My men have been amusing themselves with their wives; whilst I, you see, am trying to get what I can out of this obstinate old villain; but he will not listen to reason, and I have been obliged to make him taste hot ashes."

"Perhaps he has naught to give," said I; "at any rate he cannot speak while that bag is over his mouth; let it be removed, and we will hear what he has to say."

"Try it," said the khan; "but we shall make nothing of him, you will see."

"Remove the bag," cried I to the Pindharee who was behind him; "let him speak; and bring some water, his throat is full of ashes."

The bag was removed, and a vessel full of water, which was in a corner of the room, was brought and put to his lips; but he rejected it with loathing, for he was a Hindoo and a Brahmin.

"Drink!" cried the infuriated khan at beholding his gesture; "drink, or, by Alla, I will force it down thy throat. Kafir, to whom the urine of a cow is a delicacy, darest thou refuse water from the hands of a Moslem?"

"Blood-thirsty devil," said the old man in a husky voice, "water from thy hands, or any of thy accursed race, would poison me. I would rather drink my own son's blood, which is flowing yonder, than such pollution."

"Ha! sayest thou so? then, in the name of the blessed Prophet, thou shalt taste it. Here, Sumund Khan, get some up from the floor; yonder is a cup—fill it to the brim; the old man shall drink it, as he would the wine of paradise."

"Hold!" cried I to Ghuffoor Khan; "you would not do so inhuman an act."

"Nay, interfere not," said the khan, setting his teeth; "you and I, Meer Sahib, are friends—let us remain so; but we shall quarrel if I am hindered in my purpose; and has he not said he preferred that to pure water?"

Sumund Khan had collected the blood, and the cup was half filled with the warm red liquid—a horrible draught, which he now presented to the miserable father. "Drink!" said he, offering the cup with a mock polite gesture; "think it Ganges water, and it will open thy heart to tell us where thy treasures are."

Ghuffoor Khan laughed loudly. "By Alla! thou hast a rare wit, Sumund Khan; the idea should be written in a book; I will tell Cheetoo of it."

But the old man turned from them with loathing, and his chest heaved as though he were about to be sick.

"There's no use wasting time," cried Ghuffoor Khan; "open his mouth with your dagger and pour the draught into it."

It was done; by Alla! sahib, the two did it before my eyes,—fiends that they were! Not only did they pour the blood down the old man's throat, but in forcing open his mouth they cut his lips in a ghastly manner, and his cheek was laid open.

"Now tell us where the gold is!" cried Ghuffoor Khan. "Of what use is this obstinacy? Knowest thou not that thy life is in my power, and that one blow of my sword will send thee to Jehanum,[1] where those fools are gone before thee?" and he pointed to the dead.

"Strike!" cried the sufferer, "strike! your blow will be welcome; I am old and fit for death. Why do ye delay?"

"But the gold, the treasures!" roared the khan, stamping on the ground. "Why, are you a fool?"

"Gold, I have told ye I have none," he replied; "I told you so at first, but ye would not listen. We gave you all we had, and ye were not satisfied. Ye have murdered my sons and my wife, and dishonoured my daughters. Kill us all, and we will be thankful."

"Hear him!" cried the khan savagely; "he mocks us. Oh the wilful wickedness of age! is it not proverbial? One of you bring some oil and a light; we will see whether this humour can stand my final test, which has never yet failed."

---

1 Hell.

By this time the house was full of Pindharees, and, if I had wished it, I had not dared to interfere further. I stood looking on, determined to let him have his course; he was only hastening his own fate, and why should I prevent it?

The oil was brought, and a quantity of rags were torn from the dhotees or waist-cloths of the murdered men. They were dipped in the oil, and wound round the fingers of the old man to as great a thickness as was possible.

"Now bring a light," cried the khan, "and hold him fast."

A light was kindled, and the man held it in his hand.

"I give you a last chance," said the khan, speaking from between his closed teeth; "you know, I dare say, the use your fingers will be put to. Be quick and answer, or I will make torches of them, and they shall light me to your treasures, which, I warrant, are hidden in some dark hole."

"Do your worst," answered the old man in a desperate tone. "Ye will not kill me; and if my sufferings will in any way gratify you, even let it be so—for Narayun has given me into your power, and it is his will and not yours which does this. You will not hear me cry out, though my arms were burnt off to the sockets. I spit at you!"

"Light the rags!" roared Ghuffoor Khan; "this is not to be endured."

They were lit; one by one they blazed up, while his hands were forcibly held down to his sides to accelerate the effect of the fire. Alla, Alla! it was a sickening sight. The warm flesh of the fingers hissed under the blaze of the oiled rags, which were fed from time to time with fresh oil, as men pour it upon a torch.

The old man had overrated his strength. What nerves could bear such exquisite torture? His shrieks were piteous, and would have melted a heart of stone; but Ghuffoor Khan heeded them not: he stood glutting his savage soul with the sufferings of the wretched creature before him, and asking him from time to time, with the grin of a devil, whether he would disclose his treasures. But the person he addressed was speechless, and after nature was fairly exhausted he sank down in utter insensibility.

"You have killed him," I exclaimed. "For the love of Alla, let him alone, and let us depart; what more would you have? Either he has no money, or he will not give it up."

"Where be those daughters of a defiled mother?" cried he to his followers, not heeding what I said to him. "Where are they? bring them forward, that I may ask them about the money, for money there must be."

But they too were dead! Ay, they had been murdered also; by whom I know not, but their bodies were found in the next room weltering in their blood.

The news was brought to the khan, and he was more savage than ever: he gnashed his teeth like a wild beast; he was fearful to look on.

The old man had revived, for water had been poured on his face and on his fingers. He raised himself up, looked wildly about him, and then gazed piteously on his mutilated hands. Were they men or devils by whom he was surrounded? By Alla! sahib, they were not men, for they laughed at him and his almost unconscious actions.

"Speak!" cried the khan, striking him with his sword, "speak, kafir! or more tortures are in store for thee."

But he spoke not—he was more than half dead; misery and torture had done their utmost.

The khan drew his sword. Again he cried "Speak!" as he raised the weapon above his head. I fancied I saw the old man's lips smile, and move as though he would have spoken; he cast his eyes upwards, but no word escaped him.

The sword was quivering above his head in the nervous grasp of the khan; and seeing he got no answer, it descended with its full force on the old man's forehead almost dividing the head in two. Need I say he was instantly dead?

I was satisfied. Ghuffoor Khan's cup too was full; for my own determination was made on that spot,—I swore it to myself as I looked at the dead and rushed from the house.

———•———

Chapter XXXVII

They plied him well with wine,
  And he roared wild songs in glee:
Hurrah! cried the devil, he'll soon be mine;
  And he chuckled right merrilye.
            —*Old Ballad.*

FROM that hour I made a determination to destroy him. No sooner had I reached the camp than I assembled all my Thugs, and laid before them a scheme I had long been revolving in my mind. I spoke to them as follows:—

"You have seen, my brethren, that Ghuffoor Khan is a devil; such a person can hardly be called a man. Bad as these Pindharees are, he is the worst among them, and is unfit to live. You, Motee and Peer Khan, remember the fate of the Brahmin girl at Karinjah; you may remember my ill-suppressed indignation, which then almost impelled me to destroy this fiend; and I would have done it, but that I felt his fate was not in my hands. I felt that Alla would sooner or later urge me on to be the humble means of a retributive justice overtaking him. I have hitherto refrained, though I have sometimes fancied his hour was come. I thought that some crime blacker than any previous one would at last be committed by him, and it has been done. You all saw what it was. Can he ever do worse?"

"He cannot!" cried my men with one voice; "he has reached the mark, and he is ours."

"He shall be so," said I; "now listen. You know I have still three bottles of the sweet wine of the Feringhees, which I brought with me from Guntoor; he is very fond of it, and will easily be persuaded to come here and drink it with us. I will dose his share with opium, and after a few cups he will become stupified, and will fall an easy prey to us."

"Good!" cried Peer Khan, "it is an excellent plan. What say you to putting it into execution this very night?"

"Not to-night," I said; "we must be cautious in this immense camp. To-morrow let my tent be pitched on the utmost verge of it; nay, a short distance beyond it; and in the dead of the night, when all are overpowered by sleep, he can be despatched."

"I beg to represent," said Peer Khan, "that Ghuffoor Khan's saddle is well lined; could we not get possession of it?"

"I have been thinking about that," replied I, "but I do not see how we are to get it without much risk and fear of discovery."

Peer Khan pondered for a moment; he then said,—

"I have a plan, Jemadar, which you may perhaps be able to improve upon; and, Inshalla! we will have the saddle. What I say is this: when the khan is pretty well intoxicated, do you propose to him to sleep in your tent, and to send for his horse and saddle, so as to be near him to mount in the morning. If the saddle is brought, we can empty it of its contents and bury it with him; if not, we can only rejoice at having done a good action in having destroyed him."

"I am not sure," observed Motee, "that the omens will be good; we had better try them."

"Do so," said I; "I will think over Peer Khan's plan, and see what can be done."

We then separated for the night.

During the next morning's travel, when we were not separated by the confusion which ensued on a village or town being plundered, I purposely threw myself as much in Ghuffoor Khan's way as I could, and we conversed on the success of our expedition, and the adventures which had befallen us.

"Do you remember, Khan Sahib," said I, "the attack on the houses at Guntoor, and how we ravaged the Feringhees' storehouses in a vain search for valuables? my curses on them! They are as rich as Nuwabs, and yet not one of them has a gold or silver dish in his possession, nor a jewel or valuable of any kind,—nothing but china-ware. And do you remember how we smashed it all?"

"Ay, I remember," growled the khan; "and but for our chief's cowardice,—between you and me I say it,—we might have attacked and carried the place where the treasure was, and enriched ourselves not a little; whereas, as it was, we got nothing for our trouble. We destroyed their houses, however, and that was some satisfaction."

"True," said I, "it was, Khan; how their hearts must have burned as they saw the bright flames devouring their abodes! Do you remember, too, the precious stuff I got hold of and recommended to your notice,—the wine in the small bottles with printed papers upon them? It was rare good stuff."

"Mashalla! it was indeed," cried the khan; "the flavour of it did not leave my lips for some days. These infidels know what good wine is, that is certain. Would that I had brought some with me! a few bottles would have been easily carried, and one would have enjoyed it after a day's toil."

"I was more careful than you were, Khan; such wine is not always to be got: I brought away some bottles, and I have them still I believe, if they be not broken."

"Some with you? Nay, then, be not niggardly of your treasure; let me taste it again, for I swear to you I believe there will be no such nectar in Paradise."

"It is at your service, Khan; but to escape scandal, what do you say to coming to my tent to-night when it is dusk? that is, if any remains, of which I will give you notice. One of my fellows shall cook a good pilao, and after it we will enjoy the wine quietly."

"Your words are sweet as the wine itself, good Meer Sahib; truly I will be with thee. I will tell my saees[1] to bring my horse and picket him among yours; no one will see me, and I will bring no one with me. I might exceed, you know, and I would not be an open scandal to the faith."

My heart leaped to my mouth as he uttered the words. The saddle, then, would be ours without any trouble or risk of detection; how I blessed him for acceding so readily to my plans!

"True, Khan," said I, "it will not do to be observed: we must be secret. I will have no one in my tent but Peer Khan, whom you know; he is my foster-brother, and a rare companion: we will have a pleasant carouse. I will send him to you when the pilao is ready."

"No, no!" cried he, "do not, there is no need of it; I will stroll to your tent after dusk. And, hark ye!" said he to his saees, who was trotting after him, "mind, you are to bring my horse and saddle to the Meer Sahib's tent as soon as you see me going towards it. Remember you are to lead it after me as though I were going to ride; and when you arrive there you are to picket it among his horses."

"Jo hookum," replied the fellow; "your orders shall be obeyed."

"And mind," continued the khan, "you are not to tell any one where I am going, nor to answer any questions, if any are put to you, as you lead the horse along."

"Certainly not; since such is my lord's pleasure, I dare not disobey."

"You had better not," cried the khan, "or I will try and find a korla for you."

The fellow dropped behind again, and we resumed our desultory conversation, chatting as we rode along on the merits of the different leaders, and how they had behaved. Ghuffoor Khan was a pleasant companion, and his remarks were full of wit and satire. I had put him in good humour by the prospect of a deep carouse, and we rode on cheerfully.

---

1   Groom.

We reached our halting-place for the day, after a long and intensely hot march; and glad were we to get under the cover of our tents to screen ourselves from the noon-day heat. I had several messages from the khan in the course of the day to know whether the repast was ready; but it would not have answered my purpose to have allowed that it was, or to have had it prepared one moment before the time fixed.

"You have been riding with the khan, sahib, all the morning," said Motee to me, "and have not, I suppose, observed the omens."

"I have not," said I, anxiously; "but surely you have done so?" for I knew how much they would influence my men; nay, that without favourable ones they would have absolutely refused any participation in the matter.

"I have not been negligent," replied Motee. "Last night, after I parted with you, Peer Khan, myself, and the others, made an offering of goor to the nishān,[1] and, blessed be Bhowanee! she has vouchsafed us the thibao and pilhao;[2] you need, therefore, be under no apprehensions, for she is favourable."

"I was sure she would be, Motee, for I observe the hand of Alla guiding me; and I verily believe I should have followed the influence of my own desires in this matter even had they been unfavourable."

"Nay, say not so, Jemadar," said he laughing, "you are too good a Thug for that; but there is now no fear, for the omens were indeed cheering."

"If we succeed," said I, "I have some thoughts of further work in our own way; but of this more hereafter. There will be a stir when his disappearance is known, and we must be quiet for a time."

"Ay, that is like you, Jemadar. We have been consulting among ourselves, and had come to the determination of proposing some adventures to you, for here these dogs of Pindharees lie, night after night, and each fellow is worth some hundreds of rupees. Yet we have been content to remain inactive; and I, for one, say shame on us! We need not pass a night without some work."

"Wait, good Mootee; let us secure the khan first. And now to arrange matters; we must be our own lughaees."

"For that we are prepared, Meer Sahib; a Thug must do his duty in any grade when occasion calls for his services. We are all ready for work."

---

1   Sacred pickaxe.

2   Omen on the right hand; omen on the left hand.

"Then we must lose no time. You must join your own pall[1] to mine, and put some screen or other between them; in the empty space the grave must be prepared. It had better be ready before he comes—but no, he will perhaps suspect us; it can soon be made afterwards."

"You are right, Jemadar, he would suspect. He need not be buried deep; and there are three of our men who are old lughaees; they will prepare it in a few minutes."

"And his saees,—he must die also, Motee."

"Certainly," he replied. "Do you and Peer Khan deal with the khan, and leave the saees to us—we will manage him."

"Good; our arrangements are then complete. Remember that Peer Khan alone eats with us; you must be all outside, and see that the horses are kept saddled, for we must fly instantly if we are discovered or suspected. I have no fears, however, on either score."

"Nor have I," said Motee; "the matter will create a stir, as he is a leader of note; but it will be supposed, either that he has gone off with his plunder, or that some one has murdered him. I tell you, Meer Sahib, that many a Pindharee has died by the hand of his fellow since we left Nemawur."

"I do not doubt it, Motee. I have heard of many brawls, and men of this kind have but few scruples. They are a wicked set, and far worse than those who formed the first expedition. But now go, get the pall ready, and send Peer Khan to me."

The evening came; the calls of the faithful to evening prayers resounded through the camp with the last red streak of day. Men were assembled in knots, kneeling on their carpets, addressing their prayers to Alla,—men whose hands were scarcely cleansed from the blood they had that day shed! The ceremony over, each separated from his fellow, to lie beside his faithful horse, and to enjoy a night of repose to fit him for the toil, the rapine, and plunder of the ensuing day.

The time approached; and as I sat in my tent, awaiting the khan's arrival, my heart exulted within me, that for once in my life I should do a good action, in revenging the murdered. Peer Khan was with me; we scarcely spoke: our minds were too full of what was to follow to speak much.

"Have you drugged the bottle?" he asked.

"I have. I have put two tolas[2] of opium into it. I have tasted it, and the flavour of the drug is perceptible; but it will be the second bottle, and he will not discover it;

---

1 Tent.

2 One tola is equivalent to 11.663 grams.

and if he does, we cannot help it, we must take our chance. Do you think we can manage him between us, without any noise?"

"Shame on us if we do not, Meer Sahib; I am as strong a man as he is, and your roomal never fails. But to prevent any noise being heard, suppose we propose to admit Motee and two or three others to sing and play,—I mean when the khan has swallowed his first bottle. Motee has a sitar and a small drum with him, and its noise will drown all others."

"No, no!" said I; "others might be attracted by the singing, and come to hear it; it will not do. We must do our best, and leave the rest to Alla. However we will see when the time comes."

The evening was far advanced, and everything around us was quiet. A few fires, here and there throughout the camp, marked where, at each, a solitary Pindharee cooked his last meal of the day; the rest were already buried in profound slumber, and all nearest to us were still. I stood at the door of my humble tent looking anxiously for the khan's coming; and at length I observed a figure stealing along in the dusk, carefully avoiding the prostrate forms which lay in his path. Was it the khan! Yes. "By Alla he comes!" said I to Peer Khan; "I see him now; and there is his horse behind him, and the saees leading it."

"Shookur Khoda!" exclaimed my companion; "he has not deceived us. I feared he had, since it is so late."

"Is that you, Meer Sahib?" cried the voice of Ghuffoor Khan. "I feared I should have missed your tent in this cursed darkness."

"Here am I, Khan. Welcome to the poor tent of your servant."

"So you have found the wine, eh?" said the khan, rubbing his hands in glee. "You have not cheated me?"

"By your soul, no! Khan, I have not; there it is, you see; and Peer Khan is gone for the pilao."

"Khoob,[1] by Alla! Meer Sahib, I have fasted all day on purpose to do justice to it; and I should have been here an hour sooner, but I was summoned to the durbar about some trifle or other; and I have kept you waiting."

"And your horse, Khan?"

"Oh, he is here; my saees has picketed him among yours. I have deceived my other servants: I swore I had a headache and could not eat, and pretended to lie down to sleep, having given them all strict orders not to disturb me. The knaves knew better than to do so; and so, after lying quiet awhile, I stole out of my tent

---

1   Good.

behind, and have fairly given them the slip. I suppose your people can throw some fodder before the animal?"

"Surely; I have cared for that already."

Peer Khan now entered with the pilao; and seating ourselves, our fingers were soon buried in the midst of it.

"Now for the wine, Meer Sahib; the pilao is dry without it, and my throat lacks moisture."

"Here it is," said I, pouring it out into a cup; "see how it sparkles, like the fire of a ruby."

"Ay," said the khan, after he had drained it to the bottom, "this is wine for the houris; how one enjoys it! Think, Meer Sahib, how we true believers will quaff in paradise (if what we get there will be as good), surrounded by twenty houris, and each vying with the other to please us! But drink, man,—I would not take the whole."

"Nay, that bottle is your own share, Khan, and there is besides another for you; Peer Khan and I will divide this one between us. 'Tis a pity there is not more, or that the bottle were not larger."

"Ay, it is to be regretted certainly, Meer Sahib, but what there is, we must make the most of;" and he took another draught. "Only think," continued he, "of those infidels the Feringhees drinking such stuff as this every day. I now scarcely marvel at their doing great deeds when they are drunk. And is it not the case, Meer Sahib, that they all sit round a table, and drink and roar out songs till they fall down intoxicated?"[1]

"So I have been credibly informed, Khan. By Alla! they are jolly dogs."

"I wish I was in their service," said Ghuffoor Khan, after a short silence. "Do you think they would give one wine to drink when one wanted it?"

"I have not a doubt of it," I replied.

"Then I will take employ with them, Meer Sahib; this stuff would tempt many a better Moosulman than I am to serve an infidel. But they say Sikundur Jah drinks it also."

"So I heard when I was at Hyderabad," said I; "indeed, it was there I first tasted this liquor; and I knew the bottles again when I saw them in the Feringhees' houses at Guntoor."

"It is fit drink for a prince," sighed the khan, when he had finished the bottle, and looking at it with a most rueful countenance. "That is finished, Meer Sahib; thou saidst thou hadst another?"

"Ay, Khan! but only this one," I replied handing him the other.

---

1 The khan probably referred to proceedings of a very antiquated character. [*Taylor*]

"I feel happy now, Meer Sahib. By Alla! I could sing—I could dance I think, though it would be a scandal to do so. The Prophet, however, has not forbidden a Moslem to sing. May his name be honoured! Have any of you a sitar? People say that I have a good hand."

"Go and fetch Motee-ram's," said I to Peer Khan; "it is a good one. Shall the owner of it come also, Khan?"

"Nay, I care not, Meer Sahib; though the devil came, I would pluck him by the beard: let him come. Can he sing?"

"Like a bulbul, Khan; I have rarely heard a better voice from a man."

"Oh for some women!" sighed the khan; "one misses the glances of their antelope-eyes, and the tinkle of their anklets, in moments like these. Ah, Meer Sahib, we were happy dogs when we were encamped in the Krishna. There was one charmer—but why speak of them, Meer Sahib, why speak of them?"

"We shall enjoy their company the more when we get to Nemawur," said I. "But here is Motee with his sitar."

Motee made his salam and sat down.

"Is the instrument tuned, Motee—thou pearl of singers?" cried the khan, bursting into a laugh at his play upon Motee's name.[1] "Hast thou tuned it?"

"I have, noble Khan; though it is not worthy the touch of so exalted a person."

"Nay, 'tis a good sitar, and a sweet one," said the khan, as he ran his fingers over the frets in a manner which showed him to be a proficient.

"Wah!"[2] cried all of us at once; "play, noble Khan! the hand which could execute such a prelude as that can do wonders."

"Give me some more drink," cried he, "and I will try. Knowest thou any ghuzuls,[3] Motee?"

"I am indifferently skilled in them, Khan Sahib; nevertheless, if my lord will mention one, I will try. The tuppas[4] of my own country I know most of."

"Pah!" cried the khan, "who would sing tuppas? I will name a ghuzul which is in every one's mouth—sing 'Mah-i-Alum, Sóz-i-mun;'[5] I warrant me thou knowest it. But the wine, Meer Sahib, pour it out for me; thou art my saqee,[6] thou knowest.

---

1   *Motee* means "pearl."

2   Bravo!

3   Love songs.

4   Songs performed to the beat of a drum.

5   Moon of the world and burner of my heart.

6   Cup-bearer.

I will sing an ode to thee, as Hafiz[1] has written and sung many a one to his; peace be to his memory! Ah! that was good; but oh, Meer Sahib, it hath a different flavour from the last."

"Very likely," said I; "the bottle you see hath a different paper on it; perhaps it is a better kind."

"It is good, and that is all I care for, Meer Sahib. Now proceed, good Motee."

Motee did as he was ordered, and his voice and the khan's accompaniment were worthy of a better audience than that which heard them.

"Wah, wah! Shabash!" cried Peer Khan and I, when it was ended; "this is rare fortune, to hear two such skilful musicians in this unsainted jungle. Now it is your turn, Khan Sahib."

"More wine, Meer Sahib, 'saqee mera!'[2] more wine, for the sake of the Twelve Imams. Oh that there were a thousand bottles, that we could meet as we have done now every night! Good wine and good companions—have they not been ever the burthen of the songs of the poets?"

"Is there much left?" he continued, when he had drained the cup.

"About half the bottle," said I.

"Then give Motee a cup, Meer Sahib; he deserves it."

"Excuse me," said Motee, "but I am a Hindoo and a Brahmin."

"Thou shouldst have been a true believer, Motee; Khan would sound as well after thy name as Bam. Why, man, our blessed Prophet would have had thee to sing to him when thou hadst reached paradise!"

Ghuffoor Khan's voice was now rather thick, and he made but a poor hand of the ghuzul he attempted; but it was very laughable to see him roll his eyes from side to side like a dancing-girl, and to hear him trying to imitate their quavers and shakes.

"Pah!" cried he, when he had sung a verse, "my throat is dry—I want more wine, I think, Meer Sahib; but the truth is, I caught a cold some days ago, and am still hoarse."

He tried again after a fresh draught, but with no better success. In vain he coughed and hemmed to clear his throat; the wine, and the still better opium, were doing their work as quickly as we could desire.

"Do you sing again, Motee,—meree Motee! meree goweya?"[3] said the khan insinuatingly. "A curse on the water of this country, which spoils a man's singing.

---

1   Hafez (1315-1390), Persian poet.

2   My cup-bearer; a reference to Hafez's poem "Cup-bearer, it is morning, fill my cup with wine."

3   My pearl! my singer!

Sing, man, and I will play; it cannot spoil that, at any rate; and the Meer Sahib hath provided an antidote for this night at least."

Motee sang again; but the accompaniment was wild and irregular, and the khan at last threw down the sitar.

"It will not do, Meer Sahib, after the fatigue (a hiccup) and the trouble I have had (hiccup) all day, shouting and bullying these rascally Pindharees (hiccup). How can it be expected, Meer Sahib, that I, Ghuffoor Khan, the leader of three thousand horse, should play and sing like a goweya? By Alla I will not (hiccup)! But these hiccups, Meer Sahib, what is to cure them?"

"Some more wine, Khan Sahib; nothing but liquor can cure them. And there is more; there is still another cup."

"Then give me all!" cried the khan; "I will drink it standing like a kafir Feringhee— may their sisters be defiled, ay, and their mothers too! Nevertheless, as I said, I will serve them and drink among them, and none shall drink more than Ghuffoor Khan. Thou saidst they drink standing, and what do they say?"

"Hip, hip, hip!" said I; "I learned them from a vagabond who had been a khidmutgar[1] among them, and had seen their wild orgies."

"What, hip, hip, hip! those are the words, eh? I wonder what they mean."

"They are an invocation to their Prophet, I believe;" said I, "much as we say 'Bismilla ir ruhman ir ruheem!'"[2]

"I do not doubt it, Meer Sahib. Now help me to rise, for the stuff is in my brain, and the tent goeth round about; help me to rise, I say, and I will quaff the last drop both as a true Moslem and as a Feringhee. Ha! said I not well?"

"Excellently well, great Khan," said I, as I helped him to his feet; "now, here is the wine."

"Bismilla!" shouted the Khan, "hip! hip! hip!" and he drained the cup to the bottom. His head sank on his breast; his eyes rolled wildly; he made a desperate attempt to rush forward, and fell at his full length upon the ground.

"Bus!"[3] cried Peer Khan, as he got out of the way; "enough, great Khan! noble Khan, thou art a dead man now. Feringhee and Moslem, thou hast made rare fun for us."

"Raise him up," said I to them; "seat him on his end. I am ready, and do one of ye give the *jhirnee*."

---

1   Personal servant.

2   In the name of the most merciful and benevolent Allah!

3   Enough!

They raised him up, and as he was seated, his head sank again on his shoulder, and some froth came from his mouth.

"He is dying," said Motee; "we ought not to touch him; it is forbidden."

"Not a bit of it," said I; "all drunken men are in this way; I have seen hundreds in the same state; so hold his head up, and give the *jhirnee*;" for I had taken my post behind him.

They did so; Peter Khan uttered the fatal words, and Ghuffoor Khan wrestled out his last agony under my never-failing gripe.

"Enough, Meer Sahib," said Peer Khan, who was holding his feet; "enough! he is dead."

"Ul-humd-ul-illa!"[1] I exclaimed; "it is finished, blessed be the Prophet and Bhowanee! Go for the lughaees; he must be put underground immediately. Now for the saees."

We left the khan's body and went out; the others were waiting for us. "Where does he lie?" I asked.

"There," said one of the men; "he is fast asleep, and has been so for an hour."

"So much the better," said Peer Khan; "leave him to me."

I watched him and Motee as they approached the sleeper. Peer Khan touched him with his foot; he started up to a sitting position and rubbed his eyes, but Peer Khan threw himself upon him, and he was dead in an instant, ere he had become conscious. Nothing now remained but the disposal of the bodies and the saddle. The grave, a shallow one, was quickly dug; and while the lughaees were preparing it, myself, Peer Khan, and Motee unripped the lining and pockets of the saddle, and took out the gold. There was naught else. It was in coin, and in small lumps, as the jewels he had gotten in plunders had been melted down from time to time. We had no leisure then to speculate on its value, but we cut the saddle to pieces with our knives to make sure that none remained in it, and the fragments were buried with the bodies.

"What shall we do with the horse, Meer Sahib?" asked Motee. "We cannot take him with us, for there is not a man in the camp who does not know Ghuffoor Khan's horse; and we have no time to stain him."

I was puzzled for a while; to have retained the noble animal would have ensured our detection, and I scarcely knew what to do. At last I hit upon an expedient. "He must be destroyed," said I; "it is a splendid beast, certainly, yet our lives are worth

---

1   Praise be to Allah!

more than his. Beyond the camp, about an arrow's flight, is a deep ravine. Do any of you know it?"

"None of us have seen it," said all at once.

"Then I must go myself, and do you, Ghous Khan (he was one of my men), accompany me; we will throw him into it. Go and loosen him from his pickets."

I followed him, and we conducted the animal to the edge of the ravine; it was deep, and just suited our purpose, as the banks were precipitous.

"That will do," said I, when he had brought the horse to the edge; "now rein his head to one side; we must kill him before he falls in."

He did so; I had prepared my sword, and drew it sharply across the poor brute's throat; the blood gushed out, he reeled backwards, fell into the dark ravine, and we heard his carcase reach the bottom with a heavy fall. I looked over, but all I saw was an indistinct mass at the bottom, while a few groans of its death-agony reached my ears.

"Enough!" said I; "come away; the jackals will have a glorious feast ere morning, and no one will ever think of looking here. But it was a pity to kill the brute."

"He was worth a good thousand rupees, and would have fetched that price at Hyderabad. Why did you not send him there? I would have taken him."

"I did not think of that," said I; "but no matter now: we will earn more than that before we reach Nemawur."

"How, Meer Sahib? We get but little in this poor country."

"Trust me, Ghous Khan," said I; "we have begun, and, Inshalla! we will go on with the work."

I reached the tent, and the lughaees had done their business well: our carpets had been spread over the spot where the khan lay in his last resting-place, and we all lay down and slept soundly.

Ghuffoor Khan was missed at his accustomed post the next morning; a thousand conjectures were hazarded as to his fate, but no one could account for his disappearance. Some said the devil had taken him for his wickedness; others, that he had amassed an immense plunder, and was fearful of its being wrested from him, and he had therefore escaped with it, as it was known to be sewed up in his saddle.

When we reached our next encampment, Cheetoo sent for me: I went, and found him seated in full durbar, and the khan's servants, as prisoners, before him. I made my usual salam, and he requested me to be seated near him.

"This is a most mysterious affair, Meer Sahib," said he; "Ghuffoor Khan is gone; and Alla or the Shitan only knows whither! If he has fled, it is as extraordinary a thing as I ever heard of; for he has been attached to me from his youth, and I have ever been kind to him. What think you?"

"I am at a loss, also," said I; "your servant knows not what to say; there are a thousand conjectures afloat, but no one can give any probable solution to the mystery. But have you examined the servants? Surely they must know something."

"I have not, Meer Sahib, as yet; but here they are, and I want you to help me to question them. You may think of some things which may escape me,"

"I will do my best, Nuwab; but you had better begin—they will be afraid of you and speak the truth."

"Call one of them," said Cheetoo to an attendant.

The man came, trembling in every joint, and prostrated himself before our leader.

"What is thy name?" he asked.

"Syud Ebrahim," said the fellow.

"And what service didst thou perform to Ghuffoor Khan?"

"I am a khidmutgar, O Asylum of the World!" said the man; "I used to keep the khan's clothes, assist him to bathe, and attend him at night. I was always about his person."

"Now speak the truth, Ebrahim, and fear not. But I swear by the beard of the Prophet, if I detect thee lying, I will have thee cut to pieces before my face, as a warning to thy comrades."

"May I be your sacrifice!" cried the man, "I will not lie. Why should I? What I know is easily told, and 'tis but little."

"Proceed," cried Cheetoo, "and remember what I have said."

"Alla is my witness," said the man, "I know but little. My noble master came from your Highness's durbar late in the afternoon; we had prepared dinner for him, but he said he was ill, and would not eat, and that we ourselves might eat what we had cooked for him. He then went into his tent, took off his durbar-dress, put away his arms, and then lay down. I was with him till this time, and sat down to shampoo[1] him; but he bade me begone, and I left him. I was weary with running all day by his side, and I also lay down, and did not wake till the people roused me for the march. I went into the tent to arouse him and give him his clothes, but I found him not. The bedding was just as when he had laid down, but his sword was not there, nor a stick he always walked with. This is all I know, but Shekh Qadir knows something more, if you will call him: he saw the khan after I did."

---

1   Bathe.

Shekh Qadir was accordingly sent for, and after being cautioned and threatened as the other had been, he spoke as follows,—

"I am also a khidmutgar, but my office was not about the khan's person; I used to give him his hooka, and prepare the opium he ate. Soon after dusk I heard him moving in the tent, and I watched him; he lifted up the back part of it, and came out; I saw him walk towards the middle of the camp, and followed him; he observed me, and turned round sharp upon me. 'What!' said he, 'cannot I walk out for a few yards to breathe the air without some of you rascals following me? Begone!' Nuwab, I was frightened lest he should order me the korla, and I went away to the tent of a friend. I heard in the morning that he had not returned."

"This is very unsatisfactory," said I; "we have as yet no clue to his disappearance. If he has gone away, he must have ridden; where is his horse?"

"Ay, where is it?" cried Cheetoo. "Who can tell us?"

"May I be your sacrifice!" said Shekh Qadir; "the horse is not here, nor his saees. The khan had two horses, but the saddle of the one missing is that in which all the gold was sewed up."

"Ha!" said Cheetoo, "is it so? Where is the other saees?"

"Peer-o-Moorshid!"[1] cried an attendant; "he is waiting without."

"Let him too be called." The man entered.

"What knowest thou?" asked Cheetoo.

"I only know," said the fellow, "that the grey horse was kept saddled all the afternoon. This was contrary to custom, for its saddle was always placed in the tent, near the khan's head when he slept. I asked my fellow saees the reason of its being so; but he was angry with me, and said it was no business of mine, that the khan had ordered it, and it was his pleasure. I saw him take the horse from his picket after dark, but I asked no questions."

"There remains but one conclusion to be drawn, Nuwab Sahib," said I. "Ghuffoor Khan has fled, and made off with the booty he had got. By all accounts he had been very fortunate; and every one said his saddle was stuffed with gold."

"So I have also heard," said Cheetoo; "but yet, it is hard to think of that man's ingratitude. Here have I been associated with him from boyhood. I have raised him from obscurity, to be a leader of three thousand horse; and this has been a scurvy ending to my kindness. Go," said he to the servants, "I find no fault with any of you; take the horse to my pagah,[2] and let him be tied up among my own."

---

1   Your holiness!

2   Herd.

Thus ended this adventure; no suspicion fell upon us nor on any one. The khan was known to have friends at Hyderabad, and thither it was supposed he had fled. We alone knew his fate, and it was one he had deserved by a thousand crimes too horrible to mention.

But after this we were not idle. Having begun our work, we had constant employment; scarcely a night passed that one or two Pindharees did not fall by our hands. They were missed, too, as the khan had been, but we were favoured by the constant desertions which took place from the lubhur; for as we approached Nemawur, men daily made off in every direction to their houses, little relishing the fatigues of the camp and the constant alarms we had from reports of the vicinity of the Feringhee troops, by whom we were several times nearly surprised.

Yet I was not fated to have the uniform success which had hitherto attended me. Treachery was at work, and the blow we least feared fell with a heavy hand at last, and dispersed us. I will tell you how it happened, and what befel us.

Chapter XXXVIII

Pistol.—Trust none;
    For oaths are straws, men's faiths are wafer-cakes,
    And Hold-fast is the only dog, my duck;
    Therefore, *Caveto* be thy counsellor.
              —*King Henry V*. Act. ii., Scene 2.[1]

AMONG the men whom I had brought with me from Jhalone was one by name Hidayut Khan. I had never seen him before, but he was slightly known to Peer Khan, as having served with him, and was represented to be an able Thug. Of the extent of his accomplishments I was ignorant, as he never had any hand in the destruction of those who died in the Pindharee camp; for I preferred allowing my own men, upon whom I could depend, to do the work. But Hidayut Khan was certainly a capital horseman, a good hand with his sword and spear, and an active, enterprising fellow as a Pindharee. I have said we never employed him as a bhuttote, nor even as a shumshea;[2] why, I can hardly say; yet so it was: he acted always as a scout, and kept watch at the door of the tent while our work went on within. Many days after the death of Ghuffoor Khan, indeed, when we had again reached the Nagpoor territory, and when a few days' march would have brought us to Nemawur, Peer Khan, Motee, and one or two others came to me one evening after it was dark, with faces full of concern and alarm.

"For the sake of Bhowanee," cried I, "what is the matter? why are ye thus agitated? Speak, brothers, and say the worst; are we discovered?"

"Alas, I fear treachery," said Motee. "For some time past we have suspected Hidayut Khan, who has absented himself from us of late in an extraordinary manner, to have disclosed what we are to a person in Cheetoo's confidence. We have dogged them several times about the camp, have detected them in earnest conversation, and this night we too greatly fear he is even now in the durbar. What can be done?"

"We must fly at once," said I. "Now that you mention the name of Hidayut Khan, I, too, have my suspicions; are the horses saddled?"

---

1   Act II, Scene iii, lines 50-53.
2   The Thug responsible for holding the victim's hands.

"They are," said Peer Khan, "they are always so."

"Good," said I; "then there is no fear. Yet I should like much to satisfy myself of the fact of our being suspected,—ay, and by Alla! I will ascertain it at once."

"Ah, do not!" cried they; "for the sake of Bhowanee, do not throw yourself into peril; what can be gained by it? Our horses are ready let us mount them, leave the tent where it is, and fly."

Would to Alla that I had followed this wise counsel! matters would not have turned out as they did; but I was possessed by the idea; a headstrong man is never to be restrained, and I would hear nothing they had to say. "Is there not *one* among you," cried I, "who will accompany me? The night is dark, and we can reach Cheetoo's tent unobserved; we will lie down with our ears to the kanât,[1] and hear what passes. If the worst comes, if we really are denounced, we shall have ample time to fly before they can get from the inside."

"I will," cried Peer Khan; but no one else stirred: they were all paralysed by fear, and were incapable of action.

"That is spoken like yourself, brother," cried I; "thou hast a gallant soul. Now do ye all prepare the horses for instant flight; let their tether-ropes be loosened, and the bridles put in their mouths; do not move them from their places, and no one will suspect us: and come," cried I to Peer Khan, "there is not a moment to be lost."

"We stole out of the tent, and stealthily crept along towards Cheetoo's, which was fortunately at no great distance. No one was about it; but we could see from the outside that, by the side of a dim lamp, three persons were engaged in earnest conversation. We lay down at the edge of the kanât, and my ears eagerly drank in the words which fell on them.

"Ajaib!"[2] said a voice, which I knew at once to be Cheetoo's, "and so he murdered the khan? you said *he* did it."

"May I be your sacrifice," said Hidayut Khan (I knew his voice, too, immediately), "he did; I cannot say I saw him die with my own eyes, but they made him drunk, and they buried him, and Ameer Ali himself destroyed the noble horse."

"I do not doubt it," said Cheetoo, with a sigh; "I have done his memory foul wrong in thinking him ungrateful. And the others?"

---

1 Screen.
2 Wonderful!

"They were men of scarcely any note," said the informer, "nor do I know the names of all; one only I remember, for they had hard work to despatch him: he was a strong man, by name Hubeeb Oola, and belonged to my lord's own pagah."[1]

"I knew him well," said Cheetoo; "he was a worthy man and a brave one: and Ameer Ali slew him?"

"He did, Nuwab, with his own hands; and Motee and Peer Khan held him, or he could not have done it. This was only three nights ago, when I would fain have denounced them, but I feared no one would believe me; and as I knew Ameer Ali was in your favour, I thought no one would have listened to an accusation against him."

"Nor would I, by Alla!" cried Cheetoo, rising up, and striking his forehead in extreme agitation (I had made a hole in the cloth with the point of my dagger, and could see all distinctly). "I would never have believed your tale, but that circumstances so strongly bear out what you have said. Who could have believed that Ameer Ali, the kind, the benevolent,—one who opposed every scheme of violence, and protested against our ravages till I was ashamed of them myself,—who could have thought *him* a Thug?"

"But it is the truth, Nuwab," said the vile wretch; "when you have seized them, you will find ample evidence of what I tell, you: the sword of Ghuffoor Khan is at this moment girded to the side of Peer Khan, who threw away his own."

"That will be conclusive, indeed," said Cheetoo. "But how came you to join them?"

"I was at my village, near Jhalone," said Hidayut Khan; "I had formerly known Peeroo (as we call Peer Khan), and he asked me to join him and his jemadar, and to follow the Pindharees. I never suspected them to be Thugs,—who could, when Ameer Ali and his father were high in favour with the Rajah? and it was not till the khan's death that they began their horrible work."

"Well," said Cheetoo, "you have laid the plan; the sooner you put it into execution the better. You have prepared the horsemen, have you not?" said he to the other man, whose face I knew.

"I have," he replied; "they are standing by their horses, all ready for the signal to set on—fifty good fellows; none of the Thugs will escape us."

"Ya Alla!" cried Cheetoo; "how will he look on me? and how can I bring myself to order the punishment he deserves? Ah, Ameer Ali, how thou hast deceived me! how could any one read deceit in that honest face of thine!"

---

1 A troop (of horses); cavalry unit.

"Go," said he to Hidayut Khan and the others; "bring them to me without delay. I will not forget thy reward; thou hast asked for the saddle of Peer Khan."

"No more! no more!" cried the villain; "'tis all I want."

"Ay," said Peer Khan to me in a whisper, but he has not got it yet, and he is a cunning fellow if he does get it. Come, Meer Sahib, we must be off—they are moving."

I was almost fascinated to the spot. I could have lain there and listened to the discourse; but the peril was too imminent, too deadly for a moment's delay. I got up, and sneaking along, we saw the two figures cross the threshold of the tent, and with hurried steps direct their course to a part of the camp where the pagah was, and which was close to our tent.

Fear lent us speed; we flew to our tent, and for a few moments were engaged in tying up some valuables we had brought out for division; having done this, we hurried to our horses. Some of the men were already in their saddles; I leaped on my spirited animal, and drew my sword; ready for the worst. I wished all to move off in a body, for as yet there was no alarm; but I was deceived—we were surrounded! The instant we were in motion a body of horse dashed at us, and we were at once engaged in a conflict for life or death. What happened I know not; I cut down the only man who was opposed to me; Peer Khan was equally fortunate. I received a slight wound from another, which I little heeded; we urged our horses to their utmost speed, and the darkness favoured our escape.

I soon found, as I slackened my pace a little, that some of my men were with me. We had agreed to take a northerly direction, and rendezvous near a small village which could be seen from the camp; and by this precaution those who had escaped were soon collected together. We were not pursued, though we heard the shouts of the Pindharees, as they hallooed to each other in and about their camp, and the shots from their matchlocks; and we afterwards heard they had grievously wounded many of each other in mistake. I almost dreaded to call over the names of those who stood around me, for I could not see their faces, and no one spoke a word to his companion.

We waited for a considerable time,—for an hour or more. Gradually the noise and shouting in the Pindharee camp died away, and by the straggling watch-fires alone could one have told that a mighty army was encamped there. Now and then the shrill neigh of a horse was borne to us upon the night-wind, and when it ceased there was again a melancholy silence. The little village too was deserted: part of it had been burned, and the embers of the houses still emitted sparks, now and then sending up a flame, as portions of dry grass of the thatched huts which had escaped became ignited. Further delay was useless; I therefore broke the silence, which was painful to all.

"How many are there of us, Peer Khan?" I asked, in a low tone.

"Eleven," said he; "the rest I fear have fallen."

"I pray Alla they have: better far to fall by a sword-cut or a spear thrust, than to be exposed to torture. But who are absent? is Motee here?"

"Alas! no, Meer Sahib. Motee I saw struck down. I made a cut at the Pindharee who wounded him, but the darkness deceived me—I missed him."

"And who else are absent?" said I, stifling my grief, for Motee had been as a brother to me; "let those who are here tell their names."

They did so. Ghous Khan was away, and Nuzzur Ali and Ramdeen Singh, three of our best men; Motee was a fourth; Hidayut Khan the traitor, was a fifth, and all our attendants and grooms.

"'Tis no use staying here," said I; "we must make the best of our way to Jhalone; there we will wait the usual time, and if none return, the ceremonies for the dead must be performed for them. None of ye will grudge your share of the booty we have (blessed be Bhowanee!) brought away with us to their wives and families; swear this unto me, ye that are willing."

"We swear!" cried the whole, almost with one voice.

"I am satisfied," said I; "now let us proceed. We must turn off the main road when it is light; we all know the paths through the jungles, and by them we will travel till we are safely beyond Hooshungabad; beyond that I fear not."

"Proceed," cried Peer Khan; "we follow you."

And we rode on in silence with heavy hearts. We travelled thus for many days. Through the country we passed, we represented ourselves, as long as the Nagpoor territory lasted, to be servants of the government on a secret mission; and though we were often suspected and questioned, yet by my address I brought my band clear out of all the difficulties; and our hearts bounded with joy when at length we arrived on the banks of the noble Nurbudda, and dashing our steeds into the ford soon left its waters between us and our enemies.

Inured as we were to the fatigues of long and severe marches, and our horses also, not a day passed but fifteen or twenty coss were travelled, and at this rate we were not long in reaching our home. Blessed be Alla! we did reach it, and glad was my heart once again to see the groves of Jhalone after my weary pilgrimage. No notice had we been able to give of our approach, and I alighted at the door of my own house unattended and alone, covered with dust, and worn by fatigue and exposure to the fierce heat of the sun, and as much changed by anxiety for the fate of my poor comrades as though ten additional years had gone over my head, instead of only a few weeks. My servants scarcely knew me; but when I was recognized, the glad tidings of my return flew from mouth to mouth. I waited not even to quench my raging thirst before I was again in the embrace of Azeema, my own loved one, and peril was once more forgotten.

We assembled in the evening; and as the pockets of our saddles were one by one unripped and their contents heaped on the floor before us, a glorious pile indeed met our view of lumps of gold and silver, the produce of the jewels we had seized, which we had melted down as we got them. There were a few strings of pearls, one of which I laid aside for the Rajah; and the whole was then weighed, valued, and distributed. Those whom we supposed to be dead were not forgotten; their shares were laid aside, and afterwards delivered to their families.

I now again enjoyed peace and rest; all idea of joining Cheetoo or any other of the Pindharee leaders was out of the question; for though I might have done so under an assumed name, yet the chance of being recognised would have been too great, and I was rich enough for the present. Cheetoo, too, had reached the summit of his fame and his prosperity; his plans were all frustrated by the rash and sudden rise of the Mahratta powers. All they could do was of no avail against the skill and bravery of the Europeans; one by one they were conquered; and Cheetoo, though he might have profited by the generosity of his enemies and accepted a large estate which he was offered by them, could not curb his restless spirit. A few of his men followed his fortunes, but his standard was in vain raised for fresh adherents. These even deserted him one by one; his prospects were blasted; he became a miserable fugitive; and pursued from haunt to haunt, from fastness to fastness, he at last perished miserably by a tiger, in the dense jungles about the fort of Asseer Ghur. Peace be to his memory! he was a great man, and a skilful and brave leader; and whatever crimes he may have committed in his wild career as a Pindharee chieftain, his dreadful death has been some atonement for them.

I pass over two more years. Why should I fatigue you, sahib, with a relation of daily occurrences, monotonous in themselves, and presenting to my memory not one incident worthy of remark? I will again lead you to the road, and to further adventures.

But, Ameer Ali, said I, did you never hear aught of Motee and your other companions who were seized by Cheetoo?

I had forgotten them, sahib; theirs was a sad fate, as you shall hear.

One evening, about three months after my return home, as I was sitting in the dewan khana[1] of my house, surrounded by some friends, an attendant brought me word that a man was without, closely wrapped in a sheet, who desired to speak with me. "He will not enter," said he; "and says that you will know him when you see him."

I took up my sword and followed him. It was dusk, and I did not recognise the features of the person who had sent for me; indeed he was so closely muffled that I could hardly see them.

"What is your purpose, friend?" I asked, as the man did not speak, but motioned with his arms under his cloth for my attendant to go away. I bid him begone.

"Jemadar," cried the figure when we were alone, "do you not know me?"

"The voice," said I, "is familiar to mine ears; step into the light that I may see your face."

"No, no!" said the man in a hollow voice, "I cannot bear the light; mutilated and disgraced as I am, the darkness scarcely hides my shame: I am Ghous Khan."

"Ghous Khan!" I cried in amazement; "he is dead, he perished at—"

"It is even so," said the man with a melancholy voice; "Ghous Khan is before you: to prove it, send for a light and look at me."

I brought one myself and held it to his face. I was indeed shocked. Ghous Khan *was* before me, but, oh, how changed! His features were worn and sunken, the brightness of his eye was dimmed, his beard was matted and uncombed, and a few dirty rags covered his head; but what above all shocked me was, that his nose had been cut off close to his face, and the skin of his cheeks and mouth had been drawn together by the healed wound, so that it was tight over them, and imparted to his features a ghastly expression.

"My poor friend!" I exclaimed, embracing him; "how is this? how have you been reduced to this condition? Speak, for the love of Alla! and tell me what you have suffered."

"The disfigurement of my face is not all, Meer Sahib," said he, throwing off the dirty, ragged sheet which covered him. "Behold these!" and the poor fellow held up to my view the stumps of his arms: his hands had both been cut off between the wrist and the elbow, and the wounds were scarcely healed. Having done this, he sank down on the floor in an agony of grief and shame.

I raised him up, and comforted him as well as I could. I ordered a bath for him and clean apparel, had his wounds dressed by a skilful barber, and, after seeing him eat, or rather fed with a hearty meal, I left him to his repose.

---

1 Reception room; parlor.

I need not tell you, now that one of my lost companions had arrived, how I longed to hear the fate of the rest. That night I was sleepless and restless; but the next day closeted with me in a private room apart from observation, he gave me the following account of his adventures and sufferings: adventures indeed there were few, but sufferings many.

"You of course remember, Meer Sahib," said he, "that fatal night when, just as we were on the point of making off with our booty, we were attacked. The darkness favoured your escape, but on the first onset of the Pindharee horsemen I received a severe spear-wound in the back, which threw me from my horse. I was seized by the Pindharees, bound hand and foot, and carried to the tent of Cheetoo, where there was now a large concourse of people assembled. The wound in my back was staunched and bound up, and in a few moments afterwards other Pindharees entered bearing Motee-ram, who was desperately wounded in the head, and the two others, Nuzzur Ali and Ramdeen Singh, who were untouched. Hidayut Khan was there—the villain and traitor!—and his triumphant glance quailed under mine when I fixed my eyes on him and would not withdraw them.

"Silence was ordered, and Cheetoo demanded with a loud voice of Hidayut Khan, whether he knew any of the persons before him.

"'I do, Nuwab,' said the wretch; and he named us one by one, and pointed us out.

"'And what have you to say against them?' asked the chief.

"'I accuse them of being Thugs,' said he; 'I accuse them of murder,—of the murder of Ghuffoor Khan and of fourteen other good Pindharees: they dare not deny it.'

"'Let their jemadar, as he is called,' said Cheetoo, 'if he can speak, answer to this.' But poor Motee's spirit was fast departing, he was senseless, and never spoke afterwards.

"'I will reply,' said I; 'I say it is a lie, a base lie; I defy that man to bring proofs. Have we not served well in your camp, O Nuwab? have we not ever been foremost in danger, and more merciful than all the rest of these murdering villains?'

"'Strike him on the mouth with a shoe! cut him down for his insolence!" cried several.

"'Silence!' again exclaimed Cheetoo; 'the first man who disturbs this inquiry, by Alla! I will behead him.'

"'Go on,' he continued, addressing me; 'what more have you to say?'

"'Nothing, Nuwab; I rely on your justice.'

"'Justice you shall have; but tell me why your chief has fled.'

"'This confused me a little, but after a moment's thought I replied stoutly,—

"'Look you, Nuwab, I am a plain soldier, and cannot please your ear with fine words. My leader has fled it is true, but not from guilt. That black-hearted villain, Hidayut Khan, wanted more than his share of plunder on many occasions, and was refused it. He separated from us; we dogged him about the camp, and detected him in close conversation with a man who is known to be in your favour. This excited our suspicion. This evening we watched him to your tent; I gave the information to our jemadar; he and Peer Khan stole towards it; they laid down outside and heard his vile accusations of murder, and had only time to fly and mount their horses. We were not all prepared, and have fallen into your hands. Of what use would it have been for him to have braved your presence? the disgrace alone, to such a man as he is, would have been insupportable,—he would have destroyed himself. I know no more; do with us as you please.'

"Cheetoo seemed struck with what I had said, and mused for a moment. 'The proofs of their guilt!' cried he to Hidayut Khan; 'the proofs! bring them, or it will be worse for thee.'

"'Let their swords be brought,' said he; 'Peer Khan has made off with that of Ghuffoor Khan, but that man (pointing to Ramdeen) has one which was the property of a Pindharee who was murdered two nights ago, and other articles may be discovered in the linings of their saddles.'

"'Show me the swords,' cried a Pindharee in the crowd; 'my brother disappeared two nights ago, and I have sought him in vain since.'

"They were brought. Ah! Meer Sahib, how can I tell you that Ramdeen Singh's was instantly recognised by the Pindharee, who vehemently demanded our blood from Cheetoo?

"'This is conclusive against you,' said Cheetoo; 'what can you say?'

"Ramdeen muttered a few words in exculpation, but they were unheeded.

"'I beg further to represent, Peer-o-Moor-shid,' cried Hidayut Khan, 'that if you have any further doubts of what I have declared to be the fact, I am ready to accompany any men you may choose to select. I will guide them to the spot where that man's unfortunate brother lies in his unblessed grave; and not only him will I disinter, but march after march beyond that one will I dig up, at one place one body, at another two, until we come to where Ghuffoor Khan and his unfortunate saees lie, both in the same hole.'

"Cheetoo shuddered. 'It is too true,' said he. 'Alas! my brave men have fallen by the base hands of these stranglers—men who ought to have purchased their martyrdom by death on the battlefield. Where are the saddles and their contents? Let them be produced.'

"This was worse and worse. Nuzzur Ali's saddle, you may remember, was old and worn, and he had taken that of the Pindharee we last killed. The brother knew it and wept over it. In the lining was all the plunder he had got, just as we had received it; and around my own waist was the man's humeana,[1] with which I had replaced my own; it had his name on it written in Persian, which I had not observed. It was enough,—we were convicted; I repeated the Belief,[2] and gave myself up to death.

"Yet I once more uplifted my voice. 'Nuwab!' I exclaimed, 'it is of no use to contend further with destiny; were we a thousand times innocent, this array of facts against us would convict us. I now conceal not that we are Thugs—followers of the blessed Bhowanee, who will receive us into Paradise. We shall die by your command, but why should that vile wretch live? he who, for a greedy demand of more than his share, which he knew he could not receive according to our laws, has denounced us, has broken his oath, and been unfaithful to the salt he has eaten? Is he not a Thug? has he not joined me and a hundred others in our work ever since he was a boy? He cannot deny it; look at him, look at his cowardly features convulsed by terror,—*they* show that what I say is true. If he had been, as he says he is, an honest man, why did he not cause us to be seized when we were in the act of murder—upon the very bodies? He might have done so, for the deeds, except that of Ghuffoor Khan, were committed in the first watch of the night, when the camp was awake, and every one engaged in his own business. Why did he not then denounce us? he would have been believed. But no: he wanted half of the plunder of that man's brother; it was denied him, as similar requests had been before, and he has become a thing for men to spit at. If we die, he should not be spared, because he is a Thug as we are, because he is a traitor and a coward!'

"'Liar!' cried Hidayut Khan, scarcely able to speak between rage and fear; 'liar! I defy thee to say I ever strangled a person.'

"'No,' said I to Cheetoo, 'he was too great a coward, he dared not! and my lord may have remarked that he used the slang term to express his meaning in the last words he uttered.'

"'Vile wretch!' cried Cheetoo to him, 'thou art worse than they: they are brave and undaunted, thou art a coward; thy head shall be struck from thy body.'

---

1   Purse.

2   "La illa-il-ulla-Mahumud rusool-illa!"—"There is no God but God, Mahumud the prophet of God!" [*Taylor*]

"His cries for pardon, for life, were horrible; he besought, he threatened; but of what avail was it? He was dragged to the doorway of the tent, a Pindharee stepped behind him, and, while he still pleaded for mercy, his head was struck from his shoulders and rolled forwards.

"'Are you not dismayed?' cried Cheetoo to us; 'yours will follow.'

"'No!' cried we, one and all; 'death must come sooner or later, and ours is now—we fear not.'

"'They fear it not,' said he to another chieftain; 'death would be welcome to them; but their punishment shall be worse—they shall linger out a miserable existence. Ho!' cried he to his furashes,[1] 'out off these villains' noses and hands, and bring them to me.'

"It was done, Meer Sahib! I alone have lived to tell it; our noses were cut off—next our hands. The bleeding stumps were thrust into boiling oil, and we were driven from the camp, there and then to perish, as they thought we should, in the wild jungles. And the other two did perish; we had no one to bind up our wounds, those of Nuzzur Ali and Ramdeen broke out bleeding several days afterwards, and they died within two days of each other. So long as we were together, we supported ourselves by begging in the villages, representing ourselves to be villagers from a distant country whom the Pindharees had brought thus far and mutilated, and we procured enough to satisfy the cravings of hunger; but we could get no one to dress our wounds, which, were inflamed by the scorching heat of the weather; and, as I said, the two died. Motee we never saw; but he must have died also, for the wound in his head had cut through the brain, and he never spoke. His was a happy fate compared to ours!

"I have wandered from place to place, proceeding a few coss a day. I have been fed, and my blessings are on those who gave me food for the sake of the Prophet. What I have suffered I cannot describe; but I am now with you again, and your kindness has obliterated it all from my memory. I will live and die with you, if you will grant enough to feed your faithful slave, who will now be only a burden to you."

I was deeply affected at his story. I took the poor fellow under my care, and his wounds were healed; but he never held up his head afterwards. He died before the year was ended, I believe of shame and a sense of his helpless condition.

---

1 Servants.

Chapter XXXIX

Oh, what may man within him hide,
Though angel on the outward side.
—*Shakspeare.*[1]

THREE years, as I have before told you, sahib, passed in inactivity. My father and myself were in high favour, at least so we thought, with the Rajah, who protected us and bestowed flattering marks of kindness upon us. Our revenue business was increased: we had now the management of a large tract of country, and I believe we gave satisfaction to the people as well as to their prince. The revenue was never in arrear; and many persons from distant parts of the country, hearing of our mild and equitable mode of government, came and settled with us in our villages. Our perquisites as revenue collectors yielded a handsome income, and we lived happy and tranquilly. Still, a restless spirit was within me: I heard of the successes of various bands of Thugs in different directions; men came and boasted of their exploits; and again I longed to be at the head of my gallant fellows, and to roam awhile, striking terror into the country.

'Tis true I had gained the highest rank. I possessed fame; not a jemadar or soobehdar of Thugs could compare his actions with mine; but I vainly thought there was more to be gained, and that I had only to propose an expedition, to be joined by a larger number of Thugs than had collected together for many years. In this I was not disappointed, as you shall hear.

I have before mentioned to you the name of Ganesha Jemadar; he was always with us when not on the road, envying our quiet and respectable mode of life, which he could not attain by any means, though he left none untried. He bribed all the Rajah's court, nay, the Rajah himself, to procure employment; but there was something so harsh and forbidding in his aspect, and so uncouth were his manners, that he did not succeed in what he so much longed for.

---

1 *Measure for Measure*, Act III, Scene ii, lines 275-76.

He came in despair to us, and after rating in no measured terms the conduct of the Rajah and his officers, said that he was determined again to take to the road, for there alone he found occupation and amusement. He pressed me to accompany and join him, pictured in strong terms the booty we should gain and the glory we should win; and after many demurs and objections on my part, I finally agreed. Notice was given out to all the Thugs of that part of the country, that an expedition of great magnitude would be undertaken after the ensuing Dusera.

Accustomed as Azeema had become to my temporary absences, after the periods of quiet I had passed with her, she did not now oppose my leaving her, as she had done before. She thought it was some mercantile speculation which led me from home, and, as you may believe, I did not undeceive her.

Rejoiced at the prospect of again serving under me, all my old band, and many more, flocked to the place of rendezvous, which was at some distance from Jhalone. Ganesha had upwards of a hundred followers; and, finally, on the day of the Dusera, the usual ceremonies were concluded in the presence of upwards of three hundred Thugs, than whom a finer or more experienced band had never gathered under any leader. I was justly proud of my charge; and my father, who had accompanied me to the rendezvous, felt all his former fire kindle within him. I pressed him to accompany us, and the old man consented.

Some were for trying a new line of road, and for penetrating into Guzerat through Rajpootana. This question was fairly discussed in a general assembly, and opinions being much balanced between that route and our old one by Saugor and Jubbulpoor to Nagpoor, the matter was referred to the decision of the omens. They were consulted as I have before described; and as they decidedly pointed to the south, no further doubt could be entertained upon the subject.

Again, therefore, we moved on in our old direction, to us familiar, for there was not a man among us who did not know every step of the road, and the best places for the destruction of any persons whom chance might throw in our way.

We had proceeded nearly as far as Saugor, with but indifferent success considering our large body, having only killed fourteen travellers, and got but little booty, when, one night, as my father and myself, with a few others, sat in our little tent, we heard the ekarea—that most dreadful of all omens to a Thug. The ekarea is the short sharp bark or call of the jackal, uttered in the first watch of the night, in itself there is something peculiarly melancholy and appalling; but to a Thug the sound is one of horror. In an instant all conversation was at an end, and we gazed on each other in consternation and alarm. No one spoke, we all listened intently; it might be repeated, which would be worse than ever. It was; the sharp short bark was again heard, and there was but little time for deliberation: all started to their feet.

"We must return instantly," said my father. "Bhowanee is unpropitious, or danger threatens; at any rate, to go on is impossible, for marked you not that the sound came from the very direction of to-morrow's march?"

All agreed that it did, and were unanimous in their desire to return. Still I could not divine why the bark of a jackal should change the determination of three hundred men, and I ventured to say that I was sure it was some mistake, and that, even if it was not, we ought to proceed, since the omens had been so propitious at the commencement. "Why!" said I to my father, "were they not so? Have we not worshipped the pickaxe every seventh day according to the law? Have we not performed all the necessary ceremonies on the death of every traveller?"

"That is all true," said my father; "but it is madness to think of proceeding. Foolish boy! you have never known a reverse, thanks to your good fortune, and the excellent advice by which you have been guided; but beware how you disregard omens—it will one day lead you to destruction. As to this matter, the designs of Bhowanee are inscrutable, and she must be obeyed!"

Other Thugs too had heard the ekarea, and many came in a clamorous body to the tent, begging either to be allowed to disperse, or to be led back to Jhalone.

Any words of mine would have been useless, for the whole band seemed infected by superstitious fear; I therefore held my peace. Our encampment was broken up instantly, and, late as it was, we that night retrograded a few coss on the road by which we had come; no fresh omen of favour was vouchsafed to us, and we retraced our steps to Jhalone, disappointed, wearied and dispirited.

A month passed in idleness; but having formed my determination again to take to the road, I was not to be put off, and again I assembled my men and sought for omens. They were favourable, and I heartily prayed to Bhowanee that they might not deceive us again into a fruitless expedition. They pointed, too, to a different direction, that of the west; and we knew that between Bombay and Indoor, and indeed through all parts of Malwa, large treasures were constantly passing. We had before, as you have heard, reaped the largest booty I had ever got in that quarter, and I hoped to secure a like one again. We accordingly left our home,—one hundred and twenty Thugs under myself and Peer Khan, who still stuck to me. Ganesha had gone off in a different direction—whither I knew not; his presence was always hateful to me; why, I could not tell, and I could but ill disguise the feelings I entertained towards him.

It was too long an expedition for my father to undertake, and accordingly he stayed at our village. We met with no adventures worth recording, sahib, on our road to Bombay, for thither we were determined to proceed in quest of plunder; besides, I had heard much of its importance, and I felt a curiosity to behold the sea and the ships of the Feringhees, which came over trackless waters from their far country. But when I say that we met with no particular adventures or any worth recording, you must not think that we were idle. Thirty-one travellers died by our hands; several escaped us, the omens being against their destruction; and finally, we reached Bombay, with about four thousand rupees' worth of plunder—enough to enable us to live respectably. In Bombay we put up in the large bazar which is without the fort; and although, from the danger of detection, we could not keep together, yet a constant communication was kept up among us, and every man held himself in readiness to start in any direction on a moment's warning. I had appointed too a rendezvous, the town of Tannah,[1] which, being close to the continent, is a place where travellers congregate in large numbers previous to passing over.

I saw the sea! Day after day I went down to its edge, and gazed on its magnificence. I used to lie on the grass of the plain before the fort, and pass hours of a sort of dreamy ecstasy, looking on its varying aspect,—like that of a beautiful woman, now all smiles, again agitated by the passions of love,—or listening to its monotonous and sullen roar, as wave after wave bowed its crest, and broke into sparkling foam on the white sand.

I was lying thus one day, about the seventh after our arrival, meditating on our inactive life, and had almost determined to depart the next day, when a respectable-looking man came up to me.

"Salam Aliekoom!"[2] said he; "you are evidently a stranger, for your dress and carriage bespeak you to be an inhabitant of Hindostan. I have watched you for two days coming to this spot and gazing on the sea; have you never seen it before?"

"Never," replied I; "my home is, as you say, far inland, and in Hindostan; you have thus guessed rightly; and to me, a stranger, can it be otherwise than that I should be struck with a sight so novel and so overpowering as this expanse of water is, which seems to melt into the sky?"

"The tones of your voice are music in my ears," said the stranger; "I have heard many from my country (for that is also Hindostan), but never any which reminded me so strongly of my own home as yours. May I ask your village?"

"I lived formerly in Murnae, in the Sindousee Pergunna," said I, "but now reside in Jhalone."

"Murnae!" cried the man in astonishment; but he lowered his voice as he said, "Ah, I remember now; 'tis on the borders of Sindia's country, and belongs to him."

"Not now," said I; "the Feringhees have had it ceded to them, and they possess it."

"But," said the man, changing the topic, "you love to look on the sea; have you ever been on its surface? have you visited the ships you may have seen moored before the town?"

"I have not," replied I; "I several times determined to go, but my heart failed me when I saw the frail boat which should take me. Besides, I am a stranger; no one would have admitted me were I to have gone to them."

"Will you accompany me?" said the man. "I have an idle day before me, and shall be glad to pass it in your company."

I gladly assented, and we took our way to a stone pier which ran into the sea on the outside of the fort.

I could not divine with whom I had thus scraped an acquaintance; all the peons[1] on the bunder (for so the pier was called) paid the greatest respect to my new friend; all made low obeisances to him, and a scramble ensued among the owners of the small boats which were tied to the landing-place, for the honour of conveying us to the shipping.

He selected one, however, and pushing off, we were on the bosom of the ocean. I confess I was afraid; though Jhalone was not far from the Jumna,[2] I had never seen that river, nor had I ever seen a boat before my arrival at Bombay. Now each succeeding wave, as we descended from the top of the last one, appeared as though it would roll over us; but the men were fearless and experienced, and after a few qualms I was reconciled to our situation. We rowed, for the wind was against us, close round several of the ships which lay at anchor; and at last ascended, with the permission of a Feringhee officer who was on board, the side of an immense ship, which my friend told me was one of war, and belonged to the king of England.[3] After looking over the upper part, a small gratuity of two rupees to a sailor enabled us to proceed below to see the guns. I was astonished at their size, and at the exactness with which everything was fitted; the ropes even were twisted down into coils, like huge snakes sleeping, and the whole was a picture of neatness and cleanliness which

---

1   Porters.

2   Yamuna River.

3   King George IV.

I little expected to have seen. But these matters, sahib, are doubtless familiar to you, so I will pass them over. We returned to the shore with a fair wind, and as the boatmen spread a small sail, we danced merrily along over the heaving waters.

I was about to separate from my companion, and again protested my sense of his kindness, when he stopped me.

"No, Meer Sahib," said he, "I must have further converse with you. I am much mistaken if you are not what I was once, and am still whenever I can seize an opportunity."

I stared at him. Could he be a Thug? If he was not, he would not understand our words of recognition; if he was, I should be right. I did not hesitate.

"Ali Khan Bhaee Salam!"[1] said I, gazing intently at him.

"Salam Aliekoom!" cried he. It was enough—he also was a Thug.

"Those words I have not heard for many a year," said he; "they remind me of my early days, and the goor of the Tupounee."

"Then you have eaten it?" said I.

"I have," replied the man.

"Enough," cried I; "I have met with a friend; but who you are I am as yet ignorant."

"Have you not ever heard of Soobhan Khan Jemadar?" he asked. "You say you came from Murnae; surely I must be remembered there?"

"I have," answered I; "those who knew you have believed you dead. How is it that you are here, and a person of authority?"

"I will tell you hereafter of my situation, but at present I have many questions to ask of you; and first, is my good friend Ismail Jemadar alive?"

"My father!" said I, "surely he is; the good old man has attained a fine age, and is well."

"Shookur Khoda!" cried he; "but you said he was your father; surely he had no children—he was not even married when I left."

"Ah," said I, "so it might have been then, but here am I to speak for myself."

"And Hoosein, his and my friend, does he too live?"

"Alas, no; he died two years ago, full of age and honour." (I have not mentioned this event to you, sahib, but it had taken place soon after I returned from my Pindharee expedition.)

He continued to ask after many of his old friends, and at last inquired how many men I had with me.

---

1 Literally, "Salutation to Ali Khan, my brother." This is the phrase of recognition by which Thugs are able to make themselves known to each other in all parts of India. [*Taylor*]

I told him, and he was somewhat astonished at their number.

"Well," said he, "you are here, and it will be hard if I cannot find some work for you. I have told you I am a Thug, and have been so from my youth; my father and ancestors were Thugs before me. But, many years ago, I came here as the servant to a sahoukar of Indoor. I liked the place, and not long after got employment as a government peon, in the service of the English. They have been kind and generous masters to me; I have served them well, and have risen by degrees to the rank I now hold, which is that of jemadar. Why I left my station as a jemadar of Thugs is perhaps unknown to you?"

I replied that I did not know.

"It was in consequence of a foolish quarrel with your father," said he. "We were on an expedition, and I thought he assumed too much. We were both young men, of fiery blood, we had a sharp altercation, and both drew our swords; he was my superior, and I feared that he would condemn me to death. I fled, entered the service of the sahoukar as one of his escort from Indoor, and you see what I am. Yet I have never forsaken the Thugs whenever I have met with them. I am too old to seek adventures myself, but I put the young and active in the way of them, and thus have kept up my connection with them; not, it is true, with those of Hindostan, for a feeling of shame has hitherto prevented my doing so; but since Bhowanee has thrown you in my way, you shall not regret it. My acquaintance has been with the Thugs of the Dukhun, and I have headed one or two expeditions towards Poona, when I could get leave of absence for a while from my duties. But when I could not do this, I have secured bands of travellers for my associates, and they have been successful. I have, too, by the share of the booty I was entitled to, been able to purchase the goodwill of those who could befriend me; and your servant Soobhan Khan enjoys a high character among the Sahib-logue[1] for honesty and fidelity."

"I do not doubt it," said I: "your appearance insures respect; your manners are courtly; and how could it be otherwise?"

Thus conversing, we reached his house; it was not far from where I was residing, and, as he told me afterwards, he had discovered who we were, and had followed me from place to place, until he got an opportunity of speaking with me unobserved. From this time, as you may believe, sahib, we were sworn friends. I listened to his details of roguery (for rogue he was in his heart) with great interest, and I accompanied him several times to the durbar of the gentleman with whom his duties were connected. He was evidently a person well thought of, and as far as his office was

---

1   English gentlemen.

concerned, that of keeping the peace, was zealous and active. Still there was something forbidding to me in the way he now followed his profession of a Thug; and as we became more intimately acquainted, he unfolded to me his plans and operations. I cannot tell you, sahib, of their extent. He introduced me to the jemadars of Dukhun Thugs, who scoured the roads to Poona, to Nassuk, to Sholapoor, and Hyderabad; to others from Guzerat, who were engaged in that part of the country,—but all under his control, and from all of whom he exacted a high rate of tribute as the price of the information he was able to give them, as to the despatch of treasure in various directions by the sahoukars and merchants of Bombay.

I had remained with him a week, and our stock of money was sensibly diminishing. What was to be done? He had promised assistance in giving me information of the despatch of treasure in our direction, and I had hitherto waited in expectation that he would fulfil his promise. I was tired too of Bombay; the season[1] was advancing, and I hardly thought we should reach Jhalone before the setting-in of the rains. I therefore went to him, and frankly told him our money was running short, and that in a place like Bombay, where my men were exposed to so many temptations, they could not be expected to keep what they had; I was therefore anxious to depart, and, if he could give me no hope of any speedy booty, that I should set off in two days, and take my chance on the road.

"My plans are not quite matured in your direction," said he. "I have heard that one of the greatest traders to Indoor and Malwa is about to send not less than two lakhs of rupees thither. I know that the rokurreas[2] are hired; but as yet I cannot say whether they carry hoondees[3] or money. Three days ought to determine this; and in the meantime, as you want money, a thousand rupees are at your service, which you can repay me, with interest, at three per cent. per month, on your arrival at Jhalone. I will trust to your good faith as the son of my old friend."

"I am obliged to you," replied I; "but the money is not quite so necessary as I said. I believe every man has some twenty or thirty rupees in his possession; but it was to prevent their spending this that I spoke to you as I did. Only say that within a week we may start, and my men will be careful."

"Certainly," said he, "before a week's time. Come to me to-morrow evening after prayer-time, and you shall have further news about your bunij."[4]

---

1 Monsoon; rainy season.

2 Professional treasure-carriers.

3 Bills of exchange.

4 Merchandise; victims.

The interest-eating rascal! said I, as I left him. He a true believer! Strange I have never heard of him from my father; but I will ask him about the fellow on my return home, and doubt not I shall hear some evil or rascality of him. Not a rupee of his money will I touch, the kafir! A Thug to take interest from a Thug, who ever heard of it? I dare say he is as bad as the villainous bhutteara we killed at Saugor. Nor was I wrong, sahib. I became intimate with a Dukhun jemadar who was waiting for bunij, who told me that he ground the Thugs unmercifully, threatened to denounce them if they ever demurred, and got from them double the share he would have been entitled to had he shared the risk and the danger on the road.

"But," said the jemadar, "there is no doing without him, much as he oppresses us: he throws the most valuable booty into our hands, which we could never get scent of by ourselves; he has a number of Thugs who are his servants, and whom he pays liberally to get him information; he possesses the confidence of the sahoukars, as he assists them to smuggle; they pay him too for a kind word now and then with the Sahib-logue. In fine, he is paid both by them and us, and he contrives to sell all our valuable plunder."

"Then his receipts must be enormous," said I.

"They are," said the jemadar, "and we all grudge them to him; but still he protects us, and we could not do without him."

"Has he ever been treacherous?" I asked; for, by Alla! I was inclined to mistrust the rascal.

"There are some stories of the kind," he replied, "but in the main he is to be trusted. Still, as I said, if he were not, we could do nothing without him; he knows every jemadar of the Dukhun, and could, if he chose, blow up the whole system to-morrow; but it does not suit his interest to do so, and we are all his slaves."

"Long may ye continue to be so!" cried I to Peer Khan when he had left me; "but as for us, brother, 'tis the last time he will catch us here. What say you?"

"Certainly," said Peer Khan; "these fellows are never to be trusted; they exist everywhere, in all shapes: they are zemindars and patels of villages; and they are fakeers and bhuttearas; they are goosaens,[1] sahoukars, servants, and mutsuddees;[2] nay, the Rajah of Jhalone is one himself. They are an evil 'tis true, but we could not do without them."

"I have done so as yet," said I, "and, by Alla! I will never trust one of them."

"May you never have occasion, Meer Sahib." And the conversation dropped.

---

1 Hindu mendicants.

2 Clerks.

I went as I had promised, and found Soobhan Khan in high glee. "I have secured the bunij," said he. "Are you ready?"

"I am. What are your orders?"

"Listen," he replied. "I was right in saying the sum was two lakhs. Contrary to my expectations the sum is in gold and silver and jewels; there are about ten thousand rupees in hoondees (bills), but that is all. Now before I tell you more, we must make our bargain."

"Speak," cried I; "I am ready to give anything in reason."

"Ay, you are my old friend's son, so I must not treat you as I do the others I associate with," said he; "from them I get a third of the whole, but from you I ask only a fifth. A fifth will be twenty thousand rupees. Will you give it?"

"With pleasure," said I. "You may trust to my word; directly I get the money and reach Jhalone, I will purchase a hoondee on Bombay, and send it you."

"Capital!" cried he; "you are a man I like to deal with: no unnecessary talk, no haggling like a bunnea, but you speak like a soldier as you are. Now give me a promise under your seal that I shall have the money, and I will detail the plan to you. The paper is a mere matter of form, and I am methodical."

I objected to this, and his brow darkened. I saw it, and instantly altered what I had expressed: "Get me writing materials, and I will write it out."

"What! you write? a Thug write? But, never mind, since you are able to do it, so much the better; there will be no need of a third person."

I wrote the paper, and handed it to him, having sealed it with my seal; he folded it carefully up, and tucked it into a fold of his turban.

"Now we are all right, Meer Sahib. This treasure goes under the escort of fifteen rokurreas; they have three camels, and will be disguised as soldiers, going from Poona to Indoor. They left this place yesterday, with part of the treasure; the rest is at Poona. From Poona they will go to Nassuk, where you will fall in with them; trust me, my information is correct to the minutest particular. I know the sahoukars who send it; I have spoken with the rokurreas; and to insure your being unsuspected by them, here is a pass written in Persian and Mahratta, signed and sealed by the English officers of customs here. It represents you as persons who have come from Benares in charge of goods for a sahoukar, by name Hurree-das, and directs that no one shall molest you on your return. The men who brought the goods are still here, and likely to remain till the end of the rains. Their leader's name is Futih Mahomed, so Futih Mahomed you must be, if you please; he too is about your own age and appearance, and thus you will be better able to personate him. You see I have laid a good plan, and I leave all the rest to your own judgment. Make the best of your way to Nassuk; wait there four days, and on the fifth you will see your bunij, if you keep a proper look-out. Now go, make your preparations, and may Bhowanee send you success. Remember Soobhan Khan, and return as speedily as you like; I have no doubt I shall have found fresh work for you."

"You may depend on me, Khan Sahib," said I; "I will not be long away from you. Your plan is an admirable one; and, Inshalla! your twenty thousand rupees are as safe to you as though you even now had them in your possession."

"Remember me with many kind words to your father, Ameer Ali," continued he; "would he come thus far to see an old friend, and forgive him for the past?"

"Of that I have but little hope," said I; "he is old and infirm, and never leaves his village; but he shall write to you."

"Enough, enough," said the khan; "I have much to accuse myself of in the past; but 'tis a long time ago, and he has most likely forgotten my foolish conduct."

I left him, but made an inward determination to be guided entirely by my father's counsel as to whether one courie of the twenty thousand rupees should be paid or not. "And," said Peer Khan afterwards, "twenty thousand rupees—the old villain! He get it! Ah, Meer Sahib, we shall be the brothers of owls and jackasses if he ever sees one rupee!"

The next morning we were on our return to Jhalone, and we halted between Bombay and Tannah for the day. Our pass was of much use, for it was respected and obeyed; and the day after we passed Tannah and the different revenue guard-houses without interruption.

CHAPTER XL

1st Murd.—I am strong framed, he cannot prevail with me.

2nd Murd.—Spoken like a tall fellow that respects his reputation; come, shall we fall to work?

—*Richard III.* Act ii., Sc. 4.

"SHOOKUR Khoda!" cried Peer Khan, as he rushed into my presence on the fourth day after we had arrived at Nassuk; "Soobhan Khan was right—they are come!"

"Are you sure, Khan?"

"Certain," he replied; "the description we had of them tallies with what I have seen in every point. Come and see yourself; there are the camels, and the men are disguised. But I could have sworn, had I met them anywhere, that they were rokurreas; they have the air and bearing of the tribe."

"Enough," said I, "*you* cannot be deceived. They do not know we are here, and we will do the same as we did at Boorhanpoor. Get the men ready; we will go round the town, travel a coss or two, and enter by the same gate they did; we will then put up in the bazar with them."

We were all shortly in motion, and, as I had planned, after going round the outside of the town, we entered it on the other side, and were soon in our new quarters in the bazar.

Travellers soon get acquainted. The shop I chose adjoined the one they occupied, and I had quickly scraped an acquaintance with the jemadar of the rokurreas.

Narrayun Das, for that was his name, was a tall and very powerful man; he had small twinkling eyes, and long straight eyebrows, which, by binding his turban tightly over his temples, he had drawn up in diagonal lines to either side, and this imparted to them a very peculiar expression; long mustachios, which were twisted out to each side, and thick bushy whiskers; and his whole appearance proved him to be an experienced rokurrea, and one to whom deceit and stratagem were familiar. I shall have a cunning hand to deal with here, thought I, as I scanned his features; no common pretences will go down with him; but have him I must and will, ay, and his two lakhs too. Two lakhs! it is worth an effort, were he Roostum himself. Yet he was not slow in forming an acquaintance with me. Our salutations passed in due form, and after we had all cooked our morning meal, and sat on our carpets, we soon entered into familiar conversation.

"A pretty business Bajee Rao has made of it," said he, as I had asked him the news from Poona. "The coward! had he but put himself at the head of his army when the fight took place at Kirkee, he might have annihilated the Feringhees."

"And do you wish that he had?" said I

"Certainly; what do we know of them? While they confined themselves to the fort of Bombay it was all very well,—and I remember the time when they had hardly a foot of ground beyond it,—but now, little by little, they have advanced, until they have upset the Mahratta empire, and are in a fair way to take it."

"But," said I, "Bajee Rao has a good army, all the country is his own, and surely he will do something. The Mahrattas are good soldiers, and he has leaders of renown with him."

"He will do nothing, Meer Sahib; he will run from place to place, and his army may fight if they can or will: he will never draw a sword. The cowardly wretch has not the soul of a flea."

"Well, Jemadar, to me it matters little; I have forsworn soldiering, and find that I can get a good livelihood by escorting treasure and goods. I am just come from Benares, and the sahoukar who employed me has sent for more, which I am to bring down to him."

"Ah!" cried he, "so you are in that line. Well, it is a good one if you have plenty of men, but a sorely troublesome and difficult one if you have few. I speak from experience, for I am in the same business myself. I have been lucky, but my poor brother was otherwise: he fell by the hands of thieves between here and Indoor; we heard of him from Boorhanpoor, but beyond that we could get no tidings of him."

"Strange!" said I; "I never heard of thieves on the road, though my kafila[1] would have been worth plundering. But now I am under the protection of the Sahib-logue, I care not; they will soon have all the country, and there will be no danger in another year."

"Under the protection of the Feringhees! how do you mean? I thought you said you served a sahoukar."

"So I do," I replied; "but to insure my safe return his friend Soobhan Khan got me this pass, which he said would be respected throughout the country;" and I pulled out the document, which I had carefully folded up in wax-cloth, and showed it to him.

---

1 Caravan.

"You are fortunate, Meer Sahib, and particularly in knowing Soobhan Khan, who is a worthy man and one deservedly respected. I have known him for many years; he has always been a good friend to me, and has got me employment when I most required it, by becoming security for me to a large amount. But you said that you had given up soldiering: in this you have been wise; far preferable is it to gain an honourable livelihood than be marched in all directions, with but little pay, and hard fighting for that. With whom have you served?"

"You must not tell any one," said I; "for every man who has served the man I have would desire it to be a secret, and perhaps the knowledge of my former life might be against my present interests. I served under Cheetoo Pindharee, and led three thousand of his best horse."

"Under Cheetoo!" cried the jemadar; "this is most strange; and you are not joking?"

"I am not, I swear by your head; I dare say I could find some papers to convince you of the fact if you doubt it. But, as I said, I do not like to tell any one."

"You need not fear me," said he, "I am as close as a rokurrea, and you know the saying is proverbial. But you must have seen strange adventures and strange lands; for they say he got nearly to Madras, and left the Feringhees' country a desert behind him."

"I shall be glad to tell you some of my adventures, Jemadar Sahib, and perhaps they may interest you, though it hardly befits a man to speak of his own deeds."

"Nay, there is nothing to be ashamed of, Meer Sahib; and as for being a Pindharee, the best in the land were with him; and a gallant army they were when the first lubhur assembled at Nemawur."

"Then you were there?"

"I was. I brought some treasure from Indoor and Oojein to the sahoukars at Nemawur, and saw the whole of the preparations for the campaign; and Bhugwan[1] knows I was so taken with the appearance of the whole, that could I have got a horse, I verily believe I should have turned Pindharee myself. They say every man filled his saddle with gold and pearls."

"We were lucky enough," said I, "especially in the first expedition. Had you come to Nemawur before the second had set out, you would have heard of me; I had a good name and a high rank. In the first I was nobody, and gained Cheetoo's favour solely because I was a better swordsman than any in his camp."

---

1 Lord.

"Then I have heard of you," said the man; "but surely you cannot be that Syud Ameer Ali who was only second to Ghuffoor Khan?"

"I am the very person, and no other," I replied; "true, my rank is fallen, but whose has not? Cheetoo is dead; Ghuffoor Khan has disappeared, and is supposed to have gone to Hyderabad; Syud Bheekoo is, God knows where; and Shekh Dulla still roams about the hills between Boorhanpoor and Ellichpoor, with a price set on his head. No one knew much of me, and I suspect, so long as I behave peacefully and follow my present calling, no one will ask after me. I had enough of being a Pindharee after the second foray, and got to my home at Jhalone as soon as I could. If the others had been wise, they would have sought their safety as I did."

"Yes," said the jemadar, "Cheetoo's was a sad fate—he deserved a better; but they say the Sahib-logue offered him a jagheer;[1] is this true?"

"So I have heard," said I; "fool that he was, he would not accept it; but no wonder, his whole soul was bound up in his plans for driving out the Feringhees. He thought the Mahrattas would beat them; and when they had gained the first victory, he was to have joined them with fifteen thousand horse, and become a great commander. I should have followed him too, had they been successful; but they were not, nor ever will be, and I am what you see me."

"A strange history," said the man, "and you have told me more than I ever knew before. Had the Peshwa and the Rajah of Nagpoor played their parts as well as Cheetoo, all would have gone right; but it is useless to think of them, and I suppose we must make up our minds to our new masters. Now, however, you and I, Meer Sahib, must not separate. I am going to Indoor for some treasure, and your best way lies through it; I will keep with you for your party is a large one, and, to tell you the truth, I don't like passing those jungles by the Sindwah Ghat[2] with my own. The Bheels[3] are taking advantage of the present disturbances to be all in arms. Bands of deserters from the Peshwa traverse the country in all directions, helping themselves to what they can; and they are not over scrupulous either. So we will keep together, if you like, for mutual protection."

"I shall be glad to do so," said I; "though I have nothing to lose, except two or three thousand rupees, and whoever comes to take them will get more blows than money."

---

1   Estate.

2   The heavily forested Satpura Range in central India between the Narmada and Tapti rivers.

3   Bhils; a tribal people from central India.

"And I have still less," said he; "I have only enough to pay my expenses and feed my camels. But I am no great hand at fighting, and am not mounted as you are, to run from danger."

But the heavily laden pack-saddles belied his words. I was not to be deceived, and felt as sure that the coveted treasure was there as that the rokurrea who guarded it was before me.

We shortly afterwards separated; and when I was alone with Peer Khan I told him what I had said, and how I had deceived the rokurrea. A long and hearty laugh we had over it.

"But I fear for you, Meer Sahib," said he. "Compare his power and your own slight frame. You must risk nothing now."

I laughed. "His power, Khan!" I said; "what is it to that of many who have fallen under my hand before now? Besides, he is the brother of the rokurrea we killed beyond Boorhanpoor, and he must be mine at all hazards. I would not miss this adventure for thousands."

"I will tell you what," said Peer Khan, "it will never do to kill them so far from Indoor; let us get them as near to the city as possible, and we shall be the nearer our own home. This matter will cause a stir, and we had better not risk anything."

"Well, be it as you will. I had intended to have killed them near Boorhanpoor, and then to have turned off directly into the hills; we should never be followed."

"Ay, and risk Shekh Dulla and his party, who are out?" said Peer Khan; "that would never do. He would plunder us; and as he knows us, would most likely serve us as Cheetoo did the poor fellows who were caught."

"Astaffur Alla!"[1] cried I, shuddering. "God forbid! no, your plan is the best. We will entice them out of the towns before we have gone many marches, and then they are our own when and wherever we please."

I pass over our journey, sahib; all journeys are alike devoid of interest, and only one routine of dusty roads, parching sun (for the rokurreas would not travel by night), bad food, and discomfort of all kinds. We met with no adventure, except being robbed of trifling articles at different places; and we fully succeeded in persuading the rokurreas to encamp with us, as we adhered to our old custom of preferring the outside of the villages to entering them, where, besides the additional fear of thieves, there was more dust, more dirt, more heat, and continual squabbles with the villagers. My men had behaved admirably. No one could have told, from the broad patois they spoke, that they were aught but what they represented themselves to

---

1   Allah forbid!

be,—Benares-walas, and Bhojpoorees:[1] they looked as stupid a set of owls as could well be collected together; but they played their parts, to a man, with the extreme caution and cunning on which rested the success of our enterprise.

After all, sahib, cannot you now understand the excitement which possesses the soul of a Thug in his pursuit of men? Cannot you feel with us, as you hear my story, and follow us in my recital? Here had we kept company with these rokurreas for twenty days; we had become intimate; they told their adventures, we told ours; the evenings passed in singing or telling tales, until one by one we sank down wearied upon our carpets. Cannot you appreciate the intense interest with which we watched their every movement, nay, every word which fell from them, and our terrible alarms, as sometimes our minds misgave us that we were suspected? Yet still we stuck to them through everything; they were never lost sight of for a moment; and, above all, their minds were kept happy.

As to their leader, he was delighted with me. My accounts of my adventures as a Pindharee, the plunder we had got, the towns we had burned and sacked, all were to him interesting, and day by day I told him of new exploits. He used to sit, and the rest of his men too, listening with unfeigned pleasure to the accounts which I and Peer Khan gave. Cunning as they were, at heart they were honest and simple, and they readily believed all we told them.

But their time had drawn near. Indoor was five marches farther, and delay was now impracticable and useless; besides, to insure their safe arrival, I knew they had determined on going thirty coss in one march, and my men could not keep up with these hardy fellows.

"Come what will," said I to Peer Khan, "they die to-morrow night."

The time came. We were sitting, as usual, under some noble tamarind-trees; one by one we had sung our songs or related our adventures; and who could have guessed, had he seen us thus engaged, that a work of death was to ensue? Every tongue was employed, and the hearty laugh which broke at times from one or other of the assembly, showed how light and merry were our hearts,—we, at the certainty of our success, the rokurreas, at the thought that the peril of the road was past, and that their large amount of treasure would reach its destination in safety; there was not a grave face among us.

"There," cried the jemadar of the rokurreas, "there is the moon; when she has risen over the trees yonder we will bid you farewell, kind Meer Sahib; we have been happy in your company, and free from alarms and danger. Bhugwan grant that we

---

1 Men from Benares (Varanasi) and Bhojpur in east India.

may hereafter journey in company, and as safely as we have done! Thanks to your care in protecting us outside the villages, we have not lost a courie; and we have been taught a new mode of encamping, which we will follow in future. The moon will last us the whole night, and we shall have twenty coss of ground behind us by the time you wake from your night's sleep."

The Thugs had taken their places: to each rokurrea were four stout men allotted, and I marvelled that they should have thus allowed themselves to be separated from each other. But they had not suspected: who *could* have done so?

The moon rose majestically above the distant trees; her full, round, and yellow orb cast a mellow light upon our group. The rokurreas rose with one accord, and each turned to the men he was near to give them his parting benediction and salutation.

"Nay," said I, "we part not thus, Narrayun Das: let us separate as friends; receive my embrace; we are friends and brothers by profession." We embraced, and before the others could press forward to salute me, I gave the jhirnee: "Pān lao!" I exclaimed.

It was enough. The jemadar fell beneath my own handkerchief, and a few shrieks and groans told the rest—all had died.

"Haste ye, my good fellows," cried I to the lughaees; "the same bright moon which was to have served these fellows shines brightly upon us. Quick with your work, the camels are ready, and a few hours will see us safe from pursuit, though indeed none is to be apprehended from this small place."

The bodies were stripped; every fellow had a heavy humeana, besides what was laden on the camels. We stopped not to count our money, but hastened on when the interment was finished; and only tarrying for a few moments at the next village we came to, to purchase the goor for the tupounee, we found ourselves in the morning nearly twenty coss from the scene of our last night's adventure.

We halted till the evening, and again pushed on, but by a different road; and leaving Indoor about fifteen coss to the right, we directed our course to a small village named Dehalpoor. From this, leaving Oojein also to the right, we hastened on, always travelling by night on account of the extreme heat of the weather, and by way of Buhadoorgurh and Aorcha, we reached Jhalone in safety. No alarm had we but one. The revenue officers on the frontier of Holkar's dominions insisted on knowing who we were, and what we had with us; and so strict were their inquiries, that, had it not been for the English pass I had with me, we must have been suspected and apprehended. But, thanks to Soobhan Khan, it was not questioned; as Futih Mahomed I passed free. A duty, or rather an exaction, of fifty rupees was levied on the treasure, and a fresh pass given to us, by which we escaped further questioning and detention. Who can describe my father's joy at seeing the treasure. The old man was in ecstasy; he kissed me, he embraced me, called me by every endearing name, and extolled my conduct in glowing terms to Ganesha, who happened to be with him. It was easy to see, however, that to that worthy they might well have been spared. Jealousy possessed him, which he could ill disguise, and I verily believe, had he dared, that he would have informed the Rajah of the treasure we had secured. In the memory of the oldest Thug no such booty had ever been gained, and I was classed by the Thugs with Jhora Naek and Kuduk Bunwaree, fabled votaries of Bhowanee, of whom stories were told which, though implicitly believed by most, nay, all of our fraternity, I never credited. But it was enough for me. I had never met a reverse, and every Thug of Hindostan, I verily believe, only thought he must join me to secure to himself a booty which would support him for years.

I have forgotten, however, to mention to you an incident which befel us at Buhadoorgurh. We were encamped outside the town, and late in the evening we saw a body of men, whom we at first took to be Thugs, coming towards our camp.

"Who can they be?" said I to Peer Khan; "they look like Thugs, yet it is late for any party to be out."

"Some straggling party, I suppose," said he; "I will go and see."

"If they are Thugs and you know them," I added, "bring them, but say not a word of our booty."

"No, no, I am not such a fool," said he laughing; "but I will bring you the news."

He went, and returned with the leader of the party. I had purposely kept in my little tent, in order that my face might not be seen in case they were strangers, and to conceal it effectually I tied a handkerchief over my mouth and chin.

"Salam Aliekoom," said a gruff voice, as a man with Peer Khan entered the tent.

"You are welcome, friend," said I; "sit down." He was evidently weary with travel, and seated himself slowly.

"Your name?" said I; "and who are you?"

"My name," replied the man, "is well known, I dare say, to most people, and they are afraid of it. I am called Lall Khan, or familiarly Lalloo."

"I have not heard it before," said I; "but who are you and your men?"

"Oh, we are free traders, who help ourselves to what we can get with a strong hand."

Some wandering Pindharees, thought I; and I asked him if they were such.

"Not exactly," said he; "we are Dacoos."[1]

"Worse and worse," said I laughing; "and suppose you are from Dehli?"

---

1 Robbers.

"Ay," replied he, "even so; we know you, though you do not know us. We know you to be Thugs by your encampment; but never fear us, brethren should not interfere with each other. We have different ways of helping ourselves to spoil, but what matter? we are brothers in a general sense of the word."

"Good, we are; and if I can help you, say so."

"In no wise," said he, "but to give us room among ye for the night; we will be off early, if you do not go the same road."

"Room ye shall have, Khan, till the moon rises, and food too, but after that we are off; we travel northwards."

"Then it cannot be helped," he replied; "we will stay here till you go, and occupy your ground afterwards; we shall not be suspected."

"And where are you going?" I asked.

"To Hyderabad," said the man. "No one suspects Dacoos to be out at this time of the year, and we shall have the whole road to ourselves; we shall return after the rains, about the Dusera, by the Nagpoor road. Now we are going by Bhopal and Boorhanpoor."

"And your luck?" said I; "have you had good bunij" (for this word was understood by them, and is common to all classes of people who do their work on the roads)?

"Middling," said he; "neither good nor bad. We have had a few affairs, but nothing to boast of."

"Well," said I, "you have taken a good line: the road from Boorhanpoor to Hyderabad is a good one, and you will be in Sikundur Jah's country, where no one asks questions about the people who are left on the highways. I wish you good luck, and my friend will look after your comforts; you must excuse me, as I am in pain from a swelled face and toothache."

"Salam!" said he, as he departed; "if you were going instead of returning, we might get good plunder in company: we Dacoos are rare hands at rough work."

I had spoken in a disguised voice, and it was impossible he could recognise me again if he met me. I did this for an object which occurred to me at the moment, as you shall learn hereafter. I mentioned this meeting to my father. "What hinders us," said I, "from meeting them as they come up? they will be laden with spoil, and will be an easy prey. Brave and reckless as they are, they have no wit, and will never find us out."

"I don't know that," said my father; "they are not so stupid as you think: I know much of them, have killed some of them, and they were cunning enough. Several gangs of them have escaped Thugs by being able to detect them. However, I see nothing objectionable in your plan; and at any rate it will furnish excuse for a new expedition."

"Ay," said Ganesha, who was present, "let us go. I long to see the Meer Sahib act. We hear so much of him, that, by Bhowanee! perhaps an unlucky old Thug like myself may pick up something new. Will you let me come also?"

"Certainly," said I; "but you will see no more than you know already. Lucky I have been, but you know my pretensions to knowledge are very small, and I have never boasted of them. To my perception the whole art consists in having a smooth tongue in one's head; and a man who is a good bhuttote rarely makes a good sotha."

"Yet you are both, Meer Sahib," said Ganesha, with a malicious grin; "and your men would follow you to the death."

"So they will," said I; "for I am kind and considerate to them, and reward them handsomely."

This stung him to the quick; for he was a rough bully, and, though perhaps one of the best bhuttotes then living, was no hand at inveigling travellers; and as he always persisted in being a sotha himself, he was notoriously unlucky; but few men too would serve under him. He was preparing to retort sharply, when my father stopped him.

"Let him alone," said he; "he is a proud boy, and bickerings among us lead to no good: you must not think on what he has said."

"Nay, Ismail," said he, with the air of an offended child, "I care not what he says: pride will have its fall, and I may live to see it."

I was very angry, but there was no use in saying more. Had we been alone he should have answered for it.

So you see, sahib, out of a trifling incident a new expedition was determined on. We all prayed it might be more favourable than the former one which was planned in that direction, and I confess that my success in the last had strengthened my faith in the efficacy of the omens, though as yet by no means established it. Experience, they say, is always bought at a costly price, and is bitter when you have got it: and I had to buy mine, though the time was not yet come.

But Soobhan Khan, who was he? said I to Ameer Ali; and did you pay him his price of blood?

Not a courie of it, said Ameer Ali; but you shall hear. I asked my father who he was, and detailed the whole of my adventures with him. He remembered the man the instant I spoke of him.

"The rascal!" cried my father; "and is he so rich and honoured, the son of a vile woman? To think that he should be in such a situation, the scoundrel! But the deeds of Alla are inscrutable. Listen, my son, to his story, which can be told in a few words.

"He and I were jemadars together. I never liked him, and he had a bad reputation. He was never a good bhuttote, for the fellow was an arrant coward, but he was a capital sotha, and his smooth tongue gained him more bunij than we could gain by straightforward work. Well, many years ago we joined together, he to be sotha, and I to manage the other work. We had killed a large body of travellers near Jeypoor, for we had a numerous gang. Two were sahoukars, and the booty was large. Among it were some pearls and precious stones; they were given over to his party as their share, and he said he would go to Indoor to sell them; but I had lent him nearly a thousand rupees at different times, when he had no money to make advances to men to induce them to serve under him, and I pressed him for some of the pearls, which I wanted for my wife, in payment of the money. This was late one night, after we had divided the spoil; he said he would give me them in the morning, when I could pick out the strings I liked best; and he spoke so willingly, that I, fool as I was, never doubted him. That night he absconded, and I never heard of him till this extraordinary account of yours. Pay him!" continued my father, "not the value of a broken courie shall he ever get. In any other man I might have pardoned it, but in him the conduct was ingratitude in the highest degree; for had I not assisted and upheld him he would have been neglected and have starved."

This then was the secret of Soobhan Khan's wealth. He must have sold his pearls one by one, as he had hinted to me that he had traded in them, and raised himself by bribery to the state he was in. Of course I neither sent him his money as I had promised, nor wrote him a line to say that I had arrived safely at Jhalone. I destroyed his pass too, as it might have led to detection.

CHAPTER XLI

Prince Henry.—Where shall we take a purse to-morrow, Jack?
Falstaff.—Where thou wilt, lad; I'll make one; an I do not, call me villain
and baffle me.

—*Henry IV*. Part 1.[1]

I HAVE told you of my popularity among the Thugs; and when it became known that a new expedition was planned, and would set out after the Dusera, so many men offered themselves that I was obliged to reject numbers, and select those whom I knew, from experience and character, would be likely to behave best. Among them were a few who were excellent musicians and singers. I had before, on many occasions, felt the want of such men, to amuse travellers with whom I had fallen in; and these were particularly acceptable to me at the present time, as the expedition was a large one, and the country, being quieter and more settled than it had been for some years, we were assured that the roads would be full of persons of rank and consequence travelling to and from their homes. In order that our band might have the greater appearance of respectability, I begged of my father to accompany us, for his venerable appearance and polished manners would, I was certain, do more to insure us success than all our most cunning stratagems.

Nor was I neglectful of the Rajah. From time to time I visited his durbar, and was always received with the greatest civility and attention, as indeed I deserved; for not only was I a good servant to him, but as numbers of Thugs had settled around me in different villages, the revenue they paid for his protection and connivance at our work amounted to a handsome sum yearly; and I need not say it was punctually paid, for upon this mainly depended our concealment. In the last expedition, however, I had pleaded poverty on my return, and though I could have well spared five thousand rupees from my own share, I was content with presenting as my nuzzur a gun I had purchased in Bombay for two hundred rupees, and a small string of pearls which I had found among the treasure of the rokurreas, and he seemed satisfied; but it was merely the feigned content which precedes a violent outbreak of discontent or

---

1   I.ii.100-104.

passion. He was our bitter deadly enemy, though he cloaked his designs under the garb of friendship, and was gradually perfecting his schemes for our destruction.

We set out. I have nothing new or interesting to relate to you of the manner in which our preparations were made and completed. Azeema too, poor soul, never dreamed of what we were: it was enough for her to know that every new expedition brought her new ornaments and better clothes, and enabled her to live in a higher and more expensive manner. I had been enabled to add greatly to my house, and it was now as comfortable and spacious as I could desire. She knew too that, with increased wealth, she could look for a higher alliance for our daughter, our only child; and she had even now received proposals of marriage for her, some of which were in every way advantageous, and with persons unconnected with our profession, of which I was glad; for knowing full well that one mischance, or one traitor among us, would hurl me at once from my prosperity, I was desirous of marrying her to some one who could protect her, and be free from any dangers similar to those I was myself exposed to.

I, however, bade Azeema wait, because (as I told her) the journey I was about to undertake would be infallibly prosperous; and a fresh addition to our already ample means would enable us to have the marriage ceremony performed in a manner fitting, or perhaps exceeding our pretensions. She readily acceded to my request; for if there be one thing more than another about which a matron of Hindostan is solicitous, it is the marriage of her child; not as regards happiness, I must own, though perhaps there may be a lurking wish that she may be happy; but the main matter is, that her clothes shall be of the best and richest materials, her jewels many and of value, and the whole of the establishment which she takes to her new lord, of the most substantial description, that they may last her for years, and procure for her mother the goodwill of the female members of her husband's family. Nothing is productive of more quarrels among the females than that anything should appear indifferent; remarks are made, and reproaches are bandied about between the united families, and out of these soon grows an enmity which never cools. Many a marriage, which promised well at its outset, has been marred in its joyous termination by fault being found with the equipments of the bride, which are always submitted for inspection to her female relations before they become her own property for ever.

But I am digressing, and must return to my own adventures. We left Jhalone as before, upwards of three hundred Thugs, under my father, Ganesha, Peer Khan, and myself. We gave out along the road that we were servants of the Nizam, and were returning to our service at Hyderabad after our periodical leave of absence; this was necessary, for our numbers without it would have provoked suspicion.

Never shall I forget the first matter we took in hand; not that there was anything remarkable in the destruction of four men, but it was attended by a sad result, which damped the spirits of the party for many days afterwards, and from which one never recovered.

Peer Khan had a nephew, a boy of about ten years old, a noble little fellow, beautiful in his features, and intelligent beyond his years. As you may imagine, he was a great favourite among us all, and I had repeatedly asked Peer Khan to allow me to adopt him as my son, to supply the place of the child I had lost; but he would not hear of it, for the child was the son of a beloved sister who was dead; the boy's father had also died about two years before, and Peer Khan had taken him to his home, and loved him as his own.

The little fellow rode a spirited pony which I had given him, was always in the van of the party, and amused us by his mimic feats of horsemanship and by his intelligent prattle. He could never be kept behind; and when the time came that the four men were to meet their fate, we had given him in charge to those who brought up the rear, with strict orders that on no account was he to be permitted to come on after us. Peer Khan also had desired him to keep with these people, as he was going off the road to a village at some distance, and he had promised obedience. Yet all our precautions were of no avail; how could they be, when what followed had evidently been written in his destiny?

I had just given the *jhirnee* and the four miserable men were writhing in the agonies of death, one of them too was shrieking, when, Ya Alla! who should come galloping up but Alum Khan, the boy I have mentioned. His first exclamation was of triumph that he had caught us; but how can I tell the look of horror to which his countenance was instantly changed when he saw what was going on! His eyes became fixed, and were wide open, his tongue cleaved to the roof of his mouth, he uttered no sound, but clasped his hands in agony; and before I could dismount, or even Peer Khan, who was superintending the work, he had fallen from his pony insensible.

"What shall we do?" cried I to Peer Khan, as we raised him up and strove to comfort him, "Speak to him; a word from you may arouse him."

"My child, my child!" cried Peer Khan, in accents of terror and misery; "oh, speak to me! one word only: you are killing your father. Ya Alla!" continued he, raising his hands to heaven, "grant that this swoon may pass away, and that he may speak; I will feed a hundred fakeers in thy name, O merciful Prophet! if thou wilt but intercede and grant my prayer." But it was of no avail; the poor boy lay senseless, though his eyes were fixed and staring, and not a word could he utter. The Thugs too had left the dead, and were all around us. There was a rivulet close by, in which the bhil had been prepared; I thought of water, and bid one of the men run for some. It was brought, and I poured it into his mouth. "He revives,—his lips move!" cried Peer Khan in an ecstasy of delight—"he speaks!"

And the poor boy did speak.

"Where am I, uncle?" said he in a faint voice. "Where am I? What have I seen?"

And he passed his hands over his eyes.

"Nothing, nothing," cried his uncle; "you have fallen from your pony, that is all; you should not ride so hard, my child; you might have been killed."

"No, no," said the boy; "I did not fall. I saw—Alla, save me! save me, uncle! Oh, look at their eyes and faces—there they lie—oh, kill me, I cannot bear it!—I shall die."

Unhappy child; he had again seen their faces; we had never thought of the dead; one of the bodies lay close to us, the distorted features grinning horribly, and it had fallen against a bank, so that he saw it sitting half upright,—a dreadful spectacle for a child.

"Take it away, take it away!" he shouted in his infant voice. "I shall die—oh, bury me! I shall never forget the face and the eyes; they will be ever before me!"

"Away with them!" cried I; and as I turned again to the child, he had sunk on his face in the sand of the road, and was endeavouring to hide himself in it—he was in strong convulsions.

"Alla! Alla! what shall I do?" cried Peer Khan. "Oh, Meer Sahib, by your soul, by your mother's honour, do something! Save that child, and I will be your slave till the end of my days; I will serve you on my knees: I will be your menial!"

"What can be done?" said I. "All we can do is to stay with him, and comfort him when the paroxysm is past. He will revive soon and forget all."

Poor boy, how he strove in his convulsions! he could not speak intelligibly; he foamed at the month; his lips grew livid and contracted; his eyes, when he opened them, seemed sunk into his head. I had never seen such terror before, nor could I have believed that it would have had such an effect on any one.

We carried him to the edge of the stream, and by dint of bathing his face, and forcing water into his mouth, he partly revived. He had just opened his eyes again, when by a miserable chance they fell upon one of the turbans of the dead men, with which I had been wiping his face. It had an instantaneous effect on him; his screams broke out afresh, nothing could console him, and we were in dreadful alarm about him. What to do we knew not; we were far away from any human habitation, and even had we been near one we dared not have called in any hukeem to see him, for his incoherent ravings would have too truly exposed our doings. We sat by the boy in fearful apprehensions that every throe and convulsion would cause his death; at last we raised him up, and placed him on his pony, and had succeeded in conveying him about a coss while he was in a state of insensibility; but it was of no avail. Again he awoke from his temporary unconsciousness, and we were obliged to take him down, and lay him on a bank at the side of the road, while we fanned his face and endeavoured to compose him.

But he was greatly reduced in strength, his moans were feebler and feebler, and though he now opened his eyes and gazed calmly around him, it was but too plain to us that the delicate flower had been blighted, and was fast withering under the terror which possessed him. Peer Khan was in a dreadful state: he raved, he entreated, he prayed; he knelt down beside the poor sufferer, and bedewed his face with his tears, which were fast falling; but no mercy was shown him. We sat thus till long past midday; numerous travellers passed us, all commiserating the child's state of suffering, but they shook their heads as they left us, with a firm conviction that he must die.

And he did die. Towards evening the pure spirit fled from the suffering body, and we were left alone in the wild waste with the dead.

"It is of no use lamenting now," said I to Peer Khan, as he sat, his hands clasped in anguish, rocking himself to and fro, and moaning and sobbing as though his spirit would break. "It is of no use, brother—the boy is dead, and we must carry the body on to the stage, which is not very far distant."

"Do as you will," he replied; "as for me, my heart is broken: I shall never look up again. He was the life of my soul, and without him what shall I do? what shall I do?"

But we raised the body up, and at times carrying it, at others placing it before us on our horses, we conveyed it to the camp. Our absence had been known, but as its cause was also known, none of the Thugs had come out to meet us. We laid down our sad burden in my tent, a grave was quickly dug, and it was buried by torchlight, amidst the tears and lamentations of the whole band, for the boy was beloved by all.

Peer Khan came to me in the dead of the night, and awoke me from a restless slumber, in which the dreams of the sad scene had fearfully mingled. I was glad that he had come, but not for what followed.

"Meer Sahib," said he, after a long silence, "I am not what I was,—I never shall be again; I am broken in spirit, and am no longer fit for my profession. My fate too points against it, and after this dreadful catastrophe I should be useless to you. Permit me, therefore, to depart. You see I am calm and composed, and I do not say what I now urge on you in passion or grief; therefore let me depart. I will go to my home, and in solitude endeavour to make the remainder of my life acceptable to

Alla, who has visited me with this affliction. Nor will it be long ere the earth covers me, I feel that this blow has shaken me to my soul, and it will bow me down to the grave."

I saw it was useless to argue with him: his features were stamped with despair; and to contravene a man's fate is impossible. It is the will of Alla, and what mortal can oppose it? It must have its course.

"Go," said I, "Peer Khan; may peace be with you, and the blessing of the Prophet! I feel for you—I shall ever grieve with you; but if, in after times, your inclination leads you to join me, I need not say how gladly I shall avail myself of your services. We have been friends and brothers, and we part such, I hope, after years of a sincere and mutual affection."

He could not reply to me—he wrung my hands, while the big tears rolled from his eyes over his manly features; he made attempts to address me, but the words stuck in his throat; and at length throwing himself at my feet, he kissed them, and embraced my knees; he then arose, and after gazing on me for a moment with features working under the effects of suppressed emotion, he rushed from my presence for ever—ay, for ever! When we returned to Jhalone he was dead—his grief had killed him!

He had been more to me than any of my other companions, and deeply I sorrowed over his untimely fate.

I said this event threw a gloom over our party, which did not pass away for many days; but gradually the men assumed their wonted cheerfulness, and again the song, the jest, and the tale were heard in our merry and light-hearted camp. Nor was the more serious part of our object neglected. Within a march or two of Jubbulpoor, we had heard that a moonshee,[1] stated to be a man of great wealth, was travelling before us to Nagpoor, and we made an effort to overtake him. We effected this a march from Jubbulpoor, on the Nagpoor side, and were now entering on our best ground; I say our best, as there were but few inhabitants in that miserable country.

We overtook the moonshee; but had it not been that we were nearly three hundred Thugs in number, we should have hesitated to attack so large a party as his. He had two good-sized tents, horses, camels, a palankeen and bearers, and servants; and we deliberated long over the matter.

The omens, however, having been consulted, were found to be favourable, and therefore we hesitated no longer, but now laid our plans to effect an object which promised so much plunder.

---

1 Secretary; scribe.

We encamped close to the moonshee for two days; of course this led to inter-course. Hearing that we were respectable persons, he sent to my father and myself to come to him on the second evening, and we went. The moonshee was in the employment of the Europeans; he had served with the force at Jalna, under general Doveton, though we could not make out whether he was a servant of that officer or not; but he spoke of him in such terms as led us to suppose he was. He told us that now the country was settled, he had obtained leave to go to Hindostan, and was returning with his wife and child. We spent a pleasant evening with him, for he was a man of extensive information, and amused us with many anecdotes and accounts of the Feringhees, of whom he spoke in terms of the highest praise, and undeceived us as to many particulars we had heard of them, and materially removed many of our prejudices against them. I respected them more from what he said than I had ever done before; for though every one acknowledged they were good and brave soldiers, it was said they were vicious, and debauched, and drunken. At one or two questions of mine the moonshee laughed immoderately. I asked him once why the Europeans eat with knives and forks and spoons, instead of with their fingers, which God had given them.

"Yes," said my father, "old as I am, I have never been able to find this out. Tell us, for you know, as you have yourself seen them eat."

"Tell me what you have heard," said the moonshee, "and I will give you an answer."

"It appears so extraordinary," said I, "that I can hardly believe it; for why should not all men be the same? Nevertheless, I have heard, and from what I thought to be good authority, that their finger-nails contain poison, and therefore they dare not risk the chance of their drawing blood, nay more, of touching their food."

How he laughed! I thought he would never have ended; and I felt nettled that my remark should have given rise to such immoderate mirth. I could hear too, from the tittering behind the division of the tent, that the women were also provoked to merriment at my expense. At last he said,—

"No, no, Meer Sahib, this is folly. Who could have told you such a lie? What if their skins be white and their faces ruddy, are they not the same flesh and blood as we are? They eat with spoons and knives because it is the custom of their country, and because they do not like to soil their hands. Besides, their style of cookery is different to ours; for instance, they roast half a sheep and eat it, and how could they do so without the implements they use?"

"I confess my ignorance," said I, "and am ashamed to put any more questions to you about them, so shall believe henceforward that all I have heard are lies." Yet I longed at the same time to ask more about their drinking scenes, and the meaning of the words, Hip! hip! hip! which I fully believed to be of mystic import.

It was late when we separated, but before we did so we agreed to travel in company, and to pass our evenings together. This was what we wanted; our success was inevitable should we succeed in getting him on one or two marches farther, as the villagers there knew us, were our friends, and for a small consideration would keep themselves to their houses, and allow us to do what we liked. I have not mentioned this before, sahib, for you very well know that it is the case. We have friends wherever we go; we bribe all we can, and have our agents in every part of the country in the disguise of fakeers or merchants. Some zemindars[1] fear us, others bully us, and extort large sums from us, but they are generally faithful; and without their help and connivance do you think we could effect anything? We could not. In the Nizam's country particularly we are well aided. Many of the zemindars have Thugs in regular pay, whom they have been in the habit of sending out on the road: some are content with a certain sum every year; others, who fear so close a connexion with us, now and then pretend to arrest us, and get as much as they can; and as there is no police of any kind, they are not afraid of their dealings being brought to light. I myself know but little of how these matters are managed there,—I mean from personal experience,—but I have heard from others, and in particular from Motee, who led a gang of Thugs for some years all over the Huzoor's dominions and told me, that so long as he paid the patels of villages, the zemindars and the revenue servants *handsomely*, he had no obstruction; that hundreds of others did the same, and practised their profession so openly, that they often never took the trouble of burying the bodies of those they destroyed. You know that this is truth, sahib, and therefore I need hardly mention it. But to my story.

We reached the village we wished to gain—a miserable hamlet called Biseynee; but the patel was in our interest, and a present of twenty rupees now and then, with sometimes a new turban, gained us his silence and co-operation. I say co-operation, for he often gave over passengers to Thugs, by declaring that his village was unsafe, and that they must go and encamp outside with the rest—who were the Thugs. He knew well what would become of them; but he was, as I have said, paid for his treachery.

Well, we reached Biseynee; I had purchased for the worthy patel a handsome turban and waistband, and had prepared for him a number of other articles, one of which was an English pistol, which he had sent word by a Thug that I was to

---

1 Landowners.

purchase for him. As soon as I arrived, I went into the village to him, and in his own house tied the turban on his head, presented him with the gifts I had prepared, and added a purse of twenty rupees.

"Ha!" said he, "what now, Meer Sahib? you are not used to be so liberal. What bunij have you that you are come with it to my poor place, to give it a worse name than it has already?"

"Oh, none," said I carelessly; "you know I have not been this way for some years, and these are to prove that I have not forgotten you."

"Thanks for your kindness, may your condescension increase," said he; "but the bunij, Meer Sahib? You are a cunning gentleman; I know you of old. Who is he in the tents yonder? and why have so many Thugs collected here? You cannot conceal your designs from me."

"Nor do I wish it," said I; "but remember our old compact."

"I do, I do," said he hurriedly; "but times are changed, and with them my masters. Know you not that this country belongs to the Sahib-logue?"

"And what of that, Pateljee?" said I; "what difference does it make?"

"None," he replied, "to *me*; but have you not seen the horsemen?"

"What horsemen?" cried I.

"Six," said he, "and a duffadar.[1] My poor village it seems has a bad name for thieves, and they have sent a party here to guard it. Alla help us, and keep the bread in our mouths!"

"And the duffadar, what is he like?"

"He is a Hindoo," said the patel, "and a Bhojpooree; he is called Hittah Singh; his men too are all of his tribe."

"Bhojpoorees!" said I; "then I dare say they are Thugs. "What Bhojpooree was ever an honest man?"

"No, they are not Thugs, Meer Sahib, for I have tried them with the pass-word. But, between you and me, I think my friend Hittah Singh only wants an opportunity to be as great a rascal as I am myself,—may Alla pardon me!"

"I have no doubt of it," said I. "Where is he?"

"Shall I call him?"

"Do so," said I. "If I cannot persuade him, I will bully him; and if the worst comes to the worst, you know we are more than three hundred to six, and they would have but little chance."

---

1 Squad leader.

"True, Meer Sahib; but no violence I pray; have some consideration for my good name. If the Europeans heard of violence having been done, they would turn me out of my place."

"And you would turn Thug, I suppose. But quick, Pateljee, call the man here."

He was absent for a short time, and returned with a short mean-looking fellow, and I could plainly see that rascal was written on his countenance. You know the old proverb—"Chor ke daree men, Tinka" (there is always a straw in a thief's beard). Salutations were exchanged, and I came to the point at once.

"Look you, Duffadar Sahib," said I to him, "you may have guessed what we are?" He nodded assent. "This is good," I continued, "as perhaps you may have guessed at our object."

"Partly," said he; "but what do I know about you?"

"Exactly," said I, "the very thing I want; you need know nothing, and you will have nothing to tell if you are ever asked. Take my advice, and remain quietly within your village, and if the earth turns upside down you are not to stir out. For this you shall be well paid. But if you molest us, remember we are three hundred to seven—fearful odds, my friend."

"Nay, I am wise," said he; "what Bhojpooree is not? Nor do I wish to interfere. Do what you like; neither I nor my men will stir a foot."

"Can you depend on them?" said I; "can they be close?"

"As close as you wish them to be, Jemadar; but we must be paid."

"Certainly," said I; "I would not have it otherwise; but the reward depends on what we get."

"Say two hundred rupees," said the fellow; "it is worth your while."

"Well, it is a bargain, Duffadar," I replied, "and the patel is witness. And now I will give you further advice, which is that you are to know nothing, and see nothing, if even the Lord Sahib were to ask you. You are to know only that travellers came and departed, and you kept no account of them."

"Of course," said the fellow; "I know this of old. I have met parties of your people in my own country, and have no reason to be dissatisfied with them; they have always behaved like men of honour, and kept their words with me."

"Then we are agreed?" said I.

"Certainly; you will see nought of us, and I will come to you at night for the money."

"You had better come now, Duffadar, as I think we shall move on after it is all over."

"Do you go, Pateljee; it would not look well for me to go with the Syud Sahib. Do you go and bring the money."

"Come then," said I, "we are losing time."

"Shall you return soon?" asked the duffadar of me.

"I know not," I replied; "but it is probable. At any rate, as this country always produces good booty for us, you will see us here pretty often."

"The oftener the better," said he; "and I must continue to keep my station here; it would be hard to lose such good friends. You, Pateljee, can help me to a few low-caste rascals from time to time, to send in as thieves we have caught."

"Certainly," said the patel, "there are plenty of Gónds and Dhérs[1] in the country—every one knows they are thieves; and if they may not immediately have committed any robberies, they have been engaged in them some time or other, so that it is all the same. I will get you a few from time to time as you want them."

"Now and then I shall require a few," said he, "just to keep up my character and appearances, and a few years in irons will do none of them any harm; the Government will take care of them."

I could not help laughing heartily at the cool manner in which this was proposed and accepted. But it was the truth, and I know that it was, and is now, a matter of every-day occurrence. Many a duffadar of police has won a good name with his officers in this way, and for one guilty man, he has seized a dozen innocent people. Who cares about Mangs and Dhérs? they are always villains and robbers.

---

1 Hindus of low caste.

Chapter XLII

Good sir, you have too fair a shape to play so foul a part in.
—*Fletcher's Love's Pilgrimage.*[1]

"THAT is a bhula admee" (a respectable man), said I to the patel, as he walked to our camp; "he suits my purpose exactly."

"He has been on the look-out for some of you," said he, "for a long time. We have never spoken openly on the subject, but he has hinted as much many times. And I suspect he chose this post, if he had any choice in the matter, because he was likely to meet Thugs here. If you pay him well, he will help you materially."

"Do you think I have given enough?" said I.

"Quite," he replied; "I don't think he expected you would agree to so much."

"It is certainly a large sum," said I, "but it is the first, and the money is well spent."

"But you have forgotten me, Meer Sahib: am I not to partake of your bounty?"

"Of course, Pateljee. What I brought was only a trifle, I have more for you in the camp; you shall have your share."

"How much, Meer Sahib? I want money; my rents are in arrears, and I am in distress."

"Thirty rupees," said I.

"Make it fifty, I beseech you. You know not in what a strait I am; I cannot borrow the money, and you have been sent by Alla for my deliverance. You will lend me the money if you will not give it me? and you will have good bunij in this business."

"Well," said I, "you shall have it, but on one condition. We may not be on the road when some people whom we are looking out for pass this place: they are Dacoos; they have some tattoos[2] with them, and great wealth. If they pass either way, you must send men after us with a letter."

"I will send my own sons, well-mounted," replied he; "they will easily find you out, and you may depend on me. Where will these fellows come from?"

---

1 From Francis Beaumont and John Fletcher's play *Love's Pilgrimage* (1615-16): "Good Sir, no more; you have too fair a Shape / To play so foul a part in, as the Tempter" (V.iv.86-87).

2 Ponies.

"They have gone to Hyderabad now," said I, "and will return by Nagpoor. If we meet them, all very well; but they may escape us."

"They shall not, by Alla!" said the patel. "I will watch for them myself, and if you get them I shall hope for a handsome present."

"I will not forget you. But here we are at the camp; take care no one sees the money as you carry it away."

"Trust an old hand for that," said he, with a knowing wink. "I must go after I have got it to the moonshee, who has sent for me about fodder for his horses. I should like to see him too—to see a man whose breath is in his nostrils. And he has a wife too."

"Yes," said I, "there is no getting her out of the way, so she must die, which is a pity. He has a child also, about four years old, which I want myself; he is a pretty boy, and I have no son to bless me; he will never know the difference between me and his father after a few days."

I paid the money and dismissed him. Ganesha came to me.

"I have been looking at the ground," said he, "and there is a hole near the moonshee's tent which has been dug for some purpose or other, apparently the commencement of a well; it will save us the trouble of digging; the earth too lies close to it, and will only have to be filled in."

"Have the lughaees seen it?" said I.

"Yes," he replied, "I took Bhowanee with me; he says it is the very thing."

"Now, Ganesha," said I, "how shall we manage?"

"Oh, do you take the tent work, and leave the rest to me; I will settle all outside. You have a smooth tongue, and the moonshee is alone; I will be close at hand in case of anything going wrong; but I do not apprehend anything."

"Nor I either. None of the saeeses[1] or camel men must escape: there are many of them."

"Sixteen in all; I have counted them: let me see—eight bearers, two camel men,— one of them has a wife,—two khidmutgars,[2] one female servant, and four saeeses; how many is that?"

"Eighteen," said I.

"Ah, well, it does not matter; towards evening I will surround the whole; most of them will be listening to the songs, and the rest we must overpower in the best way we can. The night will be dark too, which is in our favour."

---

1 Grooms.
2 Menservants.

I then told him of the horsemen in the village, and what I had done. He knew Hittah Singh, the duffadar, and told me that in his excursions into the district of Arrah, in Bengal, he had met with him; and that on one occasion, when he had been arrested for murder, this Hittah Singh had got him off, by swearing to the collector that he knew him, and by being security for him to a large amount. "He is a good fellow, for a Bhojpooree," said Ganesha, "but requires to be well paid, and you have given him enough to keep him quiet."

The evening came. My father and I went to the moonshee's, but after the evening prayer-time; he had his son on his knee, and a noble little fellow he was. How I shall love that boy! said I, inwardly, as I looked on his fair beautiful features and expressive eyes; he came to me readily, and I fondled him, and displayed to his admiring eyes my beautiful sword and dagger. Azeema too will love him, thought I, and he will supply the place of our daughter when she is married and gone from us.

"You have no children?" said the moonshee; "or perhaps I ought not to ask, you may have lost them: your brow darkens at the question."

"One," replied I, "a daughter. A son, the counterpart of the Sahib Zada, it pleased Alla to take from me when he was about his age."

"It is indeed his will," said the moonshee; "there is no striving against fate. This boy is my only offspring; for many years I had been married, and my case was somewhat like that of the sultan in the 'Story of the Parrot;'[1] grey hairs were coming, and I despaired, but at last Alla was gracious, and you see the boy."

"May God grant he live a hundred years, and be prosperous," said I. "I have no hope myself."

We conversed together for some time, and on a message being given from without, I said, "You have been so pleased with the singing of some of my men, Moonshee Sahib, that they have arranged a little masque, after the manner of the byroopeas,[2] which they are anxious to perform before you. It will be absurd enough I dare say, yet it will serve to pass the evening, and your son too may be amused."

"By all means," said he; "anything in the jungle is acceptable; but for your company, Meer Sahib, we should have had a dull march. I will prepare those within, so pray call in the performers."

---

1 The *Suksaptati*, or *Seventy Tales of the Parrot*, is a ribald collection of twelfth-century Sanskrit stories about female sexual infidelity and cuckoldry.

2 Comic actors; comedians.

The men came, six stout fellows dressed fantastically, two of them as women, with sitars and drums in their hands; they personated a body of goosaeens,[1] and danced and sung in a ridiculous manner. Where they had learned their parts I know not, but the whole was well done, and the moonshee's little son laughed immoderately. As we had expected, the whole of the moonshee's people gathered round the tent, which was open on one side, to admit of their seeing the tumasha;[2] and I observed with secret exultation that every man had two or three Thugs close to him, and one in particular behind each of them. All was ready as I thought, and I was about to give the signal, when one of the Thugs called to me that I was wanted without. What it could be I knew not; but excusing myself for a moment, I went out.

"What shall we do?" said Ganesha to me in a voice full of alarm and apprehension: "Meer Sahib, the Feringhees are upon us!"

"The Feringhees!"

"Yes," he replied; "and what can we do? This good bunij will escape us. Of course the moonshee will join them, and we may then as well think of strangling the king of Dehli, as of getting him."

"But how," said I, "how are the Feringhees upon us? Have you seen them?"

"No," said Ganesha, "but I have seen their people. A long string of camels have just arrived, with I know not how many red-coated sepoys[3] to guard them,—my curse be on them all!"

"And where are they?"

"Why, they are gone into the village. They wanted this ground, but I told them I would not give it up; that the moonshee was a gentleman of rank, and could not be disturbed, and that there was better ground on the other side of the village."

"Then never fear," said I; "the work must be done immediately. I will go in and give the *jhirnee*; and if any of those prying rascals the Lascars[4] come about us, you know what to do. But I fear not; the patel will help us, and Hittah Singh too, and there need be no great noise. My father will have to personate the moonshee for awhile if necessary, but that does not matter."

"Good," said Ganesha; "but be quick, Meer Sahib, I shall be in a torment of apprehension until the whole are fairly under the ground."

---

1   Hindu mendicants.

2   Spectacle.

3   Indian soldiers serving under British command.

4   A "lascar" is a derogatory term for an Indian or Southeast Asian soldier or sailor employed by the British; it connotes "servant."

I left him, and carelessly playing with my roomal, again entered the tent.

"What is it?" asked the moonshee.

"Oh nothing," I replied; "only some Sahib-logues' tents which have arrived. Their servants wanted this ground to encamp on, but seeing us here, the Lascars have taken them to the other side of the village. The troops will be here early to-morrow."

"That will suit me exactly," said he; "I will stay with them, and bid you gentlemen farewell; but that is no reason why we should be the less merry. I warrant these good fellows have another song or two in store. Have you?" he asked of them.

"A hundred," replied one of them; "but perhaps the next will be rather a noisy one."

"Never mind," said he, "play on; you shall have as good a reward as I can afford to bestow."

I waited till the noise was at its height to give the *jhirnee*, yet I had not the opportunity I wished for. The moonshee sat with his back to the kanât,[1] and to get behind him was impossible; one of the Thugs saw my embarrassment, and relieved it, by begging him to rise and advance a few paces.

"What are they going to do?" asked he,

"I know not," I replied, "but you had as well comply."

He arose, and I slipped behind him. "Now!" I shouted; "bring the pan!" and my hand was on the moonshee's neck. One wild shriek he gave, and fell.

His wife had been looking on through a hole in the kanat; she had seen the work, and rushed out into the midst of us, with her boy in her arms. I shall never forget her—never; I shall never forget her wild look and her screams. I tore the boy from her arms, and left her in the midst of the Thugs; I ran out into the air, and the first person I met was Ganesha, his face flushed with triumph, which I saw by the glare of the torches from the tent.

"All is done!" cried he; "they have all fallen. Two I killed myself. Where are the lughaees? we must be quick."

He ran on; and I stood in the open space before the tent. Parties of Thugs passed rapidly to and fro, bearing the bodies of the dead, which were one by one thrown into the hole. But the singing and music went on as merrily as ever, and looking into the tent I saw my father sitting in the place which had been occupied by the ill-fated moonshee.

My little charge was crying terribly, imploring me, in tones and words that would have moved any one's heart but mine, to take him to his mother. I soothed him as

---

1 Screen.

well as I could, and was going to my tent; but curiosity impelled me to return, and see the hole in which the business of interment was going on. I went to the edge; Ganesha was standing by it encouraging the lughaees! he saw the boy in my arms.

"What folly is this, Meer Sahib?" said he; "you are not going to spare that boy, when we are even now in such danger!—it will be madness. Give him to me; I will silence the crying wretch, and send him with his parents."

"Never!" cried I; "the boy is mine; you may have all the spoil, but give him up to death I will not. Have I not lost a son, and is it not lawful to adopt a child of this age?"

"Madness! madness!" cried Ganesha, "the boy must die. Are you a fool, Meer Sahib, to risk such a chance?"

"He will never find out the difference between us and his parents," said I; "and I will not be interfered with."

"Fool!" said Ganesha, setting his teeth, "I spared a child once, and will never spare another; I have sworn it on the pickaxe."

"I care not for a thousand oaths," I cried: "the boy is mine, and you had better not oppose me if you wish to avoid a quarrel;" and I was going away.

He caught me by the arm.

"Let me go," I exclaimed, and I felt for my dagger, "or, by Alla! I will strike this steel into you."

"Boy," cried he, "you are mad; I fear you not; talk of daggers to others than Ganesha; he has seen too much of you to fear you. Give me the child I say, his very cries will alarm the sepoys."

I felt for my dagger or sword, but I had left them in the tent; I tried if pity could move him.

"Have you no compassion?" I said more gently; "Ganesha, have you no pity for a child? Can you bear to kill him?"

I was off my guard, and he saw his opportunity. Quicker than thought he had rudely snatched the child from, my arms, and as he hurled him into the pit, he cried scornfully, "Pity! no, I know it not. Now go and cry, Meer Sahib, for the loss of your plaything."

I started forward, and leaned over the edge of the hole, which was being rapidly filled; the poor boy lay senseless and dead at the bottom,—one shriek alone had escaped him, as he was dashed with passionate force into it. I gazed for an instant to satisfy myself that he was dead, and some of the earth which was being thrown in hid him almost instantly from my view.

I turned to Ganesha in savage anger.

"Dog!" cried I, "and son of a dog! you shall answer for this. Had I my sword now with me, I would cut you in two pieces."

"An idle threat, and one befitting what I have heard of you," said he. "Go, Meer Sahib, you are a boy and a fool: I do not fear you."

Stony-hearted villain, he had destroyed my son. Situated as I was I could then do nothing, but I was determined to have my revenge: and I took it too. I mentioned what had occurred to my father and to three of my intimate associates: they were determined to stick by me whenever I chose to attack Ganesha, and would fain have done so the next day; but this did not suit me, though his words rankled in my heart, and the deed he had done made me hate him more than ever. I deferred my revenge to the last moment, but I took it, as you shall hear.

We stayed on the ground that night; the palankeen had been broken in pieces and thrown into the hole, but my father personated the moonshee the next morning as we rode through the camp of the Feringhees, which had been pitched so near us, that indeed I have often wondered they heard not the cries of the party as we despatched them. But we had taken good precautions. The noise of the drums, and the confusion occasioned by letting loose two of the moonshee's horses, which were here and there pursued by a number of Thugs, shouting and screaming after them, had drowned the cries of our victims, and we had effected the whole without suspicion.

Our good friends, the patel and the duffadar, had kept the sepoys in conversation, and they had not noticed the noise, beyond hazarding a passing remark as to its cause.

Again therefore we were on the road. We had not got all the booty we expected, it did not indeed amount to three thousand rupees, and we earnestly looked out for the Dacoos, who were, we hoped, to be our next bunij.

We went on to Nagpoor, and sold the moonshee's camels and horses. Here the gang divided; one part, under a jemadar named Emam Buksh, took our old road towards Oomraotee, and through the valley of Berar to Khandesh and Boorhanpoor; the rest of us returned by the road we had come, after staying four days in the city of Nagpoor.

On our second or third march homewards we overtook the Dacoos. They had been seen by our spies the moment we entered the village we had encamped at; and as much caution was requisite in managing them, my father at once proposed to be alone the sotha, or inveigler.

"I shall feign to be a Hindoo," said he; "these rascals will suspect me if I go by my own name, and indeed they would know me. I will be a Rajpoot jemadar, come from Hyderabad, and you shall see I have not forgotten my old trade."

Accordingly he painted his forehead and breast after the fashion of the Hindoos, covered his eyes with wood-ashes, put on a waist- cloth and dress he borrowed from one of the men, and attended by another went into the village.

How anxiously I expected his return! I feared he would fail in his mission, but Ganesha was confident. "He never fails," said he to me; "he is one of Bhowanee's own favourites; nothing he ever did failed. Would that I had his luck!"

But he was absent so long, that I became apprehensive for his safety, and was on the point of setting out to gain tidings of him, when to my great joy I saw him approaching. I ran to meet him.

"What news?" cried I; "oh, my father, my liver has been burnt during your absence. Why did you stay so long?"

"Never mind, my son," said he, when he had dismounted, "you would have been wrong to come after me. But ah, the owls! I have entrapped them,—they are ours."

"Ul-humd-ul-illa!" cried I, "this is rare news; but how did you manage it?"

"Why," replied he, "it was done easily enough, though I feared for my success when I saw that one of the Dacoos was a fellow I had known a long time ago; however, he did not recognise me, thanks to my white beard and these marks of the infidels: he never thought I was Ismail Thug. I sat and conversed with their leader, who told me very gravely he was a servant of the English going to Hindostan on leave of absence. I said I was one also, and had come from Jalna, where I was a collector of duties on spirits. We then became intimate, and the upshot of the whole was, that we agreed to travel together; and, by Alla! if the omens are good, they shall die to-morrow. Delay is useless with these fellows, for they evidently think (from the signs I saw them making among themselves, which are known to me), that we are certain bunij to them, and if we do not attack them they will fall upon us."

"We shall need good hands," said I; "and I will take the leader."

"I will be a bhuttote also," said Ganesha: "I never killed a Dacoo. Are they stout fellows?"

"Very," answered my father; "but like all their tribe they are heavily armed, and can do but little against us, if we manage properly."

"We had better fall on them with our swords," I observed.

"Not so, my son, but we will surround them, and if there is not a good opportunity, the men can use their weapons."

We were soon agreed on this point; and in the morning the Dacoos joined us as we moved round the village into the main road. They were twenty-five in number, stout but heavy-looking men, armed to the teeth, with their heads enveloped in folds of cloth. They had with them thirteen tattoos heavily laden; and it was well they had this encumbrance, as it served to separate them, as each tattoo required a man to drive it. Had they kept in a body, we could have made but little impression on them, and dared hardly to have attacked them.

"Now, look out!" said my father to the men; "if you see them leaving their beasts and collecting in twos and threes, fall on them at once, or they will attack us; they know well enough who we are, though they pretend they do not."

We journeyed on in company; after I had ridden for some distance I dismounted, and walking beside the leader I entered into conversation with him. He did not recognize me in the least, and very gravely began telling me how he had met with Thugs on his way down; how he had fought with and overpowered a large band, and carried off their plunder, amounting to some thousand rupees.

I could have struck him on the mouth with my shoe, but I refrained; yet it was enough to have provoked me, being so barefaced a lie. Still I applauded his bravery, and he continued: "Yes, Meer Sahib, these Thugs are the greatest villians unhung; and I praise the Prophet that I have gained some information about them, which I will give to my masters the Europeans. The fool of a Thug, or rather one of his people, told me they belonged to Jhalone; I am going that way, and if I do not tell the Rajah of their being in his city, call me an owl, and a father of jackasses. I expect, too, he will reward me handsomely."

Ay, you will tell him, thought I; but you must get there first, my friend. Mashalla! words are one thing, but deeds are another.

"And were they such fools?" I asked; "all the world say that Thugs are never to be taken in."

The fellow laughed scornfully.

"Never taken in!" said he; "did not I deceive them? They are swine, they are asses; they murder poor travellers, but they have no wit, not so much as children. Their fool of a jemadar tried to deceive me by wrapping his face in a cloth; but I saw him, dark as it was, and could swear to him among a thousand."

"What was he like?" inquired I; "I am curious to know, if it were only to avoid him in future, especially as I am a constant traveller on this road; but you said you attacked them?"

"Yes," said he; "I am an old traveller too, and as we were a large body, and the Thugs not more than treble our number, I said to my companions that, though I knew we were with Thugs, they ought not to fear, and if they would only watch me, we might attack and disperse them, and get their plunder; and, by Alla! we did, sahib. Late at night we rose on them, killed some, and the rest ran away, among them the cowardly jemadar. "We got enough too to take us to Hyderabad comfortably."

So we had a narrow escape, thought I; these fellows would have attacked us, I doubt not, had we not gone on that night. But the lie, sahib, was it not an impudent one? Yet I could not help laughing heartily at his relation, which he swore was true, by Alla and the Prophet, by my beard, and by every saint in his calendar.

We trudged on till we came in sight of two trees on the road, on which travellers hung bits of rag as offerings to the guardian saint of the place. I saw very plainly that this was their bhil; one by one they began to forsake their tattoos and collect. More delay on our part would have been fatal, and my father saw this. He was as prompt as I could have desired; he had seen their movements, and just as I had disengaged my roomal from my waist, he gave the *jhirnee*. Eleven of the Dacoos fell at the same moment, the leader by my hand. I had my roomal round his throat, and before I gave the fatal wrench, I shouted in his ear that I was Ameer Ali, the leader of the Thugs he had met, and that *then* I had sworn to kill him, and had done it. The rest were cut down with swords; my men were prepared, they were not, and were heavily encumbered. Yet had we delayed for another three or four hundred paces, they would have fallen upon us, and I think, sahib, the Thugs would have run away.

As it was, however, we were victorious; we threw the bodies as they were into the jungle, and pushed on, laughing heartily, and in the highest spirits at the issue of our adventure. The booty, too, was good—thirteen thousand rupees' worth of gold, silver, and ready money met our admiring eyes, when the packages of the loaded tattoos were opened for our inspection.

Well, sahib, we had proceeded as far as Sehora on our return, when we fell in with a great European, who was also travelling. We did not fear him, but on the contrary determined to keep with him, because we well knew that he had many travellers in his train who profited by the protection of his troops; so we divided into two parties, one under myself and my father, the other under Ganesha. Our object was to separate the travellers from him, and we hoped, by representing the inconvenience they were put to by delay on account of his slow marches, and the scarcity of provisions they would experience on the road, to induce them to accompany us. I need not follow the adventure further, for it differed not from the rest; suffice it to say, that after a few marches a large party of travellers had joined with us. We left the high-road to proceed by footpaths through the jungles, and near the village of Shikarpoor we selected the bhil. The place was a favourite one, and well known to our party. The travellers fell, twenty-nine men, some women and children; all were buried in one grave, for the spot where they were killed was a desolate one. The deed was done in the night, but by the light of as fair a moon as ever shone on us. One child I saved from the general slaughter; Ganesha was not present to oppose me; and though the boy was a Hindoo, yet I determined to adopt him as my own, and to bring him up in the holy faith I professed myself, and this would enhance the merit of having spared him. But when his mother died, I could not force him away from the body; he clung to it, young as he was, with frantic force, he screamed and kicked whenever I attempted to lay hold of him, and bit me in the arms and the hands. I thought, if the body was removed from his sight, he would be quiet and submit to his fate; but no—when it was gone, he grew worse and worse; nothing would pacify or tranquillize him, and I fairly grew impatient and angry. I drew my sword, and threatened him, but he was insensible to his danger; he reviled me, he spat at me with a child's virulence. I once more raised him up in my arms, but it was of no use; he seized my ear in his teeth and bit it till the blood came. In the agony of the pain and in my rage I knew not what I did. Sahib, how shall I tell you what followed? it was the worst act of my life but one, which I have yet to tell you of.

You killed him, I suppose, Ameer Ali, said I.

Yes, sahib, I killed him: but oh, how did I do it! it was the devil's work, not mine. I never was cruel, but now the Shitan possessed me.

Here Ameer Ali put his hands to his eyes, and finding my heart sicken, I begged him to refrain from reciting the dreadful particulars. After a pause he continued.

Wretch that I was, I did this. No one was near me but the Thug who held my horse, and even he was horror-stricken, and uttered a loud scream of terror. I silenced him, and leaving the mangled body, I mounted my horse and galloped after my party.

Yes, sahib, I deserved to be hung for that deed, had I never done another; but I was spared for a different fate.

We were in full march on the third day after this happened, when we saw a body of horsemen coming after us. My mind misgave me when I observed them, and I hastened to collect the straggling Thugs and form them into a close body, in case the horsemen should prove to be enemies, or make any hostile demonstration. On they came, shouting and abusing us in every term of vile reproach their tongues could utter. There were about forty of them; and I verily believe that, had I not been at the head of the band, they would have fled as one man; however, I cheered them up, and was determined to show a good front in my retreat. I knew there was a village in our interest within a few coss, which possessed a worthy patel like him I have told you of; and that if we could but reach it, we might man the walls and towers, and bid defiance to our pursuers.

"Be not afraid," cried I to my men; "let the best of ye come behind with me, and we will stop these marauding rascals. I know they are Pindharees, and the veriest cowards in existence. Only be firm; you who have matchlocks take good aim, and when they are near enough, every one mark his man, and see if as many saddles are not emptied."

On they came; fortunately the road was narrow, and had thick thorny brushwood on each side of it, so that they could not pass us. They were within speaking distance, and I shouted,—

"Are ye friends or enemies? if the former, keep behind us; if enemies, begone, in the name of the Prophet, my friends, or ye are likely to get a sharp reception."

"Stop!" shouted the leader of the party; "who among you is leader? I would speak to him."

"I am leader," said I; "come out alone and I will meet you; but if any of ye stir, by Alla! we will fire on you." The fellow advanced, and seeing that none followed him, I rode out in front of my men. "If there is treachery," said I to them, "fire,—never mind me."

"Jemadar," said the man, "our thakoor[1] has sent for you, you may possibly have guessed why. You had better come; you will only have to pay a fine and will be released, I swear this to you on the faith of a Rajpoot."

"I will neither trust you nor your master," said I; "you are a parcel of vagabond Pindharees; I laugh at you, and spit on your beards. If you want us, come and take us; but of our own accord we come not. Are we fools? are we asses? O man! art thou one to talk thus? Go back to him that sent thee, and say, the man is yet unborn who will take Ameer Ali so long as he has a weapon in his hand, or a few gallant fellows by his side. Have you no shame to deliver such a message?"

He made no answer, but urged his horse and cut at me with his sword. Fool! he did not think that a Thug could fight, and still less that he had, engaged one whom no one had ever yet defeated. I caught the blow on my shield, and returned it on his head as he passed me;—the fellow fell from his horse a dead man.

My own men set up a shout and discharged their matchlocks—one horseman and a horse fell wounded, and struggled in the dust. Had only my own good companions in the Pindharee affairs been with me, I would have charged them and put them to flight, but I could do nothing alone. We had checked them, however, and

---

1 Village headman; chief.

retired slowly, followed by the troop, who kept out of shot, but evidently waiting for a piece of level and fair ground to charge us. In this way we retreated till the welcome walls of the village whither I had directed the main body appeared to our view. We redoubled our efforts to gain the shelter they would afford us, and the men were in some disorder as we passed over a level plain in front of the village; they were even beginning to run, but I checked them. "For the love of Alla!" cried I, "for your own sakes, keep together and have brave hearts; so long as we are firm they will not dare to come near us, but if once we separate we are lost. See, even now they are preparing to charge, as a hawk stoops on his quarry." And down they came; thundering along, brandishing their spears, and reviling us. Some of my men fled at their utmost speed to the gate, but most of them stood. Again I dashed at one of our enemies and wounded him, but the odds were against us: one of my own men fell, pierced through the breast to the backbone by a spear; another was wounded; but they could not take further advantage of us. Those who had fled, joined by others of my men and some villagers, headed by my brave old father, issued from the gate; which the horsemen seeing, they drew off, and we got within the village in safety. They kept hovering about till midday, but out of the reach of our shot; and soon after noon they all departed, and we saw no more of them. We had to pay for our shelter handsomely, however, for the patel shut the gates of his village and declared we should not pass out without having paid him a thousand rupees. I was for attacking him, plundering his village, and burning it after the Pindharee fashion, and we could have done it easily. But my father would not hear of it: "The country would rise on us," he said; "and, besides, it would ill requite the patel's hospitality and protection, even though we had to pay for it." So he paid the money; and, after a thousand protestations of mutual goodwill, we left the village in the evening, intending to push on as far as we could, to be beyond the reach of pursuit.

Nor were we followed; though this exploit made a noise in the country and was known far and wide, we were not molested. We heard afterwards that the thakoor flew into a furious passion when he heard of his men's defeat, and dismissed them from his service as a parcel of cowards, as indeed they were. Moreover he swore he would be revenged upon every Thug he might ever catch afterwards; and I believe he kept his word and put some to death. But we laughed at his beard, and many a merry jest had we over the adventure afterwards.

It seems, the day after, some herdsmen were passing the spot where the travellers had been killed, and they saw the body of the lad lying in the road; all the remains were discovered, and information was given to the ruler of the village and tract of country in which the deed had been done.

We pursued our route. Ganesha too had been fortunate; he had decoyed a large body of travellers, consisting of a jemadar who had lost an arm, and his family, with some others, along the bypaths in another direction, and he had killed them all.

You know, sahib, that it is forbidden to us to kill persons who may in any way be deformed. I was amused afterwards to hear the accounts which were given of the deliberations made upon the jemadar's fate by Ganesha and his gang: he told them to me himself when we met.

"Some, indeed most of the men," said he, "hesitated as to whether he should be strangled or not. There was no means of separating him from the party, and they said the whole ought to be abandoned on his account, as he had lost an arm, and therefore was not a fit sacrifice to Bhowanee. I replied that he was not deformed, that if he had lost an arm, he had had one once, and the losing of it was not the work of Alla but of man, and that when he died he would appear in the form in which he had been created; therefore he was not forbidden, but was true bunij; and I asked them how they would show their faces to you and to their brethren at the rendezvous with no deed to boast of, and, more than all, no plunder. I prevailed; the whole were strangled; the jemadar by my own hand, for no one else would touch him, despite of all I said to convince them there was no harm in it. The worst of all was, however, that there were two young girls of a marriageable age, the daughters of the jemadar. Two of my men took a fancy to them, and would fain have carried them off to be their wives, but they would not consent, and they were strangled with the rest."

We were now somewhat at a loss for a route, or whither to go. The omens were consulted at Saugor, which was our place of rendezvous; and as they pointed to the northward, we struck off the high-road to the north at Saugor, and took that to Seronje. But my father returned to Jhalone. We divided into two bodies, each a day's march from the other, for we were fearful of being suspected if we travelled in large numbers; and since the Europeans had got a footing in the country, we found that we were asked more questions at the different posts and guards than we had used to be. Besides, large bodies of travellers had disappeared in various directions by the hands of other bands of Thugs, and the authorities were suspicious and inquisitive to a degree. However, now with bullying, now with bribes, we contrived to pass on, leaving our fruit as we went in many a sly place, which the police never suspected; and although we got no large booty, yet scarcely a day passed but one, two, or more travellers met their death at our hands. It was at the village of Eklèra, in Holkar's dominions (alas! I shall never forget it), that our sothaees brought us word they had secured a small party of travellers, who, they had heard, were about to proceed to a village a few coss distant.

Of course our men told them of the danger of travelling alone, of the alarms there were of Thugs, and begged of them to accompany our large party for safety, which had collected for the same purpose, and they consented. The sothaees offered to introduce them to me as the leader of the kafila;[1] and accordingly, at sunset, one of them returned to the bazar, and brought two of the men to me. I received them cordially, repeated the same stories as my men had done, and frightened them quite sufficiently for my purpose.

"Listen," said one; "though I have never seen a Thug, nor know of any existing in this part, yet that they have been here there is no doubt. My wife's father was killed by them."

"How!" said I; "it is horrible to think on; how did this happen? know you aught of the particulars?"

"No," replied he, "none but what I have heard from others. I was a boy at the time, but the old men of the village know them well, and often speak of them even to this day. I will introduce you to my father-in-law, as I justly call him, and he shall tell you the tale himself. Mashalla! he tells it with much spirit, and 'tis worth hearing."

I confess I was interested; why I should have been so at a common tale of Thuggee was more than I can imagine. I rose and followed the man to his house, determined to hear the whole story from his father-in-law's mouth.

I have said it was yet day; the sun was setting, and the village was a scene of bustle and noise, as is always the case in an evening; the herds which had been out to graze were pouring in at the gates, raising clouds of dust, through which the walls were but dimly seen. Yet still as I advanced I fancied them familiar to me; I imagined I knew the names of different places near them,—one in particular, the abode of a fakeer, around which was a small garden. I almost started when I approached it, for it seemed like the face of a familiar friend one meets after a long, long absence, when one hesitates to accost him by name, though almost assured of his identity. But in spite of my desire to know the name of the garden, I walked on, for it would not have suited my purpose to have appeared to recognise any object, having represented myself to be an utter stranger. As we passed through the gate, objects more and more familiar to my eyes presented themselves,—the bazar, the little mosque, the

---

1 Caravan.

kotwal's chowree,[1] the temple of Mahadeo.[2] I could have named them all, and one house in particular,—my heart leaped within me as I passed by. There was nothing remarkable in it; but it seemed unaccountably fresh to me,—as though I had but left it yesterday.

Still I walked on silently, and my companion did not notice the agitation and surprise which must have been depicted on my features. We reached the house, a respectable one in appearance; and desiring me to be seated, he left me, to bring the old man of whom he had spoken. When he entered, Alla! Alla! I could have called him too by name, though his features were shrunken and withered. I was almost about to exclaim, Rheim Khan! but I checked myself, and as he was presented to me under another name, Futih Mahomed Khan I was silent.

The whole, after this, thought I, must be a wild dream, or I may have visited the place in my wanderings, perhaps stayed a few days at it, and it is thus familiar to me. After some desultory conversation my new friend stated what he had told me, and requested his father-in-law to relate the story of Peer Khan, with all its particulars.

———◆———

---

1   The magistrate's public hall.
2   Shiva, Hindu deity.

CHAPTER XLIII

Now o'er one-half the world
Nature seems dead, and wicked dreams abuse
The curtained sleep. . . . Now withered murder
. . . thus with his stealthy pace,
Towards his design moves like a ghost.
—*Macbeth*, Act ii., Sc. 2.

THE old man returned my salutations cordially; and when we were fairly seated, and the hookah had passed round, he related the sad history of the parents of the girl he had adopted. His version of the tale differed little from that of my new acquaintance; and indeed the whole affair appeared to have been as successful a piece of Thuggee as I had ever listened to. I wonder who they were, thought I; I will mention the story to my father; perhaps he may have heard of it, and can give me some clue to the boy whose fate is buried in uncertainty. Yet the lad may even now be among us; and as this thought flashed across my mind, a half conviction forced itself upon me that I was the man! But I checked it,—it was a foolish thought, such as one harbours sometimes upon the slightest cause, and dismisses after a moment's reflection.

"And you never heard aught of them afterwards, nor of the boy?" I asked.

"Never," said the old man; "never; years have passed since then, and the lad, if he lives, is about your own age, Meer Sahib; and—Ya Alla!" cried he, gazing on me, as a gust of wind caused the lamp to flare towards me, "those features are familiar to me!—speak, man! thou art not the son of him who was murdered?"

I confess that his earnest gaze and manner, with my previous convictions that the village was familiar to me, almost overpowered me; but I was too old an adept in deceit to be long staggered by a suspicion which he had no means of confirming, and I replied carelessly and with a laugh: "No, no, that cannot be: my father still lives, though my mother is dead; indeed I have but little remembrance of her. Besides we are pure syuds by descent, and reside in a distant country, and you spoke or your old friend as a Pathan."

"It cannot be, then," said the old man, turning away with an air of disappointment; "yet the resemblance is very striking, and I pray you, Meer Sahib, to pardon an old man's mistake; it may be that my eyes are failing me. Yet look at him, my son, and say, does he not resemble *her*?"

"He does so, certainly," replied the other, "and I was struck with the similarity of features when I first saw him; but it must be imaginary, or it is perhaps one of those unaccountable resemblances which one often sees without being able to discover any cause why it should exist."

"But you spoke of a coin," said I, "which you hold to be possessed of peculiar virtues."

"I did, Meer Sahib, and my father will tell you that I have not overrated its efficacy."

"Nor has he," said the other; "many charms have I seen, but none equal to it. "When around the neck of the wearer, no evil comes to her, no disease attacks her, and the eye of the malevolent or envious rests in vain upon her. Assuredly it possesses wonderful virtues, for if it is ever absent from her, she suffers from disease, or is unquiet in mind."

"Alla ke Qoodrut!"[1] I exclaimed; "it is the work of God. Such charms are indeed precious, and lucky is the possessor of them. I had once a son,—he became the victim of an evil glance cast by a fakeer to whom alms were denied; he cursed my house, and the boy pined and died. I was absent from my home, and you may judge, sirs, of my agony when I arrived and learned my boy was dead. I have never been blessed with another; but a girl still survives, upon whom every care is lavished, and no charm is offered for sale by the wandering fakeers, Moslem or Hindoo, but it is eagerly purchased and hung around her neck. In this manner I have spent much money, but as yet without effect; for my child is delicate, and afflicted with dreams which disturb her rest and disquiet her gentle spirit; and I would to Alla I could become the possessor of some charm similar to the one you mention."

"Keep a stout heart, Meer Sahib," said the old man; "you have bought your experience with sorrow, to be sure, yet a constant attention to the wants of the holy wanderers will no doubt have its effect in the end, and their prayers will be offered for the health of your child and her long life."

"May Alla listen to them!" said I fervently, for my heart was then with my child and my loved wife.

I arose to take my leave, and as my new friend insisted on accompanying me to our camp, we walked thither.

---

1   It is the power of God!

"You will be ready, then, at the first dawn," observed I; "we travel early for the sake of the cool morning air, and my companions bestir themselves as soon as the first blush of light spreads over the east."

"Depend on me," said he, "I will not keep you waiting: we have a long stage before us."

He left me. I will have the charm, thought I, as I lay down to rest; my child shall be protected by its extraordinary virtue, and there will be an end of the constant searchings for amulets, which do no good, and cost much money. Besides, I could not, bring Azeema a gift she would prize more highly, better far in her eyes than strings of pearls or costly jewels. Thus musing, my thoughts wandered to my home: my treasures were before me in imagination, and I compared this my wild and exciting life with the peaceful moments I enjoyed when I was there with them—Azeema lying beside me, and our child amusing us with her innocent gambols. The contrast was forcible, and appealed to my best feelings.

I fell asleep; nor did I awake until the bustle of preparation for the journey warned me that it was time to rise. Having performed my ablutions, I repeated the morning prayer and thanksgiving, and issuing from my little tent, I saw the band was in readiness to move on; but my new acquaintance and his family were as yet not with us.

"Shall we move on?" asked Laloo,—who was now my confidant, being the second of the bhuttotes,—as I stood near my horse, preparing to mount.

"Not yet," said I; "I expect some bunij from the village; they promised not to be late, yet the day advances. Send some one to hurry them."

"Ay, our friends of last night, I suppose, Meer Sahib. Of course we will wait for them, and I will send a fellow to quicken them; know you how many there will be to deal with?"

"Not I," I replied; "there are a man and his wife, but how many more I know not. We shall soon see, however."

Our messenger returned almost immediately. "They come," said he; "I had not reached the village gate when I saw them issue forth."

"And how many are there?" I asked.

"There are two women on ponies, one old one on foot; and three men armed with sword and matchlock."

"Six in all," said I. "Do you, Laloo, tell off the Bhuttotes; if we find a good place to-day I will give the *jhirnee*; if not, the business can be done to-morrow."

"True, Meer Sahib," he replied; "but we had better put it off to-day. To tell you the truth, there was an objectionable omen this morning, and you know there is no need of risking anything."

"Certainly not; we can send on the bélhas[1] to-night, and things are best done which are conducted regularly."

The village party now approached us, and salutations were exchanged. We stayed not, but pushed on at as rapid a pace as allowed the villagers to keep up with us; and we travelled thus to the end of the stage. I saw no likely place for the deed on our way, for the country was thickly peopled and the villages were close to each other. But I heard with inward satisfaction from my acquaintance, that the next march was through a lonely tract, and I was urged by him to be on the alert and careful, for that robbers were plentiful, and we might be attacked.

They rested in our camp that day and night. I watched eagerly to see, if it were possible, the face of the woman who bore the prize I so eagerly coveted, but I could not discern it: she was strictly secluded, or if she moved out of the temporary screen her husband had erected, she was enveloped in a thick wrapper, which defied my utmost attempts to discover her countenance. But she was *mine,* and I gloried in the thought that ere another day should pass over me, she would have fallen under my hand, and the charm would be mine also. You, sahib, will perhaps wonder at my eagerness to possess it; but you know us not, if you do. What mother is there in Hindostan, ay, or father, who does not covet a potent charm against the evil eye for his child or for his wife, far more than riches, nay the commonest necessaries or comforts of life? A child falls sick, the glance of some one is declared to have rested on it, ceremonies are performed without number, pepper is burned, mustard-seed placed in the room, and other things done which you would laugh at were I to relate them all; and hence comes the necessity of charms. Holy men are besought to give them, and are paid for them highly; fakeers are implored to pronounce mystic words over the suffering infant; and women will sell anything they possess, even their jewels, to purchase an amulet which is said to be efficacious. Sahib, I had lost one child; another, my sole offspring, was constantly ailing, and we were tormented by a thousand miserable anticipations regarding her. Within my reach was a sovereign remedy for all, so at least I firmly believed. Can you wonder at my eagerness, my impatience to possess it?

Laloo came to me, and with him the chief of the bélhas. "We are to go on, I suppose, as soon as we can?" said the latter.

---

1 Grave-diggers.

"Certainly," replied I; "I hear the road lies through a lonely tract, which commences a few coss from here. See that you choose a good place, and that the grave will hold six bodies."

"Jo hookum!"[1] rejoined the fellow; "but I hope the information is correct about the road, and that it is not like the last stage, cultivated ground from first to last. I would have defied the best bélha that ever drew breath to have selected a spot free from a chance of interruption."

"Rest content," said I; "the information is good, I had it from our fellow-travellers, who have passed that way a hundred times."

"Then I will start by sunset," continued he; "I suppose the nearer to this the place is selected, consistently with security, the better."

"Certainly," said I. "Go; you have your leave."

Midnight soon arrived; we had arisen and had proceeded about three coss on our way; we had passed every village, and entered on the desolate tract I have mentioned. The hot night-wind still sighed over the waste, and through the thorny bushes by which it was thinly covered. No sound broke the silence, save a shrill neigh from one of our baggage ponies at intervals, or the wild and melancholy note of the plover[2] as it piped its wailing night-song to its mate, and was answered again from afar. Once or twice the half shriek, half-howl of a hyæna might be heard, and so like was the cry to that of a wretch under the knife of an assassin, that my blood curdled in my veins as the sound thrilled through me. I rode on, first of the party, eagerly looking for the bélha, who should give me the welcome intelligence that the grave was ready, and that we were secure from interruption; nor had I long to wait for this. At a turning in the road I saw the trusty messenger seated; and as he espied me and arose, I hastened to meet him.

"Bhil manjeh?"[3] I asked in our slang language.

"Manjeh," was the reply; "'tis ready, Meer Sahib."

"And how far, Gopal?"

"Scarcely a cannon-shot from hence, a dry nulla with a sandy bed crosses the road; and a tributary streamlet's course, between high and narrow banks, was the best place we could find."

"Good," said I, "you are always careful. Now keep near me, and hold my horse when I dismount; I have a share in this affair which I would not trust to another."

---

1 Your order shall be obeyed!
2 Short-billed wading bird.
3 Have you prepared the grave?

I slackened my horse's pace, and the party soon overtook me. I stopped as they came up, and dismounted.

"A plague on these roads of yours, khan," said I to my acquaintance; "my horse has lost a shoe, and his foot is somewhat tender; so I will walk a coss or two to ease him of my weight. Surely there cannot be much more of this stony track."

"Not much; a coss or two perhaps; we ought to be near a dry nulla, if I am not mistaken, and from thence the next village is a coss and a half; after that the road is good."

"Let the Meer Sahib ride on my tattoo," said a voice like music; "I am cramped and stiff, and I shall be glad to walk awhile."

It was that of my victim! she who was to die under my hand ere a quarter of an hour elapsed. She must be beautiful with that voice, thought I; but I shall see.

"No, no, khan," said I, "that must not be; I am soldier enough to walk when I have no horse. Mashalla! my limbs are strong and supple, and I would not mind trying you at a long stage."

"As you will, Meer Sahib, but you have only to say the word, and she dismounts. Alla knows 'tis a small recompense for your safe protection over this dreary tract, which never man yet passed but with fear and apprehension. The nulla too, we shall reach it soon;—they say many a brave fellow's blood has moistened its sand."

I saw the woman shudder at her husband's speech, and I checked him.

"Shame on you, khan!" said I; "think who hears you; women's ears are not fitted to listen to tales of blood, save when they are of a battle-field and of scenes in which honour is gained and fame won at the sword's point. Here you are safe; no rascally Dacoo would dare to meddle with a kafila like ours, and we shall pass the nulla, as we have those behind us, without a thought of its dangers or what has ever happened in it. But what was that?" I eagerly asked, as something crossed our path close to my feet.

"Nothing but a hare," said the khan; "some prowling jackal has scared her from her form, and she seeks another hiding-place."

"A hare!" I repeated, the current of my blood seeming to be suddenly arrested, as I thought on the fearful omen to a Thug—one that could not be disregarded, or, if disregarded, was certain to be followed by the most dire calamities, nothing less than death? or long imprisonment.

"Yes, Meer Sahib, a hare. Why should it astonish you?"

"But across my very path," I muttered involuntarily.

"'Twas chance," said the man; "what of it?"

"Nothing," replied I; "nothing,—we have an old superstition about it in my country, but 'tis an old woman's tale, I dare say."

I paced on in silence. Ya Alla! what a conflict was raging in my heart! I have told you I disregarded omens; I cared not for them, only as they were the soul of Thuggee as far as my men were concerned; and to humour them I feigned to be particular in their observance. But my soul quailed when I was put to the proof. Every tale I had heard of the vengeance of Bhowanee at a conscious neglect of her commands and omens flashed in rapid succession across my mind: how one had died, eaten by worms; another been overtaken by what the world called justice; how another had lost his wife or children,—and I too had yet a child! I say I quailed in mental terror for awhile; but mine was a stout heart, a noble spirit; and it roused at my call, like that of a good steed, which worn and weary with travel, yet at the approach of strife or danger bears his master as gallantly as though he were fresh from his stall. Yes, my soul rallied. Away with such idle tales, fit only to be bugbears to children, said I mentally; Ameer Ali is not to be frightened by them. And to lose the charm,—the object of my anxiety, when almost within my grasp! I laughed aloud.

"You are merry, Meer Sahib," cried Laloo, who I saw was at his place; "tell us your thoughts, that we may laugh too; and, by Alla! we need it, for a more unsainted country I never saw."

"'Twas but a thought," said I. "Know you where my hookah is?"

"I do not," he replied, "but I will call for it." And the word was passed by those who followed us for it to be brought.

This was the preparatory signal. Every one heard it and took his post. The place could not be far, arid with my last words had passed away every chance of life to our companions.

Nor was it far off; a few moment's walking brought us to the brink of the nulla. I first descended into it, and disengaged my roomal. I was ready; one by one the others followed me, and we were now in the middle of the dry and sandy bed, mingled together, the victims and their destroyers. I saw the time was come, and I gave the *jhirnee*.

They fell,—ay all! and almost at the same time. There was no sound, no cry; all that I heard was a faint gurgling noise from the husband of the woman, who had writhed in her death-agony under my fatal gripe; a few convulsive throes and she was dead! I tore away the boddice which covered her bosom; I thrust my hands into it, and groped upon the still warm breast for the prize I had so earnestly longed for. I found it tied to a silk cord,—which defied my utmost efforts to break; but I unsheathed my dagger and cut it, and I hugged the treasure to my heart in a frenzy of exultation. One look at the face, thought I, and the lughaees may do their work; and I gazed on it. It was beautiful, very beautiful; but the expression and the eyes,—sahib! why did I look at it? I might have spared myself years of torment had I not done so. That face, of all that I have ever seen in death, haunts me still, and will ever haunt me, sleeping or waking.

Not that it had any particular effect on me then. No, it was afterwards, as you shall hear, and when I had discovered what I had done. Yes, she was beautiful, fair as my own Azeema, as delicate and faultless in form. The lughaees shall not behold these beauties, thought I, nor could I listen to their coarse remarks; so I covered up the bosom, folded the body decently in the sheet which had been around her, and sat down by it to await their coming.

"How, Jemadar Sahib!" said Gopal, as he came up to me, "have you not stripped the body? But let me do so; yonder sheet is worth two rupees."

"Let it alone!" cried I, "touch her not; she is too fair for the like of you to look on. And hark ye, my friend, let her be buried as you see her now. Whatever the others may say, tell them that it is my order; and for your own share, you shall have a new sheet when we reach Jhalone."

"Jo hookum," said the man, "you shall be obeyed. But have you searched for jewels?"

"I have; she had none. Away with her, and see that I am obeyed. Yet stay, I will accompany you."

I went with him. The grave was where they had described it, between the high and narrow banks of a small watercourse; it was deep, and already contained some bodies. I saw that of the fair girl laid carefully down over them, and I prevented their mutilating it with their knives as they had done the others. I waited till all had been finished, and the grave covered in; and collecting my scattered party we pursued our journey. It was well we had been so expeditious, for scarcely half a coss from the spot we met a large party of travellers, who, confident in their numbers, had pushed on by night as we had done. Short greetings were exchanged between us, a few inquiries as to the road, whether water was to be had, and where, and we passed on.

Our booty was small enough, as you may conceive: about forty rupees, a few changes of raiment, the tattoo of the deceased, and the few and simple ornaments of the women, worth perhaps a hundred rupees, were all we got, But I had the real prize, worth in my eyes thousands of rupees. No one knew I had it, and I kept it hung round my own neck, and close to my heart. A thousand times I took it out and gazed at it; there was something about it which had a mysterious effect on me: many times I thought I had seen it before, and I fancied its old and battered surface was familiar to me. But my mind gave me no clue to the idea, and I attributed the effect I have described to the influence of the charm itself, and I was assured of its potency. How Azeema will prize it! thought I;—in itself valueless, yet a treasure in her eyes and mine, for it will protect our child, and many an envious eye is upon her.

We were still far from Jhalone, and the season admitted of further wanderings; but I was sated. Strange to say, I no longer thirsted for adventure; and though it came, and men were delivered into our hands, yet I sought not for them. Those we destroyed were casual travellers who joined our party, and whose destruction was unavoidable.

We held a general deliberation at a village on the confines of Malwa; and though some were for travelling northward as far as Agra, and thence to Jhalone, I over-ruled this, and indeed had the majority on my side, who were satisfied with what we had got, and longed for their homes as I did. "However, my friends," said I, "our proceeding homewards need not bring us worse booty than we should get by going north. Roads are roads, and travellers will surely be on them wherever we go. Let us not relax in our vigilance, and do you trust in the lucky fortune of Ameer Ali. Victory has always followed him, and his star is still high in the ascendant. Above all, let us consult the omens, and by them be guided; if it is our fate soon to see our homes, they will determine our actions and proceedings."

My speech was received with plaudits; the omens were consulted, and though none remarkable were observed, yet in the opinion of the best-informed Thugs we were justified in holding our present direction, till it should be changed either by meeting with new adventures or adverse omens. Accordingly we pursued our route.

I forget how many days it was afterwards, but we were encamped at Tearee, a large town in Bundelkund, and had been there two days in the hope of bunij. We had been unlucky in not meeting with any till then; but our tilhaees[1] were actively employed, and I was determined not to quit the town without an adventure, as it was the last place on the road to Jhalone where we could hope to meet with any of consequence. The sothaees and tilhaees, however, returned in the afternoon with downcast faces, declaring they could meet with no one, except miserable creatures hardly worth the trouble of destroying; and all were for moving of the next morning.

I was piqued at our ill luck, I know not why. "Stay, however," said I to them all, "for the morrow; something tells me it will be a lucky day, and one is not of much consequence." My will was of course law to them, and early the next day I dressed myself in my best clothes, armed myself with my most showy weapons, and taking

---

1 Scouts.

some of the Thugs with me, as it were a personal escort, I rode into the town, causing my horse to caracole as I went, in order to show off my admirable horsemanship.
Twice did I ride up and down he bazar and the principal streets, but without meeting
with any hope of adventure or bunij, At last, observing three respectable-looking
Mahomedans seated on a chubootra, or terrace, under the shade of a large peepul-
tree,[1] I rode up to them, and inquired whether they could direct me to the abode of
any dealer in pearls or precious stones, as I wished to purchase some.

"Are you in earnest?" said the oldest of the three, "or do you merely ask to find
out whether our poor town would afford you such precious commodities?"

"God forbid, sirs," said I, "that one so young as I am should dare to endeavour to
jest with men of your age and respectable appearance. I do indeed seek what I have
said, and shall rejoice if any of you can direct my steps, for here I am a stranger."

"Since such is the case," replied the old gentleman, "I am happy in being able
even at this moment to present you to Shekh Nusroodeen, who sits here beside me,
and who follows the respectable calling you are in search of. But you had better dismount, and, if such is your pleasure, join our mujlis[2] for as long as you feel inclined.
My worthy friend will then, I doubt not, be happy to accompany you to his abode,
and show you the articles you require."

"You are kind," said I, "and I accept of your civil invitation." So saying I dismounted, and ascended by a few steps to where they were sitting.

A few moments were occupied in the ceremonies of being seated. My new acquaintance called for a hookah and sherbet, and in a few moments we were on
excellent terms.

"And what may be your distinguished name?" said the elder of the three, who
had first accosted me.

I named myself:—"a poor syud," said I; "an unworthy descendant of our
Prophet,—on whose name be peace!"

"Mashalla! I told you so," cried the old man. "Mashalla! there is no mistaking the
noble race; and his speech too! How say ye, my friends, is it not sweet and mellifluous like a verse of Hafiz?"

"Ameen! Ameen!" cried both, "'tis even so; the young syud is a worthy representative of his tribe, and we are fortunate in having made his acquaintance."

---

1   Fig tree.
2   Gathering.

"You overpower me, worthy sirs," said I; "I little merit these encomiums; for having spent all my days in camps and in strife, I have learned few of those courtesies which ought to adorn the manners of every true believer."

"You have served then with Sindia?" asked the pearl-merchant.

"No," said I, "not in his armies, though there has been tough fighting, enough to be seen with them. I have served in the Dukhun; and I am proud to say under the banners of Salabut Khan of Ellichpoor."

"A good name," cried all; "the noble khan too has won it bravely, though not on our side in the late contests."

"It matters not," said I; "wherever a blow was to be struck, or there was hope of a fight or a foray, Salabut Khan was ever first in the fray, and the last to leave it."

"And your destination, Syud?" asked the pearl-merchant.

"Jhalone," I replied, "Salabut Khan has reduced his force; and there being no longer hope of employment for a cavalier like myself, I returned home to my father, and have taken quiet service with the Rajah,—whom Alla preserve! for he is as generous a prince as any of Hindostan; and on his behalf I have recently been on a mission to the durbar of Doulut Rao, on some matters which have been in dispute between them. I am proud too to say that all has been quietly settled."

"Soobhan Alla!"[1] cried the third worthy; "how could it be otherwise, since our honoured guest has managed the negotiation?"

Again I bowed my head to the earth, and acknowledged the compliment. Some desultory conversation followed, and I rose to depart.

"My time is precious," said I, "and I implore you to excuse me. I have much to arrange about the men who accompany me, and I go on to the chowree to settle their accounts with the kotwal; if the worthy shekh[2] will allow one of his attendants to point out his abode, I will notice it, and visit him ere sunset."

"Nay, Meer Sahib, this cannot be," replied the shekh; "behold, I am ready, I will accompany you; my poor house is not far off, and Alla forbid I should be the means of trespassing upon your time!"

He arose, girded up his loins, threw his shawl over his shoulders, and thrusting his feet into his slippers prepared to accompany me.

"I take my leave then, worthy sirs," said I to the others; "may health be with you!"

"Not without the pān and utr, Meer Sahib," said the eider; "it cannot be that we should let you go like a dog." And calling to an attendant, the articles were brought.

---

1 Praise be to Allah!

2 Chief.

The pan was presented to me; I was duly anointed on my beard and under my arms, and after a few more salams and compliments, I was following my new acquaintance the pearl-merchant.

"Is he to be bunij?" whispered one of my attendant Thugs to me in Ramasee as I passed him.

"Hush!" said I, "speak not a word; but run all of ye before us and clear the way, as if I were a great man."

They obeyed me, and ran forward, shouting and pushing the crowd to and fro, as though I had been a nobleman of fifty descents and a hundred titles.

We soon reached the house of the merchant; and leaving our slippers at the door, he took me by the hand and led me at once into the private apartment, where I suppose he transacted his business or received his best customers. It was a dahlan, or veranda, opening into a court, in the centre of which was a small fountain; its edges were planted with red poppies and larkspur, in various figures; and a plantain tree or two flung their broad green leaves over all. The place looked cool, and was scrupulously neat and clean. The room where we sat had been newly whitewashed, and its floor covered with a white cloth, except the musnud[1] itself, which was yellow cloth bordered with blue velvet; a few large luxurious-looking pillows invited me to recline and forget the world and its cares. Such shall be my own home, thought I, after awhile; a fountain is easily made, and I will enjoy my peace and quiet even as this worthy does. I had seen a hundred such, but the unobtrusive neatness and comfort of the spot struck me forcibly; and whilst envying the possessor his peaceful lot, I was inwardly forming a plan to decoy him with me, which I had leisure to mature, for he had left me seated, and was for some time absent.

---

1 Throne.

Chapter XLIV

Hor.—What is the issue of the business there?
Ham.—It will be short, the interim is mine:
    And a man's life's no more than to say one.
        —*Hamlet.* Act v., Sc. 2.

HE returned after some time, bringing with him a small casket, and leading by the hand a noble-looking boy, whom he presented to me as his son, his first-born. He was about twelve years of age, intelligent in feature, and withal handsome, and possessing a confidence of manner I had never seen surpassed.

"Alla has been merciful to you, my friend," said I; "and the Sahib Zadah is worthy of his sire. I had a son too once, who promised to be such a one as the boy before me; but it was His will! and I have now a lonely house. Yet why obtrude my griefs upon a stranger? You have doubtless other flowers of the same tree."

"There are three of them," said the merchant, "and they are the pride of my existence; for, after all, what is wealth? what is honour? what is well-doing or respect in the world, without some one to inherit it, and to tell of his father to yet unborn generations? And you are yet young. Why be without hope? Alla will not fail to listen to the prayers of a devout syud."

"Alas," said I, "I think not of it. A girl remains to me, who is contracted in marriage to the son of a worthy neighbour, and upon her rest my hopes at present. It is on her account that I seek a few pearls for the marriage ceremonies."

"And they are here, Meer Sahib; pearls from Surat and from Serendeeb,—jewels that a monarch might be proud to wear." And he opened the casket, and displayed its beautiful contents to my admiring eyes.

"They are indeed beautiful," said I; "but a poor soldier like myself has little to do with such costly ornaments. Show me, I pray you, a few of a lower price, such as will suit my present wants, which do not reach further than three hundred rupees' worth."

He selected a string, and held them out to me; they were what I really required, and the purchase was quickly concluded.

Still however the glittering strings lay before me; and as I took up one in particular of great beauty, from the evenness of the pearls and their bright water, I said, as if involuntarily, "Would that my patron could see these!"

"Eh! what?" cried the merchant. "Do you think he would purchase them?"

"Assuredly," said I; "for shortly before I left Jhalone the Rajah was in the greatest need of pearls, and sent hither and thither for them, but without success: none were to be procured; and he was even talking of sending to Surat for some; but the length of the journey and the risk put the matter out of his head."

The merchant mused for awhile. At last he said, "And you really think he would purchase them?"

"I do. His daughter will be married next year, and he is collecting jewels for the ceremony."

"They are very beautiful," said the merchant, taking up the string, "are they not? I have had them now for two years, and no one here is rich enough to purchase them; yet they are cheap, I swear by your beard they are, and I look for but little profit upon them."

"The price?" I asked.

"From a poor man, like you, Meer Sahib, a syud and a soldier, I would take six thousand rupees; but from a Rajah and an infidel I would ask eight."

"Good," said I. "Now listen to me. I am, as you say, poor; and I have the heavy expense of this marriage coming upon me. What say you to accepting my aid and taking the pearls to Jhalone and selling them there? The Rajah is much guided by me; and if I get him to pay eight thousand rupees, you will pay me back the three hundred I now owe you for those I have purchased? Turn it over in your mind, and tell me your determination."

"Jhalone is a long way," said the merchant; "and if I sell my pearls, how am I to get back with the money? Thieves will hear of the transaction, and I may be waylaid and murdered."

"Fear not," replied I, "be at rest on that score. To one who has come so far from his home to oblige him, the Rajah will give an escort to return. Of this I am confident; and if this is all that prevents your making the determination to accompany me, you had better dismiss it from your mind at once."

"I will consult the astrologer," said he.

"Nay, Shekhjee," I replied, "this is too ridiculous. What have we true believers to do with astrologers? The man you would consult is a Hindoo, and there is abomination in the very word. Besides, what danger is there? I have some fifty men with me, my own attendants, and the Rajah's sepoys, therefore no harm can come to you; as for your return, you will have a few horsemen, who will afford you ample protection. Again, you said you have had the necklace for two years, and never had an offer for it; why, therefore, keep your money unemployed? Be wise, man, and come with me."

"Yes, father," said the lad, "listen to what the brave Meer Sahib says; and I will accompany you, and see the world beyond our town. You know you have promised to take me with you the first journey you make."

"Well, it is very tempting certainly," said the merchant. "Eight thousand rupees, you said, Meer Sahib? That is worth going for, and these baubles are useless to me here. To tell you the truth," continued he, "I got them from a Pindharee, who served with Cheetoo, or Dost Mahomed, I know not which. He kept them as long as he could, but the lubhurs[1] were broken up by the Feringhees (a sad blow to our free trade), and though a few horsemen, his own followers, stuck to him, yet he had nothing to give them; at last, when they became mutinous, and threatened his life for their pay, he was obliged to sell these, and I was the purchaser."

"And you got them cheap?" said I.

"Yes, they were not dear, Meer Sahib; a man in necessity rarely drives a hard bargain. I got them cheap; and yet I swear to you that they are cheap at eight thousand rupees. I say this from experience, for I have sold worse to Mahdajee Sindia himself for ten thousand; but he will not purchase now, and they lie heavy on my hands."

"All therefore considered, Shekhjee," said I," you had by far better accompany me to Jhalone. As to the journey, a month will see you back again; the season is favourable for travel, and as we are a strong party, and march by night, you will never be incommoded by the sun."

"Well, Meer Sahib, I have almost determined; but it will be necessary to tell those inside," said he, pointing with his thumb to the zenana; "and as you said you had to go to the kotwal on some business, if you could look in here after it is all over, about the time of evening prayer, I shall be able to give you a decisive answer. Much as we affect to despise women, you know, I dare say, Meer Sahib, that it makes one uncomfortable to undertake anything, more especially a journey, without consulting them."

"As you will," said I; "I am indifferent about the matter; it is for your good alone that I have offered this counsel; and in this world of infidelity and selfishness it is refreshing to the heart either to assist a brother Moslem, or to be assisted by

---

1 Private armies.

one without selfish motives. Alla Hafiz![1] I take my leave, and I will return by the Moghreb,[2] and bring the money for my pearls." I left him.

"Is he to be bunij?" again asked the Thug.

"Peace, fool!" said I laughing; "he has gorged the bait, but the hook is not yet struck. Wait. Inshalla! Ameer Ali is not the son of an owl or a jackass; and, Inshalla! we will yet throw dirt on his beard, for all he is so cautious."

I had no business with the kotwal, as you may have imagined. I rode to my tent, and assembling the leaders of the band developed to them my plans and gave them instructions as to their demeanour and conduct before our new guest in prospect; this done, I was easy about the rest. If he came! It was almost too much to hope for; yet I had confidence in myself and in my fate. And the boy! that beautiful boy!—I had (for once) no heart to be a participator in his death. I must not allow him to accompany us, I said to myself; enough that the house is made desolate by the death of the father. I was thus musing when Laloo came to me.

"You are mad, Meer Sahib," said he; "this plan is not feasible. Bunij met with on the road is well enough; but to drag a man out of his house, as I may say, to destroy him, is too bad; and I do not think it is justifiable."

"Ha!" cried I; "so you are turned against me. How is this?"

"God forbid that you should say so, Meer Sahib; but look at the matter. You are known in the town, people have seen you enter the house of the merchant, and they will know that he accompanies you. Will they not hunt us out?"

"You are an owl," said I, laughing; "trust me, there is no fear; and as for taking the man out of his house, I tell thee I see no more difference in it than in having met him on the road in the regular way. Let me alone, I know my work, and when we have got him, you shall applaud what I have done."

"Nay, it was but a friendly remonstrance," said he; "and as you feel confident, go on with the matter. He will be good bunij?"

"Assuredly, to the tune of some thousand rupees. By Alla! I was tired of the humdrum work we have been at lately, and my blood stagnated in my veins. This has stirred it, and I have set myself to the work. You know I seldom fail."

"Seldom indeed, Meer Sahib; but can I do aught?"

"Yes, you can," said I; "follow me at a little distance, and note the house. The fool I am after will depend on his astrologer for a good day to quit his home. I am sure of this, for he said he would; and he took my bantering against him with an ill grace.

---

1 Allah protect you!

2 Sunset.

Find out his servants, and from them the Brahmin; take money with you and pay him. There is enough of daylight yet, and remember to-morrow morning is to be a lucky one, and the next a bad one. Mind this, and do your best, for much depends upon it—nay, everything."

"On my head and eyes be it!" said he; "and therefore, Meer Sahib, I pray you accompany me even now, better in disguise perhaps, and show me the house. Leave the rest to me, and I will not fail."

"A good thought," said I. "The sun will not set for the next four hours; I can easily return and equip myself afresh. So saying, I stripped myself of my fine clothes, put on others which were soiled and dirty, tied up my face, except my eyes, and tucking my sword under my arm, looked as disreputable a brawler or smoker of ganja as any in the good town of Tearee."

"Come," said I, "our errand is soon done;" and so it was. We walked past the house, and I left my ally at the corner of the street, with a hundred rupees in his waistband, and a cunning heart in his breast.

I returned, and re-dressing myself, I mounted my horse, and took my way to the merchant's, with the money I owed him. I found him in the same spot; but as the evening was sultry, he led me to the terrace of his house, where carpets had been spread for our convenience. I paid my money, and received the pearls, and then entered upon the main object of my visit.

"You will go then, Shekhjee?" said I; "or is your mind against it?"

"Not at all, not at all," replied he. "It is my wish to go,—my great wish, Meer Sahib; but when I mentioned it in my zenana, though the proposition met with no opposing words or tears, they one and all declared that a lucky day must be fixed, without which it would be clearly of no use my going at all. You know what women are, Meer Sahib; suffice it to say, that I could not overcome their scruples; for the more I argued and persuaded, the more strongly they opposed; and in fact, the matter became so serious, that to pacify them—mind you, to pacify them—I sent ten rupees to a Brahmin who lives hard by, who is a noted astrologer, and the only one here in whom any confidence is placed. Alla is my witness, I cared not what he said; but when a message came back to say that to-morrow was an unlucky day, the whole zenan-khana,[1] wives, slaves, and asseels,[2] set up such a howl of lamentation at what might have happened, and afterwards of congratulation at my having escaped the threatened evil, that I was fairly stunned, and have given up the idea of the journey

---

1 Women's quarters.
2 Maidservants.

for to-morrow at any rate. But you know, Meer Sahib, to-morrow's conjunction of planets may have a different effect, and as you will stay—"

"Indeed, Shekhjee," said I, "I cannot stay. Here have I idled away three whole days, and I can remain no longer, for time is precious to me. My patron will even now wonder what has delayed me; and to lose his favour will be the loss of my means of maintenance. So to-morrow I start, most assuredly, whether you come or not. And as to your accompanying me, that is your matter; I am perfectly indifferent to it, except that I shall lose your pleasant society on the road."

He was fairly perplexed. He had evidently reckoned on my stay; but my careless yet determined manner of speaking left him no hope of a change in my opinions; and, as a Persian would have said, he held "the finger of deliberation between the teeth of impatient desire." There he sat for a long time, looking on the ground in silence. It was a struggle between the love of gain and superstition; for though he had wished me to believe the contrary, he was as fully imbued with the belief of lucky and unlucky days as any of his wives, slaves, or asseels. At length he said:—

"Meer Sahib, you remember our agreement—the two hundred rupees? I will make it another hundred if you stay one more day. You are a poor man, and a hundred rupees will buy many cloths for your daughter's marriage."

Here was a direct attempt to cheat me out of a hundred rupees; and, for the latter part of his speech, I could have strangled him on the spot. Yet I kept my temper: I was playing too deep a game to lose it, and for a trifle too.

"No, Shekh," said I, "it cannot be; I would not for a thousand rupees stay an hour after daylight to-morrow: you cannot tempt me. But have you ever thought that your nujoomee[1] may have played you false, and that it requires a few more rupees than ten to make the heavens propitious? I have heard of such things, ay, and proved them too, or perhaps I might believe in the aspect of the stars as you do."

"Ay! say you so, my friend?" cried he. "By Alla! I would beat the rogue with a shoe in his own temple, with a shoe of cow's leather too, if I could think he was trying to cheat me; but that is impossible. How can he help the position of the stars? And yet say, shall I send more money?"

"No," said I, "surely not: if he is honest, he will fling it in your servant's face; if he is a rogue, he will keep it, and send word that the stars have changed; in the first case you will eat dirt, in the second you will be cheated, and he will laugh at your beard. No, I see no help for you, but to go in defiance of him, the zenana, and the stars; and this will prove you to be a man."

---

1 Astrologer.

"Impossible, Meer Sahib," said he despondingly. "Putting the nujoomee out of the question, I have four wives, Alla help me!— the lawful number, you know; but oh! my friend, their wrath is dreadful, and I dare not provoke it."

"It is enough," said I; "you will not go, because you dare not,—not because you do not wish it."

"Exactly, Meer Sahib: you have hit upon the very cause. My own heart is willing, and the prospect of gain leads me; but those women—"

It was prayer-time, and the muezzin's sonorous voice proclaimed the hour from the roof of a neighbouring mosque. We performed our ablutions, and, as good Mussulmans, we spread our carpets, and turning to the still glowing west, poured forth our evening praise and thanksgiving.

I was determined to stay till the last moment I could, to give my emissary time for his proceedings, and, if no message came from the astrologer, to try some other plan, or even to agree to stay another day. Ah, gold! thought I, if thou desertest me now at my best need, I will foreswear thy worship.

Our prayers were ended, and still we sat and conversed, but no message came to suit my purpose. I had gradually led the merchant back to the subject of the journey, and was picturing to him, in terms suited to his avaricious soul, the reception he would assuredly meet with at Jhalone; and I was preparing my words to introduce a change in my opinions as to staying another day, when a servant came up the steps and whispered something in his ear at which he started, yet at the same time his face put on a joyous appearance.

"Excuse me for an instant, my friend," said he; "I am wanted below—some one awaits me in the dewan khana. Wait here, and I will rejoin you instantly."

My heart beat loud and quick in my bosom as I watched him down the steps. Could it be that I had succeeded? or was there any fear of danger to my own person? I looked over the terrace; it was far too high to leap from; escape if there was danger was impracticable. But a moment's thought rallied me; and as I disengaged my trusty sword, and held it ready for action, I laughed at my own fears, for I knew I could defend that narrow stair against a host. I looked over into the courtyard of the dewan khana, but saw no one; I could hear two voices in low and earnest conversation; and as I stretched forth my neck, and bent over the parapet of the terrace in the vain endeavour to catch a syllable, I was suddenly gratified by seeing the merchant and a figure robed in white, which I knew at once to be that of a Hindoo, while his bare and shaven head proved him to be a priest, emerge from the dewan khana; and now their words came clearly to me.

"Then there is no obstacle?" said the merchant.

"None," said the Brahmin (for so he was), "as I have said, there was a mistake in the tables and calculations which I have just discovered. My art also told me that thou wert anxious to go; am I right?"

"Right! ah, virtuous Brahmin, assuredly thou art, I am promised gain—nay, wealth."

"And thou wilt be successful," said the other. "May Narayun grant it! I will pray for thy good fortune."

"Do so, do so, good Brahmin. Good Seonath, I will not forget thee on my return. Inshalla! I can be grateful: I will make a nuzzur through thee to the temple."

"You will not fail to do so, I think, Shekhjee, for Ballajee¹ hath been propitious to thee ever since thy nuzznrs have been offered up at his shrine. But I go to present thy gift, though it is a small one. Narayun keep thee!"

"It shall be doubled—trebled, Seonath. I swear to thee by Alla I will not forget when I return. Thou goest? Well, Alla Hafiz! my friend awaits me."

He returned to me. "Rejoice with me, my friend," cried he, "my kind Meer Sahib! after all, to-morrow is the lucky day. My friend the Brahmin sent one of his disciples to say there was a mistake in the calculations upon his tablets, and that the aspect of the heavens was favourable to me for an unlimited period. Ah, how wise he is, Meer Sahib, and how honest!—you called him a rogue; but, see! he might have kept me in suspense for a month, and refused to consult the stars at all until he had been well paid. Well, after all, it is the power of Alla, and doubtless these infidels hold some communion with Him, which is denied to those of the true faith."

"So it would seem, Shekhjee," said I, humouring him; "it is no doubt wonderful that your friend, for an astrologer, is for once honest. Of course you paid him liberally for his new discovery?"

The merchant winced. "A trifle, Meer Sahib; a few pice² to purchase oil for the temple was all he wanted."

"Oh, rare disinterestedness!" cried I; "truly it is grateful to the heart to see such conduct in this selfish world, where every one appears to strive how he can overreach his neighbour. Of course he has no prospective advantage?"

"None, Meer Sahib, none! How could a true believer have dealings or connection with an infidel? Do I not take advantage of his learning for my own convenience, and then laugh at his beard?" And he chuckled.

---

1 Balaji, Hindu god.

2 Coins worth one-hundredth of a rupee.

Liar; said I to myself, as I clenched my hand and ground my teeth, thou shalt answer to Alla for this perjury before thou art many days older. Verily, this is a meritorious deed, and therefore hast thou been delivered into my hands. A Hajji[1] too! Oh, shame, shame! Yet then I remembered the Arab verse which saith, "If thy neighbour hath performed the Haj, trust him not; and if he hath done it twice, haste thee to remove thine abode from his vicinity."

"Good, O Hajji," said I, "and you do right. But the night wanes, you had better make preparation for the journey; and let me offer you counsel. Bring no one with you but a servant or two; my company is ample for your protection. I have a small pal[2] which will hold us both; and, above all, bring not your son,—he will but fatigue himself for no good purpose, and be a clog on our rapid movements, for rapid they must be."

"I will follow your advice in all things, Meer Sahib. I shall bring no servants: the man who will drive my spare tattoo can attend me when I require it; and the less show I make, the less I shall be suspected of carrying money with me."

"Remember, then," said I, "you come to my camp by the time the morning-star rises; we shall all be ready for you, and the sun will not be powerful ere we reach our stage."

He promised to be there by the appointed time, and I left him.

I found my trusty emissary waiting for me in my tent. He burst into a loud laugh when he saw me.

"Is he safe?" he asked at length. "Ah, Meer Sahib, I have had great amusement, as no doubt you have also."

"He is, he is fairly caught. The net is around him; one pull and he is a lost man. And you, my faithful friend, you have succeeded so that I marvel at your success."

"Marvel not," he replied; "the task was easier than I thought. But hear my adventures."

"Surely," said I; and I called for a chilum,[3] while he proceeded.

"You remember when you left me?"—I nodded,—"Well, it was a long time ere I could find a servant; and in despair I lay down in the shade of the wall, but kept awake. At last a fellow came out, a Hindoo, as luck would have it, and I followed him: 'Canst thou direct me to a kulal's[4] shop?' said I; 'I have travelled far, and my

---

1   A Muslim who has gone on pilgrimage to Mecca.

2   Tent.

3   Hookah.

4   Seller of liquor.

throat is dry.' I saw that the fellow himself drank, from the colour of his eyes, and they sparkled at the mention of the kulal's shop. 'There is one close by,' he replied; 'I will show it.' 'Good,' said I, 'thou shalt share my potations.' Well, we entered the shop, and went into the inner room. I called for a bottle of liquor, and paid for it. The place was somewhat dark, and I poured what I took on the ground, but he drank every drop; he finished the bottle as though it had been water, and I sent for more. At last I began by asking him who his master was, and what service he did, and, Mashalla! I heard in a wonderfully short time all about him; and, lastly, that he was going a journey, but had been prevented by an astrologer's having declared the morrow to be an unlucky day. In fine, my friend Sumbhoo (for such was his name) got very drunk, and having told me much of his master's private history, which did not redound to his credit, he fell senseless on the ground, and there I left him; but not before I had ascertained that the astrologer resided at a temple in the next street, and that his name was Seonath."

"I have seen him," said I; "a tall, fair man, a good-looking priest, and stout enough for a Thug."

"You saw him! How, and where?"

I told him, and we had a hearty laugh as I described the scene in the court-yard, and mimicked the cringing tones of the merchant and the haughty ones of the Brahmin.

"But listen," said Laloo, "and wonder, as I did. I soon found the temple and the Brahmin, and accosting him, I begged for a charm against the evil eye for my child. He looked at me—Ya Alla! how he looked! I quailed under his gaze, and my flesh crept as if I were in an ague fit; for once I was afraid, for I knew not the man, and yet he seemed as if he could read my heart. 'Follow me,' said he, 'I would speak with thee apart from these prying people.' He spoke kindly, and I followed him, though almost mechanically. He went before me. 'Leave your shoes,' said he; 'this place must not be polluted: it is sacred.' At last we were alone in a small court, where there was a shrine of the god. Again he turned on me, and looked into my face. I really knew not what to think; and oh, how glad I was when he put an end to my suspense by repeating our signal words!"

"Our signal?"

"Yes, Meer Sahib, even so; I was as much astounded as you are, but the mystery was soon solved. He proved to be a priest of our holiest of temples, Bindachul, who had travelled into these parts, and having picked up some astronomical lore at Benares, set up here for an astrologer, and found the trade so profitable that he has not returned to Bindachul. Of course I had no reservation with him; I developed our plan, from which he at first drew back; but I opened my purse, and five ashruffees[1] worked such a change in his sentiments, that he listened to my words with complacency, altered the face of the heavens as far as they concerned your friend, and, in fine, offered there and then to go and say that his calculations were wrong, and that everything boded prosperity to the poor shekh."

"He has not failed us," said I.

"No," replied Laloo, "I know that; but we have to pay handsomely. He wanted a hundred rupees more, but I represented that we were a large band, and there would not be much to divide, and I obliged him to be content with a bhuttote's share, added to whatever a general subscription might amount to when the band should be informed of the part he had played."

"And he is content?"

"You have had the best proof, Meer Sahib; has he not done the errand he promised? And when did a Brahmin of Bindachul ever break his faith? He dare not. Bhowanee would smite him on the spot, or kill him by lingering torments."

"And how," I asked, "are we to convey this share to him, whatever it may turn out to be?"

"Easily enough; we can get a hoondee on this place, and send it to him in a letter, or we can despatch a man with it."

"True, we can," said I; "and so now go; repeat to the men the lesson I taught them, and enjoin them to be circumspect and wary. We have good bunij in prospect, and, Inshalla! we will get it too. But I wish I could see the Brahmin who has done us so good a turn in this matter."

"Let him alone," said he; "he told me that, although he wished much to see you, having often heard of your conduct, it was better to avoid suspicion, and that any open intercourse between him and you would expose him to the inquiries of those with whom he was associated, and had better be avoided. And he is right, Meer Sahib; it would do no good."

———————•———————

---

1   Gold coins.

CHAPTER XLV

Cornwall.—Pinion him like a thief; bring him before us:
  Though well we may not pass upon his life,
  Without the form of justice, yet our power
  Shall do a courtesy to our wrath, which men
  May blame, but not control.
                        —*Lear.* Act. iii., Sc. 7.

FOUR days passed, and the merchant was still in our company. He was slightly attended, and we could have terminated his existence whenever we pleased; but we were anxious to carry him on as much of the journey as we could, and to baffle any traces of our route, by turning to the right and left, away from the regular tracks, and by footpaths and byways only known to ourselves. Yet we had got far enough, and I knew that the next day's march would lead us through a jungle, which was one of our favourite bhils, and where I had from the first determined that he should die.

We were on the road early on the fifth morning, and as before (indeed as was my wont) I was riding at the head of my party. It was now daylight, but we were entering the jungle, and I was merry in my heart to think that he was in my power, and that a large and valuable booty would be our prize in the course of a short hour, when I saw an animal move in the bushes on my right hand. Another instant, and a hare again crossed my path! I laughed within myself. Fools that they are, thought I, these brethren of mine! no jemadar but myself would dare to pursue this track after so dire an omen; himself and his whole band would fly, as though a hundred tigers were in their path, and would leave their bunij to escape, or to follow them, as his destiny might guide him. But I!—I laugh at it: once I have proved that the omen is harmless, and shall it deter me now? Ah, no, no! my game is sure, and within my grasp.

And so it was. Sahib, we had not gone a coss, when I saw the place I had determined on; and there the merchant died and his two servants. Yes, he died by my own hand. I pulled him off his pony and strangled him; and the servants were cared for by the others, but not before one of them had cut down one of my men; for in my eagerness to possess myself of the prize before me, I had not seen that the servants of the merchant could observe my actions. The poor fellow who had fallen was dreadfully wounded; yet he still breathed. What to do with him I knew not: we could not wait, and to transport him with us was out of the question.

"What shall we do with Anundee?" said I to Laloo; "we are far from our stage, and we cannot, with our large party, say we have fallen among thieves."

He solved my doubts at once. "Put him out of his pain," said he; "the man is dying: what matters another thrust? he can be buried with the rest. The men might not like it if they saw it, but all here are engaged, and most of the band have gone on. We can wrap him up in his sheet afterwards."

I drew my sword and stepped towards the dying wretch; he looked supplicatingly towards me and strove to speak, but my heart was hard. I was sickened by the deed I had done, and I prayed Alla to forgive me the blood of the miserable creature.

Wretch! said I, interrupting Ameer Ali, and you murdered your own companion, your brother to whom you were sworn?

I did, sahib, I did; yet why call it murder? He would have died in a short time; I did but rid him of his misery.

It was a foul deed, Ameer Ali; and one that haunts your memory, I doubt not.

Sometimes, was the careless answer of the Thug; and I bade him proceed.

We wrapped the body in the sheet which was around its waist, having taken the money from the waistband. Laloo and myself carried it to the grave, now nearly filled to the top.

"So he is dead!" cried the lughaees; "he could not have lived long after that cut: the fellow who gave it would have done for more of us had not some of us seized on him; but we have laid him quietly,—he will break no more good men's heads: and as for poor Anundee, he must be buried with the rest, for to burn him is impossible in this lonely place."

And he *was* buried; they deepened the centre of the pit, put some heavy stones over him, and covered him with earth; and I felt a load taken from my heart as he was covered from my sight for ever. Only Laloo knew what I had done, and I knew him to be faithful and silent: nevertheless I often afterwards wished either that another had done the deed, or that I had let him die.

A rare booty we had, sahib. After we had eaten the goor at the next village, we hastened on to the end of the stage; and before we ungirded our loins I opened the caskets and divided the spoil. Not only had the merchant brought the necklace I have mentioned before, but a heap of unstrung pearls; and on reckoning up their probable value, we estimated the amount at twenty-five thousand rupees. Now therefore we had no inducement to tarry away from our homes; we needed no fresh adventure to enrich us, and we pushed on to Jhalone. We reached it in safety, and again I clasped Azeema to my heart, and rejoiced to see that my child was well, and with a girl's eagerness looking forward to the time when her marriage ceremony was to take place. My father too was well, and had reached Jhalone without any adventure worth recording, so at least he told me. But of Ganesha there was no news, save that he had diverged to the eastward, and was supposed to have gone in the direction of Benares; and I little cared, except that the revenge for the destruction of the moonshee's son rankled in my heart and was not forgotten.

Two years passed at my home without care and in peace. Alas! now that I think on it, I can only compare the course of that time to the gentle stream of a river which, as it winds among peaceful scenes and between green and flowery banks, ruffled only by the soft winds playing over its bosom, is suddenly arrested, dashed among rocks, and its current changed to turmoil and furious contention with its stony opposers. I saw no mark of my future lot, no warning was given to me; destruction came upon me in one fell swoop, and I was overwhelmed—I and mine! But for that stroke of ill fortune I had lived till now an honest and gentle life, for I had abandoned Thuggee; and the more I experienced of the soothing pleasures of my home, the more I became estranged from my habits of wandering and of plunder and destruction. Nor was the least urgent reason in the meditated change of my life, that I dreaded every day more and more that some unlucky chance would reveal to Azeema the dreadful trade I had followed. I could paint to myself the effect it would have on her loving and gentle disposition, and the prostration of every faculty of her existence, under the shock of knowing that I was a murderer; and often, as she lay upon my heart in the dead of night, these thoughts have come so thick on me, that could her soul have held any mysterious communion with mine, she would have recoiled in horror from my embrace and fled from me for ever. And these fancies recurred so frequently and forcibly that sometimes I almost thought them a warning of coming evil, and I had fully determined to remove my abode and my wealth to Dehli after my daughter's marriage, there to reside for the remainder of the days which might be allotted to me.

I have said months passed without incident; I should have mentioned that an English gentleman, some time after my arrival, came to Jhalone; and in the many conferences he held in secret with the Rajah, we were given to understand that a treaty of some kind or other had been made, and that he had placed himself under the protection of the English Government. I thought not of it; yet even then a system was working silently yet surely which for a time struck at the power and confederacy of the Thugs a blow as severe, nay more so, as being more lasting, than any they had yet experienced.

The Englishman had left Jhalone some time, and his visit was nearly forgotten by us; my daughter's marriage had begun, and everything was rejoicing in my house. About noon one day one of the Rajah's hurkaras[1] came with a message that he required my presence and my father's in the durbar on particular business. In vain was it that I excused myself on the plea of the marriage ceremony. The messenger would take no excuse; and at last, seeing no alternative, we girded our loins and accompanied the hurkara.

We were ushered through the various courts to the dewan khana,[2] where the Rajah sat in durbar, surrounded by his mutsuddees[3] and soldiers. Leaving our shoes at the entrance, we were as usual advancing towards his guddee[4] to make the customary salutations, when a sudden rush was made upon us from both sides of the hall, and we were at once seized and disarmed. In vain I struggled with my captors, in vain I attempted to shake them off by the most strenuous exertions; it was useless: I was surrounded and overpowered, my turban was torn rudely from my head, and my arms were bound so tightly with it that I thought the blood would have burst from under my nails. I desisted at last, and remained passive in the hands of the soldiers. My hour is come, and my fate has led me on thus far to desert me at last! thought I; it is the will of Bhowanee and of Alla, why should I resist?

Seeing me quiet, the Rajah addressed me.

"Ah, Ameer Ali," said he, "what is this I hear of thee, that thou art a Thug, a common murderer? Can this be true of one who was looked up to in Jhalone as a merchant and a respectable man? What hast thou to say? Speak, man, and prove if thou canst to me that the accusations I hear against thee are false."

"Rajah," said I, "I know not who hath poisoned thy mind against me or mine; is there any one in your city who can speak one word against me? Have I not been fair and honourable in my dealings with all, and with thyself too? have not I managed villages and brought them to prosperity from desolation; and can any one, young or old, in this durbar say that I have ever wronged him, or defrauded him of a fraction? Rajah, none can say this; and therefore why am I and my old father thus disgraced

---

1 Messengers.
2 Reception room.
3 Secretaries.
4 Throne.

in the eyes of the city, and torn from our houses in the midst of the rejoicings of marriage?"

"*I* accuse thee not," said the Rajah; "Bhugwan alone knows whether what I hear is the truth or not; but witnesses are many against thee and the old man: let them speak, and we will afterwards decide in your case. Bring them forth!" cried he to an attendant; "one by one let them give their evidence before these unhappy men: we desire no secrecy in this matter."

There was a moment's pause in the assembly, and every eye—a hundred eyes were upon us. I looked to my father, to see the effect his situation had on him; but I read no hope in the glance he threw on me: his energy had deserted him, and he looked like a convicted felon long before he was so in reality. He returned my anxious and meaning glances by a stare of stupid apathy or extreme fear,—I know not which; and it was pitiable to behold him, for his venerable and respectable appearance but ill assorted with the disgraceful situation he was in. I turned away from him to look at the man who entered, and then I felt that my doom was sealed. I have never mentioned him, but he had been connected with our gang from the first as a tilhaee, or scout, and had afterwards assisted as a bhuttote on many occasions. His name was Sooruj; he had accompanied me on all my first expeditions, and had served under my father for some time before I became a Thug; he therefore knew every particular of my career; and until I became a Pindharee described every event with minuteness and fidelity, omitting not one nor adding in any way to those I had been so deeply concerned in. He offered to point out the spots upon which travellers had been destroyed, declared the amount of booty we had gained on many occasions, and ended by denouncing both my father and myself as the greatest leaders in Bundelkhund, as men who could take the field at any time with two hundred followers or more, and as cruel and remorseless Thugs. He dared me to disprove his words, and indeed I quailed under his accusations; for they were true, and truth searches the heart and overwhelms the guilty. But against my father he was the most bitter. "Look on him, Rajah!" cried he; "look on this hoary wretch! One would think that, old as he is, he would have ceased to deprive his fellow-creatures of life; that he would have spent the remainder of his days in propitiating Bhowanee by sacrifices, and his own Prophet by prayers! yet it has not been so. Within the last two months he has returned from an expedition laden with spoil, and the last man he strangled was one of thine own subjects, O Rajah,—one who was respected and beloved here, and whose bereaved family will rue this day that I have declared his fate in your durbar."

"One of my subjects!" cried the Rajah; "thou canst not mean it. Speak! and let not fear prevent your disclosing the truth."

"Fear! Rajah, I know it not. If I feared him, that old man, should I have dared to speak as I have done? Listen; you knew Jeswunt Mul, one of the most respectable of the shroffs[1] of Jhalone?"

"Knew him, O Messenger of ill tidings! Jeswunt Mul is not dead?"

"Ask *him*," said the man hoarsely; "or stay, ask the other man you have here; let him be brought forward, he will tell the tale: I saw it not. But Jeswunt Mul will never speak more, and let those who believe the good man safe at Saugor shave their moustachios and mourn, for he will never more be seen. Yes, he is dead, and *that* old man looked on while he writhed out his last agony under the roomal of the bhuttote;" and he pointed at my father, while he regarded him with a look of grim and revengeful pleasure.

There was a general shudder through the assembly, as the deep tones of the informer's voice fell on the ears of those who heard it; and "Jeswunt Mul dead!" was repeated by many in an incredulous tone as they drew into knots and whispered together. Nor was the Rajah himself least struck by the melancholy information. He sat on his musnud in silence, though it could be seen by the working of his features how much he was affected. But he aroused himself at last.

"Thou didst not then see this murder?" said he to the informer.

"I did not, Maha Rajah;[2] but send for Bodhee, he will relate the particulars."

Bodhee! thought I, then there is indeed no hope. Until his name was mentioned, I had a faint idea that the accusation might be a fabricated one! especially as I had heard nothing of the sahoukar's fate from my father"; but Bodhee had been with him, and he was the chief of the lughaees, and it was more than probable that he had dug the grave for the victim.

"Let Bodhee be brought forward," cried the Rajah.

He came; his fetters clanked as he moved, and it was not until he had advanced into the midst of the durbar that he beheld my father and myself bound and as criminals. The sight staggered him, and well it might; he had been trusted by us, raised to the rank he held by my father, and ever treated by him as a son, though he was of a different faith to ours. His face was convulsed by his emotions—they might have been those of a faithful heart struggling against ingratitude; and I looked with a

---

1   Bankers.
2   Great king.

breathless anxiety to the first words which should fall from him. But before he spoke the Rajah addressed him.

"Miserable wretch!" said he, "your life has been spared on the condition that you speak the truth, and reveal, without reservation of a single circumstance, every deed of murder you have been engaged in; this has been promised you by the English, and you have now to prove that you will perform your engagement. If you do perform it, well; if not, though the English are your protectors, I swear to you that you shall be dragged to death by my elephants ere a ghurree[1] of time has passed over you. Bid the elephant be brought!" cried he to an attendant; "and see that the chains are ready. By Gunga! there will be work for him ere long. And now," continued he to the approver, "knowest thou aught of the death of Jeswunt Mul of this town, he who used to manage my private affairs; or if he indeed be dead? Speak, and remember that truth alone can save you."

There was a breathless silence; my father gazed at the informer with an intense anxiety; it was evident to me that he thought one word from him would seal his fate for ever, or that, should he deny the dead, he would escape. Earnestly, imploringly he looked at him, and the informer was well nigh overcome: he trembled in every limb, and the big drops of sweat stood out on his face, while the veins of his forehead swelled almost to bursting.

"Speak, Bodhee!" said my father in a hollow voice,—yet still he smiled,—"speak, and tell the Rajah that his poor servant Ismail is not guilty of this deed."

"Silence!" exclaimed the Rajah; "gag him if he attempts to utter a word to influence the informer; we will do justice in this matter. And you, Meer Sahib (turning to a respectable-looking person who was seated near him), you shall be able to tell the Sahib-logue that justice can be done in the durbar of Jhalone. Bring up the elephant," he cried to the attendants; "and do you, Bodhee, look your last on the earth and sky, for, by Gunga! I swear thou art nigh to death if thou deceivest me. I read it in thy face that this matter is known to thee."

But still Bodhee hesitated; there was evidently a struggle within him whether he should die in defence of his old protector, or betray him to save his own life. For a moment the former feeling prevailed; he turned to the Rajah, and said distinctly and firmly, "May I be your sacrifice, Maha Rajah! I know nothing of this matter; of other murders I can tell you, but I know naught of this."

"He lies!" said the other approver; "he was with Ismail Jemadar; he is afraid to speak out, and has lied to you, O Prince."

---

1 Instant.

"You hear him," cried the Rajah to Bodhee; "you hear what your fellow Thug says; yet, much as you have deserved death, I give you a few moments more; the shadow of the verandah is now close on my musnud: till it reaches it thou shalt live; beyond it, one finger's breadth, and you die!"

There was not an eye in the crowd that was not fixed on the advancing shadow; barely a hand's breadth of light remained, and the Thug gazed on it as though he were fascinated by the eye of a tiger. My father! oh, he was fearful to look on! his eyes were glazed, his lips were tightened across his teeth, fear, *agony* was depicted in his countenance in stronger lines than I had ever before seen. I could not look on him: his face was altered, and his usual bland expression had been usurped by that I have described. I felt sick, I could have died I thought; and would that I *had* died, to have been spared what followed.

"Fool!" cried the other approver, "will you sacrifice your life for those who will be instantly put to death?" He spoke in Ramasee.

The words rallied the man to whom he addressed them, and they saved him.

"Pardon, pardon!" he cried; "O mighty Prince, I have told lies. Jeswunt Mul is indeed dead; these hands dug his grave and bore his yet warm body to it."

"Ai Bhugwan! Ai Seeta-ram!" cried the Rajah, "and is it even so? My poor friend, and art thou dead?" and for a moment or two he wept. "This is womanly," said he, rallying himself; "proceed, O kumbukht![1] let me know all, and what share *he* had in it."

"We met the sahoukar at——," said the Thug. "Ismail well knew that if we were all seen by him he would suspect us, so he sent the greater part of the band out of the village, and prevailed upon Jeswunt Mul to come and sleep in our camp, instead of remaining where he was; he went to the village and brought him away himself, else he would not have come. The grave was dug long before he arrived, and he had not been an hour with us after the sun had set, when he was strangled in the jemadar's presence by two bhuttotes, and his two servants shared the same fate. I buried them all. The sahoukar's pony we sold the next day for twenty-five rupees; and we got but little else, for he had no money but in hoondees, which we burned."

"Enough, enough," said the Rajah; "this is ample proof."

"Nay, if your Greatness requires more proof, I can give you some now," continued the approver; "look at the jemadar's hand: he wears on it a ring he took from the body himself, and it may be recognised even by you, Maha Rajah."

---

1 Miserable one!

My heart sank within me at this new and desperate stroke of fortune. I saw the ring torn from my father's finger; all examined it. A sahoukar who was in the assembly declared it to have belonged to Jeswunt Mul, and, more than all, his name was engraven on its inner surface.

"Enough!" again cried the Rajah, "I know it myself; I could have sworn to that diamond among a thousand. Away with him! chain him to the elephant, let him be dragged through the town, and proclamation made that he was a Thug."

"Stay," cried the syud, who had not as yet spoken, "he may have something to urge in his defence; ask him and hear him."

"Speak!" cried the Rajah to my miserable father; "speak, O kumbukht!"

And then my father's proud spirit broke out. With the certainty of death before his eyes he quailed not. While hope remained of life, he had clung to it as every man will; and when I had expected a grovelling entreaty for his life to be spared, from his previous demeanour, he asked it not, but gloried in the cause for which he died.

"Yes," said he, drawing himself up, while his eye glistened proudly, "I scorn to die with a lie upon my lips. I killed Jeswunt Mul because he was a villain, as you are, Rajah! because he employed Thugs, and would not reward them, but wrung from them every rupee he could, as you do. I have murdered hundreds of men because they were given into my hands by Alla, but I never destroyed one with the satisfaction I did your friend. Ay, you were friends and brothers in guilt, and you know it. My life! I care not for it. What has an old man to do with life? his enjoyments are gone, his existence is a burden to him. A short time and nature would have claimed me; you have anticipated the period. Yet, O Rajah, Bhowanee will question you for this deed—for the destruction of her votary. My blood be on your head, and the curse of a dying man be with you! You have deceived me, robbed me, shared my spoils, taken the produce of murder—nay, be not impatient, you know it is the truth, and that Alla, who is the Judge of all, knows it also. He will cast your portion in Jehanum, as a kafir; and Bhowanee will rejoice that the destroyer of her votary writhes in the torments of the damned."

"Gag him! strike the kafir's mouth with a shoe!" roared the Rajah in a fury, more like that of a beast than a man, as he foamed at the mouth. "Away with him. And let his son look on his dying agony."

And they dragged us both forth; I should not say my father, for his step was firm. I struggled against my tormentors, but it availed me not. "One word, my father!" cried I to him as we were brought near each other; "wilt thou not speak to thy son?"

He turned his head, and a tear stood in his eye. "I leave thee, Ameer Ali; but thou knowest a believer's Paradise, and the joys which await him—the seventy virgins and everlasting youth. Thou art not my son, but I have loved thee as one, and may Alla keep thee!"

"No more!" cried the rough soldiers, striking him on the mouth, and dragging him forward.

"Revenge me!" exclaimed my father in Ramasee; "tell the English of that monster's conduct to us, and when he is torn from his seat of pride, my soul will be happy in Paradise."

He spoke no more; I was held forcibly, so that I saw the end of that butchery. They secured him by a chain round his loins to the forefoot of the elephant, and they tied his hands behind him, so that he could not save himself by clinging to it. He still continued repeating the Kulma.[1] But now all was ready—the mahout[2] drove his ankoos into the head of the noble beast, which uttering a loud scream dashed forward. A few steps, and my father's soul must have been in Paradise.[3]

———•———

---

1 The Islamic declaration of faith.

2 Elephant driver.

3 *Note.*—The Rajah of Jhalone died from an inveterate leprosy, which all Thugs declare to have broken out soon after the death of the Thug in the manner described, and that it was a judgment upon him sent by Bhowanee. [*Taylor*]

CHAPTER XLVI

King Richard.—My conscience hath a thousand several tongues,
    And every tongue brings in a several tale,
    And every tale condemns me for a villain.
       *   *   *   *   *   *   *   *

    Methought the souls of all that I had murdered
    Came to my tent.
               —*Richard III.* Act v., Sc. 3.

SAHIB, can I describe to you the passions which then burned in my heart? I cannot. A thousand thoughts whirled through my brain, till I thought myself mad; perhaps I was. Revenge for my father was uppermost; and oh that I could have got loose! By Alla! unarmed as I was, methinks I would have sprung on the Rajah and strangled him. But resistance was unavailing; the more I struggled, the tighter my arms were bound, until they swelled so that the pain became excruciating, and I well-nigh sank under it. I suffered my guards to lead me away from the durbar; I was thrust into a vile hole, and at last my arms were unbound.

That day—Alla, how it passed! Men gazed at me in my cage as though I had been a tiger, and mocked and derided me. The boys of the town hooted me, and thrust sticks at me through the iron gratings. One and all reviled me in the most opprobrious terms they could devise,—me! the respectable, nay, the wealthy, to whom they had bowed before, when I basked in the sunshine of the Rajah's favour; but I was degraded now. Alas! my dreams, my forebodings had come to pass: they had been indefinite shadows; this was the reality. Alla! Alla! I raved, I called upon Azeema's name, I implored those who still lingered about my prison to fly and bring me news of her, and to comfort her; and I cursed them when they derided me, and mocked my cries. Azeema, the name that might not have been breathed by mortal out of the precincts of my zenana, became a word in the mouths of the rabble, and they jested on it, they loaded it with obscene abuse, and I heard it all. In vain I strove to stop my ears,—it provoked them the more; they shouted it close to the iron bars, and spat at me. Night came, and I was left in my loneliness. I should have been in her fond embrace; now I shared the company of the rat, the lizard, and the scorpion. It was in vain that I courted sleep, to steep my senses in a temporary oblivion of their misery; my frame was too strong, and my anguish too great for it to come to me. I wrestled with my agony, but I overcame it not, and I had to drink the bitter cup to the dregs. At last the morning broke; I performed the Namaz—the dust of the floor served me instead of sand or water for my ablutions. Water I had none; I had begged for it, for my mouth was parched and dry with anxiety, yet no one gave it. Again the court was filled; old and young, women and children, all came to look at the syud—to look at Ameer Ali the Thug—to deride him and torment him! But I was now sullen; like a tiger, when his first rage, after he has been entrapped, has subsided, I cowered into the corner of my cell, and covered my face with my waistband, nor heeded their savage unfeeling mirth, nor the bitter words they poured out against me. In vain was it that I now and then looked around to see whether one kind pitying glance rested on me. Alas! not one; every face was familiar to me; but the eyes either spoke a brutal satisfaction at my sufferings, or turned on me with the cold leaden stare of indifference. I tried to speak several times, but every murmur was hailed with shouts from the rabble before me, and my throat was parched and my tongue swelled from raging thirst.

The whole day passed—I had no food, no water. It was in the height of the burning season, and I, who had been pampered with luxuries, who in my own abode should have drunk of refreshing sherbets, prepared by Azeema, was denied a drop of water to cool my burning throat. In vain I implored those nearest to me, in words that would have moved aught but hearts of stone, to intercede with the jemadar who guarded my prison to allow me a draught of the pure element. I might as well have spoken to the scorching blast that whistled into my cage—bringing with it clouds of dust, which were increased by the unfeeling boys when they saw I shrank from them. Thus the day passed: evening came, and still no water, no relief, no inquiry into my condition. Had I been placed there to die? And no sooner had the thought flashed across my mind than I brooded over it. Yes, I was to die: to expire of thirst and hunger. And then, oh how I envied my father's fate! his was a quick transition from the sorrows and suffering he had undergone during one short hour, to Paradise and the houris.

And from evening, night. I had watched the declining sun, till its last fiery and scorching beams fell no longer on my prison-floor—I watched the reddened west until no glare remained, and one by one the stars shone out dimly through the thick and heated air—and I thought I should see the blessed day no more, for I was sick and exhausted, even to death. I lay me down and moaned, in my agony of spirit and of body, and at last sleep came to my relief. For a time all was oblivion; but horrible dreams began to crowd my prison with unsightly shapes and harrowing visions; my life passed as though in review before me, and the features of many I had strangled rose up in fierce mockery against me,—faces with protruding tongues and eyes, even as I had left them strangled.

Why describe them to you, sahib? why detain you with a description of the horrors of the scene which rose to my distempered fancy, and at last woke me, burning as though a fire raged in my bowels and would not be quenched? But morning broke at last, and the cool air once more played over my heated and fevered frame, and refreshed me. Yet I was still in agony;—who can describe the sufferings of thirst? Hunger I felt not: thirst consumed me, and dried up my bowels. How anxiously and impatiently I looked for the first man who should enter the court where my prison was! One came, he passed through and heeded not my piteous cries; another and another; none looked on me, and again I thought I was to die. Another came; I called, and he turned to regard me. He was one that I knew, one who had eaten of my bread and my salt, and had been employed about my house, and he had pity; he had a remembrance of what I had done for him: he came, and looked on me. I spoke to him, and he started, for my voice was hollow, and thin and hoarse. "Water!" cried I, "for the sake of the blessed Prophet, for the sake of your mother, one drop of water! I have tasted none since I was confined."

"Alas!" said he in a low tone, "how can it be, Meer Sahib? The Rajah has threatened any one with death who speaks to you or brings you food."

Again I implored; and I who had been his master prostrated myself on the ground and rubbed my forehead in the dust. He was moved—he had pity and went to fetch some; fortunately no one saw him, and he brought a small earthen pot full, which I drank as though it had been that of the well of Paradise. Again and again he took it and refilled it; and at last he left me, but not before he had promised to visit me in the night, bring me a cake of bread if he could, and, more than all, news of Azeema and of my house.

The next day passed, and I had no food. I treasured up the water which had been left with me and sipped it now and then; but by nightfall again I was in torment. Yet I had hopes, for I knew that the young man would not deceive me; he had sworn by his mother's head to bring me food, and he could not break his oath.

And he came. I had sat watching, with that anxiety which can only be known by those who have been in a situation like mine, listening to every distant footfall, to every noise, as though it were the step of him I looked for. I have said he came; he was muffled in a blanket, and had stolen in unobserved by the lazy sentinel at the gate; he brought me food, a few coarse cakes, and an earthen pot of milk. "Eat!" said he in a low tone; "I will sit here, and will tell you the news you bade me inquire for afterwards. I was ravenous, and I ate; coarse bread, such as I should have loathed three days before, was now a luxury, sweet and grateful; I ate it, drank the milk, and was thankful; and I called him and blessed him for his venturous daring, and for his gratitude to one who could no longer do him a kind turn. "And the news, Gholam Nubbee? can you tell me aught of *her* and my child?"

"My news is bad, Meer Sahib, and I am the unwilling messenger of tidings which will grieve your soul and add to your misery."

"Say on," said I: "tell me the worst; tell me she is dead, and you will only say what my soul has forewarned me of."

He paused for awhile. "You must know it sooner or later, Meer Sahib—she is dead."

"And my child?"

"She is with the good moolla who protected your wife when she had no longer a house to cover her, and who performed the last rites of our faith to her when she was dead."

"No home!" cried I; "they did not drive her forth?"

"They did, Meer Sahib. The Rajah sent soldiers; your house was stripped of everything, and your gold and silver, they say, was a prize he little expected; your wife and child were turned into the street, with only the clothes they had upon their persons. But to her it little mattered, for I have heard she never spoke from the time she knew of your father's fate and the cause of your imprisonment. They say she sat in stupor, like a breathing corpse, without speaking a word to say where her pain was."

"Enough!" said I, "go; may Alla keep you! I would now be alone, for grief sits heavy on me."

Then she was dead—my Azeema, my beloved! she for whom I could myself have died, she whom I had loved as man can only love once—she was dead; she had known that I was a Thug, and that had killed her. It was well—better far that she should have died, than lingered on to be scoffed at and insulted as the wife of one who was now a convicted murderer. Had she lived I could never have dared to approach her, for she was pure, and I—!

I may say I almost rejoiced at her death, sahib; I did not grieve as I should have done had the blow fallen on me while I was yet in prosperity: then it would have been hard indeed to bear; but now I was altered, and she was dead; and again I say it was well. Alla in His mercy had taken her from her scene of suffering, almost before she knew to its full extent the horrible reality. And my child too was safe; she was in friendly hands, and the moolla would be a father to her.

The day after the nocturnal visit of my humble friend, food was allowed me. It was scanty to be sure, but still I existed, though worn down by sufferings, which I have no words to express, to a shadow of what I was. Three months passed thus, and they appeared to me like years when I looked back on them.

At the end of this time I was taken to the Rajah's durbar. Few were the words he spoke to me, but those were bitter ones; for he had shared my spoil, taxed me for protection, and, after putting my father to death, he had plundered my home, and his booty was the accumulation of mine for years past. I say my father, and yet he had told me he was not my parent. But what mattered that now? He was dead, and the mystery of my birth, if any had ever existed, was gone with him. What mattered it too who was my father? I was alone in the world; not a tie, save one, bound me to existence. My daughter was with strangers, and in a few years she would forget me,—truly I might say I was alone.

I was in the Rajah's durbar—I had no friend; no one of all those by whom he was surrounded, who had formerly courted me, eaten of my bread, and flattered me that I was yet to rise to greatness under his patronage—not one spoke for me, not one interceded to avert my shame. The Rajah spoke to me.

"Ameer Ali," said he, "I had trusted thee, I had thought thee honest (how he lied as he spoke!), I had believed thee a rich and fortunate merchant; but, O man! thou hast deceived me, and not me alone, but thousands, and thou art a Thug and a murderer. Still, because I have a lingering sentiment of kindness towards thee, I do not seek thy death. Justice has been satisfied in the destruction of the hoary villain who made thee what thou art, and who led one who might have been an ornament to the world to be a wretch upon whose head is the blood of hundreds. Yes, Ameer Ali, I speak truth, and thou knowest it. And though I desire not thy death, yet thou canst not be released without a mark on thy brow that men may know and beware of. Throw him down," cried he to the attendants, "and let him be branded!"

They threw me down. Sahib, what could my attenuated and wasted frame do against men who had suffered no misery like mine? I struggled, yet it was unavailing; they held my arms, and legs, and head, and a red-hot pice[1] was pressed upon my forehead; it was held there as it burned down to the bone, and my very brain seemed to be scorched and withered by the burning copper. They took it off, and raised me up. Alla! Alla! the agony that I endured—the agony of pain, and, more than that,

---

1 Coin.

of shame: to be branded publicly that the world might think me a thief—to have a mark set on my forehead that I must carry to my grave—a mark only set on the vile and on the outcasts from society! Sahib, it was a bitter cup to quaff!

"Away with him!" cried the Rajah, "away with him! Release him at the boundary of my territory. And mark me," he continued, addressing himself to me, "I have given thee thy life, Ameer Ali: go, and be wise; learn by what has happened to be an honest man for the future; and, above all, remember that if ever thou art seen in Jhalone again, or in any of my towns or villages, nothing will be able to save thee from the feet of an elephant."

He rose and strode out of the durbar; and in pain and misery, I was conducted in two days to the frontier of his country and unbound. Two rupees were given to me, and again the wide and cruel world was before me. I hurried from my late keepers. I bound my turban over my still burning and aching brow, so that man might not see my shame, and took the road before me. I wandered almost unconscious of anything, save the pain I was suffering until night fell around me, and I directed my steps to a village, the lights of which were a short distance before me. Exchanging one of my rupees, I sat down at the shop of a bhutteara and satisfied my craving appetite; there I slept, and when I arose I was refreshed, and again believed myself to be Ameer Ali. The morning breeze blew fresh on my face as I took my way out of the town; the refreshing rest of the night had invigorated me, and I bounded along with a light heart—yes, with a light heart, for I was free! I had no thought for the past now. It was my fate which had been fulfilled; what had been written in my destiny had come to pass. As I proceeded, a jackass brayed on my right hand, and I hailed the favourable omen with a joy I can feebly express. Yes, great Bhowanee, mother of men! cried I aloud, I answer to thy omen; I am ready, and again devoted to thy service. I have sinned against thee; I had wilfully avoided thy warning omens, led on by an irresistible destiny and by a proud heart. I have been punished, and have bought a dear experience; but henceforward no votary of thine breathing shall excel Ameer Ali in devotion to thee; and therefore, great goddess, vouchsafe the thibao and pilhaoo. And they were granted: the omen on the right was followed by that on the left, and I felt that I was pardoned, and again accepted as a Thug.

And so you believe, Ameer Ali, said I, that your not observing the omens in the instances you related was the cause of your father's death and your misfortunes?

Assuredly, sahib; I was a sceptic till then, as I have told you, but I was now no longer one. Had I not cause to believe in the truth of the omens? and, had I obeyed them then, should I have the heavy crime I had committed still rooted in my heart? No, no! omens cannot, dare not be disobeyed; and I have never known an instance in which they were, or where a band has been led to destroy a person against the wishes of Bhowanee, that they were not all punished by her vengeance, either with domestic misfortune, imprisonment, or death. Ask any Thug you know, and he will tell you the same. I never doubted omens afterwards, and have allowed some rich prizes to escape me, because I feared that they were not completely propitious.

Well, sahib, to continue. I pressed forward; I again untied my roomal, for that had never quitted my waist, and I welcomed it to my grasp as I should have done the embrace of an old and valued friend. With such omens, thought I, I cannot be unsuccessful; and over any single traveller, were he Roostum himself, I can gain a victory. I had but one rupee and some pice; my clothes were in rags about me, and I must have others before I could venture to associate myself with Thugs, and hope to lead them.

But I travelled long, and met no person alone; and when noon came, and the sun's heat had overcome me, I lay down under a tree by the road side, near which was a well; and having washed and bathed and said the Namaz, I waited to see what chance would throw in my way. There I sat a long time, but no one passed me, and overcome by fatigue I dropped asleep. I was awakened by a touch from some one, and looking up I beheld a middle-aged Mussulman gazing upon me. I arose rapidly, and returned his "Salam Aleikoom" as kindly as he had given it. Fortunately my face remained well wrapped up, and the brand on my forehead could not be seen; he took me to be a traveller like himself, and as he was weary, he sat down and we entered into conversation such as usually passes between persons situated as we were. After he had been seated for a few minutes, he loosed a small wallet from his shoulder, and opening it displayed some cakes and mango pickle, to which he seemed to be inclined to do ample justice; but seeing that I looked wistfully at them he invited me to join his repast, which I was right glad to do, as I had fasted since the morning. When we had finished our meal, he said to me, "Meer Sahib, you say there is no water for some coss in the direction I am going; and therefore, if you will kindly watch my clothes and arms, I will bathe in this well."

"Surely," I replied; "I am in no hurry to be gone, and you will not delay me." As I said it he began to strip, and taking with him a lota,[1] he descended the steps of the well, and I soon after heard the splashing of the water as he poured it over himself.

Now is my time, thought I: he will be defenceless, and will fall an easy prey to me; and I prepared my roomal for work.

---

1 Drinking vessel.

He soon returned, and began to dress. I loitered near him, till I saw him take up his garment and put both his arms into the sleeves to draw it over him. It was a capital opportunity, and I closed behind him as if to assist him; he turned to me, and as he had just accomplished his purpose, I had finished mine. The roomal was about his neck, and in a few moments he was dead at my feet! I had no time to lose; so hastily stripping the band from his waist, in which there seemed to be money, I dragged the body to the edge of the well, and threw it in. I then arranged his clothes at the head of the steps, as though he had taken them off to bathe, and left them there; his lota I left also with them; and taking up his sword and shield, I girded the first to my waist, and the shield to my back, and pursued my way at as quick a pace as I could. No one will imagine he has been murdered, thought I; the clothes on the brink of the well will cause it to be supposed that he died in the water; and I chuckled over my success and strode along joyfully. But, the more to avoid detection, I struck off from the road I was travelling, and seeing the groves and white temple of a village at some distance I bent my step towards it; there I purchased some goor, and ate the tupounee, as a good Thug ought to do, and after that I opened the humeana[1] to see what my good fortune had sent me.

And so you murdered the first man who had shown you any kindness after your misfortunes. Oh, Ameer Ali, you are indeed a villain! you ate of his bread and salt, and murdered him! The recompense of a Thug certainly.

But what could I do, sahib? I should have starved most likely had I not killed him. Besides he was the first traveller I met after those good omens; he was neither blind nor lame; assuredly therefore he was bunij. It must have been his fate to die, or I should not have gone to sleep under that tree. Had I met him in the road, I should have hesitated to attack him; indeed, unarmed as I was, I dared not have done so. But, as I was saying, I examined the humeana; I found in it nineteen rupees, a gold nose-ring, and two gold rings for the fingers which were worth at least forty rupees. Ul-humd-ul-illa![2] I cried, this is rare fortune; here is enough to last me for three months, and to provide me with new clothes; and it will be hard but in that time I find out some of my brethren.

I searched around the village to endeavour to find some traces of Thugs in the mango and tamarind groves by which it was environed; and though I discovered some fire-places with the peculiar marks of my brethren in them, yet they were old, the rain had more than half washed them away, and the marks would have been

---

1   Purse.
2   Praise be to Allah!

undistinguishable to a less experienced Thug than myself. I could discover no further clue from them, though I walked for some time in the direction they pointed.

Wandering along the next day, I reached Calpee[1] on the Jumna,[2] and sitting one morning at the shop of a pan seller, some persons stopped at it, and talking among themselves, I understood that they were going to Chutterpoor.[3] Chutterpoor, thought I,—what an owl I have been! there must be Thugs there, and I had forgotten it. So I immediately determined if possible to accompany them. I watched them to a bunnea's empty shop, before which, in the street, were tied four tattoos and some bullocks; and without ceremony I told them I had overheard their conversation, that I was also going to the town to which they were journeying, and if they would allow me and pardon my intrusion, I should be glad to travel in their company, as I was alone, knew not the road, and was afraid of robbers.

"Since you are alone, you may come, and welcome," said the man I addressed. "But we are going by Bandah,[4] which is not exactly in the direct road to Chutterpoor, and our business may detain us there a day or two; if, therefore, delay is of no consequence to you, come with us; you seem to be a soldier, and we are poor merchants who will be glad of your protection."

"Such as I am, good sir," said I, "I am at your service, and will gladly accompany you to Bandah."

"Good!" replied the man; "we start early, and you had better be with us betimes; or you can spread your carpet here,—as you please."

"I will do the latter," replied I, "and be with you by the evening."

Bandah! thought I; another place full of Thugs—at least it used to be. I shall see in any case, and if I find any, I may then alter my route.

I joined them in the evening, as I had promised, and we reached Bandah in a few days by long marches. Here they declared they would stay four days, so that I had ample time before me to search the place for Thugs, should any reside there. Nor was I disappointed in my hope of meeting them. I was sauntering through the town in the evening of the day we arrived, when I met Hoormut, an old follower of Ganesha. He did not at first recognise me, as may readily be imagined, and when I gave him our token of recognition he stared as though I had been an apparition; however, he was soon convinced of my reality, and I accompanied him to his house.

---

1 Kalpi.

2 Yamuna.

3 Chhatarpur.

4 Banda.

The relation of my adventures and mishaps occupied a long time, and after I had finished them I naturally asked for an account of my old associate Ganesha. What I heard was gratifying to me: Hoormut declared him to be in misfortune, abandoned by his followers, and that he was wandering with one or two men somewhere in the neighbourhood of Saugor, preferring the precarious chance of booty in the jungles between that place and Nagpoor, to frequenting the more open and travelled country. Next followed questions as to my present plans, and when he heard I was alone and travelling with merchants, of course it naturally followed that some plan should be undertaken for their destruction.

"Look you, Meer Sahib," said he, "I believe I can muster as many as fifteen Thugs, in and near this place. I am not suspected as yet, but the country is getting too hot for us, and we must either quit it or give up Thuggee, which no man, you well know, can do after he has eaten the goor; the others are of the same way of thinking, and we had determined that we would leave this place for good after the rains, and go wherever our fate might lead us."

We soon afterwards separated for the time, Hoormut promising to collect the men by the next evening.

I joined him again by the time appointed, and found the whole assembled. I was received with exultation, for they had wanted a leader in whom they could confide, and mine was a name which, in spite of my recent misfortunes, they could look up to. I knew none of them, but they swore on the pickaxe to follow me; Hoormut vouched for their several capabilities and fidelity, and I was satisfied.

Our plan was soon formed. They were to go by two stages to a village they knew; there they were to wait for my arrival with the merchants. Beyond the village was a favourite bhil of theirs, and they would have everything prepared against our coming up.

All this being settled, we fixed the next morning (it being Monday and a lucky day) to observe the omens and open the expedition with due form. The omens were declared to be satisfactory, and by noon my new companions had started with their families for their station on the road.

Chapter XLVII

So farewell hope, and with hope farewell fear;
Farewell remorse; all good to me is lost.
Evil, be thou my good!

—*Milton.*[1]

WE strangled the merchants at the place we had fixed on, them and their bullock-drivers,—nine in all, and yet we were only seventeen Thugs; but we were desperate. In our route we had travelled towards Jhalone, and I could no longer delay my project of proceeding thither, and making over my concealed treasure to the good moolla who had charge of my child.

Hoormut volunteered to accompany me; and desiring the remainder of the band to make the best of their way to Calpee, and there to await our arrival, we pushed on to Jhalone.

Considering the risk we ran, in approaching a place where inevitable death awaited *me* should I be discovered, we did well to disguise ourselves as gosaeens.[2] We covered our bodies with ashes, matted the hair on our heads with mud, hung gourds at our waist, and in this mean and wretched disguise we entered the town—that spot where I had passed so many years of happiness, where my fairest prospects had been blighted, and the resolutions I had formed of leading a new life and forsaking Thuggee rendered alike impracticable and distasteful to me. My emotions on entering the town, and more than all on passing the house where I had resided, were overpowering; but I rallied my heart. I passed through the city, and my friend and myself took up our abode for the day near a well outside the gates, which was not far from the spot where I had buried my treasure. "We had selected the best disguise possible for my purpose; we were visited during the day by some Hindoos, who came, some out of curiosity, and a few to offer alms to us; my companion replied to their inquiries, and declared me to be under a vow of silence, which satisfied them, and they departed, leaving us to prosecute our plans.

---

1 *Paradise Lost*, Book IV, 108-110.
2 Hindu mendicants.

As the evening approached, I strolled towards the trees under which was deposited the sum I had hoarded up to serve me at any time of need. It was a deserted burial-place, overgrown by custard-apple[1] bushes and other brushwood, and the rank grass had sprung up from the frequent rain. My heart beat quick as I approached the spot; my hoard might have been discovered, and if it had been removed my child would be a beggar, dependent upon the charity of strangers; she might even be thrust into the street, to herd with the vile and worthless, when the care of her became irksome or expensive to her present protectors. But anything, thought I, is better than that she should accompany me, where a life of hardship would be her portion, and where she could not escape the contamination which scenes of guilt and murder would effect in a short time, and from which, alone as I was, I could not protect her.

I reached the tomb in which, by removing a stone, I had placed the vessel containing the money. I hardly dared look at the well-remembered spot, hardly dared attempt to remove the stone; but I did remove it, and, O joy of joys! there was my treasure undisturbed. I hastily seized the earthen vessel, and crawled with it into the thickest of the underwood ere I ventured to open and examine it. I had forgotten what it contained, and the contents surpassed my expectations. I found thirty ashruffees and four small bars of gold, a box containing two strings of pearls of some value and some jewels, and tied up in a rag were some loose stones of value, one of them a diamond of great lustre and beauty. The jewels I determined to keep, as they might be afterwards of use to me, not only from their value, but to enable me to assume the character of a dealer in precious stones, which is always a respectable calling, and for which, in the jewels before me, I had ample stock for trade. I replaced the vessel and its precious contents, which could not have been worth less than a thousand rupees; and I felt my heart lightened of a load, both at seeing my treasure safe, and at the assurance it gave me that by means of it my daughter would be decently provided for. I returned to my companion, who had been anxiously watching my proceedings, and he too rejoiced at my good fortune.

I did not proceed into the town till it was dusk: the gates, I knew, would be open until long after dark, and I went alone to avoid any chance of being remarked. I soon reached the house of the moolla, when, abandoning my character of a gosaeen, I asked for alms in a lusty voice in the name of Moula Ali of Hyderabad. Fortunately the old moolla was sitting alone in his verandah; I saw him through the open gate, and advanced rapidly, shutting it behind me. He was engaged in reading his Koran, and was rocking himself to and fro, apparently absorbed in the book before him,

---

1 Wild sweetsop; the fruit of the *Annona reticulata* tree.

so that he did not observe my approach; nor was he aware of my presence till I had prostrated myself before him.

"Punah i Khoda!"[1] he exclaimed; "what is this, a gosaeen? Thou must be mad, good friend; or what seekest thou with the old moolla? Speak, thou hast almost frightened me, and disturbed my meditations on the holy volume."

"Pardon, Moollajee!" I cried; "you see one before you who has risked his life to speak with you, and you must listen to me for a few moments. I know you well, though you do not recognise me in this disguise."

"I know thee not, friend," he said; "nevertheless, if I can do aught to serve thee, speak; yet it is seldom that the Hindoo seeks the house of the priest of the Moslem faith; and I am in astonishment at thy garb and address."

"Moolla!" I said, "I would fain speak with thee in absolute secrecy; are we secure from interruption here? Fear me not; I come with good intent, and am not what you think me, but one of thine own faith;" and I repeated the Belief.

"Strange, most strange is this," said the old man rising; "I doubt thee not—no one would do the old moolla harm; and so, as thou requirest secrecy, I will but fasten the outer gate and join thee instantly." He did so, and returned.

"Moolla," said I, when he was once more seated, and was prying into my face with a look of mingled curiosity and wonder, "Moollajee! O Wullee Mahomed![2] dost thou not recognise me?"

"Thy voice is familiar to mine ears," said the old man, "yet I remember not thy features. Who art thou?"

"Mine is a name which may hardly be pronounced in Jhalone," I replied; "but we are alone. Have you forgotten Ameer Ali?"

"Punah!"[3] exclaimed the moolla, sidling away from me to the edge of his carpet; "Punah i Khoda! do I behold that bad and reckless man?"

"Bad I may be, Moolla," said I quietly; "and reckless I certainly am; yet I wish you no harm. You were kind to one I loved—you have my child in your house—it is of them I would speak, not of myself. Tell me, for the sake of Alla, whether my child is well—tell me whether she lives, and I will bless you." I gasped for breath while he replied, lest I should perchance have to hear of further misfortune.

"This is madness, Ameer Ali," said he; "know you not that your father's fate awaits you if you are discovered here?"

---

1 The Lord protect!
2 Saint Mohammad!
3 Protect me!

"I know, I know all," said I; "and I have braved everything. I have sought you despite of danger—for my heart clove to my child, and I would fain hear of her. Ah, friend, think not of what I was, and be merciful to me."

"Unhappy man!" he cried; "thy crimes brought with them their own reward; but I will not speak of the past. Know then that thy daughter is well; but she grieves still for thee and for her mother, whom Alla in mercy removed from her sufferings before she knew her degradation."

"Shookr Khoda!" I exclaimed. "Ah Alla, Thou art merciful even to me. And my child is well, and remembers me?"

"She does, Meer Sahib; she often speaks of you, but we have told her you are dead, and she no longer thinks of you as one whom she may ever meet again."

"And you are right," said I; "you are wise in having done this. May Alla repay your kindness to a deserted child, for I cannot. I have sought you for a purpose which you must promise to agree to, even before I speak it—it is the only request I shall ever make for my child, and from henceforth you will never see my face again nor hear my name."

"Speak," said the moolla; "I promise nothing, Ameer Ali; thou hast deceived thousands, and the old moolla is no match for thee in deceit."

"Briefly then," said I, "there was a small treasure which I buried in a field here long ago; I have returned and found it safe. It is a trifle, yet it is of no use to me; and I would give it over to you, both as a portion for my daughter when she is married, and as some provision for her until that can be effected."

"The spoil of the murdered," said the old man, drawing himself up proudly, "can never enter the house of the moolla; it would bring a curse with it, and I will have none of it. Keep it yourself, Ameer Ali, and may Alla give you the grace to use it in regaining the honest reputation you have lost!"

"No, no," cried I; "the money was my wife's; she had hoarded it up for our child; she brought it with her from the Dukhun, and it has remained as she placed it in the vessel. I swear to you that it is honest money; would I curse my child with the spoil of murders?"

"Swear to me on the Koran, that it is, and I will believe you, Ameer Ali, but not else;" and he tendered me the holy book.

I raised it to my lips; I kissed it, and touched my forehead and eyes with it. I swore to what was false; but it was for my child. "Are you satisfied now?" I asked; "now that you have humbled me by obliging me to swear?"

"I am," he replied; "your trust shall be carefully and religiously kept. Have you the money with you?"

"No," said I; "but I will go and return with it instantly. Admit me alone; I will cough at your gate when I arrive."

I hastened to the spot I have before described; I hastily seized my treasure and returned to the moolla: he was waiting for me at the gate of his house, and we entered it together.

"Here is all I have," said I, pouring out the contents of the vessel on the carpet; "it is not much, but it is the only portion of my wealth which remains to me."

"Think not of the past, Meer Sahib, what happened was predestinated, and was the will of the All-powerful!"

"I have indeed no alternative but to submit, good Moolla. But my time is short, and night advances; ere morning breaks, I must be far away from this, where my associates expect me. One favour I would beg,—it is to see my child: one look will be sufficient for my soul to dwell on in after years, for I am assured that it will be the last—you will not deny me?"

"I will not, Meer Sahib; she is now at play with a neighbour's child in the zenana, and if you will follow me I will show her to you. One look must be sufficient for you; after that she is mine, and I will be a father to her. Follow me."

I did; I followed him through a court-yard to the door of a second, which was the entrance to his zenana. I heard the merry voices of the children, as they played with light and joyful hearts, and I could distinguish the silvery tones of my precious child's voice, so like those of her mother, which were now silent for ever.

"We will not disturb them, Meer Sahib," said the moolla in a whisper as he pushed open the door gently; "look in, so that you may not be seen; you will easily distinguish your daughter."

Yes, she was there, my child, my beautiful child! still delicate and fragile as she had ever been; but her face had a joyous expression, and she was as merry as those by whom she was surrounded. Long, long I gazed, and oh, my heart yearned to rush in, and for the last time to clasp her to my bosom and bless her. But I restrained myself; she would not, could not have recognised me in the disguise I wore, and I should have only needlessly alarmed and terrified her. Yet I put up a fervent prayer to Alla for her protection and happiness, and I tore myself from the spot—dejected, yet satisfied that she still lived and was happy.

"Enough!" said I to the moolla when we regained the outer apartment; "I now leave you; be kind to my child, and Alla will more than repay you for aught of care or anxiety she may cause you. What I have given you will be ample for a dowry to her in marriage with any person you may select—any one who may be ignorant of her father's shame."

"I will; and rest assured that wherever you are, whatever your after-lot in life may be, you never need give one anxious thought about Meeran; for, I again repeat it, I am now her parent, and she has also found another mother."

"I believe you," said I; "and if ever I am again favoured by fortune and in a situation to come to you without shame to her, you shall take me to her and present a father to his child: until then you hear not of me again."

I left him. I had borne up against my feelings, I had struggled against and overcome them so long as I was with him; but as I passed his threshold the fond love of a parent would not be stifled: I was overcome by bitter grief, and I sat down and wept, for I felt that I had seen my child for the last time,—and it was even so; I have never beheld her since, sahib, nor ever been able to get a clue to her fate. May Alla grant she is happy, and knows not of mine! But of this more hereafter.

I wept! yes, I sat at the threshold of what had been my own home and wept, yet not aloud. My eyes were a fountain of tears, and they welled over their lids, and coursed down my rough visage, and fell hot upon my hands. My memory was busy with the past, that period of bliss when all earthly joy was my portion, and with it wealth and fame. All was gone—gone like the fleeting dream—a mockery which, gorgeous or blissful as it may be while it possesses the sleeping senses, is broken— even the remembrance of it lost—by awakening to reality. Alla help me! I said in the bitterness of my heart at that moment; I am indeed desolate, and it matters not what becomes of me: I have no hope.

How long I thus sat I know not; but arousing myself by a sudden thought of the danger I was in, I rose up, took one long, sad survey of what was once my own, but which was now deserted, and hurrying away from the spot, I reached the gate as it was about to be shut, and soon afterwards joined my companion.

At length we reached Calpee, where we found the band and their families; and at a council of all assembled, after many plans of proceeding had been discussed and many plans proposed for our final settling-place by the different members, I opened to them one of my own which I had long entertained. It was, to proceed to Lukhnow[1] by a boat, which could be easily hired, and to remain there, as it was a city which promised an ample harvest to a Thug; and, from the not over-strict character of its government, a more likely one than any other to enable as to pursue our calling with security. The plan was agreed on; and the next morning I betook myself to

---

1 Lucknow; city in the Awadh region in north-central India.

the Ghaut,[1] to hold communication with the manjees[2] of the boats, and so strike a bargain for their conveyance of my party.

All was arranged to the satisfaction of my associates; and at the hour appointed, which had been declared a lucky moment by some astrologer employed by the boatmen, the anchor was raised, and a fair wind carried us rapidly over the smooth waters.

Day after day passed in this manner, and there was a kind of dreamy pleasure about the voyage which was indescribably grateful to me. Here I had no alarms, no fatiguing journeys, no anxiety; my mind became calm and unruffled, and I was once more at peace.

At Lukhnow we lived for some time upon the proceeds of our last booty, and I established a small traffic in precious stones upon those I had brought with me; but it yielded small returns to me, and I only delayed commencing operations till I could fix upon some settled plans. I had erred deeply in leaving my own country; if I needs must have left it, I ought to have gone to the Dukhun: there I should have succeeded; I should have risen,—for the Dukhun Thugs required leaders, and, as you may have heard, whenever a Hindostan Jemadar led them, they behaved well and became the terror of the country. Here, I was in a place of which I was ignorant, and I dared not venture to take to the roads. At length I thought I would attempt the same system we had practised so successfully at Hyderabad. No sooner had the idea possessed me than I longed to put it into execution; the more so, as my associates received it with ardour, and seemed strongly convinced of its practicability. We were unknown in that crowded and vicious city, lived in an obscure part, and could never be suspected in our daily perambulations through the bazars in search of bunij. And so it turned out: we were in great luck for two months, money flowed in upon us, and we had killed upwards of thirty persons, mostly travellers to distant parts, whom we decoyed from the serais; and as we succeeded, I had more money at my disposal and was enabled to bribe several of the serai-keepers;[3] and, by allowing them to participate to a large amount in our gains, I secured admission to the serais, and had facilities of speaking with travellers which I should never have enjoyed had I neglected to secure their goodwill. But fortune was against me despite of this cheering commencement, and we did not long enjoy our easy and profitable career.

---

1   Stone steps on the banks of a river.
2   Boatmen.
3   Inn-keepers.

We had one day taken out of the city a party of seven travellers, we being sixteen Thugs in number. I well remember it was a Friday, an unlucky day at best. Among the Thugs was an old man, one of the old Murnae stock, a capital bhuttote, who had joined us a short time before; he had known my father, and me when a child, and had recognised me in a street in Lukhnow, which led to his joining us. We had taken the travellers to a favourite bhil of ours about four coss distant, and were in the act of strangling them,—some even lay dead on the ground, and the rest were in their last agonies,—when by the merest chance a body of horse, which were on their way from the city to a distant pergunnah,[1] came upon us. We had grown too confident from our frequent success,—it was still far from morning, and we had neglected to place scouts. The horse came upon us unheard and unseen, and, as I have told you, caught us in the very act. Nine of us were seized after a faint resistance; the rest, fortunate men! made their escape. Our hands were bound behind us and we were dragged into the city, objects of wonder and terror to the inhabitants. The bodies were brought in after us; and two of the travellers who had been only half strangled, and were revived by the horsemen, gave so clear an account of our whole proceedings, how we had inveigled them and accompanied them on their march till we attacked them unawares, that no doubt remained of our guilt; and after our brief trial had been concluded before the kazee,[2] we were cast into prison, to await our fate. The old Thug and myself had been bound together, and we were in this state thrust into one of the narrow cells of the jail. There we were told we should remain till the pleasure of the king was known regarding us.

---

1   Country; district.
2   Muslim judge.

Chapter XLVIII

The sigh of long imprisonment, the step
Of feet on which the iron clanked, the groan
Of death, the imprecation of despair.
                                —*Byron.*

Queen.—O speak to me no more!
        Thy words like daggers enter in mine ears.
                        —*Hamlet.* Act iii, Sc. 4.

AGAIN I was in prison; and although not in such wretched plight as I had been at Jhalone, for the cell was roomy and tolerably clean, yet still it was a prison,—confinement to my limbs and to my spirit; a conviction which threatened my life hung over me; and as I saw no prospect of escape I was resigned to die, and to meet my fate like a man and a Thug who had been familiar with death from his childhood. We sat in silence, and my wretched companion, old as he was, clung to the idea of life with a fondness that I felt not. He had no ties on earth to bind him to it, he had never had any, yet he longed to live. I had possessed them,—they were all broken, and life had no charms for me. I could not say that I wished for death, but I was indifferent to my fate.

A week passed thus—a long, interminable week. In vain was it that I implored my jailers to relieve me from suspense, to tell me whether I was to live or die; either they knew not, or their hearts were hardened towards me—they would not tell me.

But after the expiration of this period, we were not long ignorant of our sentence. We were informed that seven of our companions had been hanged, as they had been detected in the act of strangling travellers. But there was no evidence against us so conclusive; the merchants who had escaped the fate of their associates could not swear that we had murdered any of those who had perished; and the horsemen who had captured us knew no more than that we were of the party. If this had been all, we should probably have been released; but one of the miserable men who had been executed, in a vain attempt to preserve his life, confessed his crimes; and by this last stroke of ill fortune we were convicted, and the decree went forth that we were to be imprisoned for life.

Despair seized on my faculties at the announcement of this hard sentence. Death in its most horrible shape would have been courted joyfully by me in preference to it. To linger out years and years in that wretched hole, never to be free again! I could not believe it; I tried to shut out the dreadful reality from my mind, but in vain. I implored that they would lead me to instant execution, that I might be impaled, or blown away from a gun, or hung,—anything rather than have my miserable existence protracted in the solitude and suffering of a prison. But my entreaties were laughed at or scorned. I was loaded with a heavy chain, which confined my legs, my companion the same, and we were left to our fate. Still my restless spirit held out to me hopes of escape,—hopes that only mocked me, for every plan I formed became utterly impracticable, and this only increased my misery. One day I bethought me of the money I had collected before I was seized. It was hidden, and it was not improbable that my hoard had remained undiscovered. With this I fondly hoped I should be enabled to bribe one of my jailers; and the idea comforted me for many days, while I waited for an opportunity to put in into execution.

There was one among the guards of the prison, a young man, who was always kinder in his deportment to us than any of the others. The food he brought us was better, and the water always pure, and in a clean vessel. He used to cheer us too sometimes with the hope that our imprisonment would not last so long as had been decreed; and he instanced the cases of several criminals who had been sentenced like us, but who had been released when the memory of their crimes had ceased to occupy the minds of the officers in charge of the prison. He had our clothes washed for us, and did a thousand kind acts—trifles perhaps, but still more than we experienced from any other of his companions.

It was with him, therefore, that I proposed to my fellow-captive to try our long-brooded and cherished scheme of deliverance. The next time it was his turn to attend us, I begged he would come to the cell at night or in the evening, when he would be secure from observation, for that I had something particular to communicate to him. He came in the evening of that day, and seated himself, muffled in a dark-coloured blanket, close to the bars of our cell.

"You have something to say, I think," said he in a low tone, "and I have done your bidding; I am here."

"I have, good Meer Sahib," said I (for he was also a syud); "listen, for what I would communicate to you will be for your benefit, if you will enter into my plans."

"Say on," replied the youth; "you may command my utmost exertions."

"To be brief, then," I continued, "you must endeavour to effect our escape."

"It is impossible," he said.

"Not so," cried I; "nothing is impossible to willing hands and stout hearts. You can manage everything if you will but listen to me. When we were apprehended, we had saved a round sum of money, which is concealed in a spot I can tell you of, if you will be faithful to us. Half of it shall be yours, if you will only aid us."

"How much is it?" he asked.

"Upwards of five hundred rupees," said I; "it was securely hidden, and no one can have discovered it. I repeat, half of it shall be yours if you will assist us."

"How can I?" cried he, in a tone of perplexity; "how is it possible that you can pass these doors and walls, even were you as free as I am at this moment?"

"Leave that to me," said I; "do you accept the offer?"

"I will consider of the matter, and will be here at this time to-morrow, to give you a final answer."

"May Alla send you kind thoughts to the distressed! We shall look for your decision with impatience."

The next evening he came at the same time, and seated himself as before.

"What would you have me do, Meer Sahib?" he asked; "I am ready to obey your commands if they are practicable. First, however, I must be secure of the money you have mentioned; I must receive it before I peril my situation, and, more than that, my life in your behalf."

"Listen then, Meer Sahib," said I; "I trust you,—you are a syud and I also am one; you dare not deceive me, and incur the wrath of Alla."

"I will not, by the Prophet, whose descendant I am," said he; "were the Koran in my hands this moment, I would swear upon it."

"No, no," said I, "do not swear; the word of an honest man is far more binding than an oath. I believe that you are true, and therefore it is that I trust you. First, then, as regards the money; do you remember two old tombs, one of them much broken, which stand near the river's brink over the north side of the city, about a cannon-shot from the walls?"

"I do, perfectly."

"Then," I continued, "in that broken one is an earthen vessel, containing the money; the vault where of old the body of the person over whom the tomb was erected was deposited, can be opened by removing four stones, which are loose, from the eastern side of it; they are neither large nor heavy, and you can manage the matter alone. In the cavity you will find the vessel, and the money is in it. I shall require half for my expenses. Now all I ask you for the present to do in return is, to procure us two small and sharp files and some ghee; and when we have cut through our chains, and one of these bars, I will tell you how you can aid us further."

"I will perform all you wish, said the youth; "and, Inshalla! you shall have the files to-morrow night by this time, if I find that your statement about the money is true."

He then left us, and we anxiously and impatiently awaited his coming the next day. Nor did he disappoint us.

"I have come, as you see, Meer Sahib," he said; "and, behold, here are the files for you—they are English, and new and sharp; here too is the ghee. I have fulfilled my promise."

"And the money?" I asked.

"Without it you would not have seen me to-night, I can tell you, Meer Sahib. I have got it; the amount is five hundred and fifty rupees, and you shall be welcome to your share when you have got out of this hole. And how do you intend to manage this part of your scheme?"

"Are the gates of the prison shut at night?" I asked.

"No," he replied; "that is, the gate is shut, but the wicket is always open."

"And how many men guard it?"

"Only one, Meer Sahib; the rest sleep soundly after midnight."

"It is well," said I; "we can but perish in the attempt, and I for one would gladly die, rather than linger out a wretched existence here."

"And I also," said my companion.

"I fear I cannot assist you," said the man; "yet stay, suppose you were to attempt your escape when I am on guard. I shall have the last watch to-morrow night."

"May the blessing of Alla rest on you!" said I; "you have anticipated my thoughts. We will attempt it then, and may the Prophet aid us. All night we will work at our irons and one of these bars, and to-morrow night we shall be free. Go, kind friend, you do but risk detection in being seen here."

He left us, and we set to work with a good will to cut the irons on our legs and the bar. All night we worked, and the morning's light saw the iron bar nearly cut through at the top and bottom; to cut it at the top, one of us sat down by turns, while the other, standing on his shoulders, filed till his arm was tired. Despite of the ghee however, the files made a creaking noise; we tried to prevent this by using them slowly, but in the excitement of the moment this was at times forgotten, for we worked hard for our liberty.

The morning broke and we rested from our labour; one strong shake would have separated the bar, and our irons were so nearly cut through at the ankles and the waist, that a slight wrench would have divided them. Our friend we knew was faithful, for he had proved himself so, and we enjoyed a silent anticipation of our eventual triumph.

"This time to-morrow," I exclaimed, "we shall be free, far from Lukhnow, and the world again before us, wherein to choose a residence!"

My companion was as full of hope as I was, and we passed most of the morning in debating whither we should go, and calling to mind the names of our former associates who would welcome us and join us in seeking new adventures. It was about noon, I think, that a party of the soldiers of the prison, headed by the darogha,[1] approached our cell. My heart sank within me as I saw them coming, and the haste with which they advanced towards us increased my alarm and apprehension. "We are lost!" said I to my companion; "they have discovered our plans." He did not reply, but despair was written on his countenance.

The darogha applied his key to the lock; it was opened, and the whole party rushed in and seized us.

"What new tyranny is this?" I exclaimed; "what new crime have we committed, that we are again to be ill-treated?"

"Look to their irons!" cried the darogha to his men.

"You have been busy it seems," said he to us, when they found them in the state I have described. "Let me give you a piece of advice; when you next file your irons, either use more ghee or make less noise. But you will hardly have another opportunity I think. Search them well," continued he to the men; "see where these instruments are which they have used so cleverly."

They stripped us stark naked, and the files were found in the bands of our trousers through which the string that ties them runs. The darogha examined them carefully.

"These are new, Meer Sahib, and English. Inshalla! we will find out who supplied you with them. The fellow who has done this assuredly has eaten dirt."

"We brought them here with us," said I doggedly. "Ye were sons of asses that ye did not search us when we entered your den of tyranny."

"We may be sons of asses," he replied grinning, "but we are not such owls as to believe you, O wise and cunning Syud; Thug as you are, we are not going to eat dirt at your hands. Some friend you have had among my men; one is suspected; and if these files can help us to trace him—and it is probable enough—he had better say the Kulma, for his head and shoulders will not long remain together. But come," said he to his men, "your work is only half done; examine every foot of these bars; for my worthy friends here, rely upon it, have not half done their business."

They obeyed him, and, as you may suppose, soon found the bar which had been cut.

---

1   Warden.

"Enough!" said the darogha. "You were a fool, O Meer Sahib, for this wild attempt. Had you been content to bear your deserved imprisonment, mercy might in time have been shown to you; but now, give up all hope: you have forfeited that mercy by your own imprudence, and you will long live to repent it. Bring them along," said he to his men; "we must put them into narrower and safer lodgings."

Ya Alla, Sahib, what a place they led us to! A narrow passage, between two high walls, which but just admitted of a man's passing along it, contained, about half way down, two cells, more like the dens of wild beasts than aught else. They were more strongly grated than the last we had been in, and were not half the size. Far heavier irons than those we had last worn were fastened on our legs by a blacksmith, and we were thrust into our horrible abodes.

"Now," said the darogha, "get out if you can, Meer Sahib. If walls and iron bars can hold you, you are pretty safe here, I think."

They left us, and once more we were cast into the abyss of despair; nor was there one ray of hope left to cheer our gloomy and wretched thoughts. Here am I to live, here am I to die, thought I, as I surveyed the narrow chamber,—I who have roamed for years over the world, I who have never known restraint. Alla! Alla! what have I done that this should be? O Bhowanee, hast thou so utterly forsaken Ameer Ali? I cast myself down on the rough floor, and groaned in agony. I could not weep, tears were denied me; they would have soothed my overburdened soul. A cup of misery was before me, and I was to drain it to the dregs. Hope had fled, and despair had seized and benumbed every faculty of my mind.

Months rolled on. Though only a strong grating of iron bars divided me from my old companion, we seldom spoke to each other; at most it was a word, a passing remark hazarded by the one, and scarcely heeded by the other, so absorbed were we in our misery. I ate and drank mechanically, I had no craving for food; and what they gave us to eat was of the coarsest kind. The filth which accumulated in our cells was removed only once a week, and it bred vermin which sorely tormented us. Oh that I could die! I cried a thousand times a day. Alas! my prayer was not granted.

The second year of our captivity passed—the same unvarying rotation of misery,—no change, no amelioration of our condition. We existed, but no more; the energies of life were dead within us. I used to think, were I ever released, that I could not bear the rude bustle of the world; that I should even prefer my captivity to its anxieties and cares. It was a foolish thought, for I often yearned for freedom, and occupied my mind with vain thoughts and plans for future action, should any lucky chance give me my liberty; but no ray of hope broke in upon the misery of my dungeon.

I mean not to say that my companion, the old Thug, and I never conversed; we did so now and then; we recounted our exploits again and again, and by thus recalling mine to my memory, from the beginning of my career, I stored up in my mind the adventures and vicissitudes I have related to you. One day we had been talking of my father, and his parting words to me, "I am not your father," flashed across my thoughts. I mentioned the circumstance to the old Thug, and earnestly requested him to tell me what he knew of Ismail, and of my early state.

"What!" he asked, "so you know not of it, Meer Sahib? Surely Ismail must have told you all? And yet," continued he after a pause, "he would not have done it—he dared not."

"What can you mean," cried I, "by saying he dared not? Was I his son, or did he say truly when he declared I was not?"

"He spoke the truth, Meer Sahib. I know your origin, and it is just possible there may be one or two others who do also, and who are still living: one of these is Ganesha."

"Ganesha!" I exclaimed; "by Alla! my soul has ever told me that he knew something of me. I have striven in vain to bring any scene in which he was concerned with me to my recollection, and always failed. By your soul! tell me who and what I was."

"'Tis a long tale, Ameer Ali," said the old man, "but I will endeavour to remember all I can of it; it is one too which, were you not what you are, would horrify you."

"My parents were murdered then?" said I, my heart sinking within me. "I have sometimes thought so, but my conjectures were vague and unsatisfactory."

"You have guessed truly, Meer Sahib. But listen, my memory is still fresh, and you shall know all.

"Ismail, your father, as he called himself to you, became a Thug under Hoosein Jemadar, whom no doubt you remember. I well recollect the day he joined us, at a village not very far from Dehli; I was then a youth, and belonged to the band of which Hoosein was one of the best bhuttotes."

"I know Ismail's history," said I; "he related it to me."

"Then I need not repeat it," he continued. "In time Ismail, by his bravery and wisdom, rose far above Hoosein, and became the jemadar of a band of thirty Thugs. It is of this time I would speak. We were one day at a village called Eklera, in Malwa, encamped outside the place, in a grove of trees near a well. We had been unlucky for some time before, as it was the season of the rains, when but few travellers are abroad, and we were eagerly looking for bunij.

"Ismail and Ganesha, had been into the bazar, and returned with the joyful news that a party was about to set off towards Indoor, and that we were to precede them by a march, and halt whenever we thought them secure to us. I and another Thug were directed to watch their movements, while the main body went on. The information was correct, and we dogged them till the third or fourth march, when at a village, whose name I forget, we found the band halted, and rejoined it. The party consisted of a respectable man and his wife and child, an old woman, and some young men of the village who accompanied them. The man rode a good horse, and his wife travelled in a palankeen. They were your parents, Meer Sahib."

"Go on," said I in a hoarse voice; "my memory seems to follow your narration." O sahib! I was fearfully interested and excited.

"Well," continued he, "not long after they had arrived, Ismail and Ganesha went into the bazar, dressed in their best clothes, to scrape an acquaintance with your father, and, as Ismail told us afterwards, this was effected through you. He saw you playing in the streets, gave you some sweetmeats, and afterwards rescued you from the violence of some of the village boys, who would have robbed you of them. This led to his speaking with your mother, and eventually to his becoming acquainted with your father. The end of all was, that they agreed to accompany us, and dismissed the young men by whom they had been previously attended. Does your memory aid you now, Meer Sahib, or shall I finish the relation?"

"It does," said I, "most vividly as you proceed. But go on; without your assistance, I lose the thread of my sad history." He resumed.

"Ismail in those days always rode a good horse, as also did Ganesha. He grew fond of you and you of him, and he used to take you up before him and carry you most part of the march, or till you became fatigued. This went on for some days, but we were approaching Indoor, and it was necessary to bring the matter to a close; besides, our cupidity was strongly excited by the accounts we heard from Ismail of your father's wealth, as he had told him that he carried a large sum of ready money with him. At last the bhil was determined,—I could show it you now: it was close to a river, and, before the party had crossed, the *jhirnee* was given. We strangled them all. Ganesha killed your mother, the old woman was allotted to me; Ismail had his share also, and I believe it was your father. You had been riding upon Ismail's horse all the morning, at least after the rain had ceased, and when the *jhirnee* was given you were half across the river; I saw you fall, and as you did not move afterwards, I thought you were killed. You moved, however, and Ganesha ran towards you: he threw the roomal about your neck, and was in the act of strangling you, when Ismail, who had uttered a cry of despair on seeing Ganesha's action, arrived just in time to prevent his deadly purpose. They had a serious quarrel about you, and even drew their swords; but Ismail prevailed, and led you to where the bodies were lying and being stripped by the lughaees. You became frantic when you saw your mother; you clung to her body and could hardly be torn from it; you raved and cursed us all, but terror overcame you at last, and perhaps pain also, for you fainted. Ismail, when the bodies had been disposed of, and the plunder collected, mounted his horse and took you up before him; and turning off the road, we travelled in another direction.

"How you ever bore that journey I know not; you were a thin and delicate child, and we all said you would die; but you bore it well, and when we reached a place in the jungle, I was sent to a village for milk, and you drank some. Here again Ismail and Ganesha had a second quarrel about you: Ganesha said that you were too old to adopt, that you would remember all that had happened, and that he would strangle you; and the abuse that you poured upon him made him still more savage. Again they drew their swords, and would have fought about you, but we prevented them.

"You were taken away by me to a distance; I rubbed your swollen neck, and Ismail gave you a strong dose of opium, which put you to sleep, and we again resumed our flight.

"Ganesha and he were never cordial friends after that day; they never acted in concert again until, as I heard, in your last expedition; and though they preserved an outward show of civility to each other, their hate was as strong as ever.

"Ismail took you to his home. He was married, but had no children; and as you grew up and improved under his kind and fatherly treatment, he became proud of you, and used often to say to us that he regretted your father had left your sister behind when he undertook his fatal journey to Indoor."

"My sister!" cried I, in an agony of apprehension.

"Yes, Meer Sahib, your sister. I, for one, heard your father say that he left her behind, as she was too young to be moved. You might get news of her at Eklera if you ever get out of this cursed hole."

But he now spoke to one bereft of sense—of any feeling save that of choking, withering, blighting agony. Why did not my heartstrings crack in that moment? Why did I live to drag a load of remorse with me to my grave?

Yet it has even been so. I live and I have borne my misery as best I could. To most I appear calm and cheerful, but the wound rankles in my heart; and could you but know my sufferings, sahib, you would perhaps pity me. Not in the daytime is my mind disturbed by the thoughts of the past; it is at night, when all is still around me, and sleep falls not upon my weary eyelids, that I see again before me the form of my unfortunate sister; again I fancy my hands busy with her beautiful neck, and the vile piece of coin for which I killed her seems again in my grasp as I tore it from her warm bosom. Sahib, there is no respite from these hideous thoughts; if I eat opium—which I do in large quantities, to produce a temporary oblivion—I behold the same scene in the dreams which it causes, and it is distorted and exaggerated by the effects of the drug. Nay, this is worse to bear than the simple reality, to which I sometimes become accustomed, until one vision more vivid than its predecessors again plunges me into despair of its ever quitting me.

Sahib, after that fatal relation, I know not what I did for many days. I believe I raved, and they thought me mad, but my mind was strong and not to be overthrown. I recovered, though slowly, and again and again I retraced in my memory the whole of my life till that miserable day on which I murdered my sister! It could have been no other.

I tried in vain to cheat myself into the belief that it was another; but no effort that I made could shake the conviction that it was she. My unaccountable recollection of Eklera, the relation of my father's death by the old man there, his almost recognition of me, and, more than all, the old and worthless coin for which I destroyed her, and which I now remembered perfectly,—all were undeniable proofs of my crime; and conviction, though I tried to shut it out, entered into my soul, and abode there. Alla help me, I was a wretched being! My hair turned grey, my form and strength wasted, and any one who had seen me before I listened to the old Thug's tale would not have recognised me two months afterwards. A kind of burning fever possessed me; my blood felt hot as it coursed through my veins; and the night, oh, how I dreaded it! I never slept except by day, when exhausted nature claimed some respite. Night after night, for months and months, I either rolled to and fro on my miserable pallet, or sat up and rocked myself, groaning the while in remorse and anguish. No other act of my life rose up in judgment against me—none but that one; I tried even to think on others, but they passed from my mind as quickly as they entered it, and my sister was ever before me.

You know the worst, sahib—think of me as you will, I deserve it. I cannot justify, the deed to myself, much less to you; and the only consolation I have—that it was the work of fate, of unerring destiny—is but a weak one, that gives way before the conviction of my own guilt. I must bear my curse, I must wither under it. I pray for death, and as often too pray that I may live, and that my measure of punishment may be allotted to me here, that my soul may not burn in Jehanum. I may now as well bring my history to a close, to the time when, by accepting your boon of life, I became dead to the world.

My old companion died in the fourth year of our captivity. I would fain have had him deny the tale he told me of my father's destruction, but he would not; he was dying when I urged him to do so, and again declared in the most solemn manner that what he had related was true in every particular; and again he referred me to Ganesha, my mother's murderer, for confirmation of the whole.

He died, and I was left to solitude, to utter solitude, which was only broken by the daily visit of my jailer, who brought me food, and attended me during a short walk up and down the passage. This favour alone had I extorted after those years of misery, and it was grateful to me to stretch my cramped limbs, and again to feel the pure air of heaven breathe over my wasted features.

The seventh year had half passed; the darogha of the jail was dead or had been removed; another supplied his place, and some amelioration of my condition ensued. I was removed from the lonely cell into one near where I had been first confined; it was more spacious and airy, and people passed to and fro before it. I used to watch their motions with interest, and this in some degree diverted my mind from brooding over the past.

In the twelfth year of my imprisonment the old king died, and his successor, the late monarch, ascended the musnud. Many a heart beat quickly and with renewed hope—hope that had almost died within the hearts of those wretches who were immured within the walls—and of mine among the rest. We had heard that it was customary to release all who had been sentenced to perpetual imprisonment; and you can hardly imagine, sahib, the intense anxiety with which I looked for the time when the mandate should be issued for our release, or when I should no longer dare to hope.

It came at last after some days of weary expectation, the order reached the darogha, and it was quickly conveyed to me. I was brought forth, the chains were knocked off my legs, and I was free. Five rupees were given to me, and a suit of coarse clothes in place of those which hung in rags about my person. After more than twelve weary years I issued from those prison walls, and was again thrown upon the world to seek my fortune.

"Beware, Meer Sahib," said the darogha, as he presented me with the money, "beware of following your old profession; you are old, your blood no longer flows as it used, and what you have been you should forget. Go! follow some peaceful calling, and fortune may yet smile upon you."

I thanked him and departed. I roamed through the city till night-fall, and after satisfying my hunger at the shop of a bhutteara, I begged from him shelter for the night. It was readily granted, and I lay down and enjoyed the first quiet and refreshing sleep I had known for years. I arose with the dawn and went forth,—whither I cared not,—all places in the wide world seemed alike to me. I knew no one, I could find no one who knew me in that large city, and I felt the desolation of my condition press heavily upon me. What to do, or whither to go, I knew not; but a faint hope that I might discover some of my old associates if I could reach Bundelkhund impelled me to travel thither.

A change in my dress was soon effected. From a kalundur fakeer[1] I purchased a high felt cap and a chequered garment for a small sum; and thus equipped, with a staff in my hand, I left the city by the north gate, and travelled onwards.

It was as I thought: I was never without a meal, though it might be of the coarsest food; and when I reached Jhalone, my little stock of money was nearly as large as when I had left Lukhnow. I went direct to the house of the moolla, for my thoughts were ever with my daughter, and my soul yearned to know her fate. Alas! I was disappointed. His house was inhabited by another, whom I knew not, and all he could tell me was that the old man had gone to Dehli, he believed, some years before, and that he had not heard any tidings of him since. I asked after his daughters, but the man knew nothing of them, except that one he had adopted had been married in Jhalone to a person who resided in a village of the country, but of his name or direction he was ignorant.

I turned away from the door,—I dared not pass my own, and I withdrew to an obscure part of the town where there was a small garden in which a fakeer usually resided. Him I had known of old, he had eaten of my bread and received my alms, and now I was his equal. He will not recognize me, thought I, in this dress, and changed as I am no one knows me; I will seek him, however, and if he is as he used to be, I may learn some news of my old friends.

I found the fakeer I sought; old I had left him, he was now aged and infirm; his garden, which he had always kept with scrupulous neatness, was overgrown with weeds and neglected, and he had barely strength remaining to crawl about the town for the small supply of flour or grain which sufficed for his daily wants. I was much shocked to see him thus, and representing myself to be a wandering kalundur desirous of remaining in Jhalone, I begged to be allowed to reside and share with him whatever I got. My offer was readily accepted, and there I took up my abode, in the hope that some wandering party of Thugs might pass Jhalone, to whom I could disclose myself.

---

1 Muslim ascetic.

Gradually I discovered myself to the old man: I led him to speak of old times and of persons by allusion to whom he must know I was a Thug. He did not hesitate to speak of them, and in particular of myself, whose fate he mourned with such true grief that I could control myself no longer; and to his wondering ear I related the whole of my adventures, from the time I had been released by the Rajah, to the period of my taking up my abode with him. And much had I to hear from him in return, much that distressed and grieved me: many of my old companions were dead, others had been seized and executed, and hardly one of the old leaders of Bundelkhund were in the country or in the exercise of their vocation; new leaders had sprung up, and he spoke in warm terms of a young man named Feringhea, who, when I had last seen him, was a mere boy.

Four months passed thus. To support the old fakeer as well as myself, I was obliged to perambulate the town daily, and I asked and received alms, given in the meanest portions, in the place where my hand had ever been open to the poor. A sad change in my fortune, sahib! yet I bore up against it with resignation, if not with fortitude, hoping for better days and new adventures.

New adventures, Ameer Ali! I exclaimed; had not the punishments you had received turned your heart from Thuggee?

No, sahib! cried the Thug with fervour: why should they? had not my heart become hardened by oppression and misery? They had aroused within me a spirit of revenge against the whole human race; I burned to throw off my wretched disguise and again take to the road—it mattered not whether as a leader or a subordinate, so that I could once more be a Thug. Nor was I old; true, my beard had become grizzled and grey, and care had seamed my countenance with many wrinkles; but I was still strong and powerful, and my hands had not forgotten their cunning. Four months, I have said, had elapsed, and as no Thugs came near Jhalone, I set off, with a few rupees I had saved from the produce of my daily alms, for Tearee, where I hoped to meet the Brahmin astrologer who had so materially aided me in the affair of the pearl-merchant. His share of that booty had been duly remitted to him immediately on my arrival at Jhalone, and though I had never heard from him afterwards, yet I felt assured that the letter could not have miscarried.

I reached Tearee after many days. I knew that bands of Thugs were abroad, for I saw their fire-places and marks at many villages and upon the roads; but I met with none, to my disappointment, and on my arrival I hastened at once to the temple, where I found the Brahmin; and, notwithstanding my misfortunes, I was kindly, nay, warmly, welcomed. The Brahmin still kept up his connection with Thugs, and I learned from him to my joy that a band, under a jemadar named Ramdeen, about twenty in number, had passed through the town only the day before, and were on their road towards the Nerbudda.

"You can easily overtake them, Meer Sahib," he said; "and if your old fame as a leader fails in procuring you a welcome reception, a few lines from me may aid you." And he wrote a note to the jemadar, informing him who I was, and how I had been connected with him of old. I did not long delay after I had received it, and again set off in search of my future companions. I came up with them on the second day, and warm indeed was the welcome I received; one and all were amazed to see me, whom they had long thought dead. I was clothed in decent raiment by them, admitted as one of their band, and treated as a brother. Truly their kindness was refreshing to my almost withered heart. Ramdeen insisted that I should take an equal rank with him in the band; and after the necessary ceremonies I resumed my roomal, and in a few days again ate the goor of the tupounee.

Sahib, you must by this time be weary of my adventures with travellers, and I met with none during my connection with Ramdeen's party worthy of relation. We avoided the Company's territories and kept to those of Sindia, penetrating as far as Boorhanpoor, and on our return visiting the shrine of Oonkar Manduttee, on the Nerbudda. From this latter place we were fortunate in enticing a party of pilgrims, and a large booty fell into our hands at the bottom of the Jām Ghat, whither we escorted them on their return to Oojein. Upwards of four hundred rupees was my share of this: so again you see me independent and fortune smiling upon me. But Ramdeen became jealous of me, and of my superior skill and intelligence. We had many quarrels, and at last I left him and determined, with what I had, to travel to the Dukhun, and to seek my fortune in the Nizam's country, where I knew that Thuggee still flourished unchecked.

But it was fated not to be so. My road from where I left Ramdeen lay through Saugor, and there I met with my old acquaintance Ganesha, at the head of a small band, apparently in wretched plight. I could but ill dissemble my feelings of abhorrence at meeting with him; my own misfortunes and history and the tale of my companion in imprisonment were fresh in my recollection; nevertheless I disguised the dislike I felt, though revenge still rankled in my heart, and I would gladly have seized an opportunity to satisfy it. Among his band was a Thug I had known in former days; he was weary of Ganesha, whose temper was not improved by age, and he advised me to put myself at the head of a few men he could point out to me who would be faithful, and who, he thought, would prove the nucleus of a large band; for my name was still fresh in the memory of the older Thugs, who would gladly flock to me when they heard I was determined to set up for myself without connection with others. And he was right; in a few months I was at the head of forty men; and we were fortunate. Taking a new direction we passed through the territories of the Rewah Rajah, returning to our home, which we fixed in a village not far from Hindia, in a wild and unfrequented tract, where we were secure from treachery and from the operations against the Thugs then being carried on from Saugor.

Two years passed in this manner, and I was content, for I was, as I wished to be, powerful and actively employed. Two seasons we went out and returned laden with plunder, and the name of Ameer Ali was again known and feared. Another season and it shall be my last, said I; I had discovered some clue to my daughter, and thought (vain idea!) if I could only collect a few thousand rupees, that I could dare to seek her, to live near her, and to abandon Thuggee for ever. Why was I thus infatuated? what else could it have been but that inexorable fate forbade it? The destiny which had been marked out for me by Alla I was to fulfil, and I blindly strove against it. The vain purposes of man urge him to pursue some phantom of his imagination, which is never overtaken, but which leads him on often by smooth paths and buoyed up by hope, till he is suddenly precipitated into destruction.

I had planned an expedition, on a larger scale than ever, towards Calcutta, and we had sworn to Bhowanee to pay our devotions at her shrines of Bindachul and Calcutta; the omens were favourable, and we left our home in joy and high excitement. And what cared I then, though I knew that the English had set a price of five hundred rupees upon me? It was a proof that I was dreaded and feared, and I rejoiced that Ameer Ali, the oppressed and despised for a time, had again emerged from his obscurity, and I braved the danger which threatened me. I was a fool for this, yet it was my destiny that impelled me; and of what avail would have been precautions, even had I taken any? I knew that treachery could not reach me where I was, and I trusted to my apparently lasting new run of good fortune, and to the omens with which our expedition had begun, to escape apprehension in the districts of the Company's territories, where operations against Thugs were being carried on with much success.

Saugor lay directly in the route which we proposed taking, and it was here that the greatest danger was to be apprehended. I might have avoided it, perhaps, but I trusted to the celerity and secrecy of my movements for a few days until we should pass it; and as my band were unanimous in refusing to change the route after it had been determined on and sanctioned by favourable omens, I undertook to lead them at all hazards. We travelled by night therefore, and avoided all large villages, resting either in waste spots or near miserable hamlets. Nor did we seek for bunij,—the danger was too imminent for any time to be lost; and though one or two persons died by our hands, yet this was rather to enable us to eat the goor of the tupounee, and to perform such ceremonies as were absolutely necessary for the propitiation of our patroness, and our consequent success.

———◆———

CONCLUSION

Pistol.—Trust none,
        For oaths are straws, men's faiths are wafer-cakes,
        And Hold-fast is the only dog, my duck:
        Therefore, *Caveto* be thy counsellor!
                                —Henry V. Act ii., Sc. 2.[1]

SAUGOR, I have said, lay directly in our route, and we reached a village close to it on the evening of a day of severe travel. We were fatigued already, but the town was now so close to us that we did not hesitate to push on, and we arrived at the well-known spot shortly after dark. Selecting an empty shed in as lonely a part of the town as we could, we cooked a hasty meal and lay down, determined to rise before dawn and again pursue our journey. One of our number was set to watch ere we retired to rest, and we depended upon him to give us warning should any suspicious person be observed.

The night passed, and I arose, roused my followers, and long before day had dawned we were beyond the gates of the town. "See," said I to my friend, "our much-dreaded danger is past; we are now again on our way, and we shall leave this spot at least ten coss behind us before noon; beyond that there is nothing to fear, and we shall travel with light hearts." Alas! I spoke as my sanguine hope prompted me to do; but it was not fated to be as we thought. Again treachery had been at work, and when I conceived I possessed a band free from all suspicion, two traitors, as I afterwards heard, had already laid a deep plan for my apprehension. Of this however I will tell you hereafter; you are now with us on the road, and you see us urging our course with the utmost speed.

Already had we lost sight of the town, and before us was a broad, well-beaten road, which I well remembered; yet I feared so public a route, and determined to strike off into a bye-path as soon as I could see one which diverged in the direction we were going. We might have proceeded a coss or two perhaps, and the day was now beginning to dawn; a nulla was before us a short distance, and as none of us had washed before leaving the town, I proposed that we should perform our ablutions

---

1   See Chapter XXXVIII.

there, the better to enable us to sustain the fatigue of the stage before us. My proposal was agreed to, and when we reached the running stream, one and all ungirded their loins and sat down by the water; we had not been engaged thus for more than a few minutes when a sudden rush was made upon us by a number of horse and foot soldiers, who must have been lying in wait for us on the road we were to travel.

I had left my weapons at some little distance from the water, and my first impulse was to endeavour to possess myself of them; but in this I was foiled. Two of my own men threw themselves upon me and held me, and as I vainly struggled to free myself some foot-soldiers seized me. I was thrown down and bound. The surprise was not complete. A few of my band drew their swords, and some blows were exchanged between them and the party who had come upon us, and a few of my Thugs were wounded; but we were all overpowered, and the whole affair was concluded in less time than it requires to relate it; only a few of my men escaped.

Bitterly did I upbraid the men who had prevented my getting at my weapons. Had I but possessed them, Ameer Ali would never have been taken alive; I would have sold my life dearly, sahib, and sooner than have been seized I would have plunged my sword into my heart, and ended a life which had no charms for me, and which I only wished to prolong to wreak vengeance on mankind, the source of all my misery.

As I reviled them they mocked and jeered at me. "Where is now your journey to Calcutta, O Meer Sahib?" said one; "behold, the long travel is saved thee, and thou art returning to Saugor to live in a fine house and to keep company with many old friends who are in it." "Yes," said the other, "the jemadar's day is past, and his wit deserted him when he must needs approach the den of the tiger, as if he would not be smelt out! Why didst thou come to Saugor, O Jemadar? Hadst thou forgotten the promise of reward and free pardon which was offered for thy apprehension? Truly we have done a good deed," said he to the other, "and the Sahib-logue will be pleased with us."

But their idle talk was silenced by the leader of the party, who warned them to be careful, and not to boast, lest their expectations should not be realized; and they shrank behind, unable to bear the glances of scorn and contempt which were cast on them by all; by *all*, I say, for even the soldiers who had seized us cursed the means of their success for having been treacherous and unfaithful to the salt they had eaten.

And thus, in bitter agony of spirit, and indulging vain regrets at my senseless imprudence in approaching Saugor, they led me, bound and guarded, by the road I had just travelled, free then as the morning breeze which played on me. For the third time I was a prisoner, and now I saw no hope: I had retained some on each of the former occasions, but it all vanished now. Then I was young, and a young heart is always buoyant and self-comforting; but the fire of my spirit had long been quenched, and it was only in the wild excitement of a life of continual adventure and unrestrained freedom, when I resembled what I had formerly been, that it rekindled within me. Death too was now before me; for I knew the inexorable laws of the Europeans, and that no mercy was shown to Thugs of any grade,—how much less to me for whom a reward had been offered! It was a bitter thought: I should be hung,—hung like a dog,—I who ought to have died on a battle-field! *there* death would have been sweet, and followed by an everlasting Paradise. Alas! even this hope deserted me now, and I felt that the load of crime with which my soul was oppressed would weigh me down into hell.

Who can describe the myriad thoughts which crowd into the heart at such a moment? One by one they hurry in, each striving to displace the foregoing—none staying for an instant,—till the brain reels under the confusion. It was thus with me. I walked mechanically, surrounded by the soldiers, vainly striving to collect my wandering senses to sustain me in the coming scene, the scene of death, for I verily believed I should be led to instant execution: why should the mockery of a trial be given to one so steeped in crime as I was?

A short time after our arrival at the town, I was conducted, closely guarded, to the officer who was employed by the English Government to apprehend Thugs. A tall, noble-looking person he was, and from the severe glance he cast on me I thought my hour was come, and that ere night I should cease to exist. I had prepared myself however for the worst; I saw no pity in his stern countenance, and I confess I trembled when he addressed me.

"So, you are Ameer Ali, Jemadar," said he, "and at last you are in my power; know you aught of the accusations against you, and wherefore you are here? Read them," he continued to an attendant moonshee, "read the list which has been drawn up; yonder villain looks as though he would deny them."

The man unfolded a roll of paper written in Persian, and read a catalogue of crime, of murders, every one of which I knew to be true; a faithful record it was of my past life, with but few omissions. Alla defend me! thought I, there is no hope; yet still I put a bold face on the matter.

"The proof, Sahib Bahadur;"[1] said I, "you English are praised for your justice; and, long as that list is of crimes I never before heard of, you will not deny me fair hearing and the justice you give to thousands."

---

1 Honorable sir.

"Surely not; whatever your crimes may be, do not fear that your case shall be inquired into. Call the approvers," said he to an attendant; "bring them in one by one, and the jemadar shall hear what they have told me about him."

The first man who entered was an old associate of mine in former days, before my misfortunes commenced: he had been with me in the expedition just before my father had been put to death by the Rajah of Jhalone, which I have minutely described to you; and he related the whole, from the murder of the moonshee and his child down to the last event, the destruction of the pearl-merchant. His story took a long time in relating; and the whole was so fresh in my recollection, and he was so exact and true in its details, that I could not answer a word, nor put a single question to shake his testimony. In conclusion he referred the officer to the Rajah of Jhalone for corroboration of the whole, and he appealed to me to declare whether aught he had said was false. "Not only," said he, "do you know, Meer Sahib, that it is all true, but there are others as well as myself who can speak to these facts; and know, moreover, that many graves have been opened, and the remains of your victims have been disinterred."

"Say *yours* as well as mine," I replied, thrown completely off my guard at last, and nettled by the emphasis he had placed on the words "your victims." "You had as much to do with them as myself; besides, did you not aid that villain Ganesha when I would have saved the child of the moonshee?"

"He has confessed!" cried many voices.

"Silence!" said the officer, "let no one dare to speak. Do you know, Ameer Ali, what you have said? Are you aware that you have admitted you are a Thug?"

"It is useless now to attempt to recall my words," said I doggedly; "make the most of them, for after this you shall wring no more from me; no, not by the most horrible tortures you can inflict."

The examination, however, proceeded. Others were brought forward who had known me or been connected with me in Thuggee, and at last those who had earned the reward of the Government by betraying me. They had been associated with me for the last two years, and they related what I had done, and where the bodies of the murdered were lying. After this was finished, and all the depositions recorded, I was remanded to prison; and the better to secure me, I was not only loaded with irons, but confined in a cell by myself.

After many days, which elapsed without my being sent for, and when I had concluded that my fate was decided, the moonshee whom I had seen in the court, with a jemadar of Nujeeb's[1] and two of the approvers, came to me.

"Ameer Ali," said the first, "we are sent by the Sahib Bahadur to tell you of your fate."

"I can guess it," said I—"I am to suffer with the rest. Well! many a good Thug has thus died before me, and you shall see that Ameer Ali fears not death."

"You have guessed rightly," said the moonshee, "there is no hope for you: your final trial will come on in a day or two, and there is such an array of facts against you, and the accounts from the Rajah of Jhalone so entirely agree with the statements of all the approvers, that it is impossible you can escape death; or if you do escape it, nothing can save you from the Kala Panee."

"Death!" cried I, "death at once! Ah, Moonshee! you have influence with my judges, you can prevent my being sent away over the far sea, never to behold my country more, and to linger out the remnant of my days in a strange land, condemned to work in irons. These hands have never been used to labour; how shall I endure it? Death is indeed welcome, compared with the Kala Panee."

"But why should it be either, Meer Sahib?" asked the jemadar; "your life or death is in your own hands: these men will tell you how they are treated by the master they serve, and you may be like them if you are wise."

"Never!" cried I; "never shall it be said of Ameer Ali that he betrayed an associate."

"Listen, Kumbukht!"[2] said the moonshee; "we are not come to use entreaties to one who deserves to die a thousand deaths, to one whose name is a terror to the country; you are in our power, and there is no averting your fate: an alternative is offered, which you may accept or not as you please; no force is used, no arguments shall be wasted on you. Say at once, will you live and become an approver like the rest,—have good clothes to wear and food to eat, and be treated with consideration,—or will you die the death of a dog? Speak, my time is precious, and I have no orders to bandy words with you."

"Accept the terms, Ameer Ali," said both the approvers; "do not be a fool, and throw your last chance of life away!"

I mused for a moment: what was life to me? should it ever be said that Ameer Ali had become a traitor, and, for the sake of a daily pittance of food and the boon of life, had abandoned his profession and assisted to suppress it? No, I would die first,

---

1   Military officer.

2   Miserable one!

and I told them so. "Begone!" said I; "take this message to your employer,—that the soul of Ameer Ali is too proud to accept his offer, and that he scorns it. Death has no terrors for him, yet shame, everlasting shame has!"

They left me, and I mused over my lot. I was to die; that was determined. Did I fear death? not at first: I looked at the transition as one that would lead me to eternal joys, to Paradise, to my father and Azeema. But as I thought again and again, other reflections crowded on my spirit: I was to die, but how? not like a man or a soldier, but like a miserable thief, the scorn of thousands who would exult in my dying struggles; and then I remembered those of the wretch who had been hung before my eyes when Bhudrinath was with me, and I pictured to myself the agony he must have suffered ere life was extinct—the shame of the death—the ignominy which would never leave my memory. All these weighed heavily on me. On the other hand was life—one of servitude it was true, but still it was life; I should be protected, and I might once more perhaps be free, if the Europeans relented towards me, and I did them faithful service.

Thus I debated with myself for many days. At last I was warned that my trial would come on the next day; it was clearly the crisis of my fate, and, I must confess it, the fear of the horrible death of hanging, the dread of the Kala Panee, and the advice of the moonshee, caused my resolutions of dying with the rest to give way to a desire of life. Ganesha, too, crossed my thoughts; I can revenge myself now, thought I, and his death will not lie at my door. I knew too how earnestly his capture was desired, and that I alone could tell where he was to be found, and of his probable lurking-places, in case he ever escaped from us. My determination was made, and I requested that the moonshee who had formerly spoken with me on the subject might be sent for. He came, and I told him at once that I was willing to accept the alternative he had offered.

"Ah! you speak like a wise man now," said he, "and if you exert yourself in the service you have embraced, and prove yourself faithful and trustworthy, you may rely upon it indulgences, as far as can be granted to a person in your condition, will be allowed to you hereafter; but you must first deserve them, for with the Europeans nothing goes by favour."

"I am ready," I replied, "point out what I am to do, and you will find that Ameer Ali can be true to the salt he eats."

"Then come, it is still early, and I will take you at once to the court, there you will receive your instructions."

My prison irons were struck off, and a light steel rod with a ring attached to it fastened about my right leg, so that it left me at perfect liberty to walk but not to run, and I was duly admitted as an approver, under the threat of instant execution in case I ever neglected my duty, failed to give information where I really possessed it, or abused in any way the confidence which had been reposed in me.

"Know you aught of Ganesha?" said the officer to me.

"I do, Sahib Bahadur," I replied, "I know him well: you have offered a reward for him as you did for me, and yet you know not that even at this moment he is within a few coss of Saugor."

"Can you guide my people to him?" he asked. "Remember, this is the first matter with which you are entrusted, and I need not say that I require you to use your utmost intelligence in it. Ganesha is wary, and has hitherto evaded every attempt which has been made to apprehend him."

"I will undertake it," I exclaimed. "It is possible he does not know of my capture; and if you will give me six of your own men, I will disguise them, and pledge myself to bring him to you; and not only him, but Himmut, who is, I know, with him."

"Ha!" cried the officer, "Himmut also! he is as bad as the other."

"He is as good a Thug," I replied, "and more cannot be said. But we lose time; select your men, let them be the bravest and most active you have—their weapons may be needed. I will too ask you for a sword."

"Impossible," said he; "you must go as you are; what if you were to lead my men into destruction?"

I drew myself up proudly. "Trust me or not as you will,—Ameer Ali is no liar, no deceitful villain to the cause he serves. Trust me, and you make me doubly true to your interests; doubt me, and I may doubt you."

"Thou speakest boldly," said he, "and I will trust thee. Let him have his own weapon," he added to an attendant. "And now you must begone early, Ameer Ali; the men await you without."

"This instant,—food shall not pass my lips till I have taken Ganesha."

I left him. I found the men, six resolute-looking fellows, well armed; I stripped them of their badges of office, and made them throw dust on their garments so that it should appear they had travelled far. The iron on my leg I secured so that it should make no noise, and not be visible under my trousers: and I put the party in motion.

It was nearly evening, and avoiding the town I struck at once into the open country. "If we travel well," said I to the men, "we may be up with him by midnight."

"Where is he?" asked the leader of the band.

"At ——; he lives with the patel there, and passes for a Hindoo fakeer."

"By Gunga! I have seen him then," rejoined the fellow; "he is tall, and squints, does he not?"

"That is the man," said I; "you would hardly have thought of looking for him so near you?"

"No, indeed! had we known it we might have captured him a week ago."

"Now you are sure of him," said I; "but we must be wary. Will you trust me?"

"I will, but beware how you attempt to escape or mislead me."

"I have a heavy reckoning to settle with Ganesha—he murdered my mother!" was my only reply.

We reached the village in the very dead of night; everything was still, and it was perfectly dark, which aided my purpose, for my companion's face could not be distinguished, and my own approach to the patel's house would not be noticed. "Now," said I to the Nujeeb,[1] "you alone must accompany me; let the rest of your men stay here; I will bring Ganesha here, and then you must bind him. Do you fear me?" (for he appeared irresolute); "nay, then, I will go alone, and tell your master that ye are cowards."

"That will not do either," cried the man, "I must not let you out of my sight; my orders are positive; so go I must. And if I do not return," said he to his associates, "do you make the best of your way to Saugor alone, and say that I am murdered."

I laughed. "There is no fear," said I; "in half an hour or less we shall return; are you ready?"

"I am, Meer Sahib; lead on, and remember that my sword is loose in the scabbard. I may die, but thou shalt also."

"Fool!" said I, "cannot you trust me?"

"Not yet," he replied; "I may do so hereafter."

"Remember," I continued, "that you are neither to speak to Ganesha nor the other, if he is here. I will get them out of the house; after that look well to your weapons. If they attempt to escape, or show suspicion of our real errand, fall on Himmut when I ask you how far it is to Saugor; leave me to deal with Ganesha;— we are two to two, and Ganesha is a better swordsman than the other. You will remember this."

"I will," he replied; "I will stick by you—I fear not now, for I see you are faithful."

A few more steps brought me to the patel's house, and I called for him by name. "Jeswunt! Jeswunt! rouse yourself and come out, man. Thou knowest who I am." I spoke in Ramasee, which I knew he understood. He answered me from within, and soon after I heard the bars and bolts of his door removed, and he came forth wrapped in a sheet. "Who calls me," he asked.

---

1 Soldier.

"I, your friend Ameer Ali," I replied; "where is Ganesha?"

"Asleep, within; why do you ask?"

"And Himmut?"

"Asleep also; what do ye want with either? and what brings you here, Meer Sahib, so late or so early, which you please? we thought you were half way to Calcutta."

"Ah," said I, "that matter has been given up; the Nujeebs were out, and there was risk. But go and rouse Ganesha, I have some work in hand for him, and have no time to lose; it must be finished by daylight."

"I understand," said the patel, "some bunij, eh?"

"Do not stand chattering there, or your share may be forgotten, Pateljee; bring Ganesha to me,—or tell him I am here, he will come fast enough."

He went in. "Now be ready!" said I to the Nujeeb; "do as I do, and remember the signal."

I heard the patel awaken Ganesha; I heard the growling tones of his voice as he first abused him for rousing him, and afterwards his eager question, "Ameer Ali here! ai Bhowanee, what can he require of me?" At length his gaunt figure appeared at the doorway. Ya Alla![1] how my heart bounded within me, and then sickened, so intense was my excitement on beholding him.

"Where art thou, Ameer Ali?" said he; "I can see nought in this accursed darkness."

"Here," said I, "you will see well enough by-and-by when your eye is accustomed to it. Give me your hand; now descend the step; that is right." We embraced each other.

"Are you ready for work?" I asked, "I have only two men with me, and we have picked up some bunij; there will be good spoil too if you will join us,—alone we can do nothing, there are four of them."

"Where?" he asked.

"Yonder, in the lane; I have pretended to come for fire."

"Who is that with you?"

"A friend; no fear of him, he is one of us."

"Does he speak Ramasee?"

"Not yet," said I, "he is a new hand, but a promising one; but where is Himmut?"

"Within, snoring there, you may even hear him; wait for me a moment, I will go for my sword and shoes, and rouse him up. Four men you said, and we are five; enough, by Bhowanee! we will share the spoil."

"Before you are two hours older; be quick, or they may suspect me."

---

1 Oh Allah!

He went in, and returned in a short time fully equipped; Himmut accompanied him, and we exchanged salutations.

"Now, come along," said I, "there is no time to lose."

"Hark ye!" said Ganesha, "there is a well in yonder lane, will that do for the bhil?"

"Certainly," I replied, "you will see the men directly." Soon after I had spoken we approached our party.

"Who goes there?" cried one of them.

"A friend—Ameer Ali!"

"Then all is right," was the reply, and in another instant we had joined them.

"There are your men, seize them!" cried I, throwing myself upon Ganesha with such violence that we fell to the ground together, struggling with deadly hate; but two of the Nujeebs came to my aid, just as Ganesha had succeeded in drawing a small dagger he wore in his girdle, and as I had fortunately seized his hand.

"Bind him hand and foot," said I, disengaging myself from him, "and gag him, or he may alarm the village by his cries." This was done, and he was disarmed; a cloth was tied round his mouth so that he could not speak, and we hurried our prisoners along as fast as the darkness and the roughness of the road would allow.

None of us spoke, nor was it till the day had fully dawned that I looked upon Ganesha; then our eyes met, and the furious expression of his face I shall never forget. "Take the gag from his mouth," said I to one of the Nujeebs; "let him speak if he wishes." It was done.

"You are revenged at last, Ameer Ali," he said; "may my curses cleave to you for ever, and the curses of Bhowanee fall on you for the destruction of her votary! May the salt you eat be bitter in your mouth, and your food poison to you!"

"Ameen!" said I. "You have spoken like Ganesha. I am indeed revenged, but the debt is not paid yet—the debt you owe me for my mother's life. Devil! you murdered her."

"Ay, and would have murdered you, when you were a weak puling child, but for that fool Ismail; he met his fate, however, and yours is yet in store for you."

"You will not see it," said I; "and when I behold you hung up like a dog I shall be happy."

"Peace!" exclaimed the leader of the Nujeebs; "why do you waste words on him, Ameer Ali?"

"Because I am glutting my soul with his sufferings," I answered; "and, had I my will, I would stand by and taunt him till the hour of his death. Did he not murder my mother? and, if he had not, should I have murdered my sister? Have I not cause for deep and deadly hate? Yet I will be silent now."

We reached Saugor; and the delight with which the officer received Ganesha from my hands could not be concealed. "A deep blow has been struck at Thuggee in the capture of this villain," said he, "and thou hast done thy duty well, Ameer Ali."

From that hour I rose in his confidence and estimation, and I have never forfeited it.

Ganesha's trial came on, and I was the principal witness against him. I told all I knew of the murders he had committed, and others corroborated my statements in the fullest manner. He was sentenced to die.

In vain was it that I entreated to see him before his execution; I wanted to taunt him with his fate, and to embitter his last hours, if anything I could have said might have done so. It was denied me; the officer knew of my purpose, and was too humane to allow it. But I saw him die—him and twenty others—all at the same moment. He saw me too, and cursed me, but his curses were impotent. They all ascended the fatal drop together, refused the polluting touch of the hangman, adjusted the ropes round their own necks, and, exclaiming, "Victory to Bhowanee!" seized each other's hands, and leaped from the platform into eternity. I watched Ganesha, and I joyed to see that his struggles were protracted beyond those of the others. I was satisfied,—he had paid the debt he owed me.

And now, sahib, after this event, my life became one of dull routine and inactivity. One by one I tracked and apprehended my old associates, till none of them remained at large. The usefulness of my life to you has passed away, and all that I can do is at times to relate the details of some affair I may either have witnessed or heard from others. Why should I live? is a question I often ask myself; why should an existence be continued to me in which I have no enjoyment, no pleasure, no care, not even grief? I have remorse but for one act, and that will never leave me. Yet I must support it until Alla pleases to send the angel to loose the cord which binds my life to the clay it inhabits.

I used often to think on my daughter, but her too I have almost forgotten; yet I should not say forgotten, for I love her with a parent's affection, which will last to the latest moment of my existence. But she is happy, and why should she know of me?

I fear that I have often wearied you by the minute relation of my history; but I have told all, nor concealed from you one thought, one feeling, much less any act which at this distance of time I can remember. Possibly, you may have recorded what may prove fearfully interesting to your friends. If it be so, your end is answered: you have given a faithful portrait of a Thug's life, his ceremonies, and his acts; whilst I am proud that the world will know of the deeds and adventures of Ameer Ali, the Thug.

APPENDIX

On The Thugs[1]

RECEIVED FROM AN OFFICER IN THE SERVICE OF
HIS HIGHNESS THE NIZAM[2]

By Philip Meadows Taylor

THE Thugs form a perfectly distinct class of persons, who subsist almost entirely upon the produce of the murders they are in the habit of committing. They appear to have derived their denomination from the practice usually adopted by them of decoying the persons they fix upon to destroy, to join their party; and then, taking advantage of the confidence they endeavour to inspire, to strangle their unsuspecting victims. They are also known by the name of Phanseegurs; and in the northeastern part of the Nizam's dominions, are usually called "Kockbunds." There are several peculiarities in the habits of the Thugs, in their mode of causing death, and in the precautions they adopt for the prevention of discovery, that distinguish them from every other class of delinquents; and it may be considered a general rule whereby to judge of them, that they affect to disclaim the practice of petty theft, housebreaking, and indeed every species of stealing that has not been preceded by the perpetration of murder.

The Thugs adopt no other method of killing but strangulation; and the implement made use of for this purpose is a handkerchief, or any other convenient strip of cloth. The manner in which the deed is done will be described hereafter. They never attempt to rob a traveller until they have, in the first instance, deprived him of life; after the commission of a murder, they invariably bury the body immediately, if time and opportunity serve, or otherwise conceal it; and never leave a corpse uninterred in the highway, unless they happen to be disturbed.[3]

---

1   Pronounced Túg, but with a slight aspirate. [*Taylor*]

2   "On the Thugs" first appeared in *The New Monthly Magazine* in July 1833.

3   The Thugs were known in the time of the Emperor Akbar of Delhi, by whom many were executed. They were first known to the British Government in 1812, and then many were hung in Bundelkund. Again, in 1817, they attracted notice by their horrible acts, and twelve villages in Bundelkund, which were peopled almost entirely by them, were taken by a force sent against them. They were then dispersed, but assembled in various parts in Sindhia's and the Nagpoor country,

To trace the origin of this practice would now be a matter of some difficulty, for if the assertions of the Thugs themselves are entitled to any credit, it has been in vogue from time immemorial; and they pretend that its institution is coeval with the creation of the world. Like most other inhuman practices, the traditions regarding it are mixed up with tales of Hindoo superstition; and the Thugs would wish to make it appear that, in immolating the numberless victims that yearly fall by their hands, they are only obeying the injunctions of the deity of their worship, to whom they say they are offering an acceptable sacrifice. The object of their worship is the Goddess Kalee, or Bhowanee, and there is a temple at Binda Chul, near Mirzapoor,[1] to which the Thugs usually send considerable offerings, and the establishment of priests at their shrine are entirely of their community. Bhowanee, it seems, once formed the determination of extirpating the human race, and sacrificed all but her own disciples. But she discovered, to her astonishment, that, through the intervention of the Creating Power, whenever human blood was shed, a fresh subject immediately started into existence to supply the vacancy. She therefore formed an image, into which she instilled the principles of life, and calling together her disciples, instructed them in the art of depriving that being of life by strangling it with a handkerchief. This method was found upon trial to be effectual, and the goddess directed her worshippers to adopt it, and to murder, without distinction, all who should fall into their hands, promising herself to dispose of the bodies of their victims, whose property she bestowed on her followers; and to be present at, and to preside over and to protect them on those occasions, so that none should be able to prevail against them.

Thus, say the Thugs, was our own order established, and we originally took no care of the bodies of those who fell by our hands, but abandoned them wherever they were strangled, until one man, more curious than the rest, ventured to watch the body he had murdered, in the expectation of seeing the manner in which it

---

also in Holkar's dominions. From 1817 till 1831 they were not molested; and, in consequence, increased greatly in the latter year. Measures were taken to suppress them, which have been attended with great success in this year. One hundred and eleven have been executed at Jubbulpoor, and upwards of 400 transported for life to the eastern settlement of Pinang, and upwards of 600 are now in jail at Saugor to take their trial at the next sessions at Jubbulpoor. Their apprehension, and their consequent disclosures, gave the means of those in this part of the country being pointed out. Mr. Reynolds, the officer who has the work here, has apprehended more than 100 in less than six months, and is catching others almost daily. [*Taylor*]

1 Mirzapur, in north India.

was disposed of. The goddess of his worship descended, as usual, to carry away the corpse, but observing that this man was on the watch, she relinquished her purpose; and calling him, angrily rebuked him for his temerity, telling him she could no longer perform her promise regarding the bodies of the murdered, which his associates must hereafter dispose of in the best way they could. Hence, say they, arose the practice invariably followed by the Thugs of burying the dead; and to this circumstance principally is to be attributed the extraordinary manner in which their atrocities have remained unknown, for which such circumspection and secrecy do they proceed to work, and such order and regularity is there in all their operations, that it is next to impossible a murder should ever be discovered.

Absurd as the foregoing relation may appear, it has had this effect on the mind of Thugs, that they do not seem to be visited with any of those feelings of remorse or compunction at the inhuman deeds in which they have participated that are commonly supposed to be, at some period of their lives, the portion of all who have trafficked in human blood. On the contrary, they dwell with satisfaction on the recollection of their various and successful exploits, and refer with no small degree of pride and exultation to the instances in which they have been personally engaged, especially if the number of their victims has been great, or the plunder they have acquired has been extensive.

Notwithstanding the adherence to Hindoo rites of worship observable among the Thugs, a very considerable number of them are Mussulmans.[1] No judgment of the birth or caste of a Thug can, however, be formed from his name; for it not unfrequently happens that a Hindoo Thug has a Mussulman name with a Hindoo *alias* attached to it, and *vice versa* with respect to the Thugs who are by birth Mahommedans. In almost every instance the Thugs have more than one appellation by which they are known. Of the number of Mussulman Thugs, some are to be found of every sect, Sheiks, Sezed, Mogul, and Pathan;[2] and among the Hindoo, the castes chiefly to be met with are Brahmins, Rajhpoots, Lodhees, Ocheers and Kolees.[3] In a gang of Thugs some of every one of these castes may be found all con-

---

1 Muslims.

2 Shaikh refers to an Indian Muslim of Arab descent or to a high-caste Hindu who converted to Islam; a Sayyid refers to an Indian Muslim who claims to be descended from the Prophet Mohammad; a Mughal is an Indian Muslim of Persianate descent; and a Pathan is an Indian Muslim of Pashtun or Afghan descent.

3 In the Hindu caste or varna system, Brahmins (the priestly caste) occupy the highest position; Rajputs are members of the warrior or political caste; the Lodh (grain-carriers) are a farming caste;

nected together by the peculiar plan of murder practiced by them, all subject to the same regulations, and all, both Mussulmans and Hindoos, joining in the worship of Bhowanee.

They usually move in large parties, often amounting to 100 or 200 persons, and resort to all sort of subterfuges for the purpose of concealing their real profession. If they are travelling southward, they represent themselves to be either proceeding in quest of service, or on their way to rejoin the regiments they belong to in this part of the country. When on the contrary, their route lies towards the north, they represent themselves to be Sepoys[1] from corps of the Bombay or Nizam's army, who are going on leave to Hindustan. The gangs do not always consist of persons who are Thugs by birth. It is customary for them to entice, by the promise of monthly pay or the hopes of amassing money that are held out, many persons, who are ignorant of the deeds of death that are to be perpetrated for the attainment of these objects, until made aware of the reality by seeing the victims of their cupidity fall under the hands of the stranglers; and the Thugs declare that novices have occasionally been so horrified at the sight, as to have effected their immediate escape. Others, more callous to the commission of crime, are not deterred from the pursuit of wealth by the frightful means adopted to obtain it, and remaining with the gang, too soon begin personally to assist in the perpetration of murder.

Many of the most notorious Thugs are the adopted children of others of the same class. They make it a rule, when a murder is committed, never to spare the life of any one, either male of female, who is old enough to remember and relate the particulars of the deed. But in the event of their meeting with children of such a tender age as to make it impossible they should be enabled to relate the fact, they generally spare their lives, and, adopting them, bring them up to the trade of Thugs. These men of course eventually become acquainted with the fact of the murder of their fathers and mothers by the very persons with whom they have dwelt since their childhood, but are still not deterred from following the same dreadful trade. It might be supposed, that a class of persons whose hearts must be effectually hardened against all the better feelings of humanity, would encounter few scruples of conscience in the commission of the horrid deeds whereby they subsist; but, in point of fact, they are as much the slaves of superstition, and as much directed by the observance of omens in the commission of murder, as the most inoffensive of the natives of India are in the ordinary affairs of their lives.

---

and Taylor uses the terms "Ocheers" and "Kolis" to refer to Hindus of the laboring castes.

1 Soldiers.

The chief symbol of worship among the Thugs is a khadule, or pickaxe of iron. It is known among them by the name of *hishun, kussee* and *mahee*. With every gang there is carried a *hishun*, which is, in fact, their standard, and the bearer of it is entitled to particular privileges. Previous to commencing an expedition, the jemadars[1] of the party celebrate a poojah[2] to the hishun, which is typical of the deity of their worship. The ceremonies differ little from the usual rites of Hindoos on similar occasions. A Hindoo Thug of good caste is employed in making a quantity of the cakes called poories,[3] which, being consecrated, are distributed among the assembly. The hishun is bathed and perfumed in the smoke of burning benjamin,[4] and is afterwards made over to the *hishun wulluh*,[5] who receives it in a piece of cloth kept for that purpose. It is then taken out into open fields, in the expectation of an omen being observed. This hishun is deposited in a convenient spot in the direction the party intends to proceed, and certain persons are deputed to keep watch over it. There are particular birds and beasts that are looked upon by the Thugs as the revealers of omens, to whose calls and movements their attention is, on this occasion, particularly directed. Among the number are the owl, the jay, the jackall, the ass, &c., &c. If one of these calls out, or moves to the right hand side, the omen is looked upon as favourable; but if to the left, it is considered unfavourable, and the project is abandoned. It is not unusual for the Thugs to look for a favourable omen previous to the commission of a murder, and they are frequently deterred from carrying their intentions immediately into effect by the observance of an unfavourable sign, such as a snake crossing their path when in pursuit of a victim, or the circumstances of any of the animals before mentioned calling out on their left hand sides. This, no doubt, accounts for the Thugs so often keeping company with travellers for many days previous to murdering them, although they had determined upon their sacrifice from the moment of their first joining the party. The omen is denominated *sugoor* by the Thugs, a corruption, no doubt, of the Persian *shugoôr*.

In the event of an expedition proving more than ordinarily successful, a poojah is usually made to Bhowanee, and a portion of the spoil taken by the gang is set aside for the purpose of being sent to the pagoda before alluded to, as an offering to the goddess. Propitiatory offerings are also made, and various ceremonies performed,

---

1 Captains.
2 Hindu religious ceremony in which an offering to a deity is made.
3 Puri; unleavened bread made from hard wheat flour.
4 Ficus.
5 Keeper of the sacred pickaxe.

before the *khodulee*, or *hishun*, should the Thugs have failed in obtaining any plunder for a length of time.

In every gang of Thugs there are to be found one or more jemadars who appear to hold that rank not by the choice of their followers, but in consequence of the their wealth and influence in their respective villages, and having assembled their immediate followers in the vicinity of their homes. The profits of a jemadar are of course greater than those of his followers; he receives six and a half or seven per cent. on all silver coin, and other property not hereafter specified; and then shares in the remainder in common with the other Thugs of the party. When gold is obtained in coin or in mass, the tenth part is taken by the jemadar previous to dividing it; and he has a tithe of all pearls, shawls, gold embroidered cloths, brass and copper pots, horses, &c. The jemadar acts as master of the ceremonies when the poojah is performed, and he assigns to every Thug the particular duty he is to undertake in the commission of every murder that is determined on. These duties are performed in succession by all the Thugs of the party, and to the regularity and system that exists among them is to be attributed the unparalleled success that has attended their proceedings. Next to the jemadar, the most important person is the *bhuttoat*, or strangler, who carries the handkerchief with which the Thugs usually murder their victims. This implement is merely a piece of fine, strong cotton cloth, about a yard long; at one end a knot is tied, and cloth is slightly twisted, and kept ready for use in front of the waistcoat of the person carrying it. There is no doubt but that all Thugs are expert in the use of the handkerchief, which is called boomal, or paloo; but if they are to be believed, only particular persons are called upon, or permitted to perform this office. When a large gang is collected, the most able-bodied and alert of their number are fixed upon as bhuttoats, and they are made the bearers of the handkerchief only after the performance of various and often expensive ceremonies, and only on the observance of a favourable omen. The old and experienced Thugs are usually denominated gooroo bhow, and the junior Thugs make a merit of attending upon them, filling their hookahs, shampooing their bodies, and performing the most menial offices. They gradually become initiated into all the mysteries of the art, and if they prove to be powerful men, these disciples of the *gooroo* are made bhuttoats. The Thugs say, that if one of their class was alone, and had never strangled a person, he would not presume to make use of the handkerchief until he observed a favourable omen. The ceremonies observed in making a bhuttoat are the same as those described in carrying out the hishun, in room of which the handkerchief is on this occasion substituted, and an offering of pence (copper coin), cocoa-nut, turmeric, red ochre, &c., &c., is made. When a murder is to be committed, the bhuttoat usually follows the particular person whom he has been nominated by the jemadar to strangle; and, on the preconcerted signal being given, the handkerchief is seized with the knot in the *left hand*, the right hand side being about nine inches farther up, in which manner it is thrown over the head of the person to be strangled from behind; the two hands are crossed as the victim falls, and such is the certainty with which the deed is done, as the Thugs frequently declare, that before the body falls to the ground the eyes start out of the head, and life becomes extinct. Should the person to be strangled prove a powerful man, or the bhuttoat inexpert, another Thug lays hold of the end of the handkerchief, and the work is completed. The perfection of the act is said to be, when several persons are simultaneously murdered without any of them having time to utter a cry, or to be aware of the fate of their comrades.

Favourable opportunities are given for bhuttoats to make their first essay in the art of strangling. When a single traveller is met with, a novice is instructed to make a trial of his skill; the party sets off during the night, and stops while it is still dark to drink water or to smoke. While seated for the purpose, the jemadar inquires what time of the night it may be, and the Thugs look up at the stars to ascertain. This being the preconcerted signal, the bhuttoat is immediately on the alert and the unsuspecting traveller, on looking up at the heavens, in common with the rest of the party, offers his neck to the ready handkerchief, and becomes an easy prey to his murderer. The bhuttoat receives eight annas (half a rupee) extra for every murder that is committed, and if the plunder is great, some article of value is assigned to him over and above his share. The persons intended to be murdered are called by different names, according to their sect, profession, wealth, &c. &c; a victim having much property is entitled "*niamud,*" and they are all often called bunj. To aid the bhuttoat in the preparation of a murder, another Thug is especially appointed under the denominations of samsecah. His business is to seize the person to be strangled by the wrists if he be on foot, and by one of his legs if he be on horseback, and so to pull him down. A samsecah is told off to each traveller, and he places himself in a convenient situation near him to be ready when required. In the event of the traveller being mounted on horseback, another Thug assists under the denomination of "bhugdurra;" his business is to lay hold of the horse's bridle, and to check it as soon as the signal for murder is given.

One of the most necessary persons to a gang of Thugs is he who goes by the name of tilläee. The Thugs do not always depend upon chance for obtaining plunder, or roam about in the expectation of meeting travellers, but frequently take up their quarters in or near a large town, or some great thoroughfare, from whence they make expeditions, according to the information obtained by the tilläees. These men are chosen from among the most smooth-spoken and intelligent of their number, and their chief duty is to gain information. For this purpose they are decked out in the garb of respectable persons, whose appearance and manners they must have the art of assuming. They frequent the bazaars of the town near which their associates are encamped, and endeavour to pick up intelligence of the intended dispatch or expected arrival of goods or treasure, of which information is forthwith given to the gang, who send out a party to intercept them. Inquiry is also made for any party of travellers who may have arrived, and who put up in the suraee,[1] or elsewhere. Every art is brought into practice to scrape an acquaintance with these people. They are given to understand that the tilläee is travelling the same road. An opportunity is taken to throw out hints regarding the unsafeness of the roads, and the frequency of murders and robberies; an acquaintance with some of the friends or relatives of the travellers is feigned, and an invitation from them to partake of the repast that has been prepared where the tilläee has put up, the convenience of which and the superiority of the water are abundantly praised. The result is, that the travellers are inveigled into joining the gang of Thugs and they are feasted and treated with every politeness and consideration by the very wretches who are at the time plotting their murder and calculating the share they shall acquire in the division of their property. What the feelings must be of men who are actuated by motives so entirely opposed to their apparent kindness of behaviour, it is difficult to imagine; and I know not whether most to admire the address with which they conceal their murderous intentions, or to detest the infernal apathy with which they can eat out of the same dish, and drink of the very cup, that is partaken of by their future victims!

It is on the perfection which they have attained in the art of acting as tilläees that the Thugs pride themselves, and they frequently boast that it is only once necessary to have an opportunity of conversing with a traveller, to be able to mark him as an easy victim, whenever they choose to murder him. Instances sometimes occur where a party of Thugs find their victims too numerous for them while they remain in a body, and they are seldom at a loss for expedients to create dissensions, and a consequent division among them. If all their arts of intrigue and cajolery fail in producing the desired effect, an occasion is taken advantage of to ply the travellers with intoxicating liquors; a quarrel is got up, and from words they proceed to blows, which end in the dissension of the company, who, proceeding by different roads, fall an easier prey to their remorseless destroyers. Having enticed the travellers into the snare they have laid for them, the next object is to choose a convenient spot for their

---

1 Serai; inn.

murder. This, in their technical language, is called a *bhil*, and is usually fixed upon some distance from a village on the banks of a small stream, where the trees and underwood afford a shelter from the view of occasional passengers. The Thug who is sent on this duty is called a *bhilla*, and having fixed on the place, he either returns to the encampment of his party, or meets them on the way to report the result of his inquiry. If the bhilla returns to camp with his report, the *suggaees*, or grave-diggers, are sent out with him to prepare a grave for the interment of the persons it is intended to murder. Arrangements are previously made so that the party in company with the travellers shall not arrive at the bhil too soon. At the particular spot agreed on, the bhilla meets the party. The jemadar calls out to him "Bhilla naujeh?" (Have you cleared out the hole?) The bhilla replics "Naujeh," on which the concerted signal is given that serves as the death-warrant of the unsuspecting travellers, who are forthwith strangled. While some are employed in rifling the bodies, others assist in carrying them away to the ready-prepared graves. The suggaees perform the office of burying the dead, and the remainder of the gang proceeds on its journey, having with them a certain number of the tilläees or watchmen on the look-out to prevent their being disturbed. Should a casual passenger appear, the tilläee gently throws a stone among the suggaees, who immediately desist, and crouch on the ground until the danger is averted. After the interment is completed, the suggaees rejoin their party, but it is not unusual to have one or more of the tilläees to keep watch to prevent the bodies being disinterred by beasts of prey; and if a discovery should be made by the village people, to give instant information to their companions, in order that they might have an opportunity of getting out of the way.

It often happens that the arrangements and precautions above mentioned cannot be entered into; that travellers are casually met with on the road, and hastily murdered, and as carelessly interred. In these cases, if the opportunity is afforded them, the Thugs always have some one to keep watch at the place; and rather than run the risk of detection, by the bodies being dug up by wild animals, they return, and re-inter them. If the ground is strong, they never touch the corpse; but if the soil is of that loose texture as to render it probable that the bodies, in swelling, will burst the graves, they generally transfix them with knives or spears, which effectually prevents that result.

When the Thugs may choose to strangle their victims in some more exposed situation,—as in a garden near a village where they may have put up for the night,—they resort to further precautions to prevent discovery. The grave is on this occasion prepared on the spot, after the murder has been committed; and the corpse having been deposited therein, the superfluous soil is carried away in baskets, and strewn in the neighbouring fields; the place is watered and beaten down, and it is ultimately plastered over with wet cow-dung, and *choolahs*, or fire-places for cooking, are made on the spot. If the party find it necessary to decamp, they light fires in the choolahs, that they may have appearance of having been used to cook in. Should they determine on staying, they use the choolahs to cook their food in on the succeeding day, having few qualms of conscience to prevent their enjoying the victuals prepared on a spot, the associations attendant on which might be considered too revolting for even a Thug to dwell on.

The parties of Thugs being often very large, they have many beasts of burthen in their train—as bullocks, ponies, and sometimes even camels. If they remain at a place where they have committed a murder, and do not construct fire-places, they take the precaution of tying their cattle on the spot. The Thugs say they can always recognize the fire-places of their own class, there being peculiar marks about them, which are made to serve as directions to the next party that comes that way. The Thugs always prefer burying their victims at some distance from the public road; and therefore, as soon as the bodies of the murdered persons have been stripped of the property found on them, they are carried on the shoulders of the suggaes to the spot selected for interring them. They say they are more careless about the concealment of corpses in the Nizam's country than elsewhere; for they are always so secure from molestation, that they have frequently left bodies exposed without running any risk, as no one takes the trouble of inquiring about them.

The division of spoil does not usually take place immediately after a murder, but everyone secures a portion of the property on the spot; and when a convenient opportunity occurs, each produces the articles he has been the bearer of, and a division is made by the jemadar, whose share is, in the first instance, deducted; then the bhutttoat's; next the sumseahs and bhugdurras claim the extra reward for each murder they have assisted at; the tilläee receives the perquisite which is his due for inveigling a traveller into their snares; the suggaee takes his recompense for the trouble he had in digging the grave; and the residue is divided, share and share alike, among the whole gang. It may be supposed that the cupidity of individual Thugs may occasionally lead them to attempt to defraud their comrades, by secreting an article of value at the time the murdered bodies are plundered; but they say that the whole class are bound by an inviolable oath to produce, for general appropriation to the common stock, everything that may fall into their hands while engaged with a particular party.

The division of plunder, as may be supposed, often leads to the most violent disputes, which it is astonishing do not end in bloodshed. But it might almost be supposed the Thugs have a prejudice against spilling blood; for, when pursued, they refrain from making use of the weapons they usually bear, even in defense of their own persons. The most wanton prodigality occurs when plunder is divided; and occasionally the most valuable shawls and brocades are torn into small strips and distributed amongst the gang, should any difference of opinion arise as to their appropriation. The Thugs say this is also done that every person may run the same risk, for such an article could not be shared among them until converted into money, and some danger is attendant upon the transaction. They appear invariably to destroy all hoondies[1] that fall into their hands, as well as many other articles that are likely to lead to detection. Ready money is what they chiefly look for, and when they have a choice of victims, the possessors of gold and silver would certainly be fixed upon in preference to others. In consequence, it seems to have been a general practice among the Bundelkund[2] Thugs to waylay the parties of sepoys of the Bombay and Nizam's armies, while going on leave to Hindoostan, for the sake of the specie they are usually the bearers of; and they remark, that of the many sepoys who are supposed by their officers to have abandoned the service, while their friends and relatives consider them to be still with their regiments, they alone can tell the fate, the whole number being strangled by their hands. The immense wealth that has, at various times, fallen into the hands of these miscreants, has been expended in the grossest extravagance and debauchery, and, as may be supposed, their ill-gotten gains remain but a short time in their possession.

The Thugs have in use among them, not exactly a language of their own, but they have sets of slang terms and phrases which give them the means of holding a conversation with persons of their own class, without any chance of being understood by the uninitiated. Their term of salutation, whereby also they recognise each other, if they casually meet without being personally acquainted, is, *ali khan bhaee salaam*. What appears most extraordinary is, the manner in which the Thugs recollect the names of their comrades, as well as their persons; and they declare, that though the name of any one of a gang may have escaped their recollection, they never forget the person of a Thug who has assisted with them in the perpetration of a murder. The Thugs, indeed, seem to know each other almost intuitively; and the quickness with which the recognition is made is almost enough to warrant the supposition, that a sort of Freemasonry has been established among them.

---

1   Bills of exchange. [*Taylor*]
2   In north India.

To facilitate their plan of operations, the Thugs have established a regular system of intelligence and communication throughout the countries they have been in the practice of frequenting, and they become acquainted, with astonishing celerity, with proceedings of their comrades in all directions. They omit no opportunity of making inquiries regarding the progress of other gangs, and are equally particular in supplying the requisite information of their own movements. For this purpose they have connected themselves with several persons residing in the Nizam's dominions, as patails[1] and cultivators of villages, many of the latter of whom follow the profession of Thugs in conjunction with their agricultural pursuits.

The Marwarries[2] and other bankers are also frequently the channels of communication between Thugs, and there is no doubt of their being the purchasers of the property of the murdered. The religious mendicants throughout the country occasionally assist in this measure, by becoming the receivers of messages from bands of Thugs, to be delivered to the next party that comes that way; with this view also they have adopted the practice of forming *choolahs*, or fireplaces of a particular construction, to serve as marks of their progress through the country. When a party of Thugs come to a road that branches off in two directions, they adopt the precaution of making a mark, for the guidance of their associates who may come after them, in the following manner:—the soil in a convenient spot is carefully smoothed, and the print of a foot is distinctly stamped upon it. A Thug on seeing this mark, which he naturally searches for, knows by the direction in which it points which track has been followed by those that have preceded him.

The peculiar designation by which they are known is a point in which the Thugs are particularly tenacious, and they attach an importance and even respectability to their profession, that they say no other class of delinquents is entitled to. The denomination of *thief* is one that is particularly obnoxious to them, and they never refrain from soliciting the erasure of the term, and the substitution of that of Thug, whenever it may occur in a paper regarding them, declaring that, so far from following so disgraceful a practice as theft, they scorn the name, and can prove themselves to be as honest and trustworthy as any one else, when occasion requires it.

It seems their ambition to be considered respectable persons; and with this view they expend much of their gains on their personal decoration. Even those who have been seized and admitted as approvers, or informers against their comrades, in fact, king's evidence, are more solicitous about their dress and decent appearance

---

1 Headmen of villages. [*Taylor*]
2 Inhabitants of Marwar, generally bankers and traders. [*Taylor*]

than anything else. They mostly seem to be men of mild and unobtrusive manners, possessing a cheerfulness of disposition entirely opposed to the violent passions and ferocious demeanour that are usually associated with the idea of a professed murderer.

Such is the extent to which this dreadful system has been carried that no idea can be formed of the expenditure of human life to which it has given occasion, or the immensity of the wealth that has been acquired by its adoption. When it is taken into consideration that many of the Thugs already seized confess to their having, for the last twenty-five and thirty years, annually made a tour with parties of more than a hundred men, and with no other object than that of murder and rapine; that they boast of having successively put their tens and twenties to death daily; and that they say an enumeration of all the lives they have personally assisted to destroy would swell the catalogue to hundreds, and, as some declare, to thousands[1]—some conception of the horrid reality may be formed; of the amount of the property that they have yearly made away with, it must be impossible to form any calculation; for, independent of the thousands in ready money, jewels and bullion, the loads of valuable cloths, and every description of merchandise, that continually fall into their hands, the hoondies that they invariably destroy must amount to a considerable sum.

The impunity with which the Thugs have heretofore carried on their merciless proceedings, the facility they have possessed of recruiting their numbers—which are restricted to no particular caste or sect—the security they have had of escaping detection, and the ease with which they have usually purchased their release, when seized by the officers of the weak native governments, in whose dominions they have usually committed their greatest depredations, have altogether so tended to confirm the system, and to disseminate it to the fearful extent to which it has now attained, that the life of no single traveller on any of the roads in the country has been safe, and but a slight chance has been afforded to large parties of escaping the fangs of the blood-thirsty demons who have frequented them.

---

1   Ameer Ali, an approver and noted Thug now at this place, declares and glories in having been present at the murder of 719 persons, whose property is estimated at two lacs and a half of rupees! [*Taylor*]

Confessions of a Thug

Philip Meadows Taylor

"Reader, if you can embody these descriptions, you have Ameer Ali before you; and while you gaze on the picture in your imagination and look on the mild and expressive face you may have fancied, you, as I was, would be the last person to think that he was a professed murderer, and one who in the course of his life has committed upwards of seven hundred murders."

Set in a British prison in Sagar, India in 1832, and inspired by actual events, *Confessions of a Thug* (1839) is the picaresque tale of north Indian Thug Ameer Ali, who strangled over seven hundred people in his lifetime. Kidnapped as a child by a criminal gang devoted to the Hindu goddess Kali, Ameer Ali recounts how he rose to prominence as a Thug leader, how he fell ignominiously from power, and how he took vengeance on his enemies. Hero and villain, victim and victimizer, Ameer Ali is a unique figure in Victorian literature: a charming mass murderer. The most famous Anglo-Indian novel of the ninetee *Thug* is a canonical example of British Orientalism, as well as an un ian readers to identify with an unrepentant predator.

PHILIP MEADOWS TAYLOR was born in Liverpool in 1808. Sent to India at fifteen to make his fortune, he became a lieutenant in the Nizam of Hyderabad's Army. Fluent in several Eastern languages, Taylor was named Assistant Superintendent of Police for the southwestern districts in the Nizam's Dominions, becoming responsible, at age eighteen, for the safety of over a million people. His investigations of Thuggee (*thagi*), a mysterious murder cult that claimed thousands of lives annually, inspired *Confessions of a Thug*, which drew attention to the inadequacy of native law enforcement in India. The novel was an immediate success. After serving two decades as an imperial administrator, Taylor moved to Dublin, where he devoted his remaining years to writing novels about British India, including *Tara: A Mahratta Tale* (1863), *Ralph Darnell* (1865), and *Seeta* (1872). He died in 1876.

MATTHEW KAISER is Assistant Professor of English at Harvard University.

LITERATURE

❁ cognella™

www.cognella.com 800.200.3908

ISBN 978-1-609279-95-0

90000

9 781609 279950

SKU 80076-1